THE SPINSTER'S SECRET

ANTHONY GILBERT

PANDORA

London

THE SPINSTER'S SECRET

ANTHONY GILBERT

London

First published by Collins in 1946
This edition first published in Great Britain in 1987 by
Pandora Press (Routledge & Kegan Paul Ltd)
11 New Fetter Lane, London EC4P 4EE

Set in Sabon by Input Typesetting Ltd, London
and printed in Great Britain by
Cox and Wyman Ltd, Reading

British Library Cataloguing in Publication Data

Gilbert, Anthony, *1899–*
The spinster's secret.——(A Pandora
whodunit).——(Pandora women crime writers)
Rn: Lucy Beatrice Malleson I. Title
823'.912[F] PR6013.I32

ISBN 0–86358–243–5

Pandora Women Crime Writers

Series editors: Rosalind Coward and Linda Semple

In introducing the Pandora *Women Crime Writer* series we have two aims: to reprint the best of women crime writers who have disappeared from print and to introduce a new generation of women crime writers to all devotees of the genre. We also hope to seduce new readers to the pleasures of detective fiction.

Women have used the tradition of crime writing inventively since the end of the last century. Indeed in many periods women have dominated crime writing, as in the so-called Golden Age of detective fiction, usually defined as the first novel of Agatha Christie and the last of Dorothy L. Sayers. Often the most popular novels of the day, and those thought to be best in their genre, were written by women. But as in so many areas of women's writing, many of these have been allowed to go out of print. Few people know the names of Josephine Bell, Pamela Branch, Hilda Lawrence, Marion Mainwaring or Anthony Gilbert (whose real name was Lucy Malleson). Their novels are just as good and entertaining as when they were first written.

Women's importance in the field of crime writing is just as vital today. P. D. James, Ruth Rendell and Patricia Highsmith have all ensured that crime writing is treated seriously. Not so well known, but equally flourishing, is a new branch of feminist crime writers. We plan to introduce many new writers from this area, from England and other countries.

The integration of reprints and new novels is sometimes uneasy. Some writers do make snobbish, even racist remarks.

However, it is a popular misconception that all earlier novels are always snobbish and racist. Many of our chosen and favourite authors managed to avoid, sometimes deliberately, the prevailing views. Others are more rooted in the ideologies of their time but when their remarks jar, it does serve to remind us that any novel must be understood by reference to the historical context in which it is written.

Some of the best writers who will be appearing in this series are: Josephine Bell, Ina Bouman, Christianna Brand, Pamela Branch, Sarah Dreher, Katherine V. Forrest, Miles Franklin, Anthony Gilbert (Lucy Malleson), Hilda Lawrence, Marion Mainwaring, Sara Shulman, Nancy Spain . . .

Linda Semple
Rosalind Coward

The first novels to be published during 1987 are:

Green for Danger by Christianna Brand
Death of a Doll by Hilda Lawrence
Murder in Pastiche by Marion Mainwaring
Amateur City by Katherine V. Forrest
Bring the Monkey by Miles Franklin
Stoner McTavish by Sarah Dreher
The Port of London Murders by Josephine Bell
The Spinster's Secret by Anthony Gilbert (Lucy Malleson)
and
Murder at the Nightwood Bar by Katherine V. Forrest

CHAPTER 1

'Before you set out to commit a murder,' said Arthur Crook – who was like certain Cabinet Ministers in that he rejoiced in sweeping statements – 'there's one important point to bear in mind, something like a lion in your way. And even a lion-tamer can't be sure of circumnavigating this one: that is, there's no foolproof method of murder. You can be as clever as Old Nick, as careful as a Foreign Minister, foresee every mistake to which criminals are liable and guard against 'em all; but even so, you may be tripped up, through no fault of your own, by means of The Invisible Witness. The invisible witness is the person you couldn't account for, and therefore can't protect yourself against.'

He used to quote the Burning Car Murder. Rouse didn't hang, he'd say, because he made mistakes (if you except the original murder), but because, when he had everything in train, two young men came walking over the crest of the hill at two a.m., saw him, and crashed all his carefully laid plans.

'So,' he would wind up, 'unless you're a gambler to the *n*th degree, leave murder alone and try some safer parlour game.'

Afterwards, he added Janet Martin to his list of Awful Warnings.

Every morning by ten-thirty old Miss Martin could be seen sitting at the window of her combined bed-sitting-room on the ground floor of Blakesley House looking out at the street. At seventy-four this had become her main occupation. Weak eyes made it impossible for her to read a great deal, and though she loved receiving letters, she had very few. She was old and poor and in indifferent health, and her only living relations were a prosperous married nephew residing in the north, with no time for the unsuccessful, and a niece, the daughter of her dead sister Florence. Once a month the niece wrote dutifully, telling her aunt such small-talk as she deemed suitable for one who had somehow lost her place in life; and she always said how busy she was – she ran a very popular arts and crafts shop in Southern England – and at birthday and Christmas she sent something from the shop to poor old Aunt Janet. Sometimes Miss Martin let herself go in her letters, and said how poorly she had been or how lonely it was, and the niece would say to her partner, another single woman of great dash and energy, 'I suppose I'd better go up to London and see the old thing. We don't want her grumbling to the other old ladies. Miss Fraser will say she can't keep her, and then we shall be in the cart.'

Not that Miss Blake had no sense of responsibility. From time to time she sent an old coat or jumper to her aunt when she had just got a new one, which was generous, really, considering that if you said 'No coupons' you could get a price for anything. Miss Blake was stalwart and Miss Martin was rather small, and last year she had looked a little nervously at the red and green checked spring coat her niece had given her.

'It is a little large,' she said, 'but I dare say I could get it altered.'

'Tailors are very chancy these days,' the niece reminded her, 'and very, very expensive.'

'Of course,' said Miss Martin, taking the point at once. 'Well, I expect I can take it in a little myself. A couple of inches off the hem . . .'

'Surely it's an advantage having it a little long,' said Miss Blake. 'So much warmer. And after all, Auntie' – she laughed merrily – 'at your age one doesn't bother about being fashionable.'

'I might turn it up, of course,' speculated Miss Martin, 'but it would be very bulky.'

'I don't advise you to try cutting it about,' urged the niece, looking annoyed. 'You won't get material like that again in a hurry. It came from a very exclusive shop in Winchester, and it's pre-war.'

It was on the tip of Miss Martin's tongue to ask which war; but she had realised a long time ago that dear Doreen had no sense of humour, so she said meekly that it was very good of her, and then spoiled everything by asking Doreen if she had decided to buy that new wireless yet. Miss Martin loved the wireless, and sometimes left her door open so that she could hear the wireless from the room upstairs.

'Yes; I got a real bargain through one of our regular customers – such a nice woman. Her husband was in the last Honours List. And I sold the old one for quite a good sum, so really I don't think I need accuse myself of extravagance.'

She smiled complacently. Miss Martin sat staring at her as though she couldn't believe her ears.

'You – you sold it?' she whispered.

'Of course. I didn't want two. And Agatha . . . why – Aunt Janet, what is the matter?'

Miss Martin hadn't realised till this minute how much she had counted on having the old set when Doreen bought a new one. She told herself that, of course, it wasn't possible for young people – Doreen was thirty-nine, but that was young to Miss Martin – to appreciate the position of the old and feeble. She wasn't really unkind, . . . All the same, after Doreen had gone off – saying she really couldn't wait for the late train – Agatha was so good about carrying on single-handed, but one simply couldn't take advantage of other people's good nature, could one? – Miss Martin found to her horror that there were tears in her eyes. She wiped them away and resolutely started thinking of something else; but it was no good. They kept coming back and pouring down her face, and, to crown her humiliation, Miss Fraser came briskly up and found her in a state of collapse.

'Now, come, Miss Martin, we can't have this,' she said. She was always brisk with her old ladies. She believed otherwise they yielded to self-pity, and everyone knew that was fatal. 'What's the matter? I hope you haven't had bad news.'

'N-no, of course not. It's just that I had hoped . . .'

'I don't know what Miss Blake would say if she could see you; just when she's given up a whole day to paying you a visit.'

Miss Martin hurriedly dried her eyes. She didn't want Miss Fraser writing to Miss Blake. That would be fatal. So she pulled herself together, and said there had been a little bit of bad news, but she was all right, really. She knew Doreen would be very angry if she knew of this incident, so she changed the subject; and Miss Fraser said what a splendid person Miss Blake was, and how fortunate to have a good-natured niece.

The next time Doreen came, Miss Fraser managed to meet her in the hall, and say she hoped the old lady was all right. She seemed a little feeble these days.

Doreen was shocked. Hanging over the heads of all the next-of-kin of the old ladies who lived at Blakesley House was the covert threat of expulsion. Miss Fraser's employers relied implicitly on the housekeeper's reports, and if she said that one of the tenants was getting past looking after herself they suggested that her niece or daughter, or whoever it might be, should look out for some alternative accommodation for her. This fear made Doreen more brisk than usual, and she observed that she had been wondering for some time if this big room wasn't really rather a lot for Miss Martin to manage. Miss Martin, touched by so much consideration, said she had sometimes wished she could have a little help, and Miss Fraser knew a very nice woman who obliged for two shillings an hour; but Doreen drew in her horns at once, and said, 'I don't think you can afford that sort of luxury,' and laughed merrily to show that it was a sort of joke; and then sobering up, remarked that the housekeeper had spoken of the possibility of one of the smaller rooms on the third floor shortly becoming vacant. 'And that,' said Doreen in impressive tones, 'would mean less work – and, of course, a lower rent. And she's very kindly offered to give you first refusal.'

'Oh, no,' exclaimed Miss Martin, shocked into downright speech, 'I couldn't go upstairs!'

'Why not?' demanded Doreen. 'There's nothing wrong with your heart, is there?'

'It isn't that; though, of course, my legs aren't what they were. And what with all this standing in queues, I don't feel I could face all those stairs every time I went out. But I should be too far away from people.'

'Which people?'

'The people in the street.'

Doreen stared. 'But you – don't know them.'

'They're company for me just the same. And I feel as if I know some of them. The same people come up and down several times a week and I get to know them by sight, and I make up stories about them – sometimes I think they're in love and . . .'

'Aunt Janet!' Doreen sounded appalled. 'You must be out of your mind.'

'Certainly not.' The old lady coloured. 'It's very solitary for me sitting here all day. I don't get out much in bad weather, and I can't read a great deal. These people really make up my life.'

'I hope you don't talk like that to everyone,' observed Doreen uneasily. 'They'll think you're quite odd, and you know there's always a waiting-list for these rooms. As a matter of fact,' she added heroically, 'if you're really so lonely I'll try and come a little oftener.'

But that wasn't a bit what Miss Martin wanted. Doreen came without warning as it was. She said a treat was doubly delightful if it was also a surprise, and there were days when Aunt Janet felt she really couldn't put the place in the apple-pie order she liked and Doreen apparently expected. And then without warning Doreen would come sweeping round the corner and dash straight in, and all the dust poor Miss Martin had swept so cunningly under the rug would come snaking out, and the ornaments her fluttering duster had overlooked all seemed to become more prominent. Doreen wasn't the only one who was afraid of Miss Fraser suggesting a change. Miss Martin never had the possibility out of her mind.

Of course it was a big room; the ground floor rooms were the largest in the house. Miss Martin had to have a big room because of her furniture, which had come from her mother's house. It was the sort of furniture that needs a great deal of dusting and polishing, and for sentiment's sake she had kept a number of ornaments and photographs in silver frames (that needed cleaning) and bits of silver and knick-knacks, because it made the place seem homelike. The trim Doreen fidgeted to see so much rubbish, but Agatha Turner, her partner, would console her by saying, 'Well, the old soul has nothing to do the livelong day, my dear. Let her keep the place clean. It'll stop her from brooding.'

After that, however, Doreen was careful not to seem to notice any neglect, and Miss Martin did her best to seem particularly healthy when her niece appeared. So for a little while they threw dust in each other's eyes and buried their fears. But not very deep under the surface.

CHAPTER 2

Most of all, when she sat at the window, Miss Martin liked to watch the children. Most of them were inclined to be hooligans, and belonged to the various housekeepers who lived in the basements all along the Square; but sometimes what Miss Martin called nice children went by, or babies in prams. When she was young the old lady had thought she might marry and have a baby, but there had only been herself and Florence and their mother – her brother, who was older than either of them, had married quite young and cut himself off from his family – and Florence was more robust, more pushing altogether, and was altogether resolved to get a husband. Mrs. Martin wanted one of her girls to marry and the other to stay at home and look after her. She constantly reminded them of all she had undergone in bringing them into the world, and said it wasn't surely too much for a mother to expect a little gratitude later on. Florence and her mother had been so anxious to get Florence a husband that any personable man who might have been interested was frightened away; and Florence didn't marry till she was over thirty, when she took a childless widower a good deal older than herself. After that, Mrs. Martin gave up all attempts at entertaining – and became a comfortable invalid, with Janet to fetch and carry for her. She had been quite an old lady when she died, and Janet had been more than middle-aged, and by that time her sister was also a widow with this one daughter, and not very amusing to visit, because in a way it was like being with her mother all over again. And Janet grew older and more feeble; and the war came, and her income was worth less and less, and for the past two years she had been at Blakesley House, having come when London wasn't so popular on account of bombs as it became afterwards. And she feared more than anything losing her big room and her vantage-point at the window.

One day, when she sat as usual watching the street, she saw a perfectly charming sight. A little girl in a red coat and a red tam-o'-shanter, with long dark plaits hanging to her waist, went by, accompanied by a nurse or governess – now that it was 'low' to wear any but a Service uniform you couldn't really tell – with an Aberdeen puppy in plaid braces racing on ahead. The little girl looked six or seven years old, and wore a solemn air. But she had such distinction, carried herself so beautifully and moved with such grace, that the word 'royal' flashed instantly into Miss Martin's mind. As they passed the window the child looked up and saw the old lady sitting there, and on an impulse Miss Martin waved her hand. There was a momentary pause, and then the little girl lifted her hand and sketched a kind of salute before hurrying on after her companion. From that day Miss Martin counted it a lost day if she didn't see the child. On the mornings that they exchanged their queer little silent gesture of friendship she put a red ring round the calendar of noble thoughts that Doreen had sent from the shop last Christmas, a month to a page. And as the weeks went on, Miss Martin was consumed by a desire somehow to meet and speak to the little girl. The other passers-by lost all interest for her. She tried to time her little expeditions to the shops so that she might meet the couple and the delightful dog in the street.

After a while it struck her that the little girl's companion changed with suspicious frequency. No sooner had Miss Martin got accustomed to one face than it vanished and, another – all, she noticed, painfully middle-aged – took its place. She puzzled for a long time about this. Clearly there was something wrong if no one would stay with so delightful a child for any length of time. That was her first inkling that there might be something mysterious about the affair.

She never spoke about the little girl to Doreen on her periodical visits; and once, when the couple passed the house and the child looked up as usual, Miss Martin had to pretend to be smoothing her hair, and only gave the most half-hearted wave in response. She hoped that they would understand, though how they could she couldn't imagine. Luckily, Doreen was, as usual, full of her own affairs and noticed nothing. It was about a week later that the miracle occurred. The little girl actually came into Miss Martin's room. It so happened that the housekeeper had a pet cat, a very beautiful if very wanton silver Persian. She was always talking about its value and its charm, and certainly she considered it a great deal more than she considered her old ladies. On this particular day it had escaped her vigilance, and was standing in an insolent attitude on the top step. This was naturally too much for the little dog. He came flying up the six steps in pursuit, and his paws sprawled all ways at once on the polished linoleum of the hall. The little girl paused in dismay, then started to follow him. But Miss Martin was quicker still. In an instant she had flashed open her door and had enticed the little dog inside with the aid of a biscuit. Biscuits were on points, and Doreen would have been shocked at this extravagance. In danced the little dog, all growls and excitement, saw the biscuit, decided to let the matter of the cat stand over for an instant, and at the same moment Miss Martin heard a voice say, 'You'd better go in and ask for him, Pamela. You know we ought to have him on a lead.'

'It's no fun for Roy on a lead,' said the little girl fiercely; but she walked up the steps and knocked politely on Miss Martin's door.

'You've come for your puppy,' said Miss Martin, all smiles and pleasure. 'He's in here. Miss Fraser is so fussy about her cat.' She spoke in the scornful tone of all dog-lovers who can't imagine what people see in cats. 'He's just having his elevenses.'

The little girl ran in. 'Oh, dear,' she said, 'he's making crumbs on the carpet! But he'll clear them all up. Hoover, Roy.'

The little dog obligingly licked up the remains of his biscuit. 'Won't you have one?' offered Miss Martin.

'Are you *sure* you can spare it?'

'Of course. What about your – is it your governess?'

'Oh, Terry! She's outside. Shall I call her?'

'Yes.' Terry – her full name was Teresa Lawrence – came in. Miss Martin saw that she was quite young and very pretty.

She could hardly believe it. The last one had been very angular and plain.

'I'm so sorry,' she began. 'We both are, aren't we, Pamela?'

'I'm not,' said the little girl, looking round her with fascinated eyes. 'Terry, isn't it a *beautiful* room?'

Miss Martin's heart nearly melted with delight. 'I like it,' she acknowledged, remembering how Doreen had tried to take it away from her. It had a homelike atmosphere, because of the photographs and the ornaments and the big solid furniture that had seen two generations grow up and disperse. The puppy had found a chair with fringes on it, and was making little rushes, barking and growling.

'Roy!' said the little girl warningly.

Roy lay on his back like a cat and experimented with the curly fringe.

'What an upset for you!' exclaimed Terry. 'Like being overrun. Pamela, you'd better put on his lead. We don't want any trouble.'

Miss Martin's face wore such a comical air that the girl noticed it. 'Have I said something wrong?' she asked.

'I was thinking – that's what my niece, Doreen, always says.'

'It's what Mrs Barnes says,' added the little girl.

'We're trespassers really,' added Terry.

'Not at all. You came in because I asked you. As a matter of fact, that's something I've been wanting to do for a long time. I feel, anyhow, we're not quite strangers.'

'Of course we're not,' said Terry. 'Pamela and I always come this way if we can.'

'Because we don't know many people,' explained Pamela.

'But that's all wrong. You ought to have a great many friends.' Miss Martin caught sight of a look on Terry's face and stopped. So there was a mystery – a tragedy perhaps – about the child. She went on quickly, 'Do you think one day you could both come and have tea with me? And Roy, of course.'

'We'll ask Guardy,' said Pamela before her governess could speak. 'I'm sure he'll say Yes.' From which Miss Martin deduced that someone else – probably the unspecified Mrs. Barnes – would probably say No.

'We should love to come,' Terry added. 'We live at Swan

House, that big house on the corner of the Square. You know, I've always thought when I'd got a home of my own I'd put out every single thing I possessed. Why on earth should one hide all one's bits and pieces just because they give a little trouble? I mean – why bother to be born if you're going to let a bit of trouble daunt you?'

She was years younger than Doreen, and might be expected to consider Janet Martin a relic from the neolithic age; but she talked to her as one woman to another, not dismissingly or charitably as the young so often talked to the old, but with just that shade of deference that is so appreciated once your seventieth birthday is a thing of the past.

'Then I shall look forward to seeing you,' said Miss Martin. It occurred to her that Mrs. Barnes and Doreen probably came out of the same drawer. Doreen would be shocked at the idea of asking some people to tea when you knew nothing of them beyond their appearance, and, like so many plain down-right women, she suspected charm, and she couldn't believe that any one could make an effort for no more reward than the pleasure it gave.

'Mr. Scott's an invalid,' Terry explained as they prepared to go. 'It's bound to make things rather dull for Pamela.'

'And Mrs. Barnes? Has she no children?'

'One son. But he's grown up, and if he wasn't . . .' She shook her pretty head decidedly. 'In six days God made Heaven and Earth, for a background for Mrs. Barnes and Oliver.'

'At least,' said Miss Martin, 'I'm glad she has you.'

'If I hadn't had an operation I suppose I would still be in the Services. But I've got six months certain and I might get it extended. Anyway, I hope so. They say I'm only fit for light work at the moment.'

'Am I light work?' demanded Pamela.

'You're no work at all.' And then she caught sight of the old French clock on the mantelpiece, with its pictured ladies in hoops and coiffures on its painted face and said, 'I shan't even have that job long if we don't go now.'

'I shan't say good-bye,' asserted Miss Martin; 'I shall only say *au revoir*.' She hurriedly gave Roy another biscuit and pushed one into the little girl's hand, and Pamela gave her a kiss of her own accord, and the three ran out of the house, and Miss Martin stood at the window smiling to see them, and then sighing because they seemed to have taken life with them, and reminded her of the hopes she had cherished once and that had never come to anything.

Another three weeks pased, and though Pamela and Terry often came by the window and stopped to wave, they never came in again, and Miss Martin didn't ask them until Doreen had paid her periodical visit, because it would be absolutely typical of Miss Blake to turn up the one day her aunt had a tea-party. But at last Doreen came, bringing with her some back numbers of *Woman's Own* and a really good chocolate cake with a cream filling. As a rule the cakes she brought were as plain as herself, but, as she was careful to explain, she and Agatha had given a little party the day before, and some of the guests hadn't arrived, so they had a whole cake left over.

'So you see,' she said, beaming and showing square white teeth, 'our bad fortune is your good.'

Miss Martin wondered how it was she had never noticed before that when Doreen smiled she looked exactly like the milkman's horse. However, now she could forget about Doreen and send her invitation to Pamela and the girl Terry. It occurred to her that she didn't know Pamela's other name. Guardy was Mr. Scott, but that didn't mean that Pamela was Miss Scott. On the whole it seemed better to send the invitation to Miss Lawrence. When she had written it she walked round to Swan House, where they lived, and dropped it through the letter-box. Swan House, so called because of two huge stone swans supporting a regency portico, was a big, old-fashioned affair that had been badly hit in the blitz and hurriedly patched up. The front, however, looked comfortable, even luxurious, and as she stood on the well-kept steps to push her letter through the well-polished brass letter-flap, Miss Marin could see the basement kitchen, with a fire burning, and a cook in a striped print dress and an apron, bustling about, and hear her calling to someone, presumably another servant.

'They must be very comfortably off,' thought Miss Martin. But then Pamela hadn't in the least the appearance of a neglected or poverty-stricken child. Her clothes, her puppy – clearly a pedigree beast – her governess, her whole air and manner, spoke of money, without being ostentatious. One day, thought Miss Martin, walking away from the house towards Beverley Gardens, they may ask me there – that is, if they accept my invitation. As she paused at the corner, looking anxiously right and left for oncoming traffic, a little dark-blue car came hurrying competently along the high road and turned sharply to stop opposite Swan House. It bore a number: ABC 1234. A very easy number to remember, reflected Miss Martin, and thought perhaps it was the doctor.

But if so, it was a lady doctor, and somehow Mr. Scott hadn't sounded that sort of man.

The invitation was accepted the next day, but only Pamela could come.

'You won't mind, will you?' pleaded Terry. 'But – someone I know, someone special – has embarkation leave – going out to the Far East, I'm afraid – and it seems such a wonderful chance. . . .'

Mrs. Martin, glad to know that there was 'someone' in the life of such a charming girl, said she was sorry, of course, for herself, but delighted for Terry, and she and Pamela would manage, with Roy's help, and she spent a happy morning rummaging out her nice tablecloth with the real lace trimming, and arranging a piece of plate-glass and a little wooden shepherd and some lambs and most realistic-looking May-blossom into the most fetching table decoration for Pamela's delight. And she spread the whole week's butter ration on the curly French loaf that was her sole extravagance, though Doreen was always urging her to try Procea instead, and spent all the points she had left on biscuits, and thought how wonderful it was that it should be Pamela and not Doreen who was coming to tea.

Pamela chattered away very happily, not at all shy, and Miss Martin gleaned a good deal of information about her. She was an only child; both her parents were dead. She used to live in the country till Guardy came down from London, where he had been hurt by a bomb. When he went back he asked her if she would like to come, too, and she had said she would. He was badly hurt – would never walk again. She didn't go to school, though Terry said she should some day, and had always had governesses. Until Terry came they had been quite old, but Terry was a companion and friend as well as a teacher, and both she and Guardy hoped she was going to stay.

In return Miss Martin told her about her childhood, about her sister Florence, and her mother, and a great tawny cat they had had called Marcus Aurelius. And she got down all the little bronze animals from the mantelpiece, the two foxes under a green umbrella, the mouse dressed like a housekeeper, the frog butler and the hedgehog in her spotted apron, carrying a minute dust-pan and brush. The afternoon flew for them both and it seemed no time before Terry came back to pick up her charge.

'Oh, it can't be time yet!' protested Miss Martin. 'Besides, haven't you a nice piece you could say for me?'

When she was a little girl, children had always stood up to recite in the drawing-room – 'The Wreck of the Hesperus' or – 'Beth-Gelert,' always something sad. And it seemed as though the tradition persisted, for when Pamela said obligingly that of course she would, she produced a little poem one of the elderly governesses must have taught her, called 'Little Boy Blue' –

> The little toy dog is covered with dust,
> But sturdy and staunch he stands,
> The little toy soldier is red with rust
> And his musket moulds in his hands.

Afterwards it seemed to Miss Martin that everything that happened that afternoon and on the subsequent afternoon when she paid her long-anticipated visit to Swan House was part of some mysterious jig-saw puzzle, with the most odd-shaped pieces fitting into the pattern. Nothing, not even the heartrending little recitation, was left out.

That night, shaking the crumbs off the cloth, putting away the scrap of cake they hadn't eaten, replacing the bronze animals, Miss Martin pictured the future, that hitherto had seemed no more than a slow, spiritless procession to the tomb. She would vist Pamela and Pamela would visit her, and perhaps in the fine weather they could all meet in Kensington Gardens and have tea under one of the big striped umbrellas. . . . She got out her writing-case and wrote Doreen a delightful letter, saying how much she'd enjoyed the cake and how kind it was of her to leave it, but never mentioning Pamela or Terry Lawrence. . . . And even that, it turned out, was going to prove important in times to come.

And in spite of all her anticipations, that was the last time that Pamela was to visit Blakesley House.

CHAPTER 3

Miss Martin's sole visit to the Swan House took place about three weeks later. She had gone into a stationer's shop to buy a packet of envelopes, in defiance of Doreen's consternation at the idea of an old lady with such limited means they were practically invisible, wasting money on new envelopes. She even sent her a packet of ragged envelopes of her own, and told her that for sixpence she could buy enough labels to cover them all. But Miss Martin threw the envelopes into the salvage sack and went on buying envelopes. Everyone, she said, had to draw the line somewhere. She was an old lady and couldn't accustom herself to every new trick, and patching up old envelopes was her limit. Pamela had come in to buy a birthday card for Terry, who was going to be twenty-two the following week.

'We're going to have a party,' said Pamela importantly, 'and you're to come. Guardy said we might ask someone, so we're going to ask you.'

'But – wouldn't you like to ask someone young?' exclaimed Miss Martin.

'We don't know any one young, not any one we'd like to ask,' Pamela assured her. 'Terry's going to send you a note. And it'll be someone new for Guardy. Mrs. Barnes,' she added, 'has to go to a wedding that day. Isn't it lucky?'

Miss Martin was touched almost to tears. It was years since she had been asked to a party. It took her nearly twenty-four hours to get ready. She washed her nice grey hair – she had never been to a hairdresser in her life – and she got out her best lace blouse and a black skirt, and the good old-fashioned black coat with its squirrel collar that she kept for best – for she had grown up in an era when ladies wore one set of clothes on week-days and another on Sundays – and her last pair of real skin gloves, and her glacé kid shoes, and looking like a reminder of a gentler and more gracious world, she walked slowly round to Swan House at four o' clock. She wished she knew a little more about the household, but she supposed it didn't matter really. She knew that Pamela's name was Smith, while the old gentleman was called Scott, so it seemed improbable that they were related, but perhaps something would emerge during the afternoon. Not, she reminded herself, that it was any business of hers. That's what you think, Sugar, Crook would have said; what, in fact, he did say later on. Pamela wore a scarlet frock and Terry a blue one. Roy had a plaid bow attached to his braces. Miss Martin felt she must look very sober in such a gathering, but Pamela said, 'You look simply beautiful. Doesn't she, Terry?' and that encouraged her to bring out the little present she had chosen from her own little store of treasures. It was a minute silver match-box, and both Terry and Pamela were enchanted by it.

'It opens, you see,' explained Miss Martin, pink with pleasure. 'Of course, it's too small for a match, but they tell me you could put two aspirins in; though I'm sure, my dear, you don't ever need any such things.'

Terry was enchanted. She said she had never seen anything so pretty, and she would wear it as a charm on her bracelet.

'Then it will be with me night and day,' she explained. 'It'll be like that stone in the Bible – Mizpah, or Rizpah, I never can remember which.'

Miss Martin's eyes filled with pleasure, though she winked away the tears quickly, ashamed of her weakness.

'What a charming thought! And it will be such a pleasure for me to think of your having it.'

'And if ever I'm in deadly peril,' continued Terry with mock gravity, 'I shall post it to you, and you'll recognise it as a *cri de cœur*, and you'll come and rescue me from the devil's den.'

And they all laughed.

The tea-table at Swan House made Miss Martin blink. There was an iced cake and hot buttered toast and sandwiches, and home-made scones and jam, and silver baskets of sweets. She hadn't seen anything like it since the war. She didn't suppose Doreen had either.

It was easy to see that Terry was popular here, but really, how could one help liking such an attractive girl?

'Mrs. Hubble – isn't it a delicious name? – has been keeping sugar and margarine and fruit simply for weeks,' Pamela told her. 'And then we thought, suppose that was one of the days *she* came . . .'

'She?' murmured Miss Martin.

'Mrs. Barnes. But we heard two or three days ago she couldn't come. Wasn't it luck?'

'Dear me,' said Janet Martin, 'she *does* sound like my niece Doreen.'

Mr. Scott came in then through a door opened by a male attendant, who immediately vanished. Miss Martin found herself being introduced. Her host was younger than she had anticipated, probably under sixty, though his physical disabilities might have added years to his age. From his face she realised that he had known much pain, and was probably never wholly free from it. He was still handsome – distinguished, rather – and his manner reminded her of the way men used to talk when she was a girl. Life was such a rush now; hardly any one seemed to have time for good manners any more. They pushed in shops and buses and on pavements till going out became quite a dangerous adventure. He shook hands, and said he was very glad she had been able to come; he liked to welcome Pamela's friends; and then they sat down to the wonderful tea, and the conversation, instead of dragging, as Miss Martin had secretly feared, sparkled and raced, though they were all so ill-assorted as regards age and all their backgrounds were so different. You only had to see the inside of the house to realise that Scott was a comparatively rich man. Even after six years of war you could tell. Pamela was completely at home. It made Miss Martin smile to see the motherly way she looked after her guardian, making sure he had sugar and jam and didn't have to ask for anything. Mr. Scott sounded as interested in the visitor's life as Pamela had been, and asked if she had always lived in London, and his eyes twinkled when she spoke of Doreen.

'These worthy women!' he said. 'How they harass us!'

Then they talked about cathedral cities – Miss Martin had

lived in one until her mother died, and Mr. Scott had been an architect before the Luftwaffe put an end to his active career. Gradually their conversation moved backwards until they were exchanging recollections of a world as strange as a fairy-tale to Terry.

'I'm afraid this must be rather dull for you,' apologized Miss Martin, looking so eager and shining, Doreen would have been shocked.

'Oh, but it isn't!' disclaimed Terry eagerly. 'It's lovely to think that there was ever a leisurely world. I dare say things are going to be better for everybody now, but being safe and regimented does take the colour out of things.'

Miss Martin was the older, but Mr. Scott had got about more, so they had plenty to say to one another. Presently Mr. Scott said something about his wife, so at least he had been married. But he didn't elaborate that theme, and Miss Martin was left wondering where on earth Pamela came in. She knew curiosity was vulgar, but at the same time it was perplexing. Altogether it was a very nice party, because Mr. Scott belonged to the days when hosts admitted their responsibilities, and he treated all three of them like guests, drawing out Terry to talk about her childhood and Pamela of what she had been doing that day. But nobody spoke of Pamela's past. It wasn't till a long time afterwards that Miss Martin understood why.

It was incredible how quickly the hands of the clock pointed to half-past five. Mr. Scott said he had to go down and attend to some correspondence, and the man-servant appeared as if by magic and wheeled the chair away.

'I hope you'll come again,' he said. 'We don't have many parties here. Dr. Macintosh is afraid if I have too much gaiety I shall put my heart out of action, but I feel he'd make an exception for you.' He said if she wouldn't mind calling in at the library on her way out he'd see if he could find a book they had been discussing. After he had gone, the old lady wondered how she could ever have complained about the dullness of her own life, when you realised how much tragedy there was in the world. Doreen, she supposed, would class him with the Idle Mouths, though even Doreen admitted that idle people with incomes had more right to live than those with little more than the statutory old-age pension.

After tea Pamela dragged them upstairs to her schoolroom, a delightful place, with pictures and bookcases the right height for a seven-year-old, and chairs that were comfortable instead of the hard-seated furniture Miss Martin could remember. She wondered about her more than ever, and when it occurred to the little girl that Roy might like a run in the garden and she disappeared with him, Miss Martin said 'Boo' to curiosity, and as soon as the door was shut she turned to her companion to say, 'How very sad for Mr. Scott to be such an invalid. And what a charming person he is!'

'It was an appalling tragedy,' said Terry soberly. 'He had one son, to whom he was devoted – there had been a daughter once but she died ages ago. I don't know if that was when Mrs. Scott died, because he never talks about it, it was Mrs. Barnes who told me . . . Well, this son was in the Army and he came home on leave – he wasn't married – and he came here. He had been urging his father to leave London because of the bombs, and Mr. Scott said he supposed that he went back to the base when the front-line fire started, and that closed the subject. And then, when John Scott was home on leave, there was a particularly heavy raid in this neighbourhood – you probably remember it – and a high explosive or a land-mine or something came down at the back of the house about one o'clock in the morning. John was killed outright, and Mr. Scott was buried under wreckage for thirty-six hours, and when at last they dug him out he was so badly injured they didn't think at first he could live. And there are times,' added Terry sadly, 'when I think he wishes he hadn't.'

'He doesn't seem the kind of man to be sorry for himself,' suggested Miss Martin gently.

'No. But he has so little; his wife and children all gone and he such a physical wreck – his heart's very bad – and there have been other consequences. He can't stand the dark for one thing – that was because he was buried in the cellar all that time – and I always think he brought Pamela back with him from the country because he couldn't stand the loneliness, which is only another sort of dark if you come to think of it.'

'Oh, my dear,' exclaimed Miss Martin, 'you're much too young to know that!'

'A lot of us learnt a good deal while we were young in the

war,' returned Terry soberly. 'Anyway, it's easy to see he's devoted to her. Apparently when he was sent to the country he went to stay with the people who had Pamela, and they had to make different arrangements – she was boarded out there, and perhaps her parents had been killed in a blitz; he doesn't talk a great deal about it. Anyway, when he came back he brought her with him. He said bombs didn't strike the same house twice, and an invalid must be in his own home. And I must say she seems happy enough. Only, of course, she ought to have friends of her own age.'

'Perhaps when she's a little older she'll go to school.'

'Yes. In the ordinary way there would be children here for her to know, but Mr. Scott's sister has just one son, and she a widow, and he was much too valuable to be allowed to risk his life in the Army. He's got some wonderful hush-hush government job, and he's much too busy ever to come down and see his uncle. And anyway, his mother doesn't think he ought to risk his valuable life. Oh, I know there aren't any more bombs, but there might be a train accident! It's sickening the way she talks about him.'

'I suppose if he's all she's got,' murmured Miss Martin, remembering the one about the greatest of these being charity.

'She's simply playing for Mr. Scott's money,' announced Terry in the deplorably outspoken way of her generation. 'But she needn't worry, because a good deal of it's going to Pamela.'

'Did he tell you?'

'He asked me if I would keep an eye on her, be a friend to her, after he was gone. He said he felt responsible for her because he had known her parents, and she would need someone. Then he said, "I'm afraid my sister wouldn't quite fit the bill. She doesn't understand children very well." Miss Martin, I can't bear to think of what might happen to Pamela if she were left to Mrs. Barnes' mercy. I don't mean she'd do her actual bodily harm, but – if you were to see her you'd understand. She's absolutely ruthless. Of course, she doesn't really approve of me being here. She doesn't like anyone staying very long. She's afraid of anybody getting an influence over Mr. Scott. It must be terrible to let money matter so much to you.'

But Miss Martin said nothing. The young and strong might

think money unimportant, but nobody really appreciated money until they were old and hadn't got enough. Still, she couldn't help feeling glad that Terry was there, so confident and gay, to protect the little girl's interests.

'And anyway,' Terry continued, 'look at all the things money won't buy. It can't bring back Mr. Scott's wife or children; it can't give him his health. I sometimes think Pamela is the one piece of happiness left to him. Of course, I said I'd always be glad to do anything I could, and he said in that slightly stiff way of his when he feels very strongly about things, "I'm not, of course, referring to material matters. Pamela will be all right so far as that goes, but there are more important things than money." I suppose,' added Terry. 'She'll be a ward in chancery or something. Do you understand all those things?'

'No,' confessed Miss Martin, 'but I expect he'll make it all shipshape.'

'Let's hope so,' the girl agreed. And then Pamela came running back accompanied by Roy, who was jumping ecstatically for a stick she held above his head. Then Miss Martin looked at the enamelled watch set with tiny brilliants that had belonged to her mother, and said she really must go or she'd outstay her welcome. But Terry and Pamela must come and see her again soon. On the way down she remembered what Mr. Scott had said, and she got Terry to knock on the library door, and Mr. Scott said, 'Oh, yes, do come in! I've got the book,' and he picked it off the table and gave it to her. Then, just as she was going, he went on, 'I wonder if you would be very kind and witness this for me. It's not easy for me to get members of my own household because they're implicated. I can get my doctor for one signature next time he comes if you wouldn't mind being the other.' Miss Martin said, 'Yes, of course,' and he added, 'It's my will. I always think it's a good thing to get these matters settled.'

Miss Martin wrote her neat-pointed signature and gave back the pen, and thought what a good fine signature Mr. Scott had. Then she thanked him again for the book, and said what a delightful afternoon it had been. And he said, 'You must come again soon and we'll discuss it,' meaning the book, of course, and Miss Martin went out with such a warm feeling as she hadn't known for years. It was like finding a new home quite close at hand.

But for all her hopes, that was the only time she ever went to Swan House.

It had not taken a war to teach old people with microscopic incomes the policy of make-do and mend. They knew it long before. And one of the disadvantages of being poor and old is that you have to go on wearing much the same clothes all the year round, the chief difference being that in winter you wear all you've got, and in the summer you shed some of them. For a long time Miss Martin had longed for a really warm coat, and had even envied the animals which could grow their own fur; but in the circumstances all she could do was to put on what she called an additional spencer and button up her autumn-cum-spring coat and hope for the best. But one day in November, when the wind was more than usually cutting, and she had had to wait longer than usual in the fish queue, she came home shivering, and even though she recklessly put two shillings into the gas meter it was no use. The next day she had a streaming cold, though, knowing that colds were looked on with disfavour by Miss Fraser, she tried to ignore hers, and went out as usual. The next day she couldn't even go out, and the day after she got as far as the hall and collapsed. By this time she was so ill she hardly cared what Miss Fraser thought. Miss Fraser sent for a doctor and wrote to Doreen Blake. This, she knew, was the beginning of the end. The doctor said it was pleurisy and she must go into a nursing-home. But Miss Fraser knew better than to enter into commitments on behalf of relatives who couldn't be pinned down by law to refund expenses, and so she said the nursing-homes were all packed, but managed to get Miss Martin a bed at St. Joachim's Women's Ward, and an ambulance came and carried Miss Martin away, still too bad to understand what all this meant, and Miss Fraser began a letter to the first name on the waiting-list, saying that she would shortly have a very pleasant ground-floor room to let, unfurnished.

'Here's a pretty kettle of fish,' announced Doreen when the housekeeper's letter arrived. 'Aunt Janet's been taken ill and had to go to hospital, and Miss Fraser wants me to go up to London to talk things over.'

'These people have no consideration,' agreed Agatha Turner, who was a little older than her stable companion and very downright indeed. 'It's stocktaking, and we're simply run off our feet trying to make ends meet. And if your aunt's in a hospital, what further arrangements do they expect you to make?'

'It's what I've been expecting for some time,' said Doreen darkly. 'Miss Fraser wants Aunt Janet's room. She's afraid of her getting seriously ill.'

'Very selfish!' said Miss Turner. 'What does she think you can do about it?'

'She's going to ask me to make some other arrangement.'

'That's ridiculous. Everybody knows you can't get old people in anywhere nowadays.'

'I suppose,' said Doreen slowly, 'she's thinking of our spare room.'

'Nonsense!' said the crisp Miss Turner. 'Alice Field is coming next week, and goodness knows how long she'll stay.'

'Is she? I didn't know.'

'Nor did I – till this minute. But you know she'll come like a bird if we ask her to.'

'Do you want her to?'

'No. But it's her or your Aunt Janet. And Alice is a wizard cook. Besides, once you get saddled with relatives you never get rid of them.'

Doreen saw the wisdom of that, and the invitation to Miss Field was sent without delay. Miss Blake went up to town and found that she was right in her suppositions – she always was. Miss Fraser met her with a point-blank request to find other quarters for her aunt.

'I've realised for some time that she really isn't capable of looking after herself any more,' said Miss Fraser. 'It's wonderful, really, that she's managed for so long when you think how frail she is.'

'She has an excellent heart,' said Doreen. 'As for physique, that's just a matter of chance. Some people are thin and some are not – by nature.' She herself was not.

'Still, she's a very old lady, Miss Blake.'

'Seventy-four. That's no age at all.' Doreen was a healthy thirty-nine. 'I must say, Miss Fraser, I think you're taking too serious a view of all this. I'll try and arrange for a week or two's convalescence . . .'

But it was no use. Miss Fraser could be as adamant as Doreen. It was part of her duty to keep her weather eye open for weaklings, and by hook or by crook get them out of the house before the end. Her employers intensely disliked tenants dying on the premises.

Miss Blake then scurried hither and thither in a search for some place where she could dump the hapless Miss Martin, and eventually she arranged for her to become an inmate at Beverley, advertised as a Rest-Home for old ladies requiring light attention and care. What this worked out at, in fact, was that the majority were slightly cracked; but to the hearty Miss Blake all old ladies were eccentric, and that wasn't likely to trouble her aunt. In any case, beggars can't be choosers.

Of course, the old lady would not have as much privacy as she was accustomed to, but there would be compensations. Her food would be brought and cooked for her, there would be company, there was a nice garden – something to look forward to in the spring – and the neighbourhood was pleasantly rural. Doctors were easy to come by, and there would be no question of transporting the furniture, because personal belongings of more than a portable type were discouraged.

'There is a wireless in the common room,' she told the shrinking old lady, with a false heartiness as direct as a robot bomb. 'And they have various papers and magazines.'

At first Miss Martin could not take it in. She thought it was only for a short convalescence, and she assured her niece earnestly that she really did not need to go away. She would recuperate far better in familiar surroundings. When she understood the position, she was so disheartened she almost had a relapse and died, and when she recovered she was so unreasonable that Doreen didn't think it very wicked to wish she had.

'But – what is to happen to my things?' she inquired piteously. 'You know I can't possibly afford to pay storage, and once I lose this room it may be months before I get another, and then it won't be so conveniently situated.'

'There's no question of your storing your things,' explained Doreen in patient tones. 'I will take some of the smaller stuff – we might be able to sell some of the ornaments; but the big things like the wardrobe and the wash-hand-stand and those out-of-date-chairs – well, in these days you can get a price for anything. You needn't worry about that part of it – I'll see to that.'

It was then that Miss Martin realised she was going to be parted from everything that spelt home to her and thrust into this strange house until she died there. She would never be able to get out, and if she did find another room she would have no furniture. She was going to be delivered over to the Matron body and soul, and she would be as safely shut away from Doreen as if she were in prison.

'Now that is an absurd way to talk,' expostulated Doreen when she tried to explain. 'And if you say that kind of thing when you get to Elsham, I'm afraid Matron won't allow you to stay. She particularly told me that they don't permit any depressive talk or any one with a melancholy outlook. It affects the others. Naturally, I assured her she needn't be afraid of anything of that sort where you were concerned.'

After Doreen had gone, Miss Martin lay back in bed and considered the future. So far as she could visualise it, there was nothing to look forward to but death. And surely in such surroundings death would not be long delayed.

But she had no notion of the excitements that lay between her and the grave.

Doreen had decided that she had better go straight from the hospital to Beverley, and she gave up a day to pack Miss Martin's knick-knacks; and, of course, she persisted in taking far too many. Old people are like that – sentimental and unreasonable; and she saw to the medical certificate that allowed them to hire a car for the whole journey – and that, as well as the cost of the ambulance to the hospital, came out of Doreen's pocket – and she drove the old lady down and handed her over to Matron. On the way she broke it to her that she wouldn't have a room to herself, and when she heard that, Miss Martin tried to climb out of the car.

'I can put up with a great deal,' she whispered, 'but not that – no, Doreen, not that. I'm sure if we wait a little we can find something . . . After all, it's not as if I were helpless.'

'In these days of housing shortage I was very lucky to find a place where you only have to have one other person in with you,' her niece assured her. 'Most of these homes have dormitories. As for anywhere else, the only alternative would be the infirmary, and I'm sure you wouldn't like that.'

'If I came to you for a little while, while I looked round – ' began Miss Martin.

But Doreen said in her firmest voice, 'I'm afraid that's out of the question. We have someone staying with us who may remain permanently. She is most useful . . .'

Miss Martin didn't plead any more. Naturally, nobody who wasn't useful to Doreen would be tolerated. All the same, she watched her niece with a puzzled, incredulous expression. Perhaps, she thought, it was unreasonable to expect any one who was young and strong, and could earn her own living, to appreciate the sense of helplessness, amounting to panic, that overwhelmed those no longer able to arrange their own lives. She felt as though hers had been taken away from her, and now belonged to Doreen and Matron and anyone else who might be in authority over her at Beverley, which was the name of the Home.

The house itself was a pleasant surprise, and so was Matron, both being far more human than she had anticipated. Matron really liked old people, though it was her experience that all those who came her way were slightly peculiar; but she didn't mind looking after them when they were ill, and the fact that they were a little odd made things easier from her point of view. Miss Blake had told her that her aunt was perfectly balanced but simply couldn't go on doing all her own work. But as the relations always said that, even when, as had once happened, she had been landed with a raving lunatic, Miss Webster didn't pay much attention to her. Still, it was pleasant to see such a neat old lady, obviously a gentlewoman, it seemed improbable she would cause trouble. And how was Matron to know that this same neat, unimpressive old soul was going to drag them all into the limelight before many months were past?

There was, as Doreen had said, a pleasant garden with a smooth lawn; there was a veranda where the old ladies sat out in summer; and a big parlour with a coal fire where they congregated in winter. The bedrooms were small and there was not much accommodation for one's clothes, but, as Doreen said cheerfully, Miss Martin hadn't got many, and, of course, she wouldn't think of getting any more.

Miss Martin remembered an old woman she used to visit in Winchester who, asked whether she was 'all right' for underwear, had replied haughtily, 'I can manage very well, I'm sure. I bind up me bosom with rags.'

Doreen accepted an invitation to remain to lunch, and afterwards Miss Martin took her knitting and sat with a number of desiccated old ladies in the parlour. At tea (but Doreen had gone by then) she met her room-mate, a distinctly eccentric old lady, who enlivened the nights by suddenly starting up and crying that they must get ready, for the day of the Lord was at hand, and asking Miss Martin if she too could not see signs and portents in the sky. Or she would steal out of bed, a gaunt figure with a bitsy shawl hung round her shoulders, and catch furtively at Miss Martin's sheets with skinny hands, while she hissed in a mysterious voice, 'I know that my Redeemer liveth.' Miss Martin in desperation asked Matron if she could sleep elsewhere. She was afraid of Mrs. Mount. But Matron said with determined cheerfulness, 'Oh, you mustn't mind her! She's quite harmless. It's only that she's lonely.'

And when she timidly spoke of her fears to Doreen she was met with a sharp, 'Everybody has some little idiosyncrasy, especially as they get older. I had hoped you were going to settle here.'

Miss Martin opened her mouth to protest, then remembered the infirmary and changed the subject. She knew now she was caught and she would never get away.

CHAPTER 4

At first Matron was agreeably surprised in Miss Martin. She hadn't believed Doreen when the latter assured her that there was nothing odd about her aunt. But as the days passed into weeks, Miss Webster began to think that for once she had been unduly suspicious. Of course there was the incident of Mrs. Mount; but Miss Martin seemed to accept the official decision without demur, and she didn't make a fuss about her food as most of them did, and she didn't have contrary fits or write herself letters or quarrel violently with the other occupants. She behaved as she had been brought up to believe a gentlewoman did – and yet in the end she brought more trouble to the Home than all the others put together.

One day, just before midday dinner, she went up to her room to fetch a clean handkerchief, and once there, happy for a moment in her solitude, she crossed to the window and looked out. She was remembering the days that were past, the years of her girlhood, when she had belived that something wonderful must happen some day – the long grey years of acceptance when she had looked after her mother, and the still quiet but happy years of her own independence. She remembered how glad she had been to come in from the outside to sit before her own fire; how secure she had felt. Even when she had had to give up a flat and a maid and come down gradually to a single combined room at Blakesley House she had still felt her life was her own. But now even her sense of liberty was gone. People could put constraints upon her. She must be careful, because she no longer belonged to herself. She was thinking along these lines when she saw the crocodile of little orphans from the local Home turn the corner and come walking down the street. They wore a very plain, sensible uniform that didn't need a lot of laundering, and they walked gravely – two and two. They were allowed to talk, and most of them were jabbering away nineteen to the dozen. But Miss Martin thought their existence was not so very different from her own, except that they still retained hope.

Suddenly her heart missed a beat. She leaned forward, horrified and incredulous. It must, of course, be a mistake. But it wasn't – it wasn't. She couldn't, she knew, be wrong over a thing so important. *The last little girl but two was the child, Pamela Smith, whom she had last seen walking with her governess and her Scotch puppy in Kensington!*

Her first impulse was to rush downstairs and into the street and cross over and speak to her, but she retained sufficient sense to curb it. No good would come of so rash an action. All the same, she was convinced there was something wrong. Pamela was the ward of a rich man – a man who had made provision for her in his will. Certainly Miss Martin had not read the will, but she had gleaned as much from Terry, and surely nothing could have happened in so short a time to make Mr. Scott change his mind. Mr. Scott would never have agreed to such an arrangement – of that she was convinced. So it followed that Mr. Scott must be dead. She remembered that he suffered from severe heart attacks and had not anticipated living any great length of time. But this orphanage was for destitute children, and how could such a description fit Pamela? Miss Martin remained so long upstairs, her handkerchief clutched in her hand, that Matron came to know what had happened.

'Why, Miss Martin! Wool-gathering?' she inquired, startling the old lady half out of her wits. 'Why, my dear, what's the matter? Are you not feeling well?'

Miss Martin stood up. 'I was watching the orphanage children,' she explained unsteadily. 'Miss Webster, that Home is for quite poor, unwanted children, isn't it?'

'Poor little things,' said Miss Webster. 'It's lucky for them that benevolent-minded people found such institutions. They'd never have a chance otherwise. As it is, at least they get some sort of start in life. But – didn't you hear the bell?'

'I – I don't really want any dinner.'

Miss Webster's tone insensibly took on a brisker note.

'Now come, Miss Martin, we can't have any of that. If you don't want any dinner, it means you're ill.'

Miss Martin turned quickly towards the door. 'Oh, no! Of course not. Only – there was a little girl there – she reminded me of someone I used to know in London, and I wondered . . .'

'I dare say most little girls look very much alike except to their mothers.' She smiled. She was inclined to be indulgent to her favourite.

'I suppose,' hazarded Miss Martin, 'there couldn't be any mistake. I mean . . .'

Matron's expression hardened. 'Now, you're not getting any fancies, I hope. Of course there couldn't. And your dinner's getting cold.'

Miss Martin perceived the danger signals, smiled and went downstairs. But all the same she knew there was something wrong. She had seen Pamela at home and the contrast between that cared-for child and the anonymous orphan walking soberly at the tail of a procession of social nobodies – as old Mrs. Martin would have described them – was incongruous. Oh, undoubtedly it was wrong, and something had got to be done about it!

After that the trouble began. Miss Martin kept wanting to go out on quite unsuitable days, when it was windy or rainy and she seemed to fret if she were kept indoors. Also she was perpetually going up to her room on the most trivial excuses. After all, there were plenty of chairs downstairs and free reading matter – the *Mirror* and the *Express* every day, and the *Pictorial* and the *Sunday Record* on Sundays. And sometimes people left out-of-date copies of *Picture Post* and *Everybody's* at the door. It wasn't natural to want to creep away and brood. Moreover, it presently came to Matron's ears that Miss Martin was asking all sorts of questions about the orphanage, and asking them of all kinds of people – in shops, the post office, of casual acquaintances picked up at church. When they stopped her going upstairs she used to wander up and down the garden in weather that was quite unsuited to an elderly lady who had nearly died of pleurisy, or she would linger by the gate, looking up and down the road as if she could conjure this ridiculous child out of the paving-stones.

Matron began to think she had been mistaken. Miss Blake's aunt was just the same as all the others – a nice old body, no doubt, but definitely queer.

The following week – the week after Matron had told Miss Martin she couldn't go running up and down to her room at all hours – Doreen came to visit her, and because the position was desperate and she had no other confidant, Miss Martin poured out her story.

'So you see, Doreen, we must do something,' she said. 'I know Mr. Scott never intended such a thing for Pamela and . . .' She stopped, aghast at the blank unsympathy of her niece's face.

'Aunt Janet, I really do think you've taken leave of your senses. What earthly concern is it of yours, even if something is wrong, which I don't for a moment admit? The child's no relation of yours, and anyway, what do you know of these people? It's a great mistake to pick up casual acquaintances.'

'It's you who don't understand,' said Miss Martin, a pink spot in either thin cheek. 'I'm sure we're on the track of a mystery . . .'

'I hope to goodness you're not going to be tiresome about this,' returned Doreen sharply. 'We don't want Matron to get upset, and it rests entirely with her how long you stay at Beverley.'

Miss Martin disliked Beverley so much she would not have minded leaving even under a cloud. But that would probably involve leaving Elsham altogether; and so long as Pamela remained in the orphanage she simply had to be in the locality. So she bottled up her indignation and her distress and played meek, and did not even complain when, in response to a suggestion from Matron, she had to drag one of the poor zanies from the home around with her. Matron thought old ladies were better in pairs – they exerted a restraining influence on one another. . . . Also she buttoned up her mouth about the orphanage. But perhaps she was getting slightly unbalanced, because she became convinced that Providence had allowed her to be dispossessed and tucked away in an old ladies' home with a lot of senile and crazy companions in order that she might right things for Pamela. Presently she found that, if she plumped for Mrs. Mount as a companion, the arrangement worked out excellently for them both, because Mrs. Mount never wanted to go anywhere except to the church, where she 'communed' gustily for as long as any one would permit. This gave Miss Martin an opportunity to haunt the road in front of the children's orphanage, hoping for another sight of Pamela. As the days passed she became bolder, lingering right in front of the orphanage and scanning the windows. Once a gate behind her opened sharply and a woman's voice said, 'Did you want something?' It was the wife of the doctor who attended the orphans, and to her own amazement Miss Martin heard herself rattle of a glib explanation improvised on the spur of the moment, something about a country childhood, and she asked the name of a flower growing in the doctor's wife's garden. The doctor's wife, a keen gardener, gave her a brief leture on every blossom in sight, not forgetting the grass, and Miss Martin listened intently, waiting for an opportunity to ask about the children in the house opposite.

'Oh, yes! Poor little things!' acknowledged the doctor's wife carelessly, her eye on some nameless bloom. 'I believe most of them have no position at all and no parents who care to own them.'

'I thought they were orphans,' ejaculated Miss Martin.

'A convenient description,' smiled the doctor's wife.

'And – what happens to them?'

'Oh, they're brought up to follow some useful trade – laundering or domestic work; an opportunity to earn an honest living later on. And in spite of their handicaps, I dare say some of them marry.'

While they were talking the orphans came out for their morning excursion, and Miss Martin said quickly, indicating Pamela, 'That one is rather striking.'

'Oh, some of these children are definitely pretty! Now and again one gets adopted. That one,' she added casually, 'is called Mary. She hasn't been here very long. They gave an entertainment a short time ago to raise money for some zenana mission, and that one recited quite nicely.'

'What did she recite?' Miss Martin held her breath.

'The usual pathetic thing about a dead child. I can't think why they always choose such mournful themes.'

'The Little Toy Dog Is Covered With Dust,' whispered the old lady.

'I believe it was. Why, were you there?'

'No. But we – we used to recite that when we were children. It brings everything back.'

'Poor old thing!' thought the doctor's wife kindly. 'Must be desperate to be old and alone.' And she asked, 'Are you staying here?'

'Just for a time. I've had pleurisy and I had to leave London.'

'Oh! Are you at Beverley?'

'Yes.' It was impossible to miss the drop in the atmosphere. The other turned towards her house. 'I mustn't make you late for lunch – or dinner, rather. I know Miss Webster's very particular about punctuality.'

Miss Martin went away, more convinced than ever that she was the instrument of Providence. But in that event Providence's patience far outran her own, for though she hung about in every kind of weather, she hardly ever managed to see the orphans on their peregrinations round Elsham. If she went to the Ridge they went to the town, and when she went the round of the shops they stuck to the Ridge. One day, feeling the suspense more than she could endure, she went up to the gates of the orphanage and saw a little girl hanging about sullenly in the garden. Miss Martin called to her softly. The little girl looked up. She seemed about as tame as an Exmoor pony and not nearly so pretty.

'Yah!' she jeered, when she saw who had spoken to her. 'I know who you are. You're one of the "Barmies." '

Miss Martin was shocked, though she knew that in the town all the inhabitants of Beverley were regarded as having a screw loose.

'That's not a very pretty thing to say,' she said.

The little girl pointed her finger and began to chant, 'You come from the Barmy House, from the Barmy House, from the Barmy House.'

'Don't be rude,' chid Miss Martin. 'What's happened to the little girl called Mary – the one with the long dark plaits. I haven't seen her lately.'

'She's dotty,' said the unpleasant child in indifferent tones.

'That's a wicked thing to say; and not in the least true.'

'It is then,' shrieked the child, sticking out her tongue as far as it would go. 'She's like you – barmy. So there!'

She screamed the last words so loud that she was overheard by the Matron, who was passing through the hall. She came out to see what was going on.

'Sylvia! What are you doing?'

Sylvia! thought Miss Martin. What a name for the little horror!

'It's this lady. She's asking me questions and saying funny things.' She was as cunning as a weasel, and in an instant she had rolled up her eyes and drawn down the corners of her mouth, and looked as though she was about to burst into tears.

Matron stiffened. 'What was it you wanted?' she asked Miss Martin. 'You shouldn't be talking to the children. It – it frightens them.'

'I said nothing – I was only asking . . .'

'She *said* things,' insisted the little girl. 'Funny things. I don't like her.'

'That'll do, Sylvia. You go indoors. You're not supposed to be out here anyway.' When the child had gone, Mrs. Forbes turned to the old lady. 'You come from Beverley, don't you?'

'Yes,' agreed Miss Martin, feeling humiliation strike at her with a poisoned lance. She had never expected to reach a stage where she could be examined as though she were a suspect at Bow Street.

'Does Miss Webster know you're out by yourself?'

'Of course she does. Really I . . .'

'I think I've seen you watching the children before.'

'I happen to like children,' explained Miss Martin.

'Well – but if you don't mind my saying so, it alarms them to feel they're watched.'

'There was one I noticed specially,' persevered Miss Martin. 'A very noticeable dark one, with long plaits; the one you call Mary.'

Mrs. Forbes looked at her sharply. The one you call Mary! As if she thought that wasn't really her name. It was very peculiar.

'There are several children called Mary,' she replied.

'Oh, but this one is unforgettable! I don't think she's been here very long, and I hadn't seen her just lately.'

'If you mean Mary Smith – why, no, she's had influenza.'

She smiled kindly. Poor old thing! Bella Webster's protegées were all weak in the head. 'But how observant you are! All the same, influenza's what you'll be having if you stand about in this weather.'

Miss Martin saw she wasn't going to learn anything further, and she didn't want to arouse suspicion at this stage, so she said politely she hoped the little girl would soon be better, and took herself off. Mrs. Forbes went back to the house and sent for Sylvia, whom she examined minutely, trying to find out what the old lady had really said. Sylvia, she knew, had an imagination that would have put a B.B.C. announcer to shame. Matron realised she wasn't a very reliable little girl, but all the same it was as well to discourage these old creatures from hanging about round the Home. She wrote a nice friendly note to Miss Webster, with whom she was on excellent terms, and suggested they might meet for coffee at the Rendezvous one morning to talk things over. Miss Webster and Mrs. Forbes were sensible women, and they both knew that, whatever dreamers may say, money is important, and you can't get on without it. That being so, provided you have none in your own right, you must either get it by cheating or by hard work. And it was hard work all right. But on the whole, to date, they had both found this safest, seeing that no Government was going to prevent people working for a living, while it was clearly going to become increasingly difficult to get it in any other way. What were called in the Civil Service emoluments, were either going to become wages or were going to disappear altogether.

'And if you have to earn a living,' stated Miss Webster, winding up a discussion they had had a long time ago when they first pooled their experiences, 'you've not only got to work hard, you've probably got to do something you don't much like.'

The Matron of the children's Home was more experienced in some ways than her friend, because she had been married once, though it hadn't turned out a success, and she hadn't had any children, but it had been easier to get a job as matron with 'Mrs.' tacked in front of her name. Mrs. Barnes was one of the governors of the orphanage – the late Mr. Barnes had been a children's surgeon, and was a good one until Mrs. B. wore him out and made him think more affectionately of his coffin than of his bed – and that was really how Mrs. Forbes had got the vacancy without any previous experience. There was something forceful about Mrs. Barnes – it was an alarming look-out for any little girl who had the misfortune to be at her mercy. Not that Mrs. Forbes couldn't be forceful too. She agreed with Mrs. Barnes – for the two ladies met frequently and had many a cosy chat, being contemporaries with a similar background and similar experiences of married life. Both had discovered that men were poor creatures, and both had parted from their husbands after a comparatively short married life, though Mr. Barnes had had the gentlemanliness to die and leave his widow comfortably provided for, while Mr. Forbes had taken the commoner way out by eloping with his typist and leaving his wife flat. Both women agreed that women collectively had to fight tooth and nail for their rights, and both had excellent teeth and nails, which they kept in first-class fighting trim.

Miss Webster, the spinster, was a sensible woman. She didn't want any trouble where Miss Martin was concerned, and she knew that if trouble pops up its head it must be nipped off at once. Mrs. Forbes was something of a personality, though she was only an employee, while Miss Webster owned her own home. But all the same, it was just as easy to play safe as to court trouble. So, on her return from the Rendezvous, she sent for Miss Martin at once.

'I'm sorry to tell you I've had a complaint from the Matron of the orphanage,' she announced without preamble, 'that you hang about the place and upset the children. I'm sure you don't want to do anything of the kind and that it was just thoughtlessness, but I must ask you to be more careful. You don't want to get this place a bad name, do you?'

'Perhaps,' thought Miss Martin fearfully, 'I really am going mad.' Everyone nowadays talked to her in the same strain – Doreen, Miss Webster, even the doctor's wife. It was the way they talked to the other ladies, who were admittedly a bit *non compos mentis*. She tried to explain that she hadn't meant any harm, and Miss Webster – who couldn't think of any harm she could do, unless she concealed a bread-knife under her coat and made a lunge at one of the orphans – said kindly that was just what she was saying, but she hoped that Miss Martin would make a point of staying away from Green Lane Hill in future.

'We don't want any trouble, do we?' she pointed out.

'That's always the answer,' returned the old lady with unexpected passion. 'Anything to avoid trouble. Why, I believe if it stopped at your gate and rang the bell you'd pull down the blinds and sit at the back of the house and hope it would go away. That's why things get so bad, that's why we had to have a war, because people shut their eyes – they found it easier – but you always pay in the end . . .'

To her horror she found she was shouting, and she paused aghast. 'I mean . . .' she began in more temperate tones! but Matron caught her by the shoulders and said firmly, 'Now, I'm not going to have any more of this. You're over-excited and you don't know what you're saying. I don't want to have to write to your niece, but if you don't behave sensibly I shall have to tell her.'

It was the ace of trumps and she knew it: anything rather than have Doreen descend like a Messerschmitt, raining bombs of blame and warnings of worse things to come. Miss Martin quieted at once. After that, her movements were severely circumscribed. When she went out, it was with another of the old ladies, who never wanted to look at the gardens, but wound her slow way – one step forward and two steps back – to the shopping area. She crawled round the counters at Woolworth's, never spending anything, but handling all the goods, and reminding herself and her companion of her own youth. Or she would go to Boots and have long conversations with the nurse there – who displayed an astounding patience – about laxatives and tonics.

'How you can, May!' observed the girl at the next counter.

'Poor old things!' said May tolerantly. 'They haven't much to live for, and they do love to talk about their insides.'

But one day, feeling desperate, Miss Martin managed to slip out by herself, carrying a letter and pretending she was going to the post. She was fortunate in running slap into the tail of orphans, and there was Pamela, looking paler than ever, but walking quietly enough at the end of the queue. Deliberately Miss Martin crossed the road, so that she came almost face to face with her.

'Pamela!' she breathed.

The little girl flung her a quick look and walked on. Miss Martin stood staring after her, white with dismay. Then she saw that the enterprising child had dropped out on the pretence of re-buttoning a shoe, and was half-kneeling by the kerb. As she rose to her feet she shot a glance in Miss Martin's direction, and her hand sketched a hasty parody of a salute. 'Mary!' called the woman in charge, and the child picked herself up and rejoined the rest.

CHAPTER 5

After that, Miss Martin made up her mind that something must be done. It was no use appealing to Doreen, or to either of the matrons, and she couldn't do anything more by herself. If little Pamela Smith had to count on old Miss Martin for deliverance, she might well stay in the orphanage for another five years. But there was Terry Lawrence. She at all events must know what Pamela was doing here, though why she had permitted such a thing to happen – remembering her promise to Mr. Scott – was incomprehensible.

'It seems obvious that Mr. Scott must have had a fatal attack,' she told herself. 'Then someone, I suppose Mrs. Barnes, put Pamela here. But – oh, there's a great mystery here, and I must clear it up! It's no good hoping either of the matrons will help, and the doctor's wife is married to the orphan's doctor. No, I must try and get in touch with that girl.'

The only address she had for her was Swan House, so she wrote there, marking the envelope 'Private and Urgent. Please Forward if Away.' But, unless some misfortune had overtaken her, she must surely have left a forwarding address either at Swan House or with the post office. In any case, Miss Martin could think of nothing else to be done.

She contrived to post her letter unnoticed, and then she settled back to wait. She had to allow an additional twenty-four hours in case Terry had left London, and during that time she schooled herself to stay away from the orphanage. On the morning that she calculated Terry should get her letter she was feverish with anxiety. She wouldn't go out in case a telegram arrived, though she told herself that it was absurd to expect a telegram. But a little between twelve and one came something more startling than a telegram arrived. A taxi drew up at the gate, and out of it stepped Terry herself young, confident, gay. She came running up the path and banged on the knocker in a way no inmate would dare to do, and when the door was opened she asked for Miss Martin in a ringing voice, saying she was a friend from London who had a day off and wanted to take the old lady out to lunch. The servant called Matron, and Terry exclaimed cheerfully, 'I do hope I haven't come on an inconvenient day! I didn't know where Miss Martin was till the other day. I do hope it's all right for me to take her out to lunch.'

Miss Webster couldn't think of any reason why she shouldn't, and Miss Martin, resolved that no refusal should be offered, came on the scene smiling and saying, 'My dear Terry, this is a very delightful surprise.'

And off the pair went.

'I can't tell you how thankful I was to get your letter,' said Terry as soon as they were out of earshot of the Home.

'I've been worried to death over Pamela. I couldn't discover her whereabouts, and though I wrote, the letter came back. It's absolutely outrageous, and the awful thing is – so far as I can make out – the law's on Mrs. Barnes' side.'

'It's all so dreadfully perplexing,' said Miss Martin. 'I don't understand it a bit. When I came to Swan House that afternoon I could see that Mr. Scott was quite a rich man, and he'd given Pamela everything to make a child's life happy. And I thought you said that he was providing for her. What's happened to him?'

'He died very suddenly. I told you his heart was bad, though he never would have much to do with doctors. He said they shouldn't be wasting their time on old wrecks like him when there was nothing useful they could do. As a matter of fact he had been getting worse, and Mrs. Barnes would badger him, though she must have known it was bad for him. I think the trouble was, she wanted to be sure that darling Oliver was going to get something handsome under the will. People are odious about money, aren't they? On that Tuesday he had a bad attack, and we had to call in Dr. Macintosh, and I think he must have warned him, because that evening Mr. Scott reminded me of my promise to look after Pamela as well as I could. "I know I can trust you," he said, and I told him, "I'll do everything I can. I couldn't care for her more if she were a little sister of my own." Mr. Scott laughed and said, "I'm sure you never had a sister or you wouldn't have these romantic notions about them. My sisters quarrelled like furies, always jealous of one another." The next day – it was like telepathy really, except that she always came when one hoped she wouldn't – Mrs. Barnes turned up. She started off on the wrong foot by telling him how ill he was looking, and she would go on, though she must have known it drove him mad.'

'How I can sympathise!' exclaimed Miss Martin, thinking of Doreen, who took a positive pleasure in rubbing gilt off gingerbread. Miss Martin used to think that if ever her niece got into *Who's Who* she could put that down as her recreation.

'She asked me how bad the attack had been and what the doctor had said, and suggested it might be a good thing for Pamela to go away for a while. It wasn't reasonable to expect a child never to make a noise, and she was sure noise was bad for him. I said he liked to have her about, and his serious attack of the day before was nothing to do with her. Anyhow, the doctor had brought him some new stuff, stronger than before, which would deaden the pain more quickly. He suffered a good deal, you know,' she added in sober tones.

'I could see that,' agreed Miss Martin in the same voice.

'All he wanted was to be left alone, but that was too much to ask. She would go in, and when I went down to the library she was talking nineteen to the dozen, all about darling Oliver, and how fine he was, and how much the Government thought of him, and how he didn't work for a medal, because there weren't any medals. Oh, it was sickening! Mr. Scott was saying, "It's very consoling to hear that, Eleanor. It means no one need worry about his future. It must be a great comfort to you to know you have such a steady, successful son. He'll never have to fall back on the public relief, as most of us will." She looked at him in the blackest possible way and she said, "I should have expected you to be proud of your nephew." And Mr. Scott said in his dry way, "Oh, we don't want his head to be turned." I wished I had the authority to tell her she must go, but, of course, I hadn't. I couldn't even stay, and she went on badgering him and arguing. But I think even she was a bit frightened at last, because presently she came up and said she was afraid her brother wasn't at all well, and could I tell her if the doctor had said anything definite. I reminded her he'd had a very severe attack the night before and was supposed to keep very quiet, and she jumped at that and said, "Yes. I don't think Pamela should disturb him to-night. As a matter of fact he had a sort of seizure, and I wanted to ring up the doctor. But he wouldn't let me, just asked me to give him his drops and said he'd be quite all right. I did persuade him to have a brandy and soda. That ought to pull him together. But I wish now I hadn't got to go back to-night."

'It would have been fatal if she had stayed,' exclaimed Miss Martin.

'It wouldn't have made any difference. She'd done the harm already. And I believe she knew it. Because she gave me her telephone number – a thing she'd never done before – and said, "If you should want me you can get me there at any time." I don't know if I looked at her in a queer way, for suddenly her manner changed, and she said she hoped I was being careful to check extravagance. Everyone knew that servants were extravagant when there was no real mistress on the premises. You know,' added Terry, 'she wanted to come and take charge of the house herself, but Mr. Scott wouldn't have it. She said it wasn't necessary to have such a bright light, it was brighter than Mr. Scott's own, and one should be careful about spending money, even if it wasn't one's own.'

'I'm quite sure,' put in Miss Martin, 'that Mrs. Barnes and Doreen would have a great deal in common. Anyway, children need a good light.'

'Oh, it was just an excuse to find fault! She was like that. Besides, she was really anxious about her brother. She knew she was responsible for his attack, and she made me promise that if he seemed to get worse I would ring up Dr. Macintosh. I said I would, if Mr. Scott would allow it, and she said that on her way down she would tell him what she had said to me. She went into the library, and I heard her say, "No, don't move. What you need is rest. I'll find it for you." And she opened a drawer and shut it again. I didn't hear any more. I couldn't wait. I went back to Pamela. I told myself that presently I'd go down and see if there was anything I could do, but for the moment I was sure Mr. Scott would rather be left alone. He hated to be fussed.'

'It was a great responsibility for you,' suggested Miss Martin sympathetically.

'As a matter of fact I wasn't the next person to go into the library. I took our nursery china down to the kitchen and helped Mrs. Hubble to wash up, and she said that Mrs. Barnes was like the mills of God, except that she thought Mrs. Barnes ground a bit faster. Prentice was out that afternoon, burying a grandmother or going to the pictures or something amusing. Then she said that Mrs. Barnes had been into the kitchen, and told her that Mr. Scott wasn't feeling quite himself and she must give him something very simple for supper. And Mrs. Humble said, "Yes, Mrs. Barnes. I've been with Mr. Scott for two years now and he's never been anything but satisfied." Mrs. Barnes didn't like it, but there wasn't much for her to say, and at last she went.'

'And – was it that night?'

'Yes. In a sense, you might say, she killed him, though she'll never hang for it, more's the pity.'

'Terry! My dear child, you mustn't say things like that.'

'It's the truth. I hold her responsible for his death, and he's hardly cold before she's pushed Pamela into a charity orphanage. She's no better than a criminal and you know it.'

By this time they had reached the town and found places at a small table at the Rendezvous, where Terry suggested they should lunch. It was an isolated corner, but even so, Miss Martin warned her companion to be careful as the two matrons sometimes came here, and 'walls have ears,' she said.

'I'm afraid it must have been a terrible shock to you,' said the old lady, as they managed to catch the waitress's eye and give their order.

'It was quite dramatic really – like a film. I hadn't gone down when Prentice came back. I stayed with Pamela, who was always rather out of sorts after one of Mrs. Barnes' visits. She managed to scatter a sense of insecurity round the house. The fact is, she'd have liked to make a clean sweep – Mrs. Hubble, Pamela, me. She didn't even try to conceal her feelings.'

'I wonder Mrs. Hubble stayed. I thought cooks always ruled the house these days.'

'Oh, Mrs. Hubble had her reasons. One of them was the same as mine. Neither of us minds moving on; life can't be static; but we both want to be the ones to decide when to move, and we didn't mean to be ordered about by Mrs. Barnes. And another reason was, that she said Mr. Scott had promised to remember her in his will.'

'And did he?'

'We don't know. We never found the will.'

Miss Martin looked suddenly excited. 'But, Terry, there was one. I know. I witnessed it.'

Terry put down her spoon and stared. 'You witnessed it! Then – when was this?'

'The only time I came to the house. He explained that it wasn't easy to ask any one else in the house, because of them being beneficiaries.'

'You didn't see what was in it? No, you wouldn't, of course. But he didn't tell you?'

'He only said it was important not to let these things slide. That's why I got the idea that he felt he might be nearer the end than most people suspected.'

Terry sat back. 'This makes a lot of difference,' she said. 'Mr. Merivale will be interested to know.'

'Who's Mr. Merivale?'

'The lawyer. He drew up a will some years ago, but last year Mr. Scott asked to have it back, as he wanted to re-draw it. And it seems he never sent it back. Mr. Merivale did write once, but Mr. Scott said he would be hearing from him in due course, and then Mr. Merivale himself went into the Army, and everybody forgot. Anyway, nothing more was heard of it. I suppose you didn't see where he put the will after you'd witnessed it?'

'It was on the table when I left the room.'

Terry seemed to have forgotten about the soup cooling in her bowl. 'I knew he couldn't have forgotten or put it off. It didn't make sense. He cared so much about Pamela – there was something odd there, though I dare say we shall never know what it was – and to leave her stranded . . . Miss Martin, I felt from the start there was something all wrong. *What happened to that will?*'

'Are they sure he didn't send it to the lawyer? Or perhaps he decided to make another and burnt this one?'

'Oh, but that's not the least bit likely, seeing how recently he'd made it.' She frowned. 'This is all beginning to fit together. I wondered what she'd been talking to him about to upset him so, because he was all right that morning, though a bit shaky, as he always was after one of his bad attacks. I believe she asked him outright about the money and darling Oliver's prospects, and he told her it was all going to Pamela. No wonder she shut her up in an orphanage. She'd never forgive her for ousting her son.'

'We haven't any proof,' Miss Martin pointed out, troubled and uncertain. 'And it doesn't explain why there shouldn't be a will.'

'Doesn't it? You remember her last words: "I'll get it for you?" Suppose that was the will? And suppose she tore it up in front of his eyes and put the pieces on the fire? And that upset him so that he had another attack after she'd gone . . .'

'Did he? My dear child, you mustn't speculate like this. Suppose he did have another attack, he would take his drops, wouldn't he?'

Terry lost her last grain of interest in the lunch and leaned over the table, her eyes dangerously bright. 'I wouldn't be surprised if you haven't hit on the truth, Miss Martin. No, he couldn't have taken a second dose of drops, because the phial was found on the mantelpiece – later. After the doctor arrived, I mean. And *she* must have put them there.'

'You're saying a very serious thing,' whispered Miss Martin, feeling she had been whirled into a universe where everything was violent and incomprehensible. 'If you mean she put them there deliberately . . .'

'Whether she did or not, he couldn't have got at them.'

'But surely he could have rung for someone. What about his manservant?'

'Oh, he was out that afternoon. Wasn't due back till nine o' clock. But you're right; he could have rung. He had a bell-push on the table in case of emergencies. And he didn't ring, I'm certain of that. Mrs. Hubble was in the kitchen all the afternoon and she must have heard him.'

'Tell me the rest of the story,' invited Miss Martin, and the girl went on, speaking in low, eager tones.

CHAPTER 6

This was the rest of her story, and even Miss Martin didn't guess what Arthur Crook was going to make of it in due course.

'I sat with Pamela, who was looking rather tired and disinclined to play, so we just turned over the pages of one of her favourite animal books till Prentice came back. She knew she shouldn't have gone out, and in any case she was later than she'd promised, and Mrs. Hubble has a tongue like a razor when she likes to employ it. She said to Mrs. Hubble, had the old cat said anything about her not being there to bring in the tea, and Mrs. Hubble said it wasn't likely a lady like Mrs. Barnes would notice her, and Prentice said, had Mr. Scott rung for anything, and Mrs. Hubble said no, he'd had an attack, and you couldn't wonder at it; but he hadn't wanted her, thank you. Prentice – she was quite young and pretty in a brazen sort of way and she thought Mr. Scott admired her – said anyhow she'd go and see about drawing the curtains, she didn't suppose her ladyship would have touched them, though seeing what she was hoping to get it would have been easy wages – '

'Oh, dear,' said Miss Martin. 'It all seems very vulgar.'

'I think she was rather vulgar – Prentice, I mean. But then, in her own way, so was Mrs. Barnes. And she certainly wouldn't have pulled the curtains; she was the sort to ring for someone to put a lump of coal on the fire. Well, Prentice went to the library and she said at first she thought he wasn't there at all. The room was almost dark, and sometimes if he was tired he would wheel himself into his bedroom, which opened out of the library. She must have forgotten about

Wallis being out, because he couldn't get to bed without help. She switched on the lights and walked across to the windows, saying something uncomplimentary about Mrs. Barnes, and when she turned back she realised for the first time that Mr. Scott was there after all, lying very still and quiet in his chair by the table. She said her heart went into her mouth, in case he had heard what she'd been saying, and she went towards him, saying, "I'm sorry – I'm sorry, sir. I didn't know . . ." and then she stopped, because she thought he was asleep. She went a bit closer, and then she realised it wasn't natural, and she let out a shriek that woke the whole house. Mrs. Hubble heard it in her kitchen and Pamela and I heard it in the schoolroom, and Prentice went on shrieking and shouting for Mrs. Hubble and calling on God – it was almost too real to be true, if you know what I mean.'

'How terrible!' said Miss Martin, remembering Philip Scott, that quiet man who had hated fuss and clamour.

'Mrs. Hubble came rushing upstairs and Pamela exclaimed, "It's Guardy, Terry! I know it is!" And we went along to the head of the staircase, and there was Prentice throwing herself about and shouting and clutching hold of Mrs. Hubble's arm, and Mrs. Hubble was saying, "Be quiet, you fool! Haven't you any respect at all?" And Prentice was saying it was the shock, and she couldn't help it. And Pamela said, "I'm frightened! Oh, Terry, I'm frightened!" And I told her not to be afraid till we were sure there was something to be afraid of. Then Mrs. Hubble said very firmly, "Now, my girl, you stop this instant or I'll give you something to scream for." And Pamela clutched my hand, and all of a sudden Roy put back his head and let out the most terrible howl. Prentice said, "There, you see, even the dog knows. That settle it. I'm not going to spend the night with a corpse." And Pamela said in that clear little voice of hers that carried so well, "I knew something would happen. It's all her fault." What with Prentice downstairs and Pamela up, I thought we had our hands full. But Mrs. Hubble was a tower of strength. As soon as she heard Pamela speak she forgot all about Prentice, and she came upstairs and said, "Now, dearie, poor Mr. Scott's been took very bad, and the best way we can help him is be as quiet as we can and not think about ourselves at all. We're going to ask Miss Lawrence to ring up the doctor, and you and me 'ull go back to the schoolroom and wait." She's what they call a motherly person, big and comfortable, and has the sort of voice that children can trust. Pamela said, "What's the matter with Prentice?" and Mrs. Hubble said, "You don't have to worry your head about her. She never did have any wits, and what she did have she's lost." She took Pamela's hand and led her back to the nursery, and Prentice vanished to have a pick-me-up, she said, and I went down and telephoned to Dr. Macintosh. I just said Mr. Scott had had a serious attack and seemed in a bad way, he didn't seem conscious; but I can't have done it very well, because the doctor said at once – he's a big gruff creature with no bedside manner at all – "Are you trying to tell me he's dead? Well, why don't you say so straight out?" And I said, "I'm not sure, but I think he may be." Dr. Macintosh said he'd come round at once, and be sure to keep Pamela out of the way. And then he asked, "Has that damned woman been there plaguing him?" And I said "Yes, She went about an hour ago." He said, "She's a public menace; she ought to be locked up," and rang off. I called down to Prentice to put on a kettle, and went up to tell Mrs. Hubble that the doctor was coming right away. Pamela didn't even lift her head. She said, "He can't do anything, can he?" and I could only answer that I wasn't sure and went away again to let him in. When he arrived he said Mr. Scott had died of heart disease, and he asked about the day and the attack he'd had and had I seen him. I had to say no, only Mrs. Barnes was with him. But she'd seemed to think it pretty severe, and she'd given him some brandy afterwards. He said, "Well, that shouldn't do him any harm" – as a matter of fact Prentice had broken the glass when she started throwing herself about – but you could smell the brandy all right – and he asked who found him. I explained that Mr. Scott had said he was tired and didn't want to be disturbed; and Dr. Macintosh looked almost human for once and said, "I'll say he was tired. I don't know how he stood it myself. I'd have put myself out long ago." Then he asked if there were any other relatives, and I said only Mrs. Barnes and Oliver; and he said, "You'll have to let them know, though there's nothing they can do, except gloat at the funeral." He'd met Mrs. Barnes once and they hated one another on sight. She'd tried to make Mr.

Scott change his doctor, just as she wanted him to change everyone in the house every three months or so. She was afraid he might leave any of them a legacy, and that would mean so much less for her and Oliver.'

'Oh, my dear,' exclaimed Miss Martin, putting out her hand, 'don't be so bitter! It's so sad in a young girl, and . . .'

'I am bitter,' interrupted Terry, hardly, 'I'm bitter about Mr. Scott and I'm bitter about Pamela. I couldn't do anything for him, but if I can do anything for her you may be sure I will.'

'Did Mrs. Barnes not even tell you what plans she had for the little girl?'

'Tell me? I didn't exist for Mrs. Barnes, except as someone who might defraud Oliver of fifty pounds or so. And I got worse into her bad books than ever because I didn't ring her up till late that night. Everything was so upset, you see. Prentice was storming and saying she was going that night and demanding her wages, and of course there was no one there in a position to pay them; and when I came back from trying to calm her, Dr. Macintosh was waiting in the hall, and he said, "By the way, he didn't have another attack after I left last night?" And I said, "No, nothing till this afternoon, and that was simply because . . . " But he wouldn't let me finish. He caught me by the arm and said, "Now, you look like a sensible girl. You remember that often the most important things in life – and death – are the things that people don't say. Nothing any of us do can help that poor devil now, and least said soonest mended. If you have any suspicions, keep them to yourself." '

'I think I understand,' whispered Miss Martin. 'Oh, poor Mr. Scott! Always in pain, nothing else to look forward to, and then that new medicine given to him. Still, Dr. Macintosh was right, Terry. It might have been a mistake.'

'He said, "I shall send round a certificate in the morning. He died of heart failure. I don't know what we'd do if we couldn't put heart failure on our certificates." '

'I said, "Was his heart really in a very bad state?" and he said, "It might have collapsed at any moment and he knew it." But, of course, Miss Martin, Mrs. Barnes knew it too. I can't forget that.'

'Whatever you're thinking, my dear,' Miss Martin warned

her, 'you've no proof of anything, except that his heart was in a very bad state and he had an attack and died. I know what you're thinking. That she – that she – but even if he was driven beyond endurance, and he may have been – in any case it's not for us to judge.'

Terry said hardly, 'If he'd thought of any such thing he'd have made sure about Pamela's future first. No, I think she was trying to persuade him to leave the money to Oliver, and he wasn't up to all that argument, and she must have known it. But she was so anxious to get her own way she went on and on – and then he had his attack. Oh, I dare say she was frightened then! And I know, of course, you can't call it murder! but it was indirect murder all the same.'

'Dr. Macintosh is quite right,' announced Miss Martin. 'It is most dangerous to go round saying that sort of thing. And you have absolutely no proof. Did she say anything in particular – about Pamela, I mean – when she heard what had happened?'

'She chattered with rage like a monkey when at last I got through. "When did this happen?" she said. "Why have you kept me waiting all this time? Didn't it occur to you that as his sister I had the right?" Naturally I couldn't say we wanted to protect ourselves against the chance of her coming back that evening, and besides – Dr. Macintosh had told me to postpone the call as long as possible. "I'm going to have the body taken to the mortuary," he said. "Never mind what the family thinks, someone's got to consider that little girl. I won't have her feelings harrowed by being forced to stand by the body, and that's precisely what Mrs. Barnes would do. Besides, if he's here she will live in the house till the funeral, and what with her and undertakers and so forth the place will be a nightmare. All these trappings about death," he said, "which is no more than a new development of life, and natural in any case." '

The waitress here decided they weren't going to finish their soup, and, coming forward, she slapped down two plates of boiled fish and cabbage in front of them. 'See how they like that,' she thought, but she was disappointed, because neither seemed to notice what she was eating.

'Mrs. Barnes came down as early as possible next day and took charge of everything and rang up Mr. Merivale, and together they turned over everything. Of course, she was furious about Mr. Scott having been taken away, but you might as well pepper an elephant with pebbles and expect it to be mortally wounded as think you can upset Dr. Macintosh. He simply said the living were more important than the dead, and he supposed she didn't want a highly-strung child made seriously ill for sentimental reasons. Mrs. Barnes said, "You don't really suppose that child had any feeling for my brother? Any one who gave her a home would be the same." Dr. Macintosh said, "I should warn you she has had a severe shock," and he asked me to look after her and try and stand between her and Mrs. Barnes.'

'And – didn't they find a will?' Miss Martin was breathless with excitement.

'No. They looked everywhere, and later Mr. Merivale advertised, because I was convinced Mr. Scott hadn't died without making one. But Mrs. Barnes said, though she didn't know anything for certain, he had spoken of making a will that last afternoon, and had asked for some rough notes out of his drawer. The notes were still on the table, and were just a list of names with figures or question-marks against them. Mr. Merivale said obviously he had been considering how he had best leave his money, and the names were possible legatees and the amounts what he thought of leaving them. Mrs. Barnes' name was down, and so was Oliver's, but they were both scored through. Then there were several more names, of which I recognised some as servants, and others that might have been servants belonging to the times before I went to Swan House – Florence, Hubble, Wallis, Mr. and Mrs. Howard, Prentice, and my own. Florence and Prentice were scored through, there was a figure of £500 against Wallis – he's the manservant – £500 against the Howards – they weren't servants, by the way, but the people who had been looking after Pamela – £250 against Mrs. Hubble and a query against my name. I wasn't actually there when they found the list, but even when I came in a little later Mrs. Barnes was still seething. She said she understood now why Hubble had been so anxious to stay and given herself such airs, and she talked about people blackmailing helpless people. I suppose that was a hit at Wallis, but if any one deserved a legacy he did. He was wonderful with Mr. Scott. Of course she was horrible to me, but Mr. Merivale stopped her by saying there were one or two things he wanted to ask me, if I didn't mind, and I said I didn't, of course. So he said, "Did Mr. Scott ever speak to you of a will?" and I said he'd told me he intended to provide for Pamela, and asked me if I would keep in touch with her after he was gone, but I had to agree I'd never actually seen the will and didn't know its provisions. Mrs. Barnes stuck to it that the will had never been made, that he'd been contemplating it, but that he had had a fatal attack. I asked what Pamela's position would be if no will was found, and Mrs. Barnes fired up at once and said that was a most improper question; in any case, her future would have nothing to do with me, I should have my hands full earning my own living, and she hoped she knew her duty, even though by law Pamela had no rights at all.'

'Hope is not yet taxed.' quoted Miss Martin, who was old enough to remember the publication of *The Dolly Dialogues*, and who thought them the wittiest book she had ever read.

'After that, Mrs. Barnes couldn't get rid of us quickly enough. Prentice didn't care; she went as soon as she'd got her month's wages, and so did Wallis. But Mrs. Hubble was a different proposition. She said that the master had told her he would be leaving her something in his will, and though she hoped she wasn't mercenary, it would be a help to know her position. Mrs. Barnes snapped that there wasn't any will and added something about self-interest, but Mr. Merivale said that if more people had the notion of looking after themselves there'd be fewer old men of the sea round the necks of the competent. He told Mrs. Hubble they were going to advertise for possible witnesses, and asked her if she'd ever seen the will, but she hadn't, of course, none of us had – except you.'

'Well, that ought to help,' urged Miss Martin, and was surprised at Terry's response.

'If they believe it. No, I'm not being rude, but suppose they say it's a plot we've engineered.'

'What sense would there be in my saying any such thing?' inquired Miss Martin, reasonably.

'None, on the face of it. All the same, I don't see that in law it helps much if the will can't be found now, because it could be argued that he destroyed that will, meaning to make another. . . .'

'You don't make new wills unless you mean to change everything,' protested Miss Martin. 'You add codicils. Are you sure there wasn't a secret drawer or anything?'

'We couldn't find one. And, of course, it does look odd that he should ask Mrs. Barnes to give him the notes and not the will he meant to alter or destroy. I can't help wondering if there was a will – only we shall never be able to prove it.'

The waitress took away the fish and brought two plates of sponge pudding and jam and said tersely, 'Coffee?' to which Terry replied, equally tersely, 'Presently.'

'What happens if no will is found?' Miss Martin wanted to know.

'All his money goes to the next-of-kin.'

'Meaning, Mrs. Barnes?'

'And darling Oliver. Oh, you may be sure she didn't want a will to be found. Not that I really grudge her the money, if she wanted it so desperately, but that she should clap Pamela into a charity child's home. . . . I'm going to see Mr. Merivale when I go back to London and ask if there's nothing we can do.'

'I don't see what there can be, short of someone approved by the authorities coming forward and offering to adopt Pamela.'

Terry clenched her small fist and brought it down on the fancy embroidered tablecloth. Doreen sold similar cloths; she said there was money for jam in them.

'Isn't it wicked how things work out for the wrongdoers, because I'm sure this is what Mrs. Barnes intended? Even if he hadn't made his will or had destroyed the one you witnessed, it's obvious he meant to make another one, and she was trying to find out how he meant to leave the money, and I dare say he told her, and she got into a fury and made him so ill he had an attack and she gave him drops and . . . perhaps she'd realised she'd gone too far, and that's why she gave him the brandy. But she took care to put the drops on the mantelpiece, so if he did have another attack he couldn't help himself. It's like what David says in the Psalms: the wicked flourish like a green bay-tree. As for Oliver – I hope he gets run over before he touches a penny of the money.'

'I don't see how that would help Pamela. Did you ever meet him?'

'I didn't myself, but Mrs. Hubble went to the funeral and said he was there – ever such a lah-di-dah young man, looking as if he had a bad smell under his nose. He didn't come back to the house, but Mrs. Barnes did, of course, and started making arrangements about shutting it up and so forth, till Mr. Merivale told her she couldn't do things in quite such a hurry. He looked after the immediate things, like paying Mrs. Hubble a month's wages, and he told her she could stay till she got another situation. Of course, she was snapped up at once, and she went off, leaving her address with me and Mr. Merivale in case anything fresh turned up. Then Mrs. Barnes told me I could go as soon as I liked, and I couldn't afford to be out of work, so I took a job I was offered the following week.'

'And you're a governess again?'

'No! not in a private house, that is. I've got a job in a small school, but we're having holidays at the moment, which is lucky. It meant I could come the minute I got your letter.'

The waitress brought them muddy coffee, which proved undrinkable, and Terry said, 'No reason why we should pay to be poisoned,' so they left it, and Terry insisted on settling for both of them, and they came out into the clear afternoon.

'Look here,' said the girl as they moved away, 'I've got to get into touch with Pamela somehow. Are you game to take a chance?'

'What exactly does that mean?'

'I'm going up to the orphanage.'

'To see her? But – they won't let you.'

'I shan't ask. Besides, you must think I'm a pretty poor creature if I'm so easily put off.'

'We might meet them in the street if we walked about for a little.'

'That sounds very tiring and it wouldn't be the same thing. What I want is for Pamela to recognise me in the presence of several other people. All they know so far is that she's an orphan, a friendless orphan, called Mary Smith. I want to prove her real name is Pamela and she isn't friendless. You see, you mustn't be offended, but you only met her two or three times face to face, and so they might argue you were mistaken.'

'They've already said that.'

'But I was at the house for months. I couldn't not know her and it would be bound to carry some weight.'

'Yes, that sounds very sensible,' Miss Martin agreed. 'Do you want me to come with you?'

'Not actually to the orphanage, or they may smell a rat at once. I've got to get inside before they guess why I've come.'

'Oh, dear, I wish I didn't have such a sinister feeling,' whispered the old lady. 'Do you remember Simon Tappertit? Something'll come of this. I hope it won't be human gore. I have a feeling we're in horrible danger. I almost wish I hadn't dragged you in.'

'I don't believe either of us could have done much alone,' said Terry. 'But together – you see?'

She tucked her arm into the old lady's and they turned in the direction of Green Lane Hill. Wonderful to be young, reflected Miss Martin, to be so sure of oneself. She would as soon have put her head in a lion's mouth as ring the front door-bell of the orphanage, but if Terry had any similar fears she concealed them well. She pushed open the gate without the smallest sign of furtiveness, marched up the path and pressed the bell. Miss Martin, skulking at the top of the road, watched her confront the maid who opened the door, speaking easily and with authority. A moment later the door closed and Miss Martin set herself to wait.

It seemed a long time before Terry reappeared. Her colour was high and her jaw stubborn.

'You were right,' she said, rejoining the old lady. 'It's all wrong, and it's got to be put right.'

'Did you see her?' breathed Miss Martin.

'Oh, I saw her all right. The servant left me in the hall, and I listened at the foot of the stairs and then crept up and opened a door. There was a room full of orphans and Pamela was there. The instant she saw me she stared as if she couldn't believe her eyes, and then she came plunging down the room and threw herself into my arms saying, "Terry! Oh, Terry! I thought you'd gone for ever," in a voice that nearly made me cry. Then she said, "What's happened to Roy? Do you think he's well, and misses me as much as I miss him?" By this time the creature in charge had come to and caught my arm and asked me who I was. I tried to explain, but she seemed a dull-witted female, and all she could say was, "You've no right to be here." I was still trying to explain to her and to keep Pamela quiet at the same time when Matron came blazing in, and marched up to me and said, "May I inquire what this means?" I began to tell her, but she was just as wooden-headed as her subordinate.'

'Had you just walked upstairs without permission?' asked Miss Martin, who also felt a little dazed.

'If I'd waited for permission I'd still be in the hall. She obviously wanted to deny Pamela's existence, or at all events her identity. After a minute she said, "I think you'd better come downstairs," and Pamela said, "Oh, but you'll come back, won't you? You will come back and take me away," and Mrs. Forbes said, "Don't be absurd, Mary." When we were downstairs again I said, "Why do you call her Mary here when her real name is Pamela!" Mrs. Forbes said, "Pamela is not a suitable name. When she's older she'd much rather be called Mary." I asked her what *her* name was, and she said that was beside the point, so I said, would *she* like to be called Mary if it wasn't her name, and she said that was quite different. I'm afraid I didn't make much headway, because when we got down to bedrock I had to admit I had no legal claim, and I suppose if she wanted to she could have me up for trespass. Only, naturally, she wouldn't want all that publicity. No one would.'

'One of the things I don't understand,' said Miss Martin in her temperate way, 'is whether Mrs. Forbes really knows who Pamela is.'

'I dare say she doesn't. I'm not blaming her exactly, because if Mrs. Barnes is one of the governors she probably isn't in a position to argue. And I suppose Mrs. Barnes could tell any story she pleased.'

'I was once told that if you were doing something criminal – not that Mrs. Barnes can be called a criminal really, according to law – it's always wisest to tell the truth as long as possible. It seems to me that Mrs. Barnes has only to say that Pamela had been brought up in a private home and that she was suddenly left without any means and had no home. Mrs. Forbes might think it queer, but as you say, she couldn't argue.

'Mrs. Forbes wasn't giving anything away. She stuck to the point that I hadn't any right to go bursting into the Home; I wasn't a relation or a guardian, and I couldn't produce any one who was. I said something about Pamela being adopted, and she asked me if I thought any application of mine would get past the authorities. Apparently it's easier to get into the Kingdom of Heaven than to adopt a child. Of course, I haven't any money or any backing. Any court would think Pamela better off where she is than taking a chance with me. But oh, Miss Martin, we can't leave her there. If you'd seen the way her face changed when I came in. And she's breaking her heart over her dog. That may sound absurd, but people do, particularly children.'

'What do we do now?' asked Miss Martin, sounding dismayed.

Terry said, 'I wonder what sort of a story the papers would make of it.'

'You can't do that,' said Miss Martin. 'It wouldn't be fair to Mr. Scott – or Pamela.'

'Oh, I shouldn't go to those lengths, though I dare say Mrs. Barnes would tell me she didn't care if I did. But what about darling Oliver? He wouldn't want to risk a breath of scandal if he's got such an important job.' Her eyes brightened. 'That's what I shall do. I shall go down and see Mrs. Barnes and if she won't move, then I'll ask her if she's thought of this as it affects her son? Everyone has a heel of Achilles, and Oliver is hers.'

CHAPTER 7

Terry was not accustomed to allow the grass to grow under her feet. The day after her visit to Elsham she set out for Great Baring, where Mrs. Barnes lived, resolved to take no denial, though precisely how, short of murder, she was going to move that adamantine lady she could not have told you.

'And even murder wouldn't really help, because it would simply put me in jail, and then Pamela's last hope would have gone.'

With the arrogance of the young she discounted the possibility that Miss Martin might eventually prove a more active saviour of the little girl than she herself.

Mrs. Barnes' house was a considerable distance from the station, and was served by no bus route, but Terry was a good walker, and the day was cheerful with sun and the outbreaking of spring. The newly-blown leaves waved like flags on the branches and the earth was dotted with bright green spikes swelling into buds. On the way, Terry followed her customary argument as to whether she would prefer to live in town or country, and came to the customary conclusion that when she was a rich woman she would spend the spring and summer in the country (with a car, of course) and the rest of the year in town.

When she reached The Gables – the unoriginal name of Mrs. Barnes' house – she was surprised to find a man working in the front garden. He was a tall, casual creature in a grey pullover and the shabbiest flannels she had ever seen. She paused at the gate waiting for him to speak, but he didn't seem to have noticed her.

'Can this,' she wondered, 'be darling Oliver? Surely he never did anything so strenuous or plebeian as weeding?'

She clicked the gate sharply, but he still seemed oblivious to her presence. She took a few steps forward and said in a clear voice, 'I hate to interrupt you, but – is Mrs. Barnes at home?'

The young man straightened himself casually, gave her an even more casual glance, and said, 'I'm afraid not. She did telephone the office this morning. They should have told you.'

'The office?'

'Yes. Haven't you come about the job?'

'No. I didn't know there was a job going.'

'Yes. My mother's looking for a secretary, a useful secretary.'

'To weed the garden in her spare time?'

'Why not?' He looked at her a second time. 'Of course, if you come from London you wouldn't know about weeding.'

'On the contrary,' said Terry sweetly, 'I'm an expert weeder.'

'My mother will be delighted to hear that. Hitler didn't hate the British worse than my mother hates weeds. She'd exterminate them root and branch – that is, if you can say a weed has roots and branches.'

His manner was extraordinarily irritating, what on the films is called Oxfordish.

'When do you expect your mother back?' inquired Terry.

'I couldn't say. Some time during the day, of course.'

'I suppose you're Oliver,' said the girl, and for the first time he looked at her as though he really saw her.

'You seem to know more about me than I do about you. I beg your pardon – but should I?'

'Oh, I shouldn't think so. Your mother wouldn't talk about me. But, of course, she talked a great deal about you.'

'They will do it, won't they?' he agreed complacently. 'Mothers, I mean.'

'Do what?' She was annoyed to find that he was ruffling her.

'Talk about their sons. Of course, if they had half a dozen they could divide up their enthusiasm.'

'And how you'd hate that!'

Oliver looked startled. He put down the finicky fork he was using and came a step nearer.

'How little women know men. If they understood us better they wouldn't have such wrong-headed opinions about us, and then we should not have to try to live up to their views of us. I dare say you'd never thought of it like that. Women don't, I find.'

'I thought,' said Terry, 'you were in a hush-hush job.'

'Are you an envoy from an enemy Government – if there are any left? I've never actually met a spy. . . .'

'I'm not. At least not in the sense you mean.'

'Is there another sense? How interesting! Do go on. You're not, of course, trying to tell me you came here to spy out the land so that eventually you could guide your gang here to collect my mother's valuables?'

'I never heard any one talk so much nonsense,' said Terry coldly.

'Wrong again. Ah, well – I don't think you mentioned who you were.'

'My name's Lawrence. I . . .' She stopped, surprised by the change in her companion's face. The momentary interest died out of it.

'Oh, in that case I think I do know who you are. You were employed by my uncle.'

'Yes. I was Pamela's governess.'

'And – did you want a reference from my mother? If you'd written, you know . . .'

'I don't want a reference. I wouldn't dream of asking her for a reference. I've come about Pamela.'

'The little girl? Oh, is she ill or something?'

Terry said with unexpected directness, 'Are you in it, too?'

'In . . . ?'

'Do you know where she is now?'

'I'm afraid not. It isn't any of my business, is it? Come to that, I don't quite see . . .'

'That it's any of mine? Well, I don't agree with you. Mr. Scott brought Pamela up to a certain way of living and he certainly intended to leave her provided for.'

'He told you that?'

'Practically, though not actually in those words. But he

certainly didn't mean her to be pushed into a charity home as soon as he was dead.'

'Seeing he is, as you say, dead, we can't ask him what he intended. But he had ample opportunities of making the necessary arrangements. And if he didn't . . .'

'That's just it. He did.'

'You mean . . . ?'

'I mean he made a will, the will nobody can find.'

'And he told you where it was?'

'I only wish he had. All this trouble has arisen because nobody can find it.'

'But you saw it?'

'No. But I know someone who witnessed it.'

'And knew the contents?'

'No. She just witnessed it. So, you see, it did exist.'

'And doesn't exist any more. Isn't the corollary obvious?'

'Yes.'

'Well, then' – he turned back to his weeding – 'I don't quite see what there is to be done.'

'The obvious corollary,' said Terry carefully, 'is that the will was destroyed.'

'Quite! And a destroyed will is no use to anybody. I do sympathise with your feelings for the little girl, but frankly I don't know what good you thought you could do by coming here to see my mother.'

'Your mother might. She put her into this Home, where she's probably going to be brought up to be a domestic servant.'

'From all portents, those are going to be plummy jobs for girls by the time she's old enough to start work. Home-helps, or whatever the new name is to be, practically rule the roost as it is.'

'Surely not here?' suggested Terry, sarcastically.

'Mother puts up a good fight,' Oliver agreed.

'Mr. Scott would turn in his grave if he knew where Pamela is now.'

'Then it's probably as well he doesn't.'

'You asked me just now why I came,' said Terry. 'I'll tell you. Because I don't intend that Pamela shall stay there, but I thought before I took any steps I'd make sure you knew all the facts.'

'We do. We know that there was no will found. That's the one fact of any real importance. I don't doubt the lawyers have inserted all the usual advertisements and tapped the walls for secret cupboards and taken out the seats of the chairs. My dear Miss Lawrence, do be reasonable and realise you can't blame my mother for that.'

'I do blame her for putting Pamela into a charity home.'

'What did you expect her to do? Bring her here?'

'At least she might have found her some home where she could be happy.'

'I take it you're telling me you're attached to this little girl. If your financial resources permitted, would you make a home for her?'

'Yes, until some better arrangement offered itself of course I would.'

'I believe it's a full-time job. As a bachelor, of course, I speak without the book, but . . .'

'I could have managed all that quite well.' Indeed, thought Terry, it would have been an ideal plan to establish herself with Pamela and get old Miss Martin to come and live with them to act as housekeeper. She must hate the Home she was in. . . .

'I suppose I may take it you haven't the means?' insinuated the odious Oliver.

'Of course I haven't. All Mr. Scott's money goes to your mother. . . .'

'Among others,' Oliver agreed.

'Oh, and you, of course.'

'You can't expect me to object to having a rich uncle. As for the child, I never set eyes on her, but again I don't see how I can be held responsible. Uncle Philip had every chance of arranging for her future and the sensible thing to do is to send your will to your solicitor for safe keeping. If he didn't do that, the obvious inference is there wasn't a will. Oh, I don't say he didn't make one, because there's no proof either way.'

'There is. Miss Martin witnessed it.'

'Now, look here, let's stop telling fairy-tales. We're both grown-up people and we're living in a painfully grown-up world. You must appreciate that, if you wanted to get hold of the little girl, what you've said to me is precisely the sort of story you would tell. You say the old lady witnessed the will, but – how do I know you didn't cook up that yarn between you? No, really, do let's behave like rational beings. I'm simply putting the point of view any court of law would take if you couldn't produce any proof. And I take it that you can't.'

'You mean, you're not going to do anything?'

'I can't imagine what you expected us to do. The child's not ill treated or starved, she hasn't been robbed or kidnapped.'

'This is only what I expected,' agreed Terry.

'In that case, I can't see why you bothered to come down.'

'I thought I'd give you one last chance before I took action.'

'What sort of action can you take?'

'A story like this wouldn't look very good in, say, the *Sunday Record*.'

'My dear girl' – he looked at her in amazement – 'this isn't the Lyceum stage. You're being too melodramatic altogether. As if you had a story to sell to the *Record!*'

Terry stuck to her guns. 'If you think that, you can't know the *Record* very well. It's just their cup of tea.'

'And – did you ever hear of blackmail?'

'If there isn't anything discreditable to you in the story why should you be afraid of blackmail? Besides, what proof have you got that I ever uttered any threats at all?'

'Hoist on my own petard,' acknowledged the young man. 'All the same, you may as well abandon the idea.'

Terry looked at her watch. 'If I go now I can just catch a quick train back to town.'

'Editors expect you to have appointments,' Oliver warned her.

'That depends. Good-bye. It's been very instructive meeting you.'

'From your voice one would imagine we weren't going to meet again.'

'We shan't,' snapped Terry succinctly.

'Oh, yes, we shall. Quite a lot. You'll see.'

They were so much engaged in their conversation that neither heard the click of the gate or was aware of the presence of a third person until Mrs. Barnes' crisp voice exclaimed, 'This is an unexpected pleasure, Miss Lawrence. Did you come to see me?'

'Yes. But your son's made it perfectly clear that it was a waste of time. I had hoped you'd be prepared to carry out the spirit of Mr. Scott's wishes with regard to Pamela, but it seems you're determined to leave her in the orphanage.'

'And Miss Lawrence is equally determined to get her out; and if any of us get a bit mud-bespattered in the process – well, you can't make an omelette without breaking eggs.'

'And why,' demanded Mrs. Barnes coldly, 'should you think I was responsible for the little girl?'

'Because you know that Mr. Scott meant to provide for her and – and – ' she hesitated.

'Don't funk your fences,' whispered Oliver softly.

'All right then. Because if it hadn't been for your mother's visit that day, Mr. Scott might still be alive.'

There was a moment of appalled silence. Oliver was the first to recover himself. 'If the story you propose to sell the *Record* isn't better founded than that, I don't think we've much to fear,' he observed. 'Anyway, if you have unworthy suspicions of any one, it's your duty as a citizen to talk to the police.'

'I didn't mean what you think,' stammered Terry, aware that she had gone too far. 'But if he hadn't been excited, after the shock he'd had the night before . . .'

'I really don't think it's necessary for you to involve us in all these explanations,' said Mrs. Barnes in a bored voice. 'I'm not in the least interested. . . . Oliver, if you delay Miss Lawrence she may lose her train.'

'That's all right,' said Oliver. 'I'll run her down to the station.'

'Oh, but I wouldn't like to bother you. . . .'

'It's no bother. And we should hate you to miss your train.'

'But your petrol!'

'We have a special allowance for emergencies.' He opened the gate for her and waited for her to pass through. Terry hesitated, then turned impulsively to Mrs. Barnes.

'I didn't mean by that last sentence of mine to suggest . . .'

'I'm really not interested, Miss Lawrence. As my son says, no one is likely to take such irresponsible utterances seriously.'

Flaming scarlet, Terry marched through the gate and got into the car.

'You mustn't misunderstand my mother,' observed Oliver, taking his place at the wheel. 'She is a most conscientious person, but even you would admit that you're prejudiced about this child. However, I don't wish to seem unsympathetic. I'm going to ask you a favour?'

'Do you think your mother will approve?' asked Terry.

'I think I can talk her round. Really, you know, she's a most reasonable person. I want you to promise me to take no active steps for forty-eight hours.'

'And by that time, I suppose, Pamela will have been whisked away to some other asylum?'

'I'm sure you're clever enough to keep tabs on her. No; I simply want forty-eight hours to have an opportunity to talk things over with my mother. Naturally, this was a matter that devolved on her, and I'm sure she has done what she thought best. But she might like to reconsider the position. Mind you, I make no promises. The final word is bound to lie with her, and even a prejudiced person would admit that she is more likely to carry weight with a court of law than you, if only because of her superior age and the fact that she's married. By the way' – he took a corner neatly – 'I take it you didn't really mean to accuse my mother of wilful murder?'

'Of course not. I . . .'

'I hardly thought even your enthusiasm would carry you that far. All the same, you should be careful. Your position in this affair may be said to be slightly invidious.'

'I don't understand.'

'Suppose she started an action for slander? Well, your motives may be as pure as the driven snow, but I'm afraid the man in the street might think you were on the make. After all, you did have reason to suppose you were going to be remembered in my uncle's will.'

'I don't need money. I can earn it.' Terry sounded indignant.

'You mustn't expect grown-up people to believe in fairy tales,' Oliver reminded her. 'Very few of them will understand that there's any one living who wouldn't like a bit extra if the opportunity offered. Ah, here's the station! You'll be in nice time for your train.' He stopped the car and she got out.

'I shan't say good-bye, because I'm convinced we're going to meet again.'

He drove back considerably faster than he had come. He found his mother waiting for him in the morning-room.

'What brought that girl down here?' she demanded.

'Pure altruism, if she's to be believed. However, that's beside the point for the moment. A new feature's cropped up.'

'What's that?'

'It appears,' said Oliver slowly, 'there was a will, and there's an old dame called Martin who's prepared to swear she witnessed it. That rather throws a spanner into the works.'

'If the will can't be found, there's no proof.'

'No. But it puts rather a different complexion on things. And that girl's quite capable of rushing off to some fourth-rate paper and making trouble.'

'And what exactly are you proposing?'

Oliver thought Boadicea might have looked like that before she mounted her chariot with the scythes on the wheels and went plunging into the enemy ranks.

'Just that it might be worth talking things over. She's promised to wait forty-eight hours. It occurred to me you might like to suggest seeing her again. You see' – he leaned forward, speaking in a low careful voice – 'it's just as well to be on the safe side.'

Which was why twenty-four hours later Terry received an invitation and accepted it. Before she set out she thought of ringing up Miss Martin and telling her the position. She nearly did, but the old lady was a little nervous of the telephone, and ringing up somebody in a home isn't the same as ringing up a flat or a private house. She thought of writing to her – and nearly did – but there was always the chance of Matron seeing the letter first, or so Terry feared, so she didn't do that either. She even thought of leaving a message with her landlady, telling her where she was going and leaving a telephone number, but thought Mrs. Bridges might misunderstand. So eventually she did nothing.

Crook could have told her that it's on little decisions like this that the important things of life depend.

CHAPTER 8

Miss Martin was worried almost frantic. The last thing Terry had said to her as they parted had been, 'I'll write in a day or two if I can't come down again, and let you know how things are. And you keep your eye on matters at this end.' That had been Tuesday. Miss Martin had decided that it was no good expecting to hear anything till Friday, though secretly she had hoped there might be a letter on Thursday afternoon. On Friday afternoon she said, 'I dare say she couldn't get down; Mrs. Barnes was away; there'll be a letter to-morrow.' On Saturday she said, 'Oh, well, she'll probably write on Sunday,' but by Monday she was definitely apprehensive. She tried to make herself believe that Terry would come down during the day and she refused to go out, but sat in the parlour near the window watching the gate. By four o'clock she had to admit that she wasn't coming that day, but there was still the five o'clock post. At half-past five she decided the man was late. By six she knew there was going to be no news before morning, and resolved that if there wasn't a letter, then something had happened and she must take steps. What steps she couldn't imagine. On Tuesday morning she plucked up her courage and went down to the post office in the town and rang the number Terry had given her. She was always a little afraid of telephones – like radio sets, they seemed to her diabolical instruments. She couldn't understand how any one could trap the vibrations of the air and so record the human voice. But the young lady behind the counter was unexpectedly sympathetic and told her it would be a toll number and would cost fourpence, and she put her through in no time at all. Miss Martin entered the little box that looked like an up-ended coffin, and she seized the receiver and said nervously, 'Hallo! Hallo!'

A rather hard voice said, 'Who is that?'

And she explained that she was Miss Martin ringing up from Elsham, and she wanted to speak to Miss Lawrence and –

'Miss Lawrence isn't here,' interrupted the voice.

The old lady, stemmed in the tide of her explanations, could only repeat in a shocked tone, 'Not there?' realising that her worst apprehensions were being confirmed. 'But she – gave me that number herself.'

'I didn't say she'd never been here. I said she isn't here now.'

'Then – where is she?'

'That's what I'd like to know. Went off on Friday to see a friend and not been back since. Nothing but a message that she'd been taken ill and wouldn't be back yet, and they might be sending for her things.'

'You mustn't let them have them,' cried Miss Martin. 'Don't you see, that would mean the last trace of her had vanished.'

'Here, who are you?' asked the voice.

'I'm a friend and I'm worried because I haven't heard from her. I was afraid there might have been an accident. . . .'

'Not the sort of accident that ought to happen to a decent girl,' said the inexorable voice, but the meaning of that was lost on Miss Martin.

'It may be much worse than you guess. You see, there's a matter of – of a child. . . .'

'So that's it, is it? I thought as much, the funny way she's been carrying on lately. One thing I do know, and that is, she'll never set foot inside this house again, and they can't call for her things quick enough for me.'

'She's in great danger,' whispered Miss Martin.

'She should have thought of that before,' said the unsympathetic landlady. And there was a sharp click as the receiver was replaced.

Poor Miss Martin came out, feeling utterly dazed. She couldn't think what to do now. It seemed to her she had muddled things completely. Pamela was still in her orphanage and Miss Lawrence had disappeared. People who could be callous enough to injure either of these young things obviously would have no scruples at all where an unwanted old lady was concerned. As she walked back towards the Home a fresh thought struck her. These fiends might have disposed of Pamela also. It seemed to Miss Martin that she couldn't rest until she was sure the little girl was still at the orphanage. She looked at her watch, and saw that she would have to hurry if she wasn't to be late for lunch, thereby incurring Miss Webster's further displeasure. By this time the orphans were probably back from their walk, though if she hurried she might be in time to see them whisking in through the big iron gateway.

'And if I don't,' Miss Martin said fiercely, 'I shall do what Terry did – go and ask. They may shut the door in my face, but somehow I'll get things moving, if it's the last thing I do.'

It seemed as though it might very easily be.

Panting a little, she hurried up Green Lane Hill, and as she drew near the house she knew that some instinct – only she would probably have called it her guardian angel – had led her to the orphanage that day. For there, standing in front of the Home, was a little dark-blue car, and when she looked at the number-plate she saw it bore the inscription: ABC 1234.

'A very easy number to remember,' she recalled in awe-struck tones, realising that the visitor could be none other than the redoubtable Mrs. Barnes herself. Fortunately, from her point of view, the house next door had suffered badly from a rocket bomb and was not yet habitable, so it was possible for her to creep through the gate and conceal herself behind a bush that grew close to the wall dividing the two front gardens. They were good-sized houses here, and there seemed little danger of her being seen. The bush was large and Miss Martin was small, and it was improbable that even Mrs. Barnes would come and look over the wall at that particular spot. In fact, for a long time it looked as though Mrs. Barnes wasn't going to manifest herself at all. It was a cold day, though spring was marching in merrily enough, and Miss Martin shivered as she looked yet again at her little watch. Even at the risk of being late for lunch she had got to stay where she was though it would be unfortunate if Mrs. Barnes was lunching at the orphanage. However, just before midday the front door opened, and out came Mrs. Barnes and Mrs. Forbes, in deep conversation. The semi-circular path brought them quite near the place where Miss Martin was hiding and she could hear what they said. They were both solid, upstanding women, with fresh complexions and resolute features. They were on excellent terms, and Miss Martin's heart sank at the thought of these formidable creatures banded together against such weaklings as Pamela and herself, for already she was convinced they had disposed of Terry Lawrence. Mrs. Barnes called Mrs. Forbes Flossie and Mrs. Forbes called Mrs. Barnes Eleanor. They were, in slang parlance, as thick as thieves, and they were talking about Pamela.

'We can't afford a scandal,' Mrs. Barnes was saying. 'You appreciate that, Flossie, as well as I do. This girl . . .' and then her voice dropped, and though Miss Martin strained her poor old ears she missed the end of the sentence.

'This child you can leave to me, I promise you, Eleanor. I see the difficulties, of course, but I can't agree that they're insurmountable. And if any fresh ones arise we can tackle those too.'

Miss Martin reflected, with a shudder, that she might be classed as one of the fresh ones.

Mrs. Forbes was still speaking. 'There's something in the Bible, Eleanor, about a man not going forth to battle until he's counted the strength of his opponents. I don't think we need be afraid that our opponents are likely to overwhelm us. After all, our main difficulty is past. . . .'

'Do be careful,' urged Mrs. Barnes. But Mrs. Forbes said, 'You don't think there's any one listening behind the wall, do you?' and Miss Martin had such a sense of shock that she almost passed out. Of course, she reflected, Mrs. Barnes had Mrs. Forbes in her pocket. Being Matron of the Home was probably quite a plummy job, and at her age Mrs. Forbes mightn't find it easy to get anything else nearly so good. And seeing they were much of an age they might have been friends for years, and that was how Mrs. Forbes got the position in the first place. So far as she could prove they hadn't done anything contrary to law, and suspicions weren't evidence. It *was* odd about the will and it *was* odd about Terry, but she couldn't bring either of those disappearances home to Mrs.

Barnes and her accomplice, not yet anyhow, and she didn't see how she ever would.

At last Mrs. Barnes got into her car and drove slowly off, and Mrs. Forbes went back to the house and the door closed behind her. Miss Martin saw that she'd run it fine if she was to be back in time for dinner, but all the same she waited another minute to give Mrs. Barnes a chance of getting out of sight. Whatever happened, Janet Martin didn't want Matron writing to Doreen, who would agree to any humiliation for her aunt that would keep her in Elsham or even out of Winston. So, giving Mrs. Barnes five minutes' start, Miss Martin emerged.

To her chagrin she saw that the little blue car had broken down a little way ahead, and the driver had got herself entangled with the bonnet. Green Lane Hill was a cul-de-sac and there was no alternative route, so the old lady marched on, looking neither right nor left, like one of the righteous headed for the perfect day. Only, when she was abreast of the car, she allowed herself to shoot one piercing glance at the lady standing by the bonnet to make sure she would know her again. She had had a glimpse of her over the wall, but Mrs. Barnes was wearing one of those hats with a ridiculous dipping brim and she hadn't been able to see her at all clearly.

Mrs. Barnes was muttering and doing queer things to the innards of the engine, and Miss Martin thought of Jael, who had taken a nail and driven it though the head of a sleeping man who had come to her for sanctuary. Miss Martin had never been able to admire her, and she thought Mrs. Barnes was cast in the same mould. She walked past, not changing her pace by a hairbreadth, feeling she had been rather clever. An old woman like herself, indifferently dressed, grey-haired, shabby and unobtrusive, was practically invisible, and she was so busy congratulating herself on her perspicacity and worrying about Terry and Pamela that she failed to notice that though she was walking down a straight road that had no turnings for half a mile, the blue car never passed her. And yet, when she turned for a final lightning glance before branching off to the right, it had disappeared.

The doctor's wife from over the way had been doing some

of these essential chores that everyone nowadays does in the absence of adequate domestic help, and she had been shaking a duster from an upper window when she noticed a funny little old lady crouching behind a tree in the garden of the blitzed house opposite.

'What on earth is she doing there?' she wondered, and then she recognised her as the old body who had been hanging about pretending to admire her garden not long before. Curiosity kept her where she was, though she had the sense to pull a curtain forward a little to conceal her presence if the old thing should look up. The old thing, however, behaved as though there was no such building as a house opposite. When the door of the orphanage opened and the two ladies came out, she strained even closer to the wall, and it would have been obvious to an idiot that she was eavesdropping. After the car had driven away she came through the gate, obviously quite unaware of the daft appearance she presented, with bits of twig in her hair and her hat askew, and she went pattering down the road at a great rate. Mrs. Thompson thought it no more than friendly to go across and warn Mrs. Forbes of the situation. And while she was talking, the blue car came back, and a handsome if somewhat forbidding lady emerged and joined them. She didn't seem to think much of Mrs. Thompson's story, but Mrs. Forbes said, 'There has been one of the old ladies from Beverley haunting the place lately. She's got some bee buzzing in her bonnet. Most of those old ladies have. She tries to talk to the children . . .'

'Do you know her name?' asked Mrs. Barnes, and Mrs. Forbes said she believed it was Martin. 'I'll have a word with Bella Webster about her,' she promised. 'She really must put a stop to it. She tried to talk to one of the children the other day and quite frightened her.'

Mrs. Thompson began to be sorry that she had got herself allied with two such alarming females. Her husband was always telling her that the essence of diplomacy was to let sleeping dogs lie, and she was always meaning to take his advice. It wasn't till a long time afterwards that she was able to recognise the significance of the occasion.

Miss Martin hurried home as fast as her shaky old legs could take her; but even so, she was a little late for lunch. However, no one noticed much, because Mrs. Mount had given them all a free entertainment by pointing at Matron and yelling, 'Thou fool, this night is thy soul required of thee,' after which she was hustled off to the room known as the sick bay, while all the other old ladies scuttled into the dining-room, because dinner was the most important event of the day, and if they were late, someone else would get the biggest or best portion of whatever was going. Miss Martin followed quickly, not even noticing that her helping that day was mostly skin and bone. She didn't listen to anything that was said to her – she still couldn't get used to meals at a long table – and when the meal was over and Matron had recited grace, she felt she could not, that afternoon, endure the living-room packed with soporific old ladies, so she pulled a wicker chair on to the veranda and looked round for some light reading. As a rule she didn't read newspapers, because the small print hurt her eyes, but to-day there was no choice. All the Sunday papers were left lying about until the end of the week, and as much to conceal herself as because she expected to get any amusement out of it, she took the top one off the pile. The *Sunday Record* was a paper with a huge pre-war circulation, based on its lurid true-to-life-in-every-detail reports of crimes, mysteries, perversions and oddities in general, that seemed to escape the notice or be beneath the attention of the greater part of the Sunday Press. Miss Martin had heard someone say that if a person was missing and relatives wrote to the *Record*, supplying a photograph, it was amazing how often the missing person was traced. Of course, the *Record* got all the credit. On a sudden impulse she turned the pages, half expecting to see a picture of Terry Lawrence, though common sense warned her that a young woman without relatives is hardly likely to attract any one's attention, even if she does vanish. Anyhow, there was only a woman called Hilda Brownlow, forty-one years of age, five feet in height, wearing a checked coat and cross-strapped shoes. Miss Martin turned the page. Next she read a little address by a lay preacher, called 'The Word for the Week,' and the text on this particular Sunday was 'Let There be Light.'

'Let there be light,' echoed Miss Martin earnestly, turning yet another page, and finding herself at once in a glare so dazzling that at first she didn't recognise it for what it was – the flame of pure inspiration. A gentleman called Cocky

Dowd had just been acquitted on a murder charge. The *Record* had franked his legal expenses on the understanding that he gave them the sole rights in his life-story after the trial. Since he had been acquitted, these rights were of no particular value. What the *Record* liked was the final word of a man due to hang on Tuesday week. A man in that position can let himself go. Still, Cocky had done his best (there was also a reasonable doubt that he had done the murder), and there was a picture of him saying, 'If it hadn't been for Mr. Crook, I should have swung for a murder I never done.' Miss Martin read on. The article was more about Mr. Crook, really, than Mr. Dowd. He seemed a most remarkable man – any case no one else would touch, cases where there seemed neither money nor hope, obscure cases, baffling cases, he took them all in his stride. In short, he seemed the complete answer to the spinster's prayer.

It didn't occur to Miss Martin, till after she had written and posted her letter, that she was doing anything at all unusual or rash. She had been troubled, she had prayed for light, and light had been vouchsafed her. She fetched pen and ink and settled down to a careful recital of the facts. It didn't occur to her either that any one – Mr. Crook, for example – might take the landlady's point of view in regard to Terry's disappearance rather than her own. She didn't think anything but that she needed a confidant and some advice. It was a very long letter, though she tried to stick only to essentials; but this Mr. Crook wouldn't know Terry or the child, and so it was necessary to go into a good deal of detail. She wound up by asking Mr. Crook not to write to her at Beverley, since she didn't want to be bombarded with questions, 'and as you will understand,' she wrote gravely, 'matrons are like other birds of a feather – they cling together.' Instead, she enclosed a coloured photograph of Their Majesties superimposed on a background of Buckingham Palace, self-addressed and stamped, and said that if he was interested would he please return the card to her. If she did not receive it, she would know he did not wish to be troubled further in the matter. She evaded all offers to put the letter in the post – everyone was secretly curious, for letters of that length were seldom written by the old ladies – and came back from her excursion to the pillar-box with a trouble-shared-is-trouble-halved feeling. Next morning she woke appalled at what she had done. 'I believe they are all right,' she thought. 'I am losing my wits. Why, for all I know, I have signed my death warrant.'

And when he read the letter, Mr. Crook was inclined to think so too.

CHAPTER 9

Mr. Crook was accustomed to being bombarded with letters from every corner of the country demanding his help. A good proportion of these came from the mentally unstable, and by this time he had acquired a technique which made him able to differentiate between the genuine and the hot-air-monger, and sub-divide the remainder into what might be useful to him and what he wouldn't touch with a barge-pole. Miss Martin's at first sight might appear a profitless emprise, but Crook had been, as he put it, up to the eyebrows in blood for some months past, and an aged spinster and a little girl seemed to promise a rest-cure.

'There's a dame should be in the House of Commons, supportin' private enterprise,' he observed, tossing the letter across to Bill Parsons. 'They can do with a bit of support, if you ask me. Tell me what you make of it.'

Bill read it with no change of expression, all eleven pages of it, and remarked, 'Bats in the belfry, I should say.'

'It could be, Bill, it could be. But even bats in belfries have been known to ring bells sometimes. Besides, did you notice how the yarn hung together? Letters from loonies don't do that. And, say what you like, it's queer – just queer enough to be interesting. No frills either, no screams at midnight, no white torturing face lookin' out of the window, no sinister notions about slow starvation. Why, she even admits this Barnes jane has the law on her side.'

'What does she think you are – Lord Chief Justice or something?'

'Anyway, there'd be no harm just findin' out if there ever was a kid called Pamela Smith at Swan House.'

'Or even a place called Swan House,' agreed Bill. 'Always assumin' you don't mind being had up for attempted abduction.'

'I'll take a chance,' said Crook carelessly. 'Goin' out? You might post this for me.' He threw across a postcard of Their Majesties, superimposed on a picture of Buckingham Palace. It was addressed to 'Miss J. Martin, Beverley, Elsham, Surrey.' In one corner Crook had pencilled four letters – 'O.K.A.C.'

'Think she'll tumble?' inquired Bill.

'She's not nuts,' returned Crook rudely. 'And, say what you like, it'll be nice to have a quiet job for once. My arteries aren't what they were.'

Bill reminded him of that later.

'Well, how could I tell?' demanded Crook in indignant tones. 'I'm not Moses. I couldn't know the way it was goin' to break.'

'You could have guessed,' retorted Bill unsympathetically. 'Anything you touch is screwy.'

Crook would have been hard put to it to explain why he should ever have allowed himself to be involved in so apparently tame an affair. He had remarkably little to go on: just the old lady's story, which so far couldn't be confirmed, and her fears for the girl's safety. And Crook, like Mrs. Bridges, could think of a number of reasons why an attractive girl should disappear without warning. Still, he was accustomed to looking for silver linings, and he told himself that his old enemies, the flatties, wouldn't have got in first and mucked up the whole case, because from their point of view no case existed. The police force, said Crook righteously, aren't interested in crime till it's been committed.

It was a simple enough matter to verify the earlier features of Miss Martin's story. Crook's emissary learned that there was such a place as Swan House: that its owner, Mr. Philip Scott, had died during the past few months, and the house had been listed for sale; and that there had been a little girl and a number of servants. All this Crook had anticipated. He couldn't at this stage argue about Pamela's destination. It might be cruel of Mrs. Barnes to take her from a sheltered home and thrust her into an institution, but the law allowed a number of cruel things. Philip Scott's death, however, and the lost will struck him as another matter. He thought the whole set-up phoney, and said as much to Bill. Miss Martin's letter was illuminating and very full of detail. Admittedly it was all at second hand, but it had a clarity that was impressive.

'I think I'll get around a bit here,' he told Bill. 'Or, rather, you can. Y'know, what these amateurs 'ull never believe is that there's no foolproof method for murder. Be as careful as you please, and still you may slip up. Suppose there has been dirty work here. How was Mrs. Barnes to know that Janet Martin had witnessed a will?'

'More to the point if Janet Martin could prove it,' suggested Bill.

'You're a cynic,' said Crook. 'It's no sense being on this job unless you're a romantic – like me. Now, I like the sound of Janet. I think she's got something here.'

'So what?'

'Meanin' – where do we go from here? I'll tell you. You go down and see Dr. Macintosh and get his reactions, as they say nowadays.'

'What do you expect him to tell you?'

'What I want to know,' returned Crook simply. 'Just because he brassed up with a death certificate don't mean everything's hunky-dory. It don't do a doctor any good to be mixed up in a mysterious death, any more than any one else, and if he can't prove his case he's likely to keep his mouth shut. But unless he's a fool he must have thought there was some funny business going on. Anyhow, his story'll be useful, and he'd sooner tell you than the police.'

So, shortly after seven that same evening, there called at Dr. Macintosh's house a tall man with a handsome ruined face and a slight limp, wearing a bowler hat and black coat, and carrying a small black bag. He had telephoned some time earlier for an appointment, explaining that this was not precisely a professional call, and had refused to abandon the receiver until he had received grudging permission to call that night.

Macintosh was a big, bony man with a contemptuous sort of face, a long, fierce mouth and a scornful manner.

'If you're selling something . . .' he began in threatening tones. But Bill said no, he wasn't, at least not to him. 'As a matter of fact,' he added inaccurately, 'I represent the Three Powers Insurance Company.'

'I told you . . .'

'I understand you attended the late Mr. Philip Scott of Swan House.'

The doctor's craggy brows drew together. 'Well?'

'Mr. Scott,' continued Bill fluently, 'was insured with my company and the family are preferring a claim against us. But, as is frequently the case, there is a clause in the agreement specifically agreeing that no payment shall be made in the event of suicide.'

'Who's talking about suicide?' growled the doctor.

'Naturally we have to examine all the possibilities. In a good many cases the matter doesn't arise, but Mr. Scott's is what might be called a border-line case, and I have to satisfy myself – and my Board – that the insurance should be paid.'

'I don't know what you mean about a border-line case,' snapped the doctor.

'I mean, there are some unusual features. We've seen the statements of the family, and we understand that Mr. Scott died after taking a dose of a new mixture you had given him for use when an attack came on.'

'Well?'

'The phial of drops was given him the night before his death.'

'Oh, get on with it, man!' exclaimed the doctor impatiently. 'What are you driving at?'

'Dr. Macintosh,' said Bill, not in the least moved by the other man's exasperation, 'are you satisfied that your patient had only taken the precise dose prescribed by you?'

The doctor seemed somewhat taken aback by this unvarnished candour.

'Are you querying my certificate?' he demanded.

'Your certificate states that Philip Scott died of heart failure. If we knew he'd been poisoned in the sight of all his friends the verdict would have been the same.'

'Smart,' snapped the doctor. 'What are you trying to make me do – blacken the name of a dead man?'

'I'm my company's servant. I've got to be reassured that there wasn't anything unusual about Mr. Scott's death. If you're prepared to say that he had a heart attack, took the prescribed dose but died all the same, and you're satisfied he didn't have an overdose, then that's all right.'

The doctor looked at him in great indignation. 'I have never heard a more heartless suggestion. If you ask me outright if Mr. Scott committed suicide, I tell you no; I'm convinced he did nothing of the kind.'

'That's what we thought,' nodded Bill. 'I mean, if he'd really been in that state, he couldn't have put the bottle of drops on the mantelpiece where they were found. In fact,' he added, frowning confidentially, 'that's where our query crops up. If Mrs. Barnes gave him the drops and put them out of his reach, obviously he didn't give himself an overdose. But – more than one dose had gone from the phial, hadn't it?'

'If you've ever seen a woman in a state of nerves trying to pour out drops, you'll understand how easy it is for her to pour some of them on to the carpet.'

One of Bill's eyebrows climbed like the evening star. 'New idea, isn't it?' he suggested.

'No one else was in the room when the drops were given. Damme, sir, do you realise what you're suggesting?'

'It wouldn't be the first time,' said Bill, as yet unmoved. 'Still, we aren't the law. We simply have to protect our shareholders and our funds.'

'All the same, you'd better be careful. You're sailing precious near the wind.'

'I've only asked you to agree that Mr. Scott couldn't have put the drops at the back of the mantelpiece, particularly just after he'd had a heart attack.'

'Improbable,' agreed the doctor.

'And there was more than one dose missing from the bottle?'

'I've explained how that could have happened.'

'Yes. Well, I suppose if there'd been an inquest the police surgeon would have known if Mr. Scott had had an overdose. . . .'

'If you're not damned careful you're going to make the pair of us accessories after the fact,' Macintosh warned him savagely. 'When you're as old as I am, you'll know that when a thing can't be proved there's no sense making a stink.'

'It'll be for the relatives to do that,' Bill told him.

'Meaning . . . ?'

'If they proceed with the claim, my board might ask questions, and if she – that is, the legatee – presses the case in court . . .'

'She'll be a fool if she does,' growled Macintosh.

Bill stood up. 'You've told me what I needed to know,' said he. 'Which is, that Mr. Scott didn't commit suicide. That's what I hoped to hear.'

'Hoped! That's a queer thing for an insurance agent to say. Look here!' He rose, to stand threateningly over an unperturbed Bill. 'Who are you, really – the police?'

'You ask the police and see them laugh.'

'It may be a joke to you, but to me it's a serious matter. I don't like hanky-panky in my practice.'

'No one could blame you. Still, I don't think you need be alarmed. All Mrs. Barnes has to say is that she put in the amount her brother told her. . . .'

'It's written on the phial,' snarled the doctor.

'If he was having a bad attack she might be too scared to look at the phial.'

'I know exactly what you think,' Macintosh assured him, 'but you can take it from me you're in a blind alley.'

Bill acknowledged the advice politely and went back to Crook to report.

'Well, that's how we saw it from the start,' said Crook. 'Of course it was a chance in a million for her. I dare say she only gave him the right amount in the water, but she made up for it when she persuaded him to have the brandy. Or, of course, she may have given him the whole dose in the brandy. That 'ud very likely drown the taste, supposing the infernal things have any taste.'

'And that would explain the broken glass too. The girl assumed that the maid broke it when she was barging about, but there doesn't seem to be any proof. And, of course, if a broken glass is found lying about it's cleared up at once, whereas a whole one may stand on one side for half a day. She thought of a lot, didn't she? And, as Macintosh says, it's all Lombard Street to a China orange that we could bring anything home to her.'

'Speak for yourself,' said Crook without heat. 'Have you ever noticed, Bill, that nearly every murderer slips up over some trifle even an amateur might have noticed? Strain or something, I suppose. Or they get so damned pleased with themselves they get careless. And, of course, they count on the fact that to most people murder's a word on a printed page, a yarn in the *Record;* not a thing that might happen in your family, even in your own house.'

'And yet she made a mistake?'

'Yes. She's like all these amateurs that want to play safe. She did something that proves Scott must have been dead, or, anyhow must have passed out before she went. *She turned off the light.*'

Bill digested that in silence. Crook amplified it.

'We know it was lightin'-up time, because she ticked off the girl for havin' such a high-powered light in the schoolroom. She said it was stronger than the one Scott was usin', so it sounds as though the light had been on in the library. We know he couldn't stand bein' left in the dark, and she went in to his room on her way out and spoke to him. That was to give the impression that he was alive and conscious. But, if he had been, she wouldn't have turned off the light as she left, or if she had he'd have called her back or rung for someone to put it on again, supposin' he couldn't get his chair round to the switch. Anyway, there was a readin'-lamp on the table, and he could reach that, so, seeing he didn't, the obvious reason is that he didn't want a light. And the only time Philip Scott didn't want a light at that hour of a winter evening was when he was dead, or so near it he couldn't tell the difference between light and dark. Oh, you take my word for it, Bill, she did for him all right! But she's one of the clever ones. Not even Arthur Crook can make her swing for that.'

CHAPTER 10

In the meantime there were developments at the other end. Miss Martin had remained in ignorance of the fact that her secret visit had been discovered for twenty-four hours, because Mrs. Forbes had serious toothache and couldn't think of anything else, and was pluming herself on her perspicacity and waiting in hourly anticipation of some dramatic revelation by Mr. Crook when the blow fell.

Mrs. Barnes was proposing to take Pamela away from Elsham!

It was Mrs. Forbes who passed on the information. After visiting her dentist, she met Miss Webster at the Rendezvous, and, after receiving condolence for the abscessed tooth, she said, 'There's something I must talk to you about, Bella. That old lady of yours – what's her name?'

'Miss Martin?'

'Martin?' Mrs. Forbes frowned. 'Is that it? Anyway, she's got a bit dottier than before, and now she's hiding behind walls trying to listen in on conversations in the Home. She simply must be stopped. You know how people talk, and Mrs. Thompson, the doctor's wife, saw her yesterday crouching behind a bush and came over to tell me. She thought it very peculiar.'

'So it was peculiar,' agreed Miss Webster, who didn't like Mrs. Thompson. 'She'd be peculiar herself if she hadn't thought so. But, then, old ladies are a bit odd.'

'That's all very well, Bella, but this one really is more than odd. You know what these old things are once they start talking, and if she spreads the story that she knew her – Mary, I mean – in London. . . .'

'I've been thinking, Flossie,' interrupted Miss Webster. 'It's possible she once saw her in London and . . .'

Mrs. Forbes interrupted in her turn. 'But Mrs. Barnes tells me that Mary was never in London. I do hope, Bella, that if Miss Martin starts talking to you you'll say that to her. She doesn't need any encouragement.'

'If she gives any more trouble I'll write to the niece,' promised Miss Webster. 'All the same, the old dear doesn't give the impression of being a screw loose, and that makes this obsession of hers all the more strange.'

'In any case, you can tell her that Mary is leaving us in a day or two. She doesn't fit in somehow, can't adjust herself to institutional life, and doesn't get on with the others. I did speak to Mrs. Barnes yesterday when she came to see me, and she's going to put her in the country with some woman who looks after orphans.'

'Not another home?'

'No. Mrs. Barnes thought it better. . . . So if you could keep your old lady quiet for two or three days the trouble would blow over. But you don't want her to start talking. You remember that old Mrs. Trent you had . . .'

'I remember. She went round telling everyone that I'd been paid to poison her, because she was a rich woman, really, but her relations wanted her to die so they could get all the money. Of course, no one really believes that sort of thing. On the other hand such talk grows like a snowball. I had to ask her people to take her away at last, and now she's in an asylum, still telling the same story.'

'And if your old Miss M. isn't careful she'll find herself in an asylum too. Of course, it's all psychological. They realise they're at the end of things, they're unimportant, and no one really cares what happens to them, so their obvious reaction is to court publicity – of any kind – and they go round telling these absurd stories. Don't you agree, Bella?'

'I suppose so,' returned Miss Webster slowly. 'Only – there are times, Flossie, when I wonder if some of their fantastic stories may not be true.'

Mrs. Forbes' shocked air brought her back to her senses, and she hurriedly paid for both cups of coffee, and gathered up her gloves, and said she must be going now, but Flossie needn't be afraid about Miss Martin. When she got back she felt as though the latest development was more than mere coincidence, for she found a middle-aged woman waiting to see her, begging her to take in an elderly aunt. 'She's not in the least affected mentally,' she explained in eager tones. 'It's simply that she isn't strong enough to do everything for herself now.'

'Has she seen a doctor lately? I should want his certificate, of course.'

The visitor – her name was Miss Shaw – goggled with delighted incredulity.

'Do you mean you have a vacancy?' She couldn't believe it.

'I can't say anything definite,' returned Miss Webster sharply. 'But one of the guests may be going in a week or two. I can't promise. . . .'

It wasn't like her to throw up the sponge, but she had a feeling that, just as Mrs. Barnes was removing little Mary Smith, so things would simmer down once Miss Martin was housed elsewhere.

Because she was vaguely unsettled, seeing ahead of her a prospect of one day dangerously resembling her senile charges, Miss Webster was more harsh than usual.

'I'm afraid I have something very serious to say to you, Miss Martin,' she informed the trembling old lady. 'I have warned you more than once about hanging about round the orphanage, and now I find that, so far from desisting in the practice, you were actually seen hiding in the next-door garden – a most reprehensible proceeding.'

Miss Martin by this time was getting accustomed to being spoken to as if she were wanting, and she defended herself with spirit.

'I don't think you could call it trespassing,' she replied. 'I didn't do any damage, because really there was no damage one could do; I didn't pick the flowers, because they don't exist; I couldn't injure the shrubs, because they're all dead. And there was no one in the house. . . . Who told you I had been there?' she added.

'Mrs. Forbes – Mrs. Barnes, one of the governors, knew you had been there. I'm very much afraid, Miss Martin, I shall have to ask your niece to make other arrangements for you. I simply can't have gossip. . . .'

Miss Martin merely said, 'Did Mrs. Barnes suggest that? I should quite understand if she did.'

Miss Webster said, 'Really, Miss Martin, I fail to understand . . .' and Miss Martin said, 'Only because you don't choose to believe me. There's something desperately wrong going on there and it's my duty to put it right.'

'Now you're talking nonsense,' said Miss Webster. 'Why, what can you do . . . ?'

'By myself – nothing. But I've engaged a private detective. . . .'

Miss Webster's momentary sympathy died down again. There was no doubt about it – the old lady was crazy. Paupers didn't employ private detectives, who were, Miss Webster had always understood, very expensive luxuries.

She said, therefore, 'Now you are deliberately being foolish. In any case, the little girl is being removed at once. . . .'

She had anticipated some expression of anger or frustration from her companion, but not the creeping horror that informed the old lady's face.

'So she guesses,' she whispered.

'She – Miss Martin?'

'Mrs. Barnes, I mean. That I know.'

'What do you know?' Really, this conversation was becoming absurd.

'Nothing I can prove – yet. But doesn't it strike you as peculiar that as soon as Mrs. Barnes realises I am in Elsham she decides to remove the little girl?'

'Nonsense!' ejaculated Miss Webster for about the fifth time that day. But all the same she began to wonder if everything was quite straightforward and above board. Still, goodness knew, she didn't want trouble, so she settled down to write first to Doreen and then to Miss Shaw, asking for her aunt's medical certificate and two references. When she took these down to the post, feeling superstitious about giving them to any one else, she thought, 'It may be tough on the old lady, but at least that's the end of a very tiresome incident.'

But she was right off the mark there.

In the afternoon post there was something for Miss Martin which got her into fresh trouble. This time her accuser was Miss Maynard, the sub-matron, who brought her the envelope, saying with mock severity, 'You must tell your correspondents, Miss Martin, that the Post Office isn't a charitable institution – it doesn't carry letters free.'

Miss Martin, who was deep in thought, didn't take her meaning at first, and Miss Maynard sighed for the density of these old dears.

'Unstamped!' she said, holding out a very peculiar-looking communication. Someone had taken an envelope, addressed in print to the treasurer of a well-known children's aid fund, had scrawled a great scarlet streak across the address, and in the same extraordinary red had printed Miss Martin's name and address across the back flap.

'It – it looks like a practical joke.' faltered Miss Martin. 'But who on earth would play a practical joke on me?'

'More people know Tom Fool than Tom Fool knows,' Miss Maynard reminded her archly. 'Besides, you're quite a person, aren't you?' But Miss Martin, who never went to American films, only looked at her blankly. Miss Maynard went off, wondering what it must feel like to live with normal people, and Miss Martin opened the envelope. There was no letter inside – just a torn-off scrap of newspaper wrapped round some tiny object. And when she had peeled off the newspaper she saw that it was a minute silver match-box.

Mr. Crook had been hard at it since seven a.m., and when he reached his office at ten-thirty Bill met him with a telegram and the comment, 'If you can make sense out of that you ought to be on the Council of the United Nations.'

The telegram read: –

> Very unexpected developments this end. Most urgent to see you to-day. Can you meet me Fullertons Tea Rooms Cheston three-thirty this afternoon. Will wait on chance end table if possible wearing parsley.
>
> JANET MARTIN.

'It's as plain as the nose on my face, and I can't say fairer than that,' said Crook. 'It's my girl friend from the Barmy House, and she wants me to take her to tea at Cheston this afternoon, and she'll be wearing a parsley bouquet for identification purposes. Why, a Cabinet Minister could have solved that one.'

'But why parsley?' inquired Bill.

'Because she's a woman of imagination and the sort of client any chap might be proud to have. She knows that at three-thirty this afternoon this café will be packed with aged crones, all guzzling tea and most of them wearing violets; and I ask you, Bill, how am I expected to pick her out of that Old-Age Pensioners' Party? But if she wears parsley, how can we miss? If all my clients were as enterprisin', the Chancellor of the Exchequer 'ud be a richer man than he is to-day – thanks to Arthur Crook.'

'You're going, then?' Bill's black eyebrows lifted politely.

'I may not be a gentleman, but I don't keep a lady waiting. Naturally I'm going. All the same, Bill, we've got to act like – who was that chap in the Bible who walked delicately?'

'Agag,' said Bill.

'That's the one. Well, we've got to walk same as him. Y'see, we haven't actually got anything on this Barnes dame yet. I know we suspect her of murder (once), and possible murder or abduction as well, to say nothin' of destroying a will and defrauding a little girl out of her inheritance. . . .' He paused. 'Sounds kind of handsome lumped together like that,' he suggested. 'I wonder what's happened down at Elsham. P'raps my old girl's had a warnin' – you know the kind of thing. Keep your nose out of this, if you want it to stay on your face, or – stay at home if you don't aim to go out feet first. Might be a help if she had,' he added thoughtfully.

He went down to Cheston in his infamous little red car, the Scourge. His enemies complained that even during the war he managed to get about more than most people, and, since the peace, had contrived as much freedom as a Cabinet Minister. Anyway, Cheston was only just outside the metropolitan area, and he did the journey in the snap of a beetle's wing. He didn't know the place, but it was just what he had anticipated. Call it Bramham or Petton Hill or Barbridge, and no one could have told the difference. New, smart in spite of six years of war, with a lot of tidy little houses and modern shops, mostly Co-ops. and chain stores, with an occasional hat shop or arts and crafts or Old English Tea Rooms to liven the monotony. There was a fake market-cross in the middle of the High Street, and a clock tower with doors in the base marked 'Ladies and Gentlemen.' Crook parked the car where he could see her from inside the shop and marched in. It was about half-past three, but he was shocked to see the number of people who apparently had nothing better to do in the middle of the afternoon than guzzle tea. There was a buzz of conversation that made the place as noisy as a factory, and odd phrases jumped out of the mêlée and stung his large, red ears.

'So, I said, we have to endure the privations of a peace, I said, but that's no reason for discourtesy. . . .'

'It was the button-hook that opened his eyes . . .'

' . . . and, of course, rank favouritism. Now, in Russia . . .'

Most of the people were in couples, but at a small table away from the window Crook saw a rather delicate old lady apparently trying to keep an empty chair against the combined onslaught of a pimply youth, a tartish female with a long bob and checked pants, and a waitress who was prepared to jump for the largest tip.

'There's my girl,' said Crook, perceiving a little green nosegay pinned to the shabby coat.

'I've told you,' the waitress was saying in offensive tones, 'you can't keep chairs. And, anyway, you've finished your coffee.'

'Take that chair, Gert,' said the young man. 'We'll pull up another . . .'

'My friend . . .' began the old lady unhappily, but the youth interrupted: 'Nix, sister,' and, turning, found himself face to face with a short but very solid figure in bright brown tweed, with a face and expression that might have alarmed a tank. He was so much taken aback that he side-stepped on to his girl friend's feet.

'In Russia,' said Crook pleasantly, 'they wouldn't even use you for sausage-meat.' He pushed him on one side and smiled at the old dame. 'Well, Auntie, here I am. Just on time.'

Even the waitress, who was accustomed to tossing her head and saying she'd like to see any customer try to play tricks with her (and how! said the irreverent Crook), wasn't proof against this newcomer's robust personality, and moved off to bully someone less armour-plated. Crook was left facing his latest client. Janet Martin was a very polite old lady, and the war had taught her, as it had taught most people, to conceal dismay, but Mr. Crook was almost as bitter a disappointment as the household at Elsham had been. When she visualised a private detective, which was how she thought of Crook, she had imagined someone rather like a family doctor or a solicitor – decorous, urbane, reassuring. This stout, loud-voiced creature, who now slung his common red-brown bowler hat on a hook and dropped into the chair opposite hers with a thud like a delayed-action bomb coming down, appalled her. For one thing, it was obvious that he would have none of those finer feelings absolutely essential for a case of this kind; and for another, he was clearly the sort of person to judge everything by money standards.

Crook read her mind with no trouble at all, and gave her the benefit of his most genial alligator smile.

'Now, take it easy, Auntie,' he said. 'I know just how you feel; but you stop a minute, and you'll realise all things work together for good when Arthur Crook's around. Supposin' I looked the tailor's dummy you were expecting, everyone within half a mile radius would start puttin' on his gas-mask and mannin' the stirrup-pumps. In my walk of life you can't afford to be obvious. Put chaps on their guard to think they've got a dirty spy in their midst. But when I go any place they say, "There's another of those chaps taking the spondulicks out of the Inland Revenue's pocket – racing man – see?" he added, recognising the look of mystification on his companion's face. 'Horses and dogs – that's my label. And it gets me anywhere I want to go – like having a skeleton key. Now, just suppose I looked the way you'd like me to,' he went on persuasively, seeing she was still not ready for speech, 'and I went hanging about this convent place where the little girl is, they'd start squinting down their pious noses at me right away; but they won't see me the way I am – not really see me.'

Here the waitress came sauntering up, and Crook said dubiously, 'Whatever there is,' and looked across at Miss Martin, inquiring, 'Same again?' to which she replied nervously that she would prefer a cup of tea.

'Tea!' said the languid waitress, 'Anything with it?'

'All the bundle,' said Crook, 'and there's no hurry;' which

staggered the damsel so much she returned with a laden tray within a couple of minutes. to find Mr. Crook explaining the art of camouflage in a voice that would have lured a hipppoptamus out of its pond during a heat-wave.

'There's two kinds of camouflage,' he was saying. 'One's the sort birds and animals know – you've heard the kind of thing? Look so like your background and hold your breath that nobody sees you're there. Well, I ask you, how could I melt into a background?' He slapped his comfortable paunch in a vulgar but friendly way. 'The other is to be obvious – so blooming obvious that nobody really sees you.'

'Like the "Purloined Letter?" ' suggested Miss Martin, finding her voice at last.

'I bet the poor devil who wrote that yarn has got it in hot for all the detective writers who've quoted it ever since,' reflected Crook. 'But – yes, that's the idea. Now, let's have the next instalment of our thrilling serial.'

But before she could move on to this stage there was one other point Miss Martin felt she ought to clear up. 'I feel very remiss in not saying anything before about – that is, I do begin to wonder if perhaps I've brought you down here on false pretences. You see, I was so excited when I saw that bit about you in the paper and so worred about dear Miss Lawrence, and, of course, if it had been the police – I suppose I got confused, or naturally I should have asked – should have considered . . .'

'How little my Union lets me accept *per diem*,' Crook helped her out, waving a hand like a freckled beef-steak. 'Forget it, lady. I'm one of those chaps a democratic government's going to put under Newgate flags when it's got a minute to spare – meanin', I can afford to please myself! don't have to take orders from a charge-hand. Shocking, ain't it? Still, what's the sense of having a bit if you can't give yourself a treat now and then? Anyway, I work on the hospital basis – let the rich pay for the poor. Robin Hood did the same.' He tasted the cup of tea she had passed him, and for a minute he really wondered if he was as goofy as Bill supposed, and had fallen into a trap to poison him. However, people all round him seemed to be drinking the stuff and surviving – at least no one had so far fallen flat on the floor, so he took another sip before he put the cup down.

'Now,' said he invitingly, 'Shoot!'

Miss Martin took the envelope out of her pocket. 'This came this morning,' she said, passing it across the table.

'So there are some more enterprisin' people in the world,' said Crook approvingly. 'Any idea who it's from?'

'Terry Lawrence. So, you see, things are very serious indeed.'

Crook shook the tiny match-box into his huge palm. 'Hoodoo?' he asked.

Miss Martin explained. 'I gave it her for a birthday present, and she said, just as a joke, that if ever she was in trouble she would send it back to me. And, you see, she has sent it, without a letter or anything.'

'Not very easy to write a letter in lipstick,' suggested Crook.

'Is that what it is? Oh, dear, I was afraid it was blood!'

Crook was examining the envelope first with his own keen eyes and then with a little magnifying-glass which he took out of his pocket. But even his eagle eye could make nothing of the postmark, which was a mere black smudge.

'Pity about that,' he said. 'These appeals are sent out in their thousands. Still, it shows she's still alive.'

Miss Martin gave a start. 'I never thought . . .'

'Didn't you, sugar? Well, you never know. Anything more to tell me?'

'Mrs. Barnes is taking the little girl away! and what's worse, in a sense, is that she's managed to persuade Miss Webster to ask my niece to make some other arrangements for me.'

'Didn't know you knew Mrs. Barnes,' said Crook placidly.

'I mean she's working through Mrs. Forbes, because, really, there isn't nearly enough to go on to want me out of the way unless there's something to hide.'

Crook drummed his big fingers on the table. 'Where does this niece of yours live?'

'It wouldn't be any use appealing to her,' Miss Martin assured him. 'She doesn't believe a word of what I've told her.'

'Well, but won't you go to her if you leave Elsham?'

'Oh, no! Doreen doesn't want an old aunt on the premises. No, she'll either find some other home for people who are not – not quite right, or else she'll see if she can get me into an infirmary.'

'She can't do that, can she?' said Crook. 'I mean, haven't you any control over your own cash?'

'Only the income. My mother left the capital to Doreen after I'm dead, so, you see, it wouldn't be any good suggesting selling any of the stocks. And Doreen is my executor. And I'm afraid – ' her voice sank shamefacedly – 'I'm afraid my income is now very small indeed.'

'Well, then, we've got to work fast,' said Crook. 'Anyhow, if they're goin' to move the little girl, there's no sense you stayin' at Elsham. Though as to that, I don't know. There's regulations governin' the removal of orphans, and won't this Barnes have to comply with 'em – fill up forms and what not? The Home Secretary's a tough nut, you know, and it could be that Mrs. Barnes might end up by bein' the cracked one.'

'I don't think that consideration will apply in this case – about removing Pamela, I mean. I think Mrs. Barnes has Mrs. Forbes in her pocket, as they say. And I'll tell you why.' She leaned nearer and spoke in a very low tone indeed. 'Of course, I've no proof,' she added. 'It's – it's just deduction, but it would explain so much.'

'Holy Smoke!' agreed Crook. 'I wouldn't mind betting you've stumbled on a live mine there. Well, well, isn't life interesting? Now, then, Auntie, stop looking as though the Big Bad Wolf was after you. You're not alone any more, see? And you know what they say – Union is Strength. You've got Arthur Crook on your side, and – who was that chap who said his strength was as the strength of ten because his heart was pure? Well, that's you, and if you and me together can't deal with a couple of lady crooks. . . .' His manner was so earnest that he didn't even have to explain that no pun was intended.

They came out of Fullertons and crossed to where the Scourge was standing.

'Be not afraid whate'er betide,' carolled Mr. Crook, opening the bright red door. 'Crook will take care of you.'

'It really is a weight off my mind – having told you, I mean,' acknowledged Miss Martin gratefully as she stepped in. 'Are you really going to drive me all the way back to Elsham?'

'You're valuable,' said Mr. Crook. 'Don't want to take any chances with you. And remember – when you're not under my eye, you watch your step.'

CHAPTER 11

During Miss Martin's absence Miss Webster had not been idle. She had already asked Doreen to come up the following day, and now she telephoned to Dr. Weyland, who looked after the old ladies, explaining the position, and suggesting that he might come to Beverley the following morning and get a not very comfortable business settled. Then she rang and asked for Miss Martin to be sent to her, only to be told that Miss Martin had gone out after lunch and had not yet returned. It was by this time after four o'clock and the tea-hour, and the evening was rapidly closing in. It threatened to be foggy, too, and it was early closing day in Elsham, though not in Cheston, the two towns having interchangeable free afternoons so that the employees of either could do their shopping in the other township, both sides thus benefiting from the change. Miss Martin never went to cinemas, and she wasn't like Mrs. Mount, who spent an unconscionable amount of her free time in church, where she adopted such peculiar attitudes that strangers generally thought she was about to have a fit. So it seemed obvious to poor Miss Webster that her missing charge had sneaked out to continue her maddening watch on the orphanage. Wearily she rang up Mrs. Forbes again, and Mrs. Forbes said, 'I must say, Bella, I shall be glad when you get rid of that poor lunatic. She's making our lives a burden. Anyhow, you can tell her that Mrs. Barnes called an hour ago, and she's making definite arrangements about the little girl, so your old soul won't have any further excuse for hanging about.'

'She won't have an opportunity,' said the harassed Miss Webster grimly. 'I'm asking the niece to remove her. It's either that or removing myself to the cemetery. I wish you'd see if she's hiding under a stone or anything in your garden.'

Mrs. Forbes promised that she would, but presently she rang through again to say that there was no sign of the old lady.

At four-thirty the telephone rang again and a voice said, 'Can I speak to Miss Martin, please?'

'Who is it?' demanded Matron, who had taken the call.

'This is Miss Lawrence speaking. It's most urgent.' The voice sounded flustered, and Miss Webster instantly wrote off the speaker as another of those hysterical friends of the missing old lady.

'I'm afraid you can't speak to Miss Martin just now. She's out.'

'Can you tell me when she'll be back? It's very, very important.'

The voice was, if possible, more agitated than before.

'She should be back at any time. But she's not very well, I'm afraid.'

'Surely if she's well enough to be out she's well enough to speak on the telephone,' protested the voice. 'I wouldn't bother – only it really is a matter of life and death.'

'Miss Martin's not the only one who ought to be certified,' was Miss Webster's grim comment, which, however, remained unspoken.

'Can I take any message?' she inquired grudgingly.

'No! Oh, no! It's a private call. I'll ring again later. I do hope she'll be in by then.' Suddenly the voice changed again. 'You don't think anything's happened to her, do you?'

'What should happen?'

'You can't be sure. I didn't expect anything to happen to me.' Then the telephone clicked abruptly as though the speaker had been interrupted. Miss Webster slammed her receiver back on its stand and returned to her own correspondence.

At a quarter to five a small red car stopped for about five seconds by the gate to decant an elderly passenger, and then shot on towards London. Matron, who had heard its noisy approach, was standing at the window and watched Miss Martin come nimbly up the path. She contrived to be in the hall as the front door opened.

'There you are, Miss Martin!' she exclaimed. 'We were just thinking of ringing up the police.'

'I believe there is a special charge if you ring them for nothing,' returned Miss Martin spiritedly. Wherever she had been, reflected Miss Webster, it had had a stimulating effect upon her.

'You told no one you were going to be out for tea,' resumed Miss Webster in accusing tones.

'I had an important appointment at Cheston.'

'You've been to Cheston by yourself?'

'To meet a friend.'

'And who was that who brought you back?' Matron continued.

Miss Martin told her a gentleman had very kindly offered her a lift, and as it was on his way, and the buses were very crowded at this hour, she had been glad to accept.

'From a stranger?' Miss Webster sounded scandalised.

'I hadn't seen him before to-day, if that is what you mean,' agreed Miss Martin.

'But surely you realise it is most dangerous to accept casual offers like that?'

'Seeing I am neither young nor rich, I fail to see what harm there can be in accepting such a kindness,' replied Miss Martin.

'We have been warned that there are a great many undesirable characters – notably Army deserters – on the roads.'

'This one couldn't have been a deserter. He was too old.'

'The older ones are often the most dangerous.'

'Well, he didn't try to snatch my garnet ring or my handbag.'

Miss Webster looked annoyed at this levity. 'Tea has been cleared away for some time,' she observed, but Miss Martin took that trick by saying she didn't want any tea, she had had it at Cheston.

'Someone rang you up when you were out. Wouldn't leave a message,' Matron countered loftily.

Miss Martin looked startled. 'Rang me? Did they leave a name?'

'A Miss Lawrence.'

'Lawrence!' All the satisfaction died out of the old lady's face. 'Did she say where she was speaking from?'

'No. She said she might ring again later if she had the time.'

'If she had the chance,' amended Miss Martin to herself. And aloud she asked, 'Anyhow, you would know if it was trunk or toll. It's not likely to be a local call.' But Miss Webster said she really couldn't say, as though that ended the matter.

Miss Martin went upstairs to take off her things, but she was down again in a flash, uneasily haunting the hall, looking at the telephone as though she could hypnotize it into ringing. After about a quarter of an hour, Miss Maynard, the Under-Matron, said reasonably, 'You'll catch your death of cold hanging about that cold passage, Miss Martin. The telephone won't run away. If your friend really wants you she'll ring again.'

Miss Martin couldn't believe it. Her heart pounded in her breast. She reproached herself for having stayed talking to Mr. Crook longer than was really necessary when Terry was waiting somewhere in the dark, trying to establish contact. At six o'clock, when the news was roaring in the common-room, the telephone rang, and she hurried into the hall, only to find that Miss Maynard had forestalled her.

'Who?' she was asking. 'Yes, this is Elsham 5202. Who? Yes, I think so, Who is speaking? What? Did you say Morris?'

'It's for me,' whispered Miss Martin in agony. 'I know it's for me.'

Miss Maynard waved her off with one hand as though she were a wasp or some similarly tiresome insect.

'I'm sorry,' she said into the mouth of the receiver. 'I didn't quite hear that. There was an interruption. Oh! Yes, I believe she is about.'

She pretended to look round for Miss Martin, who almost snatched the receiver out of her hand.

'Is that Terry?' whispered Miss Martin, waiting for Miss Maynard to go away.

'That is Miss Martin? Miss Martin speaking?'

'Yes, yes, Oh, Terry, I've been so worried, and when I got your little match-box this morning. . . .'

'I can't hear,' whispered the voice. 'When you did what?'

'Got the little silver match-box – I remembered our bargain, of course.'

'So it did arrive all right?'

'Yes. Oh, Terry, it was clever of you to think of addressing it in lipstick! I shouldn't have known myself, but Mr. Crook . . .'

'Who's Mr. Crook?'

'He's a sort of private investigator, and I think he's a lawyer too. I read about him in the Sunday papers, and he seemed an answer to prayer.' She tried to talk very privately down the mouthpiece, wondering why on earth Miss Maynard didn't go away. Surely she realised this was a private conversation. It didn't occur to her at the time that Miss Maynard was staying deliberately.

'And – what's he doing?'

'Oh, Terry, he's looking for you, and I showed him the match-box. Where are you, Terry?'

But nobody answered. Poor Miss Martin cried again, 'Terry, Terry!' After what seemed an age, during which Miss Maynard observed maddeningly, 'Your friend seems to have gone away,' the voice came back.

'I was afraid of being overheard. Tell me quickly about Mr. Crook. I can't speak for more than a minute. It's dangerous. And – what I wanted to say was, don't do anything. It may have fatal consequences for me and for Pamela. But, of course, if you've told this man – or can you tell him it's all right now? Because . . .'

'You don't understand,' began Miss Martin. 'He's made me realize that we've been all wrong thinking of Mrs. Barnes as unconquerable. Nobody's unconquerable once they've met their match. You and I aren't their match, but Mr. Crook will be. He's a very odd person to look at, but somehow he inspires you with faith. He . . . I met him this afternoon, – at Fullerton's, you know – we had tea, and I told him everything you'd told me, and I promised to keep in touch with him. Oh, I can't tell you what I felt like when I heard you'd telephoned while I was out! I've been in such despair, but now . . .' She got no further. There was a sudden cry from the other end of the line, and then a man's voice exclaiming furiously, 'You little fool! What do you think you're doing? I warned you . . .' And then the telephone clicked savagely, and Miss Martin was left staring into the mouthpiece and calling desperately, 'Terry, Terry! Terry, what's happened?'

She might have sat there for the rest of the evening – so stunned and aghast was she at what had just occurred – had Miss Maynard not resolutely taken the receiver from her hand and hung it up, saying in a reasonable voice, 'You've been cut off; or your friend has hung up. Now, don't look like that, dear. Any one would think you had taken leave of your senses.'

Miss Martin relinquished the receiver in a sort of daze. After a moment she said, 'Is there any way of tracing a call – I mean finding out what number . . . ?'

'No,' said Miss Maynard, who had had enough of what she called 'this nonsense.' 'The fact is, you're having waking nightmares. What you want is a nice drink of bromide and early to bed. It's a chill . . .'

Miss Martin found her voice. 'Kindly don't speak to me as though you thought I were half-witted. One day you'll understand I was right when I said something dreadful was going on. If you're sure we're not able to trace that call . . . ?'

'Quite sure.' Miss Maynard began to sound impatient. 'Now come along. You can't spend the evening in the hall, you know.'

'You don't understand,' the old lady repeated. 'It's Terry – and somebody stopped her. Oh, there'll be another death if we aren't quick.' She stretched out her hand to take the receiver.

'Who are you going to ring up now?'

'A – a friend.'

Miss Maynard shook her head. 'Oh, no! We've plenty to do here without looking after sick people, and if you want to find yourself in the infirmary you're going just the right way about it. You trot into the parlour and get thoroughly warm.' She actually had the temerity to put her hand on the old lady's arm.

'I am warm,' protested Miss Martin. 'And I shall certainly have to make another call – at once.'

'You can't ring up your niece from here. She would be horrified at the extravagance. And in any case she isn't likely to be there. She's coming to see you to-morrow. We've had a telegram.'

For a moment Miss Martin allowed her attention to be diverted.

'What for?'

'Matron has one or two things she wants to talk over with her.'

'Why can't you say outright you want to get rid of me? You must think me a fool. But, believe me, I know all about it. Which makes it all the more imperative that I should make my call now. It's only toll, and I'll pay it myself.'

'I'm afraid the telephone's wanted just now,' said Miss Maynard coolly; 'and by the time it's free, supper will be on the table.'

'Never mind about supper. This is a business call. I don't, of course, know what Matron wants the telephone for so urgently – I mean, it's been free all the afternoon – but I can't believe that whatever it is it can't wait another five minutes. That's all my call will take . . .'

'The telephone,' pointed out Miss Maynard, 'is for the use of the staff and for incoming calls. We can't allow one person to monopolise it.' Ruthlessly she shoo-ed the old lady away. Miss Martin went reluctantly into the parlour and sat near the door, listening intently. She always knew when the telephone was in use, because the lifting of the receiver caused the bell to give a single resounding ping; but there was no sound at all, she knew Miss Maynard had merely wished to prevent her from making her connection. She waited patiently till after supper, and then, when the coast seemed clear, she stole down to the hall once more. But she had no sooner lifted the receiver from its rest than Miss Webster herself appeared.

'Now, who do you want to talk to at this hour of night she inquired archly.

'I must ring up Mr Crook,' persisted Miss Martin. 'I shall only require the telephone for two or three minutes.'

'And who,' demanded Matron, 'is Mr Cook?'

Miss Martin started to correct her, then decided to let it ride. It didn't really matter. Call Crook Shepherd or Scullion and he'd remain the same person.

'He's the gentleman who very kindly gave me a lift home.' she replied. Better not to say anything about private detectives. If they believed her they'd certainly refuse to let her telephone, not wishing to get mixed up in anything unpleasant; and if they didn't, they would merely think her crazy . . . 'I really must get a connection,' she added desperately. 'He particularly asked me to let him know . . .'

'Really, the poor old thing is quite peculiar,' Miss Webster told herself. 'You can't help feeling sorry . . . if only they would die before they're reduced to this.' And aloud she said, 'He must have left his office by now. You wouldn't catch him.'

'He told me he would be there till ten o'clock to-night. He has an appointment . . .'

Miss Webster could hardly be blamed for not believing that. Ten p.m. is an unusual hour for business appointments.

'If he is as busy as all that,' she pointed out resourcefully, 'he won't want to be interrupted. Now come, Miss Martin, you must be reasonable.' Oh, there wasn't a doubt! The old lady had got a whole hive buzzing in her bonnet. It was a good thing Doreen was coming up next day. Nothing got a nursing home a bad name more quickly than having someone on the premises who made a nuisance of herself to outsiders. What went on inside the Home didn't matter, but when these old crones took it into their heads to drag strangers into their lunacies, then it was time to interfere. And how should she know – torment herself though she might in the days ahead – that the old lady was fighting like a Trojan for her life, and that if she had had her way everything might have turned out differently? She might have gone on being a problem to the practical Doreen for another ten years. And unlike Doreen, who had a fine philosophy and could on occasion agree with the American songstress who insisted that whatever is, is best, she found it very difficult to forgive herself for what happened.

Baffled, for this evening at all events, Miss Martin allowed herself to be dispossessed of the telephone. Perhaps she thought, during the nine o'clock news, to which everybody listened as intently as though the war were still in progress, and indeed in various forms it continued over half the globe, she could find an opportunity to slip down to the hall unperceived. Vain hope! The authorities, in the shape of Miss Webster and Miss Maynard, had their eye on Miss Martin, who found it difficult even to get as far as the bathroom to brush her teeth unattended. Her last thought, as she pulled the brown top blanket up to her chin, was, 'First thing to-morrow I must slip out. Never mind how, but I must. Mr. Crook must know.' It was useless to hope she could commandeer the house telephone; besides, there was no privacy at all here; and though she might be a silly old woman, she wasn't so silly that she didn't realise both Miss Webster and Miss Maynard thought her a little touched. However, the next day broke chilly, with a promise of rain, and at breakfast Miss Webster announced that the outlook was unpromising, and she thought it best that none of the old ladies should venture out before lunch. If they wanted some air, a brisk turn round the garden – or two turns, added Miss Webster humorously, for the more energetic – would suffice.

'We don't want any one starting a cold,' she added, in the bright voice so well known to the very old and the very young. 'It would only run right through the house, and Lady Instone has kindly sent up some quite recent *Picture Posts* and *Punches*, so you've plenty to amuse yourselves with.'

Mrs. Mount created a diversion by saying in a clear voice, 'If I were a seal I could have a coloured ball. Better than any *Punches*,' and began to imitate a performing seal so fantastically and yet so well that nearly everybody was put into a good temper, and forgot to sulk about the prohibition on excursions to church or town. Only Miss Martin was almost frantic. She watched her chances and made a series of futile little rushes in the direction of the front door, but as though she had been a ball tossed by a tiresome child in the wrong direction, one of the authorities fielded her every time. At last she went up to her room, and even here she met Miss Webster in the corridor outside.

'Now don't start vanishing again,' said Miss Webster in a not unkindly voice. 'You know Miss Blake may be here any time now. You wouldn't like to miss her.'

'I shouldn't mind in the least,' returned Miss Martin desperately. For the name of Doreen was synonymous with Trouble. It always had been, even before she came to Beverley. There was something about Doreen that made life seem insecure. More than ever, therefore, was it essential to contact Mr. Crook, as Doreen would have said.

'All the same, it would be most ungracious not to be on the spot when she arrives, remembering the long journey she has made to see you,' pointed out Miss Webster, patiently ignoring Miss Martin's manner. 'Did you want something out of your room?'

What Miss Martin wanted was her hat, but she said warily that she thought she had a little cold coming on and wanted another handkerchief. Because she came of a generation that disapproves of lying, she crossed to her diminutive chest of drawers and took out a clean handkerchief, and then, stooping quickly, she took her hat out of its square cardboard box.

'Now you don't want a hat in the house,' interjected Miss Webster's firm voice from the doorway.

'I wasn't going to put it on,' explained Miss Martin truthfully. 'I thought to-day was a good opportunity to – to brush it up and perhaps stitch on the ribbon a little tighter.'

'I can't see anything wrong with it,' said Miss Webster in suspicious tones. 'And as we're expecting Miss Blake . . .'

Miss Martin had anticipated this reply, and now she meekly laid the hat on the bed. 'Perhaps you are right,' she agreed.

'Besides, Doreen might think it was a hint that I wanted a new one.'

If the hat remained on the bed, where it could be seen by either Matron who chose to peep through the open door, it would naturally be assumed that she herself was in the house. Nothing would have induced Miss Martin to go into the street without a hat, and everybody knew it. But Mrs. Mount kept what she called her garden hat – a floppy black crinoline affair with red roses on it – in the hall, and Miss Martin was guilefully forming a plan by which she could escape from the house wearing the garden hat, by which trick she would, if seen, be mistaken for its owner, the two ladies being not unalike from behind, and wearing much the same sort of clothes. Though, come to that, most old ladies in homes dress very much alike.

When she came downstairs, Miss Maynard was ostentatiously seated at the telephone, ringing up the Co-op, and muttering just above her breath something about having to get on to the coal merchant and the fishmonger. Miss Martin walked past, saying cheerfully, 'I'm just going to give the birds their breakfast,' for she always collected the bits of crusty toast that were too much for the teeth of the old ladies and crumbled them on the veranda. And it was on a hook in the veranda that the garden hat hung. At this hour Mrs. Mount would be safely hidden away in some corner mumbling intercessions out of a little purple book, and the other old ladies all had matters of their own to attend to. Quietly Miss Martin collected the hat and strolled into the garden in as nonchalant a manner as she could contrive. She had pushed her purse into her pocket, and she began to weave to and fro across the little front lawn, each time coming a little nearer to the front gate. But before she was near enough to make a dash for it, a long dark car came along as silently as a magic carpet and drew up just beyond the Nursing Home. The driver, a man with dark hair and a face that just missed being handsome, got out, looked up and down the road and came to the gate.

'Excellent!' thought Miss Martin. 'He has come to arrange about an aunt or a grandmother, and while he is talking to Miss Webster I can slip out.'

The man, however, came no farther than the gate. He looked over it, saw Miss Martin and called softly. 'He has missed his road,' thought Miss Martin, 'and wants to ask the way.' It was disappointing, but at least it gave her an excuse to get as far as the gate.

'I wonder if you can help me,' said the stranger, as she had known he would. 'Is there a Miss Martin staying here?'

She looked at him in amazement. 'I am Miss Martin.'

Without another word he swung the gate open. 'Quick!' he said. 'I'm from Mr Crook. I've come down specially . . .'

She went like a bird. Not a suspicion passed through her mind. She had been brought up to believe in Providence, and here was Providence most unexpectedly coming to her rescue. 'While they are yet speaking I will answer, and before they call upon me I will hear,' promised the prophet, and Miss Martin echoed him. She slipped out like a shadow, took the seat next to the driver, and the car moved off as silently as it had come. No one saw it except Miss Maynard, who happened to look out of the window and saw the astounding hat vanish through the gate. It was a ground-floor window, so she could not see over the hedge and recognize Miss Martin; she didn't even see the stranger or the car. Mrs. Mount had a habit of slipping out to the parish church at all hours, but she could be trusted to be back in time for dinner, for dinner was the highlight of her day. Miss Maynard replaced the curtain went upstairs, looked into Miss Martin's room and saw the hat on the bed, so drew the obvious conclusion. After that, nobody thought much about Miss Martin until it became impossible to think of anything else.

CHAPTER 12

In the meantime Miss Martin was enjoying herself very much. As the car drove off she said thankfully, 'This is like a miracle – it is indeed. All last night and ever since breakfast today I have been trying to ring up Mr. Crook, but you would hardly credit the difficulties that have been put in my way.'

'Not on the telephone?' inquired her companion. 'By the way, my name's Watson.'

'Like Sherlock Holmes,' applauded Miss Martin. 'Or is it just a – a *nom de plume?*'

Mr. Watson laughed, and they talked about Sherlock Holmes for a minute or two, and them Miss Martin got back to the business in hand. She told her companion about Terry ringing up last night, and he said at once, 'She didn't give you an address, I suppose? No? Well, then, it was a trunk call perhaps?'

'I can't even tell you that,' confessed Miss Martin. 'Unfortunately, the first call came while I was out with Mr. Crook, and on the second occasion I wasn't allowed to answer the call, and though I tried to find out the source I wasn't successful. I did ask if it could be traced . . .'

'It might be possible,' said her companion thoughtfully. 'Let's see; what's your number?'

'Elsham 5202.'

'And the time of the call?'

'The second one was about six o'clock – at least it was a little later than the beginning of the news. The first was earlier – I don't quite know when.'

'I must see what can be done,' said Mr. Watson.

'If only you could find out!' Miss Martin's voice trembled with hope. 'I do feel that dear Terry is in the most dreadful danger. And the little girl too. She's being moved from Elsham, if she hasn't already gone, and of course, there's no way I can trace her once she disappears. There's something about Mrs. Barnes – really I wouldn't put anything past her. She has one of those *hard* faces. And she really behaved in the most unfeeling way about her brother.'

'I think you may safely leave all the details to Mr. Crook. By the way, he thinks you have done splendidly.'

'Oh, does he? But, really, I've done nothing. That's what's so dreadful about an affair like this. There's nothing one can do.'

'Don't let Mr. Crook hear you say that.' he warned her. 'As a matter of fact, he's on the warpath already. You may hear from him again at any time. I'm down here as his emissary to confirm one or two details in the story you told him yesterday. You'll understand that, in a case like this, nothing can be called unimportant. Now, if you could just go over what you told him yesterday . . .'

Miss Martin told him in careful detail. 'I can't show you the silver match-box, of course,' she wound up, 'because Mr. Crook has it, but that proves that things really are desperate. I mean, she clearly is being kept away from all her friends – not even a pen or a pencil. It was very enterprising of her to get into touch with me at all, and I feel I simply mustn't let her down. More than one life depends on what we can do to help her.'

'Very true,' agreed Mr. Watson. 'You may be sure we shan't let the grass grow under our feet.'

'Indeed not. The important thing is to get proof of our suspicions. Without that I suppose even Mr. Crook can't do very much.'

'Didn't he tell you his pet theory: that a good lawyer supplies proof as a shop supplies wrappings – as, thanks to the Board of Trade, they're once more allowed to do. If proof is necessary, it will be forthcoming. That's Mr. Crook's reputation. He calls it having a professional conscience.'

He was most polite, almost deferential – quite different from Crook. He was what used to be called the Old School Tie – something Crook had never met except in a comic song – or a client. People who didn't like him said there was something sinister about the way an outsider like Arthur Crook could attract such types to help him in his work. Crook said you had to be attractive to succeed in crime – charm or virtue: one of the two was essential.

'Me?' he would add simply, 'I have virtue. No one gets the whole bundle.'

Presently Mr. Watson said, 'I don't want to alarm you, but there's one thing I think you should bear in mind, and that is, that you're a danger to someone – someone who's already proved him or herself to be quite ruthless. You know the saying, "A little knowledge is a dangerous thing" (like most people, even those entitled to wear the Old School Tie, he misquoted). Now you possess that knowledge, you're safe only so long as no one realizes you've shared it. Who knows about your meeting Mr. Crook yesterday?'

'Terry. I told her on the telephone. No one else, unless . . .'

'Unless what?'

'Miss Maynard was hanging about all the time I was talking. I don't think she paid much attention, and anyway, all three of them – Miss Webster, Miss Maynard, and my niece, Doreen – treat me as though I were mentally deficient. Miss Webster even called him Mr. Cook.'

'You didn't tell any of them about Miss Lawrence?'

'They'd clap me into an asylum at once if I did. Do you mean that Mrs. Barnes may try and abduct me too?'

'It's just a suggestion you should bear in mind. After all, somebody's making strenuous efforts to get you away from Elsham. As I said before, I don't want to alarm you, but – the success of crime consists largely of being a leap ahead of your victim. Now, when you had this call yeaterday, how did you know it came from Miss Lawrence?'

'She – she told me so.'

'Quite! But suppose she hadn't, would you have known from her voice, say, who it was?'

Miss Martin looked troubled. 'I – I can't be absolutely sure. You know how the telephone distorts voices.'

'Quite! Your connection may have counted on that. Now – think a minute before you answer this – Did she tell you anything that only she could have known – I mean, take the affair of the silver match-box? Who mentioned that first?'

'I – I believe I did. I said I'd got it, and then – she said she had only a minute – I told her about Mr. Crook.'

'Precisely! Now suppose X. had an idea you might be up and doing about all this, don't you see that's exactly what he'd do – get in touch with you and then wait for you to put your cards on the table, which you seem to have done.'

Miss Martin digested that for a moment in silent horror. Then she exclaimed, 'But if that's so, she's in a worse position than before, because now the people who abducted her and are holding her a prisoner – because I'm convinced if she were a free agent she would have got in touch with me before now – now they know how great their danger is. That may hurry them into precipitate action.'

'That will give Crook his chance,' Mr. Watson tried to reassure her.

'But – he'll be in danger too.'

Mr. Watson laughed. She couldn't believe her eyes and ears. This, surely, was no laughing matter. But after a moment he said, 'No, I'm not being a brute. But Mr. Crook would tell you not to worry over him. He has a charmed life, and he needs it. Besides, he's used to this sort of game and you're not.'

Miss Martin had an instant vision of such an existence as she had never hitherto conceived – the sort of existence where daggers flashed and spears were hurled, where death and danger waited round innocent looking corners, and fat old peasant women were murderers with hand grenades in their shopping-baskets, and any moment might be your last. Of course, in a sense any moment might be your last, but it wouldn't be the same thing. Only, when you thought of that sort of life, you thought of swashbucklers and pirates and desperadoes – men in high boots and brilliantly coloured scarves and black masks, not short, fat men, with red faces, and the kind of accent you could cut with a knife.

'I do hope he'll be careful,' she whispered.

'He'll be careful. No one's ever got him yet.'

'So much depends upon him. Oh, dear! Do you really think that may have been an impersonation on the telephone?'

'It's only a suggestion,' said Mr. Watson slowly, 'and of course, I didn't hear the voice; but it does seem peculiar to me that, if it really was Miss Lawrence, she didn't begin by telling you her whereabouts.'

'But perhaps she doesn't know,' insisted Miss Martin. 'They may have taken her off in a car somewhere and have got her shut up . . .'

'She was using a telephone, remember. She must have known the exchange. And according to your story she was in a house, so she could have given you the number. Mind you, this is all speculation; but if you should get another call, insist on getting a number out of her before you give any more information.'

'I will,' promised Miss Martin fervently. 'And if I do get any such call I shall certainly let Mr. Crook know at once, no matter how many obstacles Miss Webster may put in my path.'

The poor old lady looked rather shaken, and Mr. Watson insisted on stopping at a café and giving her some coffee. By now the rain was coming down fast, thus justifying Miss Webster's contention that old ladies were best at home in such weather, but (forgetting that she was wearing someone else's hat) Miss Martin bent her head and hurried into the shop. The coffee, fetched by Mr. Watson from a Help Yourself Bar – for he insisted on waiting on her – was hot and refreshing and sweet, and Mr. Watson went to the other counter to find her a special kind of cake she fancied. He wouldn't eat anything himself, but asked if she minded his smoking, and when she said no, of course not, he produced a most fragrant Turkish cigarette, utterly different from the floor-sweepings that passed as cigarettes in the first year of the peace. He made Miss Martin promise to let Crook know her new address at once, and told her not to look so worried. Crook was already on the warpath, and Winston Churchill himself couldn't outdo Mr. Crook when it came to getting an impossibility achieved. In fact, it was quite likely he would come down to Beverley the following day.

'You won't have removed yourself before then, I suppose?' added Mr. Watson, grinding out the butt of his cigarette in the ash-tray.

'I don't wish to leave at all at the present crisis, but, unfortunately, I appear to be at an age when one's personal wishes have little weight,' Miss Martin told him. 'In fact,' she added, as back in the car they neared the Nursing Home, 'I am going to ask you to set me down just on the corner. It will only take a minute to get into the house, and really, I shall have no time to get wet. I detest anything underhand,' continued Miss Martin warmly, 'but they will no doubt be looking out for me, and my niece should have arrived by this time, and I find it so very embarrassing to be examined perpetually as to my smallest movement. I may be unreasonable, but I am not used to it, and I cannot help feeling that if people like Miss Webster and Miss Maynard had seen any service during the war beyond fire-fighting, which everyone did – even I did fire-watching, and was once able to draw the warden's attention to a fire-bomb – an incendiary, I should say – that had fallen on the roof of a public house, for which he thanked me very much, and which must have been more than one, really, considering the number of people and the time it took to extinguish it – if, as I say, they had seen the fight for freedom at close quarters, I feel sure they would be less undemocratic in their dealings.'

Mr. Watson said he quite understood, and obligingly stopped the car on the corner; Miss Martin stepped out and shook hands and thanked him profusely for all his trouble and the lovely drive – what a beautiful car, quite a treat to ride in such a vehicle. And then, fearing odious comparisons, she added, 'Of course, Mr. Crook's little open car is delightful, too. Such a cheerful colour. And calling it the Scourge. So amusing,' And she asked Mr. Watson to be sure and remember her to Mr. Crook, until at last her breathless gratitude came to a fullstop, and Mr. Watson assured her she had been more helpful than she knew, and in an atmosphere of mutual satisfaction they parted, Miss Martin, still in the fantastic hat, through the gate of the old Ladies' Home, and Mr. Watson back to make his report.

CHAPTER 13

As Miss Martin pushed open the gate of Beverley trouble came to meet her, for at the same moment the front door flashed open and a human tornado emerged. This was Mrs. Mount, who had discovered the loss of the unforgettable hat, and who now came raging down the path to snatch it forcibly from Miss Martin's head, quite prepared to tear off the hair also, so violent was her fury.

'Ruined!' she panted, looking at the monstrous erection in her hand. 'My special hat taken out into the rain! How could I ever wear it now?'

'I – it . . .' Miss Martin's faint stammer died at birth, for now it did seem to her that she had done a terrible thing – taking another lady's hat without asking permission, for reasons of her own that she could not divulge. She had to acknowledge that she would have felt outraged had she been in Mrs. Mount's shoes. In any case, she would have had no opportunity for making a defence, for Mrs. Mount was pouring forth the vials of her wrath like the angel of the Revelation.

'You're a thief!' she exploded. 'Don't you ever read the Bible? Don't you know what happens to women like you? Haven't you ever heard of the pit of fire and brimstone, where the worm dieth not?'

She was shaking the ridiculous hat in poor Mrs. Martin's face all the time, while the pair of them stood in the little porch of Beverley, and all the other inmates came creeping to the top of the stairs or the door of the parlour, enthralled or shocked by the scene. Miss Martin was ashamed to realize that her main emotion was one of shock that she could ever have put such a monstrosity on her head.

'I must have been mad,' she whispered; and Mrs. Mount catching the words repeated, contemptuously, 'Mad! I should say so. And you do know what's going to happen to you? They're going to shut you up. That's why the doctor's here. We can't have women like you in this house. We're decent women here . . .'

At this juncture, perhaps a little late in the day, Miss Webster emerged, and took Mrs. Mount by the arm, saying severely, 'We can't have all this noise. You know that perfectly well. Have you both taken leave of your senses?'

Mrs. Mount turned in fury. 'She had no right to my hat! It was mine! She took it without asking! . . .'

'It was a mistake,' said Miss Webster flatly.

'A mistake?' Mrs. Mount's voice rose in shrill derision. 'How could she mistake a hat like mine for that velvet pancake she puts on her head?'

'In any case, we can't have a scene now,' said Miss Webster. 'Miss Martin, your niece has been here for some time. I suppose you had forgotten she was coming. And if you took Mrs. Mount's hat deliberately, then it was quite wrong and most deceitful . . .'

Poor Miss Martin tried to clutch at the assurance Mr. Watson had built up in her, but without much success. They were both right. She had done wrong – she was deceitful. It *was* unpardonable to take somebody else's hat. Doreen would be very angry . . .

To say that Doreen was angry was a miracle of understatement. She was in what is sometimes described as a royal rage, though Miss Martin thought she was behaving like a fishwife. She had, of course, some grounds for her displeasure. It had been bad enough to be dragged up to Elsham as soon as she returned to her own home, and at such short notice she had had to be satisfied with a room in the annexe of her club, half a mile from a bathroom and with no private telephone. The bath water had been cold, the breakfast unsatisfactory, and, (of course, through no fault of her own) she had missed the train she intended to catch. Being later than she had agreed to arrive, she had been forced to the extravagance of a cab when she reached Elsham, and then she discovered that

Miss Martin had disappeared. She decided that this was an opportunity for losing her temper, which she did with such prodigality that the staff of Beverley – including even its Matron – began to resemble the Court of the Cardinal when the theft of His Eminence's Ring was discovered. People dashed hither and thither looking for the old lady, as though she were the piece of biblical silver. They almost reached the absurdity of looking under mats and inside empty fern-pots. But there was no sign of her.

It was then that Miss Maynard remembered seeing the feathered hat go by the window, and simultaneously recollected that Mrs. Mount, its true owner, was curled up in a corner of the parlour reading a purple book of devotions. She whispered the information to Miss Webster, who immediately had the count of the old ladies taken, and came to the obvious conclusion that Miss Martin had fooled them all, and that there would not only be trouble with Miss Blake, but also the devil to pay with Mrs. Mount if and when she discovered what had happened.

'But surely knowing I was coming, you could have kept an eye on her.' Doreen insisted. (Since it was clear that Miss Webster didn't intend to keep Miss Martin at Beverley, there was no need for further tact.) 'Where on earth can she have gone?'

'I'm afraid she is getting a little peculiar,' acknowledged Miss Webster. 'Yesterday she disappeared without warning and was brought back in a car by a strange man. She is really becoming more of a responsibility than I can accept. She is annoying some of the local people too, following them round, even spying on them from behind walls and circulating extraordinary stories . . .'

'I must say,' acknowledged Doreen brutally, 'she does sound as if she was suffering from brain-softening. Oh, dear! Why can't these old people die off when they're no longer any use to themselves or any one else?'

She had no notion how soon Miss Martin was going to oblige her.

Doreen was barely through with blowing up the unfortunate Miss Webster when Dr. Weyland arrived, He had very little feeling about the whole business. It was his experience that a good many elderly people became queer, and the best place for senile cases was the institution, unless there was some convenient relative. From what the Matron had told him, he was prepared to find Miss Martin peculiar and to sign her up, in which case there would be little difficulty in getting his opinion confirmed by another local doctor. The laity, he knew, were inclined to associate feeble-mindedness with violence. But that was a fallacy. In his own heart he agreed with Doreen – thought it a pity these old people couldn't be quietly put out of the way, instead of cumbering the earth, and needing space, attention, and food more properly expended on the young. When he reached the Home he was annoyed to find the old lady missing, and in her place a downright and voluble female, who, he gathered, was a niece. For the life of him he couldn't see why she should not assume responsibility. At forty it was ridiculous for a woman to talk of wanting to live her own life. She had neither husband nor children and an old aunt would be a sheet-anchor for her. True, she talked a lot of nonsense about her work, but it transpired that she only ran one of these catchpenny art shops which did no one but the owner any good and encouraged inflation. He was just starting to say that he couldn't stop any longer, intending to wash his hands of the whole business, when a terrific hullaballoo started in the hall, and he realized that Miss Martin had returned. The next instant Miss Webster had gone out to join the fray, and Doreen took the opportunity to say, 'I'm afraid my aunt isn't really suitable for this sort of establishment any longer,' to which Dr. Weyland, who had taken a dislike to Doreen, replied, 'One of these days I suppose the next generation will be saying that about us.'

Then the tumult and the shouting died down, Miss Maynard appeared and bore off the indignant Mrs. Mount, and Miss Webster and the old lady came in. Miss Webster said, 'This is Dr. Weyland, he has come to see you,' and Miss Martin said at once, 'I am perfectly well, except for the cold I had last month, and I believe doctors have no cure for colds.'

She spoke more tartly than usual, aware that she must present an undignified appearance after her tussle with Mrs. Mount, while the few instants she had stood in the rain after the hat was torn off her head had caused her neat hair to straggle over her ears and on the nape of her neck.

'If you've had a cold you shouldn't be out in this weather.' said the doctor carelessly. He wasn't interested in old people, but he assumed a bedside manner as casually as Miss Martin put on a pair of gloves even to go as far as the post.

'I was driving,' said Miss Martin quickly, and Miss Webster said, 'What again?' and Doreen said, 'Who with?' and the doctor remarked facetiously, 'I see your young man's brought you back all right. We were beginning to think you must have eloped.'

Miss Martin thought how absurd they all were and wondered why she had ever been nervous of them. It must be, of course, that hitherto she had had to face them single-handed, whereas now she had Mr. Crook and his nice Mr. Watson on her side. So all she said was, 'The rain's stopping, I think,' and wondered if Doreen intended to take her out to lunch.

Dr. Weyland said, 'Now, Miss Martin, these two kind ladies are getting a bit anxious about you, and they want me to take a look at you and assure them there's nothing wrong.'

'What should be wrong?' asked Miss Martin, sharply.

'The best of machines needs a bit of oiling and rest sometimes. It could be that a little change would be beneficial.'

'I don't want to leave here if that's what you mean,' cut in the old lady sharply, and the doctor laughed and said, 'Ha, ha! Unsolicited testimonial, Miss Webster, eh?'

'Anyhow,' he continued jovially, 'there's no harm in having me run the tape over you. Who knows? I may tell Matron to feed you up on chickens and champagne.'

Miss Martin disliked him at once. She felt he was treating her as though she were feeble-minded. If he could have seen how accurately she read him Dr. Weyland might have been a shade less assured. He took her into an inner room leading out of Matron's and told her to unbutton this and take off that and sounded this and tapped the other, and asked a number of questions that she answered in a dreamy sort of way, because nothing he said or did could matter any more. She was involved in a plot, of which he knew nothing, and the future spread itself before her thick with promise and perhaps even spiced with danger. When he twitted her with being picked up by young men she said coldly, 'Mr. Crook is not a young man and I dislike the expression pick-up. I have appointments – I am engaged on very important business . . .' and then she stopped, wishing she had held her tongue. He was looking at her in a very odd way, and she had no wish to become involved in explanations at this stage.

'Matter of life or death, I suppose?' remarked the doctor in the same jocose voice.

'Yes,' agreed Miss Martin. 'That's exactly what it is.'

'Why not consult the police?' He was watching her more carefully than she knew.

'Because that might be fatal. Mr. Crook says you can always tell where policemen have been because they wear such large boots.'

The doctor laughed heartily. 'He sounds an original, this Mr. Crook.' He tried to draw her out a bit further, but she shut up suddenly. She wished she hadn't mentioned his name at all. She felt the doctor was laughing at her, and anyway he would probably repeat all this conversation to Miss Webster and Doreen.

'He's doing a bit of snooping on his own, is he?' Weyland continued. 'What's he investigating? Murder?'

He was surprised at the change in her face, surprised and a little startled, though not apprehensive. When old people get an idea into their heads you can no more part them from it than you can dislodge a lobster who has caught you round the big toe.

'I won't let myself think that,' she whispered. 'I won't. I daren't. Not murder!'

She was shaking like the proverbial aspen, and Weyland thought she had had enough. Oh, she was suffering from delusions all right, and you could never tell in which direction they'd develop. There'd been a royal row when she came in a few minutes ago, and next time it mightn't stop at words. He admired Miss Webster, though he privately thought her abilities wasted on this job, but he wanted to help her, and it was as well not to have old creatures with hallucinations on the premises. He didn't think it necessary to go any farther. They'd be kind enough to her in the institution. So he said, 'Quite right! I wouldn't if I were you. Murder's quite a job, you know.' And then he said he'd get someone to come and help her to dress.

Miss Martin declared quite passionately that she was perfectly capable of looking after herself. After all, she did her own dressing every day of her life, so the doctor left her and returned to the room where Miss Webster and Doreen were anxiously awaiting him.

He shut the door carefully and walked up to the table. 'Crazy as a loon,' he said, answering the unspoken question in their eyes. 'Got persecution mania, if you ask me. Chattering about murder that mustn't be committed, all the rest of it. Who was she really out with this morning?'

'I haven't the least idea,' confessed Miss Webster. 'As a matter of fact, as I said before, she came back with a stranger yesterday, and then she wanted to ring up somebody called Cook . . .'

'Funny,' said the doctor, 'she said something to me about Cook or Crook.'

'She's got an idea in her head that there's a mystery child at the orphanage, and she hangs round there spying, and she says she's engaged a private detective – and then fancy her taking Mrs. Mount's hat. She'd never do that if she were in her right mind.'

'Oh, there's no question of that,' said the doctor heartily. 'When they start burbling about murders they're going to prevent clap 'em under hatches before they start doing the murdering themselves. Well, well, nothing for me to stay for.' He took up his hat. 'I'll have a word with Thompson, but you can take it from me you won't have much more trouble in that direction.'

'Do you think she suspects anything?'

'I've told her to be careful of her heart – not that there's anything seriously wrong, but naturally at seventy-four it's not going to be the same as it was at seventeen. Still, with these old ladies it's as well to be careful.'

He went off, as little concerned at his proposed action as a housemaid treading on a beetle.

Miss Martin emerged a few minutes later, her usual neat self.

'Did he say anything?' she inquired.

'Just that you must be careful and perhaps this is rather a

relaxing atmosphere for you.' That was Miss Webster, soothing and cool. 'Now, I believe Miss Blake was going to suggest taking you out to lunch, but in the circumstances, seeing you've been out already and the weather's so bad . . .'

'I really ought to be getting back to town,' interrupted Doreen. 'We've got a fearful pressure of work, and Agatha, my partner, has a very heavy cold. If it weren't a matter of our daily bread she would be lying up herself, but of course people with livings to get can't afford to be ill. There is an afternoon train that will get me in in time for a late supper, and Agatha can meet me at the station. Thank Heaven for basic petrol.'

'If she has such a heavy cold should she be out late?' inquired Miss Martin.

'Oh, she'll wrap up well. And then the climate down there is much less menacing.'

'I've always heard that,' agreed Miss Martin. 'I don't know how it is, but though I've several times planned to take a holiday in that part of the world something's always prevented it.'

Doreen shot a hurried glance at Matron. This was precisely the type of conversation she wished to avoid. Fortunately, at that moment the dinner bell began to ring, and there was a general movement towards the dining-room. Matron suggested that Doreen should stay for a meal, but Doreen said No, really she couldn't, her connection . . .

Miss Martin said in the same simple voice, 'I'm afraid I don't understand why you made that long journey, Doreen. Miss Webster could have sent you the doctor's report. I feel there must be something you're concealing from me!'

'You mustn't start suspecting people, Aunt Janet,' said Doreen sharply. 'It – it puts ideas into people's heads.'

Miss Martin looked at her steadily, and Doreen kissed her in a hit-or-miss manner, and went out quickly. For some reason she found herself thinking of Judas Iscariot. After she had departed Miss Martin said in a gentle voice, 'I wonder if there is something I may ask you, Miss Webster. Did the doctor say anything more to you than my niece told me? I know they often don't tell the patient.'

'He said you must be careful of your heart, not get excited.'

'I see. I am afraid what he really means is that he would

like me to abandon this inquiry I've instigated, but surely you do understand how impossible that would be. One must do one's duty, however, unpalatable or dangerous it may seem.'

Miss Webster sighed, not drearily, but with a sort of resigned satisfaction. There was no doubt about it. Dr. Weyland was right. As crazy as a coot.

When Miss Martin went up to her room to get ready for dinner she was horrified to discover Mrs. Mount sitting on the bed busily shredding her (Miss Martin's) only black velvet hat into fragments. She had a vicious little pair of scissors, and she was hacking and slicing, bending the wire that kept the brim in shape, hauling at the velvet bow, and the little bright brooch that was its sole ornament. She didn't seem to realize Miss Martin's presence, for she didn't lift her head. Her lips were moving, without ceasing. When the furious beating of her heart had subsided a little Miss Martin could make out the words. 'Vengeance is mine, I will repay, saith the Lord,' And then with a sudden cackle of laughter, 'But God helps those that help themselves.'

Miss Martin crept away, shocked and frightened. There had been such malice, such fury of purpose behind that senseless slashing, those whispered blasphemies. In the hall she found Miss Webster talking to Miss Maynard.

'You should be in at dinner, Miss Martin,' said Matron. 'Mrs. Mount will eat your share as well as hers if you're not careful.'

'No, she won't,' whispered Miss Martin. 'She's not there. She's . . .' For an instant Miss Webster's heart raced. She thought. Not another murder story, and then the old lady went on, 'She's sitting on the side of my bed, cutting my hat to pieces.'

Miss Webster was so relieved she began to laugh. 'It's not funny,' whispered Miss Martin, and there was neither indignation nor resentment in her manner. Her fear began to communicate itself to her listeners. Miss Webster capitulated hurriedly.

'No, of course it isn't funny. It was unkind to laugh. If she's really spoiled your hat naturally you shall have another.'

'Doreen won't be at all pleased,' thought Miss Martin.

'Now go in to dinner,' urged Miss Webster, but it was a few minutes before Miss Martin felt able to face the others.

When she went in at last she found Mrs. Mount already seated. She was talking in her usual excitable fashion, but she seemed no madder than usual. She was telling her neighbour about a dream she had had the previous night, a dream about death.

'My dreams,' she said mysteriously, 'always come true. There's going to be a death here before long, you mark my words.'

Her neighbour pursed up her lips to remark, 'They go by opposites, that's what I was always taught. So to dream of death means a birth.'

Mrs. Mount let out a long cackle of laughter. 'What, here, Miss Fay? Well, I never. Easy to see you're a spinster.'

Miss Maynard, who had now entered the dining-room, broke up the conversation by saying that the Vicar of St. Jude's was having a sale of work during the following month for the benefit of the heathen, and a Mrs. Ormerod created a fresh disturbance by saying thoughtfully, 'it's funny they never have sales of work for Christians, do they? Only the unconverted and girls who've gone astray. I remember my husband taking me to hear Fr. Bernard Vaughan when we were first married. He was the rage that year, and I must say he was a fine figure of a man. I can see him now, standing in the pulpit crying out, "Give me the man or woman who has sinned." Yes, I said to John on the way home, they're more interesting. No one's interested in virtue till it's been lost.'

Mrs. Mount leaned forward and her long chin almost dipped into the Scotch broth. 'It's all in the Bible, Mrs. Ormerod,' she assured her. 'It's a pity people spend so much time reading trashy papers instead of the Word. There is more joy in Heaven over one sinner that repenteth than over ninety-and-nine just persons that need no repentance.'

Miss Maynard, knowing how easily conversation on religion leads to brawling, changed the subject again, and Mrs. Mount became occupied in seeing that no one had a superior helping of pie to her own. After dinner the old ladies dispersed as usual, and Miss Martin was glad to assent to a suggestion that she should lie down for a little while in her room.

'You're looking tired,' Miss Maynard told her.

'I feel tired to death,' acknowledged Miss Martin, who had eaten nothing, and who felt, as she expressed it, quite washed-out. 'I do wish,' she added nervously, 'I need not have Mrs. Mount to sleep with me to-night. I really am afraid of her.'

'You mustn't say that. I've been talking to her and I think she's really sorry she ruined your hat. Later on she'll probably tell you so.'

Oh, I hope not, thought poor Miss Martin, feeling that any more of Mrs. Mount would be insupportable. It had been such an exhausting day already, what with her anxiety about Terry, her unexpected joy-ride, the scene with Mrs. Mount, the interview with the doctor, the conviction she had that something was being deliberately concealed from her. She wanted more than anything else to sleep – sleep for years, perhaps, drift out on the dark tides, become oblivious to the difficulties and perplexities of the present time, and wake to find that all the problems had solved themselves.

'And I needn't even feel anxious about Terry and Pamela any longer,' she reminded herself. 'Mr. Crook and Mr. Watson are looking after them.'

It never occurred to her that these two benefactors might not be batting on the same side.

CHAPTER 14

It was horribly disappointing when at last she was settled on her bed with a hot-water bottle to find that after all she wasn't going to sleep. That delicious soporific feeling she had experienced towards the end of lunch was leaving her; she felt restless, anxious even, without knowing why. She felt she was struggling in the heart of a mystery she could not solve; she knew she was surrounded by inimical influences. . . . She turned from one side to the other, and she had barely got settled when she saw the door handle slowly turn. Oh, dear, can't I be left in peace? thought poor Miss Martin. She supposed it was one of the Matrons come to make sure she was all right. It's a mistake for women to have too much sense of duty. It worries as many people into premature graves as poison or the knife.

This time, however, it was neither of the Matrons, but old Mrs. Mount. At the sight of her Miss Martin started up in bed, but the old witch put a hurried finger to her lip.

'Don't make a sound,' she mouthed. 'You know what it's like here. Like the Inquisition – the eye in the wall. You remember? People can say what they like about Henry VIIth, but he was quite right to break away from the Roman yoke.' She came closer. 'You poor dear, you do look tired.'

'I was just trying to sleep,' confessed Miss Martin, looking at those big, twitching hands.

'Quite right. Best thing for you. I only came to say I'm sorry about your hat. It was un-Christian – I see it now. I didn't at first. I thought – An eye for an eye and a tooth for a tooth. But when I looked at my gospel again – I keep it here (she smote her thin bosom) – it said, Be ye angry and sin not. Let not the sun go down upon your wrath.'

Miss Martin was feeling dazed and not like herself at all. 'There isn't any sun to-day,' she pointed out, foolishly.

'You know what I mean. My dear, I know just what you want. An aspirin.'

As a matter of fact, Miss Martin had been thinking just the same. Unfortunately she had run out of aspirins.

'I'll get you some,' offered Mrs. Mount obligingly.

'But I thought you never took them. You always say they're drugs and . . .'

'No, I haven't got any, but I know where *she* keeps hers.' *She* was Miss Webster.

'But you can't . . .' began Miss Martin, when Mrs. Mount interrupted her, saying, 'Now don't you worry. Be anxious for nothing. That's in the Book, too. But in everything give thanks. That's the other half of the text. I know she's got a bottle of aspirins in her medicine chest.'

'But you can't go to that, Mrs. Mount. It's locked, and Miss Webster wears the key round her neck.'

Mrs. Mount began to laugh in a low, rather frightening way. 'They think we're all fools here. They think we don't know anything. They forget we've lived much longer than they have, and we haven't forgotten everything we knew. That lock's child's play. Any one could open it with a bit of wire. Now, don't look shocked and say you don't want the aspirin when obviously you do. I can't go bothering Miss Webster at this hour, but I don't see why you should go without your aspirin just the same.'

She turned and marched triumphantly out of the room. Miss Martin lay quaking. Two or three minutes later old Mrs. Mount returned with two little white capsules in her open palm. 'Didn't bring the bottle,' she boasted. 'She'll never know. Now wait while I get a glass of water.'

She stood over Miss Martin while the old lady put the capsules in her mouth and washed them down.

'Some people can take them dry,' she remarked, 'but I always think they have a rather bitter taste.'

'Thank you very much,' said Miss Martin, gratefully. 'I believe now I really shall sleep.'

Mrs. Mount stood looking down at her for a minute. The

beds were rather low and Mrs. Mount looked enormous, towering above Janet's little shrinking figure. Suddenly the old lady opened her mouth and in a surprisingly sweet voice began to sing:-

'Hush, my dear, lie still and slumber,
Holy angels guard thy bed.
Heavenly blessings without number
Gently falling on thy head.

'You know, Miss Martin, I believe you're right. I believe you're going to sleep for a long, long time.'

The old ladies had what Mrs. Trent called 'a cupper' at four o'clock, and this meal was always eagerly attended. It broke the monotony of the long, dull afternoon, for in this weather it got dark too early and was at all times too cold for any pleasure to be gained from the slow crawl that constituted a walk to most of them. Besides, they had been to the shops as a rule in the morning and most of them were too blind or too deaf or too poor to go to the cinema; or else they didn't like the programmes, and in any case the afternoon show involved missing your tea, and it would take such a galaxy of stars as even Hollywood might find it difficult to produce to induce them to miss that. So as a rule they all collected in the parlour just before four o'clock when the big enamel pots of tea and the cans of milk and plates of thick bread and butter appeared, the fortunate ones clutching some little dainty sent by a relative, a small jar of honey or some seedless jam, anything that made a change and gave them that sense of superiority to their neighbours without which it is so difficult to live.

On this particular day they all arrived punctually with the exception of Miss Martin. Miss Maynard's sharp eye at once noticed her absence, and she asked if any one had seen her. At the back of her mind was a fear that the old lady might have slipped her leash once again. Mrs. Mount said the poor dear was lying down, she looked fagged out, and that was a fact, and she had said she was going to try and sleep till dinner-time. Miss Maynard, who had her own suspicions where Mrs. Mount was concerned, finished pouring out the tea and went up to Miss Martin's room. There, sure enough, she was lying fast asleep and Miss Maynard decided not to disturb her. Poor old thing, she'd little enough to look forward to and in the unusual circumstances she might have a cup of tea on her own when she awoke.

Waking, however, seemed to be something Miss Martin didn't intend to do. Miss Maynard looked in again at five and again at half-past six, and still the old lady slept. Miss Maynard might have gone over and investigated that last time if she hadn't heard the telephone just then, and had to go down to answer it, Miss Webster being out. She decided to wait till half-past seven supper and arouse Miss Martin for that. She whispered to Mrs. Mount whom she met on the stairs, that she was letting Miss Martin have her sleep out, and Mrs. Mount nodded enthusiastically and said Yes, that was what the poor dear wanted, a long, long sleep. Miss Maynard found that her telephone correspondent was Miss Shaw, whose elderly aunt was to take Miss Martin's place the following week, and to enjoy or otherwise Mrs. Mount's company, and she made tentative arrangements, covering herself by saying that these must be confirmed by Miss Webster before they could be regarded as binding. It was a little after seven when she again went upstairs to look at Miss Martin, who did not appeared to have stirred since last time. Miss Maynard crossed the room and stooped above the bed.

'Time to wake up now,' she said cheerfully, and then, when the old lady still didn't move, she put a light hand on her shoulder.

'Time for supper,' she urged, shaking the old body gently. There was no response at all, unless you can call a slight movement of the head, a falling forward, a response.

Miss Maynard was struck with a sudden suspicion. She thrust a hand inside the old lady's clothes, feeling for the heart, but there was no response there either. The lids fell back from the eyes as she moved the body slightly, and there couldn't be any doubt now what had happened. After a moment she straightened. 'Poor old thing'! she said and then, 'Well, perhaps it's all for the best. She hadn't much left to live for.'

She went downstairs, closing the door very carefully, as though afraid of disturbing the sleeper, and sought Miss Webster, who had fortunately returned by now.

In an establishment like Beverley it is impossible to keep anything dark. The old ladies, as if by instinct, always knew when fresh arrivals were expected or old hands departing. They seemed to suck in inspiration from the air, and the moment they saw the two matrons conferring in low tones just outside Miss Webster's room they realized something was afoot. They were all of them either in the parlour awaiting the call to supper or distractedly tying bows round their eldritch locks, and putting on sequined slippers, or pinning an elderly flower into their belts; for they all belonged to a generation that knew it was the right thing to change for dinner, and even if they hadn't all got as far as what Mr. Crook would have called the soup-and-fish, they had all made some embellishment to their day dress, even if the evening meal was only dried eggs and toast, with a pot of tea and cheese to follow.

Now a whisper of excitement began to run through the building. Doors opened a stealthy inch, and curious ears and eyes appeared in the resultant cracks. One or two, bolder than the rest, actually came into the upper corridor or down the stairs, causing the two ladies to retire inside Matron's room and firmly close the door. Matron echoed Miss Maynard's verdict.

'Really, a blessing for us all.'

She was never more mistaken in her life.

Leaving Miss Maynard to shepherd the old ladies into supper Miss Webster took up the telephone. Dr. Weyland was out, she was informed and no one quite knew when he would be back. Miss Webster hesitated. In emergencies there was a second doctor on call, but, since Miss Martin was clearly beyond human aid, for Matron had gone to verify her subordinate's statement, it seemed unnecessary to involve him also. But what a mercy, reflected Matron, hanging up the receiver that Dr. Weyland overhauled her this morning. Inquests never did a nursing home any good, even when the outcome was a foregone conclusion, as it was in this case. The nuisance of it was that until she had communicated with Dr. Weyland, she didn't feel able to take any steps towards removing the body, and it would obviously be advisable for the old lady to be taken to the mortuary as early as possible. You didn't want a corpse on the premises with all these scatter-brained old creatures about. Besides, it was depressing for them, reminding them of their own inevitable and probably not-long-to-be-delayed end. Still, there was no help for it. She went into the dining-room and told the assembly that she wanted everything to be kept very quiet as poor Miss Martin wasn't at all well, the doctor would be coming along later. She arranged for alternative sleeping accommodation for Mrs. Mount (another reason why the sooner the old lady was removed the better) and answered questions evasively.

'She wants a long rest,' she said in comprehensive tones. Mrs. Mount nodded. 'A long rest,' she repeated, and then in a louder voice, 'So He giveth His Beloved sleep.'

There was no keeping the old ladies quiet that evening in spite of Miss Webster's warning. They whispered and rustled, and went up and down stairs, one was even caught turning the handle of the room where Miss Martin lay, only to find the door locked. Speculations were rife. Miss Martin was dead, she's been murdered, she had the plague, they'd all have the plague and die . . . On one point they were all agreed. From the very first they'd known there was something queer about her. They reminded one another how they'd said so. At all events, it made a normally dull evening bright with sensational hopes.

The doctor rang up about nine. He sounded tired and out of sorts. He had been fighting for a boy's life and he'd lost it, so it was probably irrational of Miss Webster to mind his cursory dismissal of Miss Martin.

'Died in her sleep, has she?' he commented. 'Lucky to die so easily. This young lad I've been with . . .' He broke off. 'I'll send along a certificate in the morning,' he promised. 'I told you the heart wanted watching. She's been getting herself worked up I suppose. No, there's nothing you could have done. It's really a blessing in disguise.'

But, as Mr. Crook was to observe later, it was the sort of disguise adopted by wolves when they want to masquerade as lambs and insinuate themselves into the flock.

Mr. Crook heard of the death the next morning when he telephoned the Home and asked for Miss Martin. Miss Webster took the call and told him she was afraid he couldn't speak to the old lady, she was too ill to come to the phone. 'In fact,' she added, realizing that to make mystery about a death is to court disaster, 'she died very suddenly last night, in her sleep. It was very peaceful.'

'What did she die of?' demanded Mr. Crook, so aggressively that Matron asked who he was.

'I'm her legal adviser. I've been in touch with her recently – and she was all right then.'

'People with weak hearts often slip off suddenly, particularly when they're old,' said Matron. She felt perplexed as well she might. How could a penniless old lady with a managing niece like Doreen Blake need or achieve a lawyer? And why had they never heard of him before? It was one thing to sign up someone with practically no ties, quite another when there was a legal representative lurking in the background.

'Particularly if someone gives 'em a gentle shove.' Mr. Crook's voice recalled her to the present. 'What does the doctor say?'

'I told you – heart trouble. I think perhaps it would be best for you to get in touch with her niece, Miss Blake.'

'Not much,' said Crook, heartily. 'The weaned child may put its hand on the cockatrice's den, but I'm no weaned child.'

'But Mr. Crook . . .' Suddenly Miss Webster stopped and, strong woman though she was, almost fainted. Something in her mind had clicked all of a sudden. She had spoken slightingly of a Mr. Cook; now she realized her mistake. Miss Martin had been in earnest when she spoke of employing a private detective to make inquiries about the child at the orphanage. More, she hadn't been so crazy as they supposed. There was something in it. And her unexpected death wasn't going to be a quiet way out of an uncomfortable situation. She had never set eyes on the man now talking to her at the other end of the telephone, but she knew from his voice that he was a trouble-maker, though she had no notion how much trouble he intended to create.

'What's the name of your doctor?' Crook was demanding in so powerful a tone that the telephone wires seemed to shiver. 'And when did he last see my client?'

'Dr. Weyland. And he saw her yesterday morning when she came in from her walk.'

'Walk?' yelled Crook. 'In that downpour? Sure she didn't die of pneumonia?'

Suddenly Miss Webster remembered Miss Martin's terse explanation, 'I was driving,' and she said with her first flutter of real fear, 'She wasn't wet. She was out with someone – in a car.'

'Whose car?'

'I – really I don't know. She went out in a most secret and furtive fashion. As a matter of fact, she has recently contracted a habit of – of accepting lifts from strangers. I warned her no good could come of it, but she was inclined to be headstrong, like a lot of old people who've lived alone for years and have never had to consider any one else. This wasn't the first time. She came back the previous afternoon with some man she had never set eyes on hitherto.'

'Me,' said Crook succinctly. 'But it wasn't me yesterday.'

'The circumstances,' said Miss Webster slowly, 'were very mysterious. I can't help feeling there was something prearranged about it. And her telephone call . . .'

'Keep 'em in the bag till I come down,' begged Crook. 'Be seeing you. By the way, no thought of cremation or anything like that, I take it?'

'I am awaiting her niece's instructions. It is very trying for Miss Blake. She will only just have returned home . . .'

'Too bad,' agreed Crook. 'Still, whom the Lord loveth He chasteneth. And I know that niece.'

'She has never mentioned . . .' began Miss Webster, indignation tingeing the fear she had begun to experience. It seemed as though deceit ran in the family – first Miss Martin and now Doreen. But Crook interrupted cheerfully, 'Why, how should she? I know her but she don't know me. Thumbs up, Mother Brown,' and he rang off. But Bill, coming in an instant later, was startled by the expression on his chief's face. As a rule Crook accepted his commissions as a grocer accepts orders over the counter and 'We aim to please,' he'd say, risking his life whenever necessary without making any fuss about it, because it was all part of the day's work. He could be ruthless enough, as men who had the temerity to get up against him had discovered to their cost, but though he seldom admitted it himself he had his feelings, and both they and his professional pride were lacerated by the knowledge that Miss Martin, to whom he'd said, 'Crook will take care of you,' had been caught by the other side. For it never occurred to him that this was a natural death. You might argue it was really her own fault, putting herself into the other fellow's power, for clearly she had gone out with some stranger when he'd warned her to watch every single step she took, but that didn't materially alter the position. Crook always gets his man, was Crook's motto, and its corollary was that nobody else ever gets Crook's protégées. Bill Parsons thought he wouldn't care to be in the shoes of whoever had put Miss Martin out of the way.

But no one knew then how this extraordinary story was going to break.

CHAPTER 15

Crook was even more alarming than Miss Webster had anticipated. To begin with, she took great exception to his appearance, and she did not perceive, as Miss Martin had done almost at once, any charm or kindness under that surface vulgarity. By what she described as a lucky chance, Doreen had not, after all, returned home the previous night. When she reached her club she found a member there who could, she thought, be useful to her, so she had wired Agatha not to expect her till the next day, and by that time she had heard from Miss Webster of her aunt's death.

'Who on earth is this Crook person?' she demanded on arrival. And Miss Webster reminded her that the old lady had spoken of employing a private detective in connection with this orphan of mysterious origins.

'And who did she imagine was going to pay for him?' demanded Doreen.

'I really didn't raise the matter with her. As a matter of fact, I'm afraid I didn't take her seriously.'

'And I thought you said this Mr. Crook was a lawyer. Funny sort of lawyer if you ask me.' Doreen sniffed. 'Did you say he was coming down?'

'Yes. He seems to think there may be something – peculiar – about your aunt's death.'

'If he thinks there are any pickings for him he's going to have a rude shock. As for being peculiar, I never heard of anything so ridiculous. As a matter of fact, it's a wonderful solution to the problem. I never did like the idea of her going into the mental ward of an institution. It's not what one anticipates for one's relations, even though we are all such democrats nowadays. What's this Mr. Crook's number? I'll ring up and put him off, and at the same time I'll tell him he can whistle for his fees. It's no use talking about the estate because there isn't one. My aunt, on my advice, put all her money into an annuity.'

Miss Webster had to confess she hadn't got the number, and added she didn't think Crook was the kind of person to be put off by a telephone message.

'I'll soon show him where he gets off,' promised Doreen grimly.

But there, of course, she spoke without the book.

Crook arrived a little later, bringing his noisy little roadster to a stop outside the gate, and swinging up the path looking like Lord Bullion – Mine is the earth and you'll please get off it. As soon as he was in the Matron's room, and almost before he'd slammed down that common brown bowler which, said Doreen icily to her friend, Agatha, when she got back, marked him as being as common as they come, he announced, 'Well, this is a pretty kettle of fish. Don't blame me if you're both scalded.'

'I don't quite understand how my aunt established a connection with you,' announced Doreen in her most formal manner, the manner that intimidated nervous customers into buying something they didn't want at a preposterous price they couldn't afford, only, as Doreen had nothing that Crook wanted to buy it didn't have that effect on him, 'but it must have been obvious to you that she was not – that is, that she was non compos mentis and therefore incapable of looking after her own affairs.'

'If she was, then Heaven send a few more like her,' returned Crook, heartily. 'What lawyers hate more than anything else is the gifted amateur, the chap who thinks he knows a bit. And as for bein' incapable, that's why she came to me, and if more ladies followed her example . . .' But he stopped there, remembering what the climax of Miss Martin's visit had been. Doreen didn't notice his momentary change of manner, because she had too much to say herself.

'Naturally, I don't know what she told you,' she said, 'but if she led you to believe she was in a position to employ either a lawyer or a private detective, she misled you sadly.'

'Let it ride,' said Crook in a more cheerful voice. 'You know what they say – You cannot serve God and Mammon.'

'And which,' Doreen inquired foolishly, 'do you consider you are serving at the present time?'

'Well, lady, you've just pointed out it ain't Mammon. Remember Sherlock Holmes? Take away the impossible and whatever remains is the answer.'

Doreen decided to ignore that. 'In any case, my aunt is dead – heart failure . . .'

'You might say every death's due to heart failure,' retorted Crook, just as Dr. Macintosh had done. 'How did it happen? She was in smashin' good form the day before.'

'She was an old lady,' said Miss Webster, 'and she had had a great deal of excitement.'

'Stimulatin' as old brandy,' suggested Crook. 'Besides, hearts don't fail suddenly, Not when they're made of pure gold. Now, how about the little girl?'

'Little girl?'

'Don't she tell you anything?' asked Crook, pityingly. 'The little girl at the orphanage.'

'That was an illusion she cherished. The child resembled someone she had seen once or twice in London – why, she didn't even know any children.'

'She might not tell you that. How about the young lady?'

'The young lady?'

'This ain't the parrot-house,' Crook pointed out mildly. 'Or do you fancy yourself as Echo? Yes, there was a young lady who was also interested in the little girl, and she got a bit too interested for somebody's liking, and she disappeared. And no one seems to know what's happened to the little girl, and Miss Martin dies suddenly of a heart attack. I didn't have much schoolin',' confessed Crook handsomely, 'but they did teach me that two and two made four.'

'I never heard of any young lady,' said Doreen, stubbornly.

'Miss Lawrence,' added Crook, with his most helpful smile.

Miss Webster came suddenly to life. 'Why, that was the girl who rang her up that night.'

'Which night?'

'The night she came back from having tea at Cheston with a friend.'

'Me,' said Crook modestly.

'The first call came while Miss Martin was out, and whoever telephoned seemed very anxious to establish contact, and about six o'clock she rang up again.' Miss Webster's discomfort was obvious to them both. 'I must admit she seemed very much excited.'

'Why didn't she ring me?' demanded Crook, with a frown.

'As a matter of fact, she did try and get a connection, but the telephone was in use and afterwards it was too late . . .'

'Too right,' agreed Crook, gloomily. 'Of all sad words of tongue or pen, The saddest are these, It might have been. If she had got in touch with me she might be alive now.'

'That is quite absurd,' contradicted Doreen crisply. 'You speak as though she had been murdered.'

'Like to take a bet with me she wasn't?'

Doreen stared. 'If this is a joke, Mr. Crook . . .'

'You try gettin' murdered and see how much of a joke it is,' Crook advised her. 'By the way, where is the old lady?'

'We're waiting for the ambulance now,' Matron told him. 'You will understand that in a nursing home we can't keep the body on the premises. Miss Blake understands perfectly, don't you, Miss Blake?'

'Of course,' said Doreen.

'Glad someone does,' said Crook. 'I feel like a senior wrangler in a fog myself. Well, shall we go up?'

'I don't see any necessity,' said Doreen at once.

'Where's your telephone?' Crook asked Miss Webster.

'It's in the hall, but . . .'

'Police don't like bein' kept waiting,' explained Crook, making for the door.

'The police?'

'Anything about me give you the idea I'm not a good citizen?' demanded Crook in belligerent tones.

'I don't understand.'

'A good citizen's first duty is to help the police, in season and out, and if the aforesaid citizen thinks there's been dirty work at the cross-roads, then the least he can do it go down to the cross-roads with his magnifying glass and take a look round. But, of course, if you don't want me to see the lady, I'll have to go round and tell the police I'm not satisfied about her death.'

'You can't do that,' said Doreen at once.

'You ask the Home Secretary,' said Crook. 'It's the duty as well as the privilege of every citizen to lodge a complaint with the police and ask for inquiries if he suspects a death isn't due to natural causes. Nice for criminals if he couldn't. Think of all the chaps who'd have died comfortably in their beds – Crippen, Wainwright . . .' he reeled off a list of names.

'But who on earth could want to do an old lady like my aunt any harm?'

'You tell me who she went out with yesterday morning and I'll give you your answer.'

He ploughed upstairs and went to stand beside all that remained of Miss Martin, about as much, he reflected, as would make a good-sized bird. She had been prepared for burial, with her eyes closed and her hands crossed on her breast. Crook stooped over her and with surprising gentleness, lifted an eyelid. Then still bending, he inquired, 'Has the doctor seen her?'

'I told you, he saw her yesterday morning and said her heart was weak, and of course, all this excitement and possibly exposure to the rain, though I must admit she was scarcely wet at all . . .'

'Death certificate?'

'Dr. Weyland has just sent it up.'

'Without comin' to see the body?'

'It's quite in order. He'd seen her a few hours before.'

'Sure it is. P'raps that's what X. was counting on. Well, I'll be getting along. I dare say you'll be seein' him soon. Unless, of course, they've taken the body to the mortuary before then.'

With no further explanations he was gone, leaving the two women in a state of alarm and confusion. Miss Webster, understandably enough, thought of the reputation of the home. Doreen was uncomfortably visualizing what people in general would say if the whole story broke. How typical of Aunt Janet to be mixed up in something criminal! Only a relation would think of doing anything so tactless.

Crook went posting off to see Weyland, speculating as he went whether the two women would ring up the doctor and warn him what he was in for. Not that Crook cared; it wouldn't do the fellow any good if it got known that he was prepared to give a certificate without even seeing the body, and Crook was quite prepared to call in the police if he had to. He didn't for a moment believe that Miss Martin had come by a natural death. Life doesn't work out as simply as that. Dr. Weyland was out when Crook reached his house and wasn't expected back for the better part of an hour, but the housekeeper said he would be up at the Cottage Hospital, so, quite undaunted, Crook trekked up there and explained that one of Weyland's patients was *in extremis* and he was the next of kin. It said a good deal for his persuasiveness that within five minutes he found himself confronting Weyland, for whom he conceived an instant dislike. Just the sort of chap who would let Miss Martin be poisoned, and give a certificate of death from natural causes, he thought unfairly.

'Well, my man,' said Weyland, seeing Crook, and apparently returning the dislike in full measure, 'who are you? I was told . . .'

'It's Miss Martin,' replied Crook, unceremoniously. 'I understand you're sending along a death certificate?'

'What the hell's that to do with you?' the doctor demanded.

'Just that I thought for every one's sake it might be as well if you saw the body first.'

'When I want insolence,' began Weyland angrily, but Crook broke in, 'Better than a coroner's reprimand . . .' His voice changed, he sounded pompous and accusing. 'And I feel bound to say that I find myself in agreement with the jury in thinking the doctor greatly to blame in giving a certificate without first seeing the body. There isn't an old lady in the place who'd have you inside the house after that,' added Crook, reverting to his own voice.

'Look here, I don't know who the devil you are . . .'

'Miss Martin's legal adviser. Crook's the name, Arthur Crook.'

Weyland's face changed. 'I've heard of you,' he said.

'Honoured, I'm sure,' said Crook.

'You – you're in with the police gangs, aren't you?'

'Say we're both interested in crime and you might be nearer the mark, only the police ain't interested till it's been committed, and I like to be in on the ground floor. That's the only difference between us. And, of course, they have to keep the Home Secretary's rule, whereas, if him and me can't see eye to eye, he goes out on his ear.'

'Come outside,' said Weyland, abruptly. 'No, wait a minute. I must just have a word with Matron.' He explained to that lady that he had just been summoned to a death-bed, and he went with Crook in the Scourge. 'Now, then,' he demanded, 'What's all this about? Why should you think it's anything but an ordinary heart attack? These old ladies have 'em all the time, and they're lucky when it carries 'em off.'

'Sometimes,' suggested Crook, 'the luck's for the other people.'

'Not in this case,' Weyland assured him. 'She hasn't a bean and she was a bit dotty anyway. Matter of fact, I was going to sign her up.'

'Who suggested that?'

'It was Miss Webster, as a matter of fact. Miss Martin was always hanging about round the orphanage and spinning yarns . . .'

'About recognizing a little girl there? I know. She spun me that one, only my reaction wasn't the same as Miss Webster's. Before makin' up my mind the old lady was mad I thought I'd make a few enquiries, and I found out mighty quick why so many people were anxious to see her shut up. Know Mrs. Forbes?'

'I don't attend the House. Thompson does that. But I know her – yes.'

It might have amused a more self-conscious man to see how the doctor's manner had changed. Now he was more than civil, he was almost deferential.

'Might have a word with her presently,' brooded Crook, pulling up in front of Beverley. 'Now then – let's hope they've kept the rest of the flock out of the way.'

Doreen was waiting, half-aggressive, half-intimidated, in the hall.

'I do hope you won't find you've been brought down on a fool's errand, Dr. Weyland,' she said.

Weyland stared at her as if he'd never seen her before. 'I only hope I have,' he snapped, and pushing past he went upstairs to where Miss Martin was still sleeping.

Crook didn't offer to accompany him, but Miss Webster went up and was horrified to hear the doctor say after a brief interval, 'I'm afraid you'll have to destroy that death certificate, Miss Webster. There's been a most unlooked-for development. That fellow, Crook's right. There's something all wrong here.'

'But what is it?' asked Matron nervously.

'You didn't give her any morphia?' He threw back his head and looked at his companion keenly.

'Certainly not.'

'I thought not. All the same, that's what she died of.' He considered. 'No likelihood of her consulting another doctor?'

'I'm sure she didn't.'

'I didn't suppose so. Do you keep morphine on the premises?'

Miss Webster looked startled and a little outraged. 'There's a supply made up on your prescription during the war, in case of air raid casualties. As you know the raids never troubled us, and we have very little occasion to use the stuff here. Now and again an old lady requires a sixth of morphia to calm her down, but at very rare intervals. The supply is practically intact.'

'You could check it up then?'

'But doctor, you surely don't suppose . . .'

'Somehow, Matron, this old lady got hold of morphine or was supplied with it. If it can be shown that it couldn't have come from your store, then we shall have to start looking outside. She has none of her own, of course?'

'She told me once she had never had anything stronger than aspirin, and she certainly couldn't keep morphia on the premises without someone discovering it. There's not very much privacy here, you know, and some of the old ladies are very untidy and we keep their things in order for them. Oh, no, I should say that was quite out of the question.'

'And where do you keep your supply?'

'In the medicine chest in my room.'

'Locked, of course?'

'And the key never leaves me night or day. I don't even hand it over to my assistant.' She pulled at a slender gold chain she wore round her neck and showed him the key.

'Better check it all the same,' the doctor advised, and they left poor Miss Martin and went into Matron's room. The key went into the lock easily enough, though it was a moment before it turned.

'Sometimes it's a little stiff,' Matron explained. Then the

door swung open and she took out a little bottle. The silence that followed was so long that the doctor became apprehensive.

'Hey, what's up?' he demanded.

'I don't understand,' whispered Matron. 'No one could get at this cupboard. And yet . . .'

'Yet what?'

She turned to him in desperation. 'I unlocked it to get some aspirins for one of the old ladies about three days ago. Of course, there's nothing to prevent them buying their own, but I don't keep mine unlocked because you can do yourself harm even with aspirin if you take enough. I generally get them by the hundred, but it so happened that my chemist only had small bottles in stock last time I ordered them and, as you can see, the aspirin bottle and the bottle of morphine,' she set the two before him, 'are much of a size.'

'Well?' said the doctor, uncomprehendingly.

'Someone's been at them. I haven't touched the morphine bottle for months, but – it's the wrong cork.'

'The wrong cork?'

'Yes. The aspirin cork has a tiny white label on it bearing the chemist's name – Ainslie. The morphine bottle hasn't. But the cork in the morphine bottle has the label on it now, and the other one is plain. So you see someone has been at both bottles, and in a hurry or not noticing has replaced the corks in the wrong order. And they were all right three days ago.'

'This is infernally serious,' said the doctor, as though she had not already recognized the fact. 'You're dead sure you couldn't have left the key anywhere, even for a few minutes.'

'I tell you, it's absolutely out of the question.'

'Then – possibly someone has a duplicate.'

'It's a special lock,' said Miss Webster dully. She saw ruin staring her in the face.

'H'm. The coroner's not going to like that story much. Now, we've got to face facts. Is there any one here who had a grudge against Miss Martin?'

'Mrs. Mount had a tremendous scene with her on the day she died, but that doesn't mean anything. They all blow over.'

'This one doesn't seem to have done,' was the doctor's grim comment.

'And in any case she had no access to the morphia.'
But, as it happened, Miss Webster was wrong.

Meanwhile, Crook had wasted no time. He was at once aware that he was an object of considerable curiosity to the inmates of Beverley and, as he sometimes observed, violets were nothing but a bad example to him. When the fourth old crone had made her excuse for coming to Matron's room, and was backing out with an air of refined surprise at finding a stranger in possession, he decided on the tactics of aggression, and said cordially, 'She won't be long. Come right in and wait. Yes, really. Besides, you might be able to help me. I'm sure you were a friend of Miss Martin's.'
'The poor dear. I shared her room. Many a night we've lain awake and remembering. And I was the last person to see her alive before she fell into an eternal sleep.'
'Then you're probably just the person I'm looking for,' responded Crook, heartily. 'Cold, isn't it? Come up to the fire. She didn't say anything, I suppose?'
'Only that she thought she would sleep for a long, long time. I sang her a lullaby.'
Even Crook was a little taken aback by that, though he made a quick recovery. Miss Martin was right, he decided. Bat-house and no mistake, that was what Beverley was.
'Is that all she said?'
'I think she had something on her mind. She wasn't like herself at all. I mean, she took my hat, took it out in the rain.'
'But she went in a car so it didn't get spoilt,' Crook comforted her.
'No one takes me in cars,' mourned Mrs. Mount. 'I was very angry when I saw the hat, because she must have known it wasn't hers. I *boiled*.'
'That's known as private enterprise,' Crook assured her. 'Taking first and asking afterwards. That's the secret of the might of the British Empire.'
'Afterwards I went up to tell her I was sorry I'd lost my temper.'
'Damn nice of you,' approved Crook.
'And I found she was quite restless, so I offered to get her some aspirin.'

'Hadn't she got any of her own?'

'No. And nor had I, but I knew Matron had some in her medicine chest.'

'So you persuaded Matron to part?'

'I didn't need to bother her.' Mrs. Mount wagged her mad old head. 'Can you keep a secret?' Without waiting for a reply she leaned closer. 'I know how to open Matron's chest.'

'Do you, by George? You're wasted here, I can see that.'

'Matron doesn't know, of course. No one does – except Miss Martin and she can't tell. I had a maid once when I had my own flat. Oh, yes, I had a flat once. She'd been in prison, the maid, I mean, for theft, and she showed me how to open locks with a piece of wire. She said it was perfectly easy when you knew how.'

'Is that how you opened the chest last night?'

Mrs. Mount chuckled. 'I did want poor Miss Martin to have her aspirin, and there'd been such a lot of fuss already, and it was quite easy. All the same, I nearly made the most dreadful mistake.'

'What's that?' Crook pricked up his ears.

'Yes. Do you know, *I opened the wrong bottle*. Well, they looked very much alike, little white tablets, but luckily just in time I saw Poison on the bottle, so I put them back – and what do you think they were?'

'Morphia,' said Crook.

'How did you guess?'

'Because that's what Miss Martin died of or I'm a Dutchman.'

Mrs. Mount stared. 'Oh, no. But – I didn't give them to her.'

'I'm not saying you did. I'm saying that's what she died of.'

He spoke with no visible emotion, but he experienced a sharp twinge of dismay. Here was his beautiful case falling to pieces before his eyes. But after a minute, being trained to find silver linings, he saw that even this unexpected twist could be turned to advantage. He hadn't wanted to have to come clean with the police, repeat Miss Martin's story and hazard his own theory; this yarn the old witch had just told him might delay things a bit. There'd be an inquest, of course, and the coroner would want to know who saw the dead woman last, and Mrs. Mount was practically certain to come out with this story and there'd be a devil of a lot of doubt and speculation, but for once he was inclined to agree with Doreen that whatever is may be for the best.

Mrs. Mount was regarding him with shocked eyes. 'You do believe me, don't you? You don't think I'd give her poison just because she took my hat? Why, I'm a Christian woman. I wouldn't give any one poison.'

'I'm sure you wouldn't,' Crook agreed. 'And don't let any one jockey you out of that story. They may try and shake you, you know. They've got to explain the morphia somehow, and obviously they'll jump at any explanation that offers.'

'No one's going to frighten me,' maintained Mrs. Mount. 'I'm an innocent woman. Innocent people are safe.'

Crook thought kindly, 'No sense disillusioning the old bird.' He knew that truth is what you can make the other chap believe and innocence has precious little to do with it. They had reached this stage in their conversation when they were interrupted by Dr. Weyland and Matron who had come to speak to Crook; Miss Webster looked distinctly annoyed to find Mrs. Mount in her room.

'Were you looking for me?' she inquired crisply. 'I'm afraid I'm busy just now.'

Mrs. Mount marched up to her and held up one hand like a bishop bestowing a blessing.

'I swear I didn't do it,' she said.

'Didn't do what?'

'Give her poison.'

'Who's talking about poison?' asked the doctor.

'You see, as I was telling this gentleman, I so nearly did and then I saw the label and realized it wasn't aspirin after all, but I'd picked up the wrong bottle, so I put it back, and . . .'

'What are you talking about?' exclaimed Miss Webster.

'It was poor Miss Martin, she wanted some aspirin, and I knew you kept some in your chest, and I didn't want to disturb you . . .'

'You don't know what you're saying. My chest was locked.'

'I can open harder locks than that,' boasted Mrs. Mount.

'You don't know what you're saying,' began Matron, for

the second time, but the doctor interrupted,' I think we'll clear this up. Now then, Mrs. Mount, just begin at the beginning.'

So Mrs. Mount repeated her story, winding up with an earnest, 'But I saw the label in time. It was only aspirin I gave her, so you see that can't be the cause of her death.'

'Of course not.' said Weyland more kindly than you'd have thought possible. 'Thank you for helping us. If there's anything more we want to know we'll ask you again. And one more thing. You won't speak of this to any one else in the house, will you? You see, it's important and private, and we wouldn't want every one to hear.'

'I shan't say a word,' promised Mrs. Mount. 'Really, I shan't. I promise.'

After the door had closed behing her the three she had left looked at one another with dubious expressions on their faces.

'Look at it any way you like,' observed Weyland gloomily, 'this is going to make a stink. If the old woman gave her the morphia by mistake . . .'

'I shall be blamed,' cut in Miss Webster.

'If she did it of malice aforethought . . .'

'That cat won't jump.' said Crook. 'If she did why tell any one? The only person who knew she could open the cupboard was Miss Martin and she can't talk. And all the king's horses and all the king's men can't prove that she was responsible. People can speculate, but that's about as far as they can go.'

'I've never had anything like this happen since I started my Home,' said Miss Webster, and though her voice was calm her hands trembled. 'It's not that I don't believe Mrs. Mount – if she did give Miss Martin morphia it was sheer accident – but you can't get away from the fact that she did have a hideous scene with Miss Martin, and a few minutes later – well, an hour or so – she gives the old lady something out of a bottle which may or may not have been aspirin, and Miss Martin dies of morphine poisoning. If this comes to an inquest, as I gather it must, a coroner's jury have one conceivable verdict. It's all very horrible . . .'

'Never say die,' said Crook. 'They've only got the old lady's story, and if she sticks to what she told us no one can prove she gave Miss Martin morphia.'

'Any other source to suggest?' inquired the doctor, drily.

'It's lucky for you that Miss Martin went out with someone unbeknownst in the morning. It does provide a loophole. One of the beauties of morphine poisoning is that you can't pin it down to any particular five minutes, and how do we know that her boy-friend didn't take her out and buy her a cup of coffee and give her the stuff disguised as sugar? It has been done, y'know.'

'That explanation seems to me even more far-fetched than that Mrs. Mount's responsible,' snapped the doctor.

'It's far-fetched, but it ain't impossible.'

'But who on earth would want to poison a harmless old woman like that?'

'My point precisely,' agreed Crook. 'Maybe she wasn't so harmless.'

'Who could she conceivably harm by living?'

'She's been runnin' around tellin' a very queer story about a child at the orphanage who, accordin' to her, should be an heiress. Oh, yes, I know nobody believed her, but just supposin' there was something in it, and somebody knew there was somethin' in it and wanted to put the old lady where she couldn't be a danger to any one? Though come to that a lot of folk are more dangerous dead than livin'. That's what murderers don't appreciate.'

'Are we expected to take you seriously, sir?' demanded the doctor, who was livid at the way things had turned out.

'It's a chance,' said Crook, 'and a responsible coroner won't dare overlook it. Of course, it 'ud mean further inquiries. I take it no one saw Miss Martin's friend drive up? No, I thought as much. But it might be possible to trace him. You can thank your lucky stars – or rather, Mrs. Mount can – that the old lady did borrow that hat. You'd remember it the same way you'd remember meetin' an elephant in the High Street.'

'But even if any one should remember seeing it there's no reason why her companion should be identified.' That was Matron, troubled to the bone.

'Granted,' acknowledged Crook. 'I'm only pointing out there is such a thing as the benefit of the doubt. And if there wasn't something wrong in the first place, why am I in the picture at all?'

'If I understand you right,' said the doctor slowly, 'you think there is something fishy about this.'

Crook stared. 'Something fishy? What do you think I've been talkin' all this time? Basic English?'

'It's very ingenious,' Weyland acknowledged, 'but I don't fancy that cock would fight in the ring. We may as well bite on the bullet and admit a jury will find Mrs. Mount responsible. Mind you, the old lady's nuts in any case. It's she you should have certified, not Miss Martin.'

Miss Webster sighed wearily. 'I sometimes think a comprehensive certificate of lunacy to cover all the inmates of the house would best meet the case,' she admitted.

'Anyhow,' said Crook, preparing to take his departure, 'they can't hold the inquest till tomorrow at earliest, and we may have some more news by then. And if we don't even so there can't be much harm putting that old dame where she can't go round openin' medicine chests. Next time she mightn't notice the label till after she'd handed out the stuff, and if a thing like that becomes a habit juries have a way of gettin' nasty. And there is a bright side. Suppose they find against the old lady – now don't look so worried, there's no question of her goin' to the little covered shed – then the party really responsible may get lulled into what our bright boys at Westminster call a false security, and then they'll get careless, and they won't remember Arthur Crook waitin' like a cat in the shadows ready to pounce. Take it from me,' he prepared his noisy departure, 'most of the fellows who end up on the gallows put the rope round their own necks.'

He nodded and went downstairs to retrieve his bowler hat, after which he went off with a sound of blast and a reek of fumes that would have done credit to the Demon King.

CHAPTER 16

Leaving Beverley Mr. Crook turned in the direction of Green Lane Hill and betook himself to the orphanage. Things were not going as well as he had hoped. Three people had him for their sole barrier from ruin, and already the enemy had fatally sniped one of the three. Crook did not for an instant believe that Mrs. Mount was responsible for Janet Martin's death, and he was resolved to track down the man who was. The obvious way to give morphia, provided there was no opportunity of administering a hypodermic, which in this case seemed improbable, was to dissolve it in some liquid, when it would be tasteless, and the universal habit of 'elevenses,' which permitted people to knock off at work at what was presumably one of the busiest hours of the day and crowd into a teashop for something non-alcoholic and therefore, to Crook's prejudiced mind non-beneficial, would make the murderer's job as easy as pie.

'So all I have to do,' he reflected, looking with a sort of horrified admiration at the hat he had borne away with him, 'is discover any one who saw this monstrosity, and happened to notice the wearer's companion. I don't say it'll be easy, but all the moralists who've ever lived would tell you that nothing worth while ever is.'

He had ascertained that Miss Martin had disappeared about eleven o'clock, and presumably her murderer wouldn't give her the stuff till shortly before she was due to return to Beverley.

'So all I need to do,' calculated Crook simply, 'is call at every café within an hour's radius and exhibit the hat. They might overlook my little mouse and even the chap who was with her, but they couldn't see this even once and ever forget it.' A more self-conscious man might have shrunk from the ordeal, but Crook didn't give it a second thought. There was always the chance, of course, that X. had brought coffee with him in a thermos, but Crook discounted that. Even so innocent an old dame as Miss Martin might have found that a bit suspicious, seeing the number of cafés there were in the neighbourhood. So, patiently and with no lowering of hope when his efforts went unrewarded, Crook drew up at a café after café, restaurant after restaurant, tea-shop after tea-shop, and marched in. He attracted attention the moment he appeared, the conjunction of himself and that enormity of the milliner's art drawing all eyes. He didn't bother about good pull-ups, because no one clever enough to poison Miss Martin would imagine that she would drink anything from an open counter.

'Of course,' he realized after a while, 'the ideal thing would be a Help Yourself bar. Then he could put the stuff in the cup without any fear of detection. Plant the old lady some distance from the counter, then arrive with the coffee, hand her her cup . . . safer than offering extra sugar from a private store. Some of these old dames don't take sugar.'

It might make things easier for X., but it didn't improve Arthur Crook's position, because the girl behind the bar wouldn't notice one man any more than another, and if Miss Martin was seated the other side of the room, even The Hat might go unnoticed. Still, he wasn't accustomed, as he would have said, to drawing down the blinds till the corpse was actually on the doorstep, so on he went, in again, and out again, like the old nursery game, till even providence weakened realizing what it was up against. Crook was the sort of man who would set up a Help Yourself if necessary to get the evidence he wanted.

The hat was not, after all, recognized by the woman who sloshed the coffee into the cups out of the urns but a young woman standing at the Sales Counter at the entrance of the shop. The instant Crook entered she let out a refined squeal of entertainment, almost a titter, though titters were definitely out of date in 1945. Crook recognized his cue at once.

'Hallo,' he said wheeling right without any hesitation, 'ever seen this lid before?'

'I thought there couldn't be two,' said the young lady, tittering like anything. 'I should say I do remember it, and if you'd seen the poor old soul who wore it! Trying to hide from her creditors, if you ask me. Positively extinguished she was.'

'Ex-tinguished and dis-tinguished,' agreed Crook. 'Yes, you can't have had so much fun since last Bank Holiday.'

The tittering ceased abruptly, and a look of burnt scorn came over the young lady's face.

'No offence meant, I'm sure,' she said. 'No harm in just passing a remark, I suppose.'

'On the contrary,' Crook assured her in his politest manner. 'Did you by any chance notice the man who was with her?'

The young lady condescended to unbend. 'I don't know how a young chap like that put up with it. His favourite auntie, I suppose, and he thought she might leave him something. Lots of rich old ladies look like scarecrows, if you've noticed.'

Crook suggested gravely that only the rich could afford to look like scarecrows, and she nodded.

'That's a fact. I must say he was ever so attentive. I mean it's not natural, offering to get her more coffee and a different kind of biscuit. And she just sat there nodding and smiling like something out of Madam Tussauds. He came over to this counter, you see, because she didn't fancy anything from over there. It was as good as a film. One thing, he'll make some woman a wonderful husband one of these days.'

'I doubt it,' said Crook, but he said it to himself.

'Of course,' went on the young woman, who had no customers, which wasn't surprising since at the moment there was nothing on the counter to sell. 'if this was a film he'd be after her for her money and the body 'ud be found in a ditch.'

'Ditches,' said Crook, 'are out of date. Beds are much more comfortable.'

The young woman looked startled and said coldly she'd thank Mr. Crook to keep it clean.

'You don't understand,' sighed Crook. 'Think you'd know him again?'

She looked doubtful. 'Why are you so interested in her?' she wanted to know.

'P'raps she was my favourite aunt, too. Though as it

happens, she wasn't. Now, sugar, don't get in a taking. The fact is, your intuition was right. It wasn't natural, and she has been found dead – only not in a ditch.'

'Reely!' Her eyes sparkled for a moment. Then she took up a cloth and began to wipe down the glass counter. 'Silly old nanny-goat!' she said dispassionately. 'What did she expect? Didn't she guess there was something bogus in a young man paying her all that attention.'

'You're so cynical,' Crook reproved her. 'Think you'd know him again?'

She pursed her lips. 'Well, I didn't notice him special . . .'

'Didn't wear a button-hole? Or a tie-pin that hit you in the eye? Nothing out of the way?'

'He was tallish and dark and he had a little moustache – oh, and there was a queer sort of scar on the back of his right hand. Well, not exactly a scar 'cause it wasn't absolutely healed up. I didn't notice it till he put out his hand to pick up his change. Then I did remark on it. That's a nasty accident you've had, I told him. He said, rather quick, I remember, "That'll heal soon. It's nothing to make a fuss about," and he went off in rather a hurry. Didn't like me mentioning it. I suppose.'

'It could be that,' Crook agreed. 'Well, thanks a million. You've helped a lot. If everyone was as observant as you . . .'

'Look here, this isn't going to be a police case, is it? I mean, why are you so interested? I thought you were just having me on, but if it's serious.'

'Oh, death's always serious,' said Crook. 'You'll think so yourself one day.'

He went off, swinging the preposterous hat and whistling, 'It's the little things that matter, don't you see?'

His next visit was to the orphanage. A fog was creeping up, and he had to drive carefully, because of all the people, both pedestrians and drivers, who didn't seem to think a fog made any difference. Besides, he wouldn't put it past X. to be on his tail and crash him in some lonely place. However, he reached the institution without any mishap, and leaving the hat in the car, he went up to the front door. He asked for Mrs. Forbes, and a nervous-looking girl who had presumably been one of the former inmates, said Mrs. Forbes was away, staying with relations.

'Who's in charge?' inquired Crook, and the girl said with a gulp she'd tell Miss Wickham.

Miss Wickham, who looked very much what you would expect, interviewed him severely in the hall.

'Any way I can contact Mrs. Forbes?' Crook inquired.

'She has left no address and no correspondence is being forwarded. If it is business, I am in charge.'

'It's about an orphan.' acknowledged Crook. 'Quite sure you don't know where she is?'

'I have already told you she has left no address.'

'Not even on the strict q.t.? Suppose one of the girls dies while she's away?'

'None of our orphans would dream of doing such a thing.'

'Why don't they send all youngsters to orphanages?' wondered Crook. 'Seein' you have them in such iron control. Suppose the house catches fire?'

'Then she would see it in the papers.'

'Does she read papers when she's havin' a rest cure?'

'Even if she did not, someone would be certain to see it and tell her.'

'So she ain't travelling incog.?'

'I don't know why you are here,' began Miss Wickham freezingly, and Crook said, 'Well, I came to see Mrs. Forbes – as I said, it's about a little girl . . .'

'Where does she come from?'

'London. She . . .'

'Then I'm afraid she would be inadmissable here. This Home is for local children. We don't take Londoners.'

This was so barefaced that Crook could only gasp, 'What, never?'

'That is one of the regulations governing the policy of the Home . . .'

'Still, there are exceptions,' protested Crook. 'Why, I know of one lady, a Mrs. Barnes, whose nominee . . .'

'If you're referring to Mary Smith, that was merely a temporary arrangement. Mrs. Barnes had to find a vacancy at very short notice, but there was never any suggestion that this should be permanent.'

'Then the little girl isn't here now?'

Miss Wickham's jaws shut with a snap. 'She's a misfit. We can't have people here who don't fit in.'

'You ought to be in Ernie Bevin's shoes,' said Crook admiringly. 'He's got his work cut out tryin' to fit in all the displaced people in Europe – with a bit of help from the other Powers of course,' he added magnanimously. 'What did you do with her? Drop her in the well?'

'I really can't discuss the matter with you unless you can show me some authority. . . .'

'You win,' said Crook. 'Just one more question. Ever heard of a Miss Martin?'

Miss Wickham considered. 'No.'

'Not the old lady who snooped over the wall? Don't the boss tell you anything?'

'Oh, you mean that poor old thing from Beverley. Really, someone ought to look after her.'

'They have,' said Crook grimly.

'You mean – she's leaving the nursing home?'

'Feet first.'

Miss Wickham's brain did not register very quickly. 'You mean she's dead? Oh. Well, perhaps it's all for the best.'

'That's what someone else thought, I don't doubt. Still, they may live to change their minds. Quite sure you can't tell me any more about little Mary?'

'I suggest you ask Mrs. Barnes,' replied Miss Wickham, with the air of one scoring a point.

'Good idea,' approved Crook. 'I will.' He gave her the V-sign and took his leave.

By the time he left the orphange it was growing late and the fog was increasing in density. He drove carefully, doing mental arithmetic as he went. No sense, he decided, trying to make Great Baring to-night. Even if he got there he'd never get back, and he couldn't see Mrs. Barnes offering him a bed or himself taking it. Her family's beds were uncomfortably like coffins, he reminded himself. He reached his office to find Bill waiting for him, with his customary air of having all eternity in hand.

'There's something come in about your little bit,' he greeted Crook. 'Wilson seems to have got around quite a lot.'

'Nothing to the way you and me are going to get around to-morrow,' Crook assured him. 'I've lost one of my clients, and we're goin' to jump to it to be sure we don't lose another. D'you know the person I'm sorry for, Bill?'

'You tell me,' said the imperturbable Bill Parsons.

'Mrs. Barnes, if things are the way I think they are. Now, let's have a look at all this.'

As Bill had said, Crook's man, Wilson, had dug out a considerable amount of information about Pamela Mary Smith, though, as he also said, it could be that her future history would be even more important than her past. This was her story.

In 1942 a Mrs. Smith and her little daughter, aged four years, had arrived at Paxton Junction, a small manufacturing town engaged on munition work, set in the heart of a wide agricultural district. It was understood that she was a widow, and, as the phrase goes, she kept herself to herself. She had no visitors, and the only letters she received were from a certain Captain Scott who was serving in the Middle East. It was generally assumed that he was either her bet for a second husband or a brother, thought there were some who thought she might be a divorcee, and Scott waiting for a decree and a chance to marry her. The child, however, was called Smith like her mother. Mrs. Smith obtained work at the local factory, arranging for her little girl to be cared for at a local crèche, fetching her to and fro each day. Early in 1943 a local farmer claimed that the cottage Mrs. Smith was occupying was needed for an agricultural worker, and although she fought the claim vehemently on the ground that the child was delicate and needed country air, she was dispossessed and had to seek other quarters. She found accommodation eventually with a married couple called Howard, with three children in the Forces, two working at home on the father's farm and one still at school, but expecting to leave and be called up for war work in the following year.

To Mrs. Howard, Mrs. Smith spoke once or twice of a friend in the Middle East, who was obviously the Captain John Scott who remained her sole correspondent. For about a year she remained at the farm, but at the beginning of 1944 there was an explosion at the factory where she worked, involving a number of fatal casualties, of whom she was one. She was killed outright, and it fell to the Howards to discover some relative who could make arrangements for the funeral and for the future of the little girl, Pamela. Mrs. Howard was fond of the child, but she was a reticent little thing, and had never been encouraged by her mother to make friends. Later, the woman said she had always known there was 'something queer,' because it wasn't natural for any young woman to have no relations. It appeared, however, that she had that closest of all relations, a husband called Joseph Smith, who lived in the Midlands. Her marriage certificate dated some twelve years before was found among her papers and also a birth certificate showing that the child's father was John Scott of London. Joseph Smith was informed of his wife's death, but replied through a firm of lawyers. It appears that his wife had left him several years before and asked for a divorce in order that she might marry the man who was to be the father of her child. Mr. Smith, however, was a practising Catholic and, as such, conscientiously forbidden to institute divorce proceedings. His wife went away and all connection between the two was severed, although at intervals both Mrs. Smith and Scott himself wrote asking for a reconsideration of Smith's decision not to divorce his wife. He, however, remained adamant, and after the first two years the plea was dropped. Mr. Smith stated, through his lawyers, that he had no knowledge of his wife's whereabouts. He had offered to receive her back into his house if she would put the child into an institution, but the offer had been rejected. Since she was still his wife in law he was prepared, always through his solicitors, to meet reasonable funeral expenses though there was, of course, no question of her being buried in the Smith mausoleum. As for the child, he would not accept responsibility at all, and suggested that Mr. Howard should communicate with the father.

This Mr. Howard did, by cable and later by letter, and received a cable in reply asking him and his wife to continue looking after the little girl until John Scott could return to England and make the necessary arrangements. He enclosed a bank draft and agreed to send further sums pending his return. This was held up for operational reasons for some months, and when he did at last come back in the summer of that year conditions at the Howards had altered. The schoolgirl daughter had left school and was to work on the land, Mrs. Howard had fallen ill and had to undergo an operation, and there was no one to look after the little girl. In these circumstances, John Scott had taken his father into his confidence. It seemed obvious that hitherto he had known nothing of his grandchild's existence, but before the Howards could get further information the bomb fell that killed John Scott outright and crippled his father. After that Pamela stayed at the farm during the weeks of Philip Scott's total incapacity, but as soon as he was able to travel he went down there and arranged to bring her back to London. Although the house had been damaged it could be lived in, if some of the rooms were closed, and a little later some first-aid repairs were made.

'He seemed a man broken in mind as well as body,' Howard said. 'But there couldn't be any doubt that she was his stock. They had the same wide look between the eyes, the same shape to the head, even the same gestures.'

So Philip Scott returned to London with the little girl, and his sister, who had to be taken into the secret, found a governess, "some old hen who couldn't be expected to appeal to Grandad," ' commented Crook in his ribald way, 'and presumably became the old man's heir.'

'That must have been a nasty shock for Mrs. Barnes,' he said thoughtfully to Bill. 'After John Scott died she saw herself and darlin' Oliver as bein' brother Philip's legatees, instead of which a kid she'd never heard of, who hadn't even been born in wedlock, scoops the pie. What did he leave?'

'About fifty thousand. Quite a nice packet, even with death duties to come off it.'

'Murders,' acknowledged Crook, 'have been done for less, and if we ain't up against murder this time, Bill, I'm a Dutchman. Now then.' He settled down as if it were the beginning of the day instead of the end. 'We've got to plan for tomorrow. I shall go down to Great Baring – Mrs. Barnes' place – and if I find things the way I guess it is, I'll most likely ring you to join me – plus Mrs. Hubble,' he added, casually.

'Meaning, you're prepared to charge the lady with abduction?' Bill looked troubled. He hadn't a lot of respect for the law, but he knew that a perfect stranger can't march in from nowhere and claim someone he has never seen.

Crook elaborated. 'The important thing is first to find out if she's there. You trust your Uncle Arthur to do that. After all in these days you can't have an addition to your household without someone knowin'. The tradespeople would know if there was an extra emergency card. But when we find out she's there, next we've got to get someone to identify the girl, and the only person I can think of who can do that is Mrs. Hubble. It's lucky old Miss M. gave me her address.'

He hauled his fat shabby notebook out of his pocket and turned the pages.

'In service in Richmond,' he said. 'Well, that's all on the way to Great Baring, if it proves necessary to bring her down – and I have a hunch it will.'

'They'll scratch each other's eyes out, I should think, she and Mrs. Barnes,' remarked Bill, dispassionately.

'No sense getting her to come all that way unless we've something to show her the other end. But I fancy we shall have. You see,' he went on, his mercurial spirits rising with the spate of his words, 'if you want to hide something where you can keep an eye on it, your own house is the safest place in the world. No questions to answer, no explanations to offer. And there's another thing, Mrs. Barnes did the dirty on Mrs. Hubble, cheated her of her legacy. She'll be glad enough to see her rot. Wonder if we can get the old girl on the telephone.'

Mrs. Hubble had passed on not only the address where she was now working, but also the name of her employer, and Crook established a connection with no difficulty at all. A man's voice answered him.

'My name's Crook,' announced its owner, wasting no time on fancy introductions. 'I'm a lawyer, and I'm anxious to get into touch with Mrs. Hubble, who's your housekeeper, I understand.'

The voice at the other end of the line sounded deeply suspicious. 'What do you want her for? Offer her another fifty to come to you?'

'I wouldn't have a woman in my house for all the gold of Arabia,' Crook assured him heartily. 'All the same, it is pretty serious. Someone your Mrs. Hubble knows is in pretty bad shape, and Mrs. H. may be wanted in a hurry to-morrow. I've undertaken to get into touch. I wonder if I could speak to her for a minute.'

The voice said without any enthusiasm at all that he would

tell Mrs. Hubble. After a minute a woman's voice came through.

'Who is it?' it asked. It was unhurried and sensible, as though strange lawyers rang her up at all hours, and for all Crook knew they did.

He answered by another question. 'You were cook-housekeeper to Mr. Philip Scott of the Swan House, Kensington, for about two years, I understand.'

He heard a swift indrawing of breath. 'Yes, I was.'

'So you knew Miss Lawrence and the little girl?'

'Has something happened to them? I don't know who you are . . .'

'Just coming to that,' promised Crook. 'Do you remember an old lady coming to tea one day, a Miss Martin?'

'Of course. Pamela was always talking about her. I've often wished I could hear what happened to her, Pamela, I mean.'

'Just what we're all wishing,' said Crook.

The voice sharpened. 'I don't understand.'

'You knew Mrs. Barnes? So, of course, you know she's not a lady to let things stand in her path. You've had some experience . . .'

'Do you mean she's done any more harm to Pamela?'

'More?'

'She's done her out of her money, poor little mite. If she hasn't done worse . . .'

'It's not for want of trying.' finished up Crook. 'She's a lady that likes her own way, isn't she? Mr. Scott stood in the middle of it – her way, I mean – and he's gone. Then Miss Martin began to be troublesome, and she's gone.'

'Dead?' Mrs. Hubble sounded shocked.

'Poisoned.'

'That's the second then. Did she have a weak heart, too?'

'Mrs. Barnes wouldn't let a little thing like that stand in her way,' replied Crook, unscrupulously.

'Then Miss Lawrence? and Pamela? Do you think they're in danger?'

'Ever seen a black mamba making its way round the compound? Anything that's foolish enough to be out gets it in the neck. Well, it's the same with Mrs. Barnes. If Terry and Pamela Smith are silly enough to make difficulties, they're for it, too. Only – what Mrs. B. don't know is that Arthur

Crook's on the trail. And you're in with Arthur Crook, aren't you?'

'If you're for them, I am. Though I suppose,' she added with the sort of humour Crook could appreciate, 'I'm lining up in the poison queue myself, in saying that.'

'I wouldn't worry,' Crook told her. 'I know, of course, that murderers always follow the same procedure, but there's one point to bear in mind and that is, it ain't killin' that's so difficult, it's gettin' rid of the corpse. Even a lady as determined as Mrs. Barnes is goin' to have a job explainin' away four dead bodies, or five, if you count Mr. Scott.'

'Do you mean you know where the little girl is?'

'I've a pretty good hunch, and I hope in, say, twenty-four hours the mystery, as they say, will be solved. Now, this is where you can help. The only one of the three I ever set eyes on was old Miss Martin, and Mrs. Barnes can pin any name she likes to either of the others, and who am I to say her nay? But you – you were in the house, you're what they call a witness of importance. It would be no use her tellin' you they're refugees from Khamskatcha who don't know a word of English, because you could tell the police different, and the police, who're honest even if they ain't always so bright, do like a bread-and-butter explanation every time.'

'Are you calling murder bread-and-butter?'

'Compared with refugees from Khamskatcha. Anyway, the police have met murderers before. Now, look here, I'm going down to Great Baring, and if I find what I expect to find there I'm going to ring my partner, Bill Parsons, and he's going to come and pick you up and bring you along to The Gables, where you'll find me waiting for you. Now, can you square your boss?'

'Mr. Rivers is a most reasonable gentleman.'

'Meanin' you've got him right under your thumb. And he pays to be kept there. Well, that's how some of them like it, I suppose. Still, you can spin him some yarn . . .'

'What's wrong with the truth?' inquired Mrs. Hubble, thereby taking all the wind out of Crook's picturesque sails.

'That'll save a mort of trouble. And besides,' she added honestly, 'it'll be more interesting than any of my inventions.'

She rang off, having concluded probable arrangements with Mr. Crook, who observed to Bill, as he hung up likewise,

'Now there's a woman for you. No questions, no hysterics, just plain yes or no, and went to speak to Mr. Rivers.'

'I hope that wasn't to inform you you've been left ten thousand a year, Mrs. Hubble,' said Mr. Rivers who, unlike most of his acquaintances, didn't know what the inside of a sink looked like. 'I never have servant trouble,' he used to say. 'Give 'em a free hand and don't ask what they do with their spare time. After all, you don't want it and you don't want to go putting ideas into their heads. Then you're all right.'

Mrs. Hubble never went to any but bachelors. She said there was plenty of trouble in life anyway, and why add to it? Ladies, she said, believed that unless they make fusses three times a week they weren't getting their moneysworth, and they were always haunting the shops and telling you where you could get something a penny cheaper. Gentlemen saw brussel sprouts, say, on the table, and all they cared about was whether they were watery; ladies wanted to know if you'd given fivepence or sixpence the pound, and when they'd saved the penny they'd waste it and others like it taking a bus to the cheap markets.

'It's very queer, sir,' said Mrs. Hubble. 'You remember I was with a Mr. Scott, before I came to you?'

'Fellow who died,' agreed Mr. Rivers.

'I've never liked to say much,' continued Mrs. Hubble, carefully, 'but I was never satisfied myself that Mr. Scott's death was natural.'

'Hallo, what's that?' Rivers was startled. 'What are you trying to say?'

'There was talk at the time, but there wasn't any proof. Now someone else who might have been a nuisance has died – of poison – and she was the last sort of lady to poison herself – and the little girl's disappeared.'

'This sounds like Grand Guignol,' objected Rivers.

'That gentleman who telephoned just now thinks he knows something. He wants me to go down and see if I recognise . . .' She stopped as though something choked her. 'It was such a happy house in spite of poor Mr. Scott being a cripple,' she said. 'The little girl was so fond of him and him of her. And then suddenly to have it all broke up like that.'

Rivers spoke decidedly. 'I very much object to your getting mixed up in this, Mrs. Hubble. Have you forgotten the Professor's coming to dinner to-morrow night? If you go gallivanting off in the morning you won't be fit for a thing.'

Mrs. Hubble folded her lips together. 'I've never let down one of my gentlemen yet,' she said. 'And I'm sure my sauce wouldn't be fit to set on the table if I was still worrying – and hadn't done a thing to help.'

'If you promise to be back in time I suppose you must go,' grumbled Rivers. 'But I don't suppose any young female living is worth risking the life of a good cook.'

CHAPTER 17

Next morning bright and early saw Crook on the road to Great Baring. He took the car because he thought he might need swift movement, and when he reached the sizeable little market town he stopped to look about for a likely pub. He tried the Denmark first, but here the beer was flat, and the barmaid (who would hotly have resented the title) even flatter. Crook, who had no liking for women with about as much figure as anchovy-forks, removed himself and his custom to the Dying Duck which was a great deal jollier than its name suggested. Here the barmaid was a creature of sensible curves and bright gold hair, and she didn't think Nature had given her a tongue simply to put out at customers of whose appearance she didn't approve. Crook, having ordered a pint for himself and a large port for Gladys, settled down for a cosy chat.

Pretty soon he brought up the subject of Mrs. Barnes. The barmaid made a disparaging gesture with her hands.

'We know that lot,' she said. 'No good to us. Get all their stuff from town, and don't know the difference between beer and swipes. Or they would go to the Denmark when they do go inside a local.'

'What did Mrs. Barnes do in the Great War?' inquired Crook, and Gladys said, 'Ran the W.V.S. and pretty well ran it into the sea. Thought she was the Princess Royal most of the time.'

'You in the W.V.S.?' asked Crook, but without much hope. It was too much to expect, with those curves and that provocative eye.

'Not blooming likely. No, I did fire-fighting and got four

stripes and five bob a month for forty-two months for a gratuity to put towards my old age pension.'

'Got a biggish place, hasn't she?' continued Crook, suggesting another round.

'You'll have me tiddley at this rate,' Gladys warned him. 'Still, it all makes a change. Much too big if you ask me, for one woman, in these days when there's fellows back from the army have to live in cowsheds. There was some talk about it, not altogether friendly, if you ask me, during the Share Your Homes campaign we had the other day, and that's why she brought this Miss Smith along.'

'Who's Miss Smith?' asked Crook idly.

'Don't ask me. I've never seen her. It's a put-up job, if you ask me. Afraid she might have to have someone in one of 'er spare rooms, though you can't need a refrigerator in that house. Freeze you up, as soon as look at you, she would. Besides, I ask you, would a lah-di-dah like Mrs. Barnes have a relation called Smith?'

'What sort of a relation?'

'She calls her my poor young niece. Ever so ill, if you believe her. Got a uniformed nurse and all.'

'Been here long?' asked Crook.

'Just these last few days – the nurse, I mean. Mrs. Barnes gave out the poor girl was worse and they had to be very careful – course, she's never seen out. Probably got two heads or a tiger's tail, if you ask me. Anyway, if she is so blooming ill, why don't they ever have the doctor? Most nurses wouldn't stand for it.'

'Quite sure they don't?'

'Not unless he comes after dark. If you want to know, I wouldn't be surprised if she went out after dark, too. I do like things to be open and above-board; and the nurse has a face like the back of a taxi-cab, too.'

'You've been seeing too many pictures, Gladys,' Crook warned her.

Gladys tossed her golden head. 'If I 'aven't it's not for want of invitations, Mr. Nosey,' she assured him.

'Well, I must be getting along,' said Crook. 'Keep a couple under the counter for me if there's enough of me left to soak 'em up when Mrs. Barnes is through.'

Leaving the Dying Duck he tooled off to The Gables,

thinking, as Terry Lawrence had thought before him, that there must be some reason why Mrs. Barnes, that gregarious and managing woman, had chosen a house so far off the beaten track.

'Though she's probably got Mr. Shinwell or whoever does the petrol in her pocket,' he decided unscrupulously. 'She sounds the kind that would, which makes it all right for her. And if she's put little Miss Smith in a back room she could grow grey before any one knew anything about her. Why, if she did manage to poke her nose out of a window Mrs. B's such a good organiser she'd be sure to have a tame blackbird handy to snap it off.'

He drove noisily up to the gate – I've nothing to be ashamed of, proclaimed Crook who, difficult though it might be to credit the fact, was actually proud of his appalling little red car, The Scourge – and swung it open.

Mrs. Barnes was such a first-class organiser that even in these days of Red tyranny she had a capped-and-aproned maid wearing a 1913 expression on her plain face to answer the bell.

'Kept to keep the wolf from the door, I dare say,' decided Crook, 'and every one knows wolves are no sissies.' And, 'Can I see the lady of the house?' he inquired, hauling a notebook out of his pocket.

'We don't buy at the door,' said the Wolf-Scarer icily.

'Come from the Town Hall,' gabbled Crook. 'Housing Department. Mr. Bevan'll have something to say to your lady if you don't let me come in.'

She hesitated an instant, and while they faced one another Crook, with his air of all-grist-that-comes-to-my-mill and the W.S. stiff with dislike, Mrs. Barnes herself crossed the hall. She was like an Irish terrier; she couldn't resist a fight.

'What is it, Parker?' she inquired.

'Someone who says he's from the Town Hall, m'm,' said Parker.

Crook stuck his hand into his breast pocket. 'I have my credentials if you'd like to see them,' he said. 'Living so far from the village you might not recognise me.'

He had her on the raw there. She liked to think of herself as omniscient.

'Come in,' she told him briskly. 'Parker, when Miss Minns comes I will see her at once.'

'Old as last week's bread,' thought Crook, a little disgusted. 'Never was a Miss Minns, but she must impress on me how busy she is.'

'One of your W.V.S. handmaids?' he suggested heartily, following the lady into the morning-room.

'This Government may consider itself capable of tackling every problem from the official angle,' replied Mrs. Barnes crisply, 'but they'll find the personal touch essential for success.'

'I'm all for private enterprise myself,' agreed Crook. 'Now I'm afraid you won't be very glad to see me. If I wasn't tough-skinned I shouldn't keep this job a week, but the fact is, I have to ask you what the accommodation here consists of.'

Mrs. Barnes winced openly at his lack of grammatical chastity, but she overlooked that in her determination to prove that the local authority couldn't put one over on her.

'There are three sitting-rooms,' she said clearly. 'one of which is utilised as an office. I am a very busy woman and I am the general organiser of the neighbourhood. There are six bedrooms all at present in use.'

'Friends staying here? or residents?' asked Cróok, jotting down cabalistic signs in a ridiculous little black book.

'Residents. My son, Oliver, who is making this house his headquarters at the moment, and who expects shortly to be released from his important official position and to take up work of equal importance, my niece, who has been ill – a serious breakdown and has to live very quietly, her nurse, who naturally must live on the premises, and my two servants, Parker, who opened the door to you, and my cook, Dobson, who is at the moment away on a visit to her sick mother, but who will be back within a few days.'

'No spare room,' scribbled Crook, busily.

'Until my niece and her nurse came I had a spare room, which was invariably occupied by people doing important national work, and the other room was utilised by my son as a study. As it is, he has to share the dining-room with the household. Naturally, the nurse has her own room, and when she is off duty I look after my niece myself. I hope,' she stood up to show that the interview was over, 'that that satisfies you.'

'I'm afraid I'll have to ask you to let me see the house,' murmured Crook.

Mrs. Barnes froze. 'I thought I made it clear my niece is very ill . . . ?'

'Nothing contagious, I hope.'

'If you mean anything that should have been reported to the local authorities – certainly not. It is just that she has had this collapse and she is – well, uncontrollable. Also she is not always responsible for her actions, but sooner than agree to have her put into a private institution – I am a great believer in home life, and I am convinced that given time and proper care the trouble will abate itself.'

'I believe you,' said Crook heartily. 'All the same – if you did all that W.V.S. work you know that the human heart is deceitful and desperately wicked. You'd be surprised at the number of householders who've discovered relations neither they nor any one else knew they had twelve months ago. Funny thing,' he added meditatively, 'they're all invisible. And then they talk about the age of witchcraft bein' past.'

Mrs. Barnes looked more icy than ever. 'I hope you're satisfied . . . ?'

'I shan't ask to see the young lady's room, of course,' soothed Crook. 'But I have to hand in my report. I'm sure you'll understand.' He eyed her with a bright intent stare; he wondered if she would make the obvious correction, but clearly she was giving nothing away. Making the best of a bad job she preceded him up the stairs, indicating the various doors on the first landing – 'My room, my son's room, the nurse's room'-ah! That was because the door of the fourth room, at the back as Crook had anticipated, opened a foot or so and a woman in nurse's uniform came bouncing out.

'Oh, nurse, I hope we haven't waked the patient,' exclaimed Mrs. Barnes. 'This is a representative from the local council who appears to think that we have room for billetees.'

The nurse, a well set-up fresh-faced woman in the early fifties, said briskly, 'If you had a dozen rooms, Mrs. Barnes, you couldn't have billetees here, you know you couldn't, not with the patient in her present state. Anyway, this is too far out to be convenient to any worker, and surely the Government doesn't propose to upset private households for the sake of the slackers.'

She was like something out of a play, thought Crook, one of those slightly obvious satires that the good-natured English public always seems ready to applaud.

'Apparently the response to the appeal has been very poor, practically non-existent, in fact. Nobody seems prepared to put up with the smallest inconvenience . . .'

'I could have told them how it would be,' returned the robust nurse. 'It's the same everywhere.'

Like patball, thought the fascinated Crook. Over to you, partner. And how Partner sprinted up to the net to deliver a smasher. 'I wasn't in charge of the local W.V.S. for nothing. Personally, I find it anything but convenient to have an invalid on the premises – you understand I don't mean anything personal, Nurse . . . ?'

'I understand perfectly.' Back came the ball into the right court. 'We must hope that the absolute quiet will hasten recovery . . .'

Or alternatively, thought the unsympathetic Crook, it might persuade the undertaker's men to get a wiggle on.

'By the way,' continued Mrs. Barnes smoothly, 'were you looking for me, Nurse?'

'I was going to say there are a few things we need from the chemist. But I don't like to leave my patient.'

Crook began to feel hypnotised. In another minute he'd be offering to get them himself.

However, as usual, Mrs. Barnes beat him to it. 'Mr. Oliver will be back in a minute. Perhaps he will be able to take the car. I can't offer to relieve you. Miss Minns . . .'

'Any relation of Mrs. 'Arris?' asked Crook.

Both women stared. 'She was in the W.V.S. or something of the kind,' he hurriedly added. 'But that wouldn't be this war.'

The nurse had drawn the door of the sick-room behind her, but no light came through the narrow crack. Crook, who sometimes explained that if he believed in reincarnation he'd know he was once a cat, so keen were his sight and hearing even in the black-out, was sure he heard a sound like a groan on the farther side of the door, a groan dying away in a long sigh. Mrs. Barnes seemed to have heard it, too, for she said vexedly to the nurse, 'There, I believe we've waked her again. And you know what the doctor said. You'd better just see . . .'

The nurse slipped back. Still there wasn't any light.

'Do you wish to see the rest of the house?' demanded Mrs. Barnes, with a return to her original hauteur.

Crook shook his head. He didn't want to see anything but the inside of a telephone booth. He had undertaken to attend Miss Martin's inquest the next morning, and he wanted to be sure it wasn't a double event. 'The nurse is right. You couldn't have strangers on the premises. It wouldn't be fair to either side.'

'I'm glad you appreciate that.' Her manner became a shade more gracious as they descended the stairs. He was actually on the front step when a long dark car drew up at the door and a tall dark young man alighted. He had dark eyes and a small moustache. Crook stood his ground and watched him approach.

'Oh, Oliver,' said his mother, not, of course, offering to introduce Mr. Crook, 'Nurse wants some things from the chemist for Mary. Can you go down? I'd go myself, but Miss Minns may be here any minute.'

'I dare say I can,' agreed Oliver amiably. 'If I can put through a phone call first.'

'Of course. I hope it's not a long one. I'm expecting a trunk call any minute.'

'O.K.' Oliver seemed unruffled by her urgency. Possibly she had calls from Buckingham Palace, Downing Street and the White House at all hours of the day, reflected Crook. He pushed his ridculous little black jotter into his pocket and repeated, 'I shall report there is no available accommodation here. Sorry if my call is inconvenient.'

Mrs. Barnes became positively friendly. 'Not at all. You can tell them when you get back that I quite appreciate the necessity for such action in view of the gross lack of public spirit displayed locally. Naturally I could have told them that it was sheer waste of time coming here, but in these democratic days we all have to be treated alike. I make no complaints. Mind you, I think they're making a mistake, adopting this rather high-handed policy. But I dare say they'll find that out for themselves in due course. You can't regiment people in time of peace. . . .'

Crook, who had never had time for evening classes even when he was young, said, 'Can't you just?' and Oliver grinned unexpectedly. Mrs. Barnes, looking a little less pleasant – ten per cent off for cash, reflected the irreverent Crook – said casually to her son, 'A representative from the Town Hall,' to which he replied, 'Oh? I wondered. That your car?'

Crook bristled like a spinster whose dog is disparaged, and said with some hauteur that that was the Scourge and he'd back it against most of the Brookland exhibits, and he should know, seeing he'd watched it in action for the past ten years.

Oliver said pleasantly, 'Makes a trio with *Charley's Aunt* and Johnnie Walker, doesn't she? Still running, I mean.'

Crook said one of these days she'd doubtless run him through the Pearly Gates, and stuck out his hand in token of farewell.

Oliver looked surprised and not too pleased at the gesture, but perforce he offered his own, so that Crook saw the broad scar he had anticipated running across the back. A moment later he had stridden through the gate, leaped into the Scourge and departed as noisily as he had arrived. When he was safely round the corner he stopped the car, alighted, and came back very quietly on foot. He was pretty certain that Mrs. Barnes, Oliver and the nurse would all be conferring together over this latest development, and Mrs. Barnes would be telling him how cleverly she had circumvented those interfering local authorities. Probably they were all having a good laugh at his expense.

That was one of the occasions when Crook happened to be wrong.

Crook crept carefully in by the side door, bending double under cover of the privet hedge and reached the back garden, passing the garage and the tool-shed and the kitchen premises. It was approaching lunch-time and, in the absence of the cook, the Wolf-Scarer was presumably doing something about hashing up last night's remains for a resurrection pie. You couldn't imagine Mrs. Barnes doing her own chores, though she would, of course, know precisely how they should be done. Unperceived, he came like a small brown elephant through the bushes till he was in full view of the windows at the back of the house. He looked up and saw, as he had anticipated, that the room in which the unfortunate captive was immured was completely blacked out by some sort of curtain that covered the entire window. Beyond that were bars – probably the room had once been a nursery, unless, he reflected, resourcefully drawing on that powerful imagination of his, they had made a habit of keeping a lunatic on the premises.

'No light from without, none within,' he reminded himself. 'There's devilry going on there all right.' Taking a chance he picked up a pebble from the path and tossed it up to the window. There was a sharp click as it struck the glass, but nothing happened.

'Drugged?' he wondered. 'I wouldn't be surprised.' and shied a second pebble for luck.

This time luck was with him. Watching, fascinated and horrified, he saw thin fingers creep round the edge of the black curtain. Someone from inside was tugging to loosen it. Nailed of course. Whoever was pulling was doing it desperately, like someone in terror of her life. The phrase sprang into his mind and remained there uncomfortably. In terror of her life. How true that was, and how much might now depend on his own swiftness to act, his correct appraisal of the way the cat would jump, a minute attention to detail, for at this junction a single slip might result in at least one more death. And though death stood high on his programme he hadn't fixed on any of his side to fill the bill. Tense and motionless, he watched the invisible victim's struggle. After a minute the curtain yielded a little, a second hand was brought into play. Inch by cautious inch the black stuff yielded until at last he saw a face he wasn't to forget for weeks to come, so stamped with fear was it, so quivering with apprehension. Such rage filled him as he had rarely known, at the sight of that young panic-stricken face staring down into the garden, marked with such fear as chilled even his exuberant blood. Casting caution to the winds he stepped out into the middle of the precise little lawn, and as he came so did the sun emerge, glittering and sparkling on grass and leaf and blossom.

It was impossible to speak; no voice could penetrate those sheets of glass that separated them, and he knew that she was agog for the smallest sound from the house. He flung up his arm, making the V-sign, and he saw that frozen surface of fear break for an instant and hope gleam there. He nodded encouragingly, but inwardly he boiled with fury. What threats had they offered her? What torments had she already endured, that young helpless thing, caught in the grip of enemies as ruthless as hell?

Time was now the essence of the situation. That fellow, Oliver, had looked at him in a queer way. And what precisely had he meant by saying, 'I wondered'? It would be simple enough to make inquiries at the Town Hall (he blessed the new Government that made it possible for a man to demand entry into a private house without previous notice) and find out that his errand had been a spurious one. In fact, Mrs. Barnes, with her passion for organisation, would probably do that in any case. The curtains slid back into place as he watched, the face vanished. Had she heard some sound on the stairs? Were they even now plotting to remove her? At all events, he could do nothing more here, and as the tragic occupant of the darkened room vanished from his sight he turned and, once more bent double, made his way back to the street.

As he passed the front of the house he shot a lightning glance over the hedge. Three people were standing in the bow-window of the morning-room with their backs to the road. They were talking as though they were practising election speeches, and none of them saw him as he stole swiftly by.

They were talking about him, though, as he had surmised they might be. It was Oliver who exploded the bomb.

'Who was that chap?' he demanded, after Crook had disappeared.

'Someone from the Town Hall. I told you. He wanted to know about accommodation for billetees, but I easily persuaded him . . .'

She stopped uneasily at the sight of her son's face.

'What is it, Oliver?'

'Just a coincidence,' said Oliver in his driest voice. 'Only – Miss Martin went out with a chap in a little open red car, called the Scourge, the day before she – died. It belonged to a fellow called Crook.'

For the first time Mrs. Barnes' composure was shaken.

'Are you trying to tell me . . . ?'

'Funny if there are *two* of them, I should say. Well, makes you think, don't it?'

CHAPTER 18

Not far from the Gables was an A.A. telephone box that Crook had spotted on his way in, and thither he now repaired at top speed. Luck was with him in that he got his number without delay and that Bill Parsons answered the telephone.

'Get cracking,' said Crook, tersely.

'O.K.' said Bill.

Crook gave him brief instructions as to the quickest road to take, and the position he himself intended to occupy, and rang off at once. 'They've got her all right,' he wound up, 'but no one'll have her, bar the cemetery or the nuthouse, if we ain't quick.' As he replaced the receiver he wondered which of the two destinations was Mrs. Barnes' choice. Presumably the latter. As he had told Mrs. Hubble, corpses are the dickens.

As he rang off he reflected that one of the advantages of having Bill for a colleague was that he never wasted words. A couple of sentences and he knew what you wanted. And he could read between the lines and sense the unspoken or the unwritten word as readily as a woman. The only difference being, Crook liked to point out, that he read what was in your mind whereas women only read what they wanted to see.

Having secreted the Scourge in a convenient lane, Crook came back and took up a position whence he could watch the movements of the household without attracting attention to himself. Some kindly soul had put a seat at the top of the road, marked For Wounded Soldiers Only, and though no wounded soldier ever dreamed of sitting on it, it came in handy for less particular people. Crook took up a comfortable position and hid behind a copy of the *Times* he had thoughtfully brought with him. The *Times* is a large serious paper and can hide a small man very effectually. No copy can have been read with greater assiduity. He started on Page One with Hatches, Matches and Dispatches, worked right through the Personal Column, Kennel, Aviary, Businesses, Situations Vacant and advertisements of Crematoria. He passed on to foreign news and, with a number of Cabinet Ministers, deplored the situation in most parts of the globe. He read international and dominion snippets and became immersed in the correspondence. He read a leader on the situation in China and another on bowler hats. He noted there had been two more hold-ups, and a smash-and-grab in Davies Street, W., and two peers were in the divorce court.

At this stage in his study he noticed that someone was coming out of the side door of The Gables. She was a middle-aged woman, frumpishly dressed, and she marched up to the gate as undeviating as though she were made of wood all in one piece, and began to walk down the road. Crook watched her from behind the shelter of his paper and recognised her as the Wolf-Scarer.

'Gone down to the chemist?' he queried. 'Now, for what?'

He maintained his aloof pose, but his heart was racing madly. He knew Bill couldn't be here for another hour, even making the pace he invariably did, and he wished every evil in hell to fall on the Wolf-Scarer to prevent her returning before that time, while he brooded on the various methods Mrs. Barnes and her infamous colleagues might employ to spirit the girl away.

'One thing,' he reflected grimly, 'they can't actually take her out of the house without me seeing her.' And he was glad to remember it was more than two miles to the village, and there was no alternative transport for one without a car to Shank's mare. It was some time before it occurred to him that this might be the parlourmaid's afternoon out, and perhaps she wouldn't be returning till after dark, a reflection that brought him no satisfaction whatever. If they had seen through his disguise, what better opportunity would the three of them have for disposing of their wretched victim than an afternoon when they could anticipate no interruption.

He returned frantically to the *Times*, read a gale warning, the story of a disaster at sea, one of those rail crashes that readers were beginning to look for, so frequent had they become, and a note on the mysterious death of an actress. He became absorbed in this last, and was already framing his version when there was a second interruption.

Oliver Barnes came out of The Gables and got into his long dark car.

'Hell!' said Crook. 'What does that mean? I ought to have brought someone with me – One to go and one to stay, when Mr. Murderer drives away.'

It appeared, however, that Oliver was going no farther than the garage. So it seemed they had abandoned all thought of immediate action. The young man propped open the side door, drove the car through, stalled her, and came back to the house, whistling softly. Probably he'd whistled like that when he put the morphia into Miss Martin's coffee.

With a patience that might have put Job on his mettle Crook returned to the *Times*. By the time the car he awaited so desperately hove into view he was on the last page, absorbing details of bargains in house property, and thinking of the innumerable indirect thefts that can be perpetrated within the limits of the law.

'It's a good thing for me there's so many mugs about,' he decided. 'If they only knew it, these get-rich-quick fellows, they don't have to risk ten years hard *OR* the rope. Luckily they seem mostly wooden from the neck up. Ah, well, one man's meat . . .'

That reminded him of Miss Martin again, and he wondered uneasily what they had given that poor little prisoner for lunch. Then, when the strain was becoming too much even for his iron nerve, he heard the hum of a car and realised that the next instalment of this thrilling serial was about to begin.

Bill was driving and beside him was a tall fair man with an impassive face. In the back of the car sat a woman with a comfortable female figure and a face made for motherliness, but who looked at this moment as though she had been carved out of granite.

Crook's red brows lifted interrogatively as the car slowed down beside him, and Bill looked out, like someone asking the way.

'Seeing Mrs. Barnes hasn't thought of calling in a doctor it seemed it might be a good idea to bring our own,' Bill explained, as Crook skipped nimbly into the back, saying, 'Mrs. Hubble, I presume? I can't say how glad we are of your help.'

'It's a pleasure,' said Mrs. Hubble stiffly. Crook remembered, not for the first time, the saying that the female of the species is more deadly than the male. He reported the present situation as they drove up to the house and, at Bill's suggestion, the doctor and Mrs. Hubble remained in the car, while the other two marched up the drive.

They had to ring twice, during which period of waiting they were inspected from an upper window, before the door was torn open by Mrs. Barnes herself.

'So you're back,' she flashed at Crook. 'What's your excuse this time?'

Crook had been thinking how incongruous it seemed to connect murder with this immaculate house, with its well-hung unimaginative curtains, its well-polished window panes, its general air of prosperity and reticence. Still, that was the way it was. Murder was a thing that happened to ordinary people, and that was what most ordinary people didn't understand.

Bill, without a trace of expression, said there had been complaints about a young lady being shut up, and he had come to clear up the mystery.

'I never heard of such insolence,' exclaimed Mrs. Barnes. She laughed. It wasn't a pretty sound, but it didn't denote any sort of apprehension or fear.

'Very ingenious!' she went on. 'How many more cock-and-bull stories have you got up your sleeve?'

Bill put his hand into his breast-pocket and drew out a document. 'Search warrant,' he said, holding it out to her.

She didn't offer to take it, and he guessed she wouldn't know if it was genuine or not. Instead she called, 'Oliver,' and her son appeared from the room she called her office.

'Oliver, will you ring up the Police Station and ask if they've sent a man up here with a search warrant?'

Oliver went off to the telephone and the two men waited impassively in the hall. After a minute or two he came back.

'They don't know anything about it,' he announced.

'What did I tell you?' demanded Mrs. Barnes. 'I may seem very simple to you, but I'm not as simple as that. And I should have expected you,' she indicated Crook aggressively, 'would at least have had the wisdom to stay out of the picture this time. Do you think I don't read the papers? We all know that far more plausible stories than that are being told every day of the week by gangs of thieves.'

Neither Crook nor Bill seemed to have any answer to that.

'Well, aren't you going?' demanded Mrs. Barnes. 'If you've any sense you'll go while the going's good. The police will be here any minute.'

. . . . 'That's what we thought,' said Bill.

'I don't understand . . .'

'He told you,' said Crook impatiently. 'We think there's a lass bein' held against her will. When the police come, as of course they will, you havin' told them a gang of safe-busters is on the premises, we can explain the way we feel, and – well, you understand, don't you?'

Once again he thanked his stars that Bill Parsons was on his side and not the opposition's.

'I suppose you are quite mad,' said Mrs. Barnes after a moment. 'You don't really believe there's any one being hidden here?'

'Let's leave that to the police,' suggested Crook.

Oliver Barnes said, 'What sort of a racket is this?' and 'You'll see,' Crook told him.

'I thought this was a free country,' murmured the young man and Crook told him crisply, 'Murder's never been free.'

'Murder?' Her voice lifted shrilly. 'If you're looking for a body you're going to be disappointed. There's no one on the premises but myself and my son – and the staff of course.'

They were still exchanging compliments, Mrs. Barnes' voice becoming increasingly loud, saying perhaps he suspected her servants, when the police arrived – in duplicate. A uniformed officer was at the wheel, and he didn't come any farther than the gate. That, of course, was to watch both entrances in case any one tried to do a bolt. An inspector came to the doors and Mrs. Barnes told him contemptuously what had happened, and offered him Bill's search warrant.

'This isn't legal,' said the inspector, 'and . . .'

'You're telling us,' agreed Crook, politely. 'You see, we

had to get the police on the premises, and we thought they'd be more likely to come for Mrs. Barnes than for rats like Bill and me.'

The inspector, pardonably confused, asked for an explanation. Crook said that if he'd examine the back bedroom on the first floor, the one with the bars at the window, he might find it for himself. He added that perhaps at this very moment perhaps the nurse was making it shipshape.

'You must be out of your mind,' said Mrs. Barnes contemptuously. 'There's no nurse on the premises.'

'I wonder what could have put that idea into my head.' marvelled Crook. 'All I can asure you,' he turned to the inspector, 'is that the nurse was here this morning, and she hasn't walked out because I've been watching the house ever since.'

The inspector said, 'If you don't mind showing me round, madam . . .' and she shrugged her shoulders and said, 'I simply can't understand how you can take these men seriously. I should have thought it was obvious to the meanest intelligence that they are members of a dangerous gang.'

The inspector made no reply, but Crook said sweetly that men of mean intelligence were of no interest to the police, except, of course, in the dock.

Mrs. Barnes, ignoring him said the inspector was welcome to go anywhere he liked, and said it with such blatant assurance that even the intrepid Crook felt his heart sink. Had she, then, won yet another round against him? She'd triumphed in their first encounter, and though he knew bluff when he met it he didn't somehow believe this was bluff. Still, he could bluff pretty well himself on occasions, and no one would have believed that his heart was beating like a sledge-hammer as he joined the cavalcade now mounting the stairs. Oliver stayed where he was – the one adult member of the party in a group of children playing at dressing-up. Bill, as though something had suddenly occurred to him changed his mind and came back to wait in the hall. The others went steadily up the stairs. There was no sign of the nurse anywhere.

'Which room is it that you referred to?' the inspector asked Crook, and Crook obligingly pointed it out. Mrs. Barnes thrusting past them flung the door wide. Before he saw the interior Crook knew they were going to find nothing there.

In which he was right. The only familiar objects were the bars that were still at the window. For the rest, the dark curtains had disappered, there was no bed, no apparatus at all to suggest that a sick girl had been mewed up there, why, it wasn't even a bedroom any more.

'This,' announced Mrs. Barnes, 'is my son's study. He uses it whenever he can be spared from his Government job in the north, and now that he is hoping to be released he will, of course, make this room his headquarters.'

If she had it put on a record, thought Crook unsympathetically, it would save her a lot of breath.

'I don't know where Mr. . . .' she looked at Crook, 'where he expects to find his mythical Andromeda. In the coal-box, perhaps?'

Crook wouldn't have been particularly surprised, except that the coal-box couldn't have contained anything larger than a midget. He hadn't an idea where the girl was, but the craftsman in him admired the rapidity and thoroughness with which the metamorphosis had been achieved. So his hunch had been right – they had suspected him.

They all waited for the inspector to speak. He was courtesy itself.

'Perhaps,' he suggested to Crook, 'you have mistaken the room.'

Crook shook his head. 'Not unless there are two rooms with bars at the window, and even then I'd be right. Geography was the only subject I ever won a prize for.'

Oliver Barnes, who had tired very quickly of Bill's company, here interposed unexpectedly, 'How did you know about the bars, if you didn't see the room?' and Crook told him simply, 'I went round the back while you were holding your directors' meeting in the office.'

'Have you seen enough?' Mrs. Barnes inquired, sarcastically, but he only said, 'If you're speakin' to me – no I haven't. Y'see I probably know more about murder than any man livin', and it's my experience, and of course the inspector's, too (so he repaid courtesy by courtesy) that every criminal makes one mistake. Well, stands to reason if he's a sportsman he has to. Otherwise, how would we ever catch him? I'm just goin' to hang around till I find out the thing you've forgotten, and then everything'll be over – bar the trial, of course.'

The inspector looked a little uncomfortable. He couldn't fathom it at all. Here were two fellows trying to get into a strange house on as absurd a cock-and-bull tale as had ever come his way, who had stayed to meet the police, and didn't appear to have anything on their consciences, and who even gave the impression of believing their own story. To fill in time he began to apologise to Mrs. Barnes for inconveniencing her.

'Not at all,' said Mrs. Barnes graciously. 'I'm only too glad to have this opportunity of quieting malicious tongues.'

Crook was down on that like a ton of bricks. 'Aha!' he said. 'So I'm not the only one to talk.'

Mrs. Barnes decided that was something else that was beneath contempt.

'Do you wish to see any more of the house?' she asked the inspector, but to her annoyance it was Crook who replied.

'Well, we haven't found her yet, have we?' he demanded in some surprise. 'Of course we want to see everything.'

'Even the servants' rooms and the box-room?' asked Mrs. Barnes.

'Particularly the servants' rooms and the box-room,' insisted Crook.

The inspector, impressed against his will by this unimpressive man's assurance, said it might be as well . . . and upstairs they all traipsed.

'If you read history, criminal history, I mean,' amplified Crook, who, apparently, wouldn't have recognised tact if it had been served up on toast, 'you'd be surprised to find how unoriginal murderers are. They love box-rooms and attics.'

The inspector said rather coldly that it was a bit early in the day to talk of murder, and Crook said emphatically, No, it wasn't, and Mrs. Barnes understood if the inspector didn't.

Upstairs he was like a man possessed. He insisted on tearing open wardrobes and boxes, turning over a roll of outworn carpet, looking in cupboards and under beds and behind wardrobes.

'She's somewhere on the premises.' he asserted, in face of all the evidence to the contrary, 'and I'm going to find out where. Besides, there's the nurse. You can't get rid of two people like that. This isn't Maskelyne and Devant.'

Even Mrs. Barnes' composure was shaken. 'This is insufferable,' she protested.

'Are you telling me? All right. She isn't here. What about the kitchen?' He remembered a number of classic cases where examination of the kitchen had brought horrible disclosures to light.

'I can ssure you that you will find no one in my kitchen but my cook,' said Mrs. Barnes icily. 'But no doubt . . .'

Crook, however, had spun round at her words. 'Your cook? But she went to visit an ailing mother. She's not expected back for some days.'

He went flying down the stairs, impetuous and agile as a rubber ball. It was amazing that any one with a figure so closely resembling that of Mr. Edward Bear could hurl himself through a house with such velocity. The inspector was on his heels. In the hall Bill watched his crazy descent and prepared for the last curtains. Mrs. Barnes and her son followed hurriedly in the wake of the odious interloper.

The kitchen was a large comfortable room at the back of the house. Crook had passed it on his snooping expedition earlier in the day, but it was too well shrouded by shrubs to be seen from outside. As he flung the door open a well-built middle aged woman got quickly to her feet. Typical of Mrs. Barnes to have cooks who still wore uniform, thought Crook, but something nagged at his mind.

'Is something wrong, m'm?' she exclaimed, seeing the human avalanche pour into her kitchen.

'This person appears to think we have someone hidden on the premises, Cook.'

Cook blocked the ball neatly. 'The idea! And where does he think we've put her? In the oven?'

Crook noticed the slip but said nothing. His quick eye was examining the room. It fell on a small suitcase lying in a corner and he darted across.

'Excuse me,' said Cook in indignant tones, 'that's mine.'

'That's what I thought. Interesting to see what's inside it.'

'If you think you could get even a baby inside that . . .'

'No, I don't think that at all. All the same . . .'

'I shall have to lodge a complaint about this outrage.' stormed Mrs. Barnes. 'It's infamous.'

'Does your warrant let you ask the lady to open her case?' Crook demanded.

There wasn't a warrant and he knew it, but he felt they couldn't afford even an instant's unnecessary argy-bargy.

'I dare say the lady would have no objections,' suggested the inspector soothingly.

After a moment's hesitation the woman flung up the lid, 'I hope you're satisfied,' she flashed in venomous tones.

The case was packed with striped frocks and aprons, white caps . . .

Crook shook his head. 'I thought cooks didn't wear caps nowadays, and though I am no connoisseur I'm pretty certain they never wore hospital caps.' He pulled one out and flourished it. 'Well, that's where Nursie went.'

'Inspector, will you kindly control this – lunatic?' snapped Mrs. Barnes. 'I don't know who he thinks my cook is . . .'

'I don't think – I know,' returned Crook, simply. 'Matter of fact, it was your stand-in who told me.' He nodded to the stupefied woman on the other side of the table. "She's staying with relations" she said. 'And so you are, aren't you – MRS. FORBES?'

There was a moment during which no one spoke, the inspector because so far none of this added up for him at all, Mrs. Barnes, Mrs. Forbes and Oliver because they were too shattered. Crook had taken them all off their guard. It was Mrs. Barnes, characteristically, who recovered first.

'The situation becomes more absurd every instant,' she declared. 'Why you should imagine my cook is Mrs. Forbes, who is incidentally the matron of an orphanage,' she added for the inspector's benefit . . .

Crook didn't let her finish that. 'If she isn't, where is Mrs. Forbes?'

'How should I know?'

'I thought you might, seeing she's your sister.'

That was the second bombshell. The inspector had the look of a man who has turned to his Sunday paper expecting to find a plain cross-word and discovering himself faced with one of these fancy patterns that are all classical allusions and cockshies.

'My sister? You must be crazy.'

'Old Miss Martin rumbled that,' reflected Crook. 'She had a lot of sense, that old dame. If you'd appreciated that, you might have been a bit more careful.'

'I don't know anything about her.'

'Mrs. Forbes does, though. Don't you, Mrs. Forbes? And seeing how hard you worked to get her thrown out of Elsham, you'd be bats if you didn't. Well,' he heaved a deep sigh, 'she's gone all right, though not quite the road you planned. All we can hope is she's happier in the grave than the nuthouse.'

The inspector thought it was his turn to have a word. 'The old lady's dead?'

'Sure. The inquest is tomorrow. We'll probably all meet there, those of us who ain't under arrest, that is.'

'I know nothing about her,' almost shouted Mrs. Barnes.

'But Oliver does. Don't you, Oliver? If it was worth me giving you the tip, only it ain't because you've poisoned your last girl-friend, I'd remind you that you shouldn't take a lady out to coffee without making sure about her hat. Yes, I said hat. No one would remember her, specially, but the hat was a different matter. And the lady who remembers the hat, and is prepared to say so in court, also remembers that she was squired by a gent with dark hair and a little moustache *and a nasty-looking scar on the back of his right hand!*'

Instinctively Oliver started to thrust his hand into his pocket, but not before the inspector had seen the scar referred to. He, poor man, was trying to sort some sense out of this fandango of charges and counter-charge in which they were all involved, and being a man who believed in order he endeavoured to pluck the heart out of the mystery by turning to the self-styled cook and saying, 'I'll have to ask you to let me see your identity card.'

'I understand people no longer have to produce them at the demand of the police,' snapped Mrs. Barnes.

'In a case like this it's the easiest way to dispose of Mr. Crook's claim,' the inspector pointed out.

The lady in question retorted feebly that she hadn't got it with her; in fact, it was lost. So, decided Crook, watching the inspector's face, was her case. It was tough on an enterprising female like Mrs. Barnes that her sister should prove such a nitwit in an emergency. However, that was the inspector's pigeon and didn't worry him. Half a hundred people could identify her as Mrs. Forbes when the time came and as to why she was masquerading as Mrs. Barnes's cook – well, that was her headache and possibly her last.

'Only – they can't have got rid of the girl,' he told himself in desperation. 'They can't have put her underground since I saw her this morning.' Anxiety tore at his vitals. He flung up the kitchen window and stared at the garden. It's more difficult to dig a grave than amateurs realise, and practically impossible to do so without leaving traces. Yet there was no sign that earth or grass had been disturbed. A wind blew through the grasses, a cat mewed, there was a low humming sound, a dog barked from the other side of the house, a car went by, there was a low humming sound; behind him the voices were getting sharper, talking two or three together, the cat suddenly heard a bird move among the twigs and proceeded to stalk it. There was a low humming sound.. His senses sharpened abruptly. That was the solution, of course. That low humming sound. He cursed his denseness in not appreciating that at once. It was a matter of seconds now.

'Bill!' he yelled at the top of his voice, thrusting aside the outraged and not yet defeated Mrs. Barnes. 'Bill!'

Bill came dashing through the hall – the first time, reflected Crook, he'd ever seen Bill in a hurry, the uniformed policeman came after him, thinking that Crook and his colleague were planning a getaway; he collided with the inspector, who came bouncing out of the kitchen, looking about as cool as a kitten entangled in a ball of wool, and the two women and Oliver came hard on his heels. Crook had flung open the garden door and was making for the garage. As they got nearer the humming sound increased.

'Must be in me dotage,' said Crook. 'H'm. Padlocked? Every picture tells a story. Hey, Bill.'

Bill was at his elbow. 'No need to smash the door down,' said Oliver Barnes's voice. 'I've got the key here.' He fumbled with it from a bunch on a key-ring. 'All right, I'm getting it. Fact is, I'm running in a new car, and neighbours object to the row.'

'Barring that howling dervish of a cat I wouldn't have said you had any neighbours,' riposted Crook, 'and I can't believe that any one who can poison an old lady in cold blood is so careful of the feelings of a cat.'

Oliver continued to fumble with the key, but he released it at last and handed it to the inspector, who stopped and tried to fit it into the lock. After a moment he said, 'Sure this is the right key?' and Oliver replied, 'It's a bit stiff, but – perhaps you'd like me . . .'

And all the while that diabolical noise went on – and on.

'Here, can't you see his little game?' demanded Crook rudely, elbowing the inspector aside. 'Bill, you do your stuff.'

Bill took something out of his pocket, dropped down on his heels, did something to the padlock and the next instant it was lying in his hand. Crook had the door open in a flash. Inside was the car the young man had driven in some time ago and a catholic motley of possessions. Near the door were two sacks of potatoes, their mouths open; chopped wood was piled against another wall. There were some gardening tools, various bottles and tins, and at the far end more sacks were flung down in an untidy heap. Crook dived towards them, scattering them like a terrier sending the earth flying. The next moment he was backing furiously bringing something limp and heavy with him.

The inspector switched off the engine of the car.

In the brief period of confusion that followed only Bill had sufficient detachment to see Oliver Barnes' hand flash from his pocket to his lips. He made no move to stop him. As he said to Crook later, 'It didn't seem likely we could pin murder on him. There'd be an element of doubt where the old lady was concerned and he'd be certain to get the benefit of it. And the girl wasn't dead, so he couldn't have swung for her. And in these days of food and house shortages why should he go on taking bread and occupying space needed by better citizens than himself? Besides, we're a bureaucracy these days, and who am I to do the police's job for them?'

But he was considerate enough to move aside after that swift action on the part of the doomed man, to give him space to fall.

The police officer had fetched the doctor, and the doctor had telephoned for an ambulance, and the limp body of the missing girl lay in the room Mrs. Barnes called her drawing-room with the doctor working on it like mad. Her life, he said, hung by a thread, but he thought they'd just make it.

'If you don't,' said Crook, livid with apprehension and rage, 'I'll have such a mass murder that I'll be in Madam Tussaud's by the end of the week.' He went off to fetch Mrs. Hubble who had been waiting in the car all this time.

'You're wanted for identification,' he told her.

When she saw the unconscious figure Mrs. Hubble stared and stared. 'But – but that's not Pamela Smith,' she said, and Crook stared in turn.

'Why on earth should you think it was? There was no sense putting the little girl out of the way. What harm could she be to any one? An orphan without a name and (once Mrs. Barnes had got things settled) without a friend? That woman has practised economy all her life, and she wasn't going to waste a murder till a murder was the only card left in her hand. But – is it Terry Lawrence?'

'Yes, that's who it is. But Mr. Parsons said they called her Miss Smith.'

'Wouldn't you, in Mrs. Barnes' shoes? Then if any awkward questions should be asked later as to what happened to Miss Smith, she's only got to produce the little lass from the orphanage – because they never meant to move her, they wouldn't find anywhere else so safe from their point of view – and who'd have the last word then? I've never been afraid they'd try to get rid of her – only of her friends – Miss Martin and Terry Lawrence and – ultimately – me. Only luckily Mrs. Barnes took the K.O. before my turn came round.'

CHAPTER 19

Some weeks after the sensational developments in the Martin Murder Mystery, Mrs. Barnes paid the penalty for her crime, it being proved to the satisfaction of the court (thanks to Crook, the police and Philip Scott's doctor, in that order) that she had not merely been accessory to the murder of Miss Martin and the attempted murder of Terry Lawrence, but had actually poisoned her brother. The day following the execution Mr. Crook went to have tea with the girl whose life he had saved. To his mind – for he likes females plump, and can see no beauty in the croquet-mallet figure – she looked too thin, too pale still, but he admitted that her appearance was a considerable improvement on what it had been on that afternoon of grim suspense and terror when he had dragged her, as he picturesquely put it, from under the wheels of death.

'I wish you'd been able to come to the hospital,' said Terry frankly, putting in sugar till the tea was like syrup, which was the way Mr. Crook liked tea (I'd be a sucker for young Barnes, he acknowledged, taking the cup). 'Every one was dying to see you. The nurses kept asking . . .'

Crook grinned. 'Piece of good advice from your Uncle Arthur, free gratis and for nothing,' he said. 'Never disappoint your public. If they think you're goin' to look as if your second name was Galahad it's goin' to be a bad shock to them when they see somethin' that might have come out of the sea-lion's cage. It's what these fashion-writers tell you in the ninepennies. Mystery is woman's charm – and it's a man's best defence. Let folk go on cherishin' their illusions. I can't tell you what a shock that poor old lady, Miss Martin got when she first set eyes on me.'

'I can't think why,' said Terry, coolly. 'I wouldn't be a bit surprised to know your middle name was Galahad. And Dennis will agree with me.'

'Who's Dennis? Future Mr. Terry Lawrence?'

'I'd rather say I'm the future Mrs. Dennis Ogilvie.'

'Like that? Well, I'm not surprised. Only – what's he been doin' all this time to let you get into the jaws of the serpent?'

'It's not so easy to look after people when they're in England and you're in the Far East,' pointed out the girl, gently. 'Dennis is in India, and he's due to be demobbed this summer.'

'I suppose that's why someone thought up the theory of guardian angels,' said Crook, not in the least abashed. He caught sight of himself in a hanging mirror and grinned again. 'You know that one about entertaining angels unawares?'

'Yes. Only I'm not unawares.'

Crook took a fresh piece of toasted tea-cake and crammed it into his mouth. 'I can see you don't need to read the ninepennies,' he complimented her when it had gone down, like a rabbit down the throat of a boa-constrictor.

'There are a lot of things I want to know,' Terry continued. 'I thought about them when I was in hospital.'

'Shoot,' offered Crook in his friendly way.

'First of all, how did you know Mrs. Forbes and Mrs. Barnes were sisters?'

'Easy one that. It was obvious there must be some link between the two. It was a put-up job about the little girl, and they were both in it to the neck. It was easy to see what Mrs. Barnes stood to win by buryin' her alive in an orphanage, but how about the other? I don't say I know a lot about the rules goverin' orphans, but I do know you can't take a brat into a home without asking any questions at all. That's all right. Mean to say, you might get piled up with kidnappees or unwanted babies – anything. You have to have a birth certificate and some proof the parents are dead, and if it's a free institution, then you want proof that there's no one responsible and the kid really hasn't got a penny behind her. If Mrs. Forbes had started asking questions the whole story about Philip Scott's connection with Pamela Smith must have come out, and she might have thought it fishy to say the least. So it all goes to prove she did know what was going on, but it was worth her while to keep her mouth shut. Mrs. B. might have offered her a lump sum, of course, but I didn't think so, because that would have put the power into Mrs. Forbes' hands. I mean, no reason why she shouldn't have had the lump sum twice a year. It wouldn't suit Mrs. Barnes for the story to come out. You can only murder a man once, but you can blackmail him all your life – or his.'

'I see. And, of course, if there was no will, then the money went to the next-of-kin, and Mrs. Forbes would have as many rights as Mrs. Barnes. How did you know there'd ever been another sister, though?'

'The old lady put me on to that. The Spinster's Secret. Chance you might call it. Or feminine intuition. Or just righteousness comin' into its own. The old gentleman, Mr. Scott, happened to say something about his sisters fighting like Kilkenny cats, and Miss Martin happened to repeat it, and I happened to remember. So I thought, Yes, but we've only heard of one sister to date. But there was Mrs. Barnes going to see a lady of the right age and appearance, callin' her by her Christian name – and what a Christian name.'

Terry looked slightly bewildered.

'I don't understand.'

'Flossie – that's what Mrs. Barnes called her. And on that list of possible legatees they found in Mr. Scott's room was a name – Florence. It was scored through, but so was Mrs. Barnes and so was Oliver. Most people seemed to think it was an ex-cook or something, but nobody could explain why Mr. Scott should be considerin' a legacy to an ex-cook, and anyway he was the old Tory model, called all his servants by their surnames.'

'You do think of a lot, don't you? What made you so sure that the nurse at Great Baring was Mrs. Forbes?'

'Know what they say about a secret? A secret known to one is a secret of God; known to two is public property, or words to that effect. Whoever was lookin' after you knew there was funny business going on. Ever heard of a nurse on a dangerous case who didn't have a doctor around? And there wasn't any doctor here. Even the village had noticed that. No, the invalid at Great Baring was as phoney as the orphan at Elsham, and in each case Mrs. Barnes had an accomplice. As I've said before, she was an economical woman and she'd never spend tuppence if a penny would do. Besides, two accomplices meant more danger for her and less cash. So it seemed likely that it wasn't two women involved, but the same one in each case. Then I went to the orphanage and heard that *Mrs. Forbes was away staying with relations and hadn't left an address*. Well, as I've pointed out more than once, I may not wear the old school tie, but I do know that two and two make four, and once you've learnt that you don't really need much more education. Anythin' more?'

'Yes. Why were you so sure it was me and not Pamela in that room?'

'There wasn't any need to put Pamela out of the way. Once her friends were disposed of, what chance had a poor little kid like that? They only had to keep her at the orphanage, and to all intents and purposes she was as much buried as poor old Janet Martin in her private grave at the cemetery. In a way, she was dead already. Pamela Smith, I mean. She'd become Mary Smith, the orphan. Oh, it was a fine plot, and it might have succeeded, but for me – and Providence.'

'I like the order you put them in.'

'Remember the sayin' that Providence helps those that help themselves? That means that you've got to do something first, just as an earnest of your intentions, before you can expect Providence to intervene. Mind you, I'm not exactly blaming Mrs. Barnes. I told her every murderer makes a mistake. Hers was pittin' herself against me. She couldn't know Miss Martin was goin' to turn up at Elsham, and even when she did she couldn't know she was goin' to be one of Pamela's London buddies. Then, when she tried to cope with that by gettin' the old lady certified – and you remember how Mrs. Forbes never let Miss Webster alone till she got the doctor in – she found out there was still me. She must have telephoned Miss Martin usin' your name, and I'll say she had a fright when she heard I was on the war-path. Because if she didn't know about me darlin' Oliver did. That pepped things up a bit, because it meant Miss M. must be put out of the way before she could do any more mischief.'

'How did you know that any one had telephoned, since Miss Martin was killed the next day?'

'That inquisitive old dame at the Home listened in to Miss M.'s side of the conversation and repeated it verbatim, or so she said. Mind you, there may have been a bit of parsley round the dish, but that don't matter. You must admit they are triers, the Barnes. Oliver guaranteed to put out the old lady's light, and then they decided that they could be a bit more subtle when it came to you. Once you were both out of the way there wasn't any evidence to take into a court of law.'

'There was still Pamela?'

'Who was going to listen to what a little girl said? Besides, she was in the orphanage, and from their point of view that was as good as the grave. It was only when I began to be a nuisance to them they decided to put you where you couldn't talk. No, don't ask me what they were goin' to do. The wild wood behind the house is my notion. Safer the river really. The river has tides and bodies drift up inconveniently, and there's nothing more nosey than a policeman once you get it into his thick head that something's wrong.'

'So that was their plan? And I fell for it.'

'Oh, I don't think that was their plan from the start,' said Crook. 'They didn't mean to murder any one but Philip Scott, and they'd probably argue he signed his own death-warrant. It's a satisfaction to me to think we managed to bring it home to Mrs. Barnes. It's always the same,' continued Crook, with a blissful complacence, that had made him more enemies than all his brains, 'let a woman talk and you've got her where you want her. Luckily the doctor didn't like her, either. That was a help. Of course, she destroyed the will, either on the spot or took it home with her and burnt it there. The last most likely. Miss Martin must have been a shock to them, but they found she had no friends, as they thought, except her niece, and I'd sooner look for humanity to a pillar of salt than to Miss Doreen Blake. They decided if they could get the old girl certified they could stop worrying about her. Who was goin' to listen to her bleatin' from a padded cell? Then, when it came to your turn they couldn't think of anything better – that's always the way with criminals, stick to the same old last till even the police are bound to notice it. I dare say it was easy enough for Oliver to get hold of drugs in his hush-hush job . . .'

'That's how it began,' Terry agreed. 'I went down once, hoping they'd realise they couldn't put this thing over, and though I knew they wouldn't give Pamela the money I thought at least they'd arrange for her to be taken into some family, settle something on her, give her a chance. Oliver asked me if I'd wait forty-eight hours before I took any action, and because I thought they were weakening a bit, I agreed. Then, before the forty-eight hours were up, I got a telephone call from Mrs. Barnes asking me to go down again. She wanted to talk over a plan she'd made. She was very plausible. She said, "Everything depends now on whether you will fall in with my idea. If you are genuinely interested in the little girl's future . . ."'

'And you went like a bird?'

'What else could I do? Oliver met me at the station and took me up to the house and on the way he said, 'I've never seen mother knuckle down to any woman before. It makes her feel like murder, so be a bit more tactful this time, won't you?' I said I should do what I thought was right . . .'

'And then you're surprised they knocked you on the head? More harm's done in this world by people who want to do the right than any number of black sheep. Well, what happened?'

'Oliver pointed out again that Pamela had no legal claim, and I decided they were going to propose some arrangement I shouldn't altogether like, but should probably have to accept, because otherwise they'd say I wouldn't co-operate. And naturally I knew there wasn't any legal claim. But there's no doubt about it, Mrs. Barnes was shaken when she realised that Miss Martin had actually seen the will. At that time,' the girl added, 'Miss Martin was all right.'

'And it didn't work out the way you expected?'

'No. When I arrived Mrs. Barnes wasn't any more friendly than she had been the first time, which was clever of her really, because I should have mistrusted that. She said she'd been thinking things over and probably the best idea would be to try and get the child adopted – in any case, the orphanage had only been a temporary expedient. Though naturally I didn't believe that. I asked why they'd changed her name, and she said they wanted to protect her from publicity. Then she told Oliver to ring for drinks, and when they came he asked me if I liked a cocktail, and I said I would, and . . .'

'That's women all over,' said Crook, ungratefully. 'Never can refuse a bargain. It 'ud have been more in the picture if you'd folded your arms over your proud bosom and said, 'Drink in an enemy's house? Never!" '

'I didn't want to intimidate her. I didn't care what she thought about me so long as it came out all right for Pamela. But you're right. There must have been something in the drink, something pretty strong, too, because my memory stops there. Anyway, if it hadn't been the drink, it would have been the coffee or the food.'

'Happen you're right,' agreed Crook. 'Well?'

'When I came round I was in that room with the bars at the window. I couldn't see the bars, because there was a black curtain nailed over the window, but they warned me. No use trying to get out that way, they said. And if you screamed the house down no one would hear, but I thought perhaps a tradesman might, and be curious, or someone selling things at the door, or even the servants. But I suppose she'd squared the servants. There was only one anyway. She likes to pretend she has a cook, but none of them will stay with her and Parker combined.'

'Parker being the Wolf-Scarer?'

'What an exact description! I think she told Parker I'd had a nervous breakdown, hinted at disgraceful escapades. I didn't see her often, but when I did she looked at me as though I were a leper.'

'And then she brought in Mrs. Forbes to lend colour to things?'

'It wasn't till after Mrs. Forbes had arrived that I realised just how awful it would be for Pamela caught in her power. Because she was as hard as Mrs. Barnes, and being a nurse – I suppose it either makes you especially kind or absolutely without pity. Of the two, she was the worst. Sometimes I was sure I'd go out of my mind, the things she did – the tricks she played . . .'

'Professional versus amateur,' said Crook, his mind dwelling lovingly for a moment on some of the penalties thought suitable in the Middle Ages for wrong-doers. There was the barrel studded with nails, there was the flaming barrel of pitch, or the common or garden stake, there was the saint on the gridiron, though admittedly that was further back than the Middle Ages. Still, they probably hadn't been above taking a leaf out of the books of their predecessors.

Terry was speaking again. 'I used to try and think up ways of outwitting them, but it was no use. I was as helpless as Pamela. You see, they had so many weapons. They put stuff in the cups of tea they brought me. I don't know what it was, but I used to have nightmares in which I really was raving mad . . .'

'Maybe that was the idea,' said Crook.

'I'd refuse to drink the tea or upset the cup, but presently my throat was so parched I thought I'd go mad from thirst. And if I wouldn't obey them they'd take steps to make me – and when I was under the influence of the drugs they gave me I had no idea what I did or said. I didn't even know day from night . . .'

It was an ugly story. A young girl in the power of two unscrupulous women, and they hadn't worried about being gentle. The marks on her young body showed that.

'How did you get the match-box through to Miss Martin?' he asked. 'That put the old lady on her mettle. And I will say for her, she was a go-er. Up and down that hill on her poor old pins, hiding behind tree-trunks in March gales, facing up to first one Matron and then the other, givin' 'em the slip to meet me. I reckon if Hitler had met her, and a few like her, he wouldn't have bothered about fighting England. He'd have known he couldn't win.'

'About the match-box,' said Terry. 'It was like magic. Mrs. Forbes hadn't arrived then, and of course I was left alone sometimes. Parker had been told I was queer and mustn't be allowed to roam about alone – perhaps they thought I was a homicidal maniac, I wouldn't know, and as a rule Mrs. Barnes locked me in. But one afternoon she went down in a hurry; a man had come to look at a defective window-frame, and she forgot about turning the key. I heard them come up after a minute and go past my door, and then she went down again, and I thought perhaps this was my chance. They'd gone through my bag and taken my pen and pencil and book of stamps, but they left my powder and lipstick – "you'll want to keep up your self-respect, won't you," said Mrs.

Barnes, "and you can't do any harm with those." They'd taken my money, too, but they hadn't noticed a shilling that had slipped behind my pocket mirror, and they hadn't thought it mattered about the envelope with the printed address on it. After all, there weren't any stamps and I hadn't a pen.'

'Had they seen the match-box?'

'I wore it like a charm on a bracelet.'

'If they'd really thought you were daft they'd have taken it away in case you swallowed it. That's quite natural with lunies.'

'I put the match-box into the envelope and sealed it up, and wrote the address on the envelope with lipstick, and presently I heard the man coming down, and I listened and listened in case she was coming up, but she didn't seem to be, so I opened the door a crack and gave him the envelope and the shilling and said "Please post it. It's terribly urgent." I dare say she'd told him, too, that if he heard any one calling out not to pay any attention; he looked at me for a minute in an odd sort of way, then he put the shilling in his pocket, and took the envelope. I couldn't be sure he'd post it, of course. He might have handed it straight to Mrs. Barnes, or he might just have pocketed the shilling and thrown the envelope away. After some days I was pretty sure he hadn't given it to Mrs. Barnes, because surely she would have said something – I waited and waited and she never did – but that might just have been her cunning, to keep me in suspense.'

The imagination to which he never confessed gave Crook some insight into that long torture of not knowing she must have endured in a darkened room, ignorant of developments, fearful of her own future, racked with anxiety for Pamela. And beyond that barred and blackened window life moved, warm, tumultous, eventful, and utterly unaware.

'In any case the match-box arrived,' Crook consoled her. Miss Martin got it and contacted me, and then someone from this house must have contacted her – so perhaps they did know about the match-box, or it might have been Mrs. Forbes getting on her trail – Well, you know what happened, she tried to get me but Miss Webster sided agin the angels, and young Barnes went down the next morning to put the old lady where she couldn't do any harm. She fell for it like a stone, though it was takin' a bit of a chance. Still, if you can't ever take a risk you're best underground.'

'It must be an awful existence, never being sure from one minute to the next if you're safe. Of course, he had his remedy at hand, and once I was found in the garage he must have known he hadn't a chance . . .'

'Very bad show,' said Crook, severely. 'They should have kept their eyes on him, the police, I mean. Bill said it was written all over the fellow's face what he was goin' to do before he just stroked his chin. . . .'

'But if Bill knew, why didn't he stop him?' She sounded horrified.

'Don't you make the mistake too many women make,' Crook warned her. 'Thinkin' you know better than Providence. We couldn't have pinned any murder on to him so tight it couldn't have rubbed off, and suicide's tantamount to a confession. Why, it would have been ungrateful to try and stop him. That's the way I look at it. Anything else?' He passed up his cup for more tea. Terry refilled it in silence. Then:

'Mr. Crook, what starts people on a career of murder?' she asked. 'Or is it just that they're taken unaware? Mrs. Barnes couldn't have known her brother was going to have a heart attack, and she was going to have the chance of giving him an overdose. And yet, when the minute came, she didn't hesitate. Does one's mind work like lightning? I don't think mine would.'

'She may not have known she was goin' to murder him, but she had been thinking about his death for so long that when the chance came she took it like a flash. I don't suppose there was even a minute when she struggled with herself. She'd got beyond that. Y'see, what the average layman don't understand is that murder begins in the mind. That's why murder's so interestin' to most people. It's the amateur's crime, and most folks are amateurs. Any one might commit a murder, because you don't need any specialist knowledge, like you would for burglary, say, or embezzlement. It's only when it comes to gettin' away with it that your special knowledge comes in. That's why most murderers get hanged – just through bein' amateurs. Ever since John Scott died Mrs. Barnes had been countin' on the money coming to her and dear Flossie and darlin' Oliver. She'd got to a pitch where she practically regarded the money as her right. She'd got past thinking, if only Philip was out of the way I'd be a rich woman; instead she was thinkin', when Philip is out of the way I shall be a rich woman.' He drained his tea at a gulp and set the cup back in the saucer. 'Most people wish someone or other out of the way. Well, we're all human, and so long as it don't go farther than that, where's the harm? But it's when the thought becomes what the French call the idee fixee (he gave the words their broadest English pronunciation) that the red light snaps on, warnin' you to be careful. Like the chap who thinks, If only Jane was dead I could marry Mary, not knowing, poor sap, that at the end of six months it'll be all one to him which he's married to, and thinks it so often that presently, without his knowing it, he's saying, "Once Jane's dead I'll marry Mary." See?'

'I think I do. She was so accustomed to thinking of that money as her own she probably even thought she had a moral right to it.'

'I'll say she did. In her own mind *that was her money*, and it's natural to fight for your own. So when the chance came she tipped a double dose into the glass without winking, and if you ask me she never laid awake a single night having pangs of remorse. Murderers ain't like that. It may be popular sentiment to imagine them torn by pangs and givin' anything to have their time over again. They're only that when they think they're goin' to be caught. Because the idea that murder's something committed on the spur of the moment don't hold water. Even the chap who goes out to crack a crib and ends by cracking someone else's skull didn't do it by accident. At the back of his mind was the knowledge that things might turn out so he'd *have* to crack that skull, and when the minute came he was ready. They say that what people don't know don't hurt 'em. They're wrong. It's what people don't know that, as like as not, ends 'em up in the little covered shed. If Mrs. B. had known about Miss Martin witnessin' the will I dare say she wouldn't have taken the chance. And certainly if she'd known about her meeting the little girl and afterwards goin' to Elsham she'd have thought again. Y'see there was nowhere but Elsham she could send the little girl.'

'There was me – and Mrs. Hubble. Didn't we count?'

'You were interested parties. You had an axe to grind. See? Now Miss Martin didn't stand to gain a thing. Then – she was old and poor and a bit dotty, they thought, one of the kind that's just as well dead. Better, in fact. I'm sure that horse-faced niece of hers would tell you so. And yet there she was, sprawlin' across the path, making hay of a perfectly good murder. So – out she had to go. And – it's funny to think of it – it was through her you nearly went out, too.'

'After you'd gone that morning,' said Terry in a low voice, 'they came into my room, and Mrs. Forbes gave me an injection. She said I needed sleep. I couldn't stop her, and in a way I didn't mind. Somehow, after I'd seen you standing there in the garden, I had a most extraordinary feeling that a miracle might happen, after all. I went right out after the injection. . . .'

'And they bundled you up in a shawl and dumped you in the garage, havin' first of all sent out the Wolf-Scarer and arranged for Mrs. Forbes to go back. I don't doubt they'd got a story all ready – you'd had a fit of dementia while the Wolf-Scarer was out and they'd had to send for an ambulance and get you off to hospital, and Mrs. Forbes had gone with you, and wouldn't be coming back. Then, when I turned up unexpected, Mrs. Barnes threw a fit of temperament and shouted at the top of her voice – that was to warn Nursie, and I must say she was quick in the uptake, jumping into Cookie's shoes. I will say this for Mrs. Barnes. She don't do things by halves.'

'She certainly doesn't.'

'You see,' Crook continued – there were people who said that, next to Winston Churchill, he was Britains's best orator – 'murder's like good resolutions. One leads to another. Mrs. Barnes got started the day she gave her brother his dose; after that things went like a stone rollin' downhill. She either had to waste an unusually good, which is to say a successful murder, that could never be brought home to her, even if there was a bit of talk, or carry on and get rid of all the other obstacles that cropped up. No middle path for her. Just black or white. And so, y'see . . .' he stood up and collecting his hard brown bowler hat, clapped it over his thick red eyebrows,'Well, what would you do, chum?'

LIBRARY OF ART
PUBLISHER - DIRECTOR: GEORGE RAYAS

293 AK
PENA
MARINA

◁

Flying over the Aegean. Aerial photograph (pp. 2-3).

Karpathos, Pigadia. Partial view of the main town (pp. 4-5).

Delos. Part of the archeological site, with the lions (pp. 6-7).

Painting by G. Derpapas, inspired by the Aegean (p. 8).

Amorgos. Picturesque details of typical Cycladic architecture (p. 9).

Lesbos, Molyvos. Aerial photograph (p. 10).

Syros, Ano Meria. Terrace cultivation (p. 11).

Ancient amphoras of assorted shapes and sizes. Mykonos, Aegean Maritime Museum (pp. 12-13).

Samos, the west harbour, 1776. From the book by Luigi Mayer. Athens, Gennadios Library (pp. 14-15).

THE AEGEAN

THE EPICENTER OF GREEK CIVILIZATION

THE AEGEAN

THE EPICENTER OF GREEK CIVILIZATION

"MELISSA" PUBLISHING HOUSE

Supervision and editing:
LAMBRINI PAPAIOANNOU, philologist
DORA COMINI-DIALETI, philologist

Translation and proof-reading:
PHILIP RAMP, ALEXANDRA DOUMAS, DAVID CONNOLLY

PHOTOGRAPHERS
Kostas Manolis, Makis Skiadaresis,
Stelios Skopelitis, Yiannis Skouroyiannis,
Studio Kontos, Dimitris Trikourakis,
Manolis Vernardos, Velis Voutsas
Antonis Zervos
Aerial photographs by Velis Voutsas

Artistic supervision: SPYROS KARACHRISTOS

Phototypesetting: FASMA, P. KAPENIS
Colour separation: K. ADAM, MELISSA Publishing House
Printing: EPIKINONIA LTD
Binding: Y. MOUTSIS Co

Pages: 456. Size: 30×25 cm.
Colour illustrations: 379. Black-and-white: 191. Drawings: 23.

10 Navarinou St., 10680, tel. (01) 3611692, fax (01) 3600865

ISBN: 960-204-012-2

The Authors

ODYSSEUS ELYTIS
Poet, Nobel Prize Winner

†NIKOS SVORONOS
Historian, Professor at the École Pratique des Hautes Études, Paris

†MANOLIS ANDRONICOS
Professor of Classical Archeology at the University of Thessaloniki

CHARALAMBOS BOURAS
Architect, Professor at the National Technical University of Athens

MYRTALI ACHEIMASTOU-POTAMIANOU
Byzantinologist, Director of the Byzantine Museum, Athens

CHRYSANTHOS CHRISTOU
Professor of the History of Art at the University of Athens, Academician

ANGELOS DELIVORRIAS
Director of the Benaki Museum, Professor at the University of Athens

ANASTASIOS A. TZAMTZIS
Master, Merchant Marine

LAMBROS LIAVAS
Ethnomusicologist, Associate Professor at the University of Athens

CHRISTOS DOUMAS
Professor of Prehistoric Archeology at the University of Athens

YIORGIS YIATROMANOLAKIS
Assistant Professor in the Faculty of Letters at the University of Athens

CONTENTS

Archives, Libraries, Foundations, Institutes, Museums, Collections, Galleries, Banks, who contributed to the illustration of the volume:

Aegean Maritime Museum, Mykonos
Archeological Collection, Rhodes
Archeological Museum, Corinth
Archeological Museum, Herakleion, Crete
Archeological Museum, Samothrace
Archeological Museum, Thessaloniki
Archeological Receipts Fund (T.A.P.A.), Athens
Archive ELIA, Athens
Archives of M. Merlier, Centre for Asia Minor Studies, Athens
Benaki Museum, Athens
Byzantine Museum, Athens
Commercial Bank of Greece
Ecclesiastical Museum, Mytilene
Ekdotike Athenon
Folklore Museum, Mykonos
Gennadios Library, Athens
German Archeological Institute, Athens
Hellenic Maritime Museum, Pireaus
Historical Museum, Herakleion, Crete
Municipal Museum, Mytilene
Museum of Chania, Crete
Museum of Cycladic Art (N.P. Goulandris Collection), Athens
Museum of Folk Art, Nicosia, Cyprus
Museum of Greek Popular Art, Athens
Museum of Greek Popular Musical Instruments —
F. Anoyanakis Collection, Athens
Museum of Hydra
Museum of Milos
Museum of Spetses
Museum of Symi
National Archeological Museum, Athens
National Bank of Greece
National Gallery, Athens
National Historical Museum, Athens
Peloponnesian Folklore Foundation, Nafplion
The Monastery of Saint John the Theologian, Patmos
War Museum, Athens

Preface

Light and colour, variety and contrast, austerity and wealth are the distinctive traits of the Aegean. Here nature and man worked together in close harmony to create the very centre of Hellenic civilization.

A Greek sea, the Aegean lies between Europe and the East. With its hundreds of islands, large and small, in a remarkable unit extending from the eastern shore of the Greek Mainland to the coast of Asia Minor, for six thousand years the Aegean has been not only the bearer of messages from one continent to another, but also a source of inspiration and creativity, founding and defending its own civilization – a civilization it later bequeathed to mankind.

This volume, planned since 1978, stems from our belief in the inestimable cultural contribution of the Aegean. In compiling this multifaceted, collective work we have collaborated with Greece's leading scholars in the fields of history and art, and have sought out original and lavish illustrative material from dozens of museums and art galleries, foundations and private collections in Greece and abroad.

During the long interval which has elapsed between conception and publication, two invaluable colleagues, Nikos Svoronos and Manolis Andronicos, have passed away; their studies printed here are perhaps among their last works.

Thanks to the excellent cooperation of all who have contributed to this book, in the scholarly and the technical sphere, we are pleased to present a publication of the highest quality.

We warmly thank all those who have assisted in bringing this arduous task to fruition, and especially D. Philippides, Professor at the National Technical University of Athens, for his help on the English edition.

The Publisher

Draft for an introduction to the Aegean World

BEFORE THE RIDGE OF SERIFOS, as the sun rises, the guns of all the great world theories are silenced. The mind is surpassed by a few waves and some rocks; absurd perhaps but nevertheless sufficient to lead man to his true dimensions. And what else could be of more use to him in his life? If he likes starting off wrongly, it is because he does not want to listen. For thousands of years now and in man's absence, the Aegean has been saying again and again in the voice of its plashing along an endless length of coast: this is you! And it is repeated by the shape of the fig leaf against the sky; it is grasped by the pomegranate that clenches its fist until it bursts; it is chanted by the cicadas until they become transparent. Death may seem more or less right, by which I mean more or less an irreparable loss, depending on how you accept it. Force and number have always prevented us from accepting the one true justice, which is a "precise moment", or the one true morality, which is but a continual reference to the most simplified form of our being.

It is impossible for us to calculate the enormous gulf separating a Cycladic figurine from a pebble with the same ease that we can calculate entire aeons of light-years. And it is precisely this that constitutes our Achilles' heel, which is why we compete with knowledge in desperation. However, the Gods' portion, if it exists at all outside religions, is without doubt a form of bounty. A seagull with outstretched wings over a limitless expanse of azure. We pretend to ourselves that we can blot it out, that we have the means. But then what? The day after we are lost forever, it will still go on. Two poles of ignorance that are not linked but that at any moment could bring light; such a shame!

Is it true then that light leaps from the darkest shade of black? Love comes to confirm it in another way. When two naked bodies converse, something from the unpublicised part of their tale –the unbearable part– is wiped out. The kiss, which has not evolved in the slightest since the dawn of time, happens to be the most novel and unhackneyed thing that we possess. Some tale of love with divine dimensions must surely have preceded the tectonic tremors and the displacement of the waters when the Greek archipelago was created. The irrationality that we find in myths is sometimes redressed by nature itself. Only then do we reflect that, in spite of everything, it is we who created them perhaps even against our will. There still remains something for us to discover: this light, these clusters of islands, what are they? Are we dreaming?

While journeying in his mind's eye to Patmos and Anatolia, Hölderlin, from the distant reaches of Swabia, grasped the golden vision much more clearly than the modern passenger in a jet at a height of 11,000 feet. Not just a few turtles on the surface of the water, aber

> *Es rauschen aber um Asias Tore*
> *Hinziehend da und dort*
> *In ungewisser Meeresebene*
> *Der schattenlosen Strassen genug,*
> *Doch kennt die Inseln der Schiffer.*

The divine touch is what did not escape him. Magic has its own ways. It knows when to open a doorway even in the walls of science so that we may breathe. Such a door may prove to be an entire encyclopaedia; all we have to do is open it: the water level has only to rise or to fall by fifty or a hundred metres and the most wondrous, most vibrant achievement of matter will take place before our very eyes, and will, of course, also have its analogies –provided we are receptive enough– in the spirit.

A transformation of Picassian power in its lines and masses divides one island into two, joins another three into one, creates new clusters, causes old ones to disappear. Channels and isthmuses emerge, ridges with fresh reddish-green traces of marine life stretch out in the sun; in short, all that a living organism has to offer (together with the turmoil of its emotions) transferred by analogy to the physical world. The other aspect goes much further as we shall see.

The thought of the Ionians, the first lyrical voice in poetry, the subservience of marble to man's caress, the triangle of mountains introduced into architecture, Socrates, Jesus, everything or almost everything came from the School of this sea. How are we to explain it? If we think like millionaires do, the phenomenon is of little concern and the world certainly too big for us to discuss such matters. Yet I am afraid that the moon created by electronic technology will –whether we like it or not– always be inferior than the moon of Sappho, the beams of which, striking us as they do from the depths of one of Lesbos' olive groves, enable us to come closer to ourselves, to the things we love, «ὄττω τίς ἔραται», as the poetess put it. A simple phrase perhaps, but one that has taken on the force of a natural law in this region and has survived in the souls of the islanders, finding expression in innumerable ways, and primarily by way of the instinctive unconscious gesture that knows how to identify what is useful with what is beautiful, and, at the same time, what is beautiful with what is moral, in the most radical sense of these terms.

The parallel and simultaneous elevation of everything humble to a divine magnitude, and the bringing down of the divine to what is tangible and commonplace without the slightest trace of legerdemain called for strong resistance to the Christian superego created from the alluvium left by the superstitions of the middle ages.

Among the finds from archaeological excavations that we present-day Europeans neglected to collect and study are certain concepts which were buried in the same soil along with the products of their art. Humility, for example, which cast off the pungent and pure fragrance of aromatic herbs to become impregnated by incense, was unreservedly bequeathed to us and remained within us rather as the touch of a slave's bare feet on stone slabs than as the pride of "a footprint gathering wisdom in the sand". Nevertheless, in this corner of the earth, an invisible hand has always managed to point towards what is correct (I might even venture to say towards what is healthy) with the stubborn force of a compass needle pointing North. The inconceivable operation at every moment of this invisible mechanism whose parts are as far as the sun and as deep as the veins in the earth, or the currents of the sea depths that are in complete and harmonious correspondence, can be verified provided one dissociates it notionally from what we call immediacy. At least, to the extent that our –alas– limited intellectual abilities will allow. Unless, at such moments, the so-called poetic view (which is not a straightforward analysis, but consists in a shift from the rational to the transcendent and the search for analogies between feelings and actions) again acquires the significance it had originally.

We must not forget that only in this way did Pythagoras reach the point of declaring that the square is fire, the cube earth, the octahedron the winds and the dodecahedron the entire cosmos.

From the polypods on the Cretan vases or the flying fish in the recently discovered frescoes from Santorini; from the bare breasts of the Minoan women or the tridents in the mosaics on Delos; from the expanse of sea between two columns of a temple or the geometric embedding of a flutist in Parian marble, there rises like a light east north-easterly wind a feeling that inversely we might call "holy", which, without the slightest difficulty and as if nothing was amiss, comes to settle on the whitewash of remote churches, on the dark faces of Orthodox saints, on the arched passageways of the houses in Sifnos or Amorgos, on the blue and yellow of the humblest fishing boat. The enumeration may seem arbitrary, perhaps tiresome. It is, however, to some extent deliberately contrived so as to reveal something that takes place much more mysteriously in the souls of a community, where the forces of nature, restrained as they are on all sides by excess (the major scourge of our civilisation), always have the last word, by which I mean that they enable us to understand in what may time may be subjected.

A sun of assimilated love but always fierce? Not enough! In essence this is nothing but one aspect of the phenomenon. The other aspect, which appears to us as a direct reflection of the same feeling that comes from works of art on the works of life, acts and reactions to those daily events that we might term "human behaviour" or "conduct", is even more impressive, as it is indiscernible. It is this "conversely" that, by journeying to its other extreme, you see.

> *Enfin ô bonheur, ô raison, j'écartai du ciel*
> *l'azur, qui est du noir, et je vécus, étincelle*
> *d'or de la lumière nature.*

Once when I wrote that "diving into the sea with eyes open I had the sensation that I was bringing my skin into contact with that whiteness of memory that pursued me from some passage in Plato", it was regarded as being incomprehensible. Yet it is in the pure-blooded Greek language that the helmsman finds the equilibrium in his vessel, in precisely the same way that Ictinus found it in the Parthenon. It is in this that, for example, the actions of a great statesman approach the purity of the most noble form of marble.

It is in this that the most sublime erotic sensation approaches the bitter taste of a black grape, which might give cause to believe that poets play with words, whereas in reality, if you think carefully about it, they are more serious than is permitted by a conversation before a covered screen, with no horizon.

The Aegean has no screen; it never acquired one. It is led, whether by matter or spirit is of no importance, to what is essential. What is everything –for whatever the incomprehensible presumbably represents– is limpidity: the possibility of seeing through the first and the second and the third and the umpteenth level of one single reality, the one-dimensional and at the same time polyphonic point of their metaphorical significance.

So you see how you come to encounter morality even on the path that you take to avoid it. And perhaps then, its tap on your shoulder will appear even more persuasive.

A person waking with the dawn and gazing at a tiny mauve harbour, wishing that he'd never learned to read and write – how marvellous! He goes down to the rocks to untie the boat. Presently, one of the mountain's ridges begins to redden. Soon the Kouros will appear and behind it the outlines of the other islands, the unladen steamboat, a chapel to the Prophet Elijah. Then, everything will vanish leaving a swarthy clear face with large eyes: the fisherman with his basket, your present-day neighbour, yet at the same time, the eternal Fisherman of treasures – and of men.

Odysseus Elytis

Translated by David Connolly

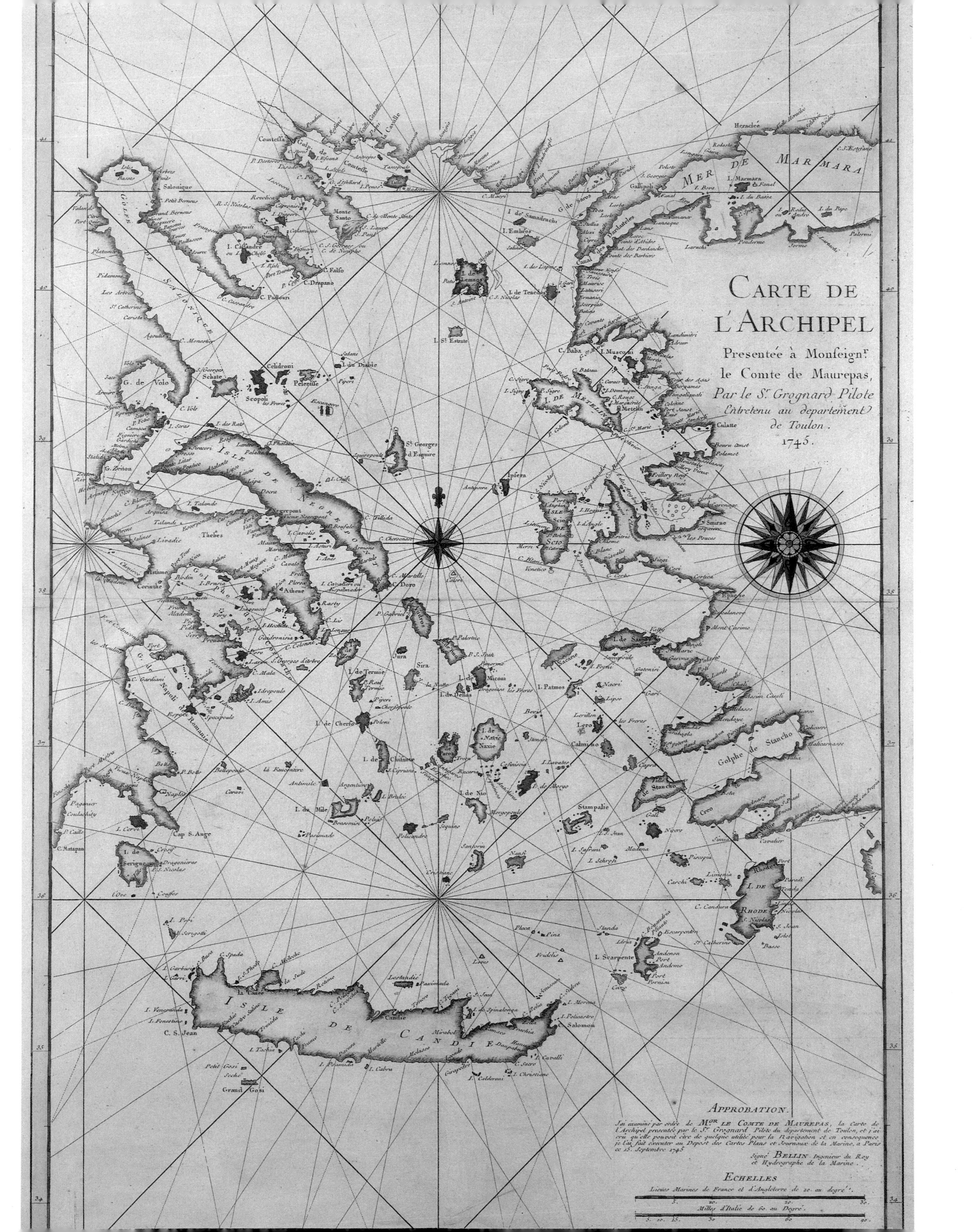
CARTE DE
L'ARCHIPEL
Presentée à Monseignr.
le Comte de Maurepas,
Par le Sr. Grognard Pilote
Entretenu au departement
de Toulon.
1745.
APPROBATION.
J'ai examiné par ordre de Mgr. LE COMTE DE MAUREPAS, la Carte de l'Archipel presentée par le Sr. Grognard Pilote du departement de Toulon, et j'ai cru qu'elle pouvoit être de quelque utilité pour la Navigation et en consequence je l'ai fait executer au Depost des Cartes Plans et Journaux de la Marine, à Paris ce 15. Septembre 1745.
Signé BELLIN Ingenieur du Roy et Hydrographe de la Marine.
ECHELLES
Lieues Marines de France et d'Angleterre de 20. au degré.
5. 10. 20. 30.
Milles d'Italie de 60. au Degré.
5. 10. 15. 30 60 90.
MER DE MARMARA
ISLE DE NEGREPONT
ISLE DE CANDIE
I. DE METELIN
ISLE DE SCIO
I. DE RHODE
Golphe de Stancho
G. de Volo
G. de Saros
Salonique
Monte Santo
I. de Lemnos
I. Embros
I. de Samos
I. de Naxie
I. Patmos
Stampalie
Santorin
Athene
Thebes
Corinthe
Napoli
Smirne
Gallipoli
Candie
C. Matapan
Cap S. Ange
Grand Gosi
Petit Gosi

◁

"Map of the Archipelago, 1745".
Copper-plate engraving by F. Grognard. Athens, Archive ELIA.

NIKOS SVORONOS

A retrospective of Aegean history

Translated by Philip Ramp

The geographical structure of the area where the Greeks lived and developed their civilization determined their historical destiny from the very moment their various peoples began to settle here.

The quadrangle which is bounded to the north by the southernmost section of the Balkan peninsula (Epirus, southern Macedonia and Thrace), to the west by the Ionian Sea, to the east by the coastal strip of western Asia Minor and to the south by Crete and Cyprus constitutes a geographical entity with the Aegean Sea at its center.

Indeed, the entire continental mass of this area which penetrates deeply into the Mediterranean and constitutes the boundary between its eastern and western sections, is oriented toward the Aegean and the East. Its principal rivers empty into the Thracian and Aegean seas.

Its eastern shores have countless natural harbors, starting points for journeys and shelters for sea voyagers. Finally, the Aegean islands have always been a chain of secure bases for the sea "bridge" which connects mainland Greece with the western coast of Asia Minor, Crete and Cyprus. In this way, the internal cohesion of this entire area has been achieved, a feature that would become more prominent over time with the development of a civilization with common characteristics so that the Aegean islands as well as the entire Aegean area would come to be seen as an extension of mainland Greece.

THE AEGEAN DURING PRE-GREEK AND GREEK ANTIQUITY

The Aegean Area and Pre-Greek Civilizations: the Allure of the East

The various Greek peoples appear already to have settled in mainland Greece before 1900 B.C. Recent research accepts that the Middle Helladic civilization (approximately 1900-1600 B.C.) was developed by Greek-speaking populations, the Proto-Greeks. The beginning of the formation of the specific Greek tribes with their special dialects, which nonetheless shared a common Greek character (Ionians, Achaeans, Aeolians, etc.), is put at the beginning of the Middle Bronze Age (1900-1600 B.C.); this process was completed by the Late Helladic or Mycenaean period (1600-1100 B.C.). During the same period, after the Greek speakers became predominant in Greece, a common civilization also began to take form, thus constituting a cohesive element in Greek nationhood and the awareness of a panhellenic idea.

The Aegean played a leading role in the development of Greek civilization up to the moment when the historical initiative came into the hands of Athens.

By way of the Aegean islands, or through direct contact with them, the Greeks would come to know the great technological and economic transformations which lay at the basis of the pre-Greek civilizations developed on the Aegean islands and Crete from the time of the Early Bronze Age.

The new techniques for the processing and the use of metals (copper, bronze, precious metals, such as gold and silver) for the manufacture of tools and weapons, utensils and jewellery first reached the Aegean (the NW coast of Asia Minor and the Aegean islands) and Crete. The consequences of these new techniques, which had spread from the valleys of Mesopotamia to the Levant and to the Nile Valley, on the economic, social, political and ideological structures can be summarized as follows: with the potential for increased production and the creation of surpluses, the previously closed, self-sufficient economy was replaced by a more highly developed open economy with commercial exchanges covering a wide area; large states, and later empires, were created with powerful

1

2

1. Schematic representation of a seal-ring from the Minoan period. Mochlos, Crete.

2. Clay "frying pan", 2800-2300 B.C. From the cemetery of Louros, Naxos. Athens, National Archeological Museum.

3. Sandstone house model, third millennium B.C. from Milos. Milos Museum.

3

organization and stable dynasties, clergy and public servants as well as social classes clearly distinguished; important urban centers where a host of artisans and merchants gathered, were also created.

Of course, during this period when Eastern civilization was exhibiting impressive growth, the Aegean world and continental Greece still presented the picture of an under-developed, peripheral economic and cultural region. However, several traits had already appeared which, through contact with the more advanced civilization, had the potential to develop and to create the pre-Greek Aegean civilizations with their marvelous achievements. These civilizations were the Minoan (Early Minoan and Middle Minoan: 2800-1600 B.C.) on Crete, the Cycladic on the Aegean islands (the first traces on Saliagos and Samos) with its variations on the NE islands (Limnos: Poliochni – Lesbos: settlement of Thermi), in the Troad and NW Asia Minor and in certain areas of Thrace, Chalkidice and eastern Macedonia (2800-1900 B.C.), and finally the Early Helladic civilization in continental Greece (2800-1900 B.C.).

The settlement of the pre-Greek populations on the shores of the Aegean, either from the interior of Asia or from the Balkans to the north, brought about certain adaptations to the new physical environment. Viniculture was added to the traditional agricultural economy. Fishing was practiced alongside stock-raising and, of course, these pre-Greek populations grew familiar with the sea and developed navigation.

Already by the Late Mesolithic period (9th millennium B.C.) the various parts of the Aegean area were in contact with each other. This communication intensified during the Neolithic period. Evidently, the Aegean islands played a special part in this. Contacts of the islands with Crete have been traced back to the first Prepalatial phase of Minoan civilization: clay pottery and Cycladic figurines have been found in Crete from the Neolithic period while obsidian is known to have been imported from Milos. The Aegean islands were further in contact with mainland Greece as is attested by the wide use of obsidian from Milos, as early as the Mesolithic period. Such contacts were also established with the coasts of Asia Minor. Crete, on the other hand, starting in the Early Minoan period, pursued communications with the SW coast of Asia Minor and commercial relations with its interior as well as Cyprus, where a distinctive Neolithic civilization had been developed. Thus, it was through the islands, during the Early Bronze Age, that the entire Aegean and eastern Mediterranean area grew aware of the new technologies and cultural achievements of the civilizations of the East. Indeed, the first important centers of the Early Bronze Age that favored relations with the East have been found on the western coasts of Asia Minor and on the Aegean islands, particularly the Cyclades, which were more densely inhabited then, as well as on Crete. A Cycladic presence, by way of the eastern Aegean islands, Samos and Limnos, has also been confirmed at Troy and Caria.

The commercial contacts of Crete, through northern Syria and from there overland to the Euphrates valley and Babylon, date from the 2nd millennium (1950-1750 B.C.), as has been documented by archeological finds: Babylonian sealstones from the time of Hammurabi were found in the Cretan palaces. During this same period, Crete had close relations with Egypt, and the influence of Egyptian civilization is strongly felt there. Some features characteristic of Minoan civilization came from Egypt: decorative elements of the Minoan palaces, hieroglyphic and iconographic writing and the use of papyrus.

These Aegean civilizations, despite the distinctiveness of each, which made them autonomous cultural units, were never sealed off from each other but sustained constant contact. The commercial relations of the Cyclades, whose ships plied the entire Aegean,

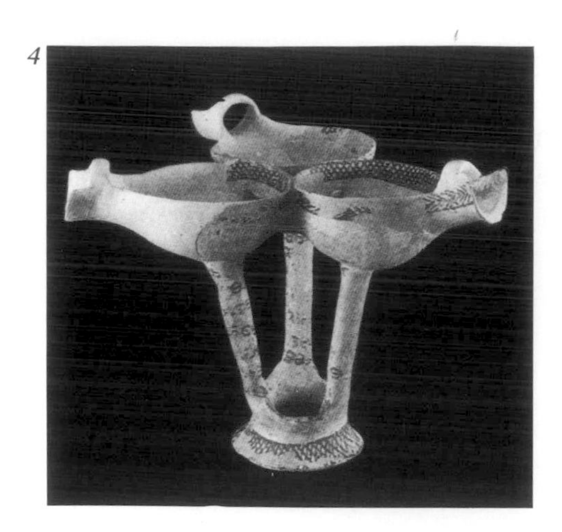

4. *Clay lamp-vessel, 2700-2300 B.C. From the cemetery of Spedos, Naxos. Athens, National Archeological Museum.*

with mainland Greece (the coasts of Attica, Boeotia, Euboea, the Argolid and Corinthia) and Crete, became stronger. The Minoan maritime empire, which from the first half of the second millennium B.C. was established in the Aegean and throughout the eastern Mediterranean (Minoan stations have been detected in Aegina, Thera, Milos and perhaps in Samos) contributed to the coalescence of various elements of these autonomous cultures. Thus, common characteristics came to the fore and evolved, in ways that would produce a degree of cultural unity. It is indeed on the Cyclades that, already by the Middle Bronze Age, Cretan civilization encountered the Cycladic and that of Greece proper; here merged the cultural elements from which the first purely Greek civilization, the Minoan (1600-1100 B.C.), would arise. Furthermore, according to the latest archeological research, many Early Cycladic indigenous elements had developed from the Neolithic period alongside the eastern influences; these elements imparted the particular character that would come to distinguish the Aegean as well as the Minoan civilization.

There is a considerable difference between the eastern figurines and the corresponding Cycladic ones. The superior execution of the latter, their unaffectedness, principally in the clarity of outline imparted by the Aegean light, and their tendency toward abstraction show their masters' intellectual command over natural models and the ideal of measure and style, elements which comprise the main characteristics of subsequent Greek art.

Despite all its eastern influences, one does not encounter in the civilization of Crete, either in its art – which always retained the human form as its basis, just as did the Cycladic – or in its ideology, the inhuman or super-human element. The content and the dimensions of the Cretan civilization remained human. These elements would be developed later by the Greek populations and would constitute the main characteristics of Greek civilization to the point that some researchers would come to speak of the Hellenizing power of the Greek space (J. Caskey).

Mycenaean Civilization and the Role of the Aegean

From around 2.000 B.C. Greek peoples would gradually spread into the area where pre-Greek civilization had already developed – certain of its common features having been outlined above. These peoples would begin to incorporate sections of the pre-Greek populations and gradually assimilate elements from the Cycladic and Cretan civilizations. A sense of Greek nationhood and its first civilization, the Mycenaean, would be created from this ethnological and cultural development.

The proto-Greek population, which had begun to settle sporadically in the Cyclades and along the western coast of the Aegean, was increased, from the 15th century B.C. onwards, by new Greek emigrants. This admixture subsequently established permanent settlements on Crete (from around 1450) and during the 13th and 14th century B.C. on Cyprus, Kos, Rhodes and Miletus. It was these Greek "phyla" (Achaeans) which conquered Crete around 1400 and further developed commercial relations with Egypt, Palestine, the Syrian coast and the coasts of Asia Minor.

It was in these circumstances that the Mycenaean world was formed and spread throughout the Aegean. All the Greek peoples contributed to the creation of Mycenaean civilization, entering its world one after the other.

The Aegean islands played an important role, for yet another time, in this new, original Greek synthesis. The features of Minoan civilization reached the Greek areas via the Aegean islands controlled by the Cretans. What is more, these features, which had merged with elements of Cycladic civilization, lay at the basis of Mycenaean civilization at its outset.

The expansion of Mycenaean civilization was also a result of its domination in the Aegean as the Mycenaeans, already well prepared, became dangerous adversaries of the Cretans during the period 1500-1425; their influence was such that this period, which scholars call the period of the Creto-Mycenaean civilization, a new synthesis of the various tendencies would come about, one to be completed later on with the conquest of Crete and the retreat of Minoan civilization to be eventually replaced by the purely Mycenaean during approximately 1400-1100.

Archeological finds and scientific research have already concluded that, from the very start, Mycenaean civilization imitated Minoan models of art. These models had been transferred to Greece, as has been shown by the finds from the palaces of Tiryns and Mycenae and from the royal tombs of the Mycenaeans and the tholos tomb of Vapheio. The writing on the tablets found at the palaces of Pylos and at Mycenae as well as inscriptions on vases from Tiryns, Thebes, Orchomenos, Mycenae and Eleusis resembling the tablets at Knossos were derived from the syllabic writing of Crete (Linear B).

According to the work of M. Ventris, whose conjectures are thought to be highly probable, this script transcribes the Greek language, having been created for that purpose, after the conquest of Crete by the Mycenaeans (Achaeans). In any case, the Greek script of Cyprus, known from the 7th and 6th century, also appears to have been derived from Minoan Linear B.

Furthermore, there are many features of Mycenaean religion that originated in Minoan Crete. Indeed, the assertion that, without the brilliant Minoan civilization of Crete, Mycenaean civilization would not have been possible appears correct. This does not mean, however, that the Mycenaeans did not develop, alongside the older Minoan features, through their Cycladic and eastern influences, new, original elements which gave Mycenaean civilization its own particular character thus justifying its being dubbed by many scholars, at least for certain of its earlier stages, as the "European version of Eastern civilization in the Mediterranean context".

Subsequent Greek Cultural Development

The new features outlined above would be further developed by the new Greek civilization which would succeed the Mycenaean after its decline. The Aegean islands and the coasts of Asia Minor would again be at the center of this formation and growth.

Establishment of the Greeks in the Aegean. During the period of the great migrations in the 12th and 11th century B.C., new waves of Greek peoples would move further south into Greece and toward the Aegean islands and the East. While the Mycenaean centers were at their most glorious and powerful, the Dorians and other Greeks – Aetolians, Boeotians, Thessalians, Aenianes, Magnetes and others – were confined to the more northerly, mainly mountainous, regions of the Greek mainland. The descent of these peoples, into the realm of Mycenaean civilization, altered the appearance of the Mediterranean area. The first great change was the spread of the Greeks throughout almost the entire region. The so-called Ionian colonization, is considered to be the most important event, after the descent of the Dorians to the south around 1000 or somewhat earlier. In about the same period, or slightly before, the conquest of the Cyclades by the Greeks is thought to have been completed. During the first millennium B.C., the Aegean became a Greek sea, all the Greek peoples taking part in the surge toward the Aegean and the East. The Ionians having set off from Attica dominated Euboea, most of the Cyclades, Samos, Chios and the coast of Asia Minor where they founded important towns such as Chios, Samos, Phocaea, Ephesus, Priene, Miletus and so on.

5. The Trojan Horse. Detail from a relief depiction on the neck of a clay amphora from the beginning of the 7th century B.C. From Mykonos.

6. Painted representation of a scene with Apollo, the Muses and Artemis on an amphora from the 7th century B.C. From Milos. Athens, National Archeological Museum.

7. Painted representation of a scene with Hercules and Deianeira from an amphora of 650-625 B.C. From Milos. Athens, National Archeological Museum.

8. Rhodian oinochoe, 7th century B.C. London, British Museum.

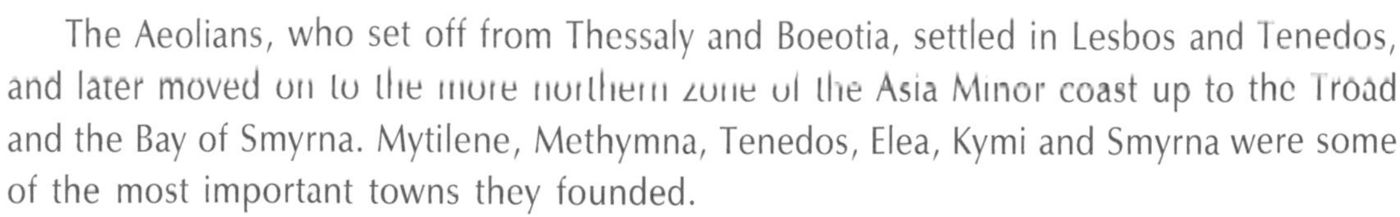

The Aeolians, who set off from Thessaly and Boeotia, settled in Lesbos and Tenedos, and later moved on to the more northern zone of the Asia Minor coast up to the Troad and the Bay of Smyrna. Mytilene, Methymna, Tenedos, Elea, Kymi and Smyrna were some of the most important towns they founded.

The Achaeans, who, from a certain point on, would be considered the fourth subdivision of Greeks, having mixed with them previously, would follow other routes. Those Dorians who had formerly settled in the more southerly continental areas set off from the Peloponnese and settled in the southern Cyclades (Milos, Thera), Crete, Rhodes, Kos and they, too, went across to the Asia Minor coastal strip. Lindos, Ialysus and Camirus on Rhodes and Halicarnassus and Cnidus on the coast of Asia Minor are among the towns founded by the Dorians.

The upheavals provoked by the shifts mentioned above, which were not always peaceful, and the archaic economic, social and political structures of these new forces as well as their archaic and still primitive skills contributed to the unsettling and the further recession of the centers of Mycenaean civilization, themselves already in decline. The initiative in economic life, particularly in trade, passed at an initial stage to the Phoenicians, who became the new ruling force in the eastern Mediterranean, while the economy of the Greek regions remained based almost exclusively on the primary sector (agriculture and stock-raising).

Economic Development of the Settlements and the New Colonization. After the period of upheaval and attendant cultural decline, there appeared the first serious indications of a renaissance with the stabilization, by the 9th century or somewhat earlier, of the new settlements at their new sites in the Aegean, a process that would intensify by the 8th century and usher in a new period.

The new colonists on the islands and the shores of Asia Minor began to familiarize themselves with the sea and to become competitors with their rivals the Phoenicians whom they would soon expel from the Aegean as they took trade into their own hands. Growth and qualitative improvement of the large handicraft industries, whose aim was commercial export-activity, soon followed. Commercial communications with the East, and later the West, spread continually. The older commercial links between Euboea, Corinth, Athens, the Cyclades and the islands of the eastern Aegean on one hand, and Cyprus, Cilicia, Syria, Phoenicia and Palestine on the other, under Phoenician control for a time, passed over to the Greeks in the Aegean from the 8th century B.C. onwards. They began to travel everywhere for the purpose of trade and for the better organization of commercial exchanges. They set up commercial stations to secure direct supplies, without the intervention of a third party, of raw materials, principally metals, which were essential to their now well-developed handicraft industry. Around 800 B.C. Rhodians settled in Tarsus of Cilicia and Euboeans in Al Mina in Syria, to obtain copper. During this same period, Aegean merchants voyaged as far as the Tyrrhenian Sea to secure metals. Around 770 B.C. the Euboeans settled on the island of Pithecussa and in Kymi in the Bay of Naples.

The "great", or second, colonization of the 8th-6th centuries is associated with this economic development and the accompanying population increase with its subsequent demographic problems in the restricted areas of the city-states, which had been created in the meantime. This colonization is also connected with the struggles related to political developments in the city-states (abolition of hereditary royalty and subsequent competition amongst the various factions). These Greek colonies, which started off either as commercial stations or as settlements with an agricultural character founded by the excess population of a town or by the defeated opponents of a social faction that had become dominant, evolved into autonomous towns, in all respects similar to the metropolises, and spread along the coasts of the entire Mediterranean and its extensions, from the north coasts of the Black Sea to the Iberian peninsula. In the eastern sector, Chalkidice, the coast of Thrace, the Hellespont, Propontis, the Bosporus, and the Black Sea were colonized, and in the west, the Illyrian coast, Sicily and southern Italy, the Mediterranean coast of present day France and the coast of the Iberian peninsula. Only the Phoenicians of Carthage on the western Mediterranean coast of Africa and the Assyrians and the Phoenicians on the coasts of Syria and Phoenicia in the East were able to stop the Greek penetration.

The Greek populations of many Greek centers participated in this colonization and the Aegean islands (Andros, Thera, Mytilene, Naxos, Paros, Rhodes, Samos, Tinos) as well as the towns on the coast of Asia Minor (Clazomenae, Cnidus, Miletus, Phocaea) played an important role.

Political and Intellectual Rearrangements. The new social, political and intellectual arrangements and reforms that would lead to the great achievements which came to characterize a common Greek civilization began in the centers of the coasts of Asia Minor and of the islands.

Indeed, a vigorous urban life was developed in these Greek centers; the concept of the city as a state institution, and of civic society was developed here; the local patriotism of the city-state was also born, long before it emerged in mainland Greece. In these centers, which were located between hostile peoples, the prerequisites were established for the cultivation (alongside an awareness of the ethnic and cultural unity of the Greeks) of a tendency toward the political union of all peoples, one that would broaden with the growth of a sense of unity within a larger concept of Greek nationhood. By the 8th century the Ionians had already established the Ionian Amphictyony with a political and religious character, the "Koinon" of Ionians, its center being the sanctuary of the Heliconios Poseidon at Mycale. The Dorian communities had the sanctuary of Triopios Apollo near Cnidus as a common center and the Aeolians most probably the sanctuary of Apollo at Gryneion.

8

In the Aegean also arose the concept of an ethically and culturally more inclusive, panhellenic, community (community and way of life); it was expressed through the tradition of the common origin of the various Greek peoples from a mythological ancestor, Hellen, through his sons Dorus and Aeolus and his grandsons Ion and Achaeus. This tradition is encountered for the first time in a fragment from Hesiod (*The Catalogues*) who, though born in Boeotia, had a father who was an emigrant from Cyme in Aeolis. In Hesiod's *Works and Days* the term "Panhellenes" is also encountered, while the oldest mention of the term "Greeks" ("Hellenes") is found in Archilochus from Paros, who travelled to many countries and took part in the great Greek colonization.

This panhellenic idea found its ultimate expression in the Homeric Epics, also creations of Ionia, the area which set the firm bases of Greek cultural unity, having moulded and consolidated the religious world of the Greeks and perpetuated the renown held in common by the heroes of all the Greek tribes in the Trojan War.

Political fragmentation notwithstanding the consciousness of the unity of one Greek people formed into one single nation spread throughout the Aegean and mainland Greece, as is shown by the unifying tendencies of the Delphic Amphictyony and the

9

9. *Bust of Homer. Roman copy, circa 150 B.C. Boston, Museum of Fine Arts.*

10. *Alcaeus and Sappho. Representation from a red-figured vase by the painter of Vrygos. Munich, Antikensammlung.*

11. *Four drachma piece from Thasos, circa 420 B.C. with a representation of a Satyr and Maened.*

12. *Four drachma piece from Rhodes, circa 375 B.C. with a rose, symbol of the island.*

10

Olympic Games. From the 6th century B.C. onward, there were not only Peloponessian participants but other Greeks as well, even those from the broader Greek world of Ionia and the colonies in southern Italy.

The opposition of the Greek towns in Asia Minor and the Aegean islands to the Lydian state and later the struggles against the Persian Empire reinforced this unifying ideology which peaked during the armed liberation struggle against Persian rule.

Except for the powerful Miletus, the Ionian and Aeolian towns on the coasts of Asia Minor were paying a tribute to the Lydians from 559. From 546 to 525 these towns, Miletus itself, as well as the Dorian towns in Asia Minor and then the eastern Aegean islands, were conquered by the Persians, who extended their rule to the southern coast of Thrace and to the kingdom of Macedonia and attempted, without success, to occupy Naxos (499).

This expansionist Persian policy soon posed a threat to Greek trade, particularly in the Ionian towns, from the moment the Persian Cambyses conquered Egypt (525) and Darius I, after the Scythian campaign (513/512), imposed Persian control on the Dardenelles, hence on Greek commercial activity in the Black Sea. In each conquered Greek city-state the Persian support of the local tyrant or of the governmental agents of the conquerors and the representatives of the local pro-Persian circles was primarily threatening to democratic political institutions and even to the internal autonomy of the towns themselves. Therefore, quite independently of the personal motives of the tyrant of Miletus, Aristagoras, and other Ionian political figures considered to be the apparent cause of the uprising, the decisive factor in the Ionic Revolt starting in 499 and lasting till 494, was (outside the economic one) its political motivation. It was this democratic incentive that gave it its liberating character and caused it to swiftly spread along the entire coast of Asia Minor, to the Greek towns of the Hellespont and on to Thrace and Cyprus. Only the Athenians and the Eretrians, among the Greeks in Greece proper, sent some assistance, if limited, for a time. These struggles of the Greeks in the eastern Aegean, however, bore a direct relationship to the large-scale attacks of the Persians against the Greeks in Greece itself which would follow and culminate in the establishment of a democratic spirit, with the victories at Marathon (490), Salamis (480), Plataea and Mycale (479) and the final repulsion of the Persians. This was the case despite the pro-Persian or neutral stance of some Greek groups and towns; a deepening awareness of the unity of the Greek nation followed the joining together of most Greek towns in the common struggle.

The First Great Cultural Achievements (Shipping–Art–Philosophy). In addition to the original thrust for developing political institutions and the growing awareness of Greek unity, one also finds, in Ionia and on the Aegean islands, the first achievements in literature, art, and more generally in the thought underlying Greek civilization, which would later constitute the basis of European civilization. First, the phonetic Greek alphabet, the first complete phonetic alphabet in the history of mankind, was created in the 10th or 9th century, most probably in Asia Minor, Crete or Rhodes, following the contact of the Aegean civilization with the Phoenicians. This was a development and application of the consonantal alphabet of the Phoenicians to the Greek language, and constituted the basis of the European alphabet. It is certainly not without significance that the form closest to this archetypal alphabet is found in the inscribed monuments of Crete and the Cyclades. The fact that this new simplified alphabet, in contrast to the old eastern writing system limited to a narrow circle of specialists, could become the property of wider sections of

11

12

society, is sufficient to show the importance of such an instrument for the development and promulgation of civilization.

Indeed, the various kinds of Greek literature took their most definitive forms on the Greek coasts of Asia Minor and the Aegean islands. Starting in the 9th century B.C., the heroic epics of Homer were composed in Ionia (Smyrna) or in Chios. The economic and social developments of the 8th-7th centuries in the Aegean also favored the apppearance of more intimate poetic forms, lyric poetry and music, because the individual became relatively independent of social and political groups, or even disagreed or conflicted with them. The oldest known and most important lyric poets, such as Callinicus from Ephesus (7th century), Archilochus from Paros (7th century), Alcaeus, Sappho and Periander from Lesbos (7th-6th century), Anacreon from Teos, Simonidis and Bacchylides from Kea (6th-5th century), came from the Ionian towns, the Cyclades, Samos and Lesbos. They all became well-known and some of them had an influence on the rest of Greece.

Ionia and the Aegean islands also produced the first prose and the first prose writers and geographers, Cadmus and Hecataeus from Miletus. In the 6th century, in this same region, human thought liberated itself from myth for the first time and rational thought had its inception with the commencement of philosophy and science. Thales, Xenophanes, Anaximander and Anaximenes, who laid the foundations for natural science were all born and worked in Miletus. Pythagoras, who was active in Croton in southern Italy, was born in Samos and Heraclitus in Ephesus.

Finally, the re-emergence of art began in Ionia, the Aegean islands and Crete in the 8th-7th century. The first examples of monumental sculpture came from the workshops of Naxos, Paros and Samos, where the technique for making hollow, bronze statues is thought to have been invented. The kouros-type of statue which had been created before the end of the 7th century, was transmitted from the Cyclades to mainland Greece. The first large examples of monumental archtecture, such as the Heraion of Samos, were also created in the same period. The second Heraion (beginning of the 7th century) was the first peripteral temple and the largest religious structure of that time, while the third Heraion (beginning of the 6th century) can be compared in size and grandeur with the temples of Egypt.

The Aegean and Athens in the Greek Civilization of the Classical Period

The Persian wars, and the resistance of the Greek people to Persian attacks, caused the center of gravity for the entire development of classical Greece to shift to Athens the city where all the elements of the Greek spirit were epitomized and which for a period became the coordinator and the regulator of Greek creativity in politics, art, literature and thought.

Even though certain historical circumstances resulted in the transfer of initiative to the Athenian Republic, a large share of the material and intellectual foundations upon which the "Athenian miracle" would be built, were still to be found in the Aegean area of the islands and the cities along the west coast of Asia Minor. Indeed, the founding (in 476) of the Athens-Delos Alliance, which was quickly transformed into an Athens hegemony, was certainly not an insignificant factor in the enormous economic expansion of Athens and its political influence. It should be stressed at this point that this alliance had an Aegean-island character right from the beginning. Most of the Ionian towns in Asia Minor, the Aegean islands and the coastal towns of mainland Greece had joined in. During the period of its peak, it stretched from the shores of Asia Minor to Euboea and from Chalkidice to Rhodes. Around 425 the number of participant states exceeded 400

13. *Bust of Epikouros. Roman copy circa 270 B.C. Rome, Barracco Museum.*

Thus, as the center of a political and economic system – large for that time – Athens had at its disposal abundant economic resources which were drawn from the Aegean for the creation of the masterpieces of the 5th and the 4th century, at the same time it had attracted a large part of the human creative potential of the Aegean (as well as from elsewhere) with its old intellectual and artistic tradition and experience. Furthermore, although the initiative and the pioneering role in cultural expression had shifted to Athens, the Aegean islands and the Asia Minor centers did not cease their remarkable activity in art and science.

There were more then a few artists and others of considerable intellectual calibre who came from the Aegean area and worked either in Athens or the long established Aegean centers. Scopas, one of the greatest and most original craftsmen of the 4th century, came from Paros; the town-planner Hippodamus from Miletus; Herodotus, the founder of History, from Halicarnassus; Anaxagoras, who brought philosophical thought to Athens, from Clazomenae and the sophist Protagoras from Abdera on the coast of Thrace. In mathematics, Chios was represented by Hippocrates (5th century) and by Eudoxus (4th century), while medical science and its ethics, based on the Hippocratic oath, was founded on Kos (Hippocrates) and Cnidus.

The movement toward the political unification of the Hellenic people, which had begun in the Aegean area, took a decisive step forward with the establishment of the Athenian alliance-hegemory. The promotion of the ideology concerning the struggle of all Greeks to repel the Persian threat was justified by the victory of Kimon at the Eurymedon, which once more transformed the Aegean into a closed Greek sea, gave Athens panhellenic authority and paved the way for the panhellenic policy of Pericles.

The unifying tendency of Hellenism that drew its resources from the Aegean was now deeper, and more firmly grounded and with a long-term perspective it found its fulfilment through the Hellenic world.

This cultural radiance would continue to act as the primary unifying factor even after the Peloponnesian War and the diminishing political influence of Athens during a period of general crisis and political discord in the Greek world. It evolved into a new ideal which, under Isocrates, promoted Greek civilization as the main component of a broader concept of Greek nationality.

THE AEGEAN DURING THE HELLENISTIC AND ROMAN PERIOD

General Observations

The new historical framework which began to be formed by the ever increasing intervention of the Kingdom of Macedonia in the Greek world was established by the ecumenical policy of Alexander the Great and was finally consolidated with the creation of the large Hellenistic kingdoms of his Successors. This meant that the Aegean, just as any other localized and limited, political formation, could no longer have any particular significance for the course of Hellenism in the general re-alignment of the economic, social and cultural physiognomy of either the countries of the eastern Mediterranean or the entire East.

Within the general structure of the Roman Empire, it is difficult to detect any pioneering initiatives carried out by limited political formations or any developments in specific cultural circles, whose function could be compared with that of the Aegean area during the Archaic and Classical periods.

By the Hellenistic period the institution of city-states, on which Greek political and cultural life had been founded during the Archaic and Classical periods, had already begun to lose its significance. The Republics and Confederations, although theoretically retained for a time, were transformed, in practice, into simple, self-governing communities, which were incorporated into the broader administrative framework of the Hellenistic kingdoms and later, the Roman Empire. Needless to say, Greek civilization continued to play a leading role in the development of the civilized world, this time enhanced and rejuvenated by the new elements it absorbed through contact with other peoples during its unprecedented expansion deep into the East. However, during the formation of the ecumenical civilization of Hellenistic and Roman times, no particular Greek area nor any specific cultural circle with distinct characteristics appears to have played a leading or coordinating role.

The large intellectual centers multiplied and they were transferred from Greece itself to the periphery, to the new centers of the East and Egypt. In addition to the Alexandria Museum, intellectual institutions of similar character were founded in other Aegean regions. The material and intellectual activities which lay at the core of Hellenism were distributed among the new important centers. They, now as capitals of large or small Hellenistic kingdoms, would become poles of attraction for intellectual figures coming from all points of both the Greek and the hellenized world. During the Hellenistic and, especially, the Roman period, the Aegean islands and its centers in Asia Minor, with their long-standing traditions, would continue to play a not insignificant role in these new developments.

The Hellenistic Period

In our summary of the role of the Aegean area in the formation of the new image presented by the world of the eastern Mediterranean and the East during the Hellenistic and Roman periods, we would note the following points.

First of all, it has been observed that the Aegean islands continued to play a unifying and stabilizing role amongst the large Hellenistic Kingdoms (Macedonia–Syria–Egypt) and thus retained their importance, both political and cultural, in the eastern Mediterranean. This was the function of the "Koinon of the Nesiotes" (Confederation of the Islanders), which was founded by one of Alexander the Great's generals, Antigonus (365 B.C.). It grew, at times under the protection of the Macedonian kingdom, at other times under the protection of the Ptolemies in Egypt. A similar role was played by the maritime empire of Rhodes through its resistance to Demetrius I Poliorcetes (the "Besieger"). Rhodes retained its independence with the peace accord of 304 and developed, alongside Alexandria, the largest center of the period, into a great naval power and the regulator of trade in the eastern Mediterranean. Some historians have characterized Rhodes as the "Clearing House" of the area. One of the oldest codifications of Naval Law, which, with variations and additions, was retained up to the Middle Ages, was called the "Rhodian Sea Law". The influence of the kingdom of Pergamum on the Hellenistic world was also important and it continued during the Roman period. It has been accurately observed that the civilization of Alexandria, after the persecution of intellectuals and artists by Ptolemy VIII (145/144 B.C.), was transplanted to Pergamum and Rhodes, from where it was transmitted to the western world.

The Roman Period

The re-alignments that took place during the Roman occupation allowed the Aegean area, particularly the Greek towns on the western shores of Asia Minor, to regain a part of their old material and intellectual vigor (with the support of the Romans, whose influence in the East was dependent on the Greek presence). Mainland Greece (with a few exceptions) became ever more marginal. Ephesus, and Pergamum and Smyrna began to flourish, the latter becoming the intellectual metropolis of Hellenism. In Ephesus and Smyrna museums were founded comparable to the Museum of Alexandria, and they, too, attracted eminent intellectual figures from everywhere. After the conquest of Macedonia by the Romans, Delos, in the center of the Aegean, replaced Rhodes as the economic coordinator in the eastern Mediterranean. Delos was declared, after the battle of Pydna (168 B.C.), a free port, where Italian merchants and bankers as well as Syrian colonists settled and competed seriously with Rhodes. The latter declined economically and politically, having lost its land holdings and its role in the protection of the Confederation of the Islanders.

Nevertheless, many of the old cultural centers of the Aegean continued to flourish and be nurseries of scientists and artists who would act as leading figures in the political and intellectual centers of the time. The Medical School on Kos still retained its old glory. The sculptural and architectural workshops in Pergamum, Miletus and Rhodes produced high quality works. Many of the great names of science, literature and art who worked in Alexandria or Athens (which continued to be the center of philosophy) came from the islands and the centers in Asia. Many of the scholar-librarians at the Museum of Alexandria also came from there. Zenodotus (285 B.C.) from Ephesus, Aristophanes from Byzantium, Aristarchus (217-145 B.C.) from Samothrace, Dionysius from Thrace; the doctor Erasistratus, director of the school of Alexandria, came from Ceos, the great astronomer Aristarchus, the founder of the heliocentric system, came from Samos and the architect and town-planner of Alexandria, Deinocrates, from Rhodes. The same is true of the most important representatives of literature of the period: the elegiac poet Psiletas (348-270 B.C.) came from Kos, Apollonius (265-215 B.C.) from Rhodes, Aratus (310-245 B.C.) from Soli in Cilicia, Nicandrus (150 B.C.) from Colophon and Asclepiades (290 B.C.) from Samos. Theocritus (305-245 B.C.) came from Syracuse and lived in Kos before he settled in Alexandia. The leaders of the philosophical schools of Athens came from the islands, Epicurus (342-271 B.C.) from Samos and Zeno (336-264 B.C.) from Citium in Cyprus.

This intellectual activity in the Aegean would continue during the succeeding centuries. Smyrna for example, would remain an important center: this is where Coindus the Smyrnian and Theon (4th century B.C.) came from; it was also the place where Antonios Polemon (2nd century A.D.) and Ailius Aristeides (129-189) worked. At the same time, several other intellectual figures came from other Aegean centers; Dionysius of Halicarnassus (1st century B.C.) and Pausanias (2nd century A.D.) from Sipylus in Magnesia and Galen (129-201) from Pergamum.

14

14. Aphrodite. Marble statuette. Hellenistic period. From Rhodes. Rhodes, Archeological Collection.

THE AEGEAN DURING THE BYZANTINE EMPIRE

The shift of the center of the Roman Empire to the East also determined a new function for the Aegean area. This shift was completed with the establishment of Constantinople as the "New Rome" and its designation as the capital of the eastern part of the Empire. In effect, it was the economic, administrative and cultural capital of the entire Empire.

The role of the Aegean islands and the Aegean in general, with its extensions into the eastern Mediterranean, would be manifold and, at least during certain periods, of some importance in this new configuration which entailed the gradual transformation of the Roman Empire into a new entity, the Byzantine Empire.

The Aegean, 4th-7th century

There was an initial transitional period, extending from the 4th to the 7th century, when the old economic, social and cultural structures were, for the most part, retained. During this period, it was the economic activity of the large urban centers on the western coast of Asia Minor and the Aegean islands that insured the relative economic vigor of the Empire. The Aegean islands, in particular, remained the vital transit centers for sea trade in the Mediterranean. Thus, they insured not only cohesion between the eastern regions of Asia Minor and its western possessions, but also economic dominance throughout the Mediterranean world. From the Hellenistic and Roman periods, Asia Minor had served as the economic foundation of the area in which the new state was to be established.

The large number of religious monuments (basilicas) continually being discovered on all the islands as well as in Greece proper, pertain to this period. These finds together with the host of seals of fiscal officials ("kommerkiarioi") or financial services bear witness to the continuous economic activity in the Aegean up to the 7th century. These seals refer not only to Constantinople and the western coast of Asia Minor (Hellespont, Lydia, Cilicia, Caria, Lycia) but also to mainland Greece (Thessaloniki, Corinth, Greece in general) and the islands (Rhodes, "Bureau of the Aegean Islands").

Furthermore, the west and southwest coast of Asia Minor, the Aegean islands and the Greek coasts supplied the Empire with naval forces, which, during certain periods, made it quite powerful. These areas constituted separate administrative entities of various sizes, whose principal aim was the expansion of the military navy on this sea which almost throughout the entire history of the Empire, had the character of a frontier region threatened by external enemies. The periods when the Empire was truly flourishing are those in which it had secured dominion over the Aegean and the Mediterranean, continually striving to enhance its naval forces within the appropriate administrative framework of the day. Such, for example, was the purpose that led Justinian to found the Questura Exercitus with Mysia, Scythia Minor, the islands and Cyprus constituting it. Indeed, particularly after the abolition of the Vandals naval state by Justinian, the maritime supremacy of Byzantium in the Aegean and the Mediterranean was firmly established and lasted until around the middle of the 7th Century. The bases of the Byzantine fleet, the Balearic islands, Septum, Sardinia, Sicily, in the western Mediterranean and in the eastern Mediterranean, Alexandria, the coasts of Asia Minor, and Crete, Rhodes and Cyprus, secured sea transport. Significant centers with substantial urban activities (commercial and light industrial) persisted in the southern Balkans and on the Aegean coasts: Heraclea, Rhaedestus, Thessaloniki and Corinth. The coastal towns of the Aegean were also included among Justianian's fortifications: Aenus, Vellaros, Trajanoupolis, Maximianoupolis, Anastasioupolis, Rhaedestus, etc.

The Arab Conquests. The Aegean as part of the Defensive System of the Byzantine Empire, 7th–11th century

By the 8th-9th century, after the formation of a powerful fleet by Muʿāwiya, the Arabs secured their supremacy in the Mediterranean. From the mid 7th century, their conquests, and especially their naval successes, greatly hindered economic activity in the Aegean, particularly on the islands – although they never interrupted it completely.

By the mid 7th century, the coasts of Africa all the way to the Atlantic Ocean were under Arab occupation, and important naval centers were falling into their hands in the eastern and western Mediterranean: in 645 they began their assault on Cyprus, which from the last quarter of the 7th century to its re-occupation by the Byzantines (965) was under a kind of "Arab-Byzantine" joint rule; they took Rhodes in 654 and from 670 to 678 and from 715 to 717, the Arab fleet was able to threaten Constantinople itself from bases at Cyzicus, Smyrna and on the SW coast of Asia Minor. At the beginning of the century they seized Crete and, in 827, Arabs would begin landing on Sicily, which became Arab in 902. At the same time, the Aegean islands suffered constant attacks and pillaging.

Despite all the Arab successes, the Byzantine presence in the eastern Mediterranean and the economic activity of the centers in the Aegean area continued, albeit reduced. The impression of exclusive Arab maritime supremacy in the Mediterranean is not supported by the sources: the seals of the "kommerkiaria" on the islands and the Aegean coast show that commercial activity continued during the 8th and 9th century. In fact, these stamps refer not only to the coastal towns of Asia Minor (Pergamum, Nicomedia, etc.) and mainland Greece (Thessaloniki, Hellas, Dysi ("West"), Corinth, Christoupolis, the Peloponnese) but also to the Aegean islands (Milos, Thera, Anafi, Amorgos, Andros and the "Aegean Sea and Islands"). Furthermore, from the 7th century, the Aegean would come to play an important role in the defensive system which the Byzantine Empire, free from other distractions, raised against its attackers. The Aegean coasts and the islands were to be covered, from the 7th century onward, by a new administrative system which the Empire set up for the defense of its sea borders. They were also to support the Empire in the counterattack that started in the 10th century. The unified command of the naval forces, the "carabisiani", was established in the 7th century. The "archons" of several islands (Cyprus, Crete, Chios) and the "droungarioi" (the droungarios of the Gulf of the Dodecanese, i.e. Cyclades and the Aegean) represented the first transitional phases in the organization of this defensive system which would be gradually consolidated from the 7th to the 9th and 10th century into the system of "themes", which eventually covered the entire Aegean. The "theme" of the Cibyrraeots (first mention in 732) centered on the SW coast of Asia Minor (with Attalia as its capital) covered the area from Seleucia to Miletus as well as the neighboring islands, among which was Rhodes. During the 9th century the following "themes" would be founded: the "theme" of the Aegean (842/843) which included a large part of the islands (Limnos, Skyros, Milos, Amorgos, Thera, Therasia, Lesbos, Chios), the "theme" of Samos (first mention in 893) which, besides Samos, contained a section of the coastal zone of Asia Minor, with its capital at Smyrna, and the islands lying along the Asia Minor coast, south of Samos. During the 10th century the "theme" of the Cyclades would also be set up.

Outside these primary naval "themes" and in line with the administrative arrangements of each period, certain coasts and islands from which forces were recruited were incorporated, into the terrestrial "themes" which surrounded the Aegean. Euboea and other islands such as Kea, Cythnos, Delos and Andros were incorporated into the "theme" of Hellas. Ephesus, Smyrna, Pergamum, Priene, Teos and Levidos were under the "theme" of Thracesion (first mentioned in 742/743), while the islands of Thasos, Samothrace, Skiathos, Skopelos were, in all likelihood, under the "theme" of the Aegean or the "theme" of Macedonia and Thrace. As for the large islands of Cyprus and Crete, which were on the front line of the Byzantine-Arab naval struggles, they were at times subject to the Arabs and at other times to the Byzantines under various forms of rule. This was the case till the 10th century when, having been definitively regained by the Empire (Crete in 961 and Cyprus in 965), they became separate "themes".

Thus, except for Cyprus and Crete, which for quite long periods were outside the imperial domain, the whole of the rest of the Aegean area, despite attacks and pillage, was always firmly incorporated into its administrative mechanism. Indeed, it played an important role in the Empire's defence: some of the crucial battles between Byzantium and the Arabs during the 7th and 8th century (674-678) were decided at sea.

15. Christ crowing the emperor Constantine VII, Porphyrogenetes. Ivory plaque, mid-10th century. Moscow, Pushkin Museum of Fine Arts.

16. Christ crowning the emperor Romanus II and his wife Evdokia. Ivory plaque, mid-10th century. Paris, National Library, Cabinet des Médailles.

15

The Cohesion of the Aegean, 11th-13th century

Such an administrative cohesion, with its various modifications, the most important of which was the continual division of administrative units by carving the larger ones into parts was to last until the end of the 12th century. During the 11th century the Aegean islands were divided up administratively: some into the maritime "themes" of the Cyclades, the Aegean, Samos, Crete and the newly founded "theme" of Chios (end of the 10th beginning of the 11th century; first mention in 1025-1028) and others into the mainland naval "themes" of the Cibyrraeots and Hellas. At the same time, the larger islands, Euboea, Cyprus and Lesbos, became autonomous governments. The large "themes" were divided into smaller ones, some including a few islands and others only one island with the "Catepano" or "Dukes" as leaders. This multiplication can be considered, from the viewpoint of administrative organization, as the main characteristic of the 12th century, during which the Dukes of Rhodes, Kos, Chios, Samos, Crete and Cyprus are mentioned.

Although somewhat looser than before, the cohesion of the Aegean area, and its incorporation into the administrative mechanism of the Empire, would last until the occupation of the islands by the Franks. This would permit the central authority to withstand two threats: the separatist insurrections which arose from the 11th century on certain islands such as Crete (11th century), Cyprus (12th century) and Rhodes (beginning of the 13th century) and repeated attacks by the Turks at sea. These attacks, from around 1050, led to the devastation of several small islands and the creation of a temporary island state by the Turkish Emir Jaha (second half of the 11th century). Smyrna was the center of this state, which also included Phocaea, Clazomenae, Chios, Samos and Lesbos.

The Ecclesiastical Administration of the Aegean, 7th-13th century

A similar picture is created from the study of ecclesiastical administration, and this is independent of the changes in the distribution of various bishoprics to the Metropolitans on the islands, mainland Greece or Asia Minor.

The continued flourishing of the Aegean world up to the end of the 7th century can be seen in the host of bishoprics founded, even on the smaller islands. Mention is made of around 11 bishoprics among the Aegean islands (Samos, Chios, Kos, Thera, Paros, Leros, Andros, Tinos, Milos, Amorgos), all subject to the Metropolitan of Rhodes. Kea and Skyros were subject to other Metropolitans and Karpathos was an archdiocese.

16

Yet, as early as the 8th century, there are indications, confirmed by other evidence, of a decline in population, the capture of towns and economic contraction. Up to the end of the 9th century, there were about the same number of bishoprics on the Aegean islands as in the catalogue of Hierocles (approximately 11 under the metropolitan of Rhodes) and several others were subject to other metropolitans. Yet, only six bishops from these communites were present at the Council of Nicaea (787). There were about 21 bishoprics in Crete before 787, but only 11 in the catalogue from the time of the Iconoclasts. The example of the autonomous Church of Cyprus is also typical. The number of its bishoprics stayed the same till the 8th century. During the Council of Nicaea (787), though, only the bishops from the eastern sector were present and none from the western, which was in the hands of the Arabs. The absence of bishops from several other islands, especially the northern Sporades, shows that at least some of the smaller ones had been laid waste.

Recovery began gradually on the islands, as well as in mainland Greece, particularly from the end of the 8th century; there are even signs from the 7th century (Methymna became an archdiocese during the middle of the 7th century). This process gained pace during the 9th and 10th centuries and, after the re-capture of Crete, in the 11th and 12th centuries as well. Aegina, for example, was promoted to an archdiocese by the end of the 8th century, Limnos probably by the 9th-10th century. The 11th and 12th centuries are considered to be the period when the Aegean islands flourished anew. During this period, many bishoprics were created, even on the small islands. The islands of the northern Sporades acquired bishoprics, the Metropolitan of Rhodes expanded to include four new bishoprics (Icaria, Astypalaia, Nisyros and Kalymnos) the ten bishoprics of Crete were re-organized and made subject to the metropolitan of Gortys. Some of them appear to have been newly established. In the 12th century some old bishoprics were promoted to Metropolitans. Methymna became a Metropolitan as did Paronaxia, when the bishoprics of Paros and Naxos were made independent of the Metropolitan of Rhodes.

Economic Inroads of the Italian Republics into the Aegean

The administrative, political and ecclesiastical re-organization of the Aegean is linked, as both cause and effect, to the economic development of the islands during the 11th and 12th century. This period is characterized by the inroads made into the economic life of the Empire (large-scale foreign trade, in particular) by the Italian Republics of Amalfi, Pisa, Genoa and, above all, Venice, which during the 12th century would take the economic initiative. At the same time, though, at least during an initial stage when imperial policy was still able to guarantee some effective control, this Italian economic activity contributed to the revival of local economy. During this period there was a certain amount of balance, economic as well as political and cultural, between the eastern and western mainland and the island regions of the empire, a balance to which the contribution of the Aegean and its islands was considerable. In fact, though the domination of the Italian cities, primarily Genoa and Venice, contributed to the decline of Byzantine commercial activity, particularly of long-distance trade, from the 12th century onward, internal short-distance trade continued during both the 11th and the 12th century. Some large monasteries organized important enterprises: the commercial fleets of Lavra and other monasteries on Mount Athos and Patmos continued to ply the Aegean and to deal with Constantinople, Crete and the other islands. The Nea Moni on Chios had economic relations with Crete. Moreover, the larger islands were not only commercial or naval stations on the trade routes of the Byzantines (for internal trade) or of the Westerners – Venice in particular, for large-scale trade, connecting Venice with Constantinople, Alexandria and later on with Syria and Palestine – but they were also important centers for import and export trade conducted by both Byzantines and Westerners. During the 11th century, Cyprus supplied the Crusaders in Syria and Palestine with food and money and had mints in Nicosia, Ammochostos and Limassol. It was also connected to Pamphylia, as can be seen from the existence of a "kommerkiarios" for Cyprus and Attalia (11th-12th century). In the 12th century the traveller Edressi characterized Limassol, Nicosia and Cyrenia as important commercial centers. In Venetian documents from the 12th century there are clear indications of economic activity in Paphos, which had connections with Syria.

17

Crete also had commercial centers till the end of the 12th century as witnessed by the seals of the "kommerkiarioi". The installation of western merchants in Cyprus, Crete and Chios, and somewhat later in Andros, is confirmed by documents from the beginning of the 12th century.

The economic development of the islands in general during these centuries is additionally witnessed by many finds of coins and the large number of ecclesiastical monuments to be found on them.

Cultural Problems in the Aegean

Of course, in a state as highly centralized as the Byzantine Empire, no one would expect to find autonomous, local cultural circles playing a leading or even modifying role in the common culture imposed to a great degree by the Empire. Art and intellectual life in general on the Aegean islands was incorporated in this common culture which was regulated by the large cultural centers, Constantinople in particular. However, the cultural contacts of the Aegean area, and even the islands, with the centers of the empire, never ceased. Important figures in political and intellectual life were to be found either as high-ranking administrative officials or political exiles on the Aegean islands or in Greece proper. Monks from the large eastern and western monastic centers, of Galicion or Athos, often visited the islands. Moreover, the monastic movement and the founding of monasteries was never interrupted. Several of these such as Nea Moni on Chios, the Monastery of Saint John the Theologian on Patmos, the monasteries of Cyprus, Egleistra, Kykkos and Machaira evolved into notable intellectual establishments. It should also be noted that, by the end of the 11th century, with the advance of the Turks, the islands had become refuges for the Christian populations of Asia Minor.

This cultural communication, alongside the economic activity, shows the participation of the islands in the common cultural movements of the Empire, a conclusion confirmed by other, albeit scant, information. It would perhaps be of interest to note, for example, that one of the most eminent figures of the first Byzantine renaissance of the 9th century, Leo the Mathematician, went from Constantinople to Andros to complete his education in Rhetoric, Philosophy and Arithmetic. There is also mention of a school of Rhetoric and Philosophy in 11th century Rhodes. The large monasteries had rich libraries (Patmos, Monastery of Leimonos in Lesbos), while on several islands, such as Cyprus and most probably Crete, there were teams trained in the copying of manuscripts.

The incorporation of the islands, into the common Byzantine civilization, and their active participation in it, is further demonstrated by the islanders' resistance to Arab influences, even in cases such as those of Crete and Cyprus which were under Arab occupation for several centuries. In Cyprus, there are minimal traces of the Arab conquest, while the continuity of the Byzantine tradition is clearly manifest: the erection of churches went on uninterrupted, even during the 9th and 10th centuries and the circulation of Greek books was free, even in the Arab-occupied areas. There are also very few traces of the Arab occupation in Crete; one can only wonder whether the degree of Arab influence on the customs and religious beliefs of the Cretans as it appears in the life of Nicon Metanoite, was any more than hagiographic exaggeration, since such a likely influence seems to have been quite ephemeral. There is the same sparsity of Arab traces on the other islands and the Aegean area in general. The architectural types which prevailed here were the typical Byzantine ones. The "common" Byzantine style was also used by painters and other artists – many of whom came from Constantinople – in painting and the other arts, discounting the range of conventional, provincial tones and variations. The traces of Arab influences in art are limited to some decorative, sculptural features in the churches of Euboea or in poetry and manuscripts. Such features also appeared outside the strictly Aegean area, as in Corfu, Corinth or Athens, and were, moreover, mixed with the Byzantine.

The incorporation of the Aegean islands into the administrative system of the Empire and the common Byzantine civilization does not, however, imply the absence of an island-specific political and cultural climate, quite strong in many cases. In addition to the decentralizing tendencies of the 11th century or the resistance of the island people to the central government, phenomena which were incorporated in the general tendencies

17. Byzantine soldiers. Drawing by Sp. Vasileiou.

18. Constantine Palaeologus. Woodcut by A. Tassos.

18

of the period or in the general opposition between provinces and capital, there were also some instances pointing to a somewhat different position on basic ideological problems. One could mention the hostile stance of the Aegean islands towards the Iconoclasts. The Cyclades as well as the "theme" of Hellas and the rest of the European areas of the empire supported the revolt (728) of Kosmas against the Iconoclast emperor Leo III. Later, around 821, the "theme" of Cibyrraeots and the European areas of the Empire supported the revolt of Thomas the Slavonian (or Slav) who is shown not only as the representative of the lower and economically weaker social classes, but as a supporter of iconolatry ("icon worship"). Moreover, Cyprus was a refuge of iconolatry. This attitude is characteristic of the islands, particularly of the more westerly ones that were closer to Greece proper and their populations are considered to have closer affinities with it. This shared resistance to the Iconoclasts who exhibited eastern influences, shows greater adherence to the spirit of Graeco-Roman civilization than one finds in the other, more easterly regions of the Byzantine Empire.

THE AEGEAN UNDER FRANKISH RULE AND DURING THE FINAL CENTURIES OF THE BYZANTINE EMPIRE (1204-1453)

Political Fragmentation

After the fall of Constantinople to the Crusaders (1204) the Aegean region experienced the same general fragmentation as the Empire. The western coast of Asia Minor from Adramyttium to Halicarnassus, from the Ionian islands (Chios – Lesbos – Samos) to the Dodecanese, the southern Aegean coast of Thrace and Macedonia, as well as the eastern coast of Greece would be found, variably, depending on political circumstances, under the rule of a Greek political formation (Nicaea, Epirus, the Byzantine Empire as reconstituted by the Palaeologus family) or, from the 14th century onward, under the Turkish emirs of Asia Minor until these, too, became subject to the Ottoman Empire. There were times when some places were under various independent or semi-independent Frankish rulers, while the Cyclades and a part of the Sporades and Crete were under direct or indirect Venetian domination, incorporated into Venice's colonial state in the East. From the 12th century Cyprus would be an independent kingdom under the Lusignan and would also come under Venetian suzerainty in the 15th century. This political fragmentation and foreign occupation did not essentially alter the ethnological composition of the population, which remained in its vast majority Greek and was able, in time, to absorb a large part of the foreign population of colonists-conquerors.

The Position of the Greeks

Thus the traditional function of the Aegean as the connecting link of Hellenism and, at the same time, a point of contact between Greek and foreign cultural elements and traditions, and a center for the fusing of these elements into new combinations, not only continued but was considerably enhanced.

In fact the harsh conditions of foreign occupation on the Greek population contributed to a bolstering of the spirit of resistance against it and to an increasingly intense development of a national consiousness, which became the main connecting element in the Greek community.

The long duration of the Frankish occupation in the Aegean widened the religious opposition between the Greek Orthodox population and the Catholics, which was no longer confined to theoretical, dogmatic disputes but took on the character of an everyday issue concerning the ecclesiastical administration and the economic foundations of the Orthodox Church. The Catholic Church made it clear right from the beginning, more so in some places than in others, that it intended to subjugate the Orthodox Church. This was the case with nearly all the occupied areas, with a few incidental exceptions which were not always applied in practice (for example, Chios under the Genoese, the duchy of the Aegean). First it organized its hierarchy (Catholic archbishops, bishops and Catholic officials); either the higher Orthodox clergy (archbishops – metropolitans – bishops) were persecuted (for example, in Rhodes, the Dodecanese and Crete), or the number of bishoprics and the jurisdiction of their bishops were reduced (in Crete from a certain period on, Cyprus). The Orthodox Church was administered by inferiors in the ecclesiastical hierarchy ("protopapades", "sakelarioi" and "megaloi oikonomoi"), who were obliged to recognize the higher Catholic ecclesiastical authorities. A large part of the Church's property was removed from the Orthodox Church and transferred to the Catholic.

19

20

The religious and ecclesiastical opposition and the resistance of the Orthodox population to the oppressive measures of the Catholic Church shaped the ideology of Hellenism and contributed to the development of a national consciousness that linked Greek identity to Orthodoxy.

Economic, social and political factors contributed to this ideological process. At least at the beginning of the occupation, the representatives of the Byzantine ruling class, all those that remained in the occupied areas, were excluded from administrative positions and were socially demoted. Even when, by the conquerors adopting a somewhat more flexible policy in the hope of securing local support, or after actual armed struggle, the ruling classes were indeed incorporated into the feudal hierarchy, they were placed (as in Crete, in the duchy of the Aegean and elsewhere) on a separate, inferior level.

The Greek middle class, too, found itself in a disadvantaged position, despite its relative development through participation in the economic activities of the rulers, particularly in the Venetian possessions where all economic activity had to pass through Venice, the supreme regulator of economic life.

19. Coat-of-arms of Sommaripa family from Naxos.

20. Coat-of-arms of Sorantsi family from Siphnos.

21. Seal of the Knights of Saint John, Rhodes.

21

As for the peasantry, to which most of the population belonged, the foreign conquest did not in essence change its legal status and social position. The large majority of farmers remained in a state of serfdom. However, there are some indications that the number of tenant farmers, in comparison to free farmers, increased and that the economic burdens of the peasantry became heavier.

Thus, all the social classes participated in the struggle of the Greek population against the forces of occupation. This struggle often took the form of rebellions, as in Cyprus and, above all, Crete where several of these rebel movements had a national as well as a social and religious character. Such was the case of the Cypriote revolt against the Templars in the 12th century and the resistance of the Orthodox clergy to the subjugating demands of the Catholic Church, which peaked with the martydom of the monks at Kandara (1231). The repeated rebellions in Crete (six in the 13th century and three in the 14th) enabled the Cretan nobility, who continually gained Venetian privileges, to improve their economic and social position in the feudal hierarchy, strengthen the status of the Orthodox Church and even secure certain protective measures for the peasantry. The economic penetration of the Italian cities into the Byzantine Empire, which began in the 11th and 12th century, grew, after the Frankish conquest in the 13th century, into a complete not only political but also economic domination of the entire eastern Mediterranean and the Near East. The whole Aegean area became the epicenter of this economic domination, with Venice and Genoa as the main competitors.

Of course, the state of Nicaea, as well as the Byzantine Empire, reconstituted after 1261, would undertake to contest the complete control of the eastern Mediterranean by these two powers through successful diplomatic manoeuvres or through military transfers, of which the Aegean would become the epicenter. They would succeed in maintaining, for a certain period, important economic centers in Thrace and Macedonia, the western coast of Asia Minor (Phocaea, Smyrna) and on the closest islands in the eastern Mediterranean (Chios, Lesbos, Rhodes and the Dodecanese); they even re-occupied certain islands (Limnos, the Sporades). These centers, however, would fall, the one after the other, into the hands of the Catholics: Rhodes and the nearby islands to the Knights of Saint John (1306); Phocaea (1275), Chios (1394) and later Lesbos (1331) and Aenus (1354) would pass into the hands of the Genoese. For a brief period Thessaloniki itself was run by the Venetians.

Economic activities

Despite the frequent destructive consequences of the military operations of hostile forces (Venetians – Genoese – Turks – Byzantines) and the continual pirate raids on towns, the economic activities in the Aegean went on. Even after the re-constitution of the Byzantine Empire in regions further than those conquered by Westerners, such activities intensified, throughout this period, with the installation of western merchants and the great expansion of western colonies (Venetian and Genoese) into the leading economic centers of the Empire: Constantinople, Galata, Smyrna, Thessaloniki and other centers surrounding the Aegean became transit stations for the large flow of trade between West and East.

Thus, in the Genoese holdings (Phocaea, Chios, Lesbos) important commercial houses were established; shipping and commercial enterprises developed under the Mahone of Chios. Rhodes, under the Knights of Saint John, became an important center for channeling trade from the West to Syria, Egypt and Asia Minor while large commercial houses from Italy, France (Montpellier, Narbonne) and from Aragon were established there. There was, moreover, substantial growth of sugar and soap industries on Rhodes. Crete, too, had a very active economic life and developed into a major station for Venetian trade in the East, a producer of raw materials for the large light-industrial plants in the West and a supplier of agricultural products. In Cyprus the development of commercial relations with the Mediterranean countries and the establishment of important urban centers had an influence even on political structures. Alongside the feudal high Court, occupied by the nobles, the Court of the Bourgesia was established, with members of the bourgeoisie participating. Of course, the most important part of all this commercial activity was in the hands of the Westerners, but the share of the local Greek population was not negligible. Evidence on this is clear and relatively abundant; Greek shipowners and merchants are mentioned in documents dealing with the economic activities of western merchants either in Crete or Constantinople or elsewhere. In some areas, such as Rhodes, large Greek enterprises are noted playing a significant role in the economic, social and cultural life of the region.

Thus, the greater Aegean area became a point of contact between the antiquated Byzantine economy and the western economy and participated in the cycle of international trade becoming familiar with the qualitatively superior economic systems of the West (more rapid monetarization of the economy, bank and credit procedures, naval insurance, etc.). This contributed to the further evolution of the structures of Greek society, at least in certain large urban centers.

Intellectual Development

The first significant consequence of the fragmentation of the Byzantine Empire was a degree of cultural de-centralization, with the establishment of intellectual centers in the districts now more or less independent from the centuries-long undisputed authority of Constantinople (Nicaea, Trebizond, Thessaloniki and Mistra). This de-centralizing movement contributed to the revival of Byzantine thought, art and literature through a continually deepening and organic encounter of the official culture with more popular elements but, primarily, by the coming into contact of traditional elements of Byzantine civilization with corresponding intellectual movements in the West. The Aegean played a leading role in this fertile contact between the two civilizations. In Chios, Rhodes, Cyprus and Crete, the urban centers which were created as a consequence of the economic growth of the Greek element, became prominent intellectual centers as well. In Rhodes, the Court of the Great Magister gathered together a host of western humanist scholars with a classical Greek education who brought along the Renaissance spirit. Greek intellectuals also took part in this atmosphere; they either continued the Byzantine tradition, such as the scholar-Metropolitan of Rhodes Neilos Diasoreinos (1357-1362), Georgios Kalivas and Emmanouil Georgilas, or drew inspiration from the new literature of the western Renaissance. The noteable collection of poems "Annals - Verses on Eros and Agape", dated to the 15th century, is set within this Rhodian climate. The new attitude created by contact between Byzantine tradition and new elements of popular and western culture can be seen even more clearly in the intellectual products of Cyprus. The chronicles of Leontius Machairas (1360-1450) and Georgios Voustronios (second half of the 15th century) or the Greek translation of "Assises", based on the local idiom of the island, can be considered as the earliest examples of a developing modern-Greek prose based on the spoken vernacular idiom; on the other hand, learned Cypriote poetry could boast of important literary achievements, influenced by the Renaissance not only indirectly but directly by the great poets such as Petrarch; at the same time, the old tradition of the Akritas cycle and the new themes inspired by Greek-Frankish society were combined in the popular works of poetasters and demotic songs. But the first outstanding literary creations, appearing originally in the 14th century and, by the 16th and 17th centuries forming the basis of modern Greek literature, were also products of a mixture of Greek tradition and the western civilization of the Renaissance. These works came from Crete and, by way of the Ionian islands, they would constitute the main factor in the formation of the new Greek literature and thought. The existence of great intellectual figures of Cretan descent, who were also active in other Greek areas shows the uninterrupted continuity of intellectual life on the island and the development of a society and an intellectual climate that gave impetus to a series of works in Cretan literature culminating in the 16th and 17th century with the works of the Cretan theater ("Erophile", "The Sacrifice of Abraham", and Cretan comedy) and the masterpiece, "Erotokritos". In the Frankish-occupied regions similar remarkable achievements appeared in architecture but, above all, in painting with the establishment of the Cretan School. The mixture of Byzantine tradition with the new styles and techniques of the Renaissance produced new forms of art which ruled from the 15th to the end of the 17th century not only in Greece but far beyond its borders through a large number of marvelous craftsmen, amongst whom great masters such as Theophanes Strelitsas Bathas, Michael Damaskinos, Georgios Klotzas and Domenicos Theotokopoulos ("El Greco") stand out.

22

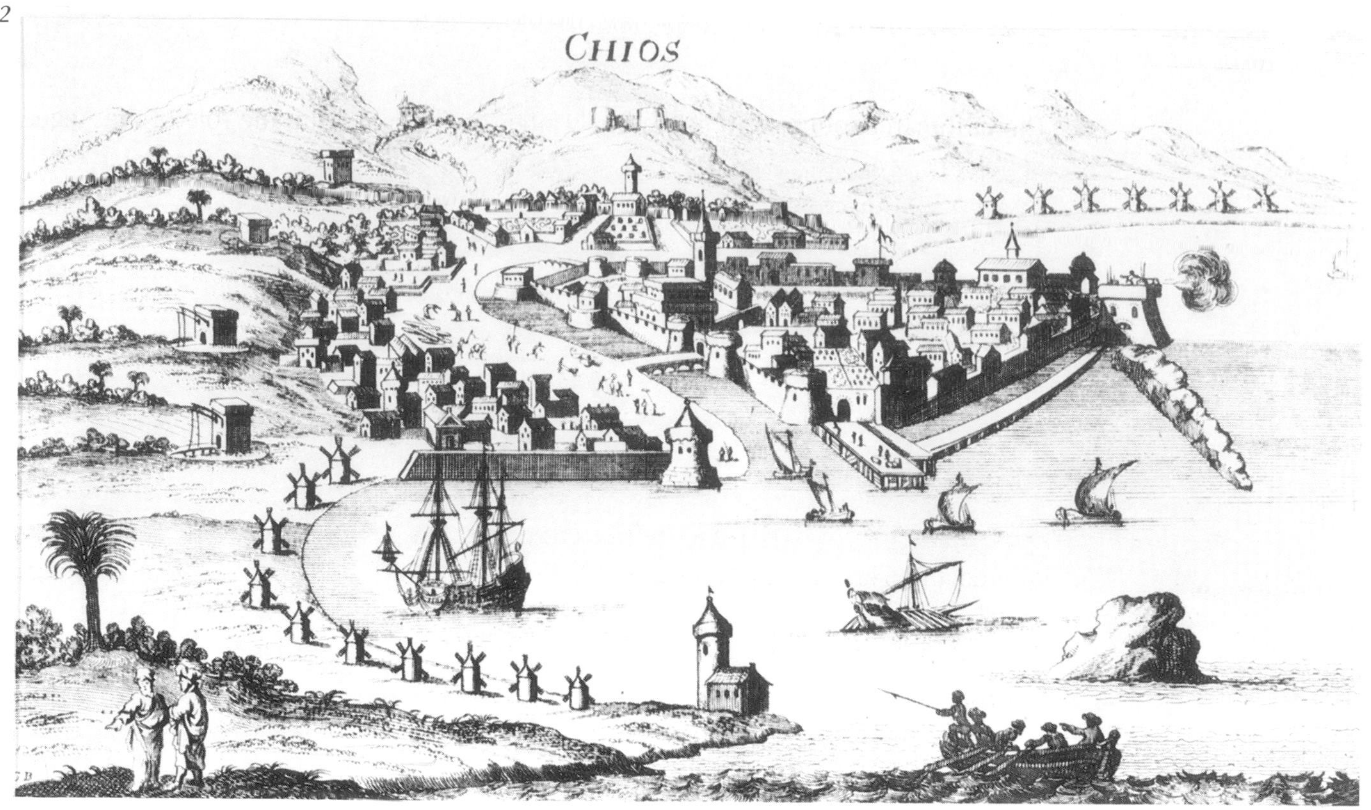

22. Chios. Engraving, end of the 17th century.

23

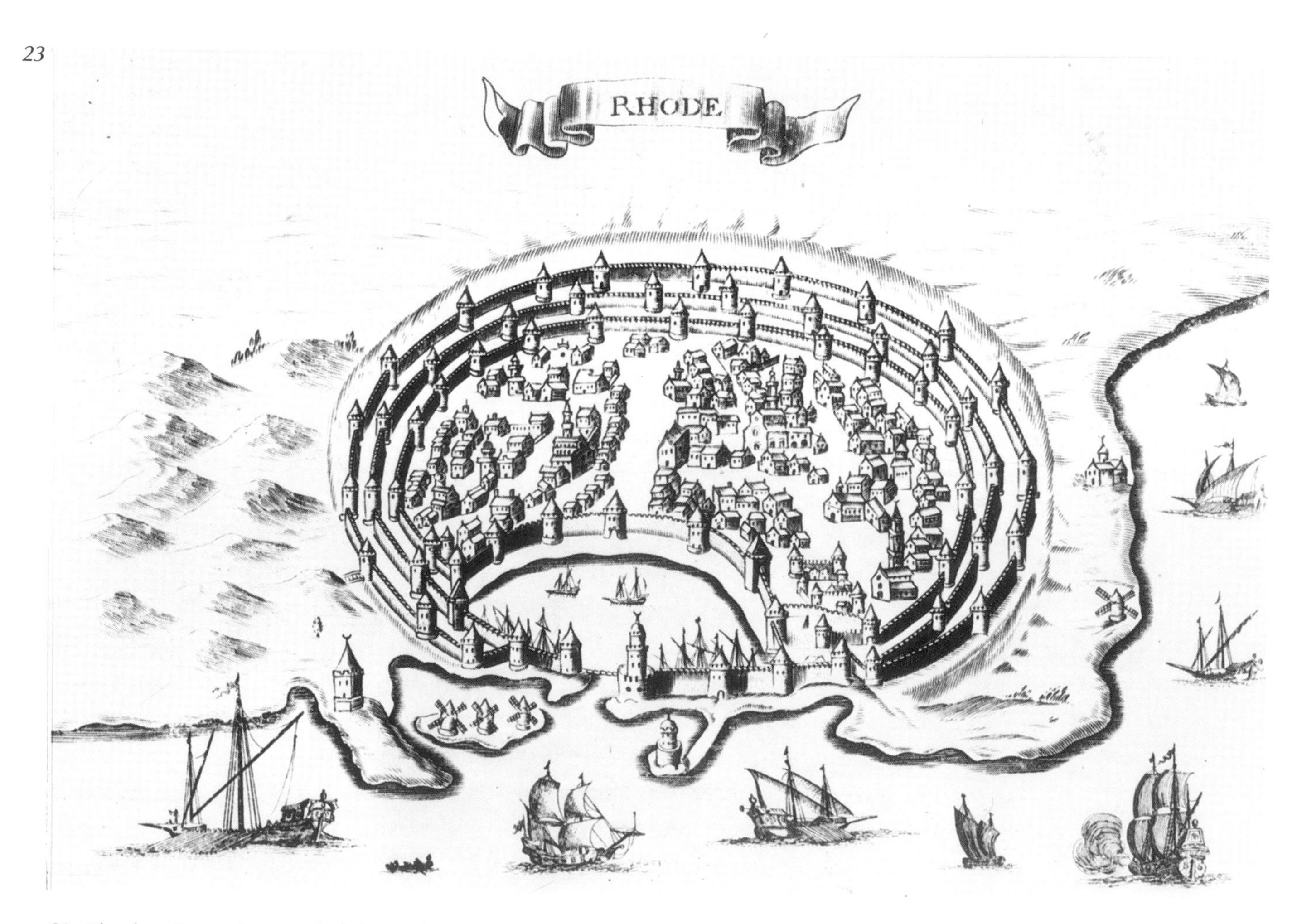

23. Rhodes. Engraving, end of the 17th century.

THE ROLE OF THE AEGEAN DURING THE TURKISH OCCUPATION

The Ottoman conquest did not radically alter, in the long term, the role of the Aegean and its extensions into the eastern Mediterranean in the history of the Hellenic world. The special conditions related to the conquest of the major part of this area as well as the international context bolstered the importance of the Aegean so that developments in this region could be considered as one of the main parameters in the economic, social and cultural history of modern Greece.

Conditions of the Conquest, Population and Ethnological Composition

The occupation of a large part of the broader Aegean area by western powers (Genoa-Venice) significantly delayed the Turkish conquest. The islands in the Thracian Sea were conquered in 1546, Lesbos in 1462 and Euboea in 1470. The Knights regime in Rhodes lasted till 1522; the conquest of Chios and the seizure of the Duchy of the Aegean only occurred in 1566, while Cyprus remained in the hands of the Venetians until 1570-71, Crete until 1669 and Tinos 1715. The struggles between the Ottoman Empire and Venice prevented the complete establishment of Ottoman suzerainty for a long time. Moreover, this took on a unique character in the Aegean region: the conquest of its largest part, principally its islands, was not accompanied by either permanent settlement by the conquerors or mass colonization of the Turkish population to a degree that would essentially have altered the ethnographic composition of the region. This is in contrast to what occurred on the western shores of Asia Minor and, in many cases, on the northern coasts of the Aegean (Thrace-Macedonia). According to the sources, only on the large islands such as Euboea, Cyprus and Crete, and to a lesser degree on Kos, did such mass colonization take place immediately after the conquest. Even there, though, the Turkish population never constituted the absolute majority. On the rest of the islands, such as on Chios, Limnos or Lesbos, the Turkish presence was small or minimal; a few high administrative officials or officers and military guards, who remained in the fortresses, was the extent of the Turkish presence. On other smaller islands, especially in the Cyclades, there may not have been any Turkish presence at all.

Of course, the Greek population in the Aegean was significantly reduced by pirate raids and continual naval wars in the 16th century, and many of the Aegean islands were laid waste. An indication of this, though perhaps a trifle exaggerated, comes from information in a Venetian report from 1563 stating that of the 16 islands in the Duchy of the Aegean, only 5 were inhabited (Naxos, Santorini, Milos, Syros and Patmos). Other sources tell us that, during the 17th century, Paros, Delos, Ios, Kimolos, the northern Sporades and Thasos were deserted or had been transformed into pirate dens.

However, the radical decline in population was quickly dealt with by the Turkish authorities themselves through colonization from other Greek areas with adequate population. Mention is made of such colonizations from the final quarter of the 16th century. In 1571 Psara was colonized and Samos in 1572. Samos seems to have been deserted since 1475, when its population was transferred to Chios by Justiniani, after it was ravaged by pirates. Having conquered the island, the Turks attempted in 1572 to attract new inhabitants from Chios, Lesbos, the adjacent shores of Asia Minor and other Greek islands. This was followed by the colonization of Ios (1575), Folegandros (1577), Ayios Eustratios (1577) and so on.

An increase in the Christian population is also observed on the western coast of Asia

24. *The Colossus of Naxos. Pencil drawing on paper, Thomas Hope, 18th century.*

25. *Naxos, as it appears through the gate of the archaic temple. Sepia drawing on paper, Thomas Hope, 18th century.*

26. *Paros, windmill. Sepia drawing on paper, Thomas Hope, 18th century.*

Minor from the end of the 16th century, when it nearly doubled, in comparison with the first quarter of the century. During the 18th century, the colonists who came from the islands and Greek areas (Epirus, the Peloponnese) reinforced the Greek populations in the centers which developed along the western coast of Asia Minor, from Adramyttium to Ephesus, Cydonia (Aivali), Pergamum, Phocaea, Maenemeni and Smyrna. This population growth also extended to the coasts of the Propontis, to Cyzicus for example, and Kios, where the founding of a shipyard, in 1789, attracted many naval workers.

Not counting local exceptions, the 17th century in general was marked by relative stagnation and decline resulting from continual wars, piracy and epidemics. However, the relative peace and economic progress which marked the 18th century insured, first of all, a certain stabilization of population movements and, from the middle of the century onward, a steady increase of the Greek population, particularly in the Aegean. This increase seems to have been the result not only of indigenous growth but also of the moving of Greek populations into the broader Aegean area, including its extensions into the eastern Mediterranean, where growing economic activity promised better living conditions. We still lack systematic general studies on the demographic development of the Greeks. However, the data that has been collected and examined by various investigators, though inconsistent and scanty, clearly indicates this rise: Psara, whose population in 1739 did not exced 1,000 people, numbered around 3,000 at the eve of the Greek War of Independence of 1821. The growth of Hydra's population was impressive due primarily to large-scale settlement on the island of colonists from the Peloponnese. The 5,000 inhabitants of the island in 1790 more than doubled by 1794, reaching 22,000 in 1809 and 28,000 in 1821, a total which subsequently fell to 16,000 in 1832, after the War of Independence. The population growth of Spetses is similarly both impressive and instructive; it developed from an insignificant settlement (up to 1730) into an important center with 21,500 inhabitants in 1808 (declining to 8,000 by 1820). The population of the islands which were subject to the jurisdiction of the Kapudan Pasha is calculated to have been about 200,000 at the beginning of the 19th century. The increase of population on other islands and the coasts of Asia Minor, Thrace and Macedonia surrounding the Aegean, was similar. The Greek population of Smyrna, for example, which was calculated, in 1721, at 7-8,000 of a total population of 60,000 more than tripled by the end of the century: 26,000 of a total population of 120,000-130,000; on the eve of the Greek War of Independence, it reached 40,000, according to some estimates.

The Greek population of Thessaloniki, about 7,000 in the 16th century, out a total of approximately 20,000, nearly tripled during the 18th: 20,000 out a total population of 60,000-70,000.

In Cyprus, the Greek population always constituted the overwhelming majority. The population of Cyprus, which was calculated at around 200,000 at the time of the Turkish conquest, dwindled considerably during the following centuries of Turkish occupation. According to some estimates, it does not appear to have been more than 100,000 during the 17th and 18th centuries. Throughout the Turkish occupation, Cyprus remained relatively sparsely inhabited. Despite the endeavors of the Turks to colonize the island with new Turkish population immediately after the conquest (as shown by a firman from 1572), the Turkish population would never constitute more than a relatively small minority on the island. A significant portion of it consisted of Cypriote converts to Islam, some of whom kept their Christian faith in secret a considerable time.

Crete followed a similar course, although the Turkish population was much bigger there. The Greeks, however, always retained the majority: 200,000 Greeks and about

100,000 Turks in 1739, 200,000 Greeks and 150,000 Turks in 1797. A part of the Turkish population here, too, consisted of Greeks who had converted to Islam.

Thus, on the whole, the ethnological composition of the broader Aegean area and the Greek islands of the eastern Mediterranean hardly changed. In the Cyclades and other small islands of the Aegean, the population remained Greek for all intents and purposes.

Public Administration and Finance System

The special administrative-financial system that was applied to a large part of the Aegean area constituted another favorable factor for the rapid growth of the Greek element. Neither the *sanjak* (prefecture) of Chios nor the *sanjak* of Naxos, to which the Cyclades were subject, nor other smaller Aegean islands had Turkish feudal lords. Most of the islands were directly subject to the jurisdiction of the Kapudan Pasha. In fact, the entire *sanjak* of Naxos was the *hass* (administrative district) of this highest officer of the Turkish fleet.

The state revenues from the other islands were given from time to time to members of the Sultans' families, to other high officials or even to Turkish philanthropic religious foundations as *vaqfs*. This was the case with Chios, Tinos, Andros, Rhodes and other islands. Thus, the Turkish administration of these regions was somewhat indirect. The beneficiaries of these concessions, who lived in Constantinople, exercised the administration of their districts and the management of their revenues through representatives who were periodically sent to the islands. In the case of the Kapudan Pasha, who had supreme authority over the islands in his administrative district (Cyclades; islands in the Argos Gulf, the Saronic Gulf; the Sporades, Psara, Patmos, Kassos, Astypalaea and Trikeri), the *dragoman* of the fleet, Kapudan Pasha's direct assistant and deputy, played the main role, an office that had been given to Greeks since its inception in 1702. In the case of other islands, whose state income had been ceded to Turkish officials or members of the Royal Family or to *vaqfs*, administration and management was in fact in the hands of the *voivodes* ("section chiefs"), who were also frequently Greeks. Furthermore, the important financial privileges given to the islands, particularly the privilege of paying taxes in a lump sum and the custom of farming them out to private parties, strengthened this system of administrative de-centralization and relative autonomy. For, frequently, these private parties were Greeks and, with the development of the communal system, particularly from the 17th century on, the right to farm out taxes or to choose parties was claimed by the communities themselves.

26

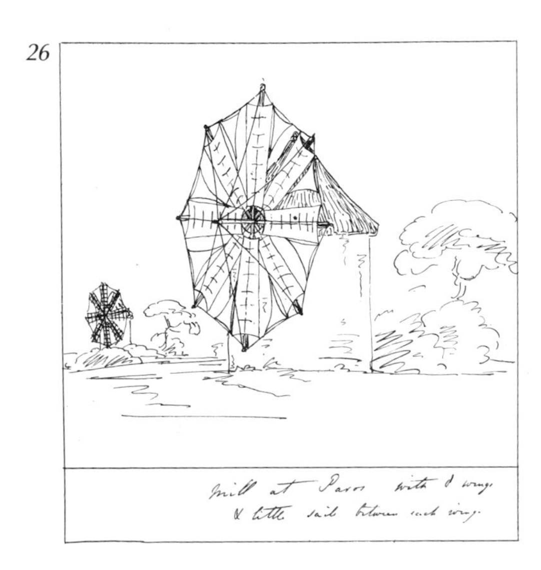

The privileged status that had originally been granted to Chios in the 16th century was extended very early on to nearly all the Aegean islands and renewed from time to time (1580, 1629, 1645: renewal of the privileges of Naxos, Andros, Milos, Paros, Santorini, Syros, Siphnos). A general framework of Islamic principles guided the position of the Ottoman authority in regard to Christians, referring primarily to freedom of worship and the jurisdiction of the ecclesiastical authorities in the judging of matters of ecclesiastical and familial law. This framework contained even more specific provisions for the islands: conscripts could not be recruited from the islands nor Janissaries installed there. The existence of such privileges, as well as other extended administrative ones, made it possible for more advanced forms to develop in the system of self-governing communities on certain islands, which, by the beginning of the 19th century and before the Greek War of Independence in 1821, resulted in a kind of administrative semi-autonomy, unlimited in practice, except by the intervention of the Kapudan Pasha, principally through his *dragoman* deputy in the fleet. In fact, many of the communities on the islands even managed to extend the jurisdiction of ecclesiastical courts and to win recognition for community courts with power to try not only cases in family law but also cases in civil law in general, and even some criminal cases, except, of course, those involving serious crimes (murder or acts against the state). Naturally, ratification and execution of the decisions and decrees of the community courts of the first instance, which were usually of an arbitrable nature, as well as judgements of the second instance belonged in principle to the Turkish authorities and, in the case of the islands, to the Kapudan Pasha and his deputy spokesman of the fleet. However certain islands, such as Tinos, managed to form a higher communal court made up of Greek elders and notables who carried out the duties of an appeals court ("Gerontocricia"). There were even ways to prevent the Christian population from taking recourse in the Turkish courts. In the communal regulations of Hydra (1818) and the codified customs of Anafi and Santorini (1797), there were provisions that penalized such recourse in certain cases.

The great degree of autonomy which the island communities had achieved on the eve of the Greek War of Independence is stressed by a French memorandum written in 1820. Its writer, after confirming that Greeks everywhere were preparing for early liberation, adds: "Indeed, one could say that this moment has already arrived for the islands which are governed by elders chosen by themselves and in accordance with their own regulations. Inhabited by seamen accustomed to being protected by the Russian flag, cultivated by hard-working private owners made rich by their protection, they do not recognize the suzerainty of the ruler in Constantinople, to whom they are adjacent, except through the yearly tax they pay to the deputy of the Kapudan Pasha".

According to this memorandum, the coasts of Asia Minor presented a similar pattern: the community of Smyrna had a remarkable organization with extensive jurisdiction. Its guilds of professionals played an important role in this organization. The community of Cydonies (Aivali) was also important. This memorandum, as well as other sources, mention examples from Aivali, Mykonos and Naxos, where the inhabitants and the communal authorities ignored both the Turkish authorities who came periodically and the consular authorities of the western powers.

Economic Development

These administrative conditions so favorable for the Greeks, along with the geographic position of the Aegean, could be viewed as important factors in the region's economic development; and this growth was of prime importance for the overall advancement of the Greek people. Their impressive economic expansion began in the Aegean area and peaked during the 18th and the beginning of the 19th century, with the growth of trade and shipping on the threshold of the Greek War of Independence.

The populations on the Aegean islands and the Aegean coasts, particularly those who for centuries had been under the domination of the Genoese, the Order of the Knights of Rhodes and the Venetians (see above) had, through taking part in their economic activities, established the pre-conditions for an even more energetic participation in this unparalleled economic activity. By the end of the 16th, but primarily in the 17th century, this activity had already been developed in the East, not only by the Italian Republics but above all by the new world economic powers – the Dutch, the French and the English.

Despite the dangers of piracy (and frequently because of the pirates, whose plunder often became an object of trade for the islanders), there was no dearth of economic and commercial activity in the Aegean during the first centuries of the Turkish occupation.

27, 28. *Women from Chios and a Greek priest. Sepia drawing on paper, Thomas Hope, 18th century.*

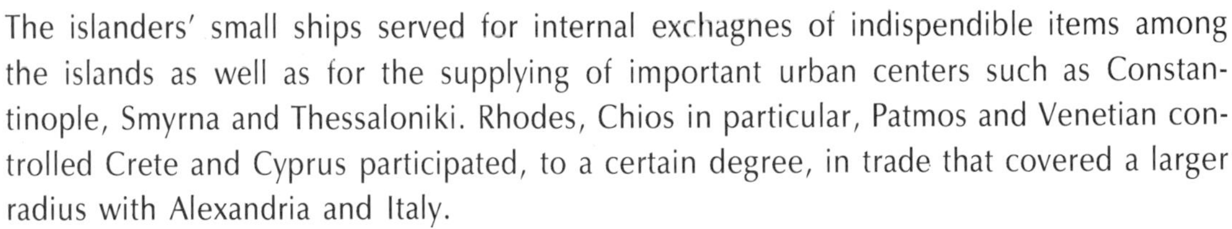

The islanders' small ships served for internal exchagnes of indispendible items among the islands as well as for the supplying of important urban centers such as Constantinople, Smyrna and Thessaloniki. Rhodes, Chios in particular, Patmos and Venetian controlled Crete and Cyprus participated, to a certain degree, in trade that covered a larger radius with Alexandria and Italy.

But the real launching of Greek commercial activity in the Aegean would occur in about the middle of the 18th century, when Western European trade routes shifted northward on account of the anarchy in the southeast provinces of the Ottoman Empire, thus passing through Greek seas. New commercial landing stages sprang up everywhere with consulates and vice-consulates of the western powers: in Cyprus, Crete, the Aegean islands, Smyrna and Thessaloniki, where prominent business communities of English, French, Dutch and Italians were active – soon to be joined by Germans and Austrians, particularly in Thessaloniki. Smyrna and Thessaloniki became the main commercial ports of the eastern Mediterranean. Crete and Cyprus also played an important role in this international commercial movement. The wealthy commercial houses of western Europe, which were continually multiplying, used these ports to export the agricultural products and raw materials of the East and the Balkans to western European industries as well as to import the industrial products of the West. An ever increasing number of Greeks – competing with Jews and Armenians (in Asia Minor) – participated in this economic activity. The Greeks played an important role in internal trade, carrying merchandise from the interior of the Balkans and Asia Minor to the large export ports, or imported industrial goods to places of consumption. They also participated, from a certain point on, in foreign overland trade with the countries of Central Europe and, from the middle of the 18th century, in foreign sea trade. The Greek commercial houses of Smyrna, Thessaloniki and other centers (such as Patmos and the Peloponnese) multiplied and became dangerous competitors of the Westerners, so that, by the end of the 18th century and the beginning of the 19th, they took a very large part of the foreign sea trade in their hands.

The Aegean area, particularly the Aegean islands, was of crucial major importance in the development of commercial shipping. Kassos, Rhodes and other, smaller islands, above all Hydra, Spetses and Psara, dominated sea transport from the end of the 18th century and had a substantial commercial fleet much of which was built in local shipyards, while other, larger, ships were purchased from the West.

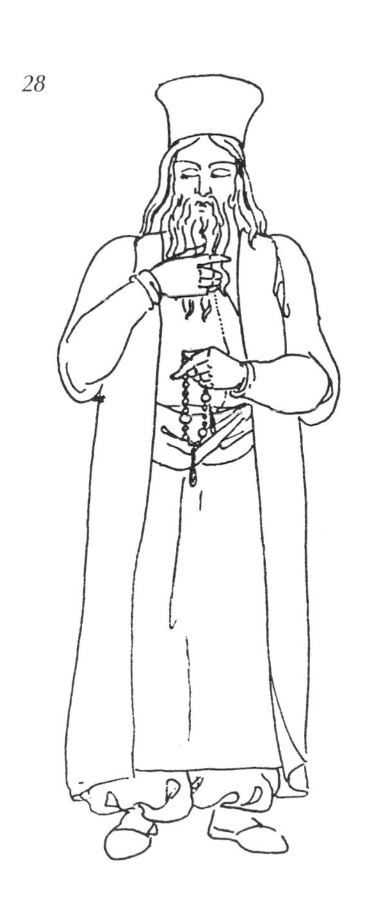

Commercial competition between the French and English for the control of the Mediterranean, and the wars between them, as well as the successes of Russia in its wars against the Ottoman Empire, presented favorable opportunities for the impressive and relatively rapid growth of Greek shipping, from the middle of the 18th century. Indeed, the hostilities between the English and French during the War of Austrian Succession (1740-1748), then again in the years 1748-1755 and, yet again, during the Seven Years' War (1756-1763) forced the French to cede "free participation" in French trade to neutrals (1751). This measure was of particular benefit to seamen on the Aegean islands who carried a significant proportion of the French trade. During this same period, the English, in agreement with the Russians, permitted the establishment of a Greek colony at Port Mahon, Minorca, and deployed Greek ships and Greek crews as corsairs, based in Minorca in the wars against the French. The Russo-Turkish wars under Catherine II (1768-1774 and 1787-1792) were of particular importance for the growth of shipping in the region. The participation of the islanders in the Russian fleet's operations in the eastern Meditarranean strengthened the island fleet. Of particular significance, in this respect, were the Treaty of Kütchük Kainardji(1774), which brought an end to the first Russo-Turkish

29

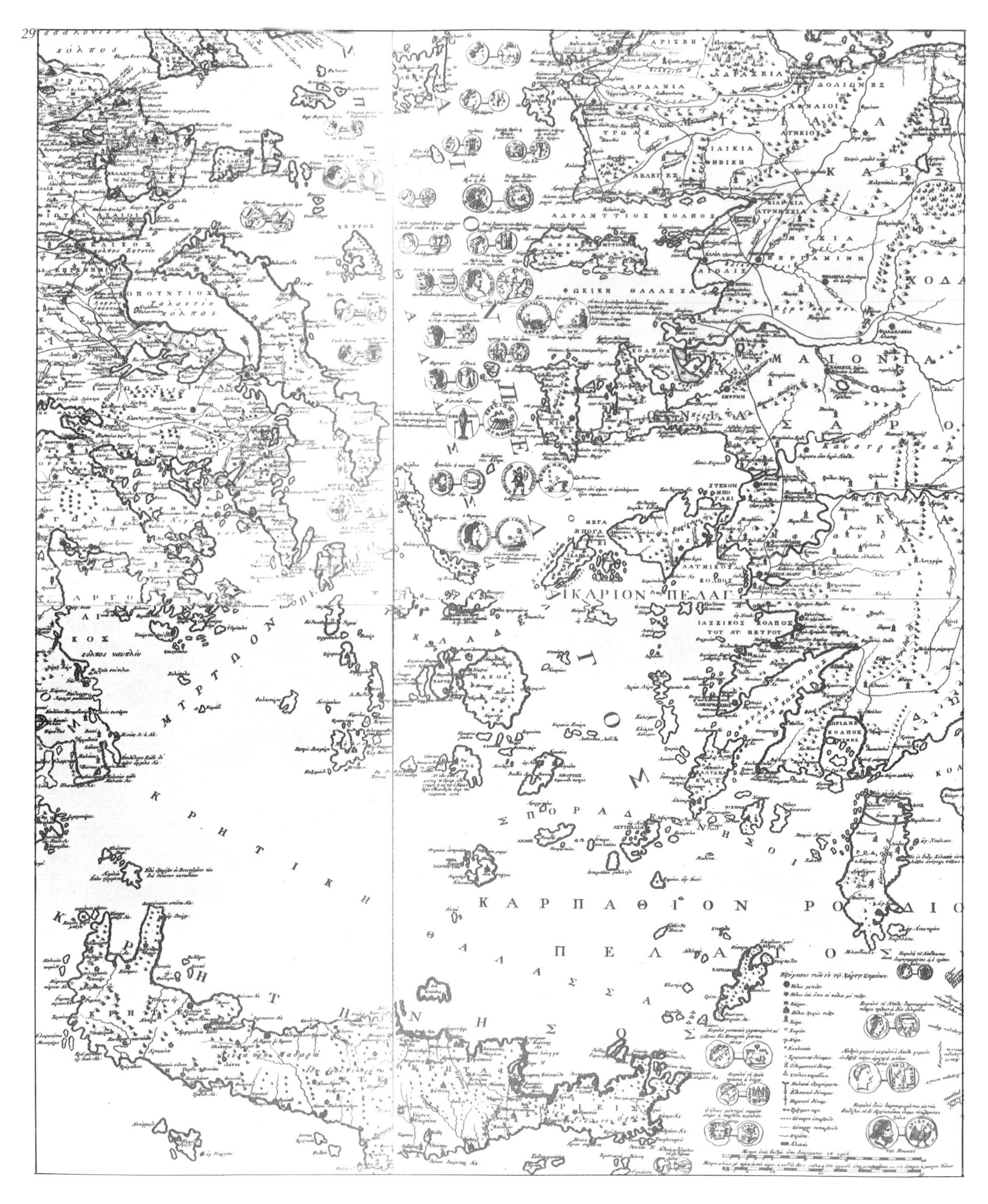
ΑΔΡΑΜΥΤΤΙΟΣ ΚΟΛΠΟΣ
ΦΩΚΙΚΗ ΘΑΛΑΣΣΑ
ΜΑΙΟΝΙΑ
ΙΚΑΡΙΟΝ ΠΕΛΑΓ
ΙΑΣΣΙΚΟΣ ΚΟΛΠΟΣ
ΤΟΥ ΑΓ ΠΕΤΡΟΥ
ΚΑΡΠΑΘΙΟΝ
ΡΟΔΙΟ
ΠΕΛΑΓΟΣ
ΘΑΛΑΣΣΑ

war, and the Treaty of Ayvalik-Kabak (1779) and the commercial agreement of Constantinople (1783) which clarified and augmented it. It was the Greeks who benefited most, particularly those involved in Aegean shipping, from the Ottoman recognition of Russia's right to protect its Orthodox subjects and the concession of free shipping rights in Turkish seas to vessels under the Russian flag, provisions contained in the above agreements. Hence, ships from the Aegean islands flying a Russian flag could travel unhindered in Ottoman seas; those "protected" by Russia multiplied; they also founded prominent Greek colonies in southern Russia.

Following the French Revolution and during the Napoleonic Wars, the hostilities in the Mediterranean between the English and French at the end of the 18th century, also proved favorable for the growth of Greek shipping. Here, too, the Aegean area played the leading role. Starting in 1792, France, faced with the English embargo, was obliged to have recourse to neutral ships in order to secure diplomatic correspondence with its consulates in the Mediterranean, to maintain whatever it could of its commercial activity and, above all, to supply its Mediterranean regions with food, principally wheat. Hydra's and Spetses' ships, as well as those from other Greek islands, and the Greek merchants in Smyrna, undertook this dangerous but profitable mission which, in order to be carried out, entailed transgressing the English blockade of the French coast. Between 1794 and 1796 Greek shipping in Marseilles held second and third place. The Greek colony in Marseilles, which consisted mainly of Smyrnian merchants, Cretans and Aegean islanders, grew continually. During the Continental System imposed by Napoleon in response to the English naval blockade, Thessaloniki became the only Mediterranean port from which English trade could be conducted with Central Europe, the Germanic countries and other countries to the north.

Scattered statistical information clearly indicates the growth of the Greek merchant navy and Greek maritime activity centered in the Aegean, during the last quarter of the 18th century and the beginning of the 19th, on the theshold of the Greek War of Independence. Hydra's ships were calculated at 120 in 1764; this number increased to about 200 by 1766; at the end of that century and the beginning of the next, it had inceased even further. Psara had only a few small ships (jigger masts), during the first half of the century engaged in local trade with the nearby islands (Chios, Lesbos), the adjacent shores of Asia Minor and some Greek coasts further away. Yet, at the outbreak of the Russo-Turkish war, it had 36 larger ships and during the war, it built 45 galiots and the first three-masted ship. In 1790 Psara had 57 ships with a total capacity of 362,820 hundredweight and crews totalling 850 men. There was an analogous increase in the fleet of Spetses where lateens and "sachtouria", small coastal sailing vessels, were built.

There was also similar activity in Greek shipping, where the islands of the Aegean always held the leading position. During the period 1776-1790, Greek ships made up, on average, 48% of the activity in the port of Alexandria. During the period 1810-1816, it rose to 64%. The Greek commercial fleet also dominated the port of Odessa from 1804-1820, having approximately 55% of the total number of ships and 44% of the total capacity, as against 22% and 27% respectively for the English. During the years 1810-1820, Greek ships represented approximately 82% of the activity in the port of Thessaloniki, against 18% for the western powers. From this and other statistical information collected to date we can conclude with certainty that most of the Greek merchant navy's international activity took place in the eastern Mediterranean and the Black Sea. For example, the Russian wheat trade through Odessa was in Greek hands. The participation of Greek shipping in the western Mediterranean was much smaller, for trade there remained in

29. Section of Regas chart showing the Aegean.

the hands of the western powers which still controlled exchanges with the West. Nevertheless, the participation of Spetses, but principally of Hydra, was not negligible in this sector. This was on account of their well-organized shipping methods and the possession of a host of ships of an average capacity of 150 tons (ships of larger capacity are also mentioned).

The Contribution of the Aegean to Social Change

The immediate consequence of the economic development of the entire Aegean region was the invaluable contribution of this area to the formation and clarification of the structures of Greek society which supported intellectual developments and determined, to a large extent, its ideological content.

Indeed, the prerequisites for a new social alignment which lay at the basis of the differentiation of Greek society and began primarily in the second half of the 18th century, were established in the main in the broader Aegean area and its immediate extensions, to a degree much greater than the rest of Greece (except for certain large urban centers).

More specifically, the first true nucleus of a merchantile middle class engaged in carrying would develop in the following places: Thessaloniki, economic capital of the Balkans and central station for overland trade with central Europe, as well as sea trade with the countries of the western Mediterranean; Smyrna, economic capital of Asia Minor; the Aegean islands, large centers of Greek shipping, and their immediate extensions in the Aegean; and Constantinople and Cyprus. This class, unlike the major Greek capitalists of the Diaspora, would remain in Greek lands and hence would play, along with the other social parameters in the nation, the leading role in the intellectual development of the Greek people and the definition of their political and national ideology.

The political struggles within the framework of communal life to be found in the Aegean, as can be seen in the examples of Smyrna, Samos, Andros, and in general in the Cyclades, to mention the most characteristic ones, just as in certain urban communities in Greece itself, reflect social contrasts more obvious than in rural communities.

Intellectual Development

The Aegean area contributed in fundamental ways to the endeavors of Turkish-occupied Greece to retain, initially, at least a part of its old intellectual heritage. At a later stage, such endeavors were aimed at improving and modernizing its education and enabling it to follow, even if from a distance, the cultural developments of the western world and to participate in the movement of ideas which were developed in "enlightened Europe".

The long-term occupation of the larger part of the Aegean area, especially the islands, by western forces – Genoa, the Knights of Saint John and Venice – permitted continuity of intellectual and cultural activities and the creation of a Greek culture renewed and enriched by the newly emerging intellectual currents in the West.

The Aegean's major contribution to the intellectual growth of all Turkish-occupied Greece can be explained on the basis of this intellectual climate as well as economic and administrative conditions favorable to the Greeks which developed in a major part of the area and were there even when the Aegean came under Turkish occupation. After nearly a century of intellectual stagnation or decline (with a few isolated exceptions) Greece as a whole began to revive in about the 16th century.

30. *Neophytos Vamvas (drawing by T. Chatzis). Prominent cleric, from Chios (1770-1855).*

Our oldest records of schools come from the Aegean area. Michael Ermodoros Listarchos taught in Chios, starting in 1533 and at intervals after that (1539-1543, 1560-1564). Theophanis Eleavoulkos and the monk and leading theologian from Zakynthos, Pachomios Rousanos also taught there (about 1535 and 1509-1533 respectively). Many of their students were later distinguished in literature and occupied high positions. Indeed, there is mention of a plan by the notables of Chios to found a university (thwarted by the attacks of the Turks). Chios, along with Constantinople, would remain the principal intellectual Greek center with brilliant schools even after the Turkish conquest. In 1577 Theodosios Zygomylas mentions the students of Ermodoros and the apparently eminent teacher, Ignatios Kaloyerakis (1581), whose students also taught Greek in Italy. A landmark in the intellectual development of Chios was the founding of a Jesuit school, in 1590, which quickly attracted around 200 students, of whom 80 were Orthodox. Many of them went on to study at Italian universities or at the college of Saint Athanasius in Rome, Leon Allatios (1585-1669) and others among them. During this same period, in the 16th century, the schools of Lesbos are mentioned: around 1545, Pachomios Rousanos taught at the school of the Leimonas Monastery, while the first girls' school was founded at the Myrsiniotissa Convent, for the nuns, by the bishop of the district Ignatios Agallianos. In the 16th century, the schools of Patmos (1596-1602) and Thessaloniki (1585) are also mentioned.

Intellectual activity continued on Cyprus during the period of the Turkish occupation as well. Schools are mentioned in Ammochostos, Nicosia and Limassol from the end of the 16th century; by virtue of hierarchs such as Philotheos and Chrysanthos they continued operating and multiplied during the 18th and 19th centuries.

We have already spoken of the intellectual activity in Crete and the great achievements in literature and art during the Venetian occupation. Let it be further noted that the large number of Greeks studying in the West came from the Frankish-controlled areas of the broader Aegean region, Crete, Chios, the other Aegean islands, and, of course, from Cyprus and the Ionian islands. They went to the Italian universities, the schools of higher education founded by the Catholic Church in Rome, the Greek Gymnasium founded by Pope Leo X at the instigation of Ianos Laskaris (1514), and, later, the College of Saint Athanasius founded by Pope Gregory XIII (1577). The registers of Greek students enrolled in the Legisti School of the University of Padua from the final decade of the 16th century to the beginning of the 19th century illustrate the Aegean's leading role in the intellectual modernization of Greece. The Greek students enrolled at the end of the 16th century did not exceed 31, most of whom came from Crete (around 25), while very few (4 only) came from Cyprus, Naxos and Corfu. During the 17th century (1622-1700) there were over 1,000 registrations. The Cretans were again in the majority, followed by the Ionian islands; but there were also a few from the Aegean islands – Chios, Syros, Siphnos – and an equally small number from other Greek areas.

Enrollments at the College of Rome present a similar picture: about 121 in the 16th century, 158 in the first half of the 17th century but only 90 in the second half; Crete and the Ionian islands held the leading place here, too, followed by Cyprus, the Cyclades and the Peloponnese; there was also a small number of students from the Dodecanese, Macedonia, Epirus, Asia Minor, Thessaly and Athens. Many of them returned to Greece and became important contributors to its intellectual development, which would expand greatly during the 18th and the beginning of the 19th century.

The Aegean's participation in the educational renaissance observed throughout Greece at the end of the 17th century, but mainly during the 18th century, was truly

31. Adamantios Korais. One of the leaders of the modern Greek Enligtenment, from Chios (1748-1833).

important. Despite the lack of adequate data concerning elementary education, some scattered numerical references are indicative: from the 16th to the beginning of the 19th century, there were about 40 schools mentioned for the Aegean area. Of these, 5 were founded during the 16th and 17th century and the other 35 were 18th century foundations (about 15 founded at the instigation of the Church and the other 20 by communities). For the sake of comparison, let us note that 35 schools are mentioned for Thessaly, of which 5 were founded during the 16th and 17th century at the initiative of the Church and the remaining 27 during the 18th century. About 49 schools are recorded in the Peloponnese: 7 in the 16th and 17th centuries, most of which were founded at the initiative of the Church; the remaining 42 were foundations of the 18th and 19th century.

The significant contribution of the Aegean to the renaissance in education becomes yet clearer in the movement for establishing intermediate schools and schools of higher education, the achievement of better organization, the modernization of education through new methods of instruction and reform programs as well as more general educational and cultural activities. These were connected to the new spirit of the Enlightenment which held away from the first quarter of the 18th century to the Greek War of Independence of 1821 and continued, though weakened, till about the middle of the 19th century. The formation of important urban nuclei, as a result of economic development, in the broader Aegean area, and its connection to the Greek diaspora played a leading role in this movement. Let us not forget that the most prestigious intellectual figure of the period and the inspiration behind this reformation movement, around which revolved a host of "lovers of learning" (large merchants and reform-minded intellectuals), was Adamantios Korais from Chios, who learned his ABCs in Smyrna.

The Aegean area became one of Greece's leading intellectual centers, inculcating the new spirit of Hellenism through the establishment or reforming of schools in Andros, Paros, Patmos and elsewhere, and, more significantly, through modernization of the higher schools on Chios, in the Cyclades and in Smyrna, along with those in the principalities south of the Danube and several other regions (Pelion, Zagora and Yiannina). It is typical that of the approximately 9 modern higher schools of education founded during this period 3 were in the Aegean area.

The school of Chios, with its magnificent buildings for teachers and students alike and fully equipped, was considered by the French diplomat Marcellus "as the most important foundation... the most renowned university in Greece." It had a remarkable library which, according to some information, contained 30,000 volumes; there were , laboratories for physics experiments and a printing office. In 1810, there were seven professors there; this figure doubled on the eve of the Greek War of Independence of 1821. It is estimated that during the same period there were six hundred students there. Neophytos Vamvas (1776-1855), an adherent of the reform program of Korais, replaced the conservative Athanasios Parios at the beginning of the 19th century in the management of the school and revised the program. By 1819 mathematics and the natural sciences were taught alongside grammar, the interpretation of texts, theology, ancient history, philosophy, rhetoric, ethics, painting and foreign languages (Turkish and French). The Lancasterian system was also introduced for the first time in the Chios School.

Cydonies (Aivali), a small fishing village inhabited by Mytilenians at the beginning of the 17th century remained a small hamlet till the middle of the 18th century (1740), but after 1759, increased its population with the influx of Epirots fleeing the persecution of Ali Pasha. Some islanders moved there, too. During the final quarter of the 18th century, Cydonies developed into an important, purely Greek urban center with the privilege of

32

32. Theophilos Kairis. Theologian, philosopher, from Andros (1784-1853).

complete autonomous government and tax exemptions (1773). At the end of the century it had a well-known school with beautiful and spacious buildings equipped with fine laboratories for teaching science as well as an important library and a printing office. Veniamin of Lesbos taught there from 1797-98 and, later, Theophilos Kairis as well. In 1817 the school had around 300 students.

Intellectual activity was particularly vigorous in the Greek community in Smyrna, which, from 1707, had a fully-organized school directed by Diamandis Rysios, the grandfather of Korais. In 1723 he founded the new school, known as the Evangelical School from 1808 and later (the beginning of the 19th century) as the "Literary Gymnasium". Here Korais, the followers of Konstantinos Koumas and his colleagues, Konstantinos Oikonomou and his brother, Stephanos Oikonomou introduced the new spirit of the Enlightenment. Mathematics and the natural sciences were taught here too, along with literature, philosophy and history. One of the terms set by Konstantinos Koumas, when in 1809 he was called upon to assume the directorship of the newly-founded Gymnasium, was an allocation by the community for the purchase of equipment needed for teaching the natural sciences. The community did, in fact, make the allocation and from the report which Koumas compiled on the school in 1810, we learn that "this year the Gymnasium conducted its first chemistry and physics experiments, the like of which have not been seen in Greece". The reforming ideas about education at the Smyrna Gymnasium provoked the reaction of the conservative circles headed by the metropolitan of Smyrna, Anthimos. He did not hesitate to incite certain guilds, as well as the Ottoman authorities, against Konstantinos Oikonomou who was charged with, among other things, preparing youth for revolutionary activities against the Ottomans. The matter was settled through the intercession of certain moderate circles of the Phanari and the Patriarchate and because of the conciliatory position taken by Oikonomou. Three printing-houses were founded in Smyrna from 1764 to the eve of the Greek War of Independence (1764, 1813 and shortly before the War of Independence). During this period Smyrna had 6-8 public schools in addition to the two schools of higher education. Enrollment in these schools is estimated at about 1,500 (300 at the Literary Gymnasium, 200 at the Evangelical School and about 1,000 at the other, ordinary schools). This total represented 37.50% of the Greek population.

Let it be further noted that the first naval training college in Greece was founded in Hydra a little before the War of Independence. At the invitation of the community, Italian and Portuguese experts taught there.

Thus, the uninterrupted intellectual tradition and continual contact with intellectual movements in the West helped make the broader area of the Aegean an important source of educated leaders for the Turkish-occupied areas as well, particularly during the first centuries of the Turkish occupation: Maximos Margounios, Pigas and later Cyril Loukaris came from Crete; Theophanis Eleavouklos, the great orator of the Ecumenical Patriarchate, came from Chios, as well as the first major interpreter-translator Panayiotis Nikousios and the generations of the Mavrokordatos family. Frangiskos Kokkos, who re-established the Patriarchal School (1604), came from Naxos.

Several of the important literary works at the end of the 17th and the 18th century could be considered as extensions of the intellectual flowering of Venetian-occupied Crete: the Rhetoric, of Frangiskos Skoufos (1681), Yerasimos Vlachos (1607-1687), Athanasios Varouchas (1631-1700), Yerasimos Palladas (1714) and Elias Miniatis (1699-1764); the metrical chronicles or translations of Italian poetic works and the theater of the Ionian islands, as produced by the Cretan Marinos Tzane Bounialis, Petros Katsaitis, Soumakis,

Antonios Stratigos, Georgios Marmoris and other anonymous ones.

On Chios we find similar "literary" endeavors connected to the students at the Catholic institutions of Rome. The verse dialogue "David" (most probably from the 18th century) can be compared favorably with the literary production of Crete.

Leading personalities and groups from the Aegean participated in the whole spectrum of Greek intellectual movements of the 18th century. Some of these, as mentioned above, stood for reform but some others despite their mixed impulses and confused ideology, manifestly bore the marks of conservatism.

The Chiote merchants in Galata were the leaders, along with certain guilds, in the discords concerning anabaptism, which began in 1750 with the decision of the Patriarch Cyril II to re-baptize the Catholics who wished to become Orthodox. The movement rapidly took on a social character setting itself against the economic privileges of the Catholic merchants as well as the liberal circles which had supported the reform efforts of Cyril Loukaris. The theoretician of anabaptism was the Christian physician-philosopher Efstratios Argentis.

The "Kollyvades movement" (conservative Orthodox monks seeking to purge the Church of foreign elements) was also connected with the broader Aegean area. The movement started in Mount Athos in 1754 at the hermitage of Ayia Anna, from a disagreement related to the performance of memorial services on Sundays or Saturdays. It evolved into a movement supporting "Orthodox tradition" against all innovation and dividing the faithful for a long time, even giving rise to bloodshed, and leaving traces right up to the present. The first leader of the movement, the director of the Athos School, Neophytos Kavsokalyvitis, after he was forced to leave Mount Athos (1759), continued his activity on Chios (1759-1763) and then elsewhere until his death in 1789. Athanasios Parios (1725-1813) his successor, had studied in Smyrna and then at the Athos School, his teachers being Evgenios Voulgaris and Nikiphoros Theotokis. He proved to be one of the most important representatives of intellectual conservatism, the enemy of every reform idea that came from the West, where he refused to continue his studies. He became a fanatical opponent of Korais and all those who studied in Western Europe. He, too, spent the major part of his life as the director of the School on Chios, where he died.

Claiming to represent pure Orthodox tradition, the "Kollyvades movement" sought to be associated with the Byzantine mystics and the Hesychasts through the works of Neophytos Kavsokalyvitis, Makarios Notaras (†1803), metropolitan of Corinth (1765-1769) and Nikodimos Ayioretis (†1809). However, its affinities lay, rather, with the ascetic theories and customs of certain western religious movements – the Jesuits in particular. The Naxian Nikodimos Ayioretis appears to have had such links. As secretary to the metropolitan of Naxos (1770-1778), he knew the Jesuits there, and wrote several works ("Invisible War", 1796 and "Spiritual Exercises", 1800) which were nothing more than adaptations of western works ("Combattimento Spirituale", 1589 by Lorenzo Scopoli and "Esercisi Spirituali" by Ignatius Loyola). Let it be further noted that the Patriarchate's failure to reconcile the conflicting parties led to the censure of Athanasios Parios and the excommunication of the movement. Then, the Kollyvades monks departed from Mount Athos and settled on the Aegean islands of Chios, Icaria, Hydra, Paros, and their continued activity found echoes in the later teachings of Makrakis and the religious populist sermons of Papoulakis.

The artistic activities of the rest of Turkish-occupied Greece can be considered as an extension of the cultural tradition developed on Crete and continued even after the Turkish conquest, particularly during the early centuries (16th and 17th) of the Turkish occupation. The fully-developed Cretan School was dominant then, and this preceded the 18th century spreading out of another School formed in northern Greece (Epirus and western Macedonia) whose main characteristic was the fusion of Byzantine tradition with folk art elements.

The Aegean islands played their traditional intermediary role at this point also. Cretan painters settled in the Cyclades, the Sporades and other centers in the Aegean and created the first nuclei of artists from which local studios would be fashioned. Paintings from these artists merged western influences with Byzantine tradition and a kind of "folk" style, while in architecture, traditional Aegean austerity and clarity of form were added to these combinations.

The Contribution of the Aegean to the Development of a National Ideology

The Aegean area and its immediate extensions in the eastern Mediterranean participated, along with the rest of Greece, in the resistance against their conquerors. This resistance was manifest from the first moment of foreign occupation and continued for centuries, thereby contributing to the preservation, further development and clarification of national consciousness. From the 18th century on, the events acted out in Aegean made a significant contribution to the precise definition of a national liberation ideology.

Already by the 13th century, resistance movements (initially, with a Christian Orthodox character) and rebellions against the Franks and the Venetians had started in Cyprus and, above all, in Crete. After the Ottoman conquest, these continued with a large number of Greeks participating in the Venetian wars and the Christian alliance against the Ottoman Empire. The Aegean islands were on the front line of operations during the Venetian-Turkish war of 1463-1479. Aegean islanders also contributed to the naval forces in the second and the third Turkish-Venetian war (1499-1503 and 1537-1539 respectively) and the Sacra Lega operations (Venice-Spain-Austria under the aegis of Pope Paul III). The activity of the Greek corsairs against the Turks continued even after the separate peace signed by Venice (1540) and was intensified by the assistance of the Spanish from 1566-1569, during the Turkish-Venetian war over Cyprus (1570-1571) and the operations of the Sacra Lega (1571-1573). A significant number of the defenders of Cyprus in the Venetian army and fleet came from Crete and the Aegean islands, on several of which, such as Lesbos, Paros, Naxos and Rhodes, the metropolitans provoked uprisings against the Turks at the instigation of the Ecumenical Patriarch Metrophanes III (1515-1572). Many of the ships that took part in the famous Battle of Navpaktos (or Lepanto, May 10, 1571) had been outfitted on the Aegean islands and Crete while the number of Greek fighters and oarsmen in the Christian fleet exceeded 35% of the total. This also represents the estimated percentage of oarsmen and Greek sailors obliged to serve in the Turkish fleet. New uprisings against the Turks throughout the broader Aegean area broke out after the destruction of the Turkish fleet at the naval battle of Navpaktos: in Thessaloniki at the instigation of the metropolitan Ioasaph Argyropoulos; in Mount Athos, in the villages of Pelion, in the Pagasitic Gulf, in Karpathos, Rhodes, Kos, Andros, Naxos, Paros, Lesbos, Ayios Evstratios, Limnos, Skiathos and even on the western coast of Asia Minor, in the region of Smyrna, and Palaea and Nea Phocaea. New anti-Turkish uprisings occurred on the Aegean islands during the Turkish-Venetian war over Crete (1648-1669); there were further disturbances during the operations in the Aegean provoked by the new Turkish-Venetian war and the entry of Venice into the Holy Alliance of Linz (1684-1699).

33

33. *Lambros Katsonis. One of the leaders of the Greek liberation movement at the instigation of Russia, 1788.*

A clearer national character and a more concrete political content was to be found in the uprisings of Greek lands during the Russo-Turkish war in the 18th century, in which the Aegean islands played an important role.

During the war of 1768-1774, the whole Greek world, from Epirus to the Peloponnese and Crete, rose up, after the descent of the Russian fleet into the Mediterranean (1770). The hope for the possibility of a free Greek state was nurtured then, both by the attempts of the Peloponnesian notables to organize the uprising politically and the temporary overthrow of Turkish occupation in the Cyclades and Samos during the Russian presence (till 1774). This occurred despite the discontent that had been created by the high-handedness of the undisciplined Russian troops, and the burdens of war and piracy. The liberal ideas promoted by Catherine II and her liberal legislative plans also reinforced these hopes; the national pro-Russian propaganda, which spread during the Orlov events in Greece, was indeed based on such thoughts. Its leading figure was Evgenios Voulgaris, who translated the Russian work "Introduction concerning the problem of a new code" into Greek and dedicated it to Catherine II, in the hope that such liberal laws could be applied to the Greeks as well. He also composed memoranda to Catherine II concerning the liberation of the Greeks and translated pamphlets by Voltaire against Ottoman despotism, inspiring hopes for the liberation of the Greek nation.

These national longings became more concrete with the unequivocal statement of the need for a free state for the Greeks. The awareness that the national problem could only be solved by a revolution initiated by the Greeks themselves became even clearer during the second Russo-Turkish war under Catherine II (1787-1792). Russian agents were sent to Greece in order to instigate uprisings in the Greek lands and to recruit Greek crews from the islands for the establishment of Russian flotillas in the Greek seas. Their propaganda was based on the plans of Catherine II to create an independent Greek state which would restore the Byzantine Empire and have her grandson, Constantine, as its emperor. The Greek colony in Trieste, which contributed to the funding of the pirate fleet of Lambros Katsonis, sent a delegation to St. Petersbourg in 1790 offering the imperial crown to Constantine, who in fact, was addressed as the Emperor of the Greeks. Lambros Katsonis and his Greek crew, who operated in the Aegean, had taken the plans of Catherine seriously and were disappointed with the Treaty of Iasi (1792) which dashed their hopes. This contributed to the idea that the organization of the struggle for the liberation of the Greek land could not come from anywhere but the Greeks themselves. Indeed, in the famous "revelation" which Lambros Katsonis "with his troops" published in May, 1792 we read, among other things: "...a considerable number of warriors representing the Greek nation, as a spearhead, had always hoped that the peace agreements would provide something for the Greek nation as well so that it might have a small, free land of its own in compensation for the burden it shouldered and is still prepared to bear, but nothing came of it ...thus they decided, leaving behind those distant and boundless lands of hope... to seek vengeance on their enemies without any protectors...".

The repeated disappointments suffered by the Greeks from their participation in the wars of the Christian forces did not prevent the Aegean islanders nor other Greeks from assisting the Russian fleet in its operations in the Aegean from 1806-1807. The idea, though, of the organization of liberation movements by the Greeks themselves had already taken hold of the broader social spectrum. It was expressed most clearly in the revolutionary activities of Regas Pheraios and, later, through the action of the Philiki Etairia which prepared, organized and declared the Greek War of Independence of 1821.

It is not without significance that the members of the Philiki Etairia, in their reasoning for the feasibility of Greek success in the suggested operarions, mentioned the feats of the Greek naval forces under the leadership of Lambros Katsonis and, of course, the endeavors of Regas himself.

THE AEGEAN ISLANDS DURING THE GREEK WAR OF INDEPENDENCE AND UNDER THE FIRST GREEK STATE

The contribution of the Greek naval forces to the Greek War of Independence of 1821 was decisive. This was through the participation of the Aegean seamen, battle-hardened after their experience in military operations, and their considerable merchant fleet (easily transformable into a war fleet in those times). Though the Greek fleet was much smaller than the Ottoman and with far less firepower, it generally accomplished its primary aim, particularly during the first stage of the revolution, and disrupted communications between Asia Minor and Greece in rebellion and, hence the supplying of the Turkish forces on mainland Greece. Through a daring and dextrous use of fire-ships, the Greek forces caused severe damage to the Turkish fleet thus compensating for its enormous superiority in number of ships and firepower. The activity of the Aegean fleet contributed decisively to the tenacity of the Revolution and forced the Great Powers of the period to intervene and bring an end to the unequal struggle. Meanwhile, the slaughter on Chios, the destruction of Kassos and Psara as well as the exodus of those besieged at Mesolongi became universal symbols of the struggle for liberty and strengthened the philhellenic movement among peoples. This had a serious influence on the position European governments took toward the Greek struggle.

The economic contribution of the Aegean islands to the common struggle was also important. According to some estimates, the contributions by three islands alone (Hydra, Spetses and Psara) almost equaled those of the rest of the country to the costs of the revolution.

The above facts as well as the existence of a strong middle class nucleus on the islands, mention of which was made above, determined the role of the Aegean islands. They contributed not only to the political evolution of the struggle itself, from the first moment a problem of authority was broached, but also to the further development of political life in the early years of the free Greek state.

Of course, it is difficult to determine either the ideological stance of each social group in an antiquated Greek society, in which the forces of reform were still weak, or their role in the political conflicts of the Revolution. The ideological contours of these groups were fluid and confused, and their conduct was still burdened by the mentality of older political formulations established during the Turkish occupation. Furthermore, the position of each group was also determined first, by the connection that each one had with the Great Powers of the period, Russia, England and France, which intervened directly or indirectly in the conflict, and, second, by the personal ambitions of its leaders.

Nevertheless, the opposition between the land-owning elders, principally in the Peloponnese, who represented the conservative spirit, and the bourgeois elements who were attempting to secure an influential position in the national leadership can be made out with a good deal of clarity, despite the temporary and opportunistic alliances between the various groups. In this opposition the island element tended to show a greater comprehension of the dual character – national and liberal – of the War of 1821; in some

34

cases the bourgeois elements of the Aegean area supported certain "liberal" movements which later found clearer expression in the period of the Kapodistrias government. Without discounting the importance and the difficulty of the work of Kapodistrias, which constituted the first serious attempt to organize the state, it is also not possible to ignore the dictatorial measures by which he chose or was forced to impose his program. Moreover, it cannot be considered an accident that the most serious opposition to him was centered in the Aegean islands, an opposition that expressed the convergent ideas of the island notables, the liberal intellectuals – among whom was Adamantios Korais, and a large part of the commercial and shipping world. The reports of the Ermoupolitans, the Psarians in Ermoupoli, the people of Mykonos, Paros, Andros, Naxos, Seriphos, Kea, Spetses, Paros and even Crete, who were all against him, kept multiplying, while the large merchants of Syros placed substantial sums at the disposal of anti-Kapodistrian propaganda.

Of course, the interests of the large shipowners on the islands as well as the notables had a part in this movement, as did the instigations of the English and the French. The fact nonetheless, that there was such an agreement amongst heterogenous elements shows that the liberal spirit, even if entangled in a confused ideological context did find some social grounding in the bourgeois elements, one of the most important centers of which were the Greek islands in the Aegean.

The establishment of the Greek State in 1832 left the largest part of the Aegean area outside its borders. Of the rebelling Aegean islands, none were included within the new state except Euboea, the northern Sporades and the Cyclades. Only Samos, which kept up its struggle till the end of the Revolution, was declared a semi-autonomous hegemony with a Christian leader appointed by the Sultan, a regime imposed, despite the resistance of the Samians, by the intervention of the Turkish fleet (1834). In 1831, Crete was ceded by the Sultan to Muhammed Ali of Egypt and remained under Egyptian rule till 1840, returning to Ottoman rule after the London Protocol, in January 1841.

It would take nearly a century of further struggle to liberate the rest of the Aegean islands, as well as the greater Aegean area, an inseparable part of the Greek State. It required a series of revolts by the Cretan people (1858, 1862 and 1866) for Crete to obtain a somewhat more privileged position, and new uprisings in 1896 and 1897 before it was declared an autonomous regime under the suzerainty of the Sultan. Finally, it took the Revolt of Therissos in Crete (1905) and the Balkan Wars of 1912-1913 for Greek suzerainty to be recognized in Crete, Macedonia, Thrace and the Greek islands of the eastern Mediterranean, except for the Dodecanese which remained under Italian occupation until 1947, and Imbros and Tenedos which remained part of Turkey.

The entire Greek population of the Aegean area, from those on the Aegean islands and the areas surrounding the Aegean in Europe and Asia Minor to the solid cohesive Greek element on Cyprus, an extension of the Aegean and an inseparable part of the Greek nation for centuries, constituted, along with the Greeks of the Diaspora, one of the main parameters in Greek history. Always in a close relationship with the population of the Greek State, as established at any given time and in a functional interdependence with it, the population of the Aegean had a major influence on its economic course and consequently the development of its social structures. In short , it determined to a large extent the internal and external policies of the Greek State and the formation of the ideological trends of modern Greece.

Indeed, the Greek element that remained within the Ottoman Empire and the most dynamic part of which lived in the broader Aegean area, did not cease its economic and

35

34. *The seal of the Philiki Etaireia.*

35. *Emmanouil Xanthos. One of the three founders of the Philiki Etaireia, from Patmos (1772-1852).*

36. *Compass of Andreas Miaoulis. Athens, Benaki Museum.*

37. *Engraving by V. Katraki.*

intellectual development even after the brief pause of the Greek Revolution. It became a formidable economic force working with the western powers in their continually growing economic penetration into the East and in many instances became the intermediary for the capitalistic penetration of the region. The role of the Greek element was important in shipping, trade and banking enterprises. Constantinople, Smyrna and Thessaloniki continued to be prominent economic centers in the eastern Mediterranean during the 19th century while the Greek economic circles with their accumulated capital had a direct relationship to the corresponding capitalists of the Diaspora in the Greek colonies of the Balkans, Russia, Egypt and Western Europe. These same circles were at the root of the economic development of the small Greek State. The Aegean would play, for yet another time in the history of the Greeks, its intermediary, connecting role between East and West. It would continue to be a link uniting the Hellenic world of the Balkan North and the East with their main Greek body.

Ermoupoli in Syros, for example, began to develop in 1822 with emigrants from Chios and Psara, and, in 1828 it numbered 13,800 inhabitants. By the middle of the 19th century, it had become one of the three important urban centers of the Greek Kingdom (along with Piraeus and Patras). Right in the center of the Aegean, Ermoupoli became the crossroads of the sea routes connecting Constantinople, Smyrna and Thessaloniki with the Black Sea and the harbors of the western Mediterranean and Western Europe. The merchants of Chios, who had settled here and were connected by kinship ties to the Greek merchants of the Diaspora (in London, Marseilles, Amsterdam, Trieste and Odessa), became the intermediaries in the exchanges between East and West. They transformed this island town into "a kind of warehouse, the commercial agency of the eastern Mediterranean" and the distribution center for the industrial products imported from the West as well as a collection point for the export of agricultural products and raw materials.

The first attempts at the founding of "industrial" enterprises in the Greek State took place in the Aegean area, in Hydra, Andros, Syros and, later, Piraeus. The initiative was again taken by the Chiotes. Ermoupoli played a leading role here, too. Shipbuilding enterprises, the first large tanneries, spinning-mills and flour mills were established here. Syros also provided the impetus for the first structural transformations of the Greek economy and the first attempts at modernizing it through the gradual introduction of the capitalist system of western economic centers, and consequently the gradual, if slow, re-structuring of Greek society, carried out in tandem with the course of liberal political movements of an bourgeois character both in Greece and the Hellenic areas of the Ottoman Empire within the framework of communal self-government and the functioning of the Orthodox Patriarchate.

36

This brief outline of the role of the Aegean area down through the centuries shows, we hope, the prime importance of this area for the entire Greek nation. The Aegean was the starting point for its cultural life and each of its cultural creations and was a prime contributor to the formation of the Greek ethnic notion and its subsequent constitution into a proper nation, in the present sense of the word. Despite the vicissitudes of the centuries acted out at this crossroads of peoples and civilizations, the Aegean unalterably remained linked with its main Greek body and was always its geographical continuation. But in many cases it was, indeed, the vital center of economic, social and political life and the connecting link between the various sections of the Greek nation which, through historical circumstance, were spread out to the North, East and West.

It took till the middle of the 20th century, with the annexation of the Dodecanese by Greece (Treaty of Paris, 1947) for a large part of the Greek quest to be realized, something that for centuries had constituted the main pursuit of Greeks everywhere: the coincidence of ethnic and state borders. Only, this event, definitive for Greek history and ideology, occurred after the Hellenic world was sharply reduced by the uprooting of approximately one and a half million Greeks, living in the lands of the Ottoman Empire, from their paternal hearths.

37

38

38. *"The shelling of the Turkish frigate by Papanikolis" by K. Volanakis. Oil on canvas, 1882. Pireaus, Hellenic Maritime Museum.*

39

40

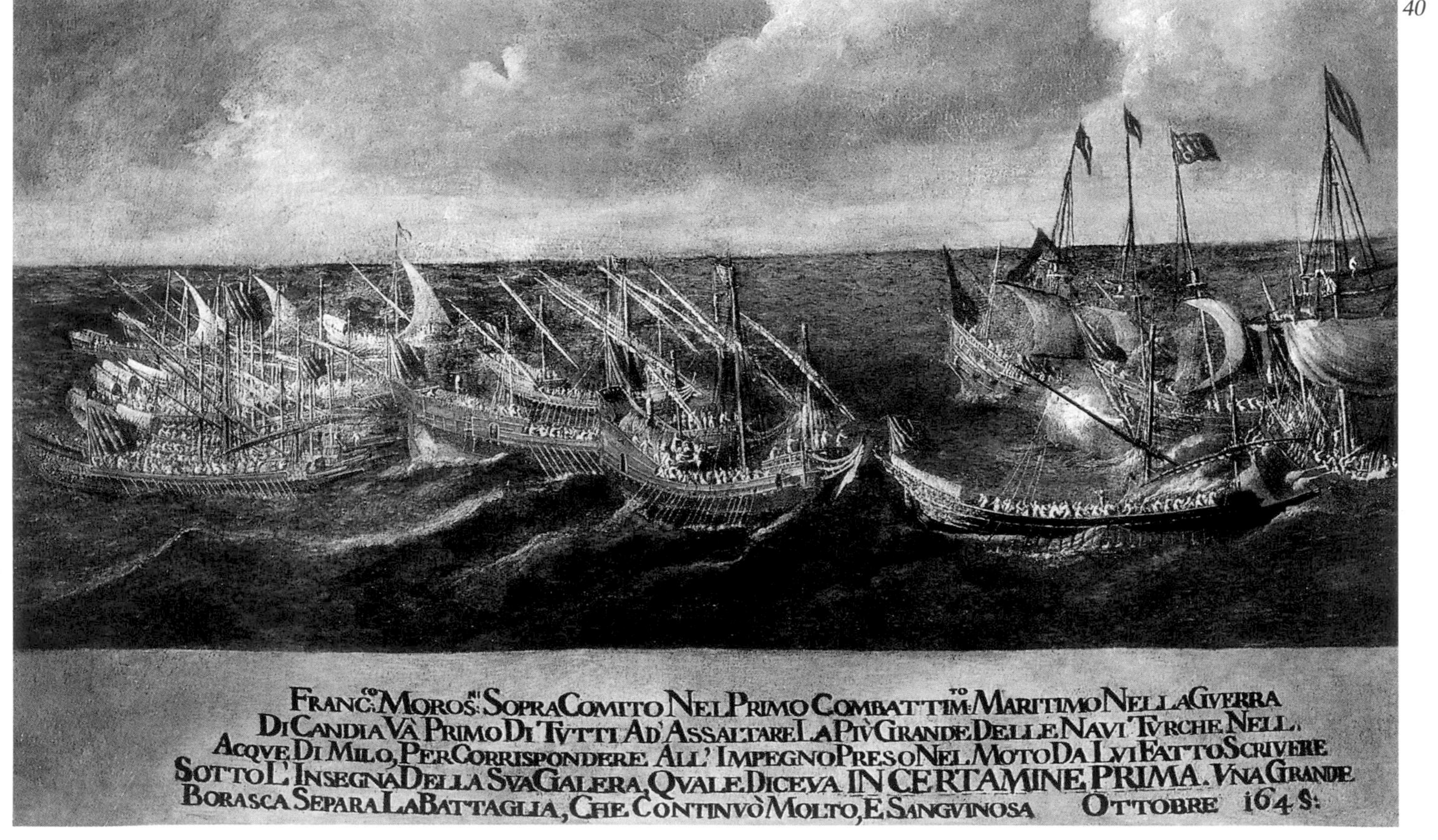

39. The battle of Samos. April 1660. Engraving. Venice, Correr Museum.

40. Naval battle of Milos. October 1645. Engraving. Venice, Correr Museum.

41

42

41. Naval battle of Tenedos. 9-10 November 1882. Colored lithograph by Johann Lorenz Rugendas. Athens, Benaki Museum.

42. The naval battle of Samos in the straits of Mycale. Water color on paper, mid - 19th century. Athens, Benaki Museum.

43

43. Map of the Archipelago and Greece by F. de Wit, Amsterdam 1680. Athens, War Museum.

MAR de MARMORA
MARE
ÆGÆUM
Hodie
ARCHIPELAGO
MARE DE CANDIA
CANDIA REGNUM
TERRANEUM
ASIÆ
PROPRIÆ
PARS
SINUS STRYMONICUS
Golfo di Contessa
PELAGICUS SINUS
SINGITICUS SINUS
Golfo de Monte Santo
TROIA
REGNUM
OLYMPENI
IONIA
CARIA
DORIS
ICARIUM MARE
CYCLADES Insulæ
MIRTOUM MARE
Sporades insulæ
CARPATHIUM MARE
RHODIENSE PELAGUS
TRIOPIUM MARE
ARGOLICUS SINUS Hodie Golfo di Napoli
LACONICUS SINUS Hodie Golfo di Colochina
SARONICUM MARE
EUBŒA Ins.
NEGROPONTE
Stalimene
Samandrachi I.
Lembro I.
Tenedo I.
Milliaria Germanica 15 in uno gradu
Milliaria Gallica sive Horæ itineris
Milliaria Italica 60 in uno gradu

44

44. *"Sea Battles of the Greeks" by D. Zographos – I. Makrygiannis. Water color on paper. Athens, Gennadios Library.*

45

45. The Greek fleet during the time of King George I. Folk engraving. Athens, National Historical Museum.

46. Nautical Atlas, "The Aegean Islands" by Batista Anieze. Painting on parchment, 1553. Venice, Correr Museum.

MACEDONIA
GRAECIA
MARE AEGAEVM
ASIA PROPIA
PELOPONESVS NVNC MOREA

MANOLIS ANDRONICOS

The contribution of the Aegean islands to the artistic development of the ancient world

Translated by Philip Ramp

1. Female Cycladic figurine. Athens, Museum of Cycladic Art (N.P. Goulandris Collection).

When one glances at a map of the ancient Greek world it is not difficult to verify that most of the important Greek towns were on the coast or only a very short distance from the sea. If the Greek world is observed from another angle, in quest of its large centers of intellectual and artistic development, one will be led to the same result. All the great, artistic centers were located in the large, naval towns. During the early centuries of Greek history the most vigorous creative forces were concentrated in Athens and Corinth, Aegina and the Cyclades, in Samos, Chios, Rhodes, Miletus and Ephesus.

But to conclude that the cultural development of the Greek world was primarily connected to the sea would be a hasty over-simplification. Still, it would be equally unjustified to deny the crucial and decisive importance of the sea in the formation of its economic, political and social character. The Aegean Sea with its archipelago of islands was, for the Greeks, the sea which united them and unlimited communication was facilitated by its open lanes. From mainland Greece to the shores of Ionia where the first Greeks, the Ionians, settled at the end of the second millenium B.C. (1100-1050 B.C.), the various sized islands of the Aegean constituted the bridge which allowed for the growth of close economic, political and cultural relations among the Ionians of the "other shore" who kept the ancient name of their race and bestowed it on their new homeland, Ionia. Thus, when we speak of the art of the Aegean, we are essentially talking about the art of the Ionian world which flourished both in the large towns of Asia Minor – Ephesus, Miletus, Smyrna, etc.–, and on the Aegean islands.

In this text we will limit ourselves to a brief account of artistic creation on the Aegean islands, excluding somewhat arbitrarily the creations of the large Ionian centers on the coast of Asia Minor. But we must not permit ourselves to forget that the art of the large islands of the eastern Aegean, Samos and Chios for example, had a close and direct relationship to the art of the coasts opposite, particularly during the Archaic period (7th and 6th century B.C.).

Just as European poetry began with a sublime creation, the Homeric epics, so did the European plastic arts have a brilliant advent: the pure and exquisite Cycladic figurines. It is no coincidence that poetry and the plastic arts were born under the Aegean sun, on that radiant sea, in the land where the god of light and music, Apollo, was born.

At the beginning of the third millenium B.C. a great revolution with enormous consequences occurred in the East; people managed to smelt the natural metallic ores which contained copper and at the same time created the large, densely populated city-states and invented writing. The use of metal passed almost immediately into the Aegean area and thus the Bronze Age began throughout nearly all of Greece. The new conditions favored the islands and the coasts and thus the "Proto-Cycladic" civilization of undreamed of brilliance and artistic wealth arose in the Cyclades. The light of a pure white stone which glorified Greece made the area sparkle. Marble, abundant in the Cyclades, crystal-like in its texture, but without the repellent hardness of the stone worked by other peoples, was a challenge to the Cycladians who worked it masterfully. Marble vases with daring and elegant shapes bear witness to the craftsmanship of the artists as well as the high cultural level of the society which used them. But figurine sculpture is where Cycladic art attained its finest, most peerless creations. There are countless marble figurines which depict a nude woman (ill. 1) with her arms resting on her belly; only the breasts and the nose are rendered plastically; the other characteristics, such as the eyes and the mouth, must have been painted on. Nevertheless, their importance for the history of art would have been limited if the artists had rendered this mysterious, female figure

2

2. Kimolos, violin-shaped Cycladic figurine. Athens, National Archeological Museum.

(Mother Earth?) only as a small figurine. But a few of the more endowed artists went on to works large in size (ills. 12, 14, 19) and superb in their plastic elaboration. The large figurine from Amorgos (ill. 15), practically life-size, is a masterpiece of monumental sculpture. The lucid form and the vibrant surface of the marble captivate the modern viewer who has studied the creations of abstract art. But besides the sensitivity of the craftsmanship, the Cycladic artists acquired remarkable wisdom and a synthetic view of volumes, as is witnessed by the astonishing harpist (ill. 16) with the complex rhythm of the modeling and the superb exploitation of the curve in the movement of the limbs and the harp. The structure rivals the sensitive treatment of the marble surface and confirms that the simple, but no less wise or captivating rendering of the flute-player (ill. 17) in another figurine was not a chance achievement, but the successful adaptation of artistic sensitivity, long-term experience and persistent endeavor.

Formerly, certain archeologists maintained the point of view that Cycladic civilization declined decisively at the end of the third millenium. However, archeological research has uncovered significant remains which bear witness not to decline, but to a fundamental transformation which was caused by the Minoan thalassocracy in the middle of the second millenium (around 1600 B.C.). This has been proved beyond all doubt by the excavations on Kea, but even more by the astonishing finds from the excavations on Thera (Santorini) which have given us some of the most spectacular wall paintings of the Minoan period. The wall painting of Spring (ill. 20) displays the deep-pitched, chromatic harmony of the rocks and the sensitivity of the supple stalks of the lilies with the crimson petals of the flowers and the swallows weaving drunkenly through all this beauty. Next to this lyrical scene we have the picture of a boxing match between two children (ill. 22), with their delightful seriousness, their enchanting glance and their wavy locks of hair and the figure of the island fisherman (ill. 23) with his two strings of fish, a vivid, Aegean form which all testify to the artistic skill of the Minoan painters on Santorini. Finally, there is the many-figured composition of the naval campaign (ill. 21) where the miniature technique is used to render the "historical" narration. A fleet composed of seven, large ships and many smaller vessels is sailing toward a well-built town, where a host of human figures are moving about. Two more towns are depicted at other points of the wall painting with warriors, and others, who appear to have drowned in the sea. Through this wall painting we have gained not simply another monument of Minoan painting but an unexpected aspect of this great art has been opened up to us which, moreover, is the first, radiant depiction of the Aegean world.

The centuries which followed were marked by the domination of the Mycenaean world. The collapse of the Mycenaean centers set the Greek world on a new course which was characterized by the creation of independent city-states throughout greater Greece. These new states had already been established by the middle of the 8th century B.C. and their creative presence was strongly felt by the end of that century and the beginning of the following one. The development of the city-states gave rise to material comfort and people acquired an awareness of their distinctive personality. An expression of this fundamental change is the birth of lyric poetry and the creation of large, permanent works, which satisfied the people's ambitions. During these years great Greek sculpture and monumental, stone temples were erected while mythology supplied inexhaustible material that would nourish vase painting for centuries. During these early years of Greek history, the Aegean islands flourished economically and culturally. Monumental sculpture would find in their soil the noblest material for the moulding of its forms: marble. From the veins of the insular earth was extracted what was needed and was given human form, the same form that was given to their gods. The first morphoplastic intervention occurred here, in the marble quarry itself, under the light of the sun, next to the Aegean sea. An imposing example of this work is the colossal statue of a bearded man (11 meters high), the bearded Dionysos (ill. 3), who is still lying in his marble womb in the village Apollonas on Naxos, as well as another unfinished colossal *kouros* (5.5 m. high) which is located in the village Flerio on the same island.

Several of the earliest dedicatory offerings on Delos also come from Naxos: the female statue that was offered by Nikandre (ill. 24), the colossal *kouros* which was offered by the sculptor Euthykartides (only the base survives) and the marvelous colossus which the Naxians offered to Apollo, only fragments of which are left though they are enough to allow us to appreciate both its size and its art. It is also significant that Nikandre and Euthykartides were among the first who carved their names on their offerings, inscribing their titles with obvious pride: the paternal name and the name of the former's husband while the latter informs us that he was the creator of what he was offering. These offerings are only a few of the archeological indications which testify to the dominance of Naxos in the Aegean and its power on the sacred island of Apollo. The imposing lions (ill. 26) which rise up next to the sacred lake can be added to these. Their austere profile and their structure, which is accentuated to the front and upwards, provoke feelings of wonder and awe in a viewer. This feeling is augmented by their number (at least nine). The remains of two impressive, archaic buildings that were erected by Naxians, the Naxos house and the Naxos stoa, are also to be found on Delos. Moreover, at the other large temple of Apollo, in Delphi, the inhabitants of Naxos erected the magnificent Sphinx on an imposing Ionic column; it still survives (ill. 25) and can be admired in the Museum. This is also a work of early Archaic art from the Naxian workshop and is another example of the economic power and the artistic activity of the island.

But the artistic creation of the island spread far beyond its own boundaries; a series of brilliant Archaic *kouroi*, which were found on Naxos itself as well as on Delos, Milos and, most importantly, in the Boeotian temple of Apollo at Ptoon, are works from the Naxian workshop and make it possible for us to affirm the special characteristics of its art, not to mention the wealth of its production. The oldest *kouros* at Ptoon and a head from Naxos, which are now in the Museum of Copenhagen, are from the beginning of

3

3. Naxos. Colossal statue of Dionysos in the village of Apollona.

the series and belong to the early 6th century B.C. The second *kouros* at Ptoon (ill. 4) and the *kouros* from Naxos in the Berlin Museum must be dated to the second quarter of the century (575-550 B.C.). The workshop carried on and reached its peak in approximately the middle of the century with a third *kouros* from Ptoon in the Thebes Museum and the *kouros* of Milos in the National Archeological Museum of Athens (ill. 28). In all of these the flesh has a certain delicacy, the skin is smooth and the curves have a calm and sweet sensitivity. The characteristic purity of the outline and the lack of animation in the pose, the love of linear rendering and the measured corporeality, which puts a limit on fleshly luxuriance, allows us to distinguish this workshop and to differentiate it from the Parian, with its fuller and more voluptuous rendering of the body. In short, there is an abundance of grace and sensitivity and a lack of dynamism and vigor.

Fewer early Archaic works have come down to us from the neighboring Parian workshop; they come from Paros itself and from the islands of Santorini, Thasos (Parian colony) and Siphnos. Other Aegean islands also had noteworthy artistic activity during the early Archaic period, such as Chios. Ancient sources inform us that sculptors with an uninterrupted family tradition lived and worked on this island. The inscribed base of the statue that was found on Delos and bears the name of the sculptor Archermos was thought to have belonged to the figure of a running Nike (ill. 29) which was found near the base. Today, this hypothesis is no longer valid; nevertheless, the Nike (or Artemis, as some others maintain) is attributed to the workshop of Chios and bears witness to a splendid feel for the flesh, a decorative and voluptuous shaping of the hair and a supple and expressive curvature of the folds and the outlines. The renowned sculptors Voupalos and Athenis, who lived in the second half of the 6th century B.C., were the children of Archermos.

But it is worth stopping at Samos more than all the other islands because during the 7th and 6th century B.C. it experienced unique prosperity and power, justifying its fame as a thalassocracy. Its ships and its sailors, daring men, roamed the sea from end to end in quest of sources of wealth for trade. One of them, Kolaios, reaching the Pillars of Hercules, the present Gibraltar, in 638 B.C. went beyond reaching Tartessos in the Gulf of Gadiz, a region with rich silver mines. The profits from the silver which was brought back to Samos must have been enormous because, as Herodotus tells us, with their "tithe", which was six talents, they made an enormous bronze krater decorated with the heads of gryphons which they dedicated to the famed temple on the island, the Heraion. They decorated the krater with three, bronze, kneeling colossuses which were about 3.5 m. high (seven cubits). Such a work must have been not only an achievement of technology, but a marvelous work of art if we can judge by the gryphon heads (ill. 31) many of which have been found in the Heraion of Samos.

The temple of Hera on Samos has an exceedingly long history, but it reached its peak during the two centuries of the Archaic period (7th-6th century B.C.). By the beginning of the 8th century the first temple of Hera had been built next to the sacred willow where there had only been an altar before then. When this was destroyed, the Samians built a second one on the same site, in the middle of the 7th century, where the first anthropomorphic statue of Hera was placed. Here, for the first time, we find the clear and practically complete form of a Greek temple, as it is enclosed by a "pteron", a colonnade which has 6 columns on the narrow side and 18 on the wide. A second row of columns was placed on the east side of the entrance, a peculiarity which all the large, Ionian temples would subsequently copy. But the temple of Samos had another important contribution to make to the history of Greek architecture. A little after the middle of the 7th century the "sacred sanctuary" of Hera was surrounded by a stone enclosure

4

4. Kouros from Ptoon. Athens, National Archeological Museum.

and the "propyleum" (entrance) of the sanctuary was built, an architectural element that would be developed by Greek architects into a glorious monument. During the same period an enormous stoa was built next to the temple, the oldest Greek stoa, 69.35 m. long and 5.91 m. wide. This architectural form, the stoa, was a valuable invention and in time became the most common and indispensable feature of every Greek temple and every agora, till at a certain moment it would give its name to one of the most famous philosophical schools, the "Stoa" (the Stoic philosophers as we call them).

The Heraion achieved its greatest glory in the middle of the 6th century B.C. when the power and the wealth of Samos reached their peak. Large and magnificent works were built by "wise" artists, as the ancients called them. The names of two famous craftsmen, Rhoecus and Theodoros, renowned throughout Antiquity are connected with the third temple of Hera, which was built in 570-540 B.C. Architects, sculptors, coppersmiths and engineers, they not only created famous works, but also came up with, for the period, noteworthy solutions to technical problems such as, for example, the construction of buildings on swampy land and the casting of bronze statues that were not solid but hollow in the middle ("cire-perdue"), a technique which opened the way for the construction of large, bronze statues. The third Heraion is their work and constituted, in both size and technique, one of the first truly outstanding architectural achievements of the ancient world. Its 104 columns, which must have been about 18 m. high, surrounded the enormous cella which was divided into three aisles. The fame of its builders travelled far and wide and thus when the Ephesians decided to build the enormous temple of Artemis, although they had their own renowned architects, they called on Theodoros as a technical consultant, as it were. This magnificent structure was destroyed almost immediately after it was completed, cause unknown, when the rule of Samos was assumed by the famous tyrant Polycrates (538-522 B.C.) who became legendary for his abilities, his power and his creative activity particularly in the construction of large, public works such as, for example, the harbor of Samos and the famous Eupalinus tunnel, approximately 1250 m. long, which was dug into the mountain to supply the town with water. He himself began the construction of a fourth temple of Hera, the remains of which still survive today (ill. 30). The experience he gained from the two previous temples in Ionia, the Heraion and the temple of Artemis in Ephesus, led to brilliant results. Its dimensions were practically the same as the temple of Artemis (112.50×55.16 m.) and it was dipteral with three rows of columns on the narrow sides, but we would say that it definitely surpassed the former in terms of unity of design and the form of the architectural members. A deep pronaos, divided into three aisles, led to an enormous cella. Sculpted friezes appear to have decorated the pronaos and the walls of the cella. Nevertheless, it proved impossible to complete the grandiose design of Polycrates within the time frame of his brief rule. Thus, the work was carried on to the end of the 4th century B.C.

This architectural activity on Samos competed most brilliantly with the sculptural creation on the island. Though the construction of the temples and other structures was owed to the care of the state, the many, marvelous sculptures that have survived are works that the pious and, of course, wealthy dedicators wanted to offer to the sanctuary, as is confirmed by the dedicatory inscriptions which record their names with pride. Ischis, Chiramyes, Leukios and Aiakes are the names of a few of these which have survived on the works that were erected in the sanctuary; along with them is the end of a name "...rchis" who dedicated one of the most respected ensemble of statues from the Archaic periods to Hera.

"Ischis dedicated the Risios" states the inscription engraved on the left thigh of a

5

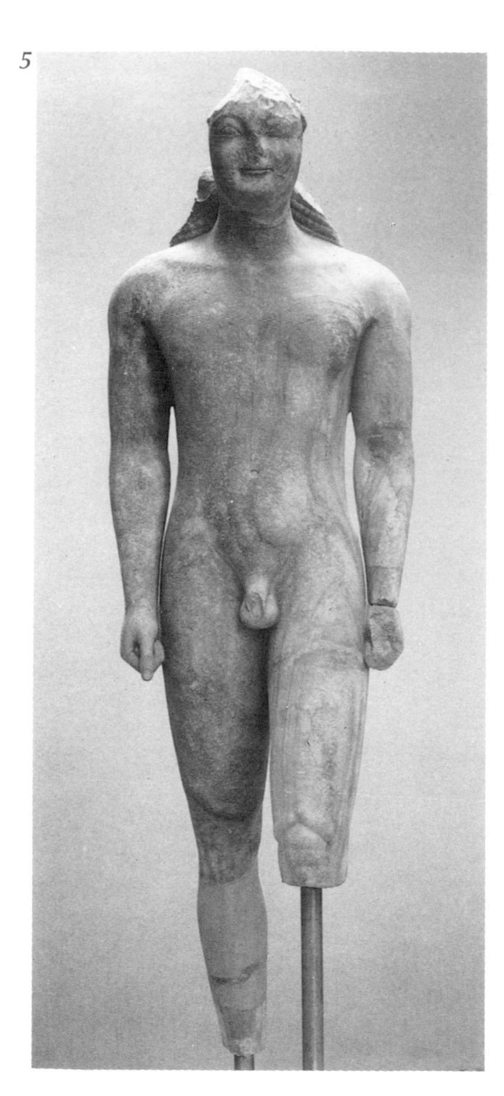

5. Samos. *Colossal* kouros.

colossal statue from the beginning of the 6th century B.C. which was found in the temple of Hera in Samos in 1974, where two parts of the left arm of a similar statue had also been found. When in 1980 German archeologists discovered the astonishing torso of an early Archaic *kouros* they had no trouble in determining that both the thigh and the arm belonged to it. Even though there is enough of the torso left for us to admire the superb art of this sculpture the lack of a head takes away a part of the satisfaction one feels in front of the "ultimate worth" shown by the form of the face. But fortune was to reward the excavators and so four years later they also found the head. Thus today in Samos this extremely beautiful youth lifts up its imposing torso (over 5.50 m. high) with its delicately fashioned flesh, the lyrical curves of the volumes of its body, moulded with extreme sensitivity, along with its luxuriant hair, divided into two with harmoniously shaped curls descending to the nape of the neck and its powerful shoulders. Together with its slightly older brothers in Sounion it now lends its charming Ionian grace and reminds us of the shores where Sappho and Alkaeus, Anacreon and Ivykos sang, the first lyric poets of Greece and, of course, Europe.

During the same period (1984) German archeologists also discovered a headless female statue with the inscription "Chiramyes dedicated this statue to Hera". And of course this immediately brought to mind the famous statue which had been found 200 m. further on and is known as the "Hera of Chiramyes", in the Louvre (ill. 32). It is exactly the same size, the inscription is identical and the form the same, with slight variations. This also brought to mind the third dedication of Chiramyes, the slightly smaller *kore* in the Museum of Berlin with the hare in her hand and the piece of a colossal *kouros* which bears the ending of the name of the dedicator "...myes". The *kores* of Chiramyes are the brilliant creations of a Samian artist who worked before the middle of the 6th century B.C. The dominance of the ripe curve and the sensitive elements of the torso with the countless, carefully made folds which are cut off at the top by the oblique straps of the tunic, terminating in the curved swell of the frontal aspect, the light but at the same time perceptible lifting of the breast, the folding of the left arm on the chest, all confirm the creator's desire for an artistic rendering and his highly sensitive perceptions concerning a pleasingly attired, female body.

A unique dedication was found in the sanctuary of Hera, consisting of six figures erected on a common base (ill. 7). This ensemble was dedicated by someone of whom only the end of his name has survived: "...rchis" and "...rchis dedicated to Hera". (Originally the name was read "...oche" and the reclining figure was thought to be female. Even though I am not certain about the reading of the figure as male, I will stick to the more recent interpretation). The statue of the same person who depicted him reclining was on the right side of the base. On the left end was the statue of Phileia, seated and an inscription with the name of the sculptor: "Geneleos made us". In the middle are the standing figures of Ornithe (ill. 6) and Philippe. (The other two figures have not been found). The seated figure of Phileia in comparison with other seated figures of the period, but above all the two erect figures, testify to the daring conception and the incomparable technical dexterity of the sculptural rendering of the volumes and the folds and confirm that Geneleos was both a creator of a high, artistic level and an inspired sculptor. Although he must not have been separated by a great interval from his fellow artist who worked on the Chiramyes dedications, he invented new, fertile solutions to the rendering of a female statue, which would open up new vistas in Greek sculpture.

All these works bear witness to the material prosperity and, above all, the great artistic activity on the Aegean islands during the Archaic period. What these works attest to is supplemented in a magnificent way by a monument which the inhabitants of Siphnos

6

6. *Samos. Ornithe from the sculptural ensemble of Geneleos. Berlin, Pergamon Museum.*

dedicated to the Sanctuary of Apollo at Delphi. This is the "Treasury of the Siphnians" which was built just before 525 B.C. by a tithe from the gold mines which had brought great wealth to this Cycladic island. It was a small, temple-shaped structure (8.55×6.14 m.) made of dazzling Parian marble. It was not the structure that was famous in Antiquity and constitutes for us a unique monument, but rather its sculptural decoration, lavish and brilliant at one and the same time. The dominance of sculpture reaches an extreme point in this monument as even the architectural members are replaced by statues. Thus, between the pilasters for the entrance, two *kores* are found instead of columns (ill. 33); they support the epistyle, a solution which would have its supreme expression in the prostasis of the *kores* (Caryatids) in the Athens Erechteion.

Above the epistyle the building has a magnificent frieze on all four sides while one of the two pediments has preserved its sculpture which depicts a charming and typical Delphic myth: Hercules attempting to take the Delphic tripod when Pythia refused him an oracle. Athena is depicted on the pediment between Hercules and Apollo trying to prevent them from coming to blows; Hercules has already taken the tripod while Apollo is trying to get it back from him. The sculptural decoration of the frieze is exceptional; more than half of it has survived and we can distinguish the hands of two artists; one worked on the west and south sides where the judgement of Paris and the abduction of the daughters of Leukippos by the Dioskouri is depicted and the other on the east and north side which is the best preserved, practically its entire length being intact.

The east frieze, which has the Trojan War as its subject, is divided into two parts: to the left (ill. 36) are gathered the gods who are on the side of the Trojans, that is, Ares, Aphrodite, Artemis and Apollo; between them and the "philhellenic" gods, Athena, Hera and perhaps Demeter, is Zeus. A battle between Greeks and Trojans (ill. 34) is depicted in the right section: Aeneias and Hector on the one side, Menelaos and Ajax on the other are battling above a dead warrior, probably Sarpidon; on the right end Nestor is making signs to his fellow warriors.

On the north side (ills. 35, 37-39) the gods are struggling against the Giants (*Gigantomachia*) who are attacking from the right and are presented as heavily armed with hel-

7

7. Samos. Heraion. The sculptural ensemble of Geneleos.

mets and shields and fighting with spears, swords and stones. On the left end, Hephestus, wearing the short tunic of the craftsman, is using his bellows to prepare his volcanic bombs; in front of him are two goddesses and opposite two giants with raised spears. On the second plane is Hercules with Cybele before him on a chariot being pulled by lions which are also attacking the Giants. We can even make out Apollo and Artemis shooting arrows at their opponents. In the middle is Zeus with his chariot; then Hera standing on top of a fallen giant, Athena, Ares, and Hermes wearing the conical hat of the shepherds of Arcadia and finally Poseidon and Amphitrite.

The difference between the sculptures on the north and east side from those on the south and west side is obvious. The artist of the *Gigantomachia* and the battle between Greeks and Trojans was most probably from Paros and must have been one of the greatest creators of his time, commanding a lofty and daring inspiration, and awareness of the difficult problems of relief and unique technical dexterity. It is sufficient if we note the exceptional rendering of the repeated levels, which often intermesh but can always be clearly distinguished. The force of the intermeshing is rendered with impressive vigor, but without detracting from the clarity of the sculpted shapes and the immediately perceived rhythm which moves us from left to right and then brings us back again with astonishing dexterity through the reversed course of the wave-like moulding.

The Treasury of the Siphnians constitutes yet one more confirmation of the artistic flourishing of the Aegean islands in the Archaic period, when the sea lanes were the great source of wealth and economic development. The radiance of the art of the Aegean islands spread throughout the area, even to the shores of northern Greece. In Thasos, where the Parians arrived in the 7th century B.C., archeological excavations have uncovered splendid monuments from the Archaic period which affirm that this island in the northern Aegean experienced a long period of flourishing, both economically and artistically. The early colossal *kouros* – Ram-bearer (ill. 40) and the mature, Archaic reliefs which decorated the civic buildings (ills. 41, 42), even the gates of the town's wall, also demonstrate that this distant island marched in step with its more southern brothers.

But the art of the Ionian islands of the Aegean also left its marks, some of them quite brilliant, on the northern coasts of the Aegean where the first Greek settlers founded their colonies at critical sites starting in the 7th century. The architectural members of Ionian structures which have been found at Neapolis (Kavala) and at Thermi (Thessaloniki), hold their own with the most important monuments of the Ionian area not only in terms of their imposing size but also their superb artistic quality. Archeological exavations over the past few years have offered us a continually growing number of elements demonstrating the close relationship between the entire area of northern Greece and Ionia and the Aegean islands in particular.

After the Persian Wars (490-479 B.C.) the Aegean islands were finally freed from the Persian threat, but were also incorporated into the Athenian alliance which exercized a determinative influence on their political, economic and intellectual life till in the end they were absorbed by the common artistic language which bore the stamp of Athens. Nevertheless, during the 5th century the character of the art from the islands was still very distinct and good fortune has brought several exceptional works from this time down to us. The "disc of Milos" occupies a special place among them (ill. 9); it is a head of a goddess in relief on a circular piece of marble which must be dated to around 460 B.C. "The main representation within this circle was the head which has survived... Today, without the dedicatory inscription and the symbol, which have been lost, we cannot be certain of the goddess' name, but can only infer the general area to which she belongs; an important local Nymph or Kore (Persephone) or Artemis or, most likely of

8

8. Ionic column capitals, archaic period. Thessaloniki, Archeological Museum.

9

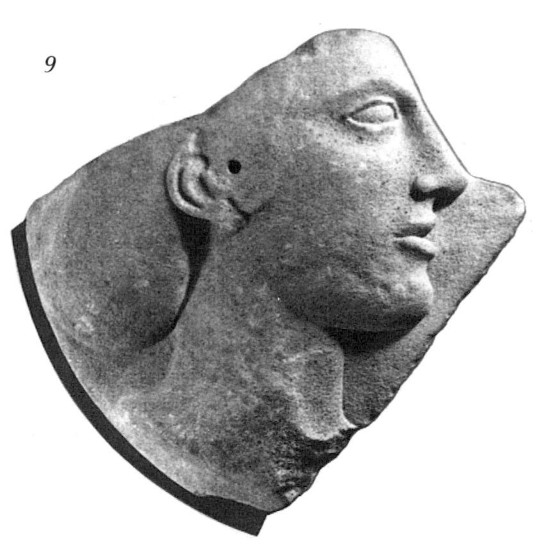

9. The disc of Milos. Athens, National Archeological Museum.

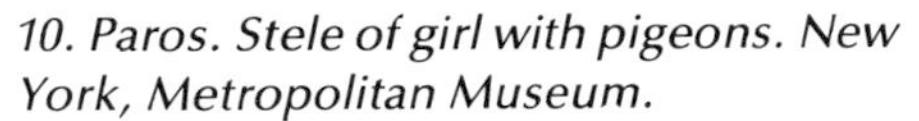

10. Paros. Stele of girl with pigeons. New York, Metropolitan Museum.

10

all, Aphrodite... the island sculptor of the relief... knew the morphological values of the curved and the rounded shape and he used them with feeling for the design and the sculptural expression of the figure, casting within their soft grace the stability of the straight line and the flat surface" (Ch. Karouzos). Archeologists believe that the creator of this masterpiece must have been from Paros.

The artists of a series of funerary steles from the 5th century B.C., which were found on the same island as well as in other parts of Greece, must also have been Parians. Three of them depict young girls with a simple, sleeveless peplos falling in sensitive folds, thus creating a sculptural symphony with infinite harmonic resonances. The one, known as the "Stele Giustiniani" is 1.43 m. high and is today in the Berlin Museum. The form of the second, smaller stele (0.80 m. high) (ill. 10), in the Metropolitan Museum of New York, is much more tender. In this one the little girl is looking sadly at the two pigeons she is holding in her hands. The *kore* in the third stele has her head bent even more (ill. 43) and is also holding one pigeon by its wings. The last one (1.55 m. high) was recently found in Nea Callicrateia, in Chalcidice, and ornaments the Museum of Thessaloniki.

Funerary steles from the early Classic period which bear witness to the high level of their art have also been found on many other Aegean islands. Nearly all the islands from Samos to Thasos and from Skyros to Nisyros and Kythnos can be represented in one panorama of sculptural production from Classical times. Though it is impossible for us to dwell on details in this brief overview, it would be unjust not to mention the masterly stele of two women, Crito and Timarista (ill. 11) in the Museum of Rhodes; it is from the late years of the 5th century B.C., and stands apart for its size (2 m. high). The influences of Attic art are now very evident, but the artistic world on the islands still had its own distinctive style, if not in the sculptural workmanship itself, at least in the iconographic formulation and the ethos of the figures. The mature Timarista is standing to the right in a frontal position turning her head to the young Crito who is depicted from the side leaning on the shoulder of the former. The delicate folds of the tunics and the heavier and more impressive ones on the himation of the young *kore* and the peplos of the mature woman compose a rich, harmonic concordance which testify to the unbelievable accomplishments of this century, which is coming to its end.

Few works from the 4th century B.C. have come down to us from the Greek islands. However, during that century one of the greatest creators of the ancient Greek world would appear in Paros: Scopas, son of the sculptor Aristandros. His creative activity spread over all of Greece, from the Peloponnese to Athens and from Boeotia to the shores of Asia Minor.

A local Greek-nurtured dynasty held power on the southeastern end of Asia Minor, at Caria in Halicarnassus, the homeland of Herodotus. Mausolus and his sister and wife Artemisia ruled it from 377 B.C. When the former died, in 353 B.C., Artemisia entrusted to two architects and four sculptors, all Greeks of course, the building of his monumental sepulchre. Two years later she also died but the work was completed and has remained in the memories of people forever, indeed, giving its name –Mausoleum– to every kind of imposing tomb monument and was considered by the people of that period to be one of the seven wonders of the world. Scopas also worked on this monument, along with Leocharis, Bryaxis and Timotheus. When Scopas and his craftsmen finished he went to Tegea where he undertook the building of the temple of Alea Athena: there he had the responsibility as both the architect and the sculptor. Quite a bit of sculpture has survived (ill. 44) from these two units, the Mausoleum and the temple of Tegea, permitting us to appreciate the pioneering contributions of Scopas to the art of the 4th century

11

11. Stele of Crito and Timarista. Museum of Rhodes.

B.C. which led to the pathos and the cosmogonic currents of the Hellenistic period.

During this new phase of the ancient world the centers of political and economic power shifted, so that the old, powerful towns lost both their authority and their cultural brilliance. Alexandria, Antioch and Pergamon, where the monarch-successors of Alexander the Great settled, were the focus of the material and intellectual vitality of this new world. But alongside these capital cities some island centers also developed which acquired wealth as commercial depots or as crucial locations for the new military and naval powers in the eastern Mediterranean. Thus Delos, which for many years had been under the control of the Athenians, managed, due to its strategic location in the middle of the Aegean, to regain its old glory. Imposing structures were once more erected on the sacred island while the private houses with their opulence and the splendid decoration of their mosaic floors (ills. 46, 47) are indisputable proof of the island's new prosperity. Statues now decorated not only the public spaces, but even the houses of the rich, such as, for example, those of Dioskourides and Kleopatra (ill. 48) which Kleopatra built in 137 B.C. in honor of her husband who had dedicated two tripods to the temple of Apollo. The most powerful work that survives from this period (around 100 B.C.) is the bronze head of a young man (ill. 45) which is today in the National Archeological Museum of Athens. The expressive power of this portrait is increased by the perfect preservation of the inlaid eyes which concentrate the inwardly restless and at the same time dynamic world of the people of this highly turbulent period, which saw the great new power, Rome, take the place of the Greeks throughout the length and breadth of the ancient world.

Nevertheless, the end of the ancient Greek world was marked by two world-renowned works both of which are in the Louvre in Paris and both of which are from the Aegean islands; the one is from the northernmost island of Samothrace and the other from one of the more southerly of the Cyclades, Milos. The first, the Winged Victory (Nike) of Samothrace (ill. 50) was found in 1863 in the sanctuary of the Great Gods in Samothrace. Its base represented the prow of a ship and the goddess is depicted as having just touched down on it, her wings still beating, her drapery swept back by the wind; she has descended in order to crown the victorious captain and his sailors. The dramatic impression is augmented by the placement of the base-prow of the boat within a basin which has two levels, while the setting of the entire work on a level above the theater of Samothrace, from where the spectator has a sweeping view of the entire sanctuary and with the sea and the shore in the background, helped complete this magnificent stage set. It is very likely that this work was the creation of the Rhodian sculptor Pythocritos, from the beginning of the 2nd century B.C. and was dedicated to the sanctuary of the Great Gods, protectors of seafarers, by the inhabitants of Rhodes after a great naval victory by their fleet. We know that in 190 B.C. the Rhodian admiral Eudamos, head of an allied fleet (Romans and the Greek opponents of Antiochus III) smashed the naval forces of Antiochus III just off Side in Cilicia and Myonnisos. So it is not impossible that the victorious admiral, upon his return to his homeland, would want to immortalize his great success by the dedication of this brilliant monument on Samothrace.

Although it was admired and is still admired as much as the Nike of Samothrace the other sculpture in the Louvre, the Aphrodite of Milos (ill. 49) is not of the same quality. Since it was found on the Cycladic island (1820) and sent to the Louvre it has been considered as the incarnation of female beauty. As a work of art it constitutes a neoclassical creation of the late years of the 2nd century B.C. which manages to combine, quite successfully, elements of the baroque of the Hellenistic period with characteristics of the classical works of the 5th and 4th century. The result of such an eclectic art corresponded to the aesthetic requirements of the Classicists of the 19th century, who considered it as a model of Greek art, but it can no longer stand up to being compared to either the creations of the pure Classical art of the Greek world or the vibrant and fertile triumphs of the Hellenistic period.

The Roman conquest essentially brought to an end the ancient Greek world. And when the new religion deposed the ancient gods from their temples the definitive end of ancient Greek art would have arrived. The new world founded its "temples" to praise the one God and his saints. The new art, which would take the name of the ancient Greek city of Byzantium, would organize its own language and find new, expressive methods. A Greek island would have an extremely crucial place in this new religion: Patmos, where inside a holy cave John would set down the divine revelations. The light of the Aegean would never cease shining.

BIBLIOGRAPHY

BARBER, R.L.N., *The Cyclades in the Bronze Age*, London 1987.

BRUNEAU, PH. – DUCAT, J., *Guide de Délos*, Athènes 1983.

DAUX, G. – HANSEN, E. – HELLMANN, CH., *Le Trésor de Siphnos*, Paris 1987 (= *Fouilles de Delphes* II).

DOUMAS, C., *The N.P. Goulandris Collection of Early Cycladic Art*, Athens 1968.

— *Thera: Pompeii of the ancient Aegean*, London 1983.

DOUMAS, C. (ed.), *Thera and the Aegean World*, I, London 1978· II, London 1980.

FITTON, J.L. (ed.), *Cycladica. Studies in Memory of N.P. Goulandris, Proceedings of the 7th British Museum Classical Colloquium*, London 1984.

FLOREN, J., *Die geometrische und archaische Plastik*, München 1987, 150-183, 328-373 (= W. FUCHS – J. FLOREN, *Die griechische Plastik* I).

FREUER-SCHAUENBURG, B., *Bildwerke der archaischen Zeit und des strengen Stils*, Bonn 1974 (= *Samos* XI).

HARDY, D.A. (ed.), *Thera and the Aegean World III*, vol. 1-3, London 1990.

HORN, R., *Hellenistische Bildwerke auf Samos*, Bonn 1972 (= *Samos* XII).

IMMERWAHR, S.A., *Aegean painting in the Bronze Age*, Pennsylvania 1990.

KAROUZOS, CHR., "An early classical Disc Relief from Melos", *Journal of Hellenistic Studies*, 71 (1951), 96-110.

KOKKOROU-ALEWRAS, G., *Archaische naxische Plastik*, München 1975.

KONTOLEON, N.M., *Aspects de la Grèce Préclassique*, Paris 1970.

ΚΩΣΤΟΓΛΟΥ-ΔΕΣΠΟΙΝΗ, ΑΙΚ., *Προβλήματα τῆς παριανῆς πλαστικῆς τοῦ 5ου αἰώνα π.Χ.*, Θεσσαλονίκη 1979.

KYRIELEIS, H., *Führer durch das Heraion von Samos*, Athen 1981.

LINFERT, A., *Kunstzentren hellenistischer Zeit*, Wiesbaden 1976, 83-100, 112-131.

MARCAD'E, J., *Au Musée de Délos*, Paris 1969.

— "Tegeatika", *Bulletin de Correspondence Hellénique*, 110 (1986), 317-329.

MARINATOS, S., *Excavations at Thera*, vol. I-VII, Athens 1968-1976.

— *Kreta, Thera und das Mykenische Hellas*, Munich 1973.

MERCER, GL., *The Hellenistic Sculpture of Rhodes*, Göteborg 1973 (= *Studies in Mediterranean Archaeology* XL.).

MORGAN, L., *The Miniature Paintings of Thera. A Study in Aegean Culture and Iconography*, Cambridge 1988.

RENFREW, C., *The Emergence of Civilisation. The Cyclades and the Aegean in the Third Millennium B.C.*, London 1972.

STEWART, A.F., *Skopas of Paros*, Park Redge 1977.

THIMME, J. (ed.), *Art and Culture of the Cyclades*, Karlsruhe 1977.

ZERVOS, C., *L' art des Cyclades du début à la fin de l' âge du bronze*, Paris 1957.

The transparancies and photographs were furnished by: the Museum of Cycladic Art (N.P. Goulandris Collection) (ills. 1, 12-14), the German Archeological Institute (ills. 3-5, 7), The Archeological Museum of Thessaloniki (ills. 8, 43) and the Archaeological Receipts Fund (T.A.P.A.) (ills. 20-31, 33-40, 44-48, 51).

12

13

14

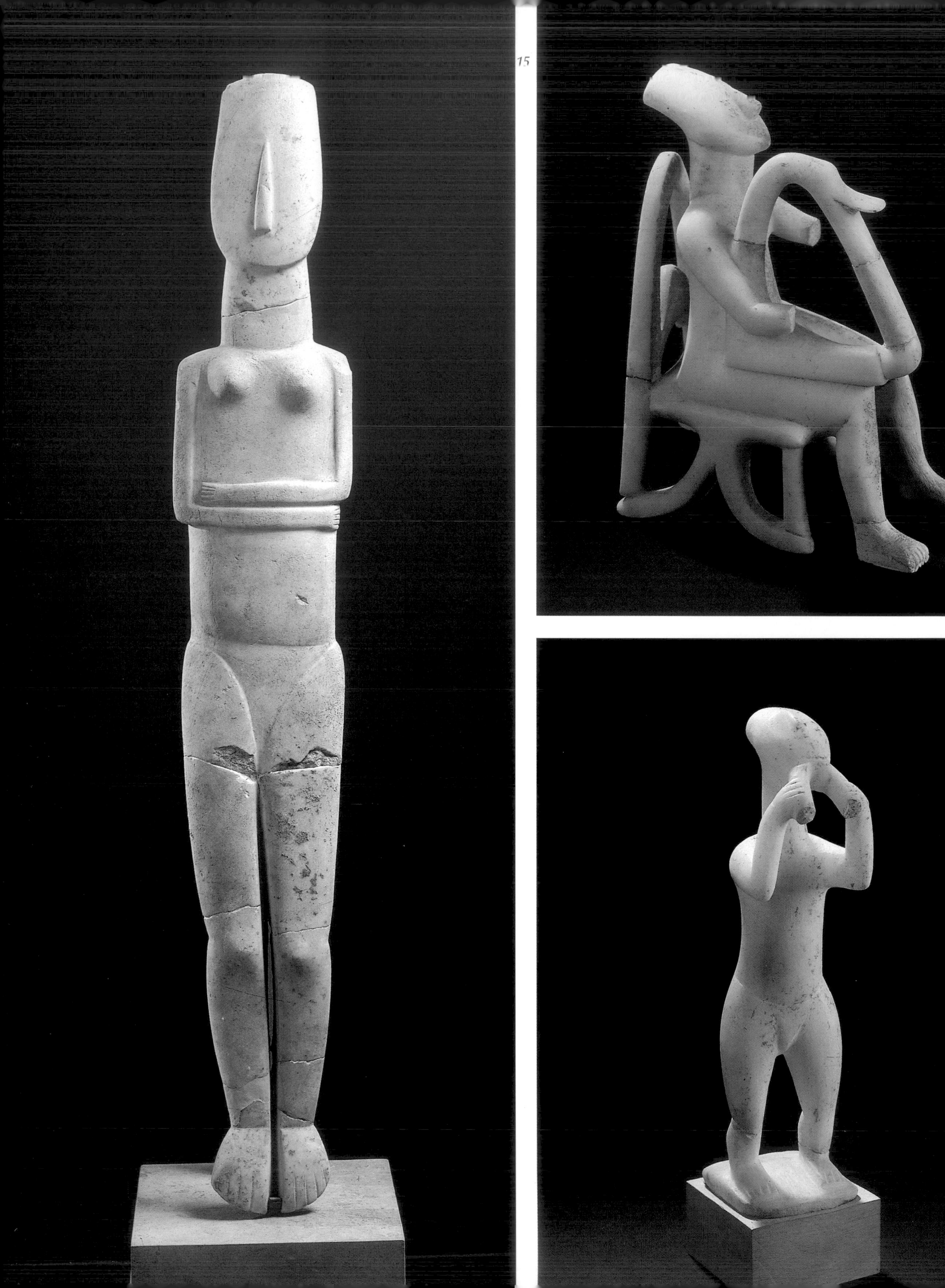

15

18

19

12. Head of a Cycladic statue. Athens, Museum of Cycladic Art (N.P. Goulandris Collection).

13. Seated Cycladic figurine. Athens, Museum of Cycladic Art (N.P. Goulandris Collection).

14. Female Cycladic statue. Athens, Museum of Cycladic Art (N.P. Goulandris Collection).

15. Amorgos. Female statue. Athens, National Archeological Museum.

16. Kéros. The harpist. Athens, National Archeological Museum.

17. Keros. The flute-player. Athens, National Archeological Museum.

18. Cycladic figurines. Athens, National Archeological Museum.

19. Amorgos. Head of statue. Athens, National Archeological Museum.

20

20. *Santorini. Section of the wall painting of spring. Athens, National Archeological Museum.*

21. *Santorini. Wall painting of the naval campaign. Athens, National Archeological Museum.*

21

22. Santorini. Wall painting of boxing children. Athens, National Archeological Museum.

23. Santorini. Wall painting of fisherman. Athens, National Archeological Museum.

24

25

26

24. The statue of Nikandre. Athens, National Archeological Museum.

25. The sphinx of Naxos. Delphi Museum.

26. The lions of Delos.

27

28

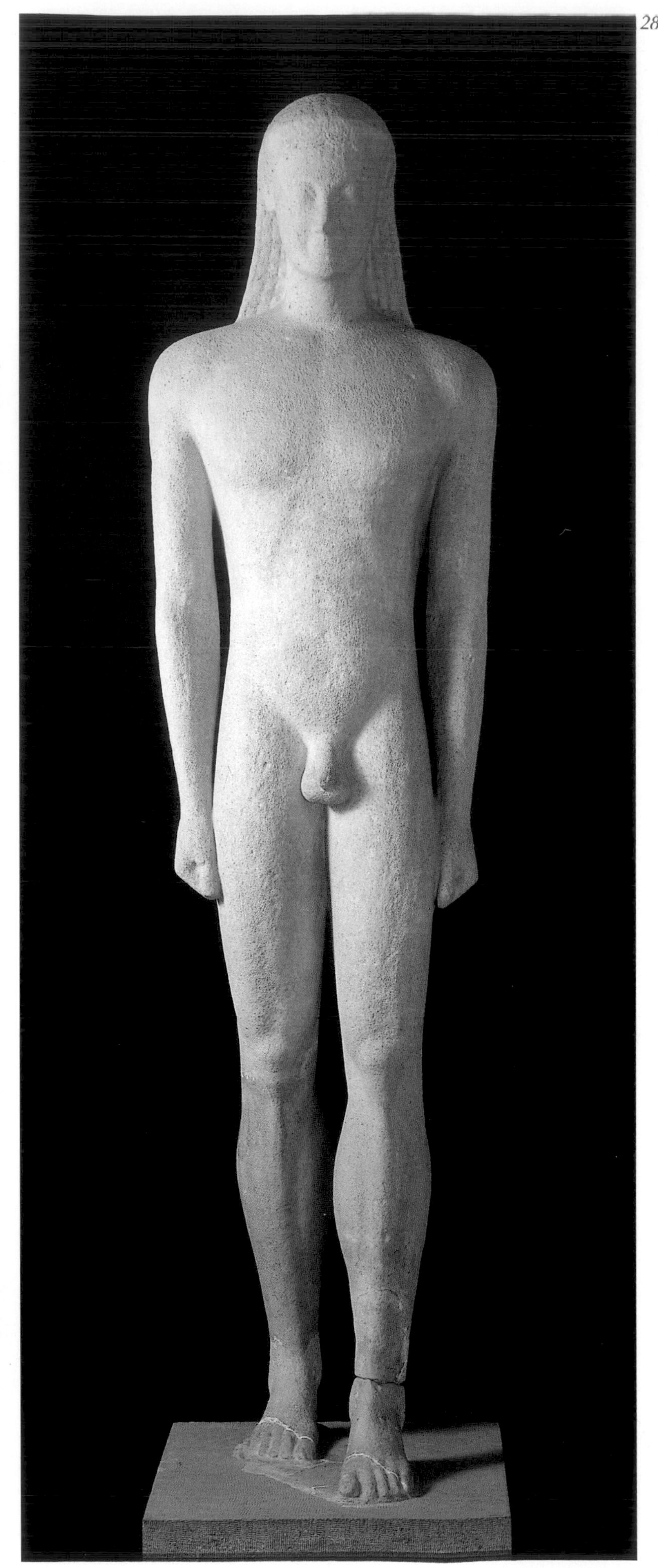

29

30

31

27. Kouros *of Thera. Athens, National Archeological Museum.*

28. The kouros *from Milos. Athens, National Archeological Museum.*

29. Running Nike (said to be by Archermos). Athens, National Archeological Museum.

30. Samos. General view of the Temple of Hera.

31. Bronze head of gryphon. Samos Museum.

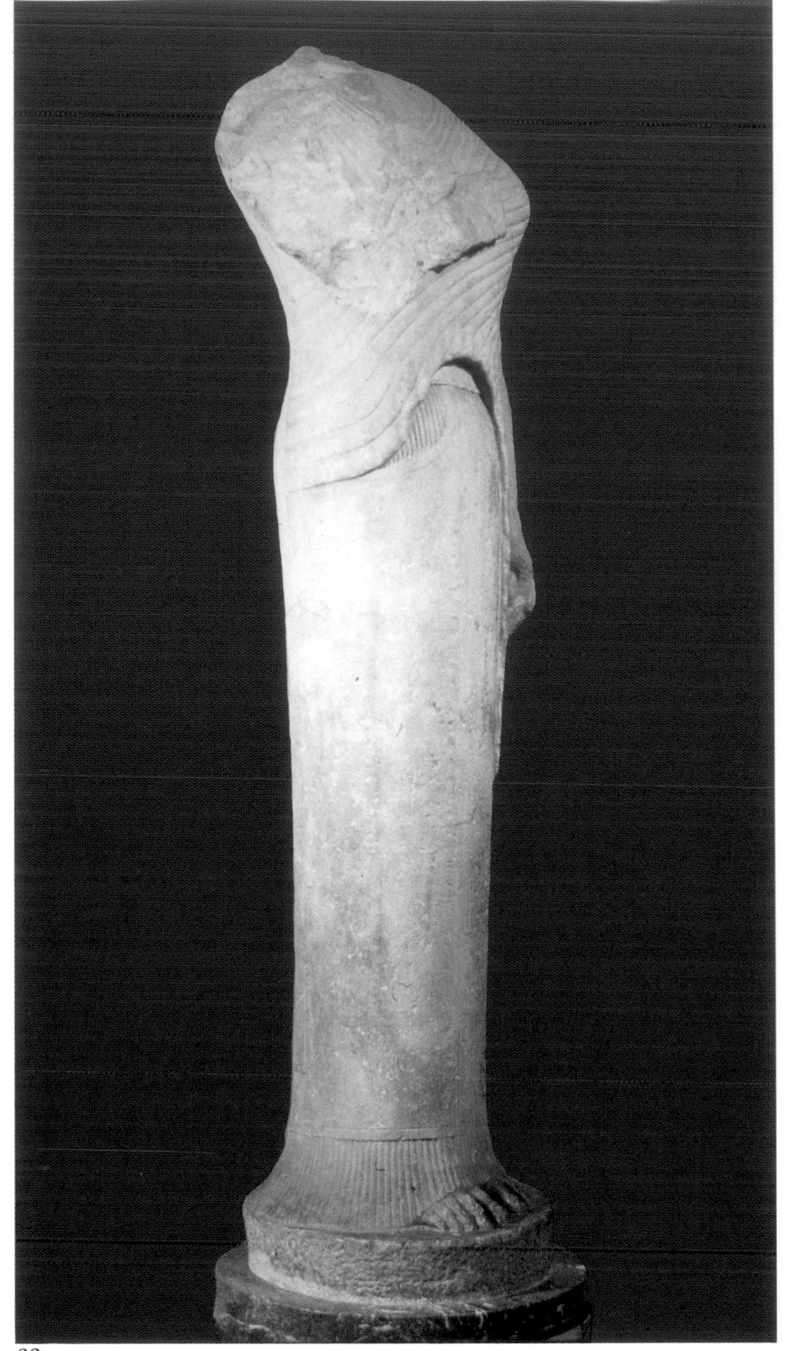

32

33

32. Samos. The Hera of Chiramyes. Paris, The Louvre.

33. The kore *from the Treasury of the Siphnians. Delphi Museum.*

34. The Treasury of the Siphnians, east frieze (detail from the battle between Greeks and Trojans). Delphi Museum.

35

36

*35. The Treasury of the Siphnians, section of the north frieze (*Gigantomachia*). Delphi Museum.*

36. The Treasury of the Siphnians, east frieze (the gods). Delphi Museum.

37

38

37, 38. The Treasury of the Siphnians, north frieze (details from ill. 35). Delphi Museum.

39. The Treasury of the Siphnians, north frieze (detail). Delphi Museum.

40. The Ram-Bearer of Thasos. Thasos Museum.

41

42

41, 42. The reliefs from the Passage of the Ambassadors in Thasos. Paris, The Louvre.

43

43. Stele from Nea Callicrateia. Thessaloniki, Archeological Museum.

44

45

44. The head of Hercules (work of Scopas). Tegea Museum.

45. Delos. Bronze hellenistic head. Athens, National Archeological Museum.

46

47

46, 47. Delos. Mosaic floors.

48. Delos. The statues of Dioskourides and Kleopatra.

49

50

49. The Aphrodite of Milos. Paris, The Louvre.

50. The Nike of Samothrace. Paris, The Louvre.

51. The Poseidon of Artemision. Athens, National Archeological Museum.

52. The «gate» of Naxos.

CHARALAMBOS BOURAS

Byzantine architecture in the Aegean

Translated by Philip Ramp

Introduction

The architectural monuments that have survived on the islands of the Aegean Sea from the eleven centuries that the Byzantine empire was in control are numerous and important. But the study of them as a single body, even in a form as brief as this article, is fraught with great difficulties because the particular inquiries into these monuments are still incomplete, scattered and, in a word, inadequate. Furthermore, for one to separate the islands of the Archipelago from the surrounding coasts is already a compromise and even more so when dealing with Byzantium which at one time joined the one to the other in the same political and cultural unity.

By examining the historical vicissitudes in correlation with artistic and architectural activity, one comfirms that while the sea truly unites, it also can divide. This is the way it was on the islands then, principally during the late period of Byzantium, when architectural ideas not only came from very far away, but were also enclosed, complete units which perpetuated local characteristics. Some examples of this, on the one hand, are the secular buildings on Thasos, Samothrace and Chios from the 14th century and, on the other, the phenomenal church building on the island of Naxos which covered a period of eight hundred years.

But the artistic and architectural activity, especially on the islands of the Archipelago, is incomprehensible without the assistance of historical knowledge. The conditions of insecurity and the lack of communication, imposed from without, as well as the productive potential of the islands themselves, also determined their fate, both under Byzantium and during the period that was to follow. Between two, large, neighboring islands, such as Chios and Lesbos for instance, there was a startling difference in terms of architecture, urban planning and culture up to the 19th century, despite the uniform origin of the population and the similarity of the natural environment, precisely because external conditions were different.

During the Middle Ages agriculture was the dominant force on all the Aegean islands and the population that was engaged with it had the simplest of needs for security, subsistence and religion. This means that even during periods of peace, poverty was endemic and building investment was on a very limited scale. What has survived from these works, also depends on a number of special factors: for example, many of the more than two hundred Byzantine churches on Naxos would no longer exist if there had been a powerful earthquake there, while the four left on Lesbos simply escaped the renovating rage which accompanied the island's flourishing during the 18th and the 19th century.

Endemic poverty also had a bearing on the character that most of the buildings in the Aegean have: even during the prosperous years of the early Christian period, the restoration of old buildings, the impovised re-building of ruins and, above all, the re-use of building material from older structures, were common practices. This reduced the significance of the design even though it occasionally increased the interest of the building. The same process was also used on a large scale, that is, in complexes and settlements, where the dynamic development and the continual modification and adaptation gradually created their particular character. During their analysis, present-day studies of island architecture and town-planning often become confused by the difficulties these matters present, given that all these things continued for five full centuries after the fall of Byzantium.

The study of the early Christian and Byzantine monuments on the Aegean islands presents other difficulties as well. Their dating is done by approximation and contains large margins for error. Few of them have founder's inscriptions and even fewer are mentioned in the written sources from that time. The formal elements of the local architectural manner on the islands do not exhibit a clear evolution; they are characterized by an exceptional degree of conservatism and trans-temporal repetitions. If one adds to all this the ambiguities that have arisen from the dynamic way of building, which have been spoken of, one can understand why many of the ecclesiastical, Byzantine monuments in the Aegean are dated only by the style of the wall paintings which decorate their interiors.

In any case, no uniform island character was established in the Aegean during the Middle Ages like the one that is found, to a degree, in more recent times. As we will see, at least three groups can be distinguished here, each with its own formal and typological character. Judging principally by the types of early Christian basilicas in the Aegean, one could not maintain the same thing for the architecture of late Antiquity.

Of course, Byzantine architecture is basically ecclesiastical architecture. The castles, the towers or the houses from the same period, which are hidden in the old settlements, are few and have scarcely been studied. There is a marked increase of these secular buildings in the Aegean area during the period after 1200, but many of their elements are at some remove from the Byzantine tradition.

As has already been noted, the economy on the Aegean islands during the Middle Ages was essentially agricultural. After the "great break" from the 7th to the 10th century, not one settlement retained the character of an urban center, not even when applying the measures of the middle Byzantine concept of production. With only a few exceptions (and very well-known ones) the monasteries were also small, with a limited potential for investment. The result of all this was that the monuments which survived are all small in scale and their structure and decoration relatively austere.

The Early Christian Monuments

The first period of the history of the Aegean, after the creation of the Byzantine state, covers the fourth, the fifth and part of the sixth century and is characterized by the continuation of the life led in late Antiquity as well as a measure of prosperity.

The lack of historical information hampers investigation somewhat but the host of monuments (and indeed large and expensive monuments) confirm the ease of life on at least several islands. It is obvious that the incursions of the Goths did not reach this far and that the decline began later, in the 7th century. Unfortunately, not one of the Aegean towns which survived up to then have been systematically excavated and subsequently

1

1. Samos. The basilica of the Heraion.

2. Delos. The basilica of Ayios Kirykos and Ioulitta.

studied to determine the form they had before there were abandoned or destroyed. Flourishing towns such as Rhodes, Mytilene, Kos and Chios, which were demonstrably ornamented with important early Christian monuments, remain unknown to us in terms of town-plan and architecture. The distribution of the monuments from that period on the various islands is assuredly connected to the mode of production and the maintenance of an old way of urban life in these towns as well as their being directly adjacent to the large centers of Asia Minor. In line with this, Kos has fourteen basilicas, Rhodes ten, Naxos four, Samos five and Lesbos fifty.

These monuments are, as a rule, in very bad condition. They have been found in excavations and have foundations, mosaic or marble laid floors, low remnants of walls and marble architectural members, sometimes whole and sometimes not. It is difficult to reconstruct them even on a simple plan, given that the building material was, to a large degree, removed after their collapse. Several of them are of quite impressively large dimensions (such as in the town of Rhodes which was recently found or the basilica of Ypsilometopos on Lesbos) while others were built on the sites of ancient temples, re-using their building material, or the existing ruins were rebuilt (the basilicas of Phana on Chios, the Heraion on Samos, ill. 1, of Sagri on Naxos, the Colona on Aegina, Ayios Kirykos and Ayia Ioulitta on Delos, ill. 2, and the Karthaia church on Kea).

In terms of typology, the early Christian monuments on the Aegean islands are, as a general rule, simple triple-aisled, wooden-roofed basilicas of the so-called "Hellenistic" type, usually with a narthex and an atrium. There is a complete lack of the usual centralized buildings found elsewhere, even in the cases of *martyria* (such as Ayios Isidoros on Chios) where this arrangement would be particularly desirable. In only a few cases can one see elements from Asia Minor, such as the *pastophoria* (basilicas of Ypsilometopos and Aphendelis on Lesbos). This uniform image of the simple, triple-aisled basilicas, without a trancept is most likely connected to complete acceptance of the Constantinopolitan prototypes in the Aegean during the 5th century with two exceptions worthy of note: the cruciform basilica on Thasos and Katapoliani on Paros.

The basilica near Limenas on Thasos, completely destroyed today, is quite well-known to us thanks to the study of A. Orlandos. It was a large building in the shape of a "free cross" with a triple-aisled arrangement of each of its arms, galleries above its side aisles and wooden roofs. The remains of its marble architectural members, columns, column capitals and an elaborate iconostasis bear witness to the wealth of the basilica. Katapoliani in Paros, also known as Ekatontapyliani (of the Hundred Gates), is one of the very few early Christian buildings which have survived practically intact. This is again a cruciform basilica with colonnades which fashion side aisles above which run galleries. During its first stage, in the 5th century, the building had a timber-roofed skylight at the intersection of the aisles, built in large part of re-used ancient marble. Later (second stage, most likely during the time of Justinian) the roofs were replaced by vaults and the skylight by a regular dome. The complex is completed by a narthex, a baptistery and the side chapel (parecclesion) of Ayios Nikolaos.

Although Katapoliani was left completely abandoned for centuries, it kept its early Christian *synthronon* and its four-columned marble ciborium in the sanctuary in perfect condition. During more recent times the Parians, in order to prevent the collapse of the church, have shored up the vaults with buttresses and interior elements and at the same time through additions, layers of plaster and countless coats of whitewash have given Katapoliani a new character with sculptural, pure white volumes more appropriate to the new architecture of the Cyclades. Extensive works were carried out during the 1960s to remove all these later elements; the church thus regained the original magnificence of its interior space but lost its picturesqueness and the poetic beauty given it by the centuries of creative interventions (ills. 50, 51).

The scientific study of the early Christian monuments of the Aegean is still incomplete and it will become continually more difficult because of the rapid deterioration of the basilicas which though excavated are not kept up. The lack of written sources renders these ruined buildings of great significance for the history of the islands of the Aegean archipelago. For the time being it is certain that the role of Constantinople was of the essence in the development of this architecture. It is characteristic that the marble parts (which were the elements of definitive importance for the appearance and prestige of the basilicas) were sometimes imported prefabricated from Proconnesos, next to Constantinople, even in the cases where the local marble was abundant (Naxos, Samos).

The Architecture of the 7th - 10th century

What is known to scholars as the "great break" in the history of Byzantium, is especially felt on the Aegean islands. It is the indirect result of the Persian incursions into Asia Minor (during the second half of the 7th century) and the direct result of the military activity of the Arabs from around the middle of the 7th century to 961, the date of the re-capture of Crete by the Byzantines. During those three centuries, as is well-known, the Aegean became the focal point of an extremely bitter war during which the seas were regularly insecure, urban life came to a standstill, the old towns were abandoned or shrank dramatically and several islands in the Archipelago were deserted for long periods of time. Furthermore, the iconoclastic movement (726-843) intensified during this period and threw the empire into disorder having a direct effect on the artistic activity of its subjects. The written sources have preserved very little information concerning this tragic period in the provinces and the repercussions of the war conditions on the cultural superstructure. The few architectural monuments that survived this period, so terrible for the islanders, are therefore valuable proofs of their endeavors to endure and to preserve their religious life as well as their cultural identity.

On Icaria, Karpathos and, above all, Naxos, churches have been located which are dated to the period under examination. This can be done with relative certainty on the basis of their wall paintings which have been extensively studied, over the past few years, to a satisfactory degree (see p. 136).

On Naxos the Panayia Drosiani has survived; it appears that it can be dated to the first half of the 7th century, that is, to a period exceptionally poor in architectural monuments throughout all Byzantium. It is a small, single-space, domed, triconch church which later, was lengthened by a vaulted room through which three, later, side chapels have their access. What strikes one is the primitive construction, the irregularity of the forms, the complete absence of sculptural decoration, except for the iconostasis (*templon*) and the use of material that was simply gathered (small, slab-shaped stones) for the erection of the church which is completely integrated into its environment. Even though the type represented by Drosiani preserves the Byzantine tradition, the exceptionally low technological level of the building makes it a prime example of the period when poverty and the suppression of contact with the large centers had their direct consequences on architecture (ill. 44).

The rest of the churches on Naxos from this period are characterized by their aniconical decoration, harking back to the time of iconoclasm. Ayios Artemios at Sagri and Ayios Ioannis the Theologian at Adisarou belong to the simple type of church, single-space with a dome and small in dimensions. Ayia Kyriaki near Apeiranthos is also a single-space domed church, but it has a vaulted narthex and a longitudinal side-chapel on its south side.

These three iconoclastic Naxian monuments belong to a very widespread type in Byzantium in which the dome is the dominant feature of the composition and together with two vaults (which cover the sanctuary and the west part of the church) house a simple, rectangular room. All three of them have common morphological and structural characteristics: a limited size, a relatively low dome, few and small openings, a lack of decorative sculpture, walls and domes that were built of small, slab-shaped stones that were simply gathered and a vivid irregularity in the layout of the architectural forms.

The rest of the churches in the Aegean from this dark period have analogous forms. In the region of Elymbos on Karpathos there are still two small churches, Ayia Anna the Catholic at Potamos and Ayios Onouphrios whose decorations are from the iconoclastic period. The architectural type here is the simple elongated room with reinforced bands (*sphendonia*) along a single barrel vault. The church of Ayios Pavlos at Akamatra, Icaria is also single-roomed, the aniconic decoration of which is dated (with reservations) to the time of iconoclasm. All these monuments have a primitive look and simplified technology which bears witness, just as on Naxos, to the poverty and the isolation of the islands during the 8th and the 9th century.

The general insecurity in the Aegean was the reason castles were built, chiefly taking advantage of natural fortification; the islanders could take refuge there in the case of danger. The remains of these fortresses, deformed and in ruins today, have not been scientifically examined. Inside Kastro on Skyros, the ruins of the Bishopric church (Episkopi) have survived, an important architectural work dated by an inscription to 895. The type used here was the inscribed cross with a dome and this bears witness, for the first time, to some relationship to Constantinople and its architecture. But the structure is still carelessly done, the walls and the domes made of rough stones, the openings kept small and the marble members second-hand.

Three other Naxian monuments, dated to the period before 961, must be noted here: Panayia Kaloritsa (a natural cave made into a church), Ayios Nikolaos at Sagri (a domed basilica, similar in type to the iconoclastic ones, but much more elegant and well-built) (ill. 47) and Ayios Ioannis the Theologian next to Apeiranthos (a large, triple-aisled basilica, vaulted, with heavy proportions, little natural lighting and careless construction, entirely of stones). This last monument could perhaps connect the architecture of Naxos to that of Asia Minor.

Middle Byzantine Architecture

The economic and cultural recovery on the islands of the Archipelago began with the re-capture of Crete in 961 by the imperial forces under Nikephoros Phocas. The Byzantine administrative system was re-instated, the coastal fortresses were restored (for example, on Rhodes, Chora and Volissos on Chios and Molyvos on Lesbos in 1085) and the sea lanes to the Dardenelles and Constantinople were made secure. Monasteries came to be founded in the countryside and production was increased.

As has already been noted, at least three definite units with their own typological and morphological characteristics could be distinguished by the middle of this period: the old, indigenous "school" which evolved; the monumental architecture of Constantinople which developed on Chios in particular and finally the "Helladic School" which influenced several islands, leaving some beautiful churches behind.

The regular evolution of the earlier condition, in indirect relationship to a uniform, middle Byzantine architecture, created noteworthy churches on the islands. Unfortunately, we are still in the dark as to what, until 1071, current church construction was during the Macedonian period in western Asia Minor. Consequently a relationship which appears plausible and which would permit the interpretation of certain phenomena, cannot be proven. Thus, churches from the 10th or the 11th century have survived on four different islands, sizeable, with narthexes, of exactly the same type (domed cruciform simple tetrastyle) with generous propotions, but still haphazardly constructed of rubble and old building material used once again. These churches are Ayios Mamas in Potamia, Naxos, the fourth stage of Ayios Isidoros on Chios, Ayios Stephanos at Mantamados, Lesbos and the Metamorphosis at Potami, Samos, all of which could be considered as representative of the new situation. While they stick to local tradition and remain at a

3. *Icaria, Kambos. Ayia Irini.*

low level of technology, they bear, at the same time, witness to an indirect relationship to Constantinople (through the large, blind arcading which constitutes their side facades) and subsequently the potential for communication between the master craftsmen and the ideas of the new period.

One could also include within this same unity of island monuments, which in many ways follows the tradition of local architecture before 961, the bishopric church of Skopelos (a small, triple-aisled church from 1078, today in ruins), Tourloti in Pyrgoi Thermis on Lesbos, Ayia Irini of Kambos on Icaria, Ayioi Apostoloi in Katomeria, Kea and even the relatively large churches of Rhodes, the Panayia of Kastro, the so-called Demirli Djami and Ilk Mihrab of Rhodes and perhaps Ayios Ioannis on the Kastro, of Lindos (ill. 34). The bishopric church (Episkopi) at Mesa Gonia, Santorini is a special case; it was built on the ruins of a triple-aisled early Christian basilica in 1177.

On Naxos, despite the spread of the inscribed cruiciform, domed churches, the practice of adhering to a local, outdated architectural idiom was still vital. In 1052 Protothronos was re-built in a third stage (?) at the expense of officials of the Byzantine state, based on the transitional cruciform, domed church with a tripartite narthex but the structure and the forms remained the traditional Naxian ones. Two more cruciform tetrastyle domed churches, Ayios Georgios Diasoritis and Ayios Georgios at Yria then appeared in Naxos made of simple rubble-masonry with small and few openings, low, cylindrical domes and a heavy structure.

It must be noted that this folk, traditional architectural idiom also characterized other "enclosed" areas around the Aegean in the 11th and 12th century, such as Kythera or Mani where it co-existed with monuments whose architecture belonged to the "Helladic School".

In the 11th century imperial interest was expressed by the erection of two important monasteries on two islands of the Aegean: Nea Moni on Chios and the Monastery of Saint John the Theologian on Patmos.

We have important, detailed studies on both of them. The monastery on Patmos, founded by Hosios Christodoulos, was endowed by the Emperor Alexios I Comnenus with land and revenues, and construction began around 1090. Its architecture is of great interest mainly from the viewpoint of the original design and the dynamic development of a monastery complex which has remained practically unaltered up to the present. The main church (*katholiko*) of the monastery, a cruciform, tetrastyle domed church with a narthex does not appear to have been designed with any special intent, but a bit later it was supplemented by an open stoa (ill. 46), a side chapel for the saint's tomb and a second one to the Blessed Virgin, which by the 12th century gave it a distinct character of its own.

Nea Moni on Chios came about as a favor paid by the Porphyrogenetes, Zoe and Theodora, as well as Constantine IX Monomachus, to a three member group of anchorites on Chios. An entire series of documents and other written information enable us to acquire complete knowledge of the conditions under which the monastery was founded and its first buildings erected. These show that an architect was sent to Chios from the Court of Constantinople with precious marble and other materials and that for the plan of the monastery he used the prototype of a specific church in Constantinople, which no longer exists today (ill. 49).

The main church of Nea Moni has survived in relatively good condition, despite the destruction and the alterations, chiefly from the last century. Its interior is decorated with mosaics of superb craftsmanship which are spoken of in another place (p. 138). The main church has a completely original plan which most likely represents the medieval interpretation and imitation of an early Christian centralized building: a square space

4. Chios, Pyrgi. Ayioi Apostoloi.

becomes, at a higher level, octagonal and is covered by a disproportionate, externally, polygonal dome. Both the sanctuary and the narthex are in keeping with this synthetic idea, being quite low with little natural light. The architectural forms and the structures verify what the texts say because they have a direct and absolute relationship to the middle Byzantine architecture of Constantinople (multiple blind arcading, small decorative niches, polygonal, externally, central apse, a structure primarily of brick).

Thus, on one of the islands of the eastern Aegean we have a work which represented the Court architecture of Byzantium during the middle of the 11th century. This is of some importance because during the immediately succeeding periods Nea Moni was used as a prototype for four or five churches on Chios (Ayios Georgios Sykousis, Panayia Krina, ills. 39, 42; Ayioi Apostoloi at Pyrgi, ill. 4; the *katholiko* of the Monastery of Ayios Menas and Ayios Ioannis at Keros near Pyrgi). These are the monuments which were characterized by modern scholars as of the "octagonal island type" because the dome had an octagonal support and they are found only on the islands of Chios and Cyprus. Today it is clear that on the one hand the churches of Cyprus are fundamentally different from those on Chios and on the other that typologically similar buildings are not unknown in the area where the architecture of Constantinople had an influence (Metamorphosis at Chortiatis, near Thessaloniki; Ayios Spyridon of Silymvria).

Ayios Georgios Sykousis has unfortunately been deformed by earthquakes and more recent additions but both Panayia Krina and Ayioi Apostoloi in the center of the medieval settlement of Pyrgi have survived in mint condition and are among the most beautiful Byzantine monuments in Greece. They are characterized by the elegance of their proportions, their natural polychromy and the plasticity of their facades, but most of all by the wealth of architectural forms. Dating is a problem with all three. The churches of Ayios Menas and Keros are buildings from the Turkish occupation and bear witness to the imposition on the island of the original prototype of Nea Moni nearly five centuries after its erection. It should be noted that the morphological characteristics of the style of Constantinople were adapted by other Byzantine churches on Chios as well: Panayia Sikelia (ills. 40, 41), Panayia Kyra-Velidaina, Sotira at Kalamoti and the chapel of the Virgin at Ayion Galas (ill. 43).

Modern byzantinologists have characterized a large group of monuments from the 10th to the 13th century in mainland Greece and the Peloponnese with special morphological and structural characteristics as belonging to the "Helladic School" of Byzantine architecture. It has now been generally accepted that a decisive role in the creation of this "school" was played by the two churches of the Monastery of Hosios Loukas in Phocis, during the late 10th and the beginning of the 11th century, and that there was also a continual development of types, forms and methods of construction for three centuries, something that can be verified and studied according to place and period. In any case, this "Helladic" idiom spread to certain islands in the Aegean which had a direct relationship to Attica during the 12th century.

Five churches have survived on Andros all belonging to the inscribed cruciform, twin-columned with a dome type which are dated from the end of the 11th century to the end of the 12th century (Taxiarch of Mesaria, ill. 36; Taxiarch of Melida, ill. 37; Taxiarch of Ypsilou; the Koimisis at Mesathouri and Ayios Nikolaos at Korthi). These monuments are distinguished for their beautiful proportions and their "Helladic" characteristics, the "cloisoné" masonry structure, the brick decorations, the externally semi-hexagonal apses of the sanctuary with elegant bifoil and trefoil windows, the eight-sided domes in the "Athenian" style or with horizontal cornices, and so on. Moreover, the first two churches have retained sculptural decoration, of exceptional quality done in white marble, which is spoken of in another place (p. 143), on the iconostases, the door frames, the columned windows and the *kosmetes*. Inscriptions on the Taxiarch of Mesaria date the monument to 1158 and the names of its proprietors, who were members of the local (?) Byzantine aristocracy, have also been preserved. Finally, the clear similarity between the monuments of Andros and the Taxiarch of Kalyvia of Karystos in neighboring Euboea, should be noted.

The Taxiarch of Elanion mountain on Aegina, a type of compact cruciform church, a part of which incorporates ancient walls, was influenced by the prototypes of Attica. The so-called "Omorfi Ekklisia" ("Beautiful Church") also on Aegina (ill. 32), is very simple typologically with its exquisite masonry made up of completely carved, massive, sandstone, represents the classicist tendencies and the perfected stone-cutting which characterize the architecture in Greece at the end of the 12th century. Two other churches influenced by the prototypes of Attica are the Koimisis and the Metamorphosis at Aianteion on Salamis.

The fact that the three islands of Andros, Aegina and Salamis belonged to the Metropolis of Athens during the middle Byzantine period is enough to warrant the spread of "Helladic" types to them. Moreover, it is obvious that itinerant craftsmen carried architectural ideas to these neighboring areas. One case that is known to us from a surviving inscription concerns the builder Theophylaktos from Kea who worked on the erection of the church of Ayios Ioannis Eleimon at Ligourio in Peloponnese, a bit after 1100.

Architecture during the Frankish Occupation and the Palaeologue Period

The political turmoil arising from the capture of Constantinople by the Crusaders in 1204 created new conditions in the Aegean. The islanders' confrontation with these new conquerors, of Italian origin and members of the Catholic faith, forged an ethnic feeling of patriotism and a tenacious clinging to traditional values. But the foreigners also brought new methods of production to the Aegean and a mobility which certainly had an effect on the life of the Greeks, at least on the larger islands. With the passage of time the foreign notables developed their construction activity, mainly through the building of fortifications and secular works which gradually changed the form of many settlements (Chios, Rhodes, Naxos, Kos). Simultaneously, the islanders became acquainted, on the one hand, with western art and architecture and, on the other, created, at least in certain areas, better economic conditions for themselves. A large number of the Orthodox faithful had the opportunity to build a church. This means that after 1204 there were a considerable number of small ecclesiastical monuments on the islands and (as in the rest of Greece) many more wall paintings in churches.

This phenomenon was particularly noticeable on Euboea which belonged to the Venetians. On Naxos the adherence to local traditions through the small, haphazardly built chapels, was brought into harmony with the new conditions. Thus, we have a large series of monuments which are dated to approximately the 13th or 14th century by the wall paintings which decorate their interiors: the Panayia Damiotissa, a type of "free cross" with a dome which retains archaic characteristics so that there is no essential difference from the buildings of the "great break" period. Ayioi Apostoloi in Kerami and the Panayia of Yiallou are single-space churches with a dome, square in plan with low, blind domes and wall paintings from the 13th century. In quite a number of other cases the type is the simplest possible, that is, a small, vaulted room (Ayios Georgios of Lathrinos, 13th century; Ayios Georgios of Noskelos, 1286; Ayios Georgios of Distomon, 1287; Ayios Polykarpos of Distomon, 1306; Ayios Sozon of Yiallou, 1314).

On Chios the Panayia of Agrelopos (ill. 38) and Ayios Ioannis Argentis, are vaulted basilicas with square narthexes which are covered by a blind, semi-spherical dome. The blind arcading on their long sides assures us that the Constantinopolitan architectural traditions had not been forgotten on the island more than three hundred years after the erection of Nea Moni. Conversely, the small church at Prasteia of Siderounta (1415) in northern Chios, has a simplified form and haphazard construction.

The image of the small, vaulted church with the heavy rubble masonry of the walls, the small openings and externally semi-circular apse of the sanctuary fits most of the Aegean islands during the period in question. As examples it is worth noting Theoskepasti at Protoria and Ayios Georgios Thalassitis on Paros, the Panayia of Kouzis on Mykonos, Ayios Nikolaos Misoskali and Ayios Nikolaos at Cheili on Tilos, Ayios Antonios on Anafi and Ayios Georgios on Sikinos (1352). Finally, during the years of the Frankish occupation it seems that a large part of the Monastery of Chozoviotissa on Amorgos was built.

During the time of the Frankish occupation and the Palaeologue period, Byzantine architecture on the Aegean islands, as can be seen from the preceding, gradually took on a "folk" character which became common everywhere. Retaining exactly the same character it would spread in the years after 1453. The custom of external white-washing which was the rule on most of the islands of the Archipelago would assist the incorporation of these small churches, Byzantine, post-Byzantine and more recent ones, into the built environment of the settlements or into the landscape of the islands: naturally and simply, as suits an architecture which serves the unvarying, centuries-long religious needs of the inhabitants of the Aegean islands.

BIBLIOGRAPHY

ΑΧΕΙΜΑΣΤΟΥ, Μ., «Ἡ ἐκκλησία τῆς Παναγίας τοῦ Κάστρου τῆς Ρόδου», *ΑΔ*, 23 (1968): *Μελέται*, 221-283.

ΒΑΣΙΛΑΚΗ, Α., «Εἰκονομαχικές ἐκκλησίες στή Νάξο», *ΔΧΑΕ*, περ. Δ΄, τόμ. Γ΄ (1962-1963), 49.

Byzantine art in Greece: Naxos, ed. "Melissa", Athens 1989.

ΔΗΜΗΤΡΟΚΑΛΛΗΣ, Γ., *Συμβολαί εἰς τήν μελέτην τῶν βυζαντινῶν μνημείων τῆς Νάξου*, τόμ. Α΄, Ἀθῆναι 1972.

DIMITROKALLIS, G., "The byzantine Churches of Naxos", *AJA*, vol. 72, 1968, 283-286.

JEWELL, H.H. - HASLUCK, F.W., *The Church of our Lady of the hundred Gates*, London 1920.

ΛΑΖΑΡΙΔΗΣ, Π., «Κατάλογος παλαιοχριστιανικῶν μνημείων Δωδεκανήσου», *Πρακτικά τοῦ Θ΄ Διεθνοῦς Βυζαντινολογικοῦ Συνεδρίου*, τόμ. Α΄, 1955, 228.

ΜΑΡΑΓΚΟΥ, Λ., *Μονή Παναγίας τῆς Χοζοβιώτισσας, Ἀμοργός*, Ἀθήνα 1988.

ΜΟΥΤΣΟΠΟΥΛΟΣ, Ν., «Ὁ Ταξιάρχης τοῦ Ἐλανίου Ὄρους στήν Αἴγινα», *Ζυγός*, 1958, τεύχ. 36-37, 37-40.

ΜΠΟΥΡΑΣ, Χ., *Ὁδηγοί τῆς Ἑλλάδος. Χίος*, Ἀθῆναι 1974.

— *Ἡ Νέα Μονή τῆς Χίου. Ἱστορία καί Ἀρχιτεκτονική*, Ἀθῆναι 1981.

— "Architecture", *Patmos, Treasures of the Monastery*, Athens 1988, 25-53.

ΟΡΛΑΝΔΟΣ, Α.Κ., «Αἱ παλαιοχριστιανικαί βασιλικαί τῆς Λέσβου», *ΑΔ*, 12 (1929), 1-72.

— «Ἡ παλαιοχριστιανική βασιλική τοῦ Χαλινάδου Λέσβου», *ΑΒΜΕ*, Γ΄ (1937), 115-127.

— «Βυζαντινά καί μεταβυζαντινά μνημεῖα τῆς Ρόδου», *ΑΒΜΕ*, ΣΤ΄ (1948), 55-215.

— «Ἡ παλαιοχριστιανική βασιλική τῆς Θάσου», *ΑΒΜΕ*, Ζ΄ (1951), 1-61.

— «Ἡ Πισκοπή τῆς Σαντορήνης», *ΑΒΜΕ*, Ζ΄ (1951), 178-214.

— «Βυζαντινά μνημεῖα τῆς Ἄνδρου», *ΑΒΜΕ*, Η΄ (1955-56), 3-67.

— «Δύο παλαιοχριστιανικαί βασιλικαί τῆς Κῶ», *ΑΕ*, 1966, 1-103.

— *Ἡ ἀρχιτεκτονική καί αἱ βυζαντιναί τοιχογραφίαι τῆς Μονῆς Ἁγίου Ἰωάννου τοῦ Θεολόγου Πάτμου*, Ἀθῆναι 1970.

ORLANDOS, A.C., *Monuments byzantins de Chios*, II, Athènes 1930.

— "Délos chrétienne", *BCH*, 60 (1936), 68-100.

PALLAS, D., "Eine anikonische lineare Wanddekoration auf der Insel Ikaria", *JÖB*, 23 (1974), 271-314.

POULOU-PAPADIMITRIOU, N., *Samos Paléochrétienne: L' apport du matériel archéologique*, doctoral thesis, Paris 1985.

ΣΩΤΗΡΙΟΥ, Γ., «Ἡ ὄμορφη Ἐκκλησιά τῆς Αἰγίνης», *ΕΕΒΣ*, Β΄ (1925), 242-276.

SODINI, J.P. - KOLOKOTSAS, K., *Thasos, Aliki II, Basilique Double*, Paris 1984.

ΧΑΡΙΤΩΝΙΔΗΣ, Σ., «Βυζαντιναί Ἐκκλησίαι τῆς Λέσβου», *Χαριστήριον εἰς Α.Κ. Ὀρλάνδον*, τόμ. Γ΄, Ἀθῆναι 1966, 72-77.

— «Παλαιοχριστιανική τοπογραφία τῆς Λέσβου», *ΑΔ*, 23 (1968), 10-69.

ZAKYTHINOS, "La grande brèche", *Χαριστήριον εἰς Α.Κ. Ὀρλάνδον*, τόμ. Γ΄, Ἀθῆναι 1966, 300-327.

Abbreviations

ΑΒΜΕ: Ἀρχεῖον τῶν Βυζαντινῶν Μνημείων τῆς Ἑλλάδος
ΑΔ: Ἀρχαιολογικόν Δελτίον
ΑΕ: Ἀρχαιολογική Ἐφημερίς
AJA: American Journal of Archaeology
BCH: Bulletin de Correspondance Hellénique
ΔΧΑΕ: Δελτίον τῆς Χριστιανικῆς Ἀρχαιολογικῆς Ἑταιρείας
ΕΕΒΣ: Ἐπετηρίς Ἑταιρείας Βυζαντινῶν Σπουδῶν
JÖB: Jahrbuch des Österreichischen Byzantinistik

The photographs were furnished by: Laskarina Boura (ills. 32-42), Charalambos Bouras (ills. 1, 2, 4), The Benaki Museum (ill. 50), St. Mamaloukos (ill. 3), The Kontos Studio (ills. 43, 51).

MYRTALI ACHEIMASTOU-POTAMIANOU

Byzantine art in the Aegean

Translated by Philip Ramp

Introduction

After the ancient world came to a close, the Aegean area grew to be the nerve center of the Byzantine empire through which it controlled the sea, communications and trade. Written sources do not give us a great deal of information on this remote and rather insignificant island province of Byzantium. Information on the cultural activities of the islanders is even more scanty, though it is supplemented in large measure by the authoritative testimony of the monuments which are continually being discovered, compared and evaluated and which frequently provide us with valuable material concerning the islands' administrative, ecclesiastical, economic and social conditions.

The special attributes of the islands, such as the isolation imposed by the sea, the degree of their ability to communicate with each other, nearby coasts on the mainland and more distant areas, their organization into small and closed societies, the self-sufficiency and the limitations of their basically agricultural economy, are all reflected in the art of the Aegean region. The particular nature, development, extent and vitality of its manifestions were also dependent on the geographical position, the size and the economic prosperity of the islands. They were dependent, more specifically, on the relationships they had with the adjacent Greek and Asia Minor coasts, the hinterland and the large island of Crete on the southern edge of the Aegean as well as their position on or close to the major sea lanes of the period, which determined their strategic value and their importance as administrative centers and transit hubs for commerce. The Aegean world's contacts with the large centers and with Constantinople itself kept it posted on the dominant ideas and artistic currents of the times. On the other hand, historical uncertainties frequently placed the islands at the epicenter of important events and not infrequently led to the destruction and ravaging of their population and temporary or more permament occupation (from the 13th century) by foreign rulers; this had repercussions on art, sometimes minor and other times negligible.

The great, monumental wealth of the Aegean area is not sufficiently well-known to make a comprehensive evaluation and categorization of its contribution to the art of Byzantium as a whole which was, essentially, religious art enlisted in the service of the Church and divine worship. Painting was the main expressive form, with certain intriguing aspects on the islands, even some of exceptional interest for their period and of particular significance for the history of Byzantine art in its entirety.

The sporadic show of interest by the central authority and the initiatives the local secular and ecclesiastic officials promoted from time to time, as well as other factors, enriched the islands with noteworthy monuments whose brilliance went beyond the boundaries of the provincial district. But these did not exclusively determine the position of the island world in the art of Byzantium, nor did they cover the entire spectrum of artistic production. Its image, which otherwise would be incomplete, is supplemented by the numerous monuments, less brilliant and of uneven value, which corresponded to the aesthetic tastes and the theoretical preferences of the population at large and which contain elements concerning the sources, the orientations and the pursuits of local art during its course down through time.

Early Christian Art

The Aegean islands, lying on the route by which Christianity spread into the West, was exposed to apostolic preaching very early on. The memory of the Early Christian centuries are preserved in the catacombs in Trypiti, Milos, a unique, for Greece, subterranean cemetery complex, with the remains of paintings on its walls.

Religious enthusiasm and economic prosperity are shown by the numerous, large, Early Christian churches, which covered the spiritual needs of the faithful after the triumph of the new religion. Constructed until the 5th and 6th century in coastal settlements, which were secure during the period of the Byzantine thalassocracy, and in the hinterland, not infrequently on the sites of abolished ancient temples, their remains are found in impressive numbers on the islands; only the majestic Panayia Katapoliani on Paros remains intact. Indicative of this are the more than 300 buildings from Early Christian times, mainly ecclesiastical, that have been located in the Dodecanese and Lesbos alone, where they have the greatest density.

The Early Christian churches were ornamented with architectural and decorative sculpture and mosaic floors, while the excavation of the large basilica at the junction of P. Mela and Cheimarras streets in the town of Rhodes has also revealed fragments of noteworthy wall paintings (ill. 5) and of a wall mosaic.

Sculpture

Many marble, sculptural parts are found *in situ* (Katapoliani) and in excavations, either scattered around the monuments or re-used in later churches and other structures. Their designs and their relief decoration, circulating throughout the Byzantine empire, the prototypes coming from Constantinople, were drawn from a reservoir of familiar types and forms, inherited from ancient tradition, which were altered in style, re-fashioned and enriched with the symbolism of Christian subject matter, in order to express the new ethos in art.

They were carved by local craftsmen in the main, but in certain cases they perhaps came from the workshops of the capital, to ornament the important buildings on the large islands. Most probably a rare type of Corinthian capital in the Archeological Collection of Pythagoreion, Samos, from the first half of the 6th century, emanated from Constantinople; its wind-blown paired acanthus leaves are folded up and open like the wings of a butterfly (ill. 6). Frequently, moreover, these pieces have interesting typological divergences and variations of decorative features, which contribute to a deeper knowledge of Early Christian plastic arts. Outstanding examples of this are the pulpits in the basilicas of Ayios Kirykos and Thesmophorion in Delos and the pulpits in Paros, the altars in Thera, Rhodes and Delos, the ciborium in Katapoliani in Paros and the episcopal throne in the Museum of Mytilene.

5. Rhodes. Early Christian basilica on P. Mela and Cheimarras Sts. Fragment of a wall painting.

6. Column capital. Samos, Archeological Collection, Pythagoreion.

5

6

Several of the most important works of Early Christian sculpture from the 4th and 5th century from the Aegean are in the Byzantine Museum of Athens. Among the best of their kind is the round, marble altar from Thera (ill. 53) decorated on its wide, finely fashioned border with a lively relief composition of wild animals which are hunting down and tearing smaller animals to bits in a forest indicated by a few, schematic trees, and also containing four male and female heads at diametrically opposite points. The same attachment to the beloved motifs of Greek antiquity is shown in the decoration on a similar altar in the Museum of Rhodes, which also has hunting scenes and heads of men and women at opposite ends of it. A fragment of another one from Milos in the Byzantine Museum shows a wounded lion with the hunter's spear stuck in its breast.

The well-known funerary stele with a statue of Orpheus on a small, four-sided base, comes from Aegina (ill. 52). Seated in front of a tree trunk, Orpheus is playing his lyre and captivating animals, mythological beasts and birds, immobile around him in a perforated ring, just like Christ did with people through the Divine Word; the musical harmony moves across the surface of the sculpture in a slow rhythm.

A rare pictorial relief of the Nativity, also in the Byzantine Museum, is from Naxos and probably from the Early Christian basilica at Lathrinos near Sagri (ill. 54). The swaddled infant, in a built manger in the middle, the two animals warming it with their breath and the two trees on the ends compose an unaffected and tranquil image. The sculptural undulations on the surface and the combination of high and low relief create the illusion of a landscape and give the impression of depth, while the intense chiaroscuro, the variation of the forms and the small divergences from strict symmetry constitute concessions to the picturesque which enliven the subject.

Mosaic Floors

The mosaic floors are an important chapter in Early Christian art in the Aegean. At least one hundred mosaic aggregates are known, most of them from the 5th and 6th century, which decorated the basilicas and other structures. The largest number, around seventy, are in the Dodecanese with Lesbos, Samos and Chios right behind. Conversely, few mosaics, or Early Christian monuments in general, have been found in the Cyclades.

Amid the decorative homogeneity of the mosaics in the Dodecanese, the floors in the buildings in Kos (ills. 55, 56, 58), stand out for their superior quality; Lesbos similarly stands out among the rest of the islands. The most important mosaic workshop, which flourished in the second half of the 5th and the beginning of the 6th century, has been located in Kos. Distinctive motifs, some uncommon, which the workshop used and which are also found in the mosaics of Rhodes, Samos and even in far-off Crete, determine the probable extent of its influences in the broader island complex. More generally, it has been observed that the decoration of the mosaic floors, which flourished on the islands, particularly in the eastern part of the Aegean, shows, in its typological formation and thematic rendering, some interesting links with corresponding works in Constantinople, Asia Minor, mainland Greece, Crete and Cyprus; links which in certain cases indicate special relationships, beyond those which the common vocabulary of the period defined, and allude to the important position of the Aegean in the moulding and the transmission of decorative features and forms.

Geometric decoration was dominant. The designs from the living tradition of Graeco-Roman art and others which contemporary sensibility and Christian thought created, compose a thematic range of forms of exceptional variety which are rendered with harmonious and vibrant colors and in a style corresponding to the urban, or the more vernacular, character of the buildings. They are primarily geometric and foliate designs; fish, animals and birds of various kinds are also found. The latter, naturalistic or schematized, convey the beauty and the motion of simple, natural life to a world of geometric order, fashioned into dense and complex shapes, hierarchic in the arrangement of their component parts and in their organic correspondence with the architectural forms of the space and infused with religious symbols which are connected to folk cosmology and reflect heavenly harmony. The holy shape of the Cross is to be found everywhere in church mosaics, in a variety of decorative forms. The symbolic representation with two facing peacocks is also common and in the beautiful mosaic of the Afendellis basilica in Lesbos constitutes the main motif in the elegant composition in the sanctuary; it has a scarab between the lithe peacocks and a vine covered in shoots which is emerging from the vase and spreading symmetrically along the surface, with birds and grapes among the spiraling vegetation.

7. Naxos. Panayia Drosiani. Ascension, angel (detail).

7

The human figure is rarely encountered, mainly in emblems and "pseudo-emblems" such as in the Tallaras bath in Astypalaia (ill. 59) and in a mosaic that was uncovered in an excavation on Demoyerontias St. in Chios (ill. 57), while on the one in the Niboreios basilica in Symi there is a hearty figure of a young man who is pulling his camel along on a rope. The mosaic in the Tallaras bath (ill. 59), from the 5th century, is of especial interest for the use of a motif from late Antiquity, one of the most beloved in the Early Christian mosaic floors in Greece: the personification of the year or the sun on the central emblem with the zodiac all around, uniquely depicted here, with the seasons and the months; this is rendered with linear simplicity and a composition almost classical in style.

Miniatures

Most of the portable objects of ecclesiastical and secular art were lost in the tempests which raged across the Aegean during various periods. Scattered finds from excavations, and treasures containing miniatures as well as coins that have come to light in Lesbos, Samos and Rhodes, give us an idea of the works that once existed on the islands.

The most important treasure was found in Krategos, Mytilene, which is dated to the beginning of the 7th century and consists of the coins of the emperors Phocas and Heracleios and the state seals for the control of the quality of silver in the "pentasfragista" vessels (those stamped with the five official seals of the controller of the quality of silver) (ills. 60-63). It consists of gold jewellery with perforated and carved decoration, silver vessels, gold coins and so forth. The designs, mostly geometric and foliate, on the jewellery and the best vessels, are in the style of the time. They have elements from Antiquity and Christianity, such as the Cross on a round, gold talisman (ill. 63) and silver trays, surrounded by shoots with leaves in the center with fluted, gilt mouldings (ill. 61) and two, tiny peacocks with a plant in the middle of one of the bands (ill. 62). The preference, moreover, of aristocratic circles for mythological and other motifs from Greek antiquity, which survived in the early Byzantine period, is shown in the decoration of a trulla with a nude female figure on the handle and other figures on the lip of the vessel (ill. 60).

Early Byzantine Wall Paintings

There are early Byzantine monumental paintings in the Aegean, specifically in Naxos, where churches are decorated with wall paintings, some of the rarest from this time.

The triconch church of the Panayia Drosiani near the village of Moni, Naxos, retains its original decoration, which was discovered by the Archeological Service, in the dome, the sanctuary and the north conch under subsequent wall paintings and whitewash, and is dated to the first half of the 7th century (ills. 7, 64-66, 68). It is perhaps the most complete surviving program of a painted church of the period and has iconographic peculiarities which are not to be found in any other. Its main areas of interest are Christ, both as a young, beardless man and more mature with a beard, in a unique double depiction on the dome, which is an interpretation of the dogma of the dual nature, divine and human, of the Lord; the Ascension in the apse of the sanctuary (ills. 7, 64) where instead of the usual four, six angels are holding Christ in Majesty; the Virgin Nikopoios and the Deesis, one of the oldest known, are in the north conch (ill. 68). The painting in the sanctuary is more intense and free in its plastic impression, where the beauty of the angel on the south side of the arch facing the main church (ill. 65) and the powerful, realistic rendering of another angel in the Ascension (ill. 7) aspire to a similar dynamic expression, which finds, in a self-composed abstract mood, more distinctive tones in the north conch with the dazzling face of the Virgin Nikopoios (ill. 66) and the delicate figures of the Deesis (ill. 68). In the main inscription, the reference to the painted figures as "sacred images", which were paid for by many Christians, "for blessing and salvation...", as is deduced from the six, dedicatory inscriptions which accompany them, is of particular interest concerning the perception the faithful had of the painted representations of the saints in their churches. The view on walls paintings – icons – dedications, was developed down through time, especially in Naxos, in the frequently repeated, partial or whole, wall paintings in Byzantine churches.

8. *Naxos. Protothroni. Aniconic decoration and traces of a hierarch from the next painting phase.*

Wall paintings from around the same time as those in Drosiani, but in another style, decorate the large, most probably episcopal, church of the Panayia Protothroni in Chalki. What remains are the Apostles from the depiction of the Ascension of Christ in Majestas Domini in the apse, of monumental size and posture with wide-open ecstatic eyes (ill. 69): a half-length Saint Isidoros on its two-lobed window on the left side, with strong characteristics on the dark-colored face and large, gleaming eyes (ill. 67); among others a difficult to distinguish representation on the north wall of the prothesis where the two layers of the painting on the tympanum of the blind vault are cut-off by its arch, which was fashioned by the interior addition of a wall during the alteration of the old church into a transitional type of cross-inscribed church with a dome.

The wall paintings we have spoken of signal the beginning of a great and virtually uninterrupted series of painted decorations, in a part of or over entire churches, up to the 15th century which bear witness, along with the other works of art, to the unbroken continuity of artistic production in the cultural unity of the Aegean island area. In their entirety they today exceed four hundred painted works of which around two hundred are in Naxos, an island of vital importance. This phenomenon on the largest island of the Cyclades is of particular import, especially the density of the decorations in the painting covering the churches of Naxos which, taking into account the island's size, is even greater than on Crete where about one thousand painted aggregates have been preserved; thus it holds first place in the map of Byzantine monumental painting, at least from the point of view of the geographical distribution of the works.

Middle Byzantine Art
Aniconic Wall Paintings

The great upheavals of the Iconoclast period (726-843/867), if in the main an affair of the Capital, appear to have set their mark on the Aegean islands as well. But while the historical sources refer to the participation of the islanders in sporadic, icon-worshipping, revolutionary movements which were organized by the outlying districts against the Capital, the aniconic wall paintings in the churches of this period, many of which in the Aegean can be dated to the 9th century, bear witness to iconoclastic tendencies which were approved of and supported by a part of the population. Through data supplied by archeological research, we find the largest part of these wall paintings are also in Naxos.

Aniconic decorations have been located in twelve and perhaps as many as fifteen churches in Naxos; they are the main church of Protothroni and in other churches which serve villages and rural settlements and cover a large and productive area of the rich island. The most important and best known are those in Protothroni (ill. 8), Ayia Kyriaki at Apeiranthos, Ayios Ioannis Theologos at Adisarou (ills. 70, 71) and Ayios Artemios, near Sagri (ills. 72, 73).

Aniconic wall paintings have also been found in Rhodes on the first layer of Ayios Georgios Chostos in Lindos and it seems the fragments of aniconic painting high up on the side walls of the sanctuary, which belong to the first of the six successive painting layers and to the oldest building stage of the *katholikon* (main church) of the Monastery of the Taxiarch Michael at Thari, near Laerma, are a work of this period. Recently aniconic wall paintings were found on Amorgos, on the first of three layers of the church of the Evangelistria near Katapola, and they probably also exist in another church on the island where a trial investigation was carried out to find them. Similar wall paintings have been found in Crete, in the church of Ayios Nikolaos at Kastelli, Merabellou (ill. 9) and even in Cyprus known as a place of exile of icon worshippers, in the eastern dome of Ayia Paraskevi, Yeroskipos, and a few on mainland Greece – Thessaloniki, Evrytania and Mani.

9. Crete. Ayios Nikolaos, Kastelli Merabellou. Aniconic decoration.

The late and rather strange non-figurative decorations in the churches of Ayios Pavlos near Akamatra, Icaria and Ayia Anna near Elymbos, Karpathos are in another category. They are one-color or two-color designs of another type, a folk-like idiom. The rather makeshift, repeated drawings with many, equally hasty inscriptions evoking "Lord assist..." on the side walls of the sanctuary of Ayios Georgios Chostos in Lindos, which belong to a more recent addition that covered in part the original, aniconic painting on the east wall, have been assigned to the same category.

Whether directly or indirectly connected to the ideological and political movement of Iconoclasm, the aniconic painting on the islands has certain programmatic principles in common, which can also be confirmed in the wall paintings from other regions, and a rich, decorative glossary, basically employing a variety of geometric and foliate designs of Early Christian art and some of Islamic derivation which are handled with facility by the painters in their design and chromatic interpretations. The holy symbol of the Cross is dominant in the painting in the apse (just as in the iconoclastic decorations of the monuments in Constantinople); it also decorates the dome of Ayia Paraskevi, Yeroskipos in Cyprus and, moreover, is practically effaced in the dense geometric formations of the designs. The single surviving representation with birds in Ayia Kyriaki, Apeiranthos is of particular interest – similar representations of iconoclastic decorations in churches were commented on in texts from that period – and for the important place it has in two panels in the lower register of the apse, left and right of the episcopal throne. The large bird with its little ones around it, with the Sassanian band ringing its neck, a symbol of royal authority in the past, perhaps stands for the Mother-Church which protects the faithful, in the sense of divine protection.

The aniconic wall painting in the apse of the sanctuary of Protothroni, with its large crosses under an arcade, is of importance (ill. 8), for the dating and the interpretation of these wall paintings (which have proven valuable for our knowledge of the ideological currents of the period), because in a second painting stage in the church this covered over the wall painting of the Apostles from the 7th century. It is obvious that the replacement of a figurative with a non-figurative representation would have not had any other motive than the clear and specific decision to have icons erased from the church. Indeed, such a decision in Naxos, with its figurative pre-iconoclastic decorations and in a church of the size and import of Protothroni would not be intelligible except within the chronological and ideological framework of Iconoclasm. The half-effaced confrontal hierarchs from the 10th-11th century, which were painted without adding plaster as a ground over the wall painting with the crosses, also supplies the oldest chronological limit for their covering, when the aniconic wave had passed, giving way to the new iconographic ideas which the restoration of the icons brought about.

Works from the 9th-10th century

Scattered works have been preserved from the following years. These are: in Naxos a section of a beautiful wall-painting of Virgin and Child vivid in appearance, a freshly and lusciously fashioned painted layer of the church of Ayios Nikolaos near Sagri, which has been dated to the 9th-10th century; the church of the Panayia Kaloritsa, in a deep and spacious cave on the mountain of Profitis Ilias, retains the original decoration of the apse in the Sanctuary which is dated to the second quarter of the 10th century (ills. 74-77). On a light blue background are depicted on a half apse the Virgin and Child enthroned with venerating archangels, the Prodrome and a prophet on the ends; on a smaller scale below, the Apostles with a roundel of the Virgin, framed above the episcopal throne, in the middle. The apostles are transported through the power of the portraiture and chromatic freedom in the rendering of their robust characters (ills. 75, 76); they are also organized in terms of their archaic iconography and the symbolic presence of the roundel of the Virgin in the center with pre-iconoclastic works such as Protothroni and Drosiani. The visible sections of figures from the original decoration of Saint John the Theologian at Aphikli near Apeiranthos, may be from the same Kaloritsa workshop. We also must mention a marble closure panel in the Archeological Museum of Andros with a relief depiction of a lion, one of the most vigorous from the 9th-10th century (ill. 10) and several important illuminated manuscripts in Patmos in the Monastery of Saint John the Theologian, from the 9th (ill. 120) and 10th (ill. 121) century.

Monumental Painting and Sculpture from the 11th and 12th century

The Panayia Drosiani, which must have been one of the most venerated churches on Naxos, owed its successive painting layers up to the 14th century to the dedications of the pious Christians on the island. Of particular interest is the Deesis which covered the original wall painting of Christ's Ascension on the half-apse (ills. 12, 14). This is the earliest of three successive layers of wall paintings in the apse with the Deesis as their subject (it was removed in 1980).

It is a fine work, perhaps from the 11th century, with expressive transparency, a drawing of clear and faultless line and nobility of color bearing important witness to the quality of the artistic dynamic during that period of the island. The representation is important because of the valuable inheritance which the Aegean has preserved; this one contains the name of its painter, Georgios, one of the few known from middle Byzantine monumental painting and the first from the islands whose work has survived. The painter of Drosiani, unknown elsewhere, is commemorated on the left, next to the Virgin, by the inscriptions which fill the space between the figures of the Deesis: "the decoration and the painting of the venerated icon of the Blessed Mother of God was done at the expense and by the hand of the sinner Georgios the painter..." and the larger, nearly illegible, inscription to the right mentions the other faithful who contributed so that the "icons" of Christ and Ioannis could be done. Most probably this Georgios would not have considered it necessary (like so many others) to have signed his work, if he himself had not undertaken a part of the cost, for the salvation of his soul.

10. Marble panel. Andros, Archeological Museum.

The middle Byzantine years are represented by artistic works of great range from the 11th century and afterward which were created on the islands through imperial grants and the contributions of prominent officials. The brilliant mosaic decoration of the Nea Moni on Chios is the supreme example (ills. 11, 78-83). One of the most costly works in Byzantine art, which the Aegean has the good fortune to possess, it is also of value for the direct testimony it supplies of the real, if only occasional, imperial concern for the island region and the protection offered by the Capital. It is dated to the years between 1049 and 1055, during the reign of Constantine IX Monomachus and owes its creation to the goodwill and the generosity shown to the monk-founders by the Porphyrogenetes daughters of Constantine VIII, Zoe and Theodora, and the third husband of Zoe, Constantine IX Monomachus, for the erection and the dedication of the Nea Moni.

The mosaics, by and large preserved, decorate the surfaces on the highest part of the *katholikon*, above the marble panels on the walls, in the sanctuary, the eight-apsed main church of unusual conception and the esonarthex. The gold background, with its otherworldly luster, makes tangible the heavenly environment of the church, having Christ Pantocrator at the peak, glorified by the angels around him which constituted the center of the iconographic system on the dome that was destroyed. The praying Virgin in the main apse of the sanctuary with the Archangels Michael and Gabriel on the apses of the *prothesis* and the *diakonikon*; the representations with the most notable events surrounding the dogma of the life of Christ (ills. 11, 77-81) and others connected to the liturgical use of the esonarthex; the Virgin on its blind dome, the Evangelists, apostles, prophets and saints of all orders (ills. 82, 83) in a hierarchal arrangement, make up this magnificent work which brought the delicate and mellow hues of the Constantinopolitan artists to the island of Chios in this sole surviving mosaic aggregate in a church from the middle of the 11th century.

11. Chios. Nea Moni. Mosaic of the Betrayal (detail).

Wall paintings from the 11th century have survived in quite a few churches on Naxos, whose important place in the Theme of the Aegean and its consequent relations with

11

12. *Naxos. Panayia Drosiani. Georgios: The Deesis, the Virgin (detail).*

the capital are confirmed by the participation of the *protospatharios* and *tourmarchis* of Naxia, Nikitas, in the renovation of the Church of Protothroni in 1052, according to the inscription on a marble *kosmetes* in the church which also mentions the Bishop Leon and the Count Stephanos Kamilaris. Protothroni (ills. 13, 84-90), Drosiani (ills. 12, 14), Ayios Georgios Diasoritis (ills. 92-97), Ayios Ioannis of Avlonitsa (ill. 91), probably the Panayia Arliotissa, on its first painted layer, and the *katholikon* of the small monastery of Ayios Dimitrios in Chalandra, Kynidaros, as well as other churches, all contain important works of art which testify to the prosperity of the island.

The inscription on the *kosmetes* concerning the renovation of Protothroni and the slightly later inscription in the northwest funerary side-chapel which commemorates the funeral of the servant of God, Anna, in 1056, led to two successive painted layers in the large dome of the church (ills. 13, 84, 85, 88) in 1052 and 1056. It is very likely that the original layer removed from the dome and the wall paintings which are preserved on the south arm of the cross and at other points (ills. 84, 85, 87, 89) belong to earlier times, in the 10th-11th century and the second layer to 1052. Archangels, cherubim and seraphim are in regular alteration with prophets on the first layer of the dome, but in a highly unusual position in a single band around the Pantocrator at the peak, while on the second layer, and in a more archaic iconographic composition, figures from the previous ones are missing so that four of the most beloved saints in the Byzantine calendar

13. *Naxos. Protothroni. Second decoration of the dome, the prophet Sophonias (detail).*

14. *Naxos. Panayia Drosiani. Georgios: The Deesis, Christ (detail).*

of feast-days can be depicted on the east part: Georgios, Nikolaos, Dimitrios and Theodoros. The oldest painting (ills. 84, 85, 87, 89), monumental in style, showing organic movement and chromatic nobility in composition, the faces sensitive and lucid, can be compared to works of the highest quality from Asia Minor and Greece itself. The subsequent painting of the dome is dense, heavy and more schematic, more anti-classical in manner of composition, with less variety of color and an emphasis on ornamentation, creating some very powerful, free and easy figures of archangels and prophets like that of Sophonias (ills. 13, 88) with an intense and dynamic presence. The large wall painting of the Annunciation on the south wall of the sanctuary has tall, noble figures in a different style (ill. 86) and is dated to the late 11th century. The saints on the east wall of the northwest side-chapel (where there are two painted layers on the south side), probably after 1056 (ill. 90), have vigorous traits, folds in their garments with formations and shapes more typical of the period, which probably indicate the hand of another painter, perhaps the same one who decorated the apse of the sanctuary in a small church of Profitis Ilias in Mesa Potamia.

In Naxos the agreement between the old and the new ideas in the iconographic programs of the churches constitutes a noteworthy characteristic, which can be verified in the unbroken continuity of monumental painting (and architecture as well) till the 14th century. In the diconch side-chapel of the cruciform church of Ayios Ioannis in Avlonitsa, whose founding pre-dates the large church, the only representation that has survived is a bust of Saint John the Prodrome in the south conch (ill. 91) which recalls the ancient tradition of the iconography of martyrs, with the representation of the venerated saint in the apse of the sanctuary. The representation of Georgios in the apse of Diasoritis (ill. 97) and probably, from the 13th-14th century, the Dormition of the Virgin in the lower register of the apse of Drosiani, the only example in this position, belong to the same tradition. Monumental in size and exceptional in craft, the depiction of the Prodrome in the side-chapel at Avlonitsa, bold and dominating in its expressive means, could be compared at certain points to the figures from the first painted stage of the dome of Protothroni. The wall painting is also of interest in terms of the method used by the richly endowed painters on the island, like the one who did Avlonitsa, who also undertook the decoration of humble buildings in the countryside with the same skill.

The modern ideas of Constantinople found in the mosaic decoration of the Nea Moni on Chios do not appear to have had an immediate effect on painting in Naxos. Near Chalki, a settlement which probably had a leading place in the administrative system of the island, the painted church of Ayios Georgios Diasoritis, which offers the most complete wall painting aggregate from a church of the 11th century in the Aegean region (ills. 92-97), displays a mixture of the typical painting program of the period, obviously dependent on the Capital in terms of the hierarchy of the figures and the clarity of the figurative language, combined with archaicism and interesting iconographic peculiarities, many of which owe their origin to the East. The former patron saint of mariners, Saint Phocas, in the *diakonikon*, a hierarch with an oar in hand, co-exists in the sanctuary with the new patron saint of sailors, Saint Nikolas, in the apse (ill. 97); a mounted Saint George killing Diocletian and Theodoros killing the dragon (ill. 96), according to an iconographic tradition which is native to Georgia, Cappadocia and elsewhere, are depicted in the main church where Saint George the Dragon-Slayer is also found in a narrative scene which perhaps constitutes the earliest known representation. Rare depictions, such as Joshua with his enigmatic escort, in the prothesis, engaged in a dialogue with the Archangel Michael, or the martyr, unknown elsewhere, Saint Teknodotos and the triptych of the great martyr Georgios on the lower register of the apse with his father

15

16

15, 16. Andros. Taxiarch of Mesaria. The Last Judgement (details).

Gerontios and his mother Saint Polychronia (ill. 97), probably based on the prototype of a portable triptych icon which reveals an unknown aspect of the worship of the widely beloved saint, constitute some other interesting points of the iconographic program, which has as its poles Christ Pantocrator on the dome (ill. 92), surrounded by four archangels and the Virgin and Child in a bust in the apse (ill. 97). There are some indications that several iconographic choices were related to the recorded migration of Asia Minor Christian populations during this time who took refuge on the islands, while the later appearances of some of these representations in churches on Crete and in mainland Greece point up the place the Aegean always held in the circulation of ideas. The wall paintings of Diasoritis are the works of good painters, which can be placed in the second half of the 11th century, balanced and symmetrical in their linear and plastic undulations with vivid colors and some of the most tender portraits of angels and young saints.

The elevation of the bishopric of Naxos into the Metropolitan of Paronaxia in 1083, at the dawn of the Comnenian dynasty, without a doubt went hand in hand with the artistic well-being of the island which also produced good subsequent examples on the second painted layer of Ayios Nikolaos near Sagri (ill. 98) and of the large church of the Panayia Archatou, probably works by the same painter. The elegant (despite later interventions) church of the Taxiarch Michael in Mesaria, Andros, which has retained parts of its sculptural and painted decoration, was built, according to its two marble inscriptions, in 1158 by Constantine Monastiriotis and his wife Eirene Prasini "under the rule of Manuel Comnenus". There are few Byzantine churches which have survived in this second largest of the Cyclades and even fewer that have uncovered sections of their pictorial decoration preserved. Among them, the precisely dated church of the Taxiarch Michael in Mesaria along with the earlier Church of the Taxiarch in Melida constitute the most important monuments of a period of prosperity and achievement on this beautiful island, which was due in large part to the production of and trade in its renowned silk.

The few wall paintings which have been preserved in the sanctuary and the main church of Mesaria must be contemporary with the building. These are representations of the life of Christ and the Mother of God and figures of saints as well as parts from the large composition of the Second Coming which were recently uncovered on the vaults of the narthex (ills. 15, 16). Dainty figures, gracefully drawn, with noble colors, bold movements and somewhat affected stances, faces that retain a memory of ancient beauty, tastefully done with sensitive spirituality, make up this valuable work of refined Comnenian art, from a period when dated paintings are rare. Most probably, this illustrates a connection of the anonymous painter of the Taxiarch with an important, artistic center. It has already been pointed out that the names of the founders are of well-known families of Constantinople and it may very well be Constantine Monastiriotis and Eirene Prasini were members of the aristocracy which ruled the island.

The sculpted, architectural members and the preserved epistyle of the marble iconostasis of the Taxiarch of Mesaria are also of exceptional workmanship. Marble door-frames, column capitals, piers, columns and epistyles of iconostases, even sections of icons, richly decorated, of the same type and analogous artistic dexterity, as well as much else, such as important parts of the epistyle of the iconostasis of the Taxiarch at Melida (ills. 17, 19) are in the Andros Museum, in the parish church of Ayios Nikolaos in Mesaria, a building from the 19th century which was ornamented with sculpture from the Church of the Taxiarch at Melida and an unknown Byzantine church, in the post-Byzantine church of the Taxiarch at Amonakleios and in other churches. Done on a "double-level" relief, with elegant and varied foliate and anthemion designs on a dense tapestry-like background where the high-relief signs of the zodiac, eagles, gryphons, wild-cats and so forth as well as the round or rectangular emblems with foliate complexes emerge at intervals and are some of the best examples of sculpture from the so-called Helladic School of the 12th century, these also give us a picture of the important artistic endeavors on the island which ecclesiastically belonged to the Metropolitan of Athens.

The Monastery of Saint John the Theologian on Patmos, founded by Hosios Christodoulos Latrenos on the deserted island, which was ceded to him by Alexios I Comnenus in 1088 for the erection of the monastery, at the instigation of his mother Anna Dalassini, was destined to know great spiritual and economic development. Preserved in the side-chapel of Hosios Christodoulos is his marble sarcophagus with relief decorations. At the end of the 12th century marvelous wall paintings of Constantinopolitan art decorated the side-chapel of the Panayia, attached to the south side of the *katholikon* and the refectory.

In the chapel are depicted the enthroned Virgin and Child with Michael and Gabriel at the side of the throne, and symbolizing the Holy Trinity; the Hospitality of Abraham on the east wall (ill. 99), the Presentation of the Virgin, Miracles of Christ, the Source of Wisdom, and an unknown hierarch and many saints (ill. 100) on the rest of the surfaces. Iconographic peculiarities of the painting program, which is preserved in large part, and more particularly the many representations of hierarchs who were bishops of

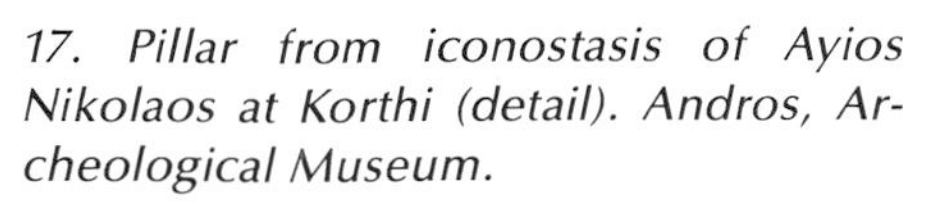

17. Pillar from iconostasis of Ayios Nikolaos at Korthi (detail). Andros, Archeological Museum.

18. Epistyle from iconostasis (detail). Andros, Taxiarch of Mesaria.

19. Epistyle from iconostasis of the Taxiarch of Melida (detail). Andros, Archeological Museum.

17

18

19

20

20. Rhodes. Ayios Ioannis in Paradeisi. The Last Judgement (detail).

Jerusalem, lead straight to the connection of the decoration with Hosios Leontios, abbot of the Monastery and later Patriarch of Jerusalem during the years 1176-1183, who, unable to exercise his duties in Jerusalem which was occupied by the Crusaders, remained in Constantinople where he continued to be in charge of the care of the Patmian monastery. According to a recent point of view, the donor of the wall paintings was not Leontios but, as had been previously maintained, his successor at the monastery, the abbot Arsenios who provided for the decoration and dedicated the side-chapel to Hosios Leontios, during a period from 1185 to the end of the century. This work of high art, which shows the level and kind of spiritual cultivation of the monks who were its receivers, is balanced and symmetrical, a pure composition in a monumental style, while the dynamic perception of post-Comnenian painting is expressed without excess in the finely drawn figures, their urgent motion and the lively folds of their garments, the serious and rather melancholic faces, the emphasis on the empty space, and the sonorous colors of the composition.

On the west side, an uncovered wall painting with fragments from the Miracles of Christ and the monk saints (ill. 101) remains from the original painting of the refectory, one of the oldest wall painting decorations that have survived. It is done in the same style as those in the chapel with a dynamic, freer moulding of the figures and must have followed them chronologically.

The figure of Ayios Vasileios in the Cave of the Apocalypse (ill. 102) is connected with the painting of the Refectory in the most recent of the two, successive painted layers on the east side, which was decorated with wall paintings. Conversely, the main representation of the Evangelist John who, divinely inspired, is dictating to his student Prochoros, standing before the cave (ill. 23), appears more conservative in the modelling

21

21. Kalymnos. Ayioi Apostoloi in Argos. Saint Peter (detail).

of the faces and in the linear shapes of the folds which recall older methods, probably influenced by the prototype.

A wall painting with a similar rendering of faces covers the aniconic decoration on the apse of Ayios Georgios Chostos, in Lindos, Rhodes (ill. 103) also of interest for its archaic iconography, with five confrontal saints on the lower register, Saint George dressed in a military uniform in the middle, hierarchs and a martyred, female saint. The linear dimension of John at the Cave of the Apocalypse, also characterizes, in another style, the Apostle Peter in the Patmian monastic estate of the church of Ayioi Apostoloi in Argos, Kalymnos (ill. 21); this is a broad and vigorous figure, with a stressed volume and a linear schematization of the formal details along with the movement of the folds in the garments in dynamic curves.

There are quite a few other examples of intense artistic activity on the islands, particularly in the later years of the 12th century. In Rhodes, in the pronaos of Ayios Ioannis Koufas in Paradeisi, whose walls are decorated with wall paintings – dedications from the 12th up to the 15th century – a section of the Second Coming of exceptional craft, with those condemned to Hell on the south side, has been preserved from the original painting of the church (ill. 20); the beautiful representation of the mounted Saint Merkourios on the west end of the same wall belongs to the following years. It is also worth noting the representations of two hierarchs and sections from the Annunciation on the east side of the originally wooden-roofed church of the Archangel Michael of Thari, Rhodes at the

22. Naxos. Panayia Damiotissa. The Dormition of the Virgin (detail).

22

end of the 12th century, and at the turn of the century the rather mediocre wall paintings on the sanctuary of Ayios Minas in Lindos which are of interest for their dynamic, if affected, manner. In Naxos stand out wall paintings such as those in Ayios Pachomios at Apeiranthos, a detached Deesis from the apse of Drosiani and above all those of the Panayia Damiotissa near Kaloxylos, where the grief of the apostles and hierarchs at the Dormition of the Virgin is expressed in passionate terms, their faces furrowed with long creases (ill. 22). The grief of the women who are accompanying the Virgin to the Crucifixion, in the church of the Panayia Krina in Chios (ill. 24), is done in a similar style but with a much more succulent, painterly rendering. The wall paintings in the Panayia Episkopi church in Mesa Gonia, Santorini are probably dated to 1176 or 1181, according to chronological data on an inscription which has been preserved in a written source from 1701. But the same source also mentions Alexios I Comnenus (1081-1118) in its reading of the inscription which accompanied the existing representation of a Byzantine emperor in the wall paintings and the donor of the Episkopi. The surviving marble iconostasis of this middle Byzantine church is a rare one with its low relief decoration on a background of mastich wax in deep red and olive colors.

Little is yet known about the original wall paintings of the Panayia Krina in Chios. Thematically they are dependent, to a certain degree, on the mosaic decoration of the Nea Moni and are of great interest, not just for their art which alone places them among the important works of post-Comnenian painting. Dated to 1197 they offer valuable information concerning the founding and the decoration of the church and the participation in the work of leading figures, probably from an aristocratic family of Constantinople.

Late Byzantine Art
Monumental Painting

The art of the Aegean in the 13th and 14th century was influenced by the disturbing political developments when Latin rulers from afar laid claim to its maritime areas after the Fall of Constantinople to the Crusaders in 1204: chief among them were the Venetians who founded the Duchy of the Aegean in the Cyclades with its capital at Naxos. Rhodes was one of the islands that escaped the conquest. Its Byzantine administrator, Leon Gavalas, as so many others in split-off Byzantine lands, declared himself an independent sovereign, "Ruler of God-defended Rhodes", with the title of Caesar.

The wall paintings decorating the Monastery of the Archangel of Thari in Rhodes, from the first half of the 13th century (ills. 104, 106, 107), can be viewed as the most important painted work from that period in the island region. The wooden-roofed church was renovated. Its transformation into a cruciform type with a dome, by the interior addition of walls in the sanctuary, sealed up the wall paintings which existed in the old church. The painting program of the 13th century was preserved to a great extent, despite the new interventions and paintings, in the sanctuary and on the dome. The Pantocrator is depicted on the imposing dome and around him, on high concentric bands, the processional line of ten angels in two hosts of figures and sixteen prophets who are divided by twos on the panels between the windows below with the evangelists on the pendentives.

This is one of the most extensive iconographic programs of this category. In the spacious sanctuary, the iconography with the Miracles of Christ on the east band of the vault and the Ascension to the west, the Last Supper and the Washing of the Feet in large, facing compositions on the side walls with hierarchs, deacons and other saints, present interesting divergences from conventional programs. Characteristic of the monumental decoration are the brightly colored, luminous bands with anthemion and other designs which separate the representations stressing the pure arrangement of the whole.

Similarly, the white outline around the well-wrought figures separates them when necessary from the colored levels on which they are projected. The fine painter of Thari has a feel for space and large surfaces. He creates an inspiring chromatic atmosphere and uses traditional, linear designs with dexterity in the shaping of figures with a contemporary air, a tranquil appearance and strong character, which claim interest as portraits. In quality and in its iconographic formulation, the work reflects ideas which must have been related to the narrow confines of the Empire exiled, from 1204, to Nicaea. Its creation during the period of the ambitious Leon Gavalas, and specifically in the period 1226-1234, when he governed Rhodes with the suzerainty of the emperor, is very likely. At the same time on Crete, the marvelous wall paintings in the church of Ayios Nikolaos of Kyriakosellia in Apokoronas (ill. 105), whose creation is connected with the campaign of the Emperor Ioannis Vatatzis on the Venetian occupied island and the stationing of Byzantine forces in the nearby fortress of Kyriakosellia in 1230-1236, very probably retain an exceptionally sensitive painted testimony concerning the aristocratic art of Nicaea, the importance of which is underlined by the absence of monuments in the Capital itself.

The large number of painted decorations, in comparison to the preceding periods, which were realized mainly in the second half of the 13th century up to the opening decades of the 14th in Venetian occupied Naxos, has been noted. This phenomenon, common on the Aegean islands, on Euboea, Crete and the Frankish areas of mainland Greece, took on an all-embracing character in Naxos where nearly all the churches in

23. Patmos. Cave of the Apocalypse. Saint John dictating to Prochoros.

24. Chios. Panayia Krina. The Crucifixion (detail).

23

24

the countryside – there have not been any Byzantine churches with wall paintings identified in the town itself – were decorated either for the first time (the new ones that were built and others that already existed) or with a few new wall paintings on top of the old ones. The partial covering of aniconic wall paintings from the 9th century, such as in Ayia Kyriaki at Apeiranthos and Ayios Ioannis at Adisarou, which had possibly been more or less abandoned during the period that intervened, were officially returned to service in the late 13th century, "consecrated" by the representation of the Deesis in the apse of the sanctuary. Also of note is the practically complete absence of visible influences of western art, as well as a revival of old iconographic themes and iconological elements of a symbolic, cosmological and glorifying nature. The brownish red of the royal purple in the cycle of the Pantocrator, in one of the "medallions" on the dome of the early Byzantine Drosiani, appeared in the middle Byzantine period, again in the Pantocrator cycle, in the second painting layer of the dome of Protothroni (ill. 88) and on the dome of Ayios Georgios Diasoritis (ill. 92); it re-appeared in the 13th and 14th century decorating the apocalyptic majesty of Christ in the Deesis in the apse of churches such as Ayia Kyriaki at Apeiranthos and Ayios Ioannis Theologos in Kaminos, in 1315, and Ayios Georgios at Oskelos or Noskelos in 1286/87, where in the apse Christ is depicted alone, with the praying figures of the Virgin, the Prodrome and of the apostles Peter and Paul on the intrados of its arch. In the wall paintings from 1270 at Ayios Nikolaos near Sagri, four-faced and six-winged seraphim are depicted on the pendentives of the dome, though its painting composition has not been preserved, and four angels with spread wings holding the celestial medallion of the Pantocrator supported on "columns" in the church of Ayios Ioannis Theologos in Kerami (ills. 108, 109).

Using the dates on the inscriptions of the churches on the island as a criterion for placing other, undated wall paintings, we find this dialectically complex phenomenon was at its height from 1281 to 1315. The donors of the wall paintings were priests and laymen who are mentioned with their families and at times many of them together undertook the expenses for a wall painting, to which even the painter of the church sometimes contributed. This intense activity, which gives interesting examples of the individual and public conscience of the inhabitants who were involved in the pious works of the churches, just as in much earlier times, were fashions in a climate of ideas where the re-awakened Orthodox feeling was expressed through an insistence on tradition and was imbued with the idea of reaction to foreign influences and impositions, deriving from several points of view the concept of a national self-awareness and resistance. Outside the situation that was created by foreign occupation certain events of local importance as well as other more important events which determined the fate of Byzantium and Orthodoxy certainly made a contribution to the fashioning of a climate of ideas such as this. Specifically, the re-occupation of Constantinople in 1261 by Michael VIII Palaeologus, the agreement on the unification of the Churches at the Synod of Lyon in 1274 and its rejection in 1282 by Andronicus II Palaeologus – as very frequently elsewhere, Andronicus is mentioned in the founder's inscription in the apse of the sanctuary of Ayios Georgios Vardas in Rhodes in 1289-1290. Of course, the more general impetus art received in the retrogressive Byzantium of the period of the Palaeologues, was very important and should not be ignored.

The quality of the painting and the techniques vary and it is not difficult to distinguish local workshops or the artistry of certain painters in various churches. The names of two painters are mentioned in cases where, it seems, they were included among those funding the decoration. They are the priest Michael at Panayia Archatou in 1285 and Nikiphoros at Theologos in Afikli in 1309. There were also a few dedicators who were

25

25. Naxos. Ayios Nikolaos of Komiaki. The Deesis, Saint John the Prodrome.

not satisfied by just a mention in an inscription and are depicted praying in the wall paintings, such as in the "depressed" Panayia Fasoulou or Theotokos "at the common" of Apeiranthos, in 1281 and in the newer layer of the Deesis in the apse of Drosiani where a miniscule dedicator is kneeling in front of the Virgin Mary and praying to Christ (ill. 110). Among the wall paintings most interesting for their art, the following stand out: the co-officiating hierarchs at Protothroni, from the fourth painted layer on the bottom register of the apse, the wall paintings from Ayios Ioannis at Kerami (ills. 108, 109); the outstanding Deesis from Ayios Georgios at Lathrinos (ills. 111, 112); Ayios Georgios at Pera Chalki (ills. 113, 114); Ayios Ioannis at Avlonitsa; the Panayia Archatou; Kaloritsa; the Panayia Monastiriotissa at Mesa Gitonia, Egares; Ayios Georgios at Potamia; Ayios Panteleimon at Pera Chalki; Ayios Stephanos at Tsikalario and Ayios Nikolaos at Troulos Skadou in Komiaki (ill. 25).

In the 13th and 14th century many other churches and monastery buildings on other islands were decorated with wall paintings: in Paros, Kea (ill. 26), Seriphos, Sikinos, Ios, Anafi, in the Cyclades; in Aegina, Chios, Patmos (ills. 115, 116), Rhodes (ills. 27-30, 117, 118), Kos, Kalymnos, Chalki and so on. Iconographic peculiarities and stylistic variations characterize their local, artistic idiom and fashion their particular style and at the same time denote the duration and the continuation of tradition and the receiving of new ideas from both large and small centers, their processing, re-moulding and transmission.

The wall paintings which decorated the vaulted dome-covered refectory of the

26

26. Kea. Ayioi Apostoloi. The evangelist Matthew.

Monastery of the Theologian on Patmos, after structural alterations during the one or two painting stages in the 13th century, are of especial interest for the iconographic program, which has been preserved to a satisfactory extent (ills. 115, 116). Scenes from the Passion and the Resurrection of Christ, Eucharistical and other depictions of a dogmatic or instructional content, such as the Ecumenical Councils and The Death of the Righteous Man, as well as figures of saints are rendered with marvelous art (which is related to the preceding painting in the monastery) frequently with vigorous movement and dramatic resonances in the moulding of the compositions, and elsewhere in more monumental tones.

Not many wall paintings from the 13th century are preserved on Rhodes. The Baptism in the pronaos of Ayios Ioannis Koufas in Paradeisi follows the technique used in the Monastery at Thari. In the church of Ayios Phanourios on Rhodes, the harmonious composition and the delicacy of the painting in the uncovered section of the Ascension gives us an idea of the superior quality of the art in the town (ill. 27). The decoration in the little church of Ayios Georgios of Vardas near Apolakkia, which was done under Andronicus II Palaelogus in 1289-1290 (ills. 117, 118) is also worthy of note. A good, provincial work with fresh figures, it shows through its iconography and technique that it was well-informed on contemporary tendencies in the Capital.

Of great interest is the painting on Rhodes in the 14th and 15th century after its seizure and during the long interval of its occupation by the western monastic order of the Knights of Saint John (1309-1522), who upon leaving Jerusalem and later Accra and Cyprus, settled on Rhodes and created a powerful little state in the Dodecanese which kept the Ottoman Turks at bay for more than two centuries. Economic prosperity, social and intellectual cultivation, the ease of communication with East and West and the tolerance, to a point, shown by the Knights in regard to the ecclesiastical affairs of the Orthodox, favored art which is demonstrated in terms of multiform points of view and tendencies and noteworthy correspondances with the painting in Cyprus and Crete where analogous conditions prevailed and an even longer occupation, and with whom Rhodes had links.

27

27. Rhodes. Ayios Phanourios. The Ascension (detail).

28. *Rhodes. Ayios Andreas at Afantou. The Nativity (Panayia tou Kastrou), the midwife with Christ (detail).*

There is mention made of around one hundred and forty works from various painting layers of churches and other buildings from this period in the Dodecanese, and more than half are in Rhodes. Only a few, and these are later, are of a purely western technique, and those are in the Knights' buildings. It is characteristic of the reciprocity of the artistic exchanges in the narrow environment of the island that the large Byzantine Cathedral church of the Panayia tou Kastrou, which was turned into a Gothic Cathedral church by the Knights, was decorated in the second quarter of the 14th century with wall paintings and some of the remaining ones are very charming, done in a mixed Byzantine and western style which, moreover, the Knights must have been accustomed to from their long service in the Christian East. During the 15th century in particular, iconographic motifs and technical elements appeared in the churches of the Orthodox and probably in the institutions of the cultivated Greek bourgeoisie, who had relations with the Knights, which show the influence of western art. But this remained limited while in most of the Orthodox churches (ills. 28-30), and particularly in the countryside, the use of western elements in the wall paintings was practically non-existent.

Important examples of painting which was attuned to the contemporary artistic currents of Byzantium are supplied in the 14th century by the decoration of the churches of Ayia Aikaterini (ill. 30) and Ayios Phanourios in the walled town, as well as fragments of the chronologically earlier wall paintings of Ayios Andreas at Afantou (ill. 28). The iconographic programs of churches such as Ayios Phanourios and Ayios Nikolaos in Fountoukli, and later on Ayia Triada in the town and Ayios Nikolaos near Trianta are also worthy of note (ill. 119). The two later churches were decorated with interesting work by one or more painters from the later years of the Knights' rule, with multi-figured representations of a narrative character and miniature figures in an elegant and succinct style with iconographic peculiarities which show the influence of western art, but also an awareness of the contemporary motifs of the early post-Byzantine years.

Contrary to Naxos and the other islands, in Rhodes during the 14th and 15th century, just as in Crete and Cyprus during the same period, the founders and the dedicators, laymen, clergy and monks, living and deceased, were frequently depicted on the wall

29. *Rhodes. Ayios Phanourios. The patrons of the church.*

30

30. Rhodes. Ayia Aikaterini. Saint Peter.

paintings in the churches. The two large representations of Ayios Nikolaos at Fountoukli (in the west conch) are impressive. Right of the entrance the "logothetis" Vardoanis and his wife are offering an effigy of the church to Christ who blesses them, with the Virgin and the Prodrome of the apocalyptic Deesis standing at the sides; in a second depiction opposite, Christ Emmanuel, accompanied by angels at the sides, blesses their three dead children, Maria Vardoani, little Georgios and the dignified youth on the right, done on a white "landscape", with vine-shoots, birds and grapes which suggest Paradise. Among others it is worth noting the representation of the founder and many deceased adults and children, in the narthex of Ayios Phanourios (which was used for funerals) in the town in a similar Paradisical landscape (ill. 29) and the beautiful figure of a young, nobly-dressed woman who is praying to the enthroned Virgin and Child in the main church to the east; there is also the tiny couple who are praying between the figures beneath the Apostles Peter and Paul at Ayios Ioannis Koufas and on the north wall opposite the deceased couple "in Paradise". The white of the ancient funeral lekythi emerges from the memory of the ages to denote here as well the surroundings of the deceased in a Christian paradise. These priceless portraits in the decorations of churches on Rhodes, a living depiction of the times and the place, offer much information concerning the inhabitants of the island, the wealthy bourgeoisie for the most part, their habits and their misfortunes, their attire and their adornment in line with the social class to which they belonged.

Middle and Late-Byzantine Portable Works

Very little has survived of the portable works of Middle and Late-Byzantine art, in comparison with all those pieces that once ornamented the monasteries and the island churches and paid honor to worship. We briefly note the portable icons, painted on wood, from the 11th to the 15th century, gold embroidery from the 15th century in the Monastery of Saint John the Theologian in Patmos and the illuminated manuscripts in the library of the same monastery from the 9th to the 15th century. Included among those is the famous Book of Job (codex 171) from the 9th century, the oldest in the monastery, which is considered to be perhaps the oldest of the illuminated Greek manuscripts which still exist in the eastern Mediterranean (ill. 121); the Sermons of Gregory Nazianzenus (codex 33) from the year 941 (ill. 120); a liturgical volumen (No. 707) from the beginning of the 13th century, one of the most important of its kind and the Tetraevangelion (four Gospels) from the year 1334-1335 (codex 81) one of the most beautiful post-Byzantine manuscripts (ill. 122). Important manuscripts with miniatures can still be found from the libraries of the monasteries of Ayia in Andros, Chozoviotissa on Amorgos, the Panayia in Lindos, Rhodes as well as others on Rhodes and on Lesbos. There are a few vessels for secular use on Rhodes and others from the 12th and 13th century which were recently found in a shipwreck near Kastellorizo.

Many of the icons are of exceptional quality and outline the relationships and the ease of communication of the island world with Constantinople and other important centers and testify to the elegance, good taste and intellectual cultivation of their receivers. Until the 13th century few survived. The small, mosaic icon of Saint Nikolas in the monastery on Patmos (ill. 124) stands apart with its delicate work from the 11th century, with contemporary silver encrustation around the border, perhaps the only mosaic which exists from those years and this category of exquisite icons produced by the workshops of Constantinople. The "devotional" icon of the Monastery, the large icon of Saint John the Theologian (ill. 125) an imperial gift according to tradition, is in all likelihood the original icon from the 12th century, mentioned in the catalogue of the treasures of the monastery from 1200, which was painted over in the 15th century. Its embossed frame of gilt silver decorated with the Deesis and depictions of the Apostles and the halo of the saint with delicate, enamel decoration, as well as the open Gospels he is holding is also from the 12th century. To the 12th century are also dated the icon of the Virgin Hodegetria in Katapoliani, Paros, and the Virgin Glykophilousa from Rhodes which today is in the like named Greek Catholic Church of Our Lady of Damascus on Valetta, Malta (ill. 31); the Virgin Glykophilousa of the Episkopi of Santorini is from the end of the century and Saint Theodore Tiro in the Patmos Monastery (ill. 127) is from around 1200.

31

31. The Virgin Glykophilousa, icon. Our Lady of Damascus in Valetta, Malta.

Let it be noted that "Our Lady of Damascus" – according to a tradition of the Knights of Saint John of Malta, some Knights saw it on Rhodes and remembered that they had noticed it earlier in Damascus – is one of the three icons of the Virgin the Knights took with them as priceless treasures when they left Rhodes in 1522. The famous Byzantine Virgin from the monastery of Philerimos was with it and is now considered lost.

The icon of the Apostle Iakovos at the Patmos Monastery, a marvelous work in a monumental style which expressed the new spirit of "renaissance" in Palaeologue art in the environs of Constantinople (ill. 126), is dated to the beginning of the Palaeologue dynasty, around 1260-1270. Oustanding works from the 13th or the 14th century by excellent painters are: the icon of Saint George in the Metropolitan Collection of Mytilene and the two double-sided icons at Kastro, Naxos; the processional icon of a Virgin and Child and the Crucifixion on the other side, in the Orthodox church of the Virgin Theoskepasti (ill. 130) and the superb full-length Virgin with Child and on the other side Saint John Prodrome, which ornaments the altar of the Catholic Church of Kastro (ill. 128). In the later, a miniature figure below right depicts "Ioannis bishop of Nicomedia" kneeling in prayer to the Virgin according to a later inscription which is written over the traces of the original. Beautiful double-sided icons of Constantinopolitan art from the first half of the 14th century have also survived in Rhodes; the Virgin Hodegetria with Saint Nikolas in the local Archeological Collection is one of the most exquisite works of the period (ills. 129, 131) along with Christ Pantocrator with the Crucifixion in the church of Ayioi Anargyroi (ill. 135) and the Virgin and Child with the evangelist Luke in the same Archeological Collection (ill. 134). The two later ones were originally in the iconostasis of an unknown church; the same painters did their first and second sides respectively. It is interesting that this constituted the prototype for the icons of Christ "Sotir" ("Savior") and the Virgin Mary "Gorgoepikoos" ("quick to hear one's prayers") works of a good painter probably from the 15th century, which are found in the Metropolitan side-chapel of the Evangelismos in Kos (ill. 140). The once double-sided icon of Christ with Saint John the Theologian on the other side, of the late 14th century, from Ayios Therapon on Lesbos (ills. 132, 133) is of exceptional interest for its artistry. A few icons still exist in Rhodes, some of them double-sided and in Lesbos, Siphnos and the Patmos Monastery as well; in the latter the icons from the first half of the 15th century are credited to Cretan workshops (ills. 136, 139).

Post-Byzantine Works

In the 15th century Crete distinguished itself as a great artistic center, the greatest since the Fall of Constantinople in 1453, and maintained its brilliance up to the time of the Turko-Venetian war and the seizure of the island by the Turks in 1669. Hundreds of painters and wood carvers, stone carvers, gold-platers, woodworkers and other artisans, who are mentioned in archival sources or are known from their works, were employed in the towns of Crete, primarily Herakleion; their creations, above all their portable icons, enriched, outside the island itself, the monasteries and the churches, as well as houses throughout the entire Orthodox, not to mention Catholic, world of the eastern Mediterranean. Painting, as the supreme expression of Cretan art, created new structures of iconography and style which would dominate the religious and artistic expression of post-Byzantine art.

Patmos, connected to Crete by its large monastic estate at Stylos, Apokoronou, which brought it important revenue, was firmly oriented to Crete for the renovation of the decoration of the Monastery of Saint John the Theologian and the churches of Chora with carved wooden iconostases and icons, as well as wall paintings. In the second half of the 15th century the Cretan painter Antonios Papadopoulos agreed to go to Naxos in order to decorate a church with wall paintings. From the 15th to the 17th century the churches of Chora and other parts of the island were decorated with Cretan icons. On all the islands, the innate good taste and love of the best from every period prompted priests, nobles, householders and shipowners to bring beautiful Cretan icons to decorate the icon-stands and the iconostases of their churches and the iconostases of their houses, many of which have been saved, most of them on Patmos. These came from Crete, Venice and elsewhere and many were painted on the islands in the 17th century by Cretan hagiographers, who had taken refuge in the Aegean area and created their own workshops, and local craftsmen.

The works of well-known artists from Crete, Angelos, Andreas Ritzos (ill. 141) his son Nikolaos Ritzos, Nikolaos Tzafouris, Michael Damaskinos, Georgios Klontzas, Thomas Bathas, Ioannis Apakas, Ieremias Palladas, Silvestros Theocharis, Frangias Kavertzas, Stylianos Yenitis, Viktor, Emmanouel Tzanes, Emmanouel Skordilis, Theodoros Poulakis and others have survived on Patmos, Naxos, Lesbos, Folegandros, Symi, Kimolos, Milos, Siphnos, Tinos, Kea, Kythnos, Seriphos, Ios and Antiparos. Among these valuable works the most priceless icon, of the Dormition of the Virgin, in the like-named church of Panayia ton Psarianon in Syros, was done by the young Cretan master (El Greco) who with pride and eloquence signed his work: ΔΟΜΗΝΙΚΟΣ ΘΕΟΤΟΚΟΠΟΥΛΟΣ Ο ΔΕΙΞΑΣ (ills. 137, 138). It was kept by good fortune on this Aegean island, perhaps brought from Venice in the 19th century, the only icon we have with the entire name of Domenicos, before the young artist took his great talent to the West.

Wall paintings in churches, icons, carved door-frames, with crosses and birds in foliage, wood and marble carvings and painted iconostases, wood-carved ecclesiastical furniture, gold-embroidered vestments and consecrated vessels were created by fine, local artists while others of superior quality were brought by ship from all parts of the world. They are treasures of the islands which gave heart to the faithful, and kept hope proud and strong in difficult times.

It is also the inestimable heritage of the Aegean, where: "the tolling winds perform sacred rites / lifting the sea like the Mother of God" (Odysseus Elytis, "Axion Esti", Athens 1980, 73).

BIBLIOGRAPHY

ΑΛΙΠΡΑΝΤΗΣ, Θ.Χ., *Θησαυροί τῆς Σίφνου, Εἰκόνες τῶν ναῶν καί τῶν μονῶν*, Ἀθῆναι 1979.

ΑΧΕΙΜΑΣΤΟΥ, Μ., «Ἀμφιπρόσωπες εἰκόνες τῆς Ρόδου, Ἡ εἰκόνα τῆς Ὁδηγήτριας καί τοῦ ἁγίου Νικολάου», *ΑΔ*, 21(1966): *Μελέται*, 62-83.

— «Εἰκών τῆς Δευτέρας Παρουσίας ἐκ τῆς Σύμης», *ΔΧΑΕ*, περ. Δ΄, τόμ. Ε΄ (1966-1969), 207-226.

— «Ἡ ἐκκλησία τῆς Παναγίας τοῦ Κάστρου τῆς Ρόδου», *ΑΔ*, 23 (1968): *Μελέται*, 221-283.

ΑΧΕΙΜΑΣΤΟΥ-ΠΟΤΑΜΙΑΝΟΥ, Μ., «Νέος ἀνεικονικός διάκοσμος ἐκκλησίας στή Νάξο, Οἱ τοιχογραφίες τοῦ Ἁγίου Ἰωάννη τοῦ Θεολόγου στ' Ἀδησαροῦ», *ΔΧΑΕ*, περ. Δ΄, τόμ. ΙΒ΄ (1984), 329-379.

— «Ἄγνωστες τοιχογραφίες στό ναό τοῦ Ταξιάρχη τῆς Μεσαριᾶς στήν Ἄνδρο», *ΑΑΑ*, XVI(1983), 106-119.

— «Ἡ Κοίμηση τῆς Θεοτόκου σέ δύο κρητικές εἰκόνες τῆς Κῶ», *ΔΧΑΕ*, περ. Δ΄, τόμ. ΙΓ (1985-1986), 125-154.

ΒΑΣΙΛΑΚΗ, Α., «Εἰκονομαχικές ἐκκλησίες στή Νάξο», *ΔΧΑΕ*, περ. Δ΄, τόμ. Γ΄ (1962-1963), 49-74.

ΒΟΚΟΤΟΠΟΥΛΟΣ, Π.Λ., «Αἱ τοιχογραφίαι τοῦ Ἁγίου Ἀντωνίου Ἀνάφης», *ΔΧΑΕ*, περ. Δ΄, τόμ. Β΄ (1960-1961), 183-194.

ΒΟΛΑΝΑΚΗΣ, Ι.Η., *Οἱ τοιχογραφίες τοῦ ναοῦ τῶν Ἁγίων Θεοδώρων Ἀρχαγγέλου Ρόδου*, Ρόδος 1982.

— *Ὁ βυζαντινός ναός τοῦ Ἁγίου Γεωργίου στά Μάσαρη Ρόδου καί οἱ τοιχογραφίες αὐτοῦ*, Ρόδος 1989.

— «Χριστιανικά μνημεῖα τῆς νήσου Κῶ, ΙΙ, Τοιχογραφημένοι ναοί τῆς βυζαντινῆς καί μεταβυζαντινῆς ἐποχῆς», *Τά Κωακά*, Γ΄ (1989), 57-118.

Ἡ Βυζαντινή Τέχνη, Τέχνη Εὐρωπαϊκή, 9η Ἔκθεσις Συμβουλίου τῆς Εὐρώπης, Ἀθῆναι 1964 (κατάλογος ἔκθεσης).

Βυζαντινές Τοιχογραφίες καί Εἰκόνες, Ἐθνική Πινακοθήκη 1976, Ἀθήνα 1976 (κατάλογος ἔκθεσης).

Βυζαντινή καί Μεταβυζαντινή Τέχνη, Ἀθήνα, Παλιό Πανεπιστήμιο 1985, Ἀθήνα 1986 (κατάλογος ἔκθεσης).

ΓΑΛΑΒΑΡΗΣ, Γ., «Πρωτοβυζαντινή Τέχνη», *ΙΕΕ*, Ζ΄, 354-397.

ΔΗΜΗΤΡΟΚΑΛΛΗΣ, Δ., *Συμβολαί εἰς τήν μελέτην τῶν βυζαντινῶν μνημείων τῆς Νάξου*, τόμ. Α΄, Ἀθῆναι 1972.

Διεθνές Συμπόσιο, Πρακτικά, 'I. Μονή 'Αγ. 'Ιωάννου τοῦ Θεολόγου, 900 χρόνια ἱστορικῆς μαρτυρίας (1088-1988), Πάτμος, 22-24 Σεπτεμβρίου 1988 (Χ. Μπούρας, Μ.Σ. Θεοχάρη, 'Ε. Παπαθεοφάνους-Τσουρῆ, Π.Λ. Βοκοτόπουλος, 'I. Βολανάκης, Γ. Οἰκονομάκη-Παπαδοπούλου, 'Α. Παπαγεωργίου), 'Αθῆναι 1989.

ΔΡΑΝΔΑΚΗΣ, Ν.Β., «Αἱ τοιχογραφίαι τοῦ ναοῦ τῆς Νάξου Παναγία "στῆς Γιαλλοῦς" (1288/89)», *ΕΕΒΣ*, ΛΓ(1964), 258-269.

— *Οἱ παλαιοχριστιανικές τοιχογραφίες στή Δροσιανή τῆς Νάξου*, 'Αθήνα 1988.

— «'Αρχαιολογικοί περίπατοι στή βυζαντινή Νάξο», *ΕΕΚΜ*, 13(1985-1990), 5-53.

ΖΙΑΣ, Ν., «'Εργασίαι εἰς τοιχογραφημένους ναούς τῶν Κυκλάδων», *ΑΑΑ*, III(1970), 223-232.

— «'Εκ τῶν ἀποκαλυφθεισῶν τοιχογραφιῶν εἰς Πρωτόθρονον Νάξου», *ΑΑΑ*, IV(1971), 368-377.

ΚΑΤΣΙΩΤΗ, Α., «Οἱ σκηνές τῆς ζωῆς τοῦ 'Αγίου 'Ιωάννη τοῦ Προδρόμου στό παλαιοχριστιανικό βαπτιστήριο τῆς Κῶ», *Ἕβδομο Συμπόσιο Βυζαντινῆς καί Μεταβυζαντινῆς 'Αρχαιολογίας καί Τέχνης: Περιλήψεις ἀνακοινώσεων*, 'Αθήνα 1987, 37.

— «Οἱ τοιχογραφίες τοῦ 'Αγίου Ζαχαρία στό Φοινίκι τῆς Χάλκης», *ΑΔ*, 40(1985): *Μελέτες*, 229-241.

ΚΟΙΛΑΚΟΥ, Χ., «'Ο ναός τοῦ 'Αγίου Γεωργίου στά Πραστειά Σιδερούντας Χίου», *ΔΧΑΕ*, περ. Δ', τόμ. ΙΑ' (1982-1983), 37-75.

ΚΟΛΛΙΑΣ, Η., «Τοιχογραφίαι τῆς 'Ιπποτοκρατίας (1309-1522) εἰς Ρόδον», *ΑΑΑ*, VI (1973), 265-276.

— *Δύο ζωγραφικά σύνολα τῆς ἐποχῆς τῆς ἱπποτοκρατίας, 'Ο Ἅγιος Νικόλαος στά Τριάντα καί ἡ 'Αγία Τριάδα (Ντολαπλί Μετζίντ) στή μεσαιωνική πόλη*, διδακτ. διατρ., 'Αθήνα 1986.

ΚΟΥΤΕΛΑΚΗΣ, Χ.Μ., *Ξυλόγλυπτα τέμπλα τῆς Δωδεκανήσου μέχρι τό 1700*, 'Αθήνα-Γιάννινα 1986.

ΚΡΙΤΖΑΣ, Χ., «Τό βυζαντινόν ναυάγιον Πελαγοννήσου-'Αλοννήσου», *ΑΑΑ*, IV(1971), 176-182.

ΛΑΖΑΡΙΔΗΣ, Π., «Συμβολή εἰς τήν μελέτην τῶν παλαιοχριστιανικῶν μνημείων τῆς Δωδεκανήσου», *ΠΘ'ΔΒΣ, Θεσσαλονίκη 1953*, IV, 'Αθῆναι 1955, 227-248.

ΜΑΣΤΟΡΟΠΟΥΛΟΣ, Γ., «Ἕνα ἄγνωστο ἔργο τοῦ Θεοτοκόπουλου», *Τρίτο Συμπόσιο Βυζαντινῆς καί Μεταβυζαντινῆς 'Αρχαιολογίας καί Τέχνης: Περιλήψεις ἀνακοινώσεων*, 'Αθήνα 1983, 53.

— «Ἄγνωστες χρονολογημένες βυζαντινές ἐπιγραφές 13ου καί 14ου αἰώνα ἀπό τή Νάξο καί τή Σίκινο», *ΑΑΑ*, XVI(1983), 121-131.

— «Ἕνας ναξιακός ναός μέ ἄγνωστο ἀνεικονικό διάκοσμο», *Ναξιακό Μέλλον*, ἀρ. φύλλου 489(25) καί 493(26), 'Αθήνα 1984.

— «Ὑπογραφές ζωγράφων σέ εἰκόνες τῆς κεντρικῆς Νάξου», *ΔΧΑΕ*, περ. Δ', τόμ. ΙΒ' (1984), 473-499.

ΜΑΥΡΟΕΙΔΗ, Μ., «Παρατηρήσεις στίς παραστάσεις τῆς πλάκας Τ.95 τοῦ Βυζαντινοῦ Μουσείου», *Ἑνδέκατο Συμπόσιο Βυζαντινῆς καί Μεταβυζαντινῆς 'Αρχαιολογίας καί Τέχνης: Περιλήψεις ἀνακοινώσεων*, 'Αθήνα 1991, 68-69.

Μητροπολίτης Μυτιλήνης Ι.Γ. ΚΛΕΟΜΒΡΟΤΟΣ, *Mytilena Sacra, Α-Γ*, Θεσσαλονίκη 1970, 1974, 1976.

ΜΟΥΡΙΚΗ, ΝΤ., «Οἱ τοιχογραφίες τοῦ παρεκκλησίου τῆς Μονῆς 'Ιωάννου τοῦ Θεολόγου στήν Πάτμο», *ΔΧΑΕ*, περ. Δ', τόμ. ΙΔ' (1987-1988), 205-263.

— *Τά ψηφιδωτά τῆς Νέας Μονῆς Χίου*, Α-Β, 'Αθήνα 1985.

ΜΟΥΤΣΟΠΟΥΛΟΣ, Ν.Κ., «Κάρπαθος, Σημειώσεις 'Ιστορικῆς Τοπογραφίας καί 'Αρχαιολογίας», *ΕΕΠΣΑΠΘ*, Ζ' (1975-1977), 39-744.

ΜΠΟΡΜΠΟΥΔΑΚΗΣ, Μ.Λ., «Οἱ τοιχογραφίες τοῦ 'Αγίου Νικολάου στά Κυριακοσέλλια», *Δεύτερο Συμπόσιο Βυζαντινῆς καί Μεταβυζαντινῆς 'Αρχαιολογίας καί Τέχνης: Περιλήψεις ἀνακοινώσεων*, 'Αθήνα 1982, 64-65.

ΜΠΟΥΡΑΣ, Χ., «Μία βυζαντινή βασιλική ἐν Χίῳ», *Νέον 'Αθήναιον*, Γ' (1958-1960), 129-144.

ΟΡΛΑΝΔΟΣ, Α.Κ., «'Η παλαιοχριστιανική βασιλική τοῦ Χαλινάδου Λέσβου», *ΑΒΜΕ*, Γ' (1937), 115-127.

— «Βυζαντινά καί μεταβυζαντινά μνημεῖα τῆς Ρόδου», *ΑΒΜΕ*, ΣΤ' (1948).

— «'Η 'Πισκοπή τῆς Σαντορήνης (Παναγία τῆς Γωνιᾶς)», *ΑΒΜΕ*, Ζ' (1951), 178-214.

— *'Η ξυλόστεγος παλαιοχριστιανική βασιλική τῆς μεσογειακῆς λεκάνης*, I-II, 'Αθῆναι 1952.

— «Βυζαντινά μνημεῖα τῆς Ἄνδρου», *ΑΒΜΕ*, Η' (1955-1956), 8-34.

— «'Ανασκαφή τῆς παλαιοχριστιανικῆς βασιλικῆς "Τριῶν 'Εκκλησιῶν" Πάρου», *ΠΑΕ*, 1960, 246-257.

— «Οἱ μεταβυζαντινοί ναοί τῆς Πάρου», *ΑΒΜΕ*, Θ' (1961), 113-223 καί Ι' (1964).

— «Δύο παλαιοχριστιανικαί βασιλικαί τῆς Κῶ», *ΑΕ*, 1966, 1-103.

— «Παλαιοχριστιανικοί ἄμβωνες τῆς Πάρου», *ΑΒΜΕ*, ΙΑ' (1969), 177-206.

— *'Η ἀρχιτεκτονική καί αἱ βυζαντιναί τοιχογραφίαι τῆς Μονῆς 'Αγ. 'Ιωάννου τοῦ Θεολόγου Πάτμου*, 'Αθῆναι 1970.

ΠΑΠΑΔΑΚΗ-OEKLAND, Σ., «'Ο κώδικας 590 τῆς μονῆς Βατοπεδίου: ἕνα ἀντίγραφο τοῦ 'Ιώβ τῆς Πάτμου», *ΔΧΑΕ*, περ. Δ', τόμ. ΙΓ' (1985-1986), 17-37.

ΠΑΠΑΘΕΟΦΑΝΟΥΣ-ΤΣΟΥΡΗ, Ε., «Εἰκόνα Παναγίας Γαλακτοτροφούσας ἀπό τή Ρόδο», *ΑΔ*, 34 (1979): *Μελέτες*, 1-14.

ΠΕΛΕΚΑΝΙΔΗΣ, ΣΤ. - ΑΤΖΑΚΑ, Π.Ι., *Σύνταγμα τῶν παλαιοχριστιανικῶν ψηφιδωτῶν δαπέδων τῆς 'Ελλάδος, I: Νησιωτική 'Ελλάς*, Θεσσαλονίκη 1974.

ΠΟΛΙΤΗΣ, Λ. - ΚΟΛΛΙΑΣ, Η., «Κατάλογος χειρογράφων ἐκκλησίας Παναγίας Λίνδου», *'Ελληνικά*, 24 (1971), 33-53.

ΠΟΥΛΟΥ-ΠΑΠΑΔΗΜΗΤΡΙΟΥ, Ν., «Παλαιοχριστιανικό κιονόκρανο μέ ἄκανθα "πεταλούδα" ἀπό τή Σάμο», *ΔΧΑΕ*, περ. Δ', τόμ. ΙΔ' (1987-1988), 151-158.

ΣΤΡΑΤΗ, Α., «Τοιχογραφία ἀπό τόν Ἅγιο Γεώργιο Λαθρήνου Νάξου», *Κληρονομία*, 14(1982), 53-67.

ΣΩΤΗΡΙΟΥ, Γ.Α., *'Οδηγός Βυζαντινοῦ Μουσείου 'Αθηνῶν*, 'Εν 'Αθήναις 1931.

— *Χριστιανική καί Βυζαντινή 'Αρχαιολογία*, Α', 'Εν ' Αθήναις 1962.

ΣΩΤΗΡΙΟΥ, Μ.Γ., «'Η πρώιμος παλαιολόγειος ἀναγέννησις εἰς τάς χώρας καί τάς νήσους τῆς 'Ελλάδος κατά τόν 13ον αἰώνα», *ΔΧΑΕ*, περ. Δ', τόμ. Δ' (1964-1965), 257- 273.

ΧΑΤΖΗΔΑΚΗΣ, Μ., «'Επιτάφια χρονολογημένη ἐπιγραφή στήν Πρωτόθρονη Νάξου», *ΔΧΑΕ*, περ. Δ', τόμ. Ζ' (1973-1974), 78.

— *Εἰκόνες τῆς Πάτμου, Ζητήματα βυζαντινῆς καί μεταβυζαντινῆς ζωγραφικῆς*, 'Αθήνα 1977.

— «'Η μεσοβυζαντινή τέχνη», *ΙΕΕ*, Η', 274-325.

— «Μεσοβυζαντινή τέχνη (1071-1204)», *ΙΕΕ, Θ', 394-423· «' Η ὕστερη βυζαντινή τέχνη 1204-1453», στό ἴδιο*, 423-458.

— «'Η μεταβυζαντινή τέχνη (1453-1700) καί ἡ ἀκτινοβολία της», *ΙΕΕ*, Ι', 410-437.

— «Πνευματικός βίος καί πολιτισμός (1669-1821): 'Η τέχνη», *ΙΕΕ*, ΙΑ', 244-273.

Χίος: 'Ιστορία καί Τέχνη (Β. Πέννα, Τ. Μανδηλᾶ), Νομαρχία Χίου, Χίος 1988.

ASSIMAKOPOULOU-ATZAKA, P., "I mosaici pavimentali paleocristiani in Grecia", XXXI *CARB* (1984), 66-72.

BALTOYIANNIS, ST., "Conservation and restoration of the wall paintings in the church of the Protothronos Naxos, Part. I. Removal of the painting", *Studies in conservation*, 21 (1976), 51-62.

BOURAS, L., "Architectural sculptures of the Twelfth and the Early Thirteenth Centuries in Greece", *ΔΧΑΕ*, περ. Δ', τόμ. Θ' (1977-1979), 63-72.

BRANDI, C., "La capella rupestre del Monte Paradiso", *Memorie*, III (1938), 7-18.

Byzantine and Post-Byzantine Art, Athens 1986.

Byzantine Art in Greece: Patmos (E. Kollias), ed. "Melissa", Athens 1990.

Byzantine Art in Greece: Naxos (M. Chatzidakis, N. Drandakis, N. Zias, M. Acheimastou-Potamianou, A. Vasilaki-Karakatsani), ed. "Melissa", Athens 1989.

CHATZIDAKIS, M., "Aspects de la peinture murale du XIIIe siècle en Grèce", *L' art byzantin du XIIIe siècle, Symposium de Sopočani 1965*, Beograd 1967, 59-73.

— "L' art dans le Naxos byzantin et le contexte historique", *XVe Congrès International des Sciences Historiques, Rapports III*, Bucarest 1980, 13-15.

— "Les aspects de la peinture monumentale byzantine en Grèce", *Class*

CCCXXXVIII de l' academie Serbe des sciences et des arts, Classe des sciences historiques, 3, Beograd 1983, 1-10.
— *Icons of Patmos*, Athens 1986.
COLLIAS, E., *The city of Rhodes and the palace of the Grand Master*, Athens 1988.
DROSSOYIANNI, P.A., "New wall-paintings from the Cyclades", *XVIII Congrès International des Etudes Byzantines, Resumés des communications*, I, Moscou 1991, 289-290.
FARIOLI, R., "Una lastra marmorea a Patmos e la tipologia dei sarcofagi mediobizantini a panelli", *Studi di storia dell' arte in memoria di M. Rotili*, Napoli 1984, 167-172.
From Byzantium to El Greco, Greek frescoes and icons, Royal Academy of Arts, London, Athens 1987 (exhibition catalogue).
GALLAS, K. - WESSEL, K. - BORBOUDAKIS, M., *Byzantinisches Kreta*, München 1983.
GHARIB, G., *Le icone mariane, Storia e culto*, Roma 1987, 148-153.
JAKOBS, P.H.F., *Die frühchristlichen Ambone Griechenlands*, Bonne 1987.
KALOPISSI-VERTI, S., "Osservazioni iconografiche sulla pittura monumentale della Grecia durante il XIII secolo", XXXI *CARB*, Ravenna 1984, 191-220.
— "Tendenze stilistiche della pittura monumentale in Grecia durante il XIII secolo", XXXI *CARB*, Ravenna 1984, 221- 253.
— "Kos tardoantica e bizantina nelle scoperte archeologiche, dal IV secolo al 1314", XXXVIII *CARB*, Ravenna 1991, 233-251.
LAFONTAINE-DOSOGNE, J., "Pour une problématique de la peinture d' église byzantine à l' époque iconoclaste", *DOP*, 41 (1987), 321-337.
MALAMUT, E., *Les îles de l' empire byzantin, VIIIe-XIIe siècles*, I-II, Paris 1988.
MOURIKI, D., "Stylistic Trends in Monumental Painting of Greece during the Eleventh and Twelfth Centuries", *DOP*, 34-35 (1980-1981), 77-124.
OEKONOMIDES, M. - DROSSOYIANNI, PH., "A hoard of gold Byzantine coins from Samos", *RN*, 31 (1989), 145-182.
ORLANDOS, A.C., "Délos chrétienne", *BCH*, LX-1936-1, 1-33.
— "Fresques byzantines du monastère de Patmos", *CahArch*, XII (1962), 285-302.
PALLAS, D.I. "Eine anikonische lineare Wanddekoration auf der Inseln Ikaria, zur Tradition der bilderlosen Kirchenausstattung", *JOB*, 23 (1974), 271-314.
— "Les décorations aniconiques des églises dans les îles de l' Archipel", *Studien zur Spätantiken und Byzantinischen Kunst*, Fr. W. Deichmann gewidmet, 10 (1968), II, 171-179.
PANAYOTIDI, M., "L' église rupestre de la Nativité dans l' île de Naxos, ses peintures primitives", *CahArch*, 23 (1974), 107-120.
— "La peinture monumentale en Grèce de la fin de l' Iconoclasme jusqu' à l' avénement des Comnènes (843-1081)", *CahArch*, 34 (1986), 75-108.
— "Les peintures murales de Naxos", XXXVIII *CARB*, Ravenna 1991, 281-306.
PAPAVASSILIOU, E. - ARCHONTOPOULOS, TH., "Nouveaux éléments historiques et archéologiques de Rhodes à travers des fouilles dans la ville médiévale", XXXVIII *CARB*, Ravenna 1991, 307-350.
Patmos, Treasures of the Monastery (E. Kollias, M. Chatzidakis, M. Theocharis, Y. Ikonomaki-Papadopoulos, D. Mouriki), Ekdotike Athenon, Athens 1988.
PENNAS, C.I., "The Basilica of St. Isidore: New evidence", *Chios, A Conference at the Homereion in Chios 1984*, Oxford 1986, 317-334.
— "Some aristocratic founders: The foundation of Panagia Krena on Chios", *Les Femmes et le Monachisme Byzantin, Actes du Symposium d' Athènes 1988*, Athènes 1991, 61-66.
POULOU-PAPADIMITRIOU, N., *Samos Paléochrétienne: L' apport du matériel archéologique*, doctoral thesis, Paris 1985.
SKAWRAN, K.M., "Stylistic cross currents in Twelfth century painting in Greece", *Πρακτικά τοῦ ΙΕ΄ Διεθνοῦς Συνεδρίου Βυζαντινῶν Σπουδῶν, Ἀθῆναι 1976*, IIB, Ἀθῆναι 1981, 697-714.
— *The development of Middle Byzantine Fresco Painting in Greece*, Pretoria 1982, 149-185 passim.
STYLIANOU, A. and J., *The painted churches of Cyprus*, London 1985.
VELMANS, T., *La peinture murale byzantine à la fin du Moyen Âge*, I, Paris 1977.
VOCOTOPOULOS, P.L., "L' évangile illustré de Mytilène", *Studenica et l' art byzantin autour de l' année 1200*, Beograd 1988, 377-382.
XYNGOPOULOS, A., "L' art byzantin du XIIIe siècle", *Symposium de Sopočani, 1965*, Beograd 1967, 75-82.

Abbreviations

AAA: Ἀρχαιολογικὰ Ἀνάλεκτα ἐξ Ἀθηνῶν
ABME: Ἀρχεῖον τῶν Βυζαντινῶν Μνημείων τῆς Ἑλλάδος
ΑΔ: Ἀρχαιολογικὸν Δελτίον
AE: Ἀρχαιολογικὴ Ἐφημερίς
ΔΧΑΕ: Δελτίον τῆς Χριστιανικῆς Ἀρχαιολογικῆς Ἑταιρείας
ΕΕΒΣ: Ἐπετηρίς Ἑταιρείας Βυζαντινῶν Σπουδῶν
ΕΕΚΜ: Ἐπετηρίς Ἑταιρείας Κυκλαδικῶν Μελετῶν
ΕΕΠΣΑΠΘ: Ἐπιστημονικὴ Ἐπετηρίς τῆς Πολυτεχνικῆς Σχολῆς Ἀριστοτελείου Πανεπιστήμιου Θεσσαλονίκης
ΙΕΕ: Ἱστορία τοῦ Ἑλληνικοῦ Ἔθνους
ΠΑΕ: Πρακτικὰ τῆς ἐν Ἀθήναις Ἀρχαιολογικῆς Ἑταιρείας
ΠΘ΄ΔΒΣ: Πεπραγμένα τοῦ Θ΄ Διεθνοῦς Βυζαντινολογικοῦ Συνεδρίου

BCH: Bulletin de Correspondance Hellénique
CahArch: Cahiers Archéologiques
CARB: Corso di Cultura sull' Arte Ravennate e Byzantina
DOP: Dumbarton Oaks Papers
JÖB: Jahrbuch des Österreichischen Byzantinistik
RN: Revue numismatique

Warmest thanks for the transfer of the transparencies and photographs are owed to the Byzantine Museum of Athens (ills. 54, 130, 131, 134, 135, 137, 138, 140, 141); the Monastery of Saint John the Theologian of Patmos and Ekdotike Athinon S.A. (ills. 99, 120-125, 127, 136, 139); the Commercial Bank of Greece (ills. 78-83); the ephors of Byzantine Antiquities, E. Kollias of the Dodecanese (ills. 5, 29, 30, 103, 117-119) and M. Borboudakis of Crete (ills. 9, 105); to the former Director of the Byzantine Museum of Athens P.H. Lazaridis (ill. 59); to the former professor of the University of Athens N. Drandakis (ill. 7); to the archeologist of the Numismatic Museum of Athens B. Pennas (ill. 57) and to the archeologist, Department Head of Archeological Sites of the Ministry of Culture, Ch. Pennas (ill. 24).

32

32. Aegina. The so-called Omorfi Ekklisia. West side.

33. Rhodes. The so-called Chourmali Mendresé church. The dome.

34. Rhodes, Lindos. Ayios Ioannis. The ruins of the church from the west.

35. Rhodes. The so-called Dolapli mosque. General view from the southwest.

34

33

35

36

37

38

36. Andros, Mesaria. The Taxiarch church. General view from the southwest.

37. Andros, Melida. The Taxiarch church. General view from the northwest.

38. Chios. Panayia Agrelopousaina. West side.

40

39. Chios. Panayia Krina. Details of the blind arcading and the brickwork on the south side.

40. Chios. Panayia Sikelia. View from above, facing south.

41. Chios. Panayia Sikelia. Details of the blind arcading.

42. Chios. Panayia Krina. General view of the north side of the church.

41

39

42

43

44

45

43. Chios. Ayion Galas. Panayia. Partial view from the south.

44. Naxos. Panayia Drosiani. Partial view from the west.

45. Naxos. Ayios Georgios Diasoritis. General view from the northeast.

46. Patmos. The Monastery of Saint John the Theologian.
The arcades of the katholikon.

47

48

47. Naxos, Sagri. Ayios Nikolaos. General view from the southeast.

48. Naxos, Kerami. Ayios Ioannis. General view from the southwest.

49

49. Chios. Nea Moni. General view (aerial view).

50

51

50. Paros. Katapoliani. Partial view of the monument from the southwest (photograph from 1948).

51. Paros. Katapoliani. The facade of the church after restoration.

53

52. *Funeral stele with Orpheus. Athens, Byzantine Museum.*

53. *Marble table (detail). Athens, Byzantine Museum.*

54. *Relief of the Nativity. Athens, Byzantine Museum.*

52

54

55

57

56

58

59

55. Mosaic floor from the basilica of Ayios Ioannis of Kos (detail). Rhodes, Palace of the Grand Magister.

56. Mosaic floor from a building on the west harbor of Kos. Rhodes, Palace of the Grand Magister.

57. Mosaic floor from the excavation on Dimoyerontias St. (detail). Chios, "Giustiniano Palace".

58. Mosaic floor from the basilica of Ayios Ioannis of Kos (detail). Rhodes, Palace of the Grand Magister.

59. Astypalaia. The bath of Tallaras. Mosaic floor, central section.

60

61

62

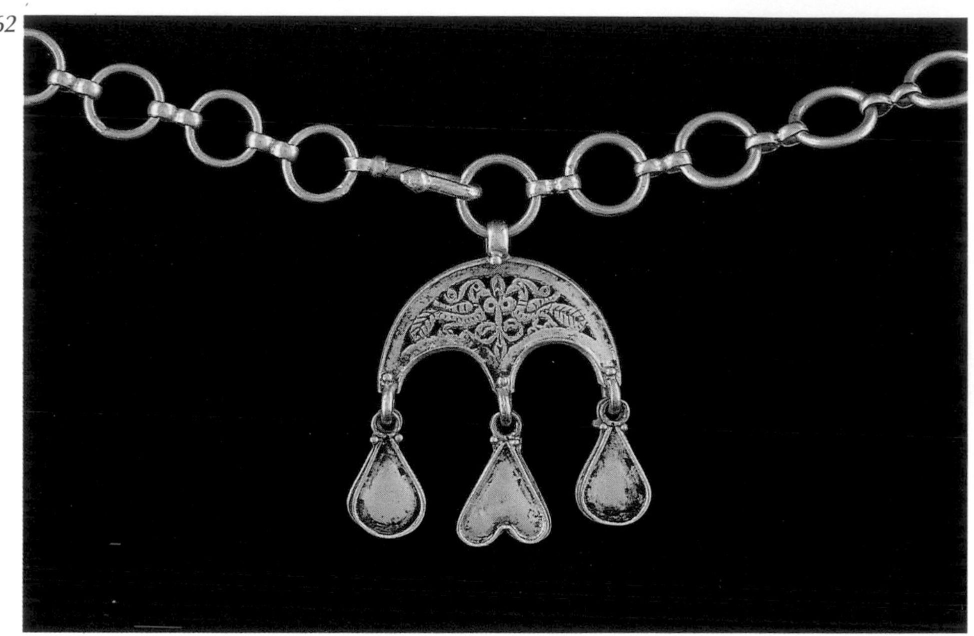

63

60. Silver vessel (trulla). Athens, Byzantine Museum.

61. Silver disc. Athens, Byzantine Museum.

62. Gold belt (detail). Athens, Byzantine Museum.

63. Gold talisman. Athens, Byzantine Museum.

64. Naxos. Panayia Drosiani. The Ascension, apostle (detail).

65. Naxos. Panayia Drosiani. Archangel.

66. Naxos. Panayia Drosiani. The Virgin Nikopoios.

67. Naxos. Protothroni. Saint Isidoros.

64
65
66
67

68

69

68. Naxos. Panayia Drosiani. The decoration of the north apse.

69. Naxos. Protothroni. Apostles.

70, 71. Naxos. Ayios Ioannis at Adisarou. Aniconic decoration.

72, 73. Naxos. Ayios Artemios near Sagri. Aniconic decoration.

70

71

72

73

74

74. Naxos. Panayia Kaloritsa. The decoration of the apse of the sanctuary.

75. Naxos. Panayia Kaloritsa. Apostle (detail).

76. Naxos. Panayia Kaloritsa. Apostle (detail).

77. Naxos. Panayia Kaloritsa. Archangel and prophet.

75

76

77

78

79

80

81

82

83

78. Chios. Nea Moni. The Resurrection.

79. Chios. Nea Moni. The Deposition, the Virgin (detail).

80. Chios. Nea Moni. Baptism (detail).

81. Chios. Nea Moni. The Resurrection (detail).

82. Chios. Nea Moni. Saint Ioakeim.

83. Chios. Nea Moni. Saint Antony.

84

85

86

84. Naxos. Protothroni. The first decoration of the dome, prophet (detail).

85. Naxos. Protothroni. The first decoration of the dome, the prophet Daniel (detail).

86. Naxos. Protothroni. The Annunciation.

87. Naxos. Protothroni. The Presentation in the Temple.

88. Naxos. Protothroni. The second decoration of the dome, archangels and prophets.

89. Naxos. Protothroni. The Annunciation, the Virgin (detail).

90. Naxos. Protothroni. NW parecclesion. Saints Philippe and Akindynos.

87

88

89

90

91. Naxos, Avlonitsa. Ayios Ioannis, parecclesion. Saint John the Prodrome.

92. Naxos. Ayios Georgios Diasoritis. The Pantocrator on the dome.

93. Naxos. Ayios Georgios Diasoritis. The Annunciation, the Archangel Gabriel.

94. Naxos. Ayios Georgios Diasoritis. Assembly of the Archangels (detail).

95. Naxos. Ayios Georgios Diasoritis. Saint Provos.

96. Naxos. Ayios Georgios Diasoritis. Saint Theodore the Dragon-Slayer.

97. Naxos. Ayios Georgios Diasoritis. The decoration of the sanctuary.

97

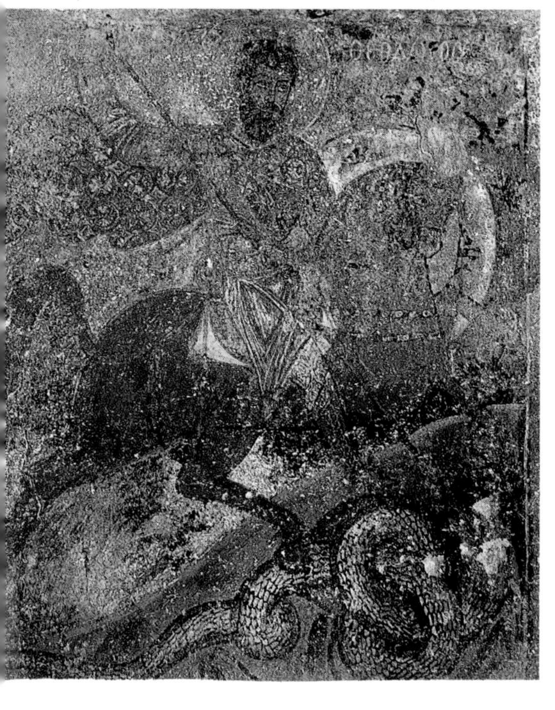

ΟΑΡ

90

99

98. Naxos. Ayios Nikolaos near Sagri. Archangel.

99. Patmos. The Monastery of Saint John the Theologian, parecclesion of the Virgin. The Hospitality of Abraham.

100. Patmos. The Monastery of Saint John the Theologian, parecclesion of the Virgin. Saint lakovos, Brother of God.

101. Patmos. The Monastery of Saint John the Theologian, Refectory. Saint Chariton.

0

101

102

102. *Patmos. Cave of the Apocalypse. Saint Basil.*

103. *Rhodes, Lindos. Ayios Georgios Chostos. John Chrysostom.*

104. *Rhodes. The Taxiarch of Thari. The Ascension, Saint Paul (detail).*

105. *Crete, Kyriakosellia. Ayios Nikolaos. The Archangel Raphael.*

106. *Rhodes. The Taxiarch of Thari. Christ with the Samaritan woman.*

107. *Rhodes. The Taxiarch of Thari. The Ascension, angel.*

103

104

106

107

108

109

110

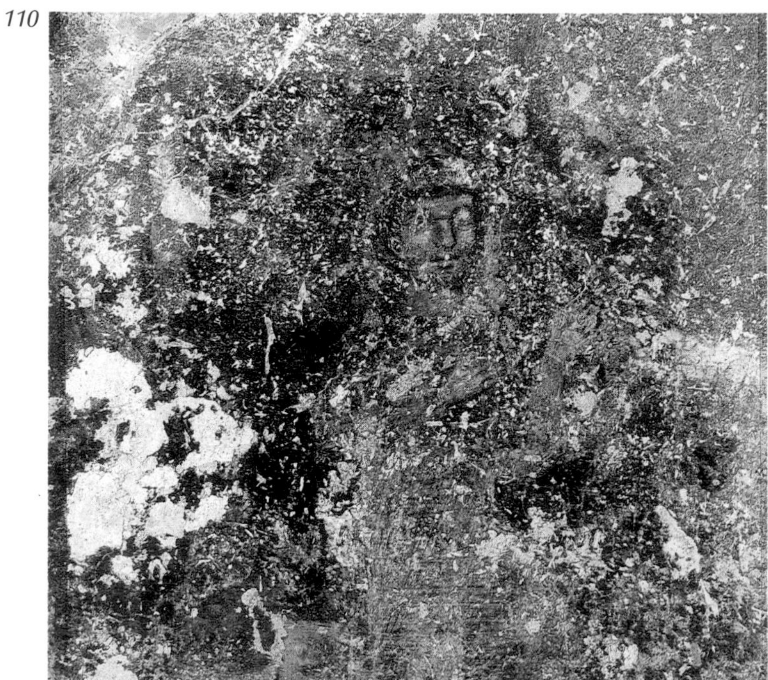

108. Naxos, Kerami. Ayios Ioannis. The decoration of the dome.

109. Naxos, Kerami. Ayios Ioannis. Archangel.

110. Naxos. Panayia Drosiani. An orant figure.

111. The Virgin from the Deesis at Ayios Georgios of Lathrino, Naxos (detached wall painting). Athens, Byzantine Museum.

112. Saint John the Prodrome from the Deesis at Ayios Georgios of Lathrino, Naxos (detached wall painting). Athens, Byzantine Museum.

113. Naxos, Pera Chalki. Ayios Georgios. Hierarch (detail).

114. Naxos, Pera Chalki. Ayios Ioannis. Hierarch (detail).

111

112

113

114

115

116

117

118

119

115. *Patmos. The Monastery of Saint John the Theologian, Refectory. View of the decoration on the west side.*

116. *Patmos. The Monastery of Saint John the Theologian, Refectory. Saint Kyprianos.*

117. *Rhodes. Ayios Georgios of Vardas near Apolakkia. Holy deacons.*

118. *Rhodes. Ayios Georgios of Vardas near Apolakkia. View of the decoration on the south side.*

119. *Rhodes. Ayios Nikolaos near Trianta. Christ carrying the Cross.*

122

123

120. *Gregory Nazianzenus, Homilies (codex 33, f. 2r). Front piece. Patmos, the Monastery of Saint John the Theologian.*

121. *The Book of Job (codex 171, p. 16). The sons and daughters of Job arrive at a banquet. Patmos, The Monastery of Saint John the Theologian.*

122. *The four Gospels (codex 81, f. 98v). Evangelist Mark. Patmos, The Monastery of Saint John the Theologian.*

123. *Liturgical scroll (no. 707). Headpiece. Patmos, The Monastery of Saint John the Theologian.*

124. *Saint Nikolas, mosaic icon. Patmos, The Monastery of Saint John the Theologian.*

125. *Saint John the Evangelist, icon. Patmos, The Monastery of Saint John the Theologian.*

126. *Saint Iakovos, icon. Patmos, The Monastery of Saint John the Theologian.*

127. *Saint Theodoros Tiro, icon. Patmos. The Monastery of Saint John the Theologian.*

124

125

126

127

128

129

130

131

128. *The Virgin Eleousa, double-sided icon. Naxos, Catholic Cathedral.*

129, 131. *The Virgin Hodegetria and Saint Nikolas, double-sided icon. Rhodes, Archeological Collection.*

130. *The Virgin Theoskepasti, double-sided icon. Naxos, Panayia Theoskepasti.*

132

133

134

135

132, 133. Christ and Saint John the Evangelist, double-sided icon. Mytilene, Ecclesiastical Museum.

134. The Virgin and Child, double-sided icon. Rhodes, Archeological collection.

135. Christ Pantocrator, double-sided icon. Rhodes, Ayioi Anargyroi.

136. The Crucifixion, icon. Patmos, The Monastery of Saint John the Theologian.

136

137

138

139

140

137, 138. Domenicos Theotokopoulos (El Greco). The Dormition of the Virgin, icon (details). Syros, Koimesis tis Panayias.

139. The Dormition of the Virgin, icon (detail). Patmos, The Monastery of Saint John the Theologian.

140. The Virgin Gorgoepikoos, icon. Kos, Evangelismos tis Panayias.

141. Andreas Ritzos. Sanctuary Doors. Patmos, The Monastery of Saint John the Theologian.

141

CHARALAMBOS BOURAS

Architecture and town-planning in the traditional settlements of the Aegean

Translated by Philip Ramp

I

Architectural creation on the Aegean islands, during more recent times, is a composite phenomenon of exceptional importance, not only for students of monuments, but for all those who take pleasure in folk culture or see architecture as art.

This phenomenon is remarkable for its wealth and multifariousness. There are hundreds of towns, villages and building complexes throughout the Aegean archipelago which bear, more of less, the same definitive hallmark: though they began to be built with simple means and the humble intents of covering the needs of survival they eventually established themselves artistically and became works unique for their aesthetic wholeness. Even though during the past fifty years this incredible, monumental wealth has been seriously degraded one is still able to ascertain its extent and above all its multifariousness: this built environment was not designed but arose dynamically and over a long period under different conditions in line with local factors and consequently is not uniform. Everywhere it is fresh and always unique.

In reality we know very little about this composite architectural phenomenon; the all-encompassing admiration for the traditional settlements in the Aegean is not based on serious scientific or aesthetic analysis, but on one's experiences, on the captivating image of "Greek towns and harbors", which were once discovered on each of them, firmly rooted in their natural environment and which in the best cases have been connected with lyrical verse and in the worst with sleek tourist advertisements. This does not mean there is an urgent need to de-mythologize things or to censure an aesthetic approach to them but it is of prime importance, now that our knowledge has improved, to interpret matters, and in all the multiplicity which they themselves present.

So the messages (not just the message) of the architecture of the traditional settlements of the Aegean will emerge from their systematic analysis. On the one hand this will be historical in order to clarify the complexes of factors which were in force during the founding of their nuclei and during their life, connecting them to the other cultural activities during the same time periods. On the other, it will be architectural, based first and foremost on the comprehension of the function of the factors which were in force during their construction: the logic, the practical methods, the economy and the respect for natural laws. Moreover, it should not be forgotten that the traditional settlements of the Aegean are also vital organisms today, which are suited to such analyses and that any endeavor to preserve them must be based on the continuence of their life and their function.

The architectural approach has been put forward with particular emphasis by modern architects, led by that great innovator Le Corbusier almost sixty years ago, with the aim of drawing forth lessons useful for their present-day work. The process involved in such "instruction" is, of course, not simple, but it is a fact that the role of architects in the study of settlements – groups of buildings and houses has been very important. The second well-known approach has been that of the folklorists who have set out to record (and thus to preserve) all anonymous activities architecture included, for they believe in the continuity of folk culture. Both of these approaches desire, in any case, to ignore the fact that in the majority of cases the Aegean has been deeply influenced by the contemporary official architecture of the large centers by processes which are only approachable through historical thought and method.

Thus one could say that the knowledge and the interpretation of the anonymous architecture of the Aegean must, of necessity, have a pluralistic character and be grounded on very broad presumptions, on an exhaustive historical analysis of the factors at work on each island and in each area, as well as a clear architectural analysis, as this was presented above.

II

The conditions under which modern Hellenism was formed, ruled by foreign powers, from 1453 to 1900, differed from place to place. On the Aegean islands in particular, one can easily perceive that their historical fortunes created completely different conditions, in each case, for the development of their civilization. In some cases, the oppressive Turkish occupation lasted for centuries (Lesbos, Euboea), in others there was long-term Venetian occupation (Crete, Tinos) while elsewhere there was self-government and yearly control by the Turkish Admiral of the Fleet (Cyclades, Nothern Sporades). The Frankish element had stong, old roots on some islands (Chios, Rhodes) while on others it continued to be preserved as a vital force right up to the Greek War of Independence (Tinos, Santorini, Syros). The privileges secured and the high demographic level created prosperity in some instances (Chios, Patmos) at the same moment when anarchy, piracy and military adventures were desolating other areas (Aegina, Cyclades). Finally, some islands (Hydra, Psara) reached their peak of prosperity relatively late through historical events which took place far beyond the borders of Greece. Economic prosperity, with its positive repercussions on architecture, appeared on the islands mainly during the 18th and the 19th century. The conditions of social life, moreover, improved with the liberation from the Turks (1830) and with the new privileges which were granted to the Turkish-occupied areas (1839). So it is not by chance that the past two centuries, 1700-1900, were definitive for the built environment of the Aegean settlements.

But let us take a brief look at these real factors which were formed within the framework of historical conditions and which had the most repercussions, both on the structure of the settlements and on church construction.

1

1. Santorini, Nimborio. The Goulas. General view from the west.

The Aegean coastline has always been plagued by security problems, disproportionately large in relation to the rest of Greece. The abnormalities of war and piracy, in all their forms, sometimes frenzied and other times more muted, forced the inhabitants to continually defend themselves under all the regimes, and ceaselessly from the Middle Ages to 1840. Architecture was forced to take on a defensive character so that it could afford security above all else (ill. 1). The choice of sites for settlements in naturally fortified locations, or near a fortified feature, town or fortress, and the squeezing of the entire settlement inside a fortified enclosure, were the most common ways in which the islanders responded to these needs. Thus, the wealthiest homes, which were built in the countryside, took the form of an enclosed, fortified tower (Andros, Lesbos, Naxos) while the monasteries also took the form of a small fortress. In any case, it should be noted that the systematic endeavors of the Venetians and the Genoese during the second half of the 15th and the beginning of the 16th century to provide security through the erection of a host of fortifications, on most of the islands, were of basic importance for subsequent developments.

The repercussions of the security factor on town-planning and architecture were always significant. Several old settlements, such as on Antiparos, Kimolos (ill. 11) and the Mastichochoria villages of southern Chios (ills. 39, 40), bear witness to an exceptional sense of purpose in the organization of the defensive part through proper design, right from the start. In other settlements, the formation of defensive lines by the external walls of the houses appears to have followed the dynamic way in which they developed (Fortress of Sifnos). Elsewhere, strong defensive towers were built in the heart of the settlements, the last refuge of the inhabitants in the event of attack (Pyrgos of Santorini). In most cases, the settlement developed directly outside the fortress providing a typical image of the Aegean (Molyvos on Lesbos, ill. 36; Astypalaia, ills. 47, 48; Skyros, ill. 45;

2

2. Hydra. Topographic drawing of the settlement (source: "Greek Traditional Architecture", monograph: Hydra).

Andros, Limnos). Within the settlements the houses, needing to adapt to the limited space, developed upward and to conceal themselves left their walls unplastered externally. The custom of the general whitewashing of the settlements in the Aegean is relatively recent.

The economy, of course, is of primary importance for the architecture of each period, not only in terms of the potential for the investment of money for the construction of each building, but also as an element which fundamentally influences both its society and its culture. In the traditional settlements of the Aegean, one can find instances of buildings corresponding to all the stages of economic development from the simplest agricultural and stock-raising economy (the small, Cycladic islands) to full-scale (for the time) capitalist systems (Chios, before 1822). One could also find houses that were built by their owners themselves mainly with collected materials (Folegandros, Anafi) all the way to houses that were erected by specialized, professional builders with expensive materials, many of which were imported, even from abroad (Hydra, Patmos, Chios). It is obvious that the more serious differentiations in the architecture we are examining are due to economic causes and that the high level of traditional architecture coincided with the economic "take-off" of the subject Greeks during the 18th century.

The factors involved in the social formation are directly connected to the preceding. The Ottoman ruling class was literally non-existent on most of the small, island societies or completely separate from them. But one could not say the same for the Venetians on Crete or the descendants of the Frankish feudal lords on the other islands. The Greek element went through a long, drawn-out process, differing from island to island, a gradual strengthening of the Greek archons–landowners, followed by the entrepreneurs, merchants and shipowners, who acquired wealth and power, principally after 1730. The social stratification had a direct impact on architecture since the archon was eager to

3. Hydra. View of the settlement west of the harbor (photograph: 1976).

3

4

promote his position through the largest or wealthiest house or through donations for the erection of churches and public works. The next was the continually increasing "urbanization" of the settlements, primarily after the Greek War of Independence.

But the exposition of the repercussions of the social factor on architecture and town-planning cannot be done in brief. Here are simply noted the astonishing wealth of traditions and customs of the islands which had a direct influence on the arts and the architecture of their houses, as well as the sense of dignity and the endeavor for a better life which will be found in even the poorest house on the Aegean islands.

In the mansions and the wealthier houses, which are at some remove from the folk perception of a house, one can isolate more clearly yet another factor in the formation of Aegean architecture: the imitation of the prototypes of official architecture. The sea unites the world; it facilitates contacts with the large centers, the arrival of craftsmen and artists, the conveyance of a complete range of everyday items and furniture as well as the importation of building materials. But once again, there are sharp differentiations: in some areas large-scale architecture had already been imported directly by the foreign rulers of the land (Crete, Rhodes ill. 56) while in others it arrived indirectly through religious relations (Tinos, Santorini) and in still others even more indirectly, principally through the copying of decorative motifs and forms which slowly acquired a new character. The third case includes the baroque and rococo style of Central Europe which was adopted in Constantinople (from 1730 on) and which became a common manner of ornamentation throughout the empire (principally in stone reliefs, wood carving and plaster decorations) including, of course, the settlements in the Aegean.

All the above, as factors connected to history, justify the multifariousness, the differentiations in the architecture of each locale and the composite phenomenon. Independent of the above, there are other conditions, ancient or natural, which have had a fundamental influence on architecture and which, in contrast to the previous ones, tend to unify the phenomenon:

—The uniform cultural heritage which has its roots in the former Byzantine empire and its fully realized culture. At the same time, there was the unified religious and ethnic consciousness of the Greeks who comprised all, or the vast majority of, the inhabitants of the islands.

—The environment. A landscape on a scale accessible to man and with impressive variety. The architectural remnants from Antiquity and the Middle Ages.

—The climate. Temperate, typically Mediterraenean, with almost continuous sunshine. The Aegean light was a fundamental factor in the architectural expression of its inhabitants.

III

Some of the settlements in the Aegean have an extremely long history. The area was prosperous during the middle of the Byzantine period and many of the larger settlements had been on the same site since Antiquity (Mytilene, ill. 35; Naxos; Paros, ills. 19, 21; Rhodes, Lindos, ill. 55; Tigani on Samos). The period after 1453 is of interest, on the one hand, for the transformations and the development of the settlements subordinate to Byzantine and Frankish rule and, on the other, for the new settlements which have been created since then. The long-term alterations undergone by the urban tissue of the Byzantine towns and villages are in reality so numerous that they cannot be distinguished from more recent ones.

In general, the growth of the traditional settlements in the Aegean follows the gradual

4. Patmos, Chora. Partial view of the settlement from the Monastery of Saint John the Theologian.

5. Mykonos. General view of the settlement (photograph: 1976).

6. Mykonos. The area of Paraportiani (photograph: 1976).

5

6

rise in population and the growth of the economy and the improvement in the security conditions. The original nucleus was, that is, nearly always something that afforded protection: the oldest fortified settlement (Naxos, Chios; Skyros, ill. 45; Chora on Kythera), a fortress (Volissos on Chios; Molyvos on Lesbos, ill. 36; Limnos), or a fortified monastery (Patmos, ill. 51; Ayios Georgios on Chios; Hydra, ill. 3). The role played by water supply was also crucial. Subsequently, the settlement grew dynamically, not according to any plan, but by meeting the day by day needs guided by the configuration of the land (ill. 13). Very often, the rudimentary road which connected the fortress gate with the work and production areas, became the main street of the settlement and at some point, different in each case, the commercial operations moved outside the fortifications while at the same time further defensive measures were taken, perhaps through the building of a new wall. Usually, the old fortress was slowly down-graded and not infrequently abandoned (Skyros, Skiathos; Astypalaia, ill. 47) or left to the exclusive use of the Turks and the Jews (Mytilene, Chios, Rhodes). On still other islands, such as Sifnos (ill. 32), the descendants of the Frankish feudal lords maintained their residence in the old, fortified nuclei and were flattered to be called "Kastrinoi" ("castle-dwellers").

The dynamic manner of growth had its reverberations in the form of the settlement. During the first stage, one finds the well-known linear development, the most typical example of which is the main complex on Sifnos (Xambela, Apollonia, ill. 15; Ano Petali, Artemonas, ill. 31). Later, a host of irregularities were created — small widenings, random angles in the plan, passageways, streets of variable width and stepped, that is, all the elements which increase the picturesqueness of the whole. Older churches could be incorporated within this grid or new ones erected, which became important features of the settlement, parish or neighborhood centers, points of reference with their tall pro-

7

7. Samos, Vathy. Partial view (photograph: 1957).

portions and bell towers. Other forms of the urban tissue, with a freer arrangement of the houses, arose from the frequently steep slope of the land, principally when the settlement went down to the harbor (Symi) or from the joining of settlements in rural areas (Phoinikia, ill. 28 and Oia, ill. 30 on Santorini). In such cases, the rapid economic development created large settlements, which were on excessively steep land without a productive hinterland and survived (Hydra) or were violently destroyed (Psara, Kastellorizo). The building of a village based on a plan is something very rare in the Aegean and bears witness to the imposition of foreign organizational initiative, such as the fortress on Antiparos and, perhaps, Kalamoti on Chios. The survival of the ancient, Hippodamian town plan, outside the medieval castle, in the "marasia" (a neighborhood-like arrangement) on Rhodes is perhaps unique.

IV

On most of the islands of the Archipelago, ecclesiastical architecture truly flourished after the fall of Constantinople, for four principal reasons : a) As in every traditional community an offering to the Divinity was a fundamental method of distinction and social promotion. b) The directives granting tax exemptions for dedications to churches or monasteries encouraged such donations. c) The erection of many, small churches was in the spirit of the older Byzantine tradition and d) The absence of Turks (in comparison to other areas of Greece and particularly in the cities) facilitated the formalities for the erection of a church.

We have already spoken about the importance of churches as elements of a town

8. Samos, Vourliotes. Facade of the Chatziyiannis house (source: "Greek Traditional Architecture", vol. 1).

9. Samos, Ano Vathy. Facade of the Chatzimanolis house (source: op. cit.).

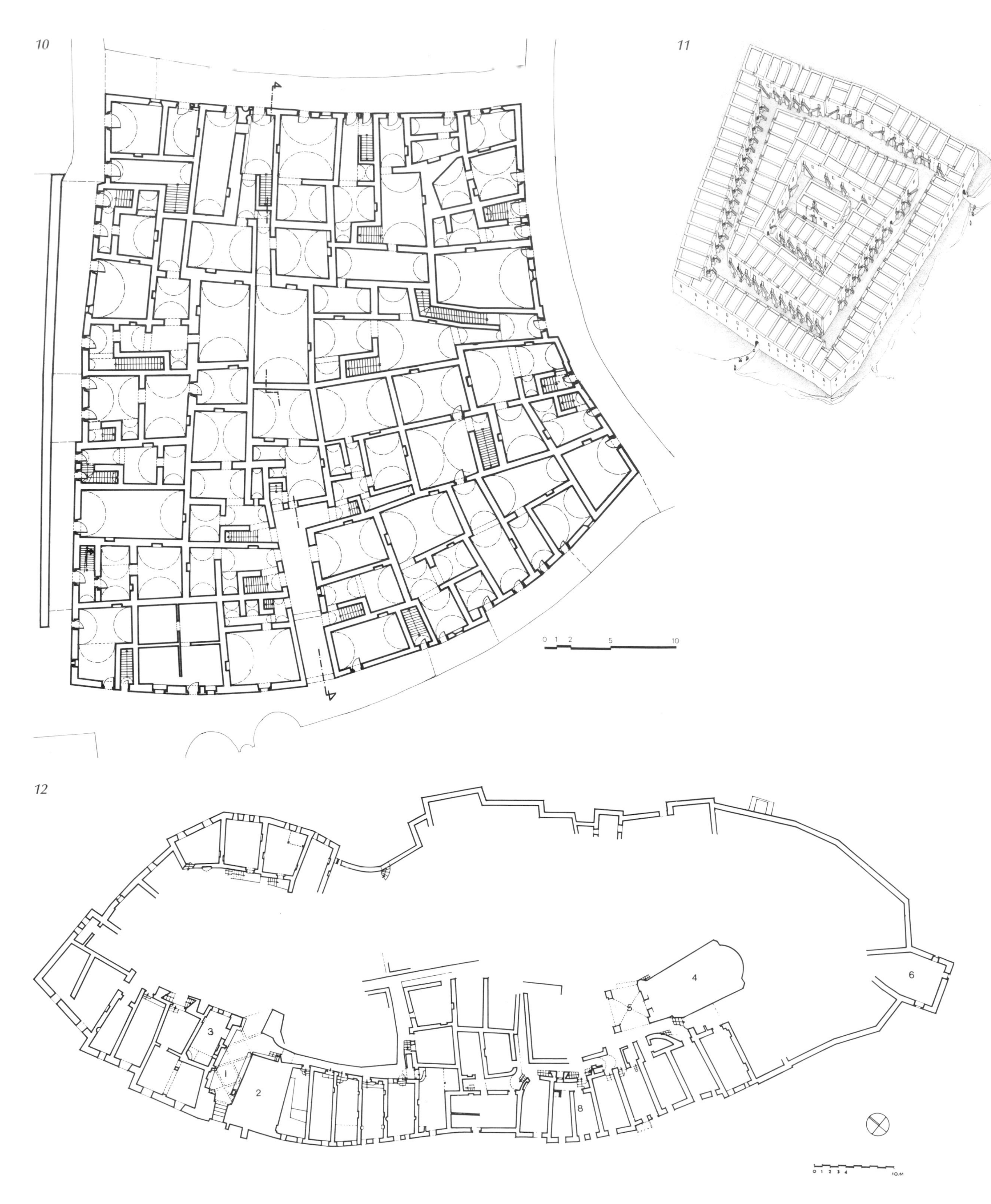
10
11
0 1 2 5 10
12
1
2
3
4
5
6
8
0 1 2 3 4
10 M

13

14

10. Chios, Olymboi. Plan of a building lot on the ground floor level (source: «Θέματα ἀρχιτεκτονικῆς μορφολογίας, Οἰκισμοί–Ἀρχοντικά–Μετόχια», Ἐργαστήριο Ἀρχιτεκτονικῆς Μορφολογίας καί Ρυθμολογίας Πολυτεχνικῆς Σχολῆς ΑΠΘ, Θεσσαλονίκη 1977).

11. Kimolos. Kastro reconstructed in its original form. Axonometric drawing (source: W. Hoepfner – H. Schmidt, "Jahrbuch des Deutschen Archäologischen Instituts", 91, 1976).

12. Astypalaia. Topographical drawing of Kastro. 1: entrance, 2: Panayia church of Kastro, 3: coffeehouse, 4: Ai-Giorgis, 5: Blatsa, 6: Serai, 7: "Yiatrou" mansion, 8: "Aga" mansion (source: "Greek Traditional Architecture", monograph: Astypalaia).

13. Karpathos, Elymbos. Topographical drawing of the settlement. The hatchings indicate the probable extent of the original nucleus with the church of the Dormition of the Virgin at the center (source: "Greek Traditional Architecture", monograph: Karpathos).

14. Kea. Built organization of the agricultural land. A ridge in Parameria (source: "Greek Traditional Architecture", vol. 2).

plan. Equally important for the organization of the countryside were the monasteries and the country churches. The small chapels give their names to and delineate capes, passages, peaks of hills and mountains or sanctify ancient ruins which retain the holiness and the memory of remains from older churches. The yearly festivals are inseparably connected to the traditional life and the customs of the islanders. The number of small shrines, chapels and dedications is enormous on some islands (Paros, Mykonos, Crete).

As is natural, church architecture was much more conservative and attached to Byzantine tradition than that of the houses or other buildings. Thus, in the majority of cases the name "post-Byzantine" is justified, not only for the churches but for the wall paintings, the icons and the vessels which were done in the same spirit. Often, however, one sees some structural of formal elements, which have been established in houses, being used in churches as well. The familiar technique used in the Aegean was, of course, more impressive in the churches. Thus we find heavy, stone-built walls, small openings, purely stereometric shapes, freely styled on the exterior, and white sculpture-like surfaces of unique harmony. The churches on Paros, Sifnos, Andros, Ios and Kythnos belong to this category. Some of these are justly considered to be peerless monuments of anonymous architecture (Paraportiani on Mykonos, Chrysopigi on Sifnos and Perissa on Santorini), along with many monastery complexes which were built using the same style (Chozoviotissa on Amorgos, the Monastery of Saint John the Theologian on Patmos).

Elements releated to the typology or the multiple and interesting foreign influences on ecclesiastical architecture in the Aegean cannot be examined here. But the increasing prevalence of the triple-aisled basilica in the late 18th and the 19th century should be noted. This type of church could, on the one hand, by adapted to a large size and thus hold the entire community and, on the other, take on a unprecedented monumental air. The Panayia of Tinos and the large basilicas on Chios and Lesbos are the most outstanding examples of this category of churches.

15. Siphnos, Apollonia. Linear development of the settlement along the main pedestrian street (source: A. Τζάκου, «Κεντρικοί οἰκισμοί τῆς Σίφνου», Ἀθήνα 1976).

15

V

What characterizes the architecture of the houses and all the other kinds of secular buildings on the Aegean islands is their superb functionality, their adaptation to needs and their potential for re-adaptation in the event of alterations. The very nature of the work, the fact (with a few exceptions) that it did not start on a drafting table, but in actual space, with a direct perception of the attainable, makes this architecture correct from its very inception. The dynamic development, particularly in old settlements with limited boundaries, demanded a process of re-adaptation, addition, modification and the re-use of sections of ruined buildings, a process of "formlessness", that is, where the original concepts had been long lost and the architectural structure arose from life itself. It would be a mistake, however, for one to generalize from this admittedly extreme position. Because on the Aegean islands there is a large number of buildings which were the crystallization of certain types, as well as no lack of dwellings in which the architectural form and not the function had the priority in their composition.

The following are several basic differentiations related to typology: the houses that are incorporated in the settlements do not usually have the size or the potential for lighting of those isolated in the countryside. There is rarely a courtyard. In most cases, they are two-storey (with auxiliary spaces and stables on the ground floor) or even three-storey. The location of the staircase either externally (Tinos; Paros, ill. 20; Antiparos; Mykonos, ills. 26, 27) or internally (towers of Lesbos, Patmos) is a fundamental typological aspect. The creation of an atrium on the upper floor is an advantageous solution, which is found in the medieval villages on Chios (ill. 10).

But fundamental typological differentiation arises from the form of the land. The problem of the staircase can also be solved on steeply inclined ground. The semi-two-storey and semi-three-storey arrangements on Tinos, as well as the subterranean houses on Santorini (ill. 29), are characteristic of such land formations. Typological differentiation also arises from the use of the spaces. The farmhouses have need of auxiliary spaces for

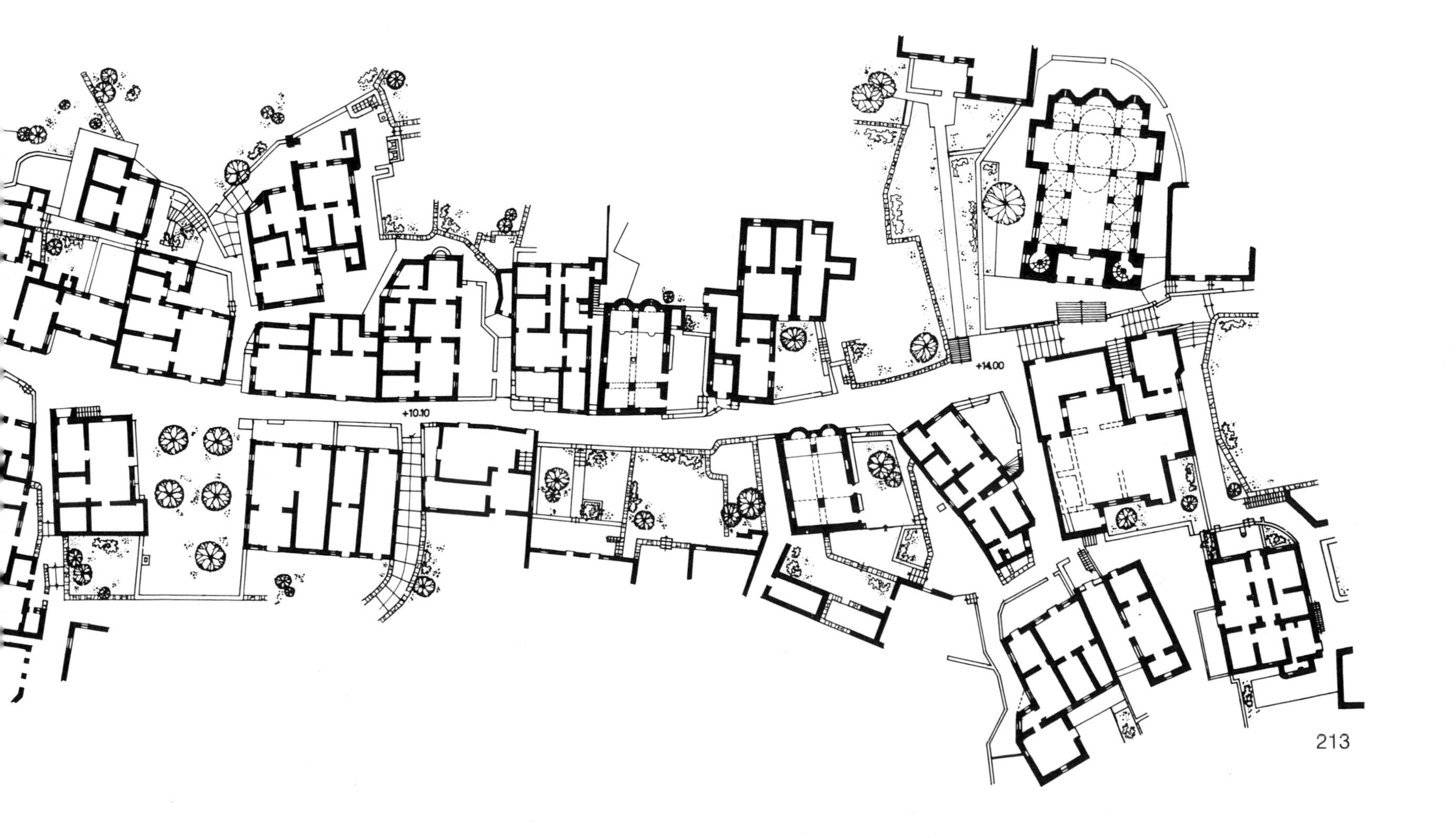

16. Chios, Mesta. A street.

the harvest and the domestic animals which frequently lead to original plans as, for example, on Aegina. Finally, economic means is a definitive factor in typology. The functions are separated through the addition of new rooms and new, more composite types are created, when the corresponding expenditures are feasible.

A hallmark of the dwellings on the Aegean islands are the arrangements for outdoor or semi-outdoor life, which is favored by the mild climate. The flat roof, the terrace, the lean-to and gallery, usually with arches, are found on nearly every island and lend even greater variety to house typology. Finally, a large chapter in the examination of the island dwelling is occupied by the organization and the furnishing of the interior spaces in which one finds, once again, functionality, knowledge of anthropometry, exceptional imagination and an elegant interconnection with the other folk arts. The achievements of several islands stand out here (Northern Sporades, Rhodes, Patmos, Crete).

The structural questions concerning the houses in the Aegean are, as has already been noted, directly related to the economy because they depend, on the one hand, on the materials used and, on the other, the abilities of the craftsmen using them. When there are very limited economic means the house is built by non-specialists, usually the owners themselves and with local, unprocessed materials: the thick walls of rubble, the cane or branches or the corbelled vaults made of thick slabs for the roofs and the tamped-down clayish soil for the floors are very common in all the purely "folk" houses throughout the Aegean. An extreme example of poverty are the subterranean houses built into the volcanic soil of Santorini. The support of the roof on a large, transverse beam, very common on nearly all the islands, is an example of technological progress which, at a different rate from place to place, led to more efficient structures. Vault construction was used on a limited scale (except for Santorini where the local materials facilitate it) despite the fact that it flourished during the Byzantine period. The widespead vault construction on Chios (ill. 16) appears to have taken its prototype from its remote Genoese past.

But one can verify the substantial progress in the structural sector, principally in the period after 1730, in the wealthy houses, the mansions. In Patmos, Hydra, Lindos on Rhodes, Lesbos, Kambos on Chios (ill. 17) and Psara one finds walls made of carved stone, stone reliefs and individual members of the structure done in marble, which bear witness to the superb quality of stone-working. One also sees vaults with daring operings, archways, cisterns of exceptional efficiency, wooden roofs and decorated ceilings, pebbled courtyards, fanlights with stained glass and wall pantings. All these constitute the pre-conditions for advanced architectural expression, but there is a need of serious study to learn how and by whom it was realized.

During this later period there was a general spread (Lesbos, Thasos; Samos, ills. 8, 9; Chora on Chios, the towns on Crete) of larger houses which on the first floor have a wooden frame structure and other characteristic structural elements (large cornices, hipped roofs, projecting upper storeys, sash windows with square fanlights above them and so on). This manner of building was generalized throughout the towns of the Ottoman empire and was based on the trade in timber for construction which reached the larger settlements in the Aegean after 1800 (?).

The morphology of Aegean architecture is an extensive and multi-faceted matter which can be analyzed by various methods. It has already become apparent that many of architectural forms have arisen from the unique way of economic development or from the structural system, while others bear witness to the concrete artistic intents of their builders and reflect the prototypes of large-scale architecture in a direct or popularized imitation. These two general categories are not unrelated to the economic and social infrastructure of their creation. They contain the results, in the first case, of

17. *Chios, Kambos. Courtyard gate of the Petrokokkinos mansion.*

the endeavor to cover vital needs on a poor, essentially improvisatory basis without any architectural pretentions and, in the second, the desire for a grander life style. This division in imperfect and schematic: the phenomenon is much more complex but incomprehensible without making certain assumptions.

The dazzling white sculptural surfaces on Mykonos (ills. 5, 6), Paros or Santorini, under the blinding light which leave us amazed by their harmony, most probably came about by chance from heterogenous structural features which were unified through repeated whitewashing. A purely architectural analysis, without preconceptions, could perhaps reveal how they emerged and why they appear so beautiful to us today: there was no intent for them to become so just as these was no artistic urge in the multitude of houses with simple cubical volumes which follow the slope of a hill and were built with thick walls and flat roofs. The common perception among the islanders themselves that there was some local architectural manner is revealed by the incorporation of their churches (where formal intentions are apparent) in the built wholes. But this was not general on all the Aegean islands nor did it rule out foreign forms if they served current needs. And it is unknown when it began.

The more recent developments are of much greater interest to the historian of architecture when, on several Aegean islands, the basic needs having been dealt with, the architectural forms were required to serve other purposes. The better way of life that the landlords and the rich procured by their participation in the new methods of production (just as in the rest of Greece) was expressed through a larger, more elegantly built and comfortable house.

The aspiration to a certain monumentality, which is expressed through symmetry or by the use of arches on the facades, which one sees on more vernacular structures (Tripotamos on Tinos, Marmara on Paros, Kythera, Symi) does not imply a specific imitation. But the frequency of contact with abroad created new conditions. As was previously noted, there was soon the possibility of copying foreign prototypes with the improvement in technique, the moving about of worthy craftsmen and the introduction of more expensive materials. The interest lies in the way the foreign forms were adapted and their final assimilation in a new artistic idiom.

In a few cases whole forms are introduced: the portals on the churches of Hydra, the Renaissance windows of Patmos, the "lionettes" (lunette-like vaults) in Chora on Chios and the baroque entrance ways on Paros. The modifications of baroque motifs, either coming directly from Central Europe or by way of Constantinople, are lacking in the restless energy and the passion of the prototypes and are reduced to simple decorative motifs (Tinos, Mykonos, Crete). The Late-Gothic motifs of the Knight architecture were flattened in Lindos, giving rise to a new look. In certain areas, the folk perception of decoration with geometrical motifs modified the originals (facades with *xysta*, a decorative technique similar to the Italian *sgraffiti*, in Pyrgi on Chios) or advanced on to striking new forms (the dove-cotes on Tinos, ills. 23, 24 and Andros). Similar modifications would appear later, after 1830, when the forms of classicism would make their appearance in the Aegean islands as well.

Architecture and town-planning, more than any other expression of civilization, reflect the social and economic reality of their time. On the Aegean islands in particular, they offer much more than their valuable historical witness. As noted above, the monuments of Aegean architecture, important monuments of folk civilization, express artistic values which still move us today and at the same time give a harmonious, human meaning to their environment. This would be a particularly difficult feat for contemporary architecture to repeat.

ΑΠΟΣΤΟΛΟΥ, ΕΛ., «Τό παλιό λεσβιακό σπίτι», *Τό Ἑλληνικό Λαϊκό Σπίτι*, Ἀθῆναι 1960, 126-146.

ΑΡΑΒΑΝΤΙΝΟΣ, ΑΘ., «Τό λαϊκό σπίτι στήν Ἄνδρο», *Τό Ἑλληνικό Λαϊκό Σπίτι*, Ἀθῆναι 1960, 105-125.

ΒΑΣΙΛΕΙΑΔΗΣ, ΔΗΜ., *Εἰσαγωγή στήν Αἰγαιοπελαγίτικη λαϊκή Ἀρχιτεκτονική*, Ἀθήνα 1955.

— «Ἡ λαϊκή ἀρχιτεκτονική τῆς Αἴγινας Α-Β», *Λαογραφία*, ΙΣΤ΄, ΙΖ΄, Ἀθήνα 1957-58.

ΓΟΥΛΑΝΔΡΗ, ΝΤ. - ΧΑΡΙΤΩΝΙΔΗ, ΤΖ., *Περιστερεῶνες στήν Τῆνο καί τήν Ἄνδρο*, Ἀθῆναι 1977.

DUSART, ET., "La leçon de Skyros", *Ekistics*, vol. 22, No 130, Athens 1966, 174-181.

EDEN, W.A., "The Plan of Mesta, Chios", *Annual of the British School at Athens*, vol. XLV, 1950, 16-20.

GOLDFINGER, MYRON, *Villages in the sun: Mediterranean community architecture*, London 1969.

Greek Traditional Architecture, ed. "Melissa", Athens, vol. 1 (1983): *Eastern Aegean - Sporades - Ionian Islands*:
E. Vostani-Koumbas, "Lesbos", 57-98; K. Papaioannou, "Samos", 99-140; Ch. Bouras, "Chios", 141-182; Chr. Arnaoutoglou, "Skyros", 183-216.

vol. 2 (1983): *Cyclades*:
A. Kharitonidou, "Andros", 9-42; A. Romanos, "Mykonos", 43-76; K. Kouroupakis et a., "Naxos" 77-110; M. Philippas-Apostolou, "Paros", 111-144; D. Philippides, "Santorini", 145-178; A. Tzakou, "Siphnos", 179-212; A. Kartas, "Syros", 213-246; R. Kloutsiniotis et. a., "Tzia", 247-272; A. Kharitonidou, "Tinos", 273-306.

and the separate issues:
E. Savvaris – V. Tsamtsouris, "Astypalaia", 1985; M. Bogdanou-Eliopoulou – A. Fetokaki-Sarandidi, "Kalymnos", 1984; D. Philippides, "Karpathos", 1985; M.A. Veniadou, "Leros", 1985; Chr. Iakovides, "Patmos", 1985; Λ. Moutsopoulou, "Rhodes", 1985; M. Filindra, "Spetses", 1986; Chr. Arnaoutoglou, "Hydra", 1986.

HOEPFNER, W. - SCHMIDT, H., "Mittelalterliche Städtegründungen auf den Kykladeninseln Antiparos und Kimolos", *Jahrbuch des Deutschen Archäologischen Instituts,* 91 (1976), 291-339.

ΘΑΛΑΣΣΙΝΟΣ, ΕΜΜ., «Τό παλιό Τηνιακό σπίτι», *Τό Ἑλληνικό Λαϊκό Σπίτι*, Ἀθῆναι 1960, 77-93.

ΙΑΚΩΒΙΔΗΣ, ΧΡ., *Χώρα Πάτμου*, Ἀθήνα 1978.

ΚΑΡΑΘΑΝΑΣΗΣ, Γ., «Τό λαϊκό σπίτι τῆς Πάρου», *Τό Ἑλληνικό Λαϊκό Σπίτι*, Ἀθῆναι 1960, 94-104.

ΚΟΝΤΗΣ, Γ.Δ., *Λεσβιακό πολύπτυχο ἀπό τήν Ἱστορία, τήν Τέχνη καί τήν Λογοτεχνία*, Ἀθῆναι 1973.

ΚΟΥΜΑΝΟΥΔΗΣ, Ι., «Περίγραμμα δημώδους θηραϊκῆς ἀρχιτεκτονικῆς: οἱ οἰκισμοί καί ἡ κατοικία», *Ἐπετηρίς Ἑταιρείας Κυκλαδικῶν Μελετῶν*, τόμ. Η΄, Ἀθῆναι 1969, 7-53.

ΚΩΝΣΤΑΝΤΙΝΙΔΗΣ, Α., *Δύο χωριά ἀπό τή Μύκονο καί μερικές πιό γενικές σκέψεις μαζί τους*, Ἀθήνα 1947.

ΛΑΣΣΙΘΙΩΤΑΚΗΣ, Κ., «Σφακιανά σπίτια», *Κρητικά Χρονικά*, ἔτ. 11ον, 1957, τόμ. ΙΑ΄, τεύχ. Ι-ΙΙΙ, 171-199.

ΜΑΡΚΟΠΟΥΛΟΣ, ΓΛ., *Ἡ λαϊκή μας ἀρχιτεκτονική*, Ἀθῆναι 1945.

ΜΕΓΑΣ, Γ.Α., «Ἡ λαϊκή οἰκοδομία τῆς Λήμνου», *Ἐπετηρίς Λαογραφικοῦ Ἀρχείου*, τόμ. 2 (1940), 3-29.

— *Ἡ λαϊκή κατοικία τῆς Δωδεκανήσου*, ἀνάτυπο ἀπό τό Β΄ τόμο τῆς μελέτης *Ἡ Δωδεκάνησος. Τό οἰκιστικό καί πλαστικό πρόβλημα*, ἀρ. 22 τῆς σειρᾶς ἐκδόσεων τοῦ Ὑπουργείου Ἀνοικοδομήσεως, Ἀθῆναι 1949 (*Λαογραφία*, 26 (1968-69, 204-264).

— «Αἱ ἀγροτικαί οἰκήσεις τῆς Ἄνδρου», *Χαριστήριον εἰς Ἀναστάσιον Ὀρλάνδον*, ἔκδ. Ἀρχαιολογικῆς Ἑταιρείας Ἀθηνῶν, τόμ. Δ΄ (1967), 83-118.

MICHAELIDES, C., *Hydra, a Greek island town, its growth and form*, The University of Chicago Press, Chicago and London 1967.

ΞΥΔΑ, ΜΑΡΙΑ, *Βοτσαλωτές αὐλές τῆς Χίου*, Ἀθήνα 1979.

ORLANDOS, A.C., "La maison paysanne dans l' île de Rhodes", *L' Hellénisme Contemporain*, Mai-Juin 1947, 224-231.

PAPAS, C., *L' urbanisme et l' architecture populaire dans les Cyclades*, Paris 1957.

PHILIPPIDES, D., *The vernacular design setting of Elymbos*, doctoral thesis, The University of Michigan, Michigan 1973.

ΣΗΦΟΥΝΑΚΗΣ, Ν. - ΠΑΠΑΪΩΑΝΝΟΥ, Κ., *Τά λιθόστρωτα τῆς Λέσβου*, Ἀθήνα 1984.

ΣΚΟΠΕΛΙΤΗΣ, ΣΤ., *Πύργοι τῆς Μυτιλήνης*, Ἀθήνα 1975.

SMITH, ARN., *The Architecture of Chios, Subsidiary buildings, implements and crafts*, ed. Ph. P. Argenti, London, Alec Tiranti, 1962, 171.

ΣΠΥΡΙΔΑΚΗΣ, Γ.Κ., «Συμβολή εἰς τήν μελέτην τῆς λαϊκῆς οἰκίας εἰς Ἰκαρίαν», *Χαριστήριον εἰς Α. Ὀρλάνδον*, ἔκδ. Ἀρχαιολογικῆς Ἑταιρείας Ἀθηνῶν, τόμ. Γ΄ (1966), 56-60.

ΤΑΡΣΟΥΛΗ, ΑΘ., *Ἄσπρα Νησιά*, Ἀθῆναι 1934.

ΤΖΑΚΟΥ, Α., *Κεντρικοί οἰκισμοί τῆς Σίφνου*, Ἀθήνα 1976.

ΤΖΕΛΕΠΗΣ, Π.-Ν., *Λαϊκή ἑλληνική ἀρχιτεκτονική*, Ἀθήνα 1971.

ΤΡΑΥΛΟΣ, Ι. - ΚΟΚΚΟΥ, Α., *Ἑρμούπολη*, Ἀθήνα 1980.

ΦΙΛΙΠΠΑ-ΑΠΟΣΤΟΛΟΥ, Μ., *Τό κάστρο τῆς Ἀντιπάρου*, Ἀθήνα 1978.

ΦΛΩΡΑΚΗΣ, ΑΛ., *Ἡ λαική λιθογλυπτική τῆς Τήνου*, Ἀθήνα 1979.

— *Οἱ Τηνιακές βοτσαλωτές αὐλές*, Ἀθήνα 1981.

ΦΡΙΣΛΑΝΔΕΡ, ΚΛΑΟΥΣ, *Περιστεριῶνες τῆς Μυκόνου*, Ἑλληνικές Τέχνες, Ἀθῆναι 1933, 1.

WACE, A. - DAWKINS, R., "The towns and the houses of the Archipelago", *Burlington Magazine*, 26 (1914-1915), 99-107.

WAGNER, F.C., *Die Töpfersiendlungen der Inseln Siphnos*, Karlsruhe 1974, 548.

ΧΑΤΖΗΜΙΧΑΛΗ, ΑΓΓ., *Ἑλληνική Λαϊκή Τέχνη, Σκῦρος*, Ἀθῆναι 1925.

The black-and-white photographs were furnished by: Charalambos Bouras (ills. 1, 4, 16, 17), Nikos Tombazis (ills. 3, 7), Maria Fine (ills. 5, 6).

19

20

21

22

18. *Kea, Chora. South side of Kastro, from Messada.*

19. *Paros, Paroikia. The Kastro neighborhood.*

20. *Paros, Naousa. Street with typical built external staircases.*

21. *Paros, Paroikia. The medieval wall of Kastro.*

22. *Naxos, Apeiranthos.*

23

24

23, 24. Tinos. Dove-cotes.

25. Mykonos. The so-called Venetia, old neighborhood of the merchant-ship captains, south of Kastro.

26, 27. Mykonos, Chora. External staircases of houses.

27

28

29

30

31

32

28. Santorini, Phoinikia. View of the central section of the settlement.

29. Santorini, Phera. Ayios Minas neighborhood, in the south section of the settlement.

30. Santorini, Oia. Partial view.

31. Siphnos. Panoramic view of the complex of settlements from the heights of Artemonas facing south.

32. Siphnos, Kastro. Section of the main street.

33

34

33. William Linton, "The harbor of Syros". Oil, 28×35.5 cm.

34. Syros, Ermoupolis and Ano Syros. General view. At the top is the monastery of Ayios Georgios.

35. Lesbos, Mytilene. Aerial view from the east with the medieval fortress.

36

36. Lesbos, Molyvos. General aerial view from the east.

37

37. Lesbos, Ayiasos. General aerial view of the settlement.

38

38. *Lesbos, Plomari. General aerial view of the settlement.*

39

39. Chios, Pyrgi. Aerial view of the medieval settlement from the south.

41

42

40. Chios, Mesta. General aerial view of the medieval settlement from the west.

41. Chios, Kambos. Newer settlements, along the main road (aerial view).

42. Chios, Anavatos. Partial aerial view of the settlement from the southwest.

43

44

43. Samos, Kokari. View of a part of the settlement from the sea.

44. Samos, Ano Vathy. Partial view.

45. Skyros, Chora. Kastro, the monastery of Ayios Georgios and a section of the settlement from the northeast.

46

46. Karpathos, Elymbos. View of the settlement from the east.

47. Astypalaia. General view of the settlement.

48. Astypalaia. The Venetian castle at the top of the hill and a section of the settlement.

47

48

49

50

51

49. *Leros, Platanos. The castle and a section of the settlement.*

50. *Leros, Ayia Marina. View of the settlement and the harbor from the castle.*

51. *Patmos, Chora. The area of Aporthiana and the Monastery of Saint John the Theologian. View from the north.*

52. *Patmos. The modern settlement of Skala. View from the south.*

53

54

55

53. Kalymnos. View of Pothia and east Marasi.

54. Kalymnos, Pothia. Section of harbor.

55. Rhodes, Lindos. View of the settlement with the acropolis to the rear.

56

56. Rhodes. Street in the medieval settlement.

CHRYSANTHOS CHRISTOU

The Aegean creators and their contribution to the fine arts

Translated by Philip Ramp

The Aegean Sea, the original "Archipelago", has always been associated with the command of the sea, with Poseidon and the father of Theseus, Aigeas, son of Pandion, which probably means raging and foaming waves, and is many more things than is commonly believed. It is the cradle of civilizations and its islands have been a bridge crossed by nations; it is the womb of the gods and the source of myth as well as the homeland of celebrated creators during all periods of history, but its greatness does not end there. The Aegean is a Greek sea stretching east and west, north and south, containing the Cyclades and the Sporades (northern and southern), the strips of Chalcidice and Euboea, the Saronic Gulf and the Dodecanese, all making up a marvelous entity which is distinguished for its muliplicity. Through one unifying sea, and islands that are no further than sixty kilometers from each other or the mainland, frugality and opulence are, in a strange way, combined. The Aegean reflects multiplicity in unity, with its islands and its coastline – the unity of the marine element which decides the fortunes of the population in this region; multiplicity is also found in the differing formation, the quality of the soil, the shape of the coast, climatological conditions, vegetation and the activities of the inhabitants: it has given and continues to give more than any other spot on our planet. The Greek sea is connected to the great moments of Greek history, to the mythical voyage of the Argonauts and the Trojan War, to the Persian wars and the Byzantine period, the struggle of the Greeks for liberation from the foreign yoke and their endeavors to achieve nationhood.

The Aegean, from the Greek mainland to the shores of Ionia, with coasts that can be inviting or forbidding, and its islands, stone masses and low-lying fertile valleys, a few of them relatively large, but most small, virtual pebbles in the sea, open to the north or the south, the east or the west, has been, one could say, condemned to be involved with everything. To be a bridge and a melting-pot for peoples and the supplier of gods, myths, civilizations and every category of creator, form and institution. The physical space with its contrasts and the need to transcend difficulties has made its inhabitants bold and daring, inventive and capable of utilizing all its potentials, open to every new idea and always free as the sea.

Right from the start the Aegean populations, those who would make it into a Greek sea, would use the common elements of the area and exploit its various characteristics. The common elements, the sea and the light, plus the unique features of each region, from the barren marble of one island which is fashioned into God and man, to the fertile soil of another which yields wine and oil, the quality of certain types of soil which could become an amphora or krater, secured the life of its inhabitants and increased their wealth. Throughout all stages of history, the Aegean islands and the areas which have been washed by the waters of the Aegean have been distinguished for their wealth of invention and the range of their intellectual accomplishments. The ceaseless motion of the sea was transformed into a permanent need for quest, for exploration, for communication with other people, civilizations, models and forms. One recognizes in all the accomplishments of the inhabitants of the Aegean, in all the characteristics of its collective and individual life, the desire for external independence and internal freedom, a belief in human dignity and personal fulfillment. The multitude of artistic workshops in Antiquity and the number of creators can be viewed as eloquent examples of the activity and the internal vigor of the Aegean population. But even today, in its vernacular architecture, closely connected to the rest, one sees in its multiplicity and its functional basis, the

1. Andreas Kriezis. "Portrait of a Noble"». 1852. Oil on zinc, 45×37 cm. Athens, E. Koutlidis Collection.

carefully weighed articulation and development of the special characteristics of each island, the entire content of the inhabitants' orientations.

The characteristics that set the tone during older periods and were found in artistic creation are also noted in the endeavors from the 19th and the 20th century. Because the role of the creators who came from the Aegean islands was definitive in the pictorial quests of the 19th and 20th century. We are not only referring to the workshops of Tinos which unquestionably set the course for modern Greek sculpture after the Greek War of Independence, but also the great teachers of modern Greek painting such as N. Lytras, N. Gyzis and G. Iakovidis who came from the Aegean islands. Creators who, with a host of others, would make endeavors which are distinguished by the very same qualities which have always been connected with the Aegean: multiplicity and personal quest, lucidity and spirituality, mobility and inner ferment, the need for freedom and a passion for the truth. Though it is not possible here to examine all the accomplishments of the creators who have their roots in the Aegean islands, we can form a good idea if we examine a few of the more important and complete endeavors: the artists of the pictorial arts from the 19th (to a greater degree) and the beginning of the 20th century who are distinguished by the range of their quest and the quality of their expression, particularly in painting and sculpture.

The first major figure in Aegean painting is Andreas Kriezis (ills. 1, 34, 35) who was born in Hydra in 1813 and studied painting in Paris. A member of an old, well-to-do family of sailors, Kriezis was involved with portraiture and historical scenes, mainly dealing with the sea. Within a climate of academic realism, the works of Kriezis are distinguished for their clarity of design and character of color, their accuracy of depiction and, in some cases, an excess of supplementary forms and decorative elements.

Another distinctive figure, despite the fact that her works are not known, was the first Greek woman painter, Eleni Altamoura-Boukoura who was born in Spetses in 1821, the mother of one of our most important seascape painters, Ioannis Altamouras. In order to study painting at the Academy of Fine Arts in Rome, Eleni Altamoura disguised herself as a man. A mother beset by tragedy, she destroyed most of her works and among them her best, after the death of her son Ioannis from tuberculosis at the age of 26.

2. Ioannis Altamouras. "Coastal Landscape of Spetses". Oil on canvas, 24×41 cm. Athens, E. Koutlidis Collection.

Nikiphoros Lytras (ills. 39-42) was born in Pyrgos, Tinos in 1832 and was unquestionably a definitive figure for modern Greek art. Nikiphoros Lytras "the patriarch" of Greek painting, as he is correctly referred to, was distinguished both as a creator and a teacher whose work asserts itself with expressive force and inner wealth. A student at the Athens School of Fine Arts, he completed his education at the Academy of Fine Arts in Munich and in 1886 became a professor at the latter School of Fine Arts where he remained until 1904, the year he died from slow poisoning caused by the fumes from his paints. He produced works and left behind students who set the course for modern Greek painting. Involved in all thematic areas, he was an exceptional portrait and a marvelous genre painter, as well as a painter of historical scenes. He was not limited to the framework of the attainments of the academic Munich School. He forged ahead with his own personal quests, creating paintings in which design elements were combined with chromatic values, well-planned organization with the active role of space and external fidelity with inner truth. Definitive works of his, such as "Lament for the Dead of Psara" are distinguished by their inwardness which is reminiscent of Rembrandt's style. "The Kiss" is noted for its purely poetic tone and the portraits "Lyssandros Kaftantzoglou" and "The Painter's Wife" for their convincingness and verity. A painter who was more interested in painting values than in description, Lytras was the creator who gave truly new dimensions to modern, Greek art and enriched it with his sensibility.

3. Nikolaos Gyzis. "The Inspection of the Dogs". Oil on canvas. Private collection.

3

Nikolaos Gyzis (ills. 3, 43-46), who was born ten years later, in 1842 in Sklavochori, Tinos, was another important figure in modern Greek art. Both a creator and a teacher, Gyzis also studied at the School of Fine Arts and completed his studies at the Academy of Fine Arts in Munich where he became a professor in 1882 and enriched modern, Greek painting with new insights. Despite the fact that his residence in Munich had negative repercussions on the Greek painting of his time, he produced works that combined, in a personal way, the achievements of academicism and his personal quests. Though excessively adhering to the academicism of the Munich School, he nevertheless managed in several of his more distinctive endeavors to produce works which are notable for their wealth of expressive content. Furthermore, it should not be overlooked that most of his mature works with their peculiar idealistic orientation and romantic atmosphere, their symbolic content and mystical tendencies, also contain elements which characterize the endeavors of other important creators in European painting. One of the chief traits of Gyzis' artistic creation is the multiplicity of his stylistic quests and the uneveness of his formulations. Thus, in his genre and historical work as well as his still lifes he achieves exceptional expressive results, while in his works based on literary and allegorical themes he is not convincing and moves us a great deal less. But unquestionably, his most creative moments are to be found in his studies and drawings, particularly from the final years of his artistic career. These, with their freedom and eloquence, their poetic spirit and

4. Georgios Iakovidis. "Girl with Basket". 1874. Charcoal on paper, 110×70 cm. Athens, E. Koutlidis Collection.

5. Polychronis Lembesis. "Portrait of Old Man". Charcoal on paper, 78×58 cm. Athens, National Gallery.

4

5

inner truth, their expressive power and sincerity, are achievements which break out of the framework of both academicism and realism and make him a great creator.

In Polychronis Lembesis (ills. 5, 47-49), who was born in 1848 in Salamis and who also studied at the School of Fine Arts and completed his studies at the Academy of Fine Arts in Munich, we find another artist who managed to transcend the academicism of the Munich School. For this reclusive artist and friend of Alexandros Papadiamantis, who lived in seclusion and died unknown, managed in his mature ventures not only to transcend the limitations of the Munich School, but to achieve a purely personal, morphoplastic idiom, so true and eloquent that N. Gyzis admired him and, if we can believe certain rumors, N. Lytras was actually jealous of him. Thus, while in a number of his early works, genre scenes, still lifes and nudes, he based himself on the well-known formulations of the Munich School, in his mature and later works he showed development which approached the work of the outdoor landscape painters and the Impressionists. In his works after 1890, particularly his genre work and landscapes, he gives us painting which is distinguished by a limiting of the extraneous, supplementary themes and a rejection of academic models with an emphasis on lucidity and the inwardness of the forms, along with an incorporation of the achievements of Impressionism. In several of the most characteristic of his late endeavors, Lembesis anticipates, through his purely personal quest, the insights of German Impressionism, as illustrated by F. von Uhde and Max Lieberman. Furthermore, he gives us works that marvelously combine warm and vibrant color with a naturalness in the rendering of the themes, a convincing development of space with a clarity of light and, frequently, a pure, poetic spirit.

In Georgios Iakovidis (ills. 4, 50-53), who was born in 1852 in Chydira, Lesbos and was a student of Lytras at the School of Fine Arts completing his studies at the Munich Academy as well, we also have an artist who played an important role in the preservation of the academic spirit of the Munich School. An artist who in 1900 was called upon by the Greek government to organize the National Gallery and who was a professor at the School of Fine Arts after the death of Lytras in 1904, becoming its director from 1910 to 1930, he only managed to transcend the limitations of the Munich School and its formalities of academicism in a few instances. Thus, in many of his works he kept to external characteristics and a somewhat shallow sentimentality, heavy colors and a superficial, theatrical tone, as well as idealistic features and a vague atmosphere. Iakovidis advanced somewhat further, in his scenes from childhood; even though he seems to have been influenced by similar motifs in F. von Uhde, he does achieve personal expression. In these, he combines his marvelous design with his love for narrative themes and manages to convincingly convey to the viewer the reactions and the state of a child's psyche. In several of his more complete ventures in which academic models are rejected, such as the portrait "Wife and Son of Artist", Iakovidis gives us true masterpieces which bring him very close to Eduard Manet, one of the great teachers of European painting.

But undoubtedly one of the most important and most highly endowed Greek artists of the 19th century was Ioannis Altamouras (ills. 2, 36-38) who was also born in 1852; it is not certain precisely where he was born but he died in Spetses at the age of 26. He was one of the most important painters of seascapes in all of European painting who also studied at the Athens School of Fine Arts, a student of Lytras, and completed his studies at the Academy of Fine Arts in Copenhagen. More a seascape painter than anything else – he did few landscapes that dealt with dry land – and aware of the accomplishments of the Dutch seascape painters of the 17th century, Ioannis Altamouras came to produce works which are distinguished for their inwardness and their painting verity. In his most characteristic works, one always finds supplementary themes spurned and the stress placed on the fundamental, with an emphasis on the rendering of the atmosphere and a free, impressionistic treatment, combined with a few light, bright colors and the inwardness of the whole. Altamouras always managed to give us the particular character of the moment, with the passing clouds, the sea which answers their motion, the vibrating atmosphere and the inner motion from contact with the marine element. The death of the creator at the age of 26 must be considered as one of the great losses to modern Greek art, for he had an exceptional feel for pure, painting values and his life-based contact with his subject matter, his use of impressionistic models and his personal idiom, produced works with astonishing, expressive extensions.

The work of Konstantinos Panorios (ills. 6, 7, 54), who was born in Sifnos in 1857 and died young as well, at 35, in an asylum, is also of importance. Through his studies at the Athens School of Fine Arts and the Munich Academy, a student of Lytras and influenced by the painting of Lembesis, it was natural Panorios would adopt the models of academicism. But despite his studies in Munich, Panorios managed in his most distinctive works to retain an inner independence and to produce works which are noted for their genuineness and immediacy. In these the artist combined, in a personal way, a precision of design with a plastic purpose, the monumentality of the forms with a generosity of

6. Konstantinos Panorios. "Titika". Oil on canvas, 140×80 cm. Athens, E. Koutlidis Collection.

7. Konstantinos Panorios. "Portrait". Oil on canvas, 125×94 cm. Athens, V. Kalkanis Collection (formerly).

6

7

color, external fidelity with an emphasis on inward quality. Though in his portraits the characteristics of German academicism play an important role, in his genre works and still lifes a purely personal, painting language holds sway. Uniform, large surfaces, a strict organization based on geometric elements, unaffected colors in harmonious cooperation and a combination of realistic description with generic models are his personal, formal characteristics which set the tone. Panorios, in his most important and personal endeavors marvelously combines synthetic fullness and distinctive colors, monumentality and inwardness, which lend exceptional expressive extensions to the whole.

Georgios Chatzopoulos (ill. 55) was born on Patmos in 1859 – though some doubts have been expressed about this – and was one of the most highly endowed students of Gyzis in Munich. Chatzopoulos played a very important role because though he studied in Munich, he was not only less influenced than anyone else by the conservatism and the academic climate of the Munich School, but did not hesitate to forge ahead, and with success, into the new, progressive quests of the period. His work, both thematically (with his almost exclusive focus on landscape) and technically, moved with assurance and competence in the climate of Impressionism. What is particularly noteworthy in the most distinctive works (all undated) of Chatzopoulos (who worked for many years as a restorer in the Greek National Gallery) is his use of the accomplishments of French landscape painting and impressionistic formulations; light, vivid colors and exceptionally subtle tones, shadows which can barely be seen along with the dissolution of the outlines, an emphasis on atmosphere and a rendering of the momentary together with a kind of immaterialization of the figures, set the tone. Beyond the bright colors and a purely subjective handling of the theme, through a stressing of the role of light and his short, abrupt brushstrokes, he manages to imbue the painting surface with inner life.

The Hydriote, Nikolaos Vokos (ill. 56), was born in 1861 and studied at the Athens School of Fine Arts and the Munich Academy of Fine Arts, under Gyzis. He was one of the most noteworthy painters of still lifes and "breakfast pieces" as they were called in the 16th and 17th century. An artist who was influenced by his teachers at the Munich Academy of Fine Arts and his personal study of the works of the important creators of the Low Countries, principally from the 17th century, Vokos has given us works which are impressive for their realism. The study of the works of artists of the past, such as Franz Snyders and Alexander Andrianssen, is obvious not only in the thematic compositions with fishermen and the still lives with lobsters and all kinds of fish and seafood, but also in his treatment of his themes. In a few of his more completely realized works in this category, as well as in his other still lives, he manages to avoid the rigidity of the academic tradition and its limitations and to create wholes which are exceptionally expressive. These are works which are distinguished for the correct design and the precision of the description, the synthetic assurance and the inwardness of the color as well as the expressive force and the opulence of the whole.

Loukas Geralis (ill. 58) was another Aegean painter who, even though he did not go beyond certain limits, has also given us some important works. A student of Iakovidis, Loukas Geralis was born in Mytilene in 1875 and had a particular interest in genre painting and landscapes; in his best work he strived for a combination of academic models with the attainments of outdoor painting. He was interested in precision and clarity of description and rendered the life of simple people with particular emphasis on anecdotal themes and graphic details, and tended to beautify events. He was also distinguished by his preference for subtle, warm colors and uniform light, nobility of form and idealistic temper, the way he handled space and his somewhat sentimental mood.

Vassilios Ithakisios was also more of a landscape painter than anything else. He was born in 1878 in Akrotiri, Lesbos and studied at the Athens School of Fine Arts, a student of Nikiphoros Lytras and Georgios Roilos. An artist closely bound to the earth and its people, Ithakisios travelled to various areas of Greece and painted landscapes and scenes from rural life as well as occasional portraits. His works are distinguished for their emphasis on realistic, descriptive characteristics and the precision of the design, the avoidance of supplementary forms and strict composition. Though in his earlier works academic features played a significant role, in the mature, later years of his creative life he not only availed himself of the achievements of Impressionism, but in several cases even made use of Fauvist forms.

Stelios Miliadis (ills. 8, 57), who was born in Chios in 1881 and studied in France, was an artist who clearly worked in an impressionist mode. More given to landscapes, Miliadis was distinguished by an absolute dedication to the accomplishments of French Impressionism as one can see in his works painted while he was still in France. But his ventures which came after his permanent settlement in Greece, display a fertile approach to the painting forms of Cézanne. Certain of his characteristics come from here, such as his tectonic organization and chromatic perspective with the succession of warm, neutral and cool hues, which set the tone in his later works.

Another direction is represented by Apostolos Geralis (ill. 59), who was born in Plomari, Samos in 1886 and studied at the Athens School of Fine Arts and the Julien Academy in Paris. Primarily an artist of genre themes, Apostolos Geralis is distinguished by his emphasis on descriptive characteristics and realistic forms. But in several of his ventures one can spot a rather superficial, sentimental temperament which weakens his works.

8

8. Stelios Miliadis. "Landscape". Oil on canvas, 25×31 cm. Athens, M. Zachariou Collection.

9

10

9. Iakovos Malakates. Tomb of hero in the region of the Achilleio. Gastouri, Corfu.

10. Iakovos Malakates. Tombstone on the grave of Pavlos Skalistiris. First Cemetery of Athens.

But undoubtedly the sculptors who came from the Aegean islands played a more pre-eminent role. The sculptors who entered the world throughout the 19th and continued their endeavors at the beginning of the 20th century produced the most distinctive and accomplished work in modern Greek sculpture. The sculptors who came from Tinos led the way creating funerary monuments, statues, busts, architectural sculpture and decorative wholes – works of all categories. It began with the Malakates brothers (ills. 9, 10, 20, 21), who were born in Ysternia, Tinos – it is not known precisely when – and who came to Athens in 1835 to set up the first sculpture workshop with the proud name "Hermoglyfeion". The workshop unquestionably was a bearer of all the great traditions and the wealth of experience of the Tinian workers in stone and acted as an incubator for modern Greek sculptors. Born sculptors, it appears that in Athens Iakovos and Fragiskos Malakates were involved with all areas of the plastic arts, but their best known and most complete creations were their funerary monuments, especially their tomb reliefs. A stroll through the First Cemetery of Athens will convince one of the range of their talent and the wealth of their expression. Their sculpture has provided us with a marvelous synthesis of their study of ancient Greek sculpture, the use of the models of the European Classicism and the characteristics of folk art.

The four Fytalis brothers (ills. 11, 12, 22) were also born in Ysternia, Tinos. In 1860 they founded the "Andriantopoieion" in Athens, the other great incubator for the creations of modern Greek sculpture where, among others, Vitalis, Vitsaris, Philippotis and Iakovidis studied. Two of the brothers, Georgios Fytalis (b. 1830?) and Lazaros (b. 1831?) gave us some of the most important work of the period, while Dimitrios gave up sculpture in favor of architecture and Markos was more involved with painting and decoration. After studying at the Art School, the Fytalis brothers (Lazaros continued his studies in Paris and was appointed a professor at the Art School in 1859) produced the first sculpture in the round in Athens. The two brothers collaborated on several of their works while on others they worked separately and were involved with every category of the plastic arts – statues, free compositions, funerary monuments and decorative wholes. What can be quite easily confirmed in the work of the two Fytalis brothers, in those which are signed separately by each one – Georgios and Lazaros – and are not creations done in common in the workshop, is the superiority of Georgios in sculptural imagination and content. In all his important ventures, the purely plastic values, with an emphasis on the tectonic characteristics, the equilibrium of the volumes, the interaction of the planes, the preference for large surfaces and the rejection of classicist forms, are dominant. In the works of Lazaros, conversely, we find a preference for smaller surfaces and design elements which are accompanied by an emphasis on classicist characteristics and idealistic forms. We can confirm these differences if we examine and compare two works on the same subject, the "Shepherd Carrying a Goat" which have survived, the one in its final material, marble and the other in gypsum. The virtues of the sculpture of Georgios Fytalis can be better seen in his statues, such as "Patriarch Grigorios V" in front of the University of Athens, with its combination of realistic forms and generalized elements, small and large surfaces, a controlled posture and gestures, tectonic organization and the monumentality of the whole. The statue of Konstantinos Kanaris in Kypseli (Athens) is distinguished for a different plastic language with an emphasis on idealistic features, small surfaces, the design elements and the superficial, theatrical stance.

Yet another sculptor came from Pyrgos, Tinos. He also established a workshop in Athens but his only well-known work is the statue of Gillford in Corfu. Kosmas Apergis (ill. 14) born around 1830, studied at the Athens School of Fine Arts and in Rome and taught plastic arts for a brief period – just six months – at the School of Fine Arts. He has not left us any other works that we know of but it is believed that quite early on he was led astray by worldly pursuits and died a pauper.

Georgios Vitalis (ills. 13, 23, 24), another of Greece's important sculptors, was born in Ysternia, Tinos in 1838. He also studied at the School of Fine Arts and the Fytalis workshop, completing his studies at the Munich Academy of Fine Arts. After his return to Greece he decided to settle on Syros where he opened a studio, rejecting proposals that he become a professor at the Athens School of Fine Arts. Vitalis concentrated his efforts on statues and was influenced by the Fytalis brothers, who were his uncles, and by his studies in Munich. He produced works which combined the accomplishments of ancient Greek plastic art and the forms of classicism. In some of his more distinctive and relatively early ventures, such as "Achilles or Paris" and "Theseus" – now in the Museum of Tinian Artists in Tinos – one finds the classicist prototypes which set the tone, particularly his acquaintance with the work of Thorvaldsen. A more personal dimension can be seen in the statue of "Byron" in Messolongi, a sculpture in which are combined a romantic temperament and fine calligraphic work. His busts in Ermoupolis, Syros and in Athens convey a more realistic dimension, a typical example being the bust of "Spyridon Trikoupis" in the National Historical Museum with the emphasis placed on the individual, physiological characteristics and the small details. Among his most important works are the statue "Gladstone" in front of the University of Athens where one finds a combination of idealistic and realistic forms, established features and personal expressions.

Dimitrios Philippotis (ills. 15, 25, 26), who was born in Pyrgos, Tinos in 1839, one year after Vitalis, marks a turn of Greek sculpture to themes of everyday life and a taste for realism. He studied at the Athens School of Fine Arts, under Georgios Fytalis, and completed his studies at the Academy of Fine Arts in Rome. After his return to Greece in

11

12

13

14

11. Lazaros Fytalis. "Konstantinos Kanaris". 1876. Athens, Kypseli Square.

12. Georgios Fytalis. "Shepherd with Kid". Kontostavleio Prize, Athens School of Fine Arts.

13. Georgios Vitalis. War Memorial. 1880. Ermoupoli, Syros.

14. Kosmas Apergis. "Gillford". 1893. Corfu.

15. Dimitrios Philippotis. Tombstone on the grave of D. Drosinis. Messolongi Cemetery.

16. Giannoulis Chalepas. "The Sleeping One". Tombstone on the grave of Sophia Afentaki. 1875. First Cemetery of Athens.

1870 he also opened his own workshop and had many students. "Marmarofagos" ("Marble-Eater") as he was dubbed by his colleagues, Dimitrios Philippotis was involved with scenes from everyday life even when he was still a student, as is shown by his sculpture "The Harvester" which won the first prize in a contest at the Academy of Rome. This involvement was truly something new for Greek sculpture, as it was, more generally, for European sculpture as well, which remained closely tied to funerary monuments and statuary or architectural works which had a somewhat impersonal character. Even in his early efforts, Philippotis was producing sculpture in the round for public spaces, gardens, streets or even interiors without any connection to architecture or dependence on a specific commission. From this point of view Philippotis belonged to a group of avant garde artists of the 19th century, both in terms of subject matter and treatment with an emphasis on work that had not been pre-commissioned, opening the way to the future. Despite the fact that his morphoplastic vocabulary was centered in an area where idealistic forms were combined with realistic characteristics, his work is distinguished by its immediacy and its expressive truth. We recognize the realistic orientation of Philippotis' sculpture in his works like the well-known "Wood-Splitter" in the Zappeion, the "Little Fisherman" also in the Zappeion, the Funerary Monument of Maria Kasimati in the First Cemetery, the "Child with Grapes" in Syntagma Square as well as in other works of his. In all these cases Philippotis, through a development of levels and a rendering of volumes, the flexibility of the oultines and the various axes of the forms, managed, by placing his emphasis on purely plastic values, to give us the entire content of his subject. Thus, his sculpture combines eloquence and expressive force, clarity and truth.

Giannoulis Chalepas (ills. 16, 17, 27–31), the most important voice in Greek sculpture at the end of the 19th and the beginning of the 20th century, was born in Pyrgos, Tinos in 1851. A tragic figure, but without a doubt a great creator, Chalepas was to produce sculpture which compared favorably with the creations of his great fellow artists through-

17

17. Ioannis Chalepas (father of Giannoulis Chalepas). Tomb of Taroula and Nikolaos Kagadis. 1895. Tinos Cemetery.

out Europe. Chalepas also studied at the Athens School of Fine Arts and at the Munich Academy of Fine Arts, where he made works which left no doubt concerning his potential. Because, despite the tragic aspect of his life, his works prove that he was indeed a truly great creator: in his quests and his realizations, the impact and the wealth of his form, the range of his inspiration and the quality of his treatment. For Chalepas, despite his mental illness and the suspension of his creative activity for nearly forty years, produced in both his early, accomplished work and his mature and later work, not to mention his studies – drawings and models – some of the most inventive plastic creations of the entire period. What makes the greatest impression is doubtlessly his formal richness and expressive force, the strict plastic character and the inner truth of his treatment. Works of his such as "Satyr Playing with Eros" and the "Sleeping One", his series based on the fairy tale of Sleeping Beauty, Medea, the Satyr and Eros as well as a host of other efforts enable us to comprehend the potential and the wealth of his sculpture. This applies even more to his movement from the outer to the inner, from the supplementary elements to strictly plastic values, the transfer of the center of gravity from narrative characteristics to the essential content of the subject. A sculptor who was more interested in the profound character of the plastic form than anything else, Chalepas gave us isolated figures and complexes which assert all their expressive truth. One notes that as the years pass there is an ever growing austerity and simplicity, an ever developing emphasis on structural characteristics and plastic values, and an ever increasing domination of the inner over the outer. Thus, Chalepas, who set off by assimilating and freely exploiting the accomplishments of the past and the present, quickly arrived at a series of purely personal, plastic formulations. Indeed, in his endeavor to produce works with a marked nobility of character, he arrived at a form of sculpture which is distinguished for its avant garde character and its expressive wealth.

Georgios Kaparias was born in Pyrgos, Tinos in 1860, a student of Leonidas Drosis at the Athens School of Fine Arts before completing his studies abroad. A sculptor who worked in Patras and in Tinos, where he finally settled and opened an atelier, Kaparias was not able to transcend the climate of classicism and the spirit of his teachers, particularly Drosis. In his few works, principally his funerary monuments and decorative wholes, Kaparias stayed within strictly classicist tendencies lacking the potential to bring forth the essential content of his subjects.

Lazaros Sochos (ills. 18, 19, 32) was born in Ysternia, Tinos in 1862 and studied at the Athens School of Fine Arts, a student of L. Drosis and N. Lytras, completing his studies at the Paris School of Decorative and Fine Arts in the company of sculptors who were idealistically oriented. A romantic by nature and raised with the irredentist vision of the "Megali Idea" ("Great Idea") of a Greek nation, Sochos was not slow in organizing a group of Hellenophiles and Greek fellow students and friends of his in Paris, where he was studying, and to take part in the Battle of Domokos in the ill-fated war of 1897 – of particular interest for its historical side. The most important and distinctive of his works is the "Mounted Statue of Kolokotronis" in front of the old Parliament building in which he managed to achieve a purely personal manner of expression. The more personal elements in this work are in the free combination of realistic and idealized forms with an epic tone, the wealth of forms and the equilibrium of volumes, the assured organization and the unity of the whole. Through the reliefs on the pedestal, where narrative characteristics and descriptive values are combined, he managed to avoid classistic neutrality and academic elements, bringing the conception of the subject and the charac-

18

18. Lazaros Sochos. Tomb of hero Pavlos Melas. 1910. Athens, Rigillis Square.

ter of the statue to consummation. He presented Kolokotronis not so much as a victor, but as a leader of the people, with his arm raised showing the way, while at the same time looking back to see if they are following him. A sculptor with a complete mastery of classicist models, Lazaros Sochos appears in some of his works to have been hesitating over the road he should follow. In any case, in the "Mounted Statue of Kolokotronis" he managed to achieve an effective combination of classicist elements and realistic forms, which leave no doubt as to his capabilities.

Konstantinos Foskolos was born in Tinos in 1875 and studied sculpture at the Polytechnic School under Y. Vroutos. A sculptor of limited abilities, Foskolos was more involved with decorative sculpture of no particular character, primarily reliefs.

Antonios Sochos (ill. 33) was born in Ysternia, Tinos in 1888, the nephew of Lazaros Sochos and whose father, grand-father and great-grandfather had also been sculptors. Antonios Sochos began his studies at his father's marble cutting-workshop in Patras and continued at the Athens School of Fine Arts, a student of Vroutos as well, completing his studies in Paris at the School of Fine Arts with A. Bourdelle as his teacher. After his return to Greece and his de-mobilization in 1922, he was appointed Professor at the Architecture School of the National Technical University, where he taught until 1959. In his wood and stone sculptures we find both the development of the expressive potential of the material and the utilization of a personal, plastic idiom, which is distinguished by its folk technique and its archaic, practically hieratic characteristics. It is easy to discern in the artistic creations of Antonios Sochos a rapid movement away from the sculptural conceptions of his teacher, Vroutos, and the adoption of a strictly personal, expressive language. His works, either fashioned in wood or stone, or those cast in bronze, are always ruled by his personal characteristics which are the tendency toward schematization and the use of a strict geometric vocabulary, a concern for austere outlines and well-designed composition, an emphasis on the clarity of the form and hieratic immobility and finally a stressing of the structural features of the theme. His works in the National Gallery of Greece such as "Head of Kore" in sandstone, the "Girl" in wood and the "Digenis" leave not a shadow of a doubt about the purely personal character of his treatment.

Polygnotos Vagis was also from the Aegean; he was born in Potamia, Thasos in 1884 and died in New York where he spent the major part of his life. Vagis studied in New York, in the sculptural department of the Cooper Union and later at the Beaux Arts Institute and he began to exhibit his sculptures with success in 1922. Shortly before he died, he bequeathed his works, which were in his studio in Bethpage, Long Island, to the Greek State with the express wish they be placed on exhibit in his native Thasos or the town nearest to it. A museum of his work is now operating in Kavala, where one can study his entire artistic career. In Vagis' most characteristic efforts one can easily see both an assimilation of classicist forms and personal quests based on modern currents. In his early works Vagis was primarily interested in the motifs of ancient tradition and allegorical form, works such as "Universe", "Sleep", "Prayer" and "Night", without making a great deal of progress. Among his most important works are those containing animals, where he achieves a more personal and accomplished rendering. In works such as "Snake" at the Museum of Modern Art in New York, "Owl" in the Public Library of the same city, "Birds", "Dog" and "Fish", now in Kavala, he achieved his own personal vision. This was based on a combination of realistic description and an emphasis on the typical, a stressing of purely plastic elements and schematization, which are all striking. Polygnotos Vagis produced several memorable sculptures of animals but he appears to have been somewhat limited in the rest of his efforts.

The review of the course and the creative achievements of the Aegean creators, who entered the world in the 19th century, leaves no room for doubt as to the extent and the wealth of their achievements. The definitive role played by the artists from Tinos, primarily the sculptors but the painters as well, should be stressed. The 20th century, though not lacking in important artists from Tinos, includes creators from nearly all the islands. Though it is not possible to list the names of the artists, because we would be running the danger of just compiling a catalogue of names, we can state that the important creators of modern Greek art have come from all the islands. Thus, we have painters and sculptors from the northern islands as well as the southern Aegean, creators who have moved in all stylistic dimensions and are distinguished by their quests and the expressive wealth of their endeavors. Artists have come from Mytilene and Symi, from Chios and Icaria, from Paros and Lesbos, from Syros and Limnos, from Hydra and Naxos, from Nisyros and Andros, from Kalymnos and Milos, from Spetses and Thasos, from Amorgos and Skopelos, from Kythera and Patmos, from Folegandros and Santorini, from Skyros and Skiathos: in short, from all the islands in the Aegean, small and large, rich or poor. There is not another area in Greece which has turned out such a great number of artists and one, moreover, that was so open to every form of inquiry in the 20th century. These are works which are distinguished for the multiplicity of their achievements and the wealth of their formulations, their contact with modern reality and the sincerity of their expressive language. Despite the fact that most of them are today living and working in the large centers, Athens, Thessaloniki and abroad, their endeavors still supply us with something of the character and the spirit of the Aegean. Its austerity and its inwardness, its light and its freedom, its belief in Humanity and its love of truth.

19

19. Lazaros Sochos. Mounted Statue of Theodoros Kolokotronis. Athens, Old Parliament.

BIBLIOGRAPHY

We are not aware of any study which mentions the definitive role of Aegean artists in the overall development of modern Greek art. But there are related entries in dictionaries and histories of modern Greek art as well as monographs on various creators. The following are of especial note:

ΛΥΔΑΚΗΣ, ΣΤ., *Ἡ Ἱστορία τῆς Νεοελληνικῆς Ζωγραφικῆς*, ἔκδ. «Μέλισσα», Ἀθήνα 1976 (= *Οἱ Ἕλληνες Ζωγράφοι* 3).

— *Λεξικό τῶν Ἑλλήνων ζωγράφων καί χαρακτῶν*, ἔκδ. «Μέλισσα», Ἀθήνα 1976 (= *Οἱ Ἕλληνες Ζωγράφοι* 4).

— *Ἡ Νεοελληνική Γλυπτική: ἱστορία - τυπολογία - λεξικό γλυπτῶν*, ἔκδ. «Μέλισσα», Ἀθήνα 1981 (= *Οἱ Ἕλληνες Ζωγράφοι* 5).

ΣΠΗΤΕΡΗΣ, Τ., *3 αἰῶνες Νεοελληνικῆς Τέχνης*, Ἀθήνα 1979.

ΧΡΗΣΤΟΥ, ΧΡ., *Ἡ Ἑλληνική Ζωγραφική 1832-1922*, Ἀθήνα 1981.

ΧΡΗΣΤΟΥ, ΧΡ. - ΚΟΥΜΒΑΚΑΛΗ-ΑΝΑΣΤΑΣΙΑΔΗ, Μ., *Νεοελληνική Γλυπτική 1800-1940*, Ἀθήνα 1982, where there is particular emphasis placed on the role of Cycladic workshops in the development and the application of all types of modern Greek sculpture.

From the monographs and studies of Aegean artists we again note the following for painters:

ΑΘΑΝΑΣΟΓΛΟΥ, Ν., *Νικηφόρος Λύτρας 1832-1904*, διδακτ. διατρ., Ἀθήνα 1974.

— «Νικηφόρος Λύτρας», *Ἀπό τό 19ο αἰώνα στόν 20ό*, ἔκδ. «Μέλισσα», Ἀθήνα 1974, 100-137 (= *Οἱ Ἕλληνες Ζωγράφοι* 1).

ΚΑΛΛΙΓΑΣ, Μ., *Νικόλαος Γύζης, ὁ ἄγνωστος, 1842-1901*, Ἀθήνα 1980.

ΠΑΠΑΪΩΑΝΝΟΥ, Γ.Χ., «Νικόλαος Γύζης», *Ἀπό τό 19ο αἰώνα στόν 20ό*, ἔκδ. «Μέλισσα», Ἀθήνα 1974, 138-187 (= *Οἱ Ἕλληνες Ζωγράφοι* 1).

Ν. Γύζης, Ν. Λύτρας, Κ. Βολανάκης, Γ. Ἰακωβίδης καί ἡ Ἐποχή τους, Ἀθήνα 1973 (κατάλογος ἔκθεσης).

ΧΡΗΣΤΟΥ, ΧΡ., «Γεώργιος Ἰακωβίδης», *Ἀπό τό 19ο αἰώνα στόν 20ό*, ἔκδ. «Μέλισσα», Ἀθήνα 1974, 230-267 (= *Οἱ Ἕλληνες Ζωγράφοι* 1).

For sculptors: On the Malakates brothers:

MOURELLOU, K., *Die griechische Bildhauerei des 19. Jhdts*, doctoral thesis, Munich 1972, 9, 14.

ΣΠΗΤΕΡΗΣ, Τ., *3 αἰῶνες Νεοελληνικῆς Τέχνης*, Ἀθήνα 1979, τόμ. Α΄, 221-222.

On the Fytales:

ΧΡΗΣΤΟΥ, ΧΡ. - ΚΟΥΜΒΑΚΑΛΗ-ΑΝΑΣΤΑΣΙΑΔΗ, Μ., *Νεοελληνική Γλυπτική 1800-1940*, Ἀθήνα 1982, 198, with bibliography.

On Georgios Vitalis:

ΓΙΟΦΥΛΛΗΣ, Φ., *Ἱστορία τῆς Νεοελληνικῆς Τέχνης*, τόμ. Α΄, Ἀθήνα 1962, 250-251.

On Giannoulis Chalepas:

ΚΑΛΛΙΓΑΣ, Μ., *Γιαννούλης Χαλεπᾶς*, Ἀθήνα 1972, with an extensive bibliography.

20

21

20. Fytales brothers. Detail from the base of the monument of Michael Tositsas. First Cemetery of Athens.

21. Iakovos (Giakoumis) Malakates. Tomb relief. First Cemetery of Athens.

22

23

22. Georgios Fytalis. "Patriarch Grigorios V". 1872. Facade, University of Athens.

23. Georgios Vitalis. "Gladstone". Propylaia, University of Athens.

24. Georgios Vitalis. "Paris". Plaster. Tinos, Museum of Tinian Sculptors.

24

25

26

27

25. Dimitrios Philippotis. "Wood-Splitter". Athens.

26. Dimitrios Philippotis. "The Harvester". 1870. Athens, The Zappeion.

27. Giannoulis Chalepas. "Satyr playing with Eros". 1877. Athens, National Gallery.

28

28. Giannoulis Chalepas. "The Fairy Tale of Sleeping Beauty". Tinos, Museum of Tinian Sculptors.

29. Giannoulis Chalepas. "The Final Repose". 1931. Clay. Athens, National Gallery.

30. Giannoulis Chalepas. "Satyr and Eros". 1933. Tinos, Chalepas family.

31. Giannoulis Chalepas. "Satyr and Eros". 1918. Tinos, Museum of Tinian Sculptors.

29

30

31

32

33

32. Lazaros Sochos. "Kolokotronis Speaking". One side of the base of the Statue of Kolokotronis (ill. 19). Athens, Old Parliament.

33. Antonios Sochos. "Regas Pherraios". Wood. (Photograph from the Archives of I. Manolikakis).

34. Andreas Kriezis. "Portrait of Kyria Konstantinou". Oil on canvas, 100×82 cm. Athens, E. Koutlidis Collection.

35. Andreas Kriezis. "Captain of Psara". Oil on canvas, 95×71 cm. Athens, E. Koutlidis Collection.

36. Ioannis Altamouras. "The Harbor of Copenhagen". 1874. Oil on canvas, 30×43 cm. Athens, National Gallery.

34

35

36

37

38

37. Ioannis Altamouras. "Caique at Spetses". 1877. Oil on canvas, 29×39 cm. Athens, National Gallery.

38. Ioannis Altamouras. "Seascape". 1874. Oil on canvas, 28×40 cm. Athens, National Gallery.

39. Nikiphoros Lytras. "The Firing of the Turkish Flagship by Kanaris". Oil on canvas, 141×112 cm. Athens, I. Serpieris Collection (formerly).

40

42

41

40. Nikiphoros Lytras. "Return from Fair on Pendeli". Oil on canvas, 98×64.5 cm. Athens, E. Koutlidis Collection.

41. Nikiphoros Lytras. "The Kiss". Oil on canvas, 88×69 cm. Athens, E. Koutlidis Collection.

42. Nikiphoros Lytras. "The Lady in White" (portrait of Marianthi L. Charilaou). Oil on canvas, 155×78 cm. Athens, National Gallery.

43. Nikolaos Gyzis. "Behold the Celestial Bridegroom". Oil on canvas, 200×200 cm. Athens, National Gallery.

43

44

45

46

47

44. Nikolaos Gyzis. "Koukou". Oil on canvas, 100×75 cm. Athens, National Gallery.

45. Nikolaos Gyzis. "Artemis Gyzis". Oil on canvas, 137×100 cm. Athens, E. Koutlidis Collection.

46. Nikolaos Gyzis. "The Betrothal of the Children". Oil on canvas, 104×157 cm. Athens, National Gallery.

47. Polychronis Lembesis. "Still Life" or "Basket with Fruit". 1878. Oil on canvas, 35×44 cm. Athens, E. Koutlidis Collection.

48

49

50

48. *Polychronis Lembesis. "The Rabbits". 1879. Oil on canvas, 132×103 cm. Athens, National Gallery.*

49. *Polychronis Lembesis. "The Aeropagus Hill". 1880. Oil on canvas, 62.5×94.5 cm. Athens, National Gallery.*

50. *Georgios Iakovidis. "The First Steps". Oil on canvas, 140×110 cm. Athens, E. Koutlidis Collection.*

51

51. Georgios Iakovidis. "The Artist's Family". 1898. Oil on canvas, 110×75 cm. Athens, E. Koutlidis Collection.

52. Georgios Iakovidis. "Springtime". 1927. Oil on canvas, 120×168 cm. Athens, E. Koutlidis Collection.

53

53. Georgios Iakovidis. "Children's Concert". 1900. Oil on canvas, 177×250 cm. Athens, National Gallery.

54. Konstantinos Panorios. "Village Girl with Basket". Oil on canvas, 114×76 cm. Athens, E. Koutlidis Collection.

54

55

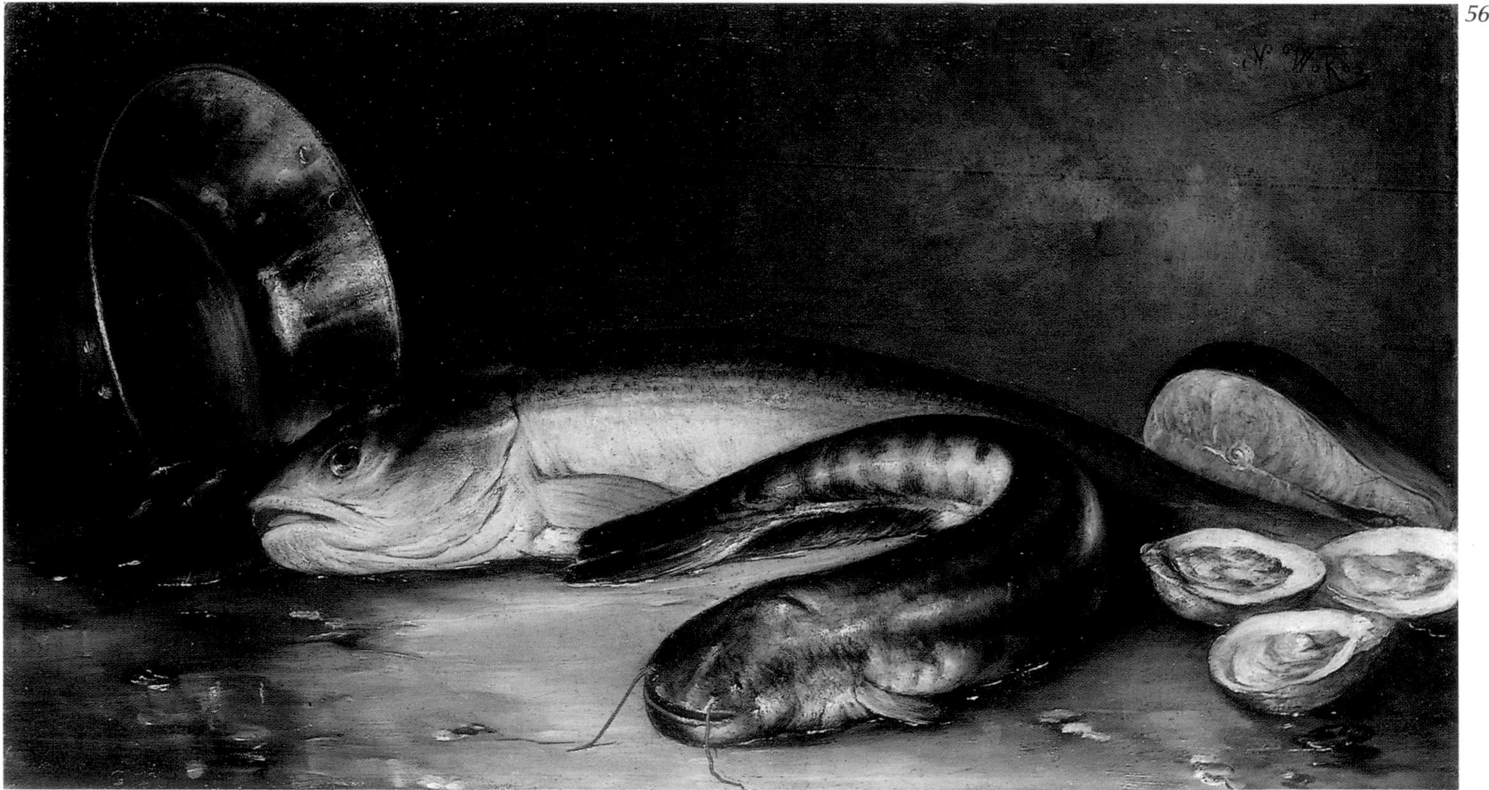

56

55. Georgios Chatzopoulos. "Aigion Landscape". Oil on canvas, 80×110 cm. Athens, E. Koutlidis Collection.

56. Nikolaos Vokos. "Still Life with Fish". Oil on canvas, 54×110 cm. Athens, National Gallery.

57

58

57. Stelios Miliadis. "Greek Landscape". Oil on canvas, 50×65 cm. Athens, National Gallery.

58. Loukas Geralis. "Fruit". Oil on canvas, 41×72 cm. Athens, National Gallery.

59

59. Apostolos Geralis. "Village Woman Watering Flowers". Oil on canvas.

ANGELOS DELIVORRIAS

Traditional art on the Aegean islands

Translated by Alexandra Doumas

The particular quality of artistic phenomena in the Aegean islands in post-Byzantine times follows the coordinates of historical circumstances far more assiduously than in any previous periods of Greek civilization. One would reach this axiomatic conclusion even without the tangible evidence of cultural documents, even if preliminary research were based exclusively on theoretical criteria. After all, it would have been difficult for the basic factors implicated in this artistic process to have been mobilized independently of the continuous stratification of components which had already begun to accumulate after the Fourth Crusade (1204) and which were mainly inspired by Western influences. Despite independent development in certain areas, or even the singularity of events, the fundamental factor of national consciousness – that is collective memory – seems to have served as a connective tissue, activating the heritage of the past at those crucial moments when uncontrolled changes in historical fate should rather have caused the irrevocable plunge into oblivion. This was what one would logically have expected, for example, during those tragic periods of persecution and bondage, with their violent mass displacements of populations and their inhuman resettlement elsewhere, which left the indelible marks of Ottoman expansionism on the body of the islands. However, the unyielding orthodoxy of rationalist appraisals, in other words the one-sided application of historical laws, does not always facilitate our understanding of phenomena; indeed, more often than not, it would seem to operate in inverse proportion to their impenetrability. For, as can be easily ascertained in the case of ecclesiastical painting, it was precisely this historical consciousness and the needs of collective memory, rather than the demands of dogma or the supposed inability of artistic expression to advance to new, revolutionary achievements, which encouraged the maintenance, but also the gradual transformation, of many art forms inherited from the Byzantine period of the Greek past.

By the middle of the seventeenth century, but chiefly from the eighteenth century onwards when the Ottoman conquest of Greece was complete, more and more components of the Ottoman cultural tradition, re-fashioned and assimilated, can be detected in the existing reserves of aesthetic orientations. Taking the flower as the principal element, together with influences from late European Baroque and Rococo, Greek aesthetic sensibility proceeded to "weave" a whole world of remarkable effloresence which does not just reflect a deep-rooted decorative disposition, or an imperative need to invest certain eugenic wishes with symbolism, it is the absolute affirmation of life itself, the optimism of an unwavering conviction in its ultimate prospects. From the beginning of the nineteenth century, and throughout the period of the struggle for liberation from the Turks, alongside the gradual expansion of the borders of the newly formed Greek state, the influences of the already crystallized aesthetic of mainland Greece on island artistic expression are obvious. It is to the dynamic synthesis of all these parameters, to the amazing facility of Greek tradition to assimilate and re-fashion, that the exceptionally interesting and truly captivating artistic production of the islands, which describes a rising curve that reached its peak in the late eighteenth century, is due. Since then the descending curve has followed, as it were in reverse, the conquests of Hellenism in revolt, the creation of the Modern Greek state, the radical restructuring of the shipping industry in the second half of the nineteenth century and the historic adventures of the twentieth, to peter out in the paranoid pace with which contemporary "civilization" has invaded the degraded Greek world.

There is no doubt that the aesthetic dimension of artistic phenomena is determined by a large number of disparate factors and variously charged stimuli, by the polymorphism of their components and the multiple meanings of their vocabulary, by the not always clearly circumscribed limits of their original aims. The Neohellenic artistic creation of the island world presents, despite the infinite penetration and infiltration of its formal transmutations and the distilled sensibility of the many chronological levels in the fabric of its expressive manifestations, a wonderful unity of spirit and uniformity of style. However, even a schematic recording of it, observing the principles of methodological validity, would necessitate division of the geographical unity and the cutting up of historical sequence into smaller units. Thus the artistic production of Crete, the Dodecanese and the Cyclades, of the islands of the East and the North Aegean, of the Sporades and Euboea would be presented as relatively complete wholes, so that the importance of the integrity of the part to the cohesion which characterizes the internal discourse of the overall may be immediately perceived. However, such a structure would be contrary to the conventional specifications of this volume, just as extending the process of inquiry to neighbouring regions is likewise contrary, even though the sea – the supreme unifying factor in the history of civilization – explains the presence of analogous art forms and associated expressive manifestations in many of the coastal towns of mainland Greece, the islands of the Saronic Gulf and the Ionian Sea, Kythera, and, above all, Cyprus.

In addition, however, to broadening the scope of investigation in order to understand the artistic creation of the Aegean islands, as well as to follow its gradual transformations in post-Byzantine and later times, a more penetrating examination of the chronological parameters is essential: that is a more thorough peeling away of the layers of stylistic stratigraphy. This would presuppose a "knowledge" of island art far more substantial and extensive, far more detailed and complete than Modern Greek scholarship could claim to have acquired, or than my own intellectual faculties have managed to absorb. The irresolute bibliography, the absence of relevant studies – even when these do exist they are overburdened with a "folklorism" quite unacceptable to modern scholarship – the non-existence of catalogues in which the collected material is recorded and evaluated, the indifference of the State to the continuing plundering of local evidence, and the lack of comparanda for investigating the horizontal and vertical coordinates of the problem, make any effort extremely difficult, if not discouraging it completely. So my conviction that every endeavour to sketch, even superficially, the character of recent art in the Greek islands is foredoomed to reach an impasse, is not due to excessive modesty on my part but to the lack of sufficent evidence. This is even more valid when the aims are more ambitious, that is when a more serious scrutiny of the substrate and heartland, as it were, of artistic phenomena is embarked upon, with an overt attempt to move from the specific and partial to the generic but authoritative.

From the remnants which have survived, from whatever is accessible – even if the bibliographical documentation is unorthodox –, from whatever traces can still be located beyond the malice of time, from whatever it is possible to evaluate without any deviation towards the enticement of basic research, one ascertainment of indisputable authority is deduced: the islands of the Archipelago are governed by a single artistic tradition, born of a common cultural component which reflects both their racial unity and shared historical fate. Disregarding the veneer of ignorance laid down by the ingratitude of the times and the ambivalence of the facts, I shall attempt a "restoration" of the incompletely preserved and scattered components to their archetypal forms of expression, in the hope that the reader too will find the tracking of the spoor beyond the bounds of oblivion a fascinating, exploratory adventure.

Before proceeding to present my views, I feel that one clarification is absolutely necessary: the social circumstances existing in the islands of the Archipelago, and indeed in all other areas of Hellenism, were not favourable – with the exception of ecclesiastical painting and architecture, both religious and secular – to creative expression on a large scale, in open space and of autonomous substance. In this Byzantine tradition must also have played a part – the long period during which art remained primarily the servant of religion –, as well as Greece's isolation from the spirit of the Renaissance, which irrevocably emancipated art, establishing its social destiny. Consequently, in my efforts to perceive and record the indices of artistic sensibility, given the absence of "great" art, I shall, of necessity, confine myself to those manifestations which, even if located in the limited private domain, express with lucidity and immediacy the overall disposition of society to live with beauty and to produce creatively. In qualifying this art I shall avoid using the adjective "folk", not only because it misleadingly refers us to a system of class relations with uncertain equivalents, but also for the equally serious reasons I have maintained repeatedly on other occasions.

THE ISLAND COSTUME: THE INDEPENDENCE OF ITS EXPRESSIVE VARIATION AND THE SOURCES OF ITS COMMON SPECIFICATIONS

Perhaps no other artistic manifestation reveals the artistic taste of the Greek islands more strikingly and fully than the female costumes with their virtually inexhaustible formal variations and quite independent chromatic gradations. This unusual phenomenon of sartorial diversity, both quantitative and qualitative, essentially unknown in other geographical areas and cultures, would be difficult to interpret were it not for the existence of a robust dynamic of imagination in its provisioning and reproduction, as well as a deeply rooted need for independence, that is a conscious desire to maintain a distinct local identity even in the cases of closely related neighbouring regions. Of course, the number of local variations, as well as the more recent components gradually accrued as fashions have changed, is extremely large, while the extant genuine examples are rarely earlier than the beginning of the nineteenth century, and more specifically the years of the Greek Struggle for Independence. These data would be meagre indeed without the testimony of foreign travellers who, from around the middle of the sixteenth century, began to draw as well as describe their impressions. Thus, one finding of fundamental importance emerges from comparative study: the island, female costume is governed by an internal homogeneity.

The basic costume type consists of a multipleated dress with shoulder straps, close-fitting over the bosom, the length and many of the partial details of which changed according to place and time, just as the quality of fabrics changes in direct proportion to the oldness of the surviving examples. The torso was covered by a sleeved or sleeveless bodice, showing off the needlework of the long sleeves of the chemises worn underneath, just as their more lavishly embroidered hem showed below the dress. These general features, varying in the degree of their correspondance to the basic abstract schema, define the costumes of Limnos (ill. 56), Psara (ill. 57), Thasos in the North Aegean, Skyros (ill. 64), Skiathos (ill. 61) and Skopelos (ill. 63) in the Sporades, Trikeri in Thessalian Magnesia, and Kymi in Euboea (ill. 65). Despite easily discernible stylistic differences and some minor divergences, the costumes of Megara, Salamis and Aegina in the region of the Argosaronic Gulf – according to the testimony of Karl Krazeisen (1826) (ill. 2) – and the costumes of Embona on Rhodes, Tilos, Nisyros (ill. 68) and Astypalaia (ill. 69) in the Dodecanese are classified in the same costume group.

1. N. Nicolay. Girl from Paros, engraving.

According to Ioanna Papantoniou, whose summary of the characteristics of island costume is based principally on the drawings of seventeenth and eighteenth-century travellers, the immediately antecedent form of this costume style is handed down to us in the now-vanished white costumes of the Cyclades. Of course, there are many intervening gaps which make it difficult to follow the successive phases smoothly, but as Papantoniou stresses, the basic type would not have differed significantly from island to island and comprised the following garments: a short chemise or shift (*poukamiso*) with narrow sleeves, a long chemise with voluminous sleeves – usually tucked up on the shoulders –, a small bodice (*bousto*), a dickey (*trachilia*), and a kind of apron (*podia*) worn over a deeply pleated, short white skirt. Nevertheless, if I am not misled by the pictorial evidence, that is if my reading of the old drawings is correct, in place of the skirt I can make out a dress with straps, exactly like the one found in all the islands cited so far. I would also like to propose a revision of the *terminus ante quem* for the appearance of the dress in the Cyclades, lowering it to an earlier date, judging from the Paros costume in 1551, as shown in an unequivocal drawing by Nicolas de Nicolay (ill. 1). Since exactly the same costume type is encountered on Mykonos, Ios, Amorgos, Milos, Santorini, Kimolos, Kythnos and Kea, it would be reasonable to assume its presence also on those islands for which we have no information, such as Anafi, Sikinos, Folegandros, Seriphos and Syros.

We could have had some idea of the form of the Syros costume at the beginning of the nineteenth century if the Benaki Museum had acquired the complete set of water colours by John Collings or Collins, originally included in an album dated 1810, entitled *Costumes of Turkey*. Besides the water colours of the costumes of Naxos (ill. 55) and Paros (ill. 52), which still kept their original form, as well as the costume of Tinos (ill. 53), which had changed somewhat in the meantime, the relevant correspondence informs

2. K. Krazeisen. Woman from Aegina, lithograph (detail).

3. Th. Hope. Women from Mykonos, sepia drawing. Athens, Benaki Museum, Inv. No 27138.

us that two other water colours were offered for sale at the same time, showing the costumes of Santorini and Mykonos. The latter, as painted by an anonymous artist of the same period (ill. 54), retained the morphological features known from between 1787 and 1795, thanks to the testimony of Thomas Hope (ill. 3). Hope's drawing of the earlier Mykonian costume is placed alongside an obviously newer and more "modernized" type with a coat, not dissimilar to the costume of Tinos, as depicted by John Collins at the beginning of the nineteenth century (ill. 51), as well as by an unknown traveller in the late eighteenth century (ill. 50). It would seem from authentic examples from Ios (ill. 58) and Amorgos (ill. 59), Siphnos and Andros (ill. 66), that this new composition, with a chemise, a skirt of silk brocade, a sleeveless bolero and a brocade coat began to be established towards the end of the eighteenth century.

The costume of Santorini – which fell to the Turks in 1579 – was recorded in 1806 by Jacques Grasset de Saint-Saveur with an additional morphological element of Ottoman origin, namely the baggy trousers known as *salvari.* This same drastic intervention in the purity of the traditional type is observed on other islands after the Ottoman conquest, though by no means with the regularity of an infrangible code of dress. The surviving evidence from the East Aegean, where changes in fashion follow the cycles of historical fate more obviously, points also to this conclusion. Comparing, for example, a marvellously preserved nineteenth-century costume from Lesbos (ill. 60) with a water colour by the unknown traveller mentioned above (ill. 49), we can see what limited significance the *salvari* had by the end of the eighteenth century in the make up of a costume in which the long dress was the dominant feature. As Maria Anagnostopoulou has pointed out, the record of the same costume without the *salvari*, painted by the artist who accompanied Joseph Pitton de Tournefort to the Aegean islands *circa* 1700/1702 (ill. 4), confirms the sporadic appeal of this Ottoman element in the garment repertoire of the islands even in the seventeenth century, although a previous, transitional, period, after the imposition of Turkish rule in 1462, also seems likely.

The same evolutionary process may be conjectured for the costume of Samos too, from where a late nineteenth-century urban costume of European style has survived. Judging from a water colour by the same traveller as recorded the costume of Lesbos (ill. 49), it seems that towards the end of the eighteenth century the established costume type combined the baggy trousers with those older elements still retained after the Turks had settled there, *circa* 1550 (ill. 57). What happened in Icaria, which was subjugated in 1567, is a matter for speculation since we have only one surviving drawing from 1806. The costume of Samothrace, which fell in 1462, remains unknown, even though the difficulties of communication with this island should have contributed to the preservation of some testimony.

The further development of this line of reasoning is facilitated by the example of Chios, which was conquered in 1566, since the special conditions prevailing there and the island's relative autonomy appear to have kept Ottoman influences at bay. Thus the fact that the *salvari* is absent from the costumes of Pyrgi and Kalamoti (ill. 62) is explained. It would seem from a large number of drawings, as well as a water colour by the same anonymous traveller as mentioned elsewhere (ill. 48), that during the late eighteenth century the costumes of Chios were not essentially different from the type depicted in 1648 by Georges de la Chapelle, and, moreover, in 1551 by Nicolas de Nicolay (ill. 5). And though the densely pleated dress and inner chemise places them in the costumes group of the North Aegean, the Sporades, Trikeri, Kymi, the Saronic Gulf, the Cyclades and many of the Dodecanese, the predominance of white in their coloration, as Ioanna Papantoniou has observed, more clearly attests their affinity with the earlier, large family of lost costumes from the Archipelago, than is the case with the other islands.

This wide diffusion reinforces from other angles too the restitution of the island costume's family tree to a common archetype, even where the baggy trousers were in fact worn. That is not only in the islands of the East Aegean and the Cyclades mentioned above, but also on Patmos, Kos (ill. 71), Kastellorizo (ill. 70) and Kalymnos – even if the example in the Benaki Museum has survived without the *salvari* – (ill. 72) in the Dodecanese. The same situation must have obtained on Crete, on Cyprus and wherever the skirt with coat held sway – Siphnos, Andros (ill. 66), Ios (ill. 58) and Amorgos (ill. 59) in the Cyclades, and on Symi (ill. 67) in the Dodecanese. In these cases the skirt seems to have represented a simplified form of the dress, while the coat, originally a winter garment, was established when its most luxurious version was adopted as the official urban costume of the Ottoman world.

From the costumes of Crete (which finally surrendered to the Turks in 1669), the costume of Anogeia with its baggy trousers (*vraka*) must have taken shape in the eighteenth century, that is after the capture of Candia and after a period of coexistence with an older costume type, known from many pieces dispersed in collections in Greece and abroad. These are a series of very deep embroidered hems with riotous floral decoration and an inexhaustible wealth of colour. They do not, however, come from chemises, as is usually said and written, but from dresses, the original form of which is attested by a few intact specimens (ill. 76). Thanks to these examples, with their white cloth, densely pleated skirt and high bosom, an assemblage akin to the older costume type from the Cyclades and other islands is re-established: with an inner wide-sleeved chemise and an outer garment, sometimes longer sometimes shorter. Indeed, in accordance with certain instances of dated embroideries, it seems very possible that the older Cretan costume had been elaborated well before the fall of Candia. This hypothesis is reinforced by an analysis of the embroidery style (permitting us to make a preliminary schematic classification of the existing material), in which examples such as that in the Benaki Museum (ill. 76) are assigned to the seventeenth century. In the immediately following development stage, monochromy evidently came to the fore and a more conventional rendering of themes, as a survival of the same tradition during the period of Turkish rule. The most splendid of these creations, such as the "*phelonion* (chasuble) of Kassiani", which is embroidered all over and must have been taken to Siphnos by Cretan refugees (ill. 74), can be dated to the early seventeenth century, if not to the sixteenth, the age when artistic production in Crete in general was at its zenith.

The costume of Karpathos is equally interesting. Altered with the passage of time, it is best known in its most recent phase and from the study by Tatiana Oikonomidi. On this same rather remote island a special kind of "chemise" occurs, of simple line, with dense, austere embroidered decoration and which is unquestionably from an earlier period (ill. 73). Without belonging morphologically to the groups of chemises worn under the pleated dresses, this type is characterized by its excessive length, which is considerably reduced, however, by a horizontal overfold, which gives the impression of two separate garments. It would seem that in days gone by this was used as an outer garment, in the way that Otto Magnus von Stackelberg depicted the kindred costume of Kassos, sometime between 1810 and 1814 (ill. 75), thus providing a *terminus ante quem* to the quest for its genetic code, which was certainly before the nineteenth century. No matter

4

5

4. J. Pitton de Tournefort. Woman from Lesbos, engraving.

5. N. Nicolay. Woman from Chios, engraving.

how elusive the precise chronological moment of its first appearance is, the Byzantine tradition surely lived on in the "chemises" of Karpathos, on account of the island's geographical isolation, which is also the reason why many other extremely old cultural traits have survived there.

Among the chemises from the other islands, those of Astypalaia (ill. 69) are outstanding for the imaginative inventiveness of their embroideries. The abstract charm of the alternation of human figures and floral symbols, of strange beasts and boats on their hems is dictated by the same geometric conception of motifs as found on the shifts of Karpathos (ill. 73), which are the most replete expression of this principle. Furthermore, the embroidery technique – though the actual stitches differ – is distinguished by the same dense texture characteristic of Dodecanesian needlework in general, with the exception of the finely drawn "column" (*kolonato*) decoration of the Kalymnos chemises (ill. 72). Finally, the pictorial embroideries on the hem of the Skyros shifts, impressive for their naturalistic inclination and vibrant colours, are in aesthetic harmony with the weighty floral motifs, densely embroidered in gold thread at the ends of the sleeves (ill. 64). Other accessories of the island costumes are gold-embroidered – executed in a technique from Byzantine tradition –, such as a bridal veil (*bolia*) from Astypalaia, the edges of which are embellished with a dance of schematic women (ill. 6). The pearl-encrusted headdress of the Astypalaia costumes – derived from a diadem – and the several diaphanous veils (ill. 69) enhance the sense of imperial majesty, the crystallization of elements from the Byzantine East and the Renaissance West, nowadays impossible to extricate and decipher. In other costumes too, the headdress, fashioned from successive layers of such fabrics and often inordinately large, recalls representations of courtiers from the Byzantine period. This type of headdress, known from the costumes of Psara, Ios and Amorgos (ills. 57-59), Kalamoti, Skopelos, Skyros and Kymi (ills. 62-65), according to the drawings of travellers (ills. 2, 3, 5, 45-50, 52-54) and many modern paintings (ills. 115-117, 121), must have been widely disseminated throughout the island area up until the beginning of the last century.

The male costumes of the islands, in contrast to the female ones, repeat, without any fundamental variations and divergences, a common prototype, comprising wide trousers (*vraka*), a shirt and a waistcoat (*gileko*). Exceptions are the white costume of Pyrgi on Chios, of enigmatic origin, and the white-embroidered bridegroom's shifts from Skyros with their interesting decoration. The sleeves of one such shift, altered in later years (ill. 77), embellished with a vertical row of female figures, are quite outstanding. The monumental dimension of the design and the expressive simplicity of its symbolism places this embroidered decoration among the major achievements of the humble inquiries of Neohellenic art.

6

6. Bridal veil from Astypalaia. Athens, Benaki Museum, Inv. No EE 2781.

THE DISCOURSE OF JEWELLERY: IN THE STRATIGRAPHY OF ITS SUCCESSIVE LAYERS AND THE BRILLIANCE OF ITS ORIGINAL GRANDEUR

The theoretical model used in the approach to the history of costume proves to be more effective in the case of island jewellery than I had formerly imagined, when studying the relevant problems for the first time. As I take up again the threads of the same line of reasoning, in the meantime enriched with both the reserves of material available and the reserves of scholarly experience acquired through repeated consideration of the subject, I feel the need to stress once more certain points of basic significance, in order to give impetus to the investigative process.

The term jewellery is used of all the partial components of a system of adornment which, through the employment of the same materials, the same technique and the same stylistic manner, reveals beauty – primarily female –, aesthetically setting off the forehead, ears and neck, the bosom, waist and hands. Just as today, so in post-Byzantine times, jewellery, though an autonomous entity, was an essential accompaniment to apparel, its morphology changing mainly in response to the dictates of fashion. Nevertheless, the fact that many of the members of the old "families" of goldwork have disappeared, leaving no "descendants" – or even if they have survived their original purity has been altered by a host of foreign admixtures and innovative traits – is not due solely to changes in fashion, but also to the troubled succession of historical circumstances. This demands the careful distinction between their layers, by stylistically related unities, and the determining of the chronological parameters, with the least possible leeway for misinterpretation.

A typical example of a confused image with superimposed influences from other periods and forms of diverse origins is the resplendant parure of Karpathos, as recorded in the inter-war years by Marica Monte Santo (ills. 7-8). Outstanding among its individual elements and worthy of closer examination is a nineteenth-century frontlet of interlinked rosettes, a type which is also found in the veritable "treasure trove" of votive offerings (*tamata*) in the church of the Dormition of the Virgin (Koimisis tis Theotokou) in Elymbos (ill. 10). Thus there is no doubt that this is a specifically Karpathian kind of diadem, essentially unknown in the other islands and quite unlike the host of frontlets, bridal as a rule, found on the Greek Mainland. However, because in its composition and workmanship some dim recollections of the recurring components of a large assemblage of gold jewellery from the eighteenth century can be discerned, such as the rosettes on the famous dangle earrings (*kambanes*, lit. bells) of Kos (ill. 13), the assumption that analogous frontlets were also part of the earlier parure in the rest of the Dodecanese is highly plausible. The same applies to a kind of necklace of interlinked biconical beads and pendant crosses, which must have disappeared around the turn of the present century. It was at this time that the *kolaines*, sewn with gold coins, began to be worn on Karpathos, projecting, as in their Mainland counterparts, an illusion of economic prosperity as a counterbalance to the first wave of emigration to America. In the general climate of confusion that prevails, this type of necklace is frequently recorded as being of Macedonian provenance. However, its attribution to Karpathos is consolidated by two pieces of gold jewellery, of kindred inspiration, from Tilos and now in the Benaki Museum, and, above all, by a silver piece in the Manto Oikonomidi Collection (ill. 11), embellished with the same drop-shaped pendants as feature in the typical Karpathian ornaments for the temples (ill. 7).

7

8

9

Of the jewellery worn by Karpathian women in the inter-war years (ill. 8) the precious pectoral with its successive rows of hanging foliate elements and central pendant rosettes, belongs morphologically to a type which, though primarily known from the *kordonia* of Attica, can be traced throughout Greece and even as far as the remotest reaches of Hellenism in Safranboli. This is obviously a very old type which in the nineteenth century had been preserved on both Karpathos and neighbouring Kassos, as can be seen in Isavella Sidirourgou's valuable set of gold jewellery, a family heirloom (ill. 80). The presence of the very same type in Crete, during the same period (ill. 87), bolsters the assumption that in previous periods this item of jewellery was widespread in the Dodecanese, if not in the rest of the Aegean islands too. Then, of course, the form would have been less "diluted" than it was in the nineteenth century.

The same holds true for an earring which has been rather oddly hung on the chains of the frontlet of the Karpathian woman in this picture (ill. 7) from the inter-war years, perhaps because its original purpose has been forgotten. The few known examples of this unstudied type, with its flat circular hoop, breast-like protuberances and schematic double-headed eagle at the centre, are clearly more recent and more crudely made, by casting. In an exceptional, unique and older example (ill. 9), the ring of bosses recalls the globules enclosing certain kinds of Byzantine earrings in fan-shaped arrangement, while the abstract decorativeness of the eagle motif is vaguely reminiscent of the aesthetic of Dodecanesian embroidery (ill. 90). This superb piece of jewellery, at present suspended in time and space in the realm of Neohellenic goldwork – its relationship to a specific parure still unknown – may originate from pre-eighteenth-century Rhodes.

Other pieces of Dodecanesian jewellery are also difficult to understand, such as the fabric belt on the Nisyros costume with its appliqué signs of the Zodiac in gilt, and the cast ornaments (ill. 68), which though reminiscent of filling motifs on Dodecanesian embroideries, could well have come from Africa. The necklace with coins on the same costume – in view of the foregoing remarks on the *kolaines* of Karpathos – refers to the final stage in Dodecanesian adornment. The parure of Nisyros also includes a metal belt with rosettes and mermaids on the clasp, from which chains with various pendant ornaments frequently hang. Exactly the same kind of belt accompanies the Astypalaia costumes too, as well as the type of earrings with large hoops and transverse spherical elements (ill. 69). In the earrings of Astypalaia, with their more restrained proportions and alternation of seed pearls and delicately wrought tiny spheres, an earlier family of jewellery survives, the presence of which can be traced to Kassos (ill. 80), Crete (ill. 79), Cyprus (ill. 12) and to many of the Cyclades (ills. 81, 82).

The large gilt buckles from Symi (ill. 67), as well as a stylistically related dorsal ornament from Astypalaia (ill. 78), are included among the more recent set of Dodecanesian jewellery from the nineteenth century, created in the same workshop and clearly displaying the decorative spirit of the Greek Mainland. Judging, however, from the austere filigree buckles worn in exactly the same way on Kastellorizo (ill. 70), we may legitimately hypothesize the pre-existence of a typologically analogous piece as part of an earlier parure. Taking the buckles of Kastellorizo as a pretext, it should be noted that the technique of fashioning jewellery from fine sheet gold and affixed filigree decoration reflects both the aesthetic preferences and economic affluence of the eighteenth century, manifest in a large group of examples scattered throughout most of the Greek islands. The spherical elements on the earrings of Astypalaia (ill. 69), as well as the biconical beads on more recent necklaces from Crete, from which hang schematic bows with crosses (ill. 79) also belong to this group. The more naturalistic rendering of the bow with the cross in the

10

11

7. Woman from Elymbos, Karpathos, photograph by M. Monte Santo.

8. Woman from Elymbos, Karpathos, photograph by M. Monte Santo.

9. Earring with a representation of a double-headed eagle. Athens, Benaki Museum, Inv. No 31397.

10. Frontal ornament with interconnected rosettes. Elymbos, Karpathos, church of the Koimisis tis Theotokou.

11. Silver necklace. Athens, collection of Manto Oikonomidi.

12. Necklace and earrings from Cyprus. Athens, Benaki Museum, Inv. Nos Ea 1884, Ea 1885.

earlier enamelled gold jewellery of the seventeenth century (ill. 83), as well as the confirmed existence of earlier Cretan necklaces with gold *botonakia*, of spherical shape, enable us to date the biconical beads with schematic crosses, and made of the cheaper gilded silver, to the nineteenth century. Corresponding jewellery from Cyprus (ill. 12), the artistic tradition of which was, in general, imbued with certain aesthetic principles diffused throughout Crete and the Dodecanese, is also dated to that period. The correctness of the proposed chronological scheme is verified by the *botonakia* of Kassos (ill. 80), and by an even earlier segment of a gold necklace, probably from Siphnos (ill. 81), clearly showing the distribution of this fragmented unity of island adornment already in the eighteenth century, but also the exceptional quality of its early examples.

A different type of gold necklace occurs in the Cyclades, made of flattened, perforated rhomboid elements and large pendant amulets which originally covered the entire torso in imbricated layers. However, since these were gradually divided up from mother to daughter and generation to generation, none of them has kept the original length intact (ill. 82). Though there are missing links in the chain of continuity, it would be worth exploring the hypothesis that a group of more recent, nineteenth-century pectorals found on Karpathos (ill. 7), Kassos (ill. 80) and Crete (ill. 87), and considered to be parts of an older, panhellenic family of jewellery, may have originated from a necklace of this kind. Analogous Dodecanesian necklaces, though with enamelled details on the filigree decoration, could date from the seventeenth or even the sixteenth century and be the surviving descendants of a primal parure which formerly existed throughout the island world. One is led to this conclusion by perhaps the most brilliant piece to have survived; its original length is much reduced and its provenance is Patmos (ill. 83). As has already been noted, the schematic nineteenth-century pendants on the necklaces of Crete (ill. 87) are also included in the typology of crosses with bow, demonstrating the persistence of traditional forms through time, as well as the duration of their continuous alterations and transformations. The fact that precisely the same type of cross is repeated in the earlier pectoral jewellery of Corfu, though perhaps casting doubts on the certainty of the Dodecanesian origin of the Patmian necklace, dispels any margin of ambiguity concerning the common roots of island adornment in the periods prior to the eighteenth century.

Among the older enamelled pieces of island jewellery, the well-known caravel pendant from Patmos (ill. 84), originally part of a necklace in similar style, is outstanding. Thanks to a pair of earrings from Siphnos, featuring the same motif and in the same technique (ill. 85), the presence of these ornaments in all the islands of the Archipelago is once again confirmed, while at the same time an assertion I made a few years ago is also validated: that those pieces that have survived singly as independent objects once belonged to a complete parure with a uniform style and thematic content. It is worth comparing the earrings from Siphnos (ill. 85) with another pair, probably from Folegandros, in the possession of Augi Proukaki (ill. 86). The schematization of the formal elements, particularly in the tiny hanging boats, must have taken place during the period between the seventeenth and the nineteenth century. Identical little boats are also found in a group of earrings recorded as coming from Lefkas (ill. 87), though it is quite possible they originate from Crete, since the main accessories on the later necklaces with several rows of pendant elements (ill. 87) are executed in exactly the same technique. Thus the Folegandros earrings add their own testimony to the growing body of evidence pointing to the locating of the unknown centres of early island goldsmithing on Crete. It is no mere coincidence that these earrings belonged to the Varouchas-Venieris family which, after the fall of Candia and before finally settling on Paros, had gone to other islands. A

13

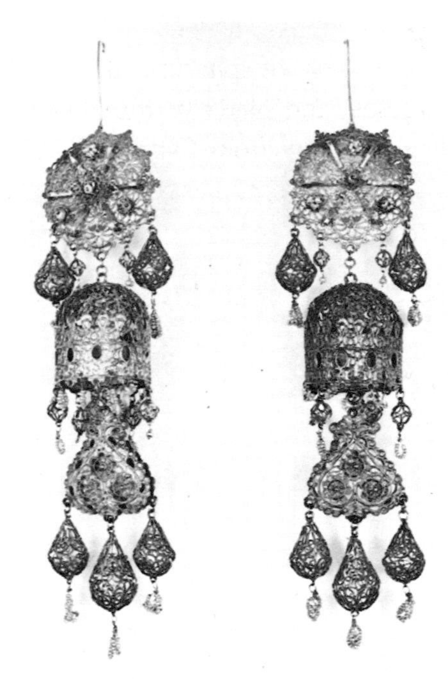

13. Gold earrings from Kos. Athens, Benaki Museum, Inv. No Εχρ. 265.

large group of composite Dodecanesian earrings of developed forms, outstanding among which are the famous *kambanes* of Kos (ill. 13), is dated to the eighteenth century. Simpler earrings in the same style are encountered both on Karpathos and Cyprus, combining both the imposing majesty of Byzantine tradition with the predilection for intricacy of the late Baroque.

The lack of early jewellery on some islands may be due to inpropitious historical circumstances, such as the tragic destruction of Chios and Psara, or to a premature turn towards Europe, on account of the Catholic faith, not to mention the demands of a maritime economy, as in the cases of Syros, Tinos, Andros and Naxos. From Mykonos come two bracelets in the Benaki Museum, of knitted gold thread in the shape of a snake, imported from abroad. Other jewellery found at random in the islands comes from abroad, but there are no detailed studies of it, just are there are none on the incidental information contained in dowry contracts. Those pieces referred to in this brief presentation as Greek, though by no means covering the entire spectrum of a very wide range of types, do, nevertheless, represent certain categories, the numerical frequency of which is truly impressive. Impressive too is their smooth development, that is the internal cohesion running through the various stages of their stylistic transformations. It is precisely this, in conjuction with the undoubted localism of the examples from the nineteenth century, which, in my opinion, decisively increases the likelihood of their manufacture in Greece, despite the widely held view that they were made in Venetian workshops or those of some unknown centre in the Adriatic.

I consider it superfluous to reiterate the reasons and arguments which demonstrate the Greekness of the island jewellery, and insist that its origins should be sought in Crete. During the protracted period of the Venetian occupation, the artistic tradition of that island – as has already been said – managed to successfully exploit many of the precepts of Western experience, while preserving many legacies of the Byzantine heritage. After the capture of Candia by the Turks, the highly competent local goldsmiths evidently followed the stream of refugees to the Ionian and the Aegean islands, where they transplanted their craft – as did the icon-painters contemporary with them – grafting new potentials onto the trunk of Neohellenic sensibility.

THE CODED MESSAGES OF EMBROIDERY AS DISTILLATES OF SENSIBILITY AND IMPRINTS OF SENSITIVITY

The island embroideries are, without exaggeration, the most original of all the creations of Neohellenic expression, not only because they illustrate fully the content of its aesthetic objectives, but also because they lucidly record the particularly high level of its cultural values. Developmentally reproducing a very old tradition and gradually systematizing the principles of a sensibility forged by time, the island embroideries had already begun to deteriorate by the beginning of the nineteenth century, and had finally disappeared by the end of it. It was then that they began to be dispersed, on account of the recognition – initially intuitive – of their importance by foreigners, especially collectors. This took place before any recording in the field of those relevant testimonies which would have nowadays delivered us from the confusion of conflicting evaluations; that is the chaos which prevails concerning the geographical distinction of the stylistic assemblages, as well as the marking of the boundaries delimiting partial affinities and differences. The foreigners should be commended for providing the first scientific approach to the embroideries, in other words the first attempt to combine the then surviving information with the evidence of their provenance and other desiderata, which constitute the basis of any critical reappraisal of the related problems.

It is not fortuitous that many of the most important island embroideries are now in museums abroad. That is why Antonis Benakis should be extolled for his timely formation of the valuable collection in the Benaki Museum, as well as Popi Zora, thanks to whose efforts all the embroideries later gathered in the Museum of Greek Folk Art were repatriated. However, both of these assemblages, barring a few select exceptions, remain unpublished, in effect inaccessible to research, which continues to rely almost exclusively on the fundamental studies of Alan J.B. Wace and Pauline Johnstone. Indeed, Wace's monograph – grounded in a broad education, the well-tried method of another discipline and an acute sensitivity – does not end simply with the acknowledgement of the exceptional quality and artistic value of island embroideries, but in the formulation of basic questions, on the clarification of which any further investigation of the subject depends: How are local expressions distinguished from each other and what is their correspondence to the geography of the Aegean area? What is the role of the historical parameter in the complexities of the chronological problem and what is the importance of the availability of raw materials – silk, cotton, linen – in the formation of the separate, local traditions?

Artistic phenomena are certainly far more complex than the sum of the complexity of the data constituting their creation. The fact that many of the Cycladic islands – such as Andros, Tinos and Syros – have no embroideries to exhibit may be due to special reasons, for the moment inexplicable, if not to an early urbanization of society and the consequent imposition of Western models. That is, something analogous to the striking absence of costumes and jewellery in these very same areas. However, the dearth of information, which, as Wace concedes, obfuscates discernment of the different units, in combination with the spectacular divergences of needlework, leaves a margin of hope that there will be a future redistribution of the existing material, preceded, of course, by the necessary publication where all the extant evidence will have been presented.

With regard to the difficulties inherent in the dating of embroideries in terms of the over-stressed factor of traditional insistence on the replication of the same decorative motifs, I believe that a more exhaustive analysis would be beneficial to understanding style, and consequently to achieving a chronological evaluation of their layers. And this because it is difficult for even the so-called "folk" arts – an unhappy term indeed – to be completely freed from the evolutionary currents of the laws of history. No matter that, for example, the earliest embroideries of the Dodecanese, which are mentioned in written sources from the late fifteenth and the early sixteenth century, remain unknown at the moment, Pauline Johnstone's rather instinctive conviction that the best of the surviving examples are creations of the seventeenth century appears to be correct. Her conclusion not only finds support in the dated Cretan embroideries – mentioned in the chapter on costumes –, but also in the demise of the embroidery tradition round the beginning of the nineteenth century. In the rare instances of a confirmed continuity, as in the embroidery of Skyros, the gradual degeneration of the motifs, the dulling of the colours, as well as a progressive weakening, also apparent in the laxness of technical workmanship, is observed. That is, whereas during the eighteenth century the embroidery was infused with a naturalistic spirit and a remarkable freedom in the dynamics of its inspirations, the examples from the nineteenth century are characterized by stylization and repetitiveness – even more striking in those of twentieth century date –, in other words the natural deterioration resulting from over-use and the redundancy of decrepit ideas. The evolutionary course in colour preferences – from the vibrant shades of the eighteenth century to the enfeebled harmony of the more mature stages – describes a similar curve. On the contrary, in the embroideries from the seventeenth century the keen distinction of the colours, the clear description of the separate forms and the compositions rich in content, prompt us to conjecture an even earlier stage in which the abstract tendency in the geometric density of the compositions is more overt, consistent with certain principles, evidently of general validity, visible in many examples of the embroidery of other islands.

Unless there is a flaw in my line of reasoning, the renowned Skyrian pillow with the schooner (ill. 91) must have been embroidered around the middle of the seventeenth century, antedating the piece of a bridal towel with two female figures, which could be dated to the closing years of that century (ill. 88). While in both these examples the dense texture of the central motifs is in accord with the geometric purity governing the organization of the components of the composition, the *horror vacui* is more obvious in the first, where the surface is entirely covered with a host of supplementary motifs, in constrast to the situation in the latter, where the representation "breathes" much more easily in the free space. The dating of the piece to the later years of the seventeenth century is also vindicated by the approximate time surely required for certain elements, inspired by the weaving of Prussa and the pottery of Iznik, such as the carnations and tulips, to have been fully assimilated. In the embroideries from the eighteenth century the decoration becomes more and more elaborate, the floral motifs are enriched by many variations of oft repeated themes and in the choice of colours pale tones become more general, at the expense of the striking contrasts which enliven the gamut of earlier preferences.

As is the case with island jewellery, so island embroidery, even though it has survived in a fragmented state, must have originally been part of sets, with the bridal bed as the axis, with a uniform spirit in the decorative theme, as well as a uniformity of style and choice of colours. Each geographical unit, and each island individually, must have had its own particular system for the decoration of the bed, but embroidered sheets, valances and bedspreads, pillows and towels, would have existed everywhere. On Rhodes, where the bridal bed is covered by an embroidered baldachin, the *sperveri*, it is reasonable not to find embroidered sheets and bedspreads, except for the *bandes*, that is the bed valances which were visible through an opening (*portadela*) in the side of the canopy (ill. 89), as well as pillows stacked in piles on chests. This must have been the case in other Dodecanesian islands, such as Patmos, from where the central opening of an analogous *tenta* (bed curtain) of astonishing artistry has survived (ill. 90), despite local differentations imposed on the morphology of the embroideries by the way in which the bed was incorporated, and isolated, within the single room of the island house. Thus the wooden columns which demarcate the balustrades of the usually elevated place for the bed, were invariably covered with impressive long, narrow embroideries, such as the *stylomantiles* of Astypalaia (ill. 94), or bear densely embroidered hangings, like curtains.

The arrangement of the bridal bed on Naxos is not known, despite the large number of embroideries preserved from that island, offering us perhaps the most complete Cycladic example of a set of sheets (ill. 92), bedspreads (ill. 93) and pillows (ill. 95), but no hangings or canopies. What was happening in Crete before the fall of Candia (1669) is difficult to deduce from the few pillows that have survived (ill. 14). Certainly some of the narrow embroidered strips incorporated into the valances may well have originally embellished the edges of sheets. Even though this hypothesis has not been confirmed, the very logic of things leads to the conclusion that in Crete too there was initially a set of bed embroideries, which has been lost with the passage of time.

In the light of my remarks in the first chapter, the example of Crete permits, prima facie, the trial formulation of a rule, the application of which would be beneficial for any future re-examination of the problem of embroidery: that in each centre with an embroidery tradition both the embroideries in the home and the embroideries on the costumes must have been initially characterized by a uniform style. If this rule is of general validity, as the example of Skyros would suggest, as well as the obvious affinity of corresponding embroideries in many of the Dodecanese, than the course of investigation could be based on another well-founded working hypothesis: that where embroideries have survived from only one of the two categories, it is highly probable that the second category originally existed as well.

It appears that the pillows of Thasos belonged to a set of bed linen, the specific components of which have been lost. Their geometric decoration is distinguished by an impressive inventiveness, an astonishing variety and a strangely modern conception in composition and use of colour (ill. 96). In the abstract designs covering the entire surface of the fabric, it is impossible to detect the floral origins of the motifs, which are, for example, quite easy to discern in the equally densely embroidered examples from Naxos (ills. 92, 93, 95). The entirely different naturalistic spirit imbuing the dispersed floral motifs on the sleeves of a Thasian chemise dated to 1775 (ill. 15) – one of the rare examples of a dated embroidery – would seem to conflict with what has been said above concerning the relationship between the embroideries in the home and those on the costumes. The evident contradiction would only be abrogated if the chronological precedence of the pillow were certified, and indeed that its was created no later than the early eighteenth century. However, this would presuppose another unproven principle: that the functions of the internal mechanism in the evolution of Neohellenic embroidery lead – with the inevitability of law – from an earlier stage of generalized abstraction to the summational concreteness of the later naturalistic tendencies.

To test the validity of the theoretical model on which the organization of the data and the solution of the associated problems is based, is certainly fraught with difficulties, for with the exception of the complete evolutionary schema for Skyrian embroidery (ills. 16, 64, 77, 88, 91), the rest of the groups of island embroidery have only survived in fragments. So, summoning up all my courage and casting caution to the wind, I posit that the early aesthetic of geometric decoration may be due to the chronologically closer influences of Byzantine weaving, which, for technical reasons, preferred straight lines and angular outlines. Recollections of Byzantine weaving can be seen in the survival of decorative motifs, but primarily in the frequent presence of the double-headed eagle (ills. 17, 90, 94, 101). In order to back up my reasoning – despite the unorthodox method – I would like to insert here the example of a white bedspread, woven in the well-known "relief" technique of carded flax, most probably on Crete from where it must have been taken to Milos (ill. 17) after the capture of Candia in 1669. This superb piece of weaving, undoubtedly, I believe, a seventeenth-century creation, facilitates the relative dating of many white embroideries of a kindred decorative spirit: an early towel from the Cyclades with ships and sailors (ill. 102), a somewhat later one from Samos with the same design (ill. 18), the column curtain from Astypalaia (ill. 94), and the border of a sheet, probably from the Dodecanese (ill. 101), where, in a truly monumental manner, spectacular female

14. Pillow from Crete. Athens, Benaki Museum, Inv. No 6690.

15. Sleeve from bridal shift with the embroidered date 1775. Athens, Benaki Museum, Inv. No EE 838.

16. Towel from Skyros. Athens, Benaki Museum, Inv. No 6398.

17. White bedspread from Crete, woven in the skoulati technique (fluffy or looped weaving). Athens, Benaki Museum, Inv. No 22418.

figures alternate with winged griffins, ships with sailors and double-headed eagles. In all these works the partial differences may be due to slight chronological gradations or to the independence of local traditions, but the component of expressive objectives is common. The same spirit, moreover, animates the aesthetic of many of the coloured embroideries from the Dodecanese (ill. 90), a fragment of a gold-embroidered chemise from Milos (ill. 99), the edge of a curtain from Siphnos (ill. 100) and the "frieze" on a sheet from Anafi (ill. 98).

The geometric rendering of motifs, albeit with a varying degree of abstraction, is not only distinctive of the embroidery of the Dodecanese and the Cyclades, but also of a group of embroideries attributed to the Ionian islands, among which those from Lefkas are of exceptional quality. Conversely, the few extant examples of embroidery from the islands of the East Aegean, with the exception of the white embroideries of Samos (ill. 18), are distinguished for their faithful adherence to the naturalistic rendering of floral themes. The embroideries of the East Aegean do not, however, facilitate redirecting the research process towards the unexplored field of "Asia Minor" embroideries, with their uncertain nationality and contentious geographical distribution. For precisely this reason it is worth drawing attention to a unique piece, recorded as being from Asia Minor, on which the rare subject of female figures in the ideal setting of a garden in bloom (ill. 97), alludes to corresponding painted creations, which not only argues for its Greekness but also its probable place of origin, namely Mytilene.

Without entering into the problems of dating on the basis of technique, that is the extraordinarily large variety of stitches, and avoiding embroiling the reader in the issues concerning the relationship between technique and style, I wish to stress the inventiveness of the thematic repertoire and chromatic sensibility of the embroideries of Skyros, which frequently exalt the human figure (ills. 16, 77, 88), and to take this opportunity to note that the embroideries of the island home were part of the dowry, which is why their intellectual content mainly derives from the sentimental world of women. This is an entire cosmos, inspired by a vision of the ideal state, of which marriage is the culmination, and narrated according to certain inviolable principles, of which strict symmetrical

18

18. White-embroidered towel from Samos. Athens, Benaki Museum, Inv. No 6420.

organization is the most important. The symmetry of Greek embroideries reflects the wish for stability in the logical distribution of "given" factors within a "given" space, which, nevertheless, is not static, since the more or less perceptible rhythmical interplay of its components imbues its internal articulation with the vitality of real life. Over the centuries the coding of the expectation of fertility has crystallized a large number of symbols of differing timbre, unequal frequency of appearance and varying value, the deciphering of which is not always easy and consequently a "reading" of the narrated text not always possible.

Among the ideograms which compose the "language" of the island embroideries, from the perspective of both quantitative frequency and qualitative importance, those which signify the cycle of plant-natural life stand out. Focused on the sacred tree (ills. 74, 89, 90, 98-100, 102), they are often disguised by and hidden behind the decorativeness of a vase of flowers (ills. 16, 88), or compressed into the "succinct" formula of the flower and the leaf (ills. 14, 15, 91, 92, 94, 95). The tendency to generalization, which is a natural concommitant and consequence of this symbolic script, in conjunction with the inexhaustibly inventive imagination and the repetitiousness of a profoundly musical need, leads to remarkable compositions based on themes and their variations. Just one of its vocal elements, when multiplied, can cover the entire available surface, creating the impression that the wish for fertility is being proclaimed by a thousand voices. In the embroideries of Naxos (ills. 92, 93, 95) and Thasos (ill. 96), as has already been pointed out, this is achieved through an abstract force of exemplary purity. The insertion of the human figure, very often in the discreet and allusive representation of the lovers' tryst – the couple is understood as both the recipient and guarantor of the ideal state – strengthens the explicit vitality of the more realistic "painterly" genre of the embroideries from Skyros (ills. 16, 77, 88, 91), as well as those from Crete (ills. 14, 74, 76). The same holds true for the embroideries of Siphnos, impressive for their geometric conception (ill. 100), and of Anafi (ill. 98), where the birds warbling in the branches of the tree of life are the veritable heralds of happiness.

The tree of life, that is the fertile promise of efflorescence, whose origins are lost in the ancient convictions of the East and whose connotations were renewed through the sensibility of Byzantine times, presents an incredible longevity as a symbol of vocal value, which features in virtually all the designs on the island embroideries. On the white-embroidered towel from the Cyclades (ill. 102), interposed – with the disarming austerity of great inspiration – between the ships with sailors, it mitigates, like a prayer for a pleasant trip and a safe return, the anguish of the unknown and the perils of the voyage. Very often the abstract mode in which it is rendered stamps its form with the eloquent purity of a protective symbol par excellence, the cross (ill. 98). On the column curtain from Astypalaia the cross is flanked by two mermaids (ill. 94), thus ensuring the sanctification of the sea and the benevolent co-operation of its elements, just as in a wall-painting from Mytilene (Lesbos) (ill. 112). The messages of the marine world are condensed and fomalized mainly through the allusive depiction of the ship, not only on the white-embroidered towels from the Cyclades (ill. 102) or Samos (ill. 18), or on the white-embroidered sheet border (ill. 101), nor only on the *portadela* from Patmos (ill. 90), or on the gloriously magnified projection on the Skyrian pillow (ill. 91), but in all the other expressions of island art too (ills. 18, 19, 22, 46, 84-87, 103, 107, 109-111, 128, 129, 133).

The discourse of symbols never ends. The frequent message of the double-headed eagle (ills. 17, 76, 90, 94), for example, repeated across the entire spectrum of island artistic production with constant intensity, conveys to us, beyond the certainly apotropaic significance of a standardized motif, echoes lost among ecclesiastical survivals where memories of the Byzantine past and awareness of continuity in its protective dimension are interwoven. Consequently, any attempted "reading" should not be considered definitive, nor should it discourage new exploratory endeavours. The fascinating multiplicity of meanings and the limitless possibilities of approaching the motifs from different perspectives constitute the very nature of embroidery, in a manner not unknown to us in the constitution of great works of art as well. Thus it would be worthwhile, sometime, to try to decipher analytically the story "narrated" by two of the most impressive embroideries from the Greek islands: the *portadela* of Patmos (ill. 90) with the female figure gazing out from her house and wishing for concord between the opposing elements of the environment, and the column curtain from Astypalaia (ill. 94) with the central praying figure which protects an entire value system. Man and his world are integral parts of an indivisible unity, the dialectical constitution of which also determines the canonically small scale in the codification of the human figure. Indeed, the abstract disposition which is the foundation of the essence of existence, even when tempered by a naturalistic spirit, expresses the deep-seated Greek need for generalization at the expense of the circumstantial particularity of individual characteristics.

THE WORLD VIEW IN PAINTING: GUIDE TO THE BOUNDARY BETWEEN REALITY AND FANTASY

The secular painting which flourished on the Greek islands in post-Byzantine times – as opposed to ecclesiastical painting – remains largely unknown and neglected by scholarship. Neither the quantity nor the quality of the very few surviving, or, more accurately, located examples is sufficient to furnish the necessary reserve, the exhaustive distillation of which would enable some conclusions to be drawn, even if of limited authority. So, may I be excused yet again for deviating from the prescriptions of methodological consistency and permitted to direct my own course for the exploratory path, starting from a creation essentially alien to the rules of conscious artistic expression: the rough scratchings in the side chapel of Saint Basil in the Monastery of Saint John the Theologian on Patmos. In these, with the immediacy of a child's drawing, the catastrophic raid by Morosini and the Venetians in 1659 is recorded (ill. 19). The scientific unorthodoxy of this choice is justified by the significance of the Patmian "incisions" as spontaneous expressions of awareness in the rendering of a momentous historical event, in which there is, of course, confusion in the organization of the facts into a composition, but which has, nevertheless, the charm of experimentation in a *terra incognita*. I should add, how-

19. "The Invasion of Patmos by the Venetians" (1659). Patmos, Monastery of Saint John the Theologian, chapel of Saint Basil.

19

ever, that the historical messages transmitted are much weaker in their make up than the psychological impulses which the marine world, with its dangers of the unforeseen and the allure of the unknown, with the struggle and the anguish of the whirlpools of existence through the never-ending cycle of the great adventure, incites in the island imagination generally.

Of course, we should not forget that sometime between 1571 and 1608 an accomplished iconographer from Crete, Georgios Klontzas, had already rendered, using the canons of early post-Byzantine icon-painting, perhaps the most important historical event of that period: the routing of the Turkish fleet at the Battle of Lepanto (ill. 104). However, both in the majestic eponymous creation and the humble "scratchings" of Patmos (ill. 19) the boundaries between reality and fantasy are difficult to discern, because the ingredients of the subject matter are remodelled, filtered through the basic need for generalization, which, as has already been noted, also governs the art of embroidery. The same spirit can also be detected in the votive icons of miracles at sea, that is showing specific events, such as that depicted on a well-known icon of 1619 in the Monastery of Panayia Chozoviotissa on Amorgos (ill. 105). However, the degree of fidelity in reproducing the facts of the real world in the secular painting of the seventeenth and eighteenth centuries, is better illustrated in a familiar wall-painting from the destroyed *konak* (mansion) of Fazil-bey in Herakleion, Crete, where, with almost cartographic accuracy, the town and harbour of Candia are depicted at some peaceful-idyllic moment during turbulent historical times (ill. 103). The wall-painting from Herakleion is the creation of a gifted professional artist, who must have been working *circa* 1800, though it has not been established with certainty whether he was also involved in ecclesiastical painting. This anonymous painter knew how to design and organize the partial elements of the subject into a well-balanced, unified composition with a stylized, "narrative" manner and a pristine sense of colour, undoubtedly influenced by the traditional aesthetic of the wall-paintings of mainland Greece.

In the Herakleion mural the stability of the land balances the instability of the sea, conveying a sense of security. Indeed, it is not without significance that the intellectual weight of the composition is focused on the safety of the harbour, towards which, indicatively, all the ships still at sea are heading. Here the pre-eminent absolute value – of the age and of the art which is its expression – of the concept Earth, is made abundantly clear: that is the allusive juxtaposition of the bounties of the inhabited environment and the security of social organization to the uncertainty of the tempting promises of the irrational watery element. The rest of the wall-paintings in the *konak* (ills. 106-108), presented here thanks to the eager response of Luisa Karapidaki-Kalokairinou, draw their subjects from the same cognitive cycle. The inspiring vision of an ideal earthly domain, which is also the central idea in the poetic creations of the folk (demotic) songs, strikes the same meritorious balance in the painting of Mytilene. In the wall-paintings of the Vareltzidaina mansion, which is dated to between 1790 and 1800, that is roughly contemporary with the wall-paintings in Herakleion (ill. 109), the earthly domain is rendered in a more romantic genre, easily discerned in the more naturalistic drawing of the landscape, the architectural elements and the sailing ships. The fragments of wall-paintings from a destroyed mansion must be slightly earlier, judging from the fervour of their chromatic vigour and the mature vitality of their drawing (ill. 110). But, the thematic objectives remain constant, the ship being the dominant element as *pars pro toto* of the concept Sea, its symbolic content being juxtaposed to the likewise symbolic beauty of the flower-filled settings, to the attraction of the organized settlements of the human community, to the promises of security concealed behind the façades of the buildings. In opposition to the instability and the threatening uncertainty of the watery element, the stability and certainty of earthly reality is projected like a dream. The same ideological statement can be detected in similar painted compositions from the same period, on the lid of a chest, for example, in the collection of Theodoros Mintzas (ill. 111), where the absence of the human figure – the peculiar silence which envelopes the representation – makes its message more clearly heard.

The painting tradition of Mytilene continued during the nineteenth century, the most representative example being the wall-paintings which decorate the Krallis mansion in Molyvos, dated to 1833. Among them a heraldic representation with mermaids – benevolent spirits – stands out. A strange mixture of pagan memories and religious symbols (ill. 112), they are guarantors of a successful voyage and a safe return for seafarers. In other parts of the decoration the familiar theme of the seascape is repeated, always seen from the vantage point of the prosperity on land, large bouquets of flowers and a marvellously drawn female figure (ill. 113). Indeed, this figure, in conjunction with a representation from another wall-painting in the same mansion, depicting an extensive architectural complex (ill. 114), could be used as a guide for the hypothetical restoration of the fragments of a small chest in the Benaki Museum (ill. 117). Some differences in the details of the garments, the *salvari* for example, which characterize the female costume in the wall-painting – in accordance with what has been said in the relevant chapter – reveal the antecedence of the chest. The same is true of the extraordinary miniaturist quality of the drawing, while the stylistic tradition of Eastern influence, chiefly in relation to Mytilene's proximity to Asia Minor, indicates that its painter was probably local.

A more chronologically complicated case involves another chest, also from Mytilene, on which are portrayed, with exemplary emphasis, the most complete and perhaps the most spectacular rendition of a male and female figure (ill. 121). In the symmetrical organization of the composition, with the dominant floral element in the middle, the type of the couple framing the tree of life – familiar from embroidery – survives. The lute in the man's hands emits an equally familiar love song, while the woman's gesture unequivocally expresses a positive response. The amorous overture, the joyous efflorescence and the impressive fruitfulness of the vegetal elements are infused with such optimism that only the worn-out soul of a dessicated critic would fail to find it uplifting. That the work is earlier finds support in – besides the indicative picturing of the female costume without a *salvari* – the use of colours, uninfluenced by the tonal gradations of the early nineteenth century, and the rendering of the subject without recourse to the naturalism apparent both in the wall-paintings of the Krallis mansion (ills. 112-114) and in the "escutcheon" of the *Council of Elders of Metylina*, dated 1828, from Samos (ill. 120). All things considered, a date in the second half of the eighteenth century seems most likely, consonant with the vegetal decoration on the chest's main face, where themes familiar from marble fountains of the same period are repeated (ills. 43, 44, 47).

The thematic content and the stylistic singularity of painting in Mytilene, notwithstanding certain Eastern influences, recall the painting tradition of northern Greece. The same can be said for all the other islands of the Aegean where examples of painting, however fragmentary, have survived, such as a unique example from Samos where, with an impressionistic freedom of drawing, the typical subject of female figures in front of an imaginary architectural complex is shown (ill. 115). The sartorial elements, the absence of a *salvari* and the large headdresses – in line with the remarks in the chapter on costumes – would lower the date of the work to around the middle of the eighteenth cen-

20

20. The school teacher Photeini Ch. M. Boyatzi. Museum of Symi.

tury. This conclusion is strengthened when the work is compared with an equally rare example of Cycladic painting from Siphnos in the collection of Olga Karatza, which bears the date 1804 (ill. 116). This exceptional piece, probably the leaf of a closet door – from a piece of furniture something like the *ambataro* in the Patmian mansion of the Kourkoulas family (ill. 126) – even though it has not been cleaned and its bright colours are now dulled, allows us to form a faint picture of the aesthetics of decoration in the wealthier Cycladic mansions of the eighteenth century. The representation belongs iconographically in the tradition of subject cycles showing the couple in an ideal environment full of flowers and with the prospect of a happy home. Moreover, the enthroned figures in their formal attire reflect the high social status of the persons depicted, indeed we venture to suggest that we may well see in them "portraits" of the owners. What is of interest here is the rendering of the facial features, in that folk vein distinctive of nineteenth-century artistic expression in general and which is particularly overt in painting. The lower part of the composition, with its large bouquet of flowers, reminiscent of similar motifs on island iconostases, strengthens the innermost certainty that the creator was an experienced icon-painter and, if I am not mistaken, one known from two later works of 1825 – *Blind Eros between the Sirens* and *The History of Suzanna* – namely Deuterevon of Siphnos (ill. 119).

The exceptionally powerful, if not always easily discernible bonds, the reciprocal influences and mutual interchange between ecclesiastical and secular painting in the islands, from about the middle of the eighteenth to the middle of the nineteenth century, are confirmed by other creations too, such as a wooden architrave, probably from Syros, in the collection of Maria Argyriadi (ill. 118). The rebirth of Greece after the National Struggle of 1821 is dominant here, with the figure of the goddess Athena standing forth in all her glory between the symbols of the War of Independence, while in the lower part of the composition is Constantinople with a dumbfounded Mohammed, his sword falling from his hands. The work's obvious stylistic and chronological affinity with the corresponding symbolic depiction of the "Escutcheon" of Metylina (ill. 120) shows that its painter had totally assimilated the more widespread currents of an expressive idiom common throughout Greece during the second quarter of the nineteenth century. Peloponnesian painters used this same idiom to depict the historical testimonies and visions of Makryyannis, and it was also used by an anonymous artist, probably Dodecanesian, to render the features of the schoolmistress Photeini Ch. M. Boyatzi from Symi, in what is, to my knowledge, the only example of a portrait (ill. 20). This work, from around the middle of the nineteenth century, rounds off what is – as I hope I have demonstrated – a single tradition, which runs through the artistic creation of the Aegean islands from the eighteenth century onwards, not least in painting.

In the development of the subject so far, one question of fundamental importance has emerged: to what point did the contact, if not the identification, of the icon-painter's art with contemporary folk, secular art – as Manolis Chatzidakis has so succintly put it – follow in depth the temporal levels of island painting prior to the middle of the eighteenth century too? This question could be confronted in connection with a group of Dodecanesian works which have either remained unpublished in the Folk Museum of Rhodes or are found scattered in various mansions of Patmos, essentially inaccessible to research. Therefore I shall resort to three examples from Rhodes which have been preserved in the inexhaustible "treasure trove" of the Benaki Museum (ills. 122-124). These are three oblong wooden panels on which the badly effaced decoration has been painted directly, without the gesso preparation characteristic of icons. It would appear from a drawing by Athena Tarsouli (ill. 21) that they probably originally framed the place reserved for the bed, though not in regions such as Lindos where the *sperveria* are encountered (ill. 89). Italian post-Renaissance influences in the style of the painting are obvious, though assimilated along with Eastern inputs from the ornaments of compositions, in a pleasing, refreshing manner and with boundless chromatic sensitivity: with riders, couples, vases with carnations and tulips, medallions with heraldic cupids and many-petalled rosettes, lions, leopards, monkeys and deer, partridges, peacocks, doves and hawks alternating in the rectangular partitions. They evoke the odd sensation that they belong to the same world as inspired the creations of Dodecanesian embroidery, such as the elaborate *portadela* of Patmos (ill. 90). It is precisely this sensation, in combination with the solid design and the clear colours of the representations, which places them on a time level antecedent to some late eighteenth-century examples in Rhodes, as well as to the painted Patmian *ambataros* in the Kourkoulas mansion (ill. 126).

The Rhodian panels do not, of course, represent isolated instances but the lost artistic production of an entire "School". This can be deduced from observing the same tradition in some painted cupboards on Patmos, one of which is presented here for the first time, thanks to a photograph supplied by Euthalia Konstantinidi (ill. 125). Indeed, from some traces on the painted ceilings of Lindos, it could be maintained that this "School" was already flourishing by the seventeenth century, that is during the period of great building activity to which this historic village (ill. 39) owes its most important architectural achievements. We are also led toward such a dating by the mature phase of the Iznik ceramics which were, after all, once considered to be Rhodian and which, for not inexplicable reasons, also influenced the style of Dodecanesian painting. However, even if the dating of the "School" does not go back to the seventeenth century, what is practically certain is that the secular and the ecclesiastical tradition are not united in its expressive idiom. It seems more likely that it developed autonomously from preceding periods, in accord-

21

21. Ambataros, *wooden partition of a Rhodian house, drawing by A. Tarsouli.*

ance with the example of Crete, where, through the archival research of Maria Konstantoudaki, it has been confirmed that an independent tradition was already flourishing by the sixteenth century. These creations, for the time being at least, can only be approached via the later echoes of them in the works of other islands.

THE SHATTERED COHESION OF TRADITION IN THE FRAGMENTARY IMAGE OF CERAMIC CONTINUITY

If the secular painting of the islands is composited of numerically limited testimonies in relation to the percentages of the hypothetical reasoning which activates them, the extant examples of pottery define a gnostic scale of far more diminished quantitative components. This observation does not refer to the better studied categories of large storage vessels, nor to the less studied (or unstudied) assemblages of undecorated domestic vessels, often with interesting and inspired forms. Just as it does not refer to all the more recent production from the workshops of Skyros, Chios, Mytilene, Siphnos, Samos and other islands which are connected up in the valuable work of Vasilis Kyriazopoulos on the more recent history of Greek pottery, from the opening decades of the twentieth century onwards. The pessimism of the opening remark is due to the dire dearth of evidence concerning the preceding pottery tradition which, even allowing for the vicissitudes of the island area during the post-Byzantine period, could not have died out and disappeared without trace of the passage of time.

Comparative study of other civilizations teaches us that pottery is one of those basic areas of human activity which harmoniously combines aesthetic and practical needs through practically automatic processes and far more directly than the other manifestations of man's artistic inquiries. It could be said, of course, that the pot, as a utilitarian vessel of the highest priority, more than any other human creation, not only follows the course of the cycle of life, but also the unity of the social group in the course of its acculturation and progress. This rule acquires a particularly significant force in those cases of historical periods, and in the coincidences of adverse social circumstances, during which the use of metal or glass was difficult and certainly not economically viable for the wider consumer public. There is, however, yet another reason which compels us to accept, even if only theoretically, the existence of island pottery in the periods prior to the nineteenth century, even if its overall picture still eludes us, even if its characteristics still remain unclear: the fact that pottery objects covering entire surfaces in the reception areas are still used as decorative features in the island home.

On Skyros and on Rhodes (ill. 21), on Karpathos, Astypalaia and wherever else such decorative assemblages have survived intact – though unfortunately not systematically recorded so that they could be the subject of more detailed study in the future – we are dealing with ceramics imported from Europe, various regions of Asia Minor in the Ottoman Empire and North Africa. The pace of the imports followed the development of shipping and trade from around the middle of the seventeenth century, with the large quantities of Iznik pottery which were diffused throughout the Dodecanese and elsewhere, with the orders received from many places by the workshops of Kutahia in the eighteenth century, with the Pesaro ware which, from the end of the eighteenth century, covered the needs of Skyros in particular, and with the variety and abundance of Çanak-Kale ceramics, which inundated the entire island area during the nineteenth century. The decorative use of imported pottery – as can be observed in the embellishment of the exteriors of many churches, even in earlier periods, as in the examples recorded by Yorgos Nikolakopoulos – reveals the widespread distribution of the phenomenon, as well as the depth to which its roots delve. However, since only the more prosperous sectors of the population could afford pottery creations of such value, it may be readily conjectured that the poorer and more populous classes satisfied the same aesthetic needs with cheaper products of local manufacture, even before the seventeenth century.

The working hypothesis which directs the quest for the early pottery of the Aegean islands via its more recent survivals is based on the deep-seated conviction that its origins must go back to Greece's Byzantine past. For example, taking as a guide the technique of *badanas*, the viscous white slip still in use, reproducing in the run-of-the-mill tourist creations of Skyros (ill. 127) something of the aesthetics of white embroidery (ills. 18, 77, 94, 101, 102), it would not be unreasonable to end up back in the late Byzantine period when precisely the same technique was used for the reserved decoration on the less important faces of many vessels. Unfortunately, only a few of the intermediary stages of this long evolutionary process are documented with some degree of certainty. The output of the inter-war years is classed in the latest stage, when there was a spectacular spread of the *badanas* technique, though without analogous artistic interest. The opposite could be said of the marvellously preserved basin with marine motifs, in the Benaki Museum, a creation from some Cycladic workshop from the turn of the nineteenth century (ill. 128). The entire decorative genre, having here absorbed, shortly before the demise of traditional inspirations, a considerable legacy of earlier aesthetic experiences, does allow us to refer back to the previous stages of the craft, even though the potter has difficulty in concealing the attraction the uneasy prospects of future developments exerts on him. Though it may not be strictly legitimate to compare two creations from different "genera", it is worthwhile doing so for the edge of the white-embroidered sheet – cited in the chapter on embroidery – with the large female figures, griffins, boats and eagles (ill. 101), because *vis-à-vis* the dissolved painted figures on the basin, the disciplined design of the embroidery, as well as the eurrhythmy of its composition, assist us in arriving at intuitive assumptions concerning the unknown technique of *badanas* in the periods before the nineteenth century.

An analogous retrogressive course through the unexplored field of island pottery, though starting off from the technique of incised and glazed surfaces, seems to offer more hope for at least a future solution to the relevant problems. Here the continuance of Byzantine tradition is confirmed in an obvious and indisputable way by a platter with inscription from Siphnos (ill. 129), dated to 1860, which ought to have already prompted the search for other examples from the same workshop, both in Siphnos and the rest of the Cyclades. The simplifying disposition of the decorative spirit of course presages the gradual expiry of the traditional dynamic that took place towards the end of the nineteenth and at the beginning of the twentieth century. There is no doubt, however, that in more or less this same period, that is around the middle of the nineteenth century, the technique – of Byzantine derivation – of glazed incised pottery would have been in use in other workshops too. This conclusion is strengthened by a humble example with green glaze, purchased on Skyros (ill. 130), the place of manufacture of which could be sought on some other island, were it not for the fact that the incised wavy line from which sprout forked branches – a schematic rendering of the blossoming bough – also features in Skyrian embroideries, as well as on Skyrian pottery creations painted with *badanas* (ill. 128). The wide diffusion of incised technique is also confirmed by a small jug with inscription, from Samos, dated 1846 (ills. 131, 132). This paultry piece of Neohellenic pottery does not promise much for a responsible morphological and stylistic analysis, nevertheless, the schematic human figure on which the optimism of the decoration is centred – though rendered with the slapdash vagueness of a child's drawing –, the vegetal motifs which frame it, as well as the large many-petalled rosette on the back, all obediently follow expressive canons of the island vocabulary. The same optimism is also embodied in the conception of the figures within an idealized, flower-filled environment on yet another pottery creation, but in a manner incredibly more monumental and the pretensions of important achievements (ills. 22, 133, 134).

Once again the piece in question is in the Benaki Museum – being one of its most valuable possessions –, yet another link in the chain of components of Neohellenic self-awareness which had been furtively inserted into the assemblages of Islamic art. When I first published it, I not only supported its Greekness but strongly advocated its origin in a Skyrian workshop of the seventeenth-eighteenth century, basing my arguments primarily on the astonishing affinity of its decorative motifs with those in the repertoire of Skyrian embroidery (ills. 16, 77, 88). Without overlooking this affinity, I now believe that the creation should be dated to the mid-eighteenth century. I would like once again to stress the impact of the compositional development, the quality of the design and the symbolically charged subject with the two patron saints of Hellenism, on horseback, guaranteeing auspicious prospects for the voyage (ill. 22). The boldness of the many-figured representation, with the ship as the central symbol, just like the optimism of the efflorescence, reflects an attitude to life which, along with the simplicity of the rendering, perceptibly augments the scale of the theme's inspiration.

It is impossible at present to trace incised pottery back to the periods before the eighteenth century. Its presence in many other parts of Greece as early as the sixteenth century – confirmed by excavations –, and the invaluable contribution of Angeliki Charitonidi in this field, gives me hope that a more serious research effort would prove of benefit in filling the gaps in the continuity of tradition in the Aegean. Spurred on by this hope I would like to make more widely known one last example, even though its origins in the obscure reaches of time and space on the Greek islands are, for the moment, based on reasons which are largely intuitive (ills. 135, 136). This is a large jug with

22

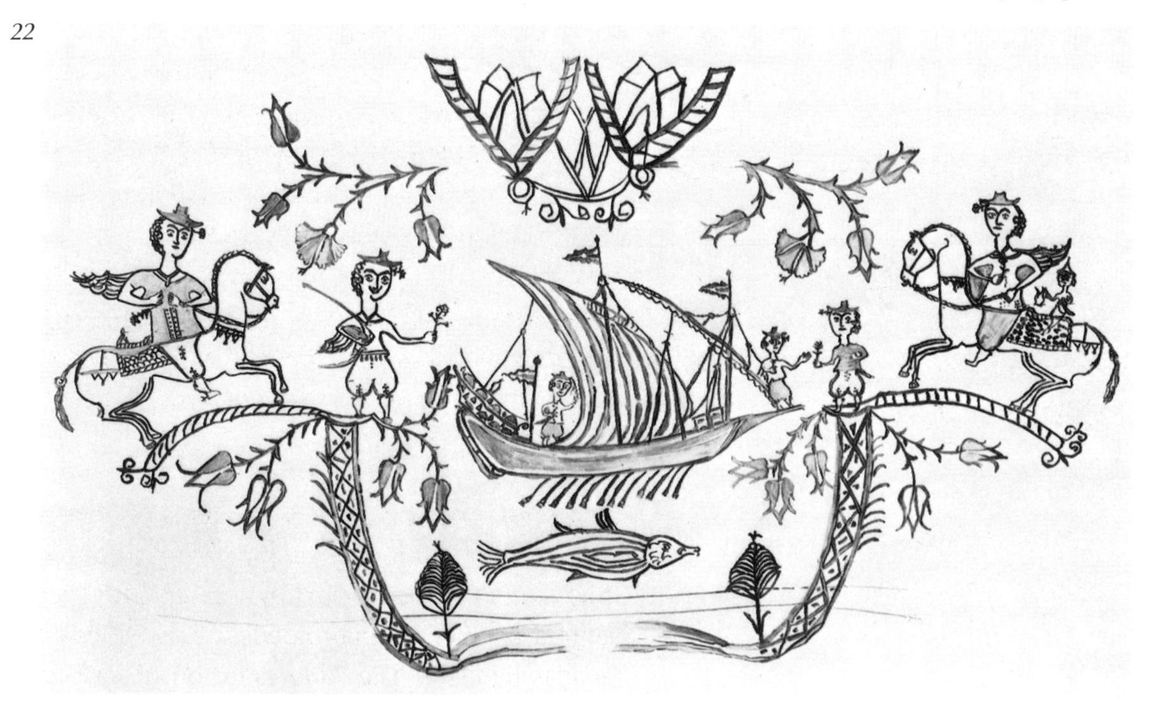

22. Drawing of the representation on a jug with incised decoration (also see ills. 133, 134). Athens, Benaki Museum, Inv. No 8682.

23

a greenish-yellow glaze and incised with a remarkable representation of a dance, in which the individual female figures are rendered as if inspired by the abstract geometric charm of Early Byzantine pottery, while the psychological timbre of the whole is well attuned to the rhythm of Neohellenic strains. The motif itself is repeated with unusual frequency in the embroidery of the Aegean islands (ills. 6, 94), as well as in Cretan weaving, generating the idea that the work probably comes from Crete, in the thematic repertoire of which the circles with inscribed many-petalled rosettes – supplementary motifs on the vase – are frequently encountered. But Cyprus too could claim paternity of the piece, in line with the similar spirit which governs the rendering of the human figure in the local pottery tradition of Late Byzantine times.

24

THE CHARACTER OF WOOD CARVING AS REVEALED THROUGH THE PRACTICAL AND THE AESTHETIC NEEDS OF THE HOME

25

Being completely ignorant of the actual material of secular wood carving on the islands, as well as of the corresponding bibliography, I am bound to confess that any attempt at even the most rudimentary classification of works that have only come to my attention by chance is more than difficult. And it would be even more risky to formulate any conclusions concerning their stylistic character and attribution to specific workshops, which presupposes, among many other intellectual resources, a more complete scholarly grasp of ecclesiastical wood carving too. However, with the exception of the iconostases of the Dodecanese, which have been recorded by Charalambos Koutelakis – and those only up to *circa* 1700 – none of its other creations has been set down in an easily readable manual or at least illustrated in an album. I should, moreover, observe that we cannot be at all certain that the ecclesiastical wood carving of a particular area was executed by local craftsmen and not itinerant ateliers, as was the case with the Cretans who worked in the Dodecanese before 1700. By the same token, it is not at all certain that the same craftsmen as carved wood for the needs of the Church also served the needs of the home, which were, in any case, as limited on the islands as in the rest of Greece. Thus we may comprehend the affinities as well as the difference in the workmanship of two secular wood-carvings from Rhodes: the seventeenth-century octagonal "heaven" which holds up the *sperveri* in the Benaki Museum (ill. 137), and the leaf of a door, probably from Lindos, in the collection of Theodoros Mintzas, from about the same period (ill. 25). In the former the floral decoration is freely developed on the flat surfaces of the wood, recalling certain decorative elements in the house of Irini Chaska on Symi, which was probably built in the first half of the eighteenth century (ills. 23, 24). In the latter the floral motifs, executed in a similar manner, are articulated within a system of small, independently worked panels, which seem to derive from earlier Islamic wood carving. The same technique and the same decorative spirit of geometric shapes characterizes many of the wood carvings of Symi (ills. 23, 24) and of Karpathos (ill. 26), in combination with floral ornaments and rosettes of inscribed radiating, foliate or horseshoe-shaped motifs (ill. 27). Indeed, the type of rosette displays a certain degree of affinity, if not a common stylistic origin, both with the rosettes recurring in the painted works from the Dodecanese (ills. 122, 125) and with the incised rosettes which characterize the wood carving and stone carving of Crete, with its Doric austerity (ills. 143, 145). Conversely, the technique used for the diamond-shaped panels is not confined to the islands of the

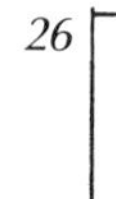
26

27

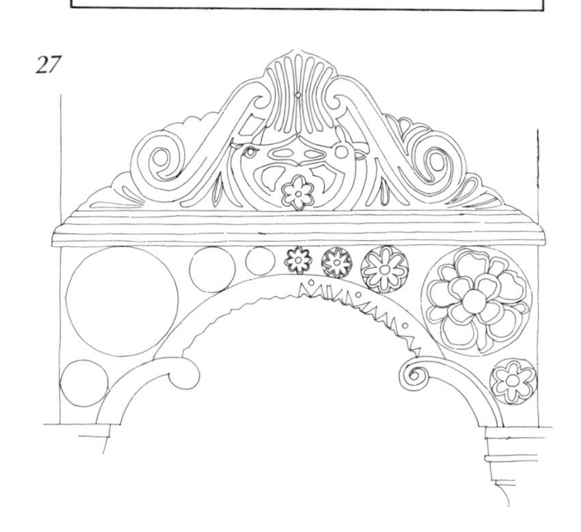

East Aegean or to Crete, but is encountered in the rest of Greece as well, and is not exclusively representative of the aesthetic of the islands.

Of course, we must not forget that at least the wealthiest of the island mansions were furnished with carved wooden European furniture, as well as luxurious chests brought from abroad, while, as has already been said, in certain of the homes of the more prosperous classes, painted rather than wood-carved decoration was preferred. Many of the chests in Mytilene, which have been published by Charilis Binos, bear dates from the middle of the eighteenth century, and floral motifs frequently combined with schematic representations of architectural structures. But despite the exceptional quality of their workmanship, either in embossed or incised technique, it is difficult to attribute them to a single stylistic tradition. The reverse holds true for a large number of the carved wooden chests, often of monumental dimensions, the conventional provenance of which is the Greek islands, though this has not been confirmed (ill. 28). Here not only the unity of the style can be easily observed, but also the subordination of the decorative motifs to the crystallized, or rather predetermined cycles which are only explicable in terms of a common workshop. However, no matter how often it has been maintained that they originate from the Dodecanese, the difference in workmanship from that of confirmed Dodecanesian chests is obvious (ills. 25, 137). The same applies to the Cyclades, where their origin has also been sought, despite the impressive example which has survived in the Siphnian mansion of Olga Karatza. Finally, their appearance in Crete is followed by the gradual weakening of the emphasis on relief and the transformation of the floral motifs into lifeless, schematic memories, which took place during the late nineteenth and the early twentieth century.

The chests of this type are distinguished by the division of the main face into a row of rectangular panels framing vases of flowers in relief (ill. 28), a motif often repeated on the painted panels of the island iconostases, as well as on other painted works of the seventeenth to eighteenth century, from the Dodecanese and the Cyclades. The depressing monochromy of the carved wooden surface, so contrary to the strident vitality of the island decorative spirit, leads us to suspect that there has been a subsequent drastic intervention. This may have occurred during the opening decades of the present century and in the inter-war years, when the prevailing urban aesthetic aspired to "upgrade" "folk" art through its forced immersion into whatever it considered to be a component of the Byzantine mode of expression. Familiar processes such as the barbarous scraping and staining black of the originally polychrome and lavishly gilded Kozanian *ondás* of Eleni Stathatou, in the Benaki Museum, or the fake aesthetic of "Byzantinesque" Skyrian furniture, flourished during this period.

28

23. The interior of the Irini Chaska house in Symi, drawn by K. Kaiger.

24. The interior of the Irini Chaska house in Symi, drawn by K. Kaiger.

25. Single-panelled door of a house from Lindos. Athens, collection of Theodoros Mintzas.

26. Single-panelled door of a house from Elymbos, Karpathos, drawing by D. Philippides.

27. Arched frontpiece of sofas from Elymbos, Karpathos, drawing by D. Philippides.

28. Carved wooden chest. Athens, Benaki Museum, Inv. No 8715.

29 a

b

29. Carved wooden chairs from Skyros. a. Athens, Benaki Museum, collection of Eleni Eucleidi, b. Athens, Benaki Museum, Inv. No 8723.

In contrast to the gloom provoked by the chromatic monotony of the chests "from the Greek islands" (ill. 28), the *kanavetes* of Skyros glow with their vibrant colours (ill. 139). And yet the two apparently different entities contain some common characteristics, not only with respect to the technique of working the wood, but also to the choice of subjects for their decoration. Therefore we hazard the assumption that the colourful *kanavetes* originate from the same workshop circle. Its centre, however, could not possibly be related geographically to Skyros because their style bears absolutely no relationship to the little low chairs found in the home, made in local workshops, and which are, moreover, the only indisputed examples of Skyrian wood carving (ill. 29).

The questions which remain unanswered concerning the island chests and the indications of their original brilliance, are answered to a degree by the folk-style wood carving of Cyprus, in which the polychrome feast is still intact (ill. 138). More eloquent, however, is the case of an early armchair from Paros in the possession of Augi Proukaki, not only because it preserves its original colouring, but also because the quality of its decoration strengthens the hypothesis of the existence of an island wood-carving centre, though the place and time of its activity remain unknown. To this same unit also belongs a series of similar high-backed chairs (ills. 140, 141), on which the floral decoration, as it is developed with a vertical thrust, is vaguely reminiscent of the marble Cycladic door frames of the eighteenth century (ills. 36, 151, 152). Although, in this case too, any evidence of provenance is lacking, there are some oblique indications that the producing workshop was located in one of the centres in the Cyclades, the only region of the Greek world, along with the Dodecanese, where household furniture is found, whether brought from Europe or influenced by Western prototypes.

The aesthetic of wood carving in Crete, judging from the mainly nineteenth-century furniture recorded by Ch. Vallianos, Y. Pervolarakis and Y. Neroladakis, is completely different. As a rule the motifs are single, incised and with a pronounced tendency to abstraction: rosettes predominate numerically. The vegetal foundation of the motifs, as well as their close stylistic relationship to the stone carving on the same island, is easily detected (ill. 145). However, with the data available today it is difficult to evaluate the course of the abstractive process in absolute chronological terms. Considering the affinity displayed by the corresponding motifs in the wood carving of the Dodecanese (ill. 27), it would not be overly bold to date a Cretan armchair in the Benaki Museum (ill. 143) to the early nineteenth century. The incised designs on a loom must have been executed in more or less the same period, while both the attributing and the probably earlier dating of a unique – as far as I know – lamp-stand in the same Museum (ill. 142), remains uncertain for the present.

Those examples of wood carving cited here, as well as those which have certainly escaped me, though not betraying the basic aesthetic components of the island area, would have difficulty in claiming a prominent place among the other units of artistic creation. This is not only because they lack a monumental dimension, but also because their decorative character is stressed more than it should be. Conversely, of all the figureheads that have survived, the "size" of which would direct us to large-scale wood carving, only a few can be unequivocally atrributed to specific shipyards in the Aegean islands, and most of them do not date back further than the turn of the eighteenth to the nineteenth century. With great hesitation, I would mention just one female head, of rare beauty, from Symi (ill. 30), if I did not have my doubts concerning its Greekness. The best known figureheads in the National Historical Museum, from the ships of Spetses, Hydra and Psara, transmit a feeling of Greekness which has nothing to do with

30

30. Female head from ship's figurehead. Museum of Symi.

the antiqueness and the symbolic connotations of their representations, nor with the burden of associations, that is the emotional impulses generated by their connection with the Greek War of Independence. This feeling is related to the crystallized aesthetic perception which marks the rendering of a new type of man, with an easily discerned heroic dimension in the animation of the human figure, filtered through the psyche and the poetic sensitivity of the general public of the period. In its most expressive example, the valiant figure of Themistocles, from the prow of Chatziyiannis Mexis' sailing ship (ill. 144), we sense that the vision imbuing it, having come full circle during the historic time of Modern Hellenism, will not be long in dying. Just as the fire will be extinguished which smoulders in the conscience at that crucial point where anonymous creation meets eponymous behaviour, between tradition and modernization, the past but also the future of the expressive values of the last champion of the Greek idea, Theophilos Chatzimichail.

THE RESISTANCE OF MARBLE, THE ENDURANCE OF STONE AND THE ANXIETIES OF SCULPTED EXPRESSION

Up until now in our exploratory journey through the *terra incognita* of island art, we have been groping in the dark, relying mainly on instinct and certain chance encounters. In our investigation of stone carving we are able to seek assistance through consulting Popi Zora's scientifically sound consideration of the problems and the expert studies of Antonis Stephanou, Alekos Florakis and Marina Karagatsi. Until this important preparatory work on the material from Chios, Tinos and Andros functions as a paradigm, encouraging the collection and publication of all the other carving dispersed throughout the islands of the Archipelago, it at least enables us to draw certain conclusions with a smaller degree of erroneous appraisals.

Stone carving – just like wood carving, not only in the Aegean but all over continental Greece – is always dependent on architecture and constrained by the two-dimensional demands of relief formulae. Three-dimensional creations are either totally absent or only encountered as rare exceptions to a rule, the validity of which must be in large part due to the persistence of Byzantine memories, the Orthodox faith's ban on statues in churches and, perhaps, to the unconfessed need to resist dangerous confrontations with Catholicism. But such an explanation would be one-sided if certrain other determinant factors were not taken into account, predominant among which is the "painterly" view of the environment which is abundantly clear throughout the entire development of Neohellenic artistic production, wherein many assimilated aesthetic experiences from the Byzantine past can be traced. Consequently it would be worthwhile making a detailed study of certain sculptures in the round of problematic interpretation, not so much because they lead to uncertain conclusions, as for the beneficial influence they would almost certainly exert during the search for other equivalent examples in the virgin territory of the Archipelago.

The only island sculptures known to me depict wild beasts – mainly lions –, and human heads, and crown small pilasters decorated with relief vegetal motifs on the most elaborate of the monumental staircases in the mansions of Chios. What the original purpose of a male stone head from Limnos may have been is difficult to ascertain without the aid of comparanda (ill. 31). Bringing to mind the ancient figurines of prehistoric times

31

32

33

and the apotropaic "mason's" heads incorporated in architectural structures of mainland Greece, it is not possible at the moment to make a chronological assessment of this piece, even through the confirmed presence of a local stone-carving workshop leads us to suspect that it was fashioned some time around the middle of the nineteenth century. Equally difficult to date is another male head of island marble, in a private collection (ill. 33), the facial features of which are vaguely reminiscent of the figures depicted on Chian reliefs of the mid-nineteenth century (ill. 34). Of interest is the easily discernible deviation from the traditional canons of symmetry in the modelling of the partial forms, something which could have been avoided if, of course, it did not stem from a specific and conscious inner need for a starting point corresponding to that which animated ancient Greek sculpture in Archaic times: that is a desire to register movement, the essence of life, through a differentiation which rejects a uniform description of the two sides of the face. The same applies, to a lesser degree, to a third male head, of obscure origin, carved on soft stone (ill. 32). Discernible in its facial features, in barely perceptible relief, is that folk spirit which also governs painting, becoming increasingly standardized in manner as the nineteenth century progressed. For inexplicable reasons, perhaps related to the romantic treatment of the wavy hair, one has the feeling that here we see the hero of 1821, Athanasios Diakos.

The rendering of the human figure in island sculpture, and indeed more generally in Neohellenic art, composes one of the most fascinating, as well as the most difficult chapters in the issues being explored, which is why it cannot be dealt with exhaustively here. It is sufficient to note some interesting facets exemplified by certain works, selected more or less at random, but in relation to what has already been said in the examination of embroidery and painting. The relief from Chios mentioned above, for example (ill. 34), "urbanizes", in the middle of the nineteenth century, the almost emblematic symbolism in the depiction of the couple, the ideal crystallization of which is that painted on the closet from Siphnos, from the beginning of the same century (ill. 116). More closely akin to the spirit of the painted creation is the section of a splendid relief of the late eighteenth century, portraying a notable, in the Folklore Museum of Mykonos (ill. 35). The status of the eminent person is recorded in the formal attire and the worry beads, denoting that he has time on his hands, a privilege not enjoyed, for example, by the ploughman represented in a rare relief on the floor of the church of the Holy Trinity (Ayia Triada) at Gyrla on Tinos. The most interesting creations in this unit are those which make up the impressive relief decoration on the bell-tower of the Panayia Tourliani Monastery at Anomera on Mykonos, though they do not in fact constitute a continuous narrative: the metropolitan with his deacon, a church-warden with his purse, the cook with his implements (ill. 149), the "icon" of the Holy Virgin and various decorative motifs, mainly cypress trees. On the dedicatory inscription of the monumental composition the date of construction (1806) is inscribed with precision, but there is no information about the craftsman, whose sensitivity is such that Popi Zora assigns him to the stone-carving tradition of Tinos. The monastery fountain, with a representation of a crowned Sun (Helios)? (ill. 150) is evidently from the same atelier and of the same period.

If the carvings of Mykonos can be understood as examples of a large family of analogous works scattered through more or less all the Aegean islands, the same is not, alas, true, of two relief figures, in secondary use, incorporated in the wall of Evanthia Damia's house in Paroikia on Paros. It is difficult to deduce, only from photographic evidence, their date and what they represent, but from the explicit message of fertility in the emphatic rendering of the sexual characteristics, I suspect a couple is depicted, as in the

34

35

unique case, as far as I know, of the door frame in the house of Sophia Petrou Theologitou in Chora, Amorgos, which bears the date 1730 (ill. 152).

The example from Amorgos belongs to a type of door frame, of Renaissance origin, found in the Cyclades from as early as the sixteenth century, though without the splendid vegetal decoration, the wide variety of thematic variations and the stylistic expressions observed in the eighteenth century. In certain cases the same decorative motifs are repeated with such amazing accuracy on the door frames of most of the islands, that one can easily attribute their workmanship to the circulation of set patterns for the designs or to itinerant craftsmen from ateliers which for the moment remain unknown. The door frames in the Folklore Museum of Mykonos (ill. 151), that of a mansion (now demolished) on Ios, now in the Benaki Museum, from where a window frame decorated in an identical manner also comes, as well as another window frame from the Papadatos mansion (formerly Theocharides) in Paroikia, Paros (ill. 36), repeat a common decorative model without any divergences whatsoever. The door frame of the church of Saint George (Ayios Georgios) at Merovigli on Paros, as well as those in many other Cycladic churches, must be attributed to the same atelier. So, once again, the dividing line between ecclesiastical and secular stone carving should be regarded as completely conventional, even though the latter has not yet presented us with examples of developed compositions, such as the relief icons or the still unstudied – to our chagrin – marble iconostases of the island churches.

Of the relief icons which are encountered in most of the Cycladic islands, placed, as a rule, above the main entrance to the church, only the examples on Tinos and Andros have been systematically recorded. Despite the obvious stylistic differences and the variable quality of their workmanship, and despite their general classification into two broad units, of which the later is distinguished by the folk-style rendering of motifs, their iconographic dependence on the repertoire of ecclesiastical painting is direct. The same holds true for the marble iconostases, which transcribe the current models of ecclesiastical wood carving with impressive results and are of exceptional interest for the study of the internal relations of wood carving to stone carving. The marble iconostases on the islands are monumental creations on a large scale, of complex technical specifications, and despite the differences in their morphological constitution can be admirably compared to the corresponding structures from Byzantine times. In the well-preserved example in the cemetery church of the Agias Monastery on Andros, the simplified rendering and the quality of the generalized motifs verge on the folk genre which, as in the case of painting, from *circa* 1800 followed the unfolding of the nineteenth century. Their dating to the late eighteenth century is reinforced by the more "modelled" formulation in an undoubtedly earlier section of a corresponding Cycladic iconostasis with a representation of a mermaid (ill. 40).

There can be no doubt that the combination of skill in the chiselling of marble with ability in drafting the depicted motifs defines a relationship directly proportional to the age of the works of island sculpture. Thus is explained the sappier substance of the vegetal decoration, as well as the more balanced aesthetic, which characterizes, in the early seventeenth century, the iconostases of the Katapoliani church in Paroikia, Paros – recorded by Anastasios Orlandos (ill. 37) – leading us to speculate that the acme of the workshop in which they were made must have reached back to previous periods. The marble iconostasis in the Panayia Septemvriani, in the same region, dated to 1590 or 1596, confirms that island stone carving was already flourishing by the sixteenth century.

The evolutionary course of stone carving, from the more complex and luscious to

31. Male stone head from Limnos. Athens, Benaki Museum.

32. Male stone head. Athens, Benaki Museum.

33. Male marble head. Athens, private collection.

34. Marble relief from the Chatzi Konstantis Papazis mansion. Vrontades, Chios.

35. Section of a relief with the representation of a notable. Mykonos, Folklore Museum.

36

37

38

simple, repetitious and stylized forms is confirmed by the dated door frames of the church of Saint Antonios on Folegandros (1709) and Saint Sozon at Apollonia on Siphnos (1768). The door frame of Saint Nicholas at Mesaria on Andros, intermediate to them, adds its own testimony to the further development of this line of reasoning (ill. 38). It is dated to 1734, because of the inscription recording the repair of the church by artisans from Chios, which also makes its attribution to a Chian workshop more plausible. Nevertheless, the possibility that local craftsmen were also involved in carving the marble, in conjunction with the absence of similar works on Chios itself, entwines the stylistic and the geographical problems into a string of different questions. However, regardless of the doubts overshadowing its origins, the example from Andros is valuable because it allows us to comprehend the creative personality of a craftsman, albeit anonymous, in another of his works on a different island: the coat of arms of Bernardo Barozzi on his towel at Chalki on Naxos, dated to 1742 (ill. 41), where the fleshy rendering of the dense vegetal decoration coexists with the selfsame decorative spirit and the same description of the details.

Examples of door frames with a dense arrangement of the decorative elements and frequently an earlier date of construction are encountered on nearly all the Cycladic islands. However, given the unlikelihood of carrying out a thorough comprehensive study, the assembling of similar units and the observation of their stylistic evolution would seem to be insuperably difficult, at least for the present. Thus the counting and the locating of workshops becomes a problem, while a question of basic importance remains unanswered: to what degree are these works the result of a single widely diffused artistic tradition or of quite independent centres in the island area? Of the contributors which helped fashion the carving of the Cyclades, Chios can be excluded, since neither this type of door frame nor its typical decoration are found there. For the same reasons Tinos must also be ruled out, since its workshops were experimenting in other directions. It would, however, be permissible to conjecture that parallel with the main tendencies others were operating autonomously, on a smaller scale, local in character and with independent aesthetic orientations, judging from a folk-style lintel in Kea (ill. 42), the simpler lintels with incised rosettes on Crete (ill. 145), and the seventeenth-century "Gothic" style decoration of the door frames of Lindos (ill. 39).

The difficulties inherent in distinguishing local workshops are more apparent on Tinos where two ostensibly independent tendencies existed alongside one another: the flat, carved fanlights, some of the most important Greek stone-carvings (ill. 146), and the reliefs in *alto rilievo*, which mainly feature on fountains (ills. 43, 44). In the first group the sparse linear rendering of the motifs is governed by an abstract generalization akin to the aesthetic of white embroidery. In the latter the chiefly vegetal motifs are imbued with an explosive temperament by the extravagance of their components and their confused articulation within the interwoven anthithetic arcs of the frames. The differences between the two tendencies are so obvious that if they were not found on the same island it might be thought that they represented two totally independent traditions. But an elementary respect for the ethics of scholarship cautions against simplifying solutions. For there are also striking differences between the fanlights known to date, which range from the schematic to a more luscious rendering of motifs, from the planar *rilievo stiacciato* to high relief, from a plethora of diverse idosyncratic currents to personal approaches. Furthermore, a large part of the plundered material of Tinos remains inaccessible and disparate, such as the unpublished piece in an Athenian collection (ill. 45). If to this body of material are added all the fanlights already existing on Andros and other

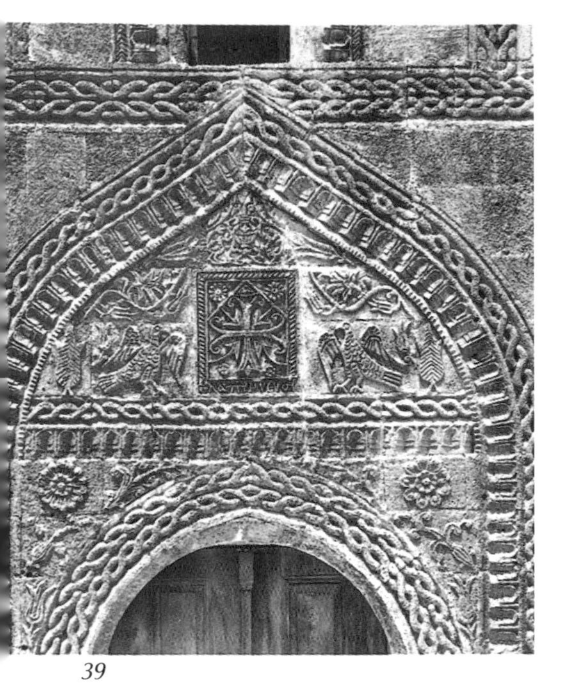

39

40

41

42

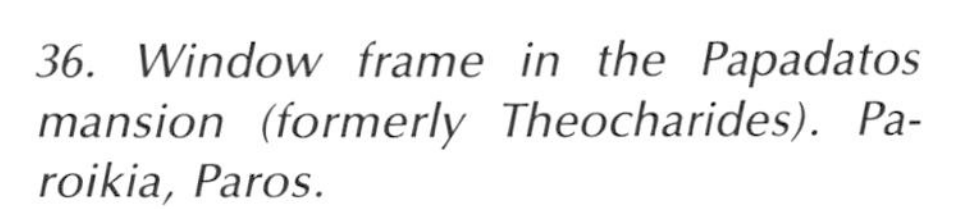

36. Window frame in the Papadatos mansion (formerly Theocharides). Paroikia, Paros.

37. Section of the iconostasis from the church of Panayia Katapoliani in Paroikia, Paros, drawing by A.K. Orlandos.

38. Detail from the door frame of the church of Ayios Nikolaos. Mesaria, Andros.

39. Exterior relief decoration of a house. Lindos, Rhodes.

40. Section of a marble iconostasis. Athens, Benaki Museum, Inv. No 29066.

41. Marble coat-of-arms on the Vernardos Barotzis tower (Gratsias tower). Chalki, Naxos.

42. Lintel over courtyard gate. Chora, Kea.

islands by the mid-eighteenth century, then the provisional nature of any conclusions weighs depressingly upon us.

The solutions to the problem of chronological assessment, without the assistance of inscriptions, are equally provisional. Nevertheless, judging from the most mature fanlights of the middle of the nineteenth century, with the confused aesthetic of inarticulate floral – as a rule – motifs and some emphasis on the third dimension, I would venture to date all those governed by the principle of spare, planar austerity and the rational assemblage of clearly drawn motifs to the periods prior to the end of the eighteenth century. This conclusion is reinforced by the well-known tombstone of 1804 in the cemetery of Pyrgos on Tinos (ill. 46), with the pronounced isolation, or rather elevation, of the principal motif and a barely perceptible realistic nuance in its description, marking the turning point in this same aesthetic perception, heralding the subsequent eponymous creations of Tinian stone carving.

The more naturalistic tradition of the *alta rilieva* reliefs, with the over-ornate floral "baroque" decoration, is represented by the Kato Vrysi (Lower Fountain) of 1798 in Chora, Tinos (ill. 43), as well as by another fountain, most probably from the same atelier, on the old road which led to the Monastery of the Evangelistria (ill. 44). The same stylistic spirit of the late eighteenth century is expressed by the reliefs on the Mavrogenis fountain in Paroikia on Paros, dated to 1777 (ill. 47). The "fraternity", however, brings us back to the vexed question of local ateliers, of their movements and of distinguishing their works, principally with regard to the information gathered by Nikos Kephalliniadis concerning the parallel activity of Tinians, Parians and local stone carvers on Naxos, where stone carving also flourished. It is through such a nexus of various tendencies and traditions, their intersections and reciprocal influences, that the unity of style in the stone carving of the Cyclades, as well as the unity of its choice of decorative subjects, is explained. This same unity, evidently for the same reasons, also characterizes the corresponding creations of other islands, as is easily confirmed, despite the self-evident differences, by many examples from Samos, Chios (ills. 147, 148) and Mytilene.

43. Fountain with the date 1798. Chora, Tinos.

44. Fountain on the way to the Panayia church of Tinos.

45. Fanlight from Tinos. Athens, collection of Irini Kalliga.

46. Marble tombstone relief in the Pyrgos cemetery. Tinos.

47. The Mavrogenis fountain. Paroikia, Paros.

EPILOGUE

The need to include in my exposition as many examples as possible, in order to back up my arguments, has inevitably resulted in a conventional and insipid, an awkward and inarticulate presentation. This is exacerbated by my luckless attempt to maintain a sense of balance, that is to accord equal treatment to the earlier stages of the art of the Greek islands, by resorting to clichéd and synoptic expressions, without exceeding the permitted number of pages. Thus I have not avoided an inordinate amount of illustration, not so much because of an inability to follow the faint impressions of continuity and cohesion in a different way, but because of a deep belief that our eyes should become more accustomed to the artistic creations and cultural documents of more recent times.

More light would, of course, have been shed on our investigation of the aesthetic dimension of the artistic production of the islands by juxtaposing the works of visual art with other forms of cultural expression, with first and foremost the poetic values of Greek folk (demotic) songs. But such a venture would "overstretch" the text still further beyond the specified limits. Despite this serious omission, I sincerely hope that the all-pervasive joy of life governing the thematic choices of island art will have been perceived. I also hope it has clearly emerged that the painterly view of the world distinctive of it, voluntarily rejects the third dimension as an expendable component in man's relationship to an ideal environment, which is conceived of as an attainable reality and not as an ephemeral illusion. After all, it is from here that the optimism of this art springs, the preference for the general as opposed to the specific, the abstraction of its geometric constructs and its concommitant tendency to refer it to an organized stable system of decoration. The human figure, even when not depicted in this system, is understood as part of a closed, indivisible and complete whole.

The constant need for improvisation on already crystallized forms leads the art of the islands – contrary to what is said and written – to a single artistic tradition, which was retained intact till around the middle of the eighteenth century. Its subsequent differen-

46

47

tiations, as well as the increasingly dynamic autonomy of local idioms, together with their admirable expressive variety, was to bring about, a century later, a gradual dissipation of its activating force.

Warm thanks are addressed to the following friends for allowing the use of unpublished photographic material, without which this text could not have been completed, and for their generous and unreserved assistance; Maria Argyriadi, Myrtali Acheimastou-Potamianou, Peggy Zoumboulaki, Eirene Kalliga, Marina Karagatsi, Luisa Karapidaki-Kalokairinou, Eleni Karastamati, Olga Karatza, Vasilis Kyriazopoulos, Euthalia Konstantinidi, the Right Reverend Ioannis Lambrinos, Yannis Mazarakis-Ainian, Andreas Malekos, Lila Marangou, Theodoros Mintzas, Manto Oikonomidi, Ioanna Papantoniou, Dionysis Photopoulos, Augi Proukaki, Youla Riska, Isavella Sidirourgou, Stelios Skopelitis. Special thanks are due to Marilena Masoura for the hardships she endured during the continual revisions and annotations of the manuscript.

This article is dedicated to my friend Popi Zora, for her contribution to the study of Modern Greek culture and in gratitude for all she has given me.

BIBLIOGRAPHY

General

ΑΙΚΑΤΕΡΙΝΙΔΗΣ, Γ.Ν., «Λαϊκός πολιτισμός», *Κρήτη: Ἱστορία καί πολιτισμός*, Κρήτη 1988.

ARGENTI, PH.P. – ROSE, H.J., *The folk-lore of Chios*, vol. 1-2, Cambridge 1949.

DELIVORRIAS, A., *Guide to the Benaki Museum*, Athens 1980.

ΔΗΜΗΤΡΙΟΥ, Ν.Α., *Λαογραφικά τῆς Σάμου*, τόμ. Α-Β, Ἀθήνα 1983.

Ἑλληνική Παραδοσιακή Ἀρχιτεκτονική, ἔκδ. «Μέλισσα», τόμ. 3, Ἀθήνα 1984.

Greek Handicraft, ed. National Bank of Greece, Athens 1969.

Greek Traditional Architecture, ed. "Melissa", vol. 1-2, Athens 1982.

HAGIMIHALI, A., *L' art populaire grec*, Athens 1937.

Κατάλογος Μουσείου Φιλίππου Ἀργέντη, Πινακοθήκη καί λαογραφική συλλογή, Βιβλιοθήκη Χίου Κοραῆς, [Ἀθήνα] χ.χ.

ΜΙΧΑΗΛΙΔΗΣ-ΝΟΥΑΡΟΣ, Μ.Γ., *Λαογραφικά Σύμμεικτα Καρπάθου*, τόμ. Β΄, Ἀθήνα 1934.

MONTE SANTO, M., *La Città Sacra (Lindo)*, Rome 1930.

— *L' isola dei Gigli (Stampalia)*, Rome n.d.

OHNEFALSCH-RICHTER, M.H., *Griechische Sitten und Gebräuche auf Cypern*, Berlin 1913.

ΠΑΠΑΔΑΚΗ, Ε., *Ἡ λαϊκή τέχνη τῆς Θάσου σάν ἐκδήλωση τοῦ λαϊκοῦ πολιτισμοῦ*, Θεσσαλονίκη 1964.

ΠΙΕΡΙΔΗ, Α.Γ., «Κυπριακή λαϊκή τέχνη», *Δημοσιεύματα τῆς Ἑταιρείας Κυπριακῶν Σπουδῶν*, 6 (1980).

ΠΡΟΒΑΤΑΚΗΣ, Θ.Μ., *Κρήτη. Λαϊκή τέχνη καί ζωή*, Ἀθήνα 1990.

ΡΗΓΑΣ, Γ.Α., *Σκιάθου λαϊκός πολιτισμός*, τόμ. Δ΄, Θεσσαλονίκη 1970.

ΣΕΤΤΑΣ, Δ.Χ., «Εὔβοια, Λαϊκός πολιτισμός, Γ: ἡ Κύμη», *Ἀρχεῖον Εὐβοϊκῶν Μελετῶν*, παράρτημα ΚΖ΄ τόμου (1988).

ΣΙΜΟΠΟΥΛΟΣ, Κ., *Ξένοι ταξιδιῶτες στήν Ἑλλάδα*, τόμ. Α΄, 2η ἔκδ., Ἀθήνα 1972· τόμ. Β΄, Ἀθήνα 1973· τόμ. Γ, Ἀθήνα 1975.

SMITH, A.C., *The architecture of Chios, subsidiary buildings, implements and crafts*, Ph. P. Argenti (ed.), London 1961.

Σύντομος ὁδηγός τοῦ Μουσείου Λαϊκῆς Τέχνης Κύπρου, Λευκωσία 1973.

ΤΑΡΣΟΥΛΗ, Α., *Δωδεκάνησα*, τόμ. Α΄, [Ἀθῆναι] 1947· τόμ. Β΄, [Ἀθῆναι] 1948· τόμ. Γ΄, [Ἀθῆναι] 1950.

— «Ἡ Κυπριακή λαϊκή τέχνη», *Ἑλληνική Λαϊκή Τέχνη*, 1 (1970).

The Greek Merchant Marine, ed. National Bank of Greece, Athens 1972.

TSIGAKOU, F.-M., *Thomas Hope: Pictures from 18th century Greece*, Athens 1985.

ΧΑΤΖΗΜΙΧΑΛΗ, Α., *Ἑλληνική λαϊκή τέχνη. Σκῦρος*, Ἀθῆναι 1925.

— «Ἑλληνική λαϊκή τέχνη. Σάμος», *Ἑλληνικά Γράμματα*, Γ΄, τχ. 3 (1928).

— *Ἑλληνική λαϊκή τέχνη. Ρουμλούκι, Τρίκερι, Ἰκαρία*, Ἀθῆναι 1931.

— «Αἱ ἐκδηλώσεις καί ἡ μορφή τῶν ἔργων τῆς λαϊκῆς τέχνης στίς Κυκλάδες», *Ἐπετηρίς τῆς Λαογραφικῆς καί Ἱστορικῆς Ἑταιρείας Κυκλαδικοῦ Πολιτισμοῦ καί Τέχνης*, Α΄ (1935).

— «Ἡ λαϊκή τέχνη τῆς Κύπρου», *Νέα Ἑστία*, 56, τχ. 659 (1954) ἀνάτυπο.

— «Ἡ λαική τέχνη τῆς Εὔβοιας», *Ἀρχεῖον Εὐβοϊκῶν Μελετῶν*, Ζ (1960) ἀνάτυπο.

— «Ἡ λαϊκή τέχνη τῆς Κύπρου», *Ἑλληνική Λαϊκή Τέχνη*, 2 (1971).

ΧΑΤΖΗΦΩΤΗΣ, Ι.Μ., *Ὁ λαϊκός πολιτισμός τοῦ Καστελλόριζου*, Ἀθήνα 1982.

Costumes

GRASSET DE SAINT-SAUVEUR, A., *Voyage Historique, Littéraire Et Pittoresque Dans Les Îles Et Possessions Ci-Devant Vénitiennes Du Levant...*, vol. I-III and album, Paris 1797.

GRASSET DE SAINT-SAUVEUR, J., *Voyages Pittoresques Dans Les Quatre Parties Du Monde...*, vol. I-II, Paris 1806.

KRAZEISEN, K., *Bildnisse ausgezeichneter Griechen und Philhellenen, nebst einigen Ansichten und Trachten...*, Munich 1828-31.

NICOLAY, N., *Der erst Theyl von der Schiffart und Rayss in die Türchey...*, Nuremberg 1572.

PITTON DE TOURNEFORT, J., *Relation D' Un Voyage Du Levant Fait Par Ordre Du Roy...*, Paris 1717.

STACKELBERG, O.M. BARON VON, *Costumes Et Usages Des Peuples De La Grèce Moderne*, Rome 1825.

WHELER, G., *A journey into Greece...*, London 1682.

ΑΝΑΓΝΩΣΤΟΠΟΥΛΟΥ, Μ.Α., «Μία λεσβιακή φορεσιά τοῦ 17ου αἰώνα μέ τίς παραλλαγές της», *Δελτίο τῆς Ἑταιρείας Λεσβιακῶν Μελετῶν*, Θ΄ (1985) ἀνάτυπο.

— «Ἡ παραδοσιακή φόρεσιά τοῦ Πλωμαρίου», *Μνήμη καί Παράδοση τοῦ Συνδέσμου Πλωμαριτῶν Ἀττικῆς*, 1 (1986) ἀνάτυπο.
— «Τό σαλβάρι στή γυναικεία ἐνδυμασία τῆς Λέσβου», *Ἐθνογραφικά*, 7 (1989).
ARGENTI, PH. P., *The costumes of Chios. Their Development from the XVth to the XXth Century*, London [1953].
HATZIMICHALI, A., *Hellenic National Costumes*, Benaki Museum, vol. I, Athens 1948; vol. II, Athens 1954.
— *The Greek Folk Costume*, ed. "Melissa", vol. II, Athens 1983.
ΚΑΠΕΤΑΝΑΚΗ, Σ. - ΚΩΤΣΟΥ, Μ., «Ἡ ἔρευνα γιά τή νεοελληνική φορεσιά ἀπό τό 15ο ὥς τό 19ο αἰώνα», *Ἐθνογραφικά*, 4-5 (1983-85).
ΚΕΦΑΛΛΗΝΙΑΔΗΣ, Ν., «Ἡ παλιά γυναικεία φορεσιά τῶν Κυκλάδων», *Ἑλληνική Λαϊκή Τέχνη*, 14 (1974).
ΚΟΡΡΕ-ΖΩΓΡΑΦΟΥ, Κ., *Νεοελληνικός κεφαλόδεσμος*, 2η ἔκδ., Ἀθήνα 1991.
ΚΟΥΡΙΑ, Α., «Ἡ παράσταση τῆς ἑλληνικῆς φορεσιᾶς στά χαρακτικά τῶν εὐρωπαϊκῶν περιηγητικῶν ἐκδόσεων (15ος - 19ος αἰ.)», *Ἐθνογραφικά*, 7 (1989).
MONTE SANTO, M., "Costumi et gioielli del Dodecaneso e di Castelrosso", *Dedalo*, X (1932).
— "Gemme della forematica neoellenica; visioni del costume classico ellenico", *Rassegna della Istruzione Artistica*, 9-10, 11-12, (n.d.) off-print.
ΟΙΚΟΝΟΜΙΔΗ, Τ., «Ἡ γυναικεία φορεσιά τῆς Καρπάθου», *Λαογραφία*, ΚΔ΄ (1966).
ΠΑΠΑΝΤΩΝΙΟΥ, Ι., «Συμβολή στή μελέτη τῆς γυναικείας ἑλληνικῆς παραδοσιακῆς φορεσιᾶς», *Ἐθνογραφικά*, 1 (1978).
— «Οἱ τοπικές φορεσιές στό Αἰγαῖο ἀπό τήν ἅλωση μέχρι τήν ἀπελευθέρωση», *Ἐθνογραφικά*, 4-5 (1983-85).
PAPANTONIOU, I., *Creek Costumes*, vol. 1, Athens 1973; vol. 2, Athens 1974.
— *Greek Costumes*, Naïplion 1981.
ΤΑΡΣΟΥΛΗ, Α., *Ἑλληνικές φορεσιές*, [Ἀθήνα 1941].
TARSOULI, A., *Embroideries and Costumes of Dodecanese*, Athens 1951.
ΤΣΕΝΟΓΛΟΥ, Ε., «Τά καστελλοριζιακά γυναικεῖα ἐνδύματα», *Ἐθνογραφικά*, 4-5 (1983-85).
ΦΙΛΙΠΠΑΚΗΣ, Μ., «Ἡ γυναικεία φορεσιά τῆς Σίφνου», *Σιφναϊκή Φωνή*, φύλ. 13-15, 17-22, (1966).
— «Ἡ ἀνδρική φορεσιά στήν παλιά Σίφνο», *Σιφναϊκή Φωνή*, φύλ. 25-26,28, (1967).
ΦΡΑΓΚΑΚΙ, ΕΥ. Κ., *Ἡ λαϊκή τέχνη τῆς Κρήτης: ἀνδρική φορεσιά, γυναικεία φορεσιά*, τόμ. Α-Β, Ἀθήνα 1960.
ΧΑΒΑΚΙΣ, Ι., «Ὁ κρητικός ἀργαλειός καί τά κρητικά μεσαιωνικά καί μεταμεσαιωνικά ροῦχα», *Κρητικά Χρονικά*, Θ΄, Α΄ λαογραφικό παράρτημα, (1955).
ΧΑΤΖΗΜΙΧΑΛΗ, Α., *Λεύκωμα ἐθνικῶν ἐνδυμασιῶν*, τόμ. Α΄, Ἀθῆναι 1948· τόμ. Β΄, Ἀθῆναι 1954.
— *Ἡ ἑλληνική λαϊκή φορεσιά*, ἐπιμέλεια ἔκδοσης Τ. Ἰωάννου-Γιανναρᾶ, ἔκδ. «Μέλισσα», τόμ. Β΄, Ἀθήνα 1983.
ZORA, P., *Embroideries and Jewellery of Greek National Costumes*, Athens 1981.

Jewellery

ΑΝΤΩΝΙΑΔΗ, Σ.Α., «Πλοῦτος τοῦ ἀστικοῦ πληθυσμοῦ τῆς Κρήτης πρίν ἀπό τό 1669, χρυσοχοΐα», *Πεπραγμένα τοῦ Β΄ Διεθνοῦς Κρητολογικοῦ συνεδρίου*, τόμ. Β΄, Ἀθῆναι 1968.
CHATZIDAKIS, M., "Bijoux des XVIe et XVIIIe siècles rehaussés d'émail et de pierreries", *Collection Hélène Stathatos*, vol. II, Limoges 1957.
DELIVORRIAS, A., *Greek Traditional Jewelry*, Benaki Museum, Athens 1980.
ΠΑΠΑΜΑΝΩΛΗ, Λ., *Τό παραδοσιακό κόσμημα στά Δωδεκάνησα*, ἔκδ. ΕΟΜΜΕΧ, [Ἀθήνα] 1986.
ΠΙΕΡΙΔΟΥ, Α., «Δείγματα νεώτερης Κυπριακῆς Ἀργυροχοΐας», *Κυπριακαί Σπουδαί*, ΚΖ΄ (1963).
ΧΑΤΖΗΜΙΧΑΛΗ, Α., «Ἑλληνική Ἀργυροχοϊκή Τέχνη», *Νέα Ἑστία*, 14 (1933).

Embroideries

ΑΝΑΓΝΩΣΤΟΠΟΥΛΟΥ, Μ.Α., «Παραδοσιακές πετσέτες τῆς Μυτιλήνης», *Μυτιλήνη*, Β΄, (1983) ἀνάτυπο.
ΑΡΦΑΡΑΣ, Μ.Ε., *Ἡ κεντητική καί ὑφαντική τέχνη τῆς Νισύρου*, Ἀθήνα 1984.
Burlington Fine Arts Club, *Catalogue of a collection of old embroideries of the Greek islands and Turkey*, London 1914 (exhibition catalogue).
GENTLES, M., *Turkish and Greek Island Embroideries from the Burton Yost Berry Collection in The Art Institute of Chicago*, Chicago [1964].
JOHNSTONE, P., *Greek Island Embroidery*, London 1961.
— *A guide to Greek island embroidery*, Victoria and Albert Museum, London 1972.
MACMILLAN, S.L., *Greek Islands Embroideries*, Museum of Fine Arts, Boston.
Mediterranean embroideries, lent by professor Alan J.B. Wace, Liverpool Public Museums, Liverpool 1956 (exhibition catalogue).
MONTE SANTO, M., "Il ricamo nelle Meridionali", *Dedalo*, VIII (1930).
PIERIDOU, A.G., *Cyprus embroidery*, Nicosia 1976.
POLYCHRONIADIS, H., *Greek embroideries*, Benaki Museum, Athens 1980.
WACE, A.J.B., *Mediterranean and near eastern embroideries*, London 1935.
— «Broderies grecques des XVIe, XVIIe, XVIIIe siècles», *Collection Hélène Stathatos*, vol. II, Limoges 1957.
WEALE - BADIERITAKI, J.-A., "A new approach to Greek island embroideries", *Ἐθνογραφικά*, 7 (1989).
ΦΑΛΤΑΪΤΣ, Μ., «Σκυριανή κεντητική», *Βόρειοι Σποράδες*, 27 (1972) ἀνάτυπο μέ προσθήκη καί ἄλλων κεντημάτων.
ΦΡΑΓΚΑΚΙ, ΕΥ. Κ., *Ἀπό τήν κεντητική στήν Κρήτη*, Ἀθῆναι 1979.
ΧΑΤΖΗΓΙΑΣΕΜΗ, Α., *Τό λευκαρίτικο κέντημα: Ἱστορική ἐξέλιξη – σχέδια – τεχνική*, Λευκωσία 1987.
ΧΑΤΖΗΜΙΧΑΛΗ, Α., «Μεσογειακά καί Ἐγγύς Ἀνατολῆς κεντήματα, τά ἑλληνικά κεντήματα – Ἤπειρος, Σκύρος», *Byzantinisch – Neugriechische Jahrbücher*, vol. XII (1936) off-print.
— *Κεντήματα τοῦ Τρίκερι*, Ἀθήνα 1951.

Lace

Cinque secoli di merletti europei: I capolavori, Burano 1984 (exhibition catalogue).
IOANNOU-YANNARA, T., *Greek Threadwork*, ed."Melissa", vol. I: *Lace*, Athens 1986; vol. II: *Bobbin Lace*, Athens 1990.

Weaving

ΑΝΑΓΝΩΣΤΟΠΟΥΛΟΥ, Μ.Α., *Τά ὑφαντά τῆς Λέσβου*, Ἀθήνα 1990.
ΒΑΟΣ, Ζ., *Ἡ παραδοσιακή ὑφαντική τῆς Μήλου*, ἔκδ. ΕΟΜΜΕΧ, [Ἀθήνα] 1986.
ΔΗΜΗΤΡΙΟΥ, Ν., «Ἡ ὑφαντική τέχνη στή Σάμο», *Λαογραφία*, ΚΗ΄ (1972).
Λαογραφικό Μουσεῖο Μυκόνου, 30 χρόνια, Ἀναμνηστικό λεύκωμα δήμου Μυκόνου, Μύκονος 1988.
ΣΤΑΘΑΚΗ-ΚΟΥΜΑΡΗ, Ρ., *Τά ὑφαντά τῆς Κρήτης. Διακόσμηση καί σύμβολα*, Ἀθήνα 1987.
Ὑφαντά Νάξου, ἔκδ. ΕΟΜΜΕΧ, [Ἀθήνα] 1982.
ΦΡΑΓΚΑΚΙ, ΕΥ. Κ., *Ἡ λαϊκή τέχνη τῆς Κρήτης. Ὑφαντική καί Βαφική*, τόμ. Γ΄, Ἀθῆναι 1974.
ΧΑΡΒΑΛΙΑΣ, Γ. – ΑΝΤΩΝΟΠΟΥΛΟΥ, Λ., *Τά Κρητικά Ὑφαντά*, ἔκδ. Μουσείου Κρητικῆς Ἐθνολογίας, Ἀθήνα 1986.

Painting

ΚΩΝΣΤΑΝΤΟΥΔΑΚΗ, Μ.Γ., «Οἱ ζωγράφοι τοῦ Χάνδακος κατά τό πρῶτον ἥμισυ τοῦ 16ου αἰῶνος, οἱ μαρτυρούμενοι ἐκ τῶν νοταριακῶν ἀρχείων», *Θησαυρίσματα*, 10 (1973).
— «Μαρτυρίες ζωγραφικῶν ἔργων στό Χάνδακα σέ ἔγγραφα τοῦ 16ου καί τοῦ 17ου αἰῶνα», *Θησαυρίσματα*, 12 (1975).

— «Νέα ἔγγραφα γιά ζωγράφους τοῦ Χάνδακα (ΙΣΤ αἰώνας) ἀπό τά ἀρχεια τοῦ Δούκα καί τῶν Νοταρίων τῆς Κρήτης», *Θησαυρίσματα*, 14 (1977).
ΜΑΡΑΓΚΟΥ, Λ., *Ἀμοργός, Μονή Παναγίας τῆς Χοζοβιώτισσας*, ἔκδ. Ὑπουργείου Αἰγαίου, Ἀθήνα 1988.
ΠΑΛΙΟΥΡΑΣ, Α.Δ., *Ὁ ζωγράφος Γεώργιος Κλόντζας (1540 ci- 1608) καί αἱ μικρογραφίαι τοῦ κώδικος αὐτοῦ*, Ἀθῆναι 1977.
ΣΚΟΠΕΛΙΤΗΣ, Σ.Β., *Ἀρχοντικά τῆς Λέσβου. Τοιχογραφίες*, Ἀθήνα 1977.
ΧΑΤΖΗΔΑΚΗΣ, Μ., *Ἕλληνες ζωγράφοι μετά τήν ἅλωση (1450-1830)*, τόμ. 1, Ἀθήνα 1987.

Pottery

ΒΑΒΥΛΟΠΟΥΛΟΥ-ΧΑΡΙΤΩΝΙΔΟΥ, Α., «Νεοελληνική κεραμική στήν Ἄρτα ἐπί Τουρκοκρατίας», *Ἐθνογραφικά*, 3 (1981-82).
ΔΕΛΗΒΟΡΡΙΑΣ, Α., «Στά χνάρια τῆς παραδοσιακῆς κεραμικῆς τῶν χρόνων τῆς Τουρκοκρατίας», *Ζυγός*, 21 (1976).
— «Γύρω ἀπό τήν ἀντοχή τῆς παράδοσης στή νεοελληνική κεραμική τοῦ ὄψιμου 19ου αἰώνα», *Ἁρμός*, τιμητικός τόμος στόν καθηγητή Ν.Κ. Μουτσόπουλο γιά τά 25 χρόνια πνευματικῆς του προσφορᾶς στό Πανεπιστήμιο, τόμ. Α, Θεσσαλονίκη 1990.
ΚΥΡΙΑΖΟΠΟΥΛΟΣ, Π., *Ἑλληνικά παραδοσιακά κεραμεικά*, ἔκδ. ΕΟΜΜΕΧ, [Ἀθήνα] 1984.
MONTE SANTO, M., "La ceramica di Lindo (Rodi)", *Rivista delle Colonie Italiane*, VII, nos. 6-7 (1929) off-print.
ΝΙΚΟΛΑΚΟΠΟΥΛΟΣ, Γ., *Ἐντοιχισμένα κεραμεικά στίς ὄψεις τῶν μεσαιωνικῶν καί ἐπί τουρκοκρατίας ἐκκλησιῶν μας, Ι. Εἰσαγωγή· ΙΙ. Τά κεραμεικά τῶν Ἁγίων Θεοδώρων*, Ἀθῆναι 1978· *ΙΙΙ. Τά κεραμεικά τῆς Παναγίας τοῦ Μέρμπακα τῆς Ναυπλίας*, Ἀθῆναι 1979· *IV. Τά κεραμεικά τοῦ Καθολικοῦ τῆς Παναγίας τῆς Φανερωμένης τῆς Σαλαμῖνος*, Ἀθῆναι 1980.
ΠΙΕΡΙΔΟΥ, Α.Γ., «Κυπριακή λαϊκή ἀγγειοπλαστική», *Κυπριακαί Σπουδαί*, ΚΔ΄, (1960).
ΤΡΟΥΛΟΣ, Α.Γ., *Ἡ Ἀγγειοπλαστική στό νησί τῆς Σίφνου*, Σίφνος 1991.
ΦΑΛΤΑΪΤΣ, Μ., «Σκυριανή κεραμική», *Βόρειοι Σποράδες*, 29 (1972).
ΧΑΡΙΤΩΝΙΔΟΥ, Α., «Μορφές μεταβυζαντινῆς κεραμικῆς: Ἀθηναϊκά ἐργαστήρια», *Ἀρχαιολογία*, 4 (1982).
ΧΑΤΖΗΔΑΚΗΣ, Μ., «Κεραμουργήματα μέ ἑλληνικές ἐπιγραφές», *Ζυγός*, 16 (1957).
ΨΑΡΟΠΟΥΛΟΥ, ΜΠ., *Τελευταῖοι τσουκαλάδες τοῦ ἀνατολικοῦ Αἰγαίου*, Ναύπλιο χ.χ.

Wood carving

ΒΑΛΛΙΑΝΟΣ, Χ. - ΠΕΡΒΟΛΑΡΑΚΗΣ, Γ. - ΝΕΡΟΛΑΔΑΚΗΣ, Γ., *Τά Κρητικά ἔπιπλα*, ἔκδ. Μουσείου Κρητικῆς Ἐθνολογίας, Ἀθήνα 1986.
HADJIMIHALI, A., "La sculpture sur bois", *Collection de l'Hellènisme Contemporain*, 1950 (= *L'art populaire de la Grèce* II).
ΘΕΜΕΛΗΣ, Π., «Σκύλλα Ἐρετρική», *Ἀρχαιολογική Ἐφημερίς*, (1979).
ΚΟΥΤΕΛΑΚΗΣ, Χ., *Ἡ ἀνάπτυξη τῆς ξυλογλυπτικῆς στό Αἰγαῖο καί ἰδιαίτερα στά Δωδεκάνησα*, Ἀθήνα 1985.
— *Ξυλόγλυπτα τέμπλα τῆς Δωδεκανήσου μέχρι τό 1700*, Ἀθήνα 1986.
ΜΠΙΝΟΣ, Χ., «Ξυλόγλυπτες λεσβιακές κασέλλες», *Ζυγός*, 2 (1965).
ΦΑΛΤΑΪΤΣ, Μ., «Σκυριανή ξυλοτεχνία», *Ἑλληνική Λαϊκή Τέχνη*, 10 (1973).

Stone carving

ΒΑΒΥΛΟΠΟΥΛΟΥ-ΧΑΡΙΤΩΝΙΔΟΥ, Α., *Νεοκυκλαδικά λιθόγλυπτα Λαογραφικοῦ Μουσείου Μυκόνου*, Θεσσαλονίκη 1989.
ΖΩΡΑ, Π., «Συμβολή στήν μελέτη τῆς Ἑλληνικῆς λαϊκῆς γλυπτικῆς», *Ζυγός*, 5 (1966).
ΚΑΡΑΓΑΤΣΗ, Μ., *Λίθινες εἰκόνες τῆς Ἄνδρου*, Ἄνδρος 1990.
ΚΕΦΑΛΛΗΝΙΑΔΗΣ, Ν., «Ἡ μαρμαρογλυφική στή Νάξο», *Ἑλληνική Λαϊκή Τέχνη*, 6 (1972).
ΜΑΘΙΟΠΟΥΛΟΣ, Π., *Πάρος. Ἕνα ἱστορικό νησί στήν καρδιά τοῦ Αἰγαίου*, Ἀθήνα 1963.
ΜΟΥΤΣΑΤΣΟΣ, Γ., *Αὐλόπορτες Κάμπου Χίου*, Χίος 1986.
ΟΡΛΑΝΔΟΣ, Α.Κ., «Οἱ Μεταβυζαντινοί ναοί τῆς Πάρου, Ἡ γλυπτική διακόσμησις», *Ἀρχεῖον τῶν Βυζαντινῶν Μνημείων τῆς Ἑλλάδος*, Θ΄, τχ. 2 (1961).
ΣΤΕΦΑΝΟΥ, Α.Π., *Δείγματα νεοελληνικῆς τέχνης*, Α: *Γλυπτά*, Χίος 1972.
ΦΛΩΡΑΚΗΣ, Α.Ε., *Ἡ λαϊκή λιθογλυπτική τῆς Τήνου*, Ἀθήνα 1979.

48

49

50

51

52

48. Woman from Chios, watercolor. Athens, Benaki Museum, Inv. No 23299.

49. Woman from Lesbos, watercolor. Athens, Benaki Museum, Inv. No 23300.

50. Woman from Tinos, watercolor. Athens, Benaki Museum, Inv. No 23138.

51. Woman from Samos, watercolor. Athens, Benaki Museum, Inv. No 23295.

52. J. Collins. Girl from Paros, watercolor. Athens, Benaki Museum, Inv. No 23074.

53

54

53. J. Collins. Girl from Tinos, watercolor. Athens, Benaki Museum, Inv. No 23071.

54. Artist unknown. Woman from Mykonos, drawing. Athens, Benaki Museum, Inv. No 24015.

55. J. Collins. Girl from Naxos, watercolor. Athens, Benaki Museum, Inv. No 23073.

56. Female costume from Limnos. Athens, National Historical Museum.

57. Female costume from Psara. Athens, National Historical Museum.

58. Female costume from Ios. Athens, National Historical Museum.

59. Female costume from Amorgos. Athens, National Historical Museum.

55

56

57

58

59

61

62

60. Female costume from Lesbos. Athens, Benaki Museum, costume No 115.

61. Female costume from Skiathos. Athens, Benaki Museum, costume No 225.

62. Female costume from Kalamoti, Chios. Athens, Benaki Museum, costume No 192.

63

64

65

63. Female costume from Skopelos. Athens, Benaki Museum, costume No 53.

64. Female costume from Skyros. Athens, Benaki Museum, costume No 46.

65. Female costume from Kymi. Nafplion, Peloponnesian Folklore Foundation.

66

67

68

69

66. Female costume from Andros. Athens, Benaki Museum, costume No 54.

67. Female costume from Symi. Athens, Benaki Museum, costume No 209.

68. Female costume from Nisyros. Athens, Benaki Museum, costume No 112.

69. Female costume from Astypalaia. Athens, Benaki Museum, costume No 95.

70. Female costume from Kastellorizo. Athens, Benaki Museum, costume No 158.

71

73

72

71. Female costume from Kos. Athens, Benaki Museum, costume No 23.

72. Female costume from Kalymnos. Athens, Benaki Museum, costume No 134.

73. Female costume from Karpathos. Athens, Benaki Museum, Inv. No EE 923.

74. "The phelonion of Kassiani". Siphnos, Monastery of the Panayia Vrysiani.

75

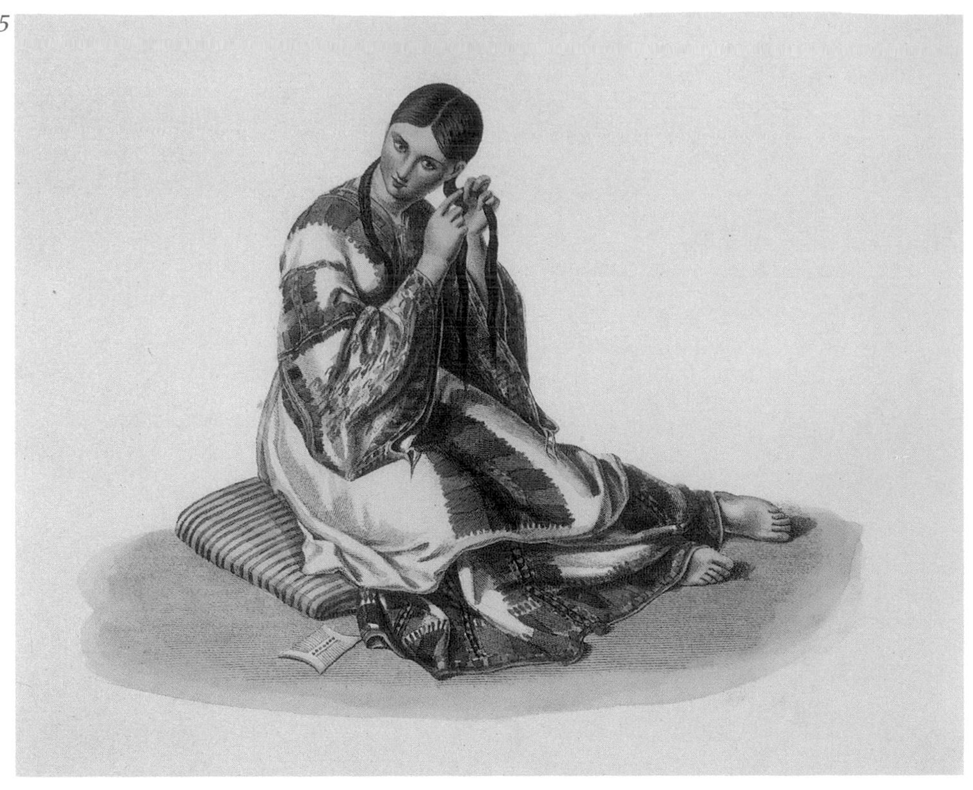

75. O.M. von Stackelberg. Woman of Kassos, engraving.

76. Female dress from Crete. Athens, Benaki Museum, Inv. No EE 872.

77. Detail from the sleeve of a male shirt. Skyros, private collection.

78. Jewellery for the back from Astypalaia. Athens, Benaki Museum, Inv. No Ea 2038.

79. Gold necklace from Crete. Athens, Benaki Museum, Inv. No Ea 470.

80. Jewellery from Kassos. Athens, collection of Isavella Sidirourgou.

76

77

78

79

80

81

82

83

81. Gold necklace from Siphnos. Athens, Benaki Museum, Inv. No 31147.

82. Gold necklace from Siphnos. Athens, collection of Olga Karatza.

83. Gold necklace from Patmos. Athens, Benaki Museum, Inv. No Εχρ. 626.

84. Gold pendant from Patmos. Athens, Benaki Museum, Inv. No 7669.

85. Gold earrings from Siphnos. Athens, Benaki Museum, Inv. No 7670.

86. Gold earrings from Folegandros. Athens, collection of Augi Proukaki.

87. Gold necklace from Crete and gold earrings from Lefkas. Athens, Benaki Museum, Inv. Nos Εχρ. 629, Εχρ. 612.

84

85

86

87

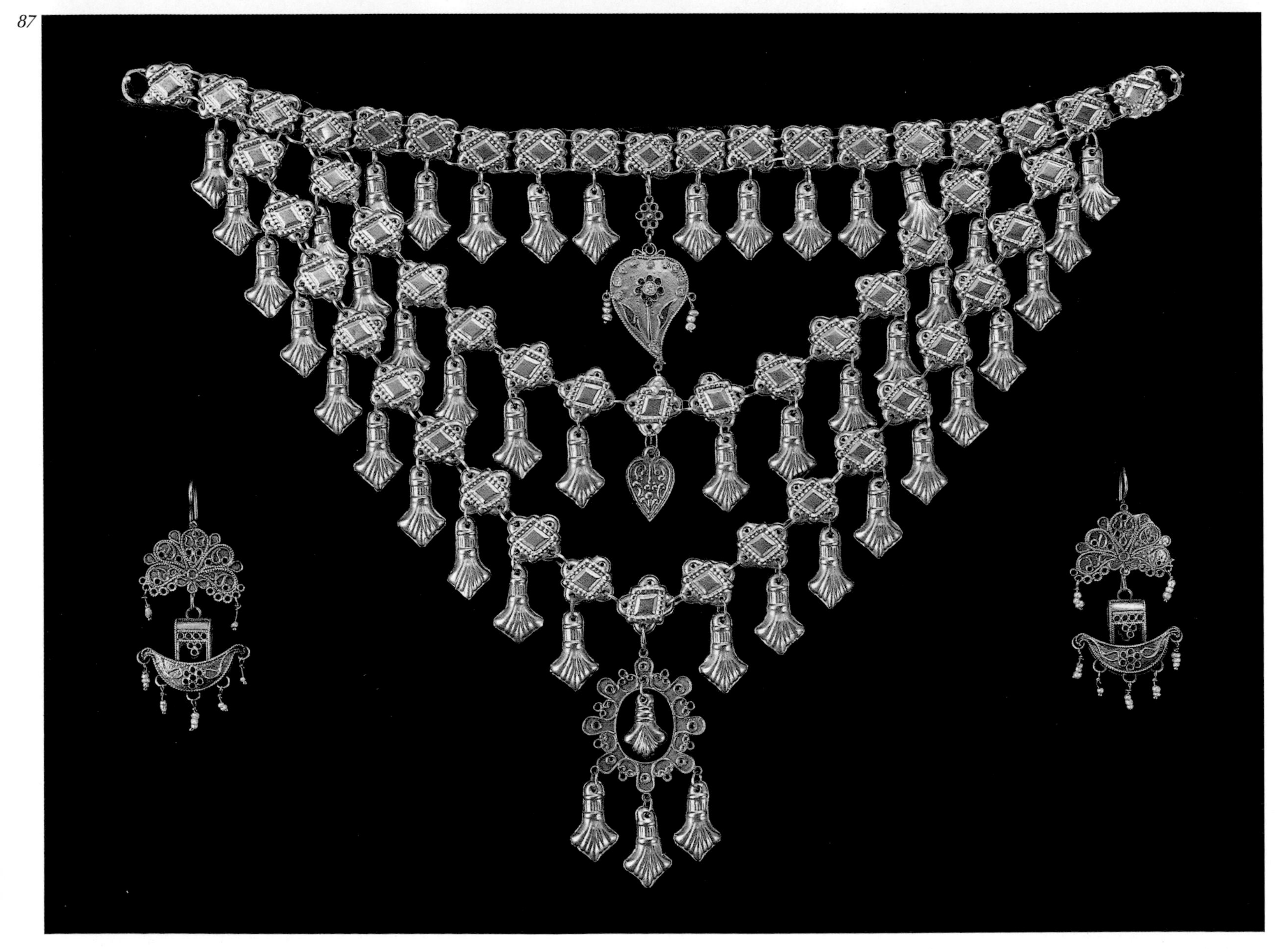

88

90

89

88. Piece of bridal towel from Skyros. Athens, Benaki Museum, Inv. No 11225.

89. Rhodian sperveri. *Athens, Benaki Museum, Inv. No 7650.*

90. Portadela, *central opening of a curtain from Patmos. Athens, Benaki Museum, Inv. No 6654.*

91. Skyrian pillow with a galley. Athens, Benaki Museum, Inv. No 6389.

92

93

94

95

96

92. Sheet from Naxos (detail). Athens, Museum of Greek Popular Art.

93. Bedspread from Naxos. Athens, Benaki Museum, Inv. No 21932.

94. Column cover from Astypalaia. Athens, Benaki Museum, Inv. No 6820.

95. Pillow from Naxos. Athens, Benaki Museum, Inv. No 11299.

96. Pillow from Thasos. Athens, Benaki Museum, Inv. No 11352.

97

98

100

99

97. Embroidery from Asia Minor. Athens, Benaki Museum, Inv. No 6736.

98. Bed-valance from Anafi. Athens, Benaki Museum, Inv. No 6536.

99. Part of gold-embroidered shift from Milos. Athens, Benaki Museum, Inv. No 6518.

100. Curtain border from Siphnos. Athens, Benaki Museum, Inv. No 6526.

101. Border of a white-embroidered sheet (detail). Athens, Benaki Museum, Inv. No 31353.

102. White-embroidered towel from the Cyclades. Athens, Benaki Museum, Inv. No 6570.

103. Herakleion and its harbor, wall painting from the Fasil-bey mansion. Herakleion, Historical Museum.

104

104. G. Klontzas. The destruction of the Turkish fleet at the Naval Battle of Lepanto. Icon. Athens, National Historical Museum.

105

105. Icon with a miracle at sea. Amorgos, Monastery of Panayia Chozoviotissa.

106

107

108

106. Wall painting from the Fasil-bey mansion. Herakleion, Historical Museum.

107. Wall painting from the Fasil-bey mansion. Herakleion, Historical Museum.

108. Wall painting from the Fasil-bey mansion. Herakleion, Historical Museum.

109

110

111

109. Wall painting from the Vareltzidaina mansion. Petra, Lesbos.

110. Fragment of a wall painting from Lesbos. Athens, collection of Peggy Zoumboulaki.

111. Chest lid from Lesbos. Athens, collection of Theodoros Mintzas.

112

113

114

112. Wall painting from the Krallis mansion. Molyvos, Lesbos.

113. Wall painting from the Krallis mansion. Molyvos, Lesbos.

114. Wall painting from the Krallis mansion. Molyvos, Lesbos.

115. Chest lid from Samos. Athens, Benaki Museum, Inv. No 21005.

116. Painted panel of a cupboard. Siphnos, collection of Olga Karatza.

117. Two sections of a chest from Lesbos. Athens, Benaki Museum, Inv. Nos 8908, 8909.

115

116

117

118

118. *The Rebirth of Greece. Painting on wood. Athens, collection of Maria Argyriadi.*

119. *Deuterevon from Siphnos. "Blind Eros Between the Sirens". Icon. Athens, Byzantine Museum.*

120. *Coat of arms of the Municipality of Metylinoi of Samos. Athens, Benaki Museum, Inv. No 25866.*

121. *Painted chest from Lesbos. Athens, Benaki Museum, Inv. No 31165.*

119

120

121

122

123

124

125

122. Section from the wood-panelling of a Rhodian house. Athens, Benaki Museum, Inv. No 8728.

123. Section from the wood-panelling of a Rhodian house. Athens, Benaki Museum, Inv. No 8726.

124. Section from the wood-panelling of a Rhodian house. Athens, Benaki Museum, Inv. No 8727.

125. Painted cupboard from Patmos. Patmos, collection of Euthalia Konstantinidi.

126. Ambataros in the Kourkoulas mansion, Patmos.

127

128

129

127. Jug from Skyros. Athens, Benaki Museum.

128. Basin from the Cyclades. Athens, Benaki Museum, Inv. No 26000.

129. Platter from Siphnos. Athens, Benaki Museum, Inv. No 8643.

131

132

130

130. Vase from Skyros. Athens, Benaki Museum, Inv. No 23615.

131, 132. Small jug with incised decoration from Samos. Athens, Benaki Museum, Inv. No 8646.

133
134
135
136

137

138

139

133, 134. Large jug with incised decoration. Athens, Benaki Museum, Inv. No 8682.

135, 136. Large jug with an incised representation of a dance. Athens, Benaki Museum, Inv. No 31355.

137. Carved wooden mylospervero *from Rhodes. Athens, Benaki Museum, Inv. No 8907.*

138. Carved wooden souvantza *from Cyprus (detail). Nicosia, Folk Art Museum.*

139. Kanaveta, *painted chest from Skyros. Athens, Benaki Museum, Inv. No 8719.*

140

141

142

143

140. Carved wooden armchair from the Cyclades. Athens, Benaki Museum, Inv. No 21181.

141. Carved wooden armchair from the Cyclades. Athens, Benaki Museum, Inv. No 21182.

142. Carved wooden lamp-stand. Athens, Benaki Museum, Inv. No 21952.

143. Carved wooden armchair from Crete. Athens, Benaki Museum, Inv. No 21180.

144. Figurehead from the "Themistoklis", the sailing ship of Chatziyiannis Mexis. Athens, National Historical Museum.

144

145

146

147

148

145. Lintel with inscribed rosettes, Crete.

146. Low relief fanlight from Tinos. Athens, Byzantine Museum.

147. Lintel with coat-of-arms from Pyrgi, Chios.

148. Built-in relief in the Leriotis residence (formerly Cappari). Kambos, Chios.

149

150

151

149. Reliefs on the bell tower of the Panayia Tourliani church. Anomera, Mykonos.

150. The fountain of the Panayia Tourliani church. Anomera, Mykonos.

151. Door frame in the Folklore Museum of Mykonos.

152. Door frame in the house of Sophia Petrou Theologitou. Chora, Amorgos.

ANASTASIOS TZAMTZIS

Shipping, a brief consideration through the ages

Translated by Philip Ramp

When did the people who inhabited the coasts and the islands of the Aegean begin to communicate with each other via the sea? The answer to this question, at least with the facts at hand, is exceptionally difficult. In all his actions, primitive man took his most important steps toward progress and civilization before he began to leave behind anything that would, in some way, record what he had done. For example, human beings discovered how to make fire, how to sow wheat and to harvest it, and how to manufacture tools and weave mats, but they only wrote about these things much later on. Thus it is up to us to speculate about primitive man's way of life and his work, based on the remains and the fragments left behind which have been found by archeologists, either buried in the places where these people lived or sunken in the sea. But based on only these elements we would be able to present this way of life in nothing more than a partial and incohesive manner. The early shipping and navigation we are interested in, is no exception to this rule.

Prehistoric Shipping in the Aegean

Sea communications in the Aegean date back to the Neolithic period. This period used to be described by specialists "as a period of simple farming life, where several independent communities were fashioned into villages, and where people lived in practically complete isolation"[1]. But today, after the latest archeological finds, "there is clear evidence which confirms the existence of extensive trade in raw materials in the Aegean from the beginning of the Neolithic period"[2].

Everyone has now accepted that we were mistaken in assuming that the primitive farmers were static peoples, rooted to a piece of land, as is the case with many later farming communities.

The first exchanges in the Aegean world seem to have had obsidian as their object. This volcanic glass, so esteemed by prehistoric man, with its sharp edges caused by breakage, is one of the most valuable indications of the early sea voyages. It is now certain that the first positive testimony concerning the existence of shipping in the world is given to us by the obsidian from prehistoric Greece.

The Aegean has only three sources of obsidian and all three of them are on islands. The first is on Milos, from the Nychia quarry, another is on the other side of the same island, at Demenegaki and the third is on Antiparos. Finally, there is a considerable variety of obsidian at Gyiali, near Nisyros, but very little information as to whether it was locally exploited before the Bronze Age. Outside Greece, obsidian can be found in Turkey, Hungary, Czechoslovakia and the Lipari islands near Sicily.

Obsidian artifacts have been uncovered in many of the early Neolithic settlements in Greece, such as blades that were used as knives and scrapers. Obsidian has been found in the Neolithic pre-ceramic layers of the important Neolithic settlement of Seskio in Thessaly and the same is true of Argissa, Soufli Magoula and many other settlements in the region. Pieces of obsidian were also found in many of the Neolithic settlements of southern Greece and even, in small quantities, in regions far to the north, such as Nea Nicomedia in Macedonia.

At Knossos, obsidian tools were found in the lowest layers of the Neolithic period, when pottery was not yet being made. These finds chronologically correspond to the period before 6500 B.C.

There are numerous repercussions from these verifications but what is of interest in our case is that we now have a positive indication concerning the image of the oldest sea trade in the world: "...not only in the Aegean, but in the western Mediterranean and the Near East we have categorical indications of sea voyages over long distances... Perhaps even more important is the fact that these voyages were taken by the inhabitants of mainland Greece to Milos during the earliest Neolithic times (6000 - 5200 B.C.) which pre-supposes a previous knowledge of the existence of the material. We do not know precisely how they learned of the existence of obsidian on Milos for the first time, but it must have been during voyages taken for other reasons, or perhaps in search of something like it. This in its turn brings us, in some manner, to the conclusion that there were controlled sea voyages"[3].

But the most surprising thing of all are the finds of obsidian which were discovered in the Mesolithic layers of the Phragchthi cave in Argolida, dated to around 8000 B.C. The indication that obsidian was transported by sea from Milos to Phragchthi during such an ancient period is astonishing. Milos is about 70 miles from the cave by sea. Furthermore, these two-way voyages must have been made many times, because the Milos obsidian appears in successive layers. Experts now believe that "the obsidian at Phragchthi can be considered as the oldest positive indication of the transport of goods by sea, in any part of the world"[4].

This discovery is of enormous importance. This makes it clear that sailors crossed the Aegean and arrived at Milos to obtain obsidian long before 7000 B.C., that is, before the beginning of agricultural life.

So today obsidian constitutes the first and surest indication of the extent of contacts between the inhabitants of the various regions of Greece before 6000 B.C. with the emphasis on sea communications.

However, the Mesolithic finds from Phragchthi also present something else of interest: they show that the existence of obsidian is not the only proof of a knowledge of the sea. From the oldest layers, it appears that the inhabitants of the cave were hunters who lived chiefly on deer meat. But later, in the layers with obsidian, a large number of fish bones appear. Obviously by the 7th millennium B.C. these people had become fishermen and had grown so familiar with the sea as to travel to Milos.

The above conclusions bring archeologists face to face with a problem. What kind of craft did these first sailors of the Aegean use to transport obsidian from the islands to mainland Greece? What were they made of or, at least, what form did they have or what did they look like? The answers to these questions are purely conjectural since we have to go forward quite a few thousand years, specifically to 2000-1500 B.C., to find the earliest depictions or models of ships which give us some idea of what these primitive vessels may have looked like.

1. Reed raft (drawing by I. Pantazopoulos). Institute for the Preservation of Nautical Tradition.

A consideration of these later representations and a study of the primitive vessels in general have led us to the conclusion that these vessels must have been dug-out canoes or something similar. But if we accept this, a new problem arises. The tools that were found in the cave are the typical microlithic ones, that is, it would be difficult to use them to build something like a dug-out canoe. The problem as to how easy or difficult it would be to build a dug-out canoe with an assortment of microlithic tools is not one of those that has been solved.

There is, however, another view. Namely, that these first sailors used a kind of vessel made of reeds tied together. This type of boat is the easiest to make of all the primitive craft, since only very simple tools are required. The use of such craft in Egypt and Mesopotamia, where there was an abundance of reeds and a lack of wood, is well-known. But craft that are constructed in this manner are of limited potential. If they are too long, they break in half during bad weather or when heavily loaded. They have almost no sides and overturn easily in a storm. Consequently, they are primarily meant for rivers and not the sea. Despite all that, there is little doubt that for the transport of valuable cargo both in Mesopotamia and Egypt, these boats were the most important means of transport.

Recently (1989) such a craft was built by the Institute for the Preservation of Nautical Tradition and on one voyage of experimental archeology it travelled from Lavrion to Milos with relative success (ills. 1, 26, 27).

Minoans and Mycenaeans

Thucydides, in his history[5] of the Cretans during the Minoan period, notes: "Minos, as we learn from oral tradition, was the first to acquire a naval fleet, which ruled the largest part of the Greek sea"[6] and later Strabo adds, "There are legends of the thalassocracy of Minos and the sea-faring Phoenicians". These observations by Thucydides and Strabo have been confirmed by archeological finds. The merchants of Minoan Crete appeared to have played an important role in the international spirit which developed because of trade during the period of the XII Egyptian Dynasty (1999-1786 B.C.). The vases of the Middle Minoan II period (1800-1700 B.C.) travelled as far as Byblos and Ras Shamra on the Syrian coast, to northern Cyprus and to Qatna on the river Orontes, as well as to Egyptian towns. At the same time, the excavations on Crete revealed Egyptian statues and Egyptian scarabei, Cretan commercial contacts with the Middle East were further confirmed when the archives of ancient Babylon, written in cuniform, were read.

Cretan naval activity is depicted better than anywhere else in the lavishly decorated tombs of Egyptian Thebes. Among the painted representations the processions of foreigners bearing valuable gifts to Egypt, almighty at that time, stand out; among these appear the "Keftiou". The "Keftiou" are wearing Minoan clothes and offering metal vessels, *rhyta* in the shape of animal heads, metal inpigs or bolts of expensive cloth.

The foodstuffs and raw materials exported from Minoan Crete to Egypt appear to have been olive oil, olives, wine and perhaps raisins and certainly timber, more specifically cypress. Sesame was one of the odder things exported from Greece to Egypt where it was used to make bread. Sesame from Greece was found at El Assasif in Thebes and in the tombs of the Middle Dynasty.

The long-term education of the youth of Crete in athletic competitions and naval matters led it to being the ruler of the sea and to having contacts not only with the East but also with mainland Greece. Of all the Cretan towns, Knossos, for around three generations, had the closest relations with the Greek Peloponnese. It was the best harbor on the north coast of Crete facing Greece and it developed regular communications with it, using Kythera, Milos and Aegina as intermediary stations. Mycenae and, to a lesser degree, Pylos, appear to have been the towns that were regularly visited. The Cretans of Knossos and the Greeks definitely shared mutual interests which appear to have been based on profit. Crete offered its advanced technology, luxury goods and an extensive knowledge of Egyptian commerce and the harbors of the eastern Mediterranean. Mainland Greece, in return, offered horses, soldiers and a variety of other assistance to Cretan enterprise. Intermarriage between Knossos and Mycenae must be considered probable.

The Cyclades also developed commercial relations with Crete and mainland Greece. There is a good deal of evidence that the peoples were not strangers to each other in origin and civilization and it appears that they could communicate without interpreters in their commercial or piratical exchanges. Cycladic handicraft production must have been extremely good and the islanders would certainly have looked forward to spring, the season when the voyages began. Cycladic products could be found all the way from Bulgaria to Crete and from Troy to the Dalmatian coast and Sicily. Some weapons and ornaments must have passed through many hands before they reached their final tomb, where they were uncovered by archeologists. What the sailor-merchants from the islands brought back is not so clear. Their tombs contain practically nothing that could have come from abroad. Perhaps they brought back pure copper from Cyprus, zinc from the Black Sea for bronze alloys, cloth and meat from Crete and wheat from mainland Greece.

One should not think that a fleet of Cycladic merchant ships (ill. 28) were waiting for spring to set off. The voyages appear to have been unconnected to each other. Two or three local shipowners, using their family or some of the poorer farmers as their crew, either went up to Aegina or down to Mochlos with the few things they had produced over the winter. These handmade articles were those attractive household items that are today found buried in the earth, such as frying pans, small clay or marble vessels with covers, trays and flasks, figurines and pins, obsidian, copper and silver wares. The jewellery and the tools were loaded in their final form but the pieces of obsidian and the ore from which metal was extracted were probably loaded in their original form, to be processed by the buyers – or in accordance with their wishes – by the sailors-craftsmen while the customers waited on the shore. This custom of sailors-craftsmen seems to have been in force throughout the Bronze Age.

After 1460 B.C., the Mycenaeans, who appear to have ruled Crete, carried on the naval tradition of the island and because the center of their power was further west, in mainland Greece, they conducted their sea trade even further away in the Mediterranean, going beyond Sicily to Marseilles and the Spanish coast.

The Mycenaeans even appear to have capably replaced the Cretans, in the period 1400-1200 B.C., in the commercial relations between Ugarit and Minoan Crete. The tombs in the harbor (Minet el Beida) proved to be full of Mycenaean vessels.

During the early Mycenaean period, captains and merchants must have travelled to the Lipari islands and southern Italy in the west, to Troy and Syria in the east and Egypt and Palestine in the south. In all the areas where examples of Mycenaean trade were found, it is clear that the contacts were limited to the coastal regions and a few rivers in the interior. It is very unusual to find Mycenaean objects deep in the hinterland.

This emphatically shows that these objects arrived there via the sea lanes. The cargo that was exported consisted principally of the marvellously worked Mycenaean vases that

2

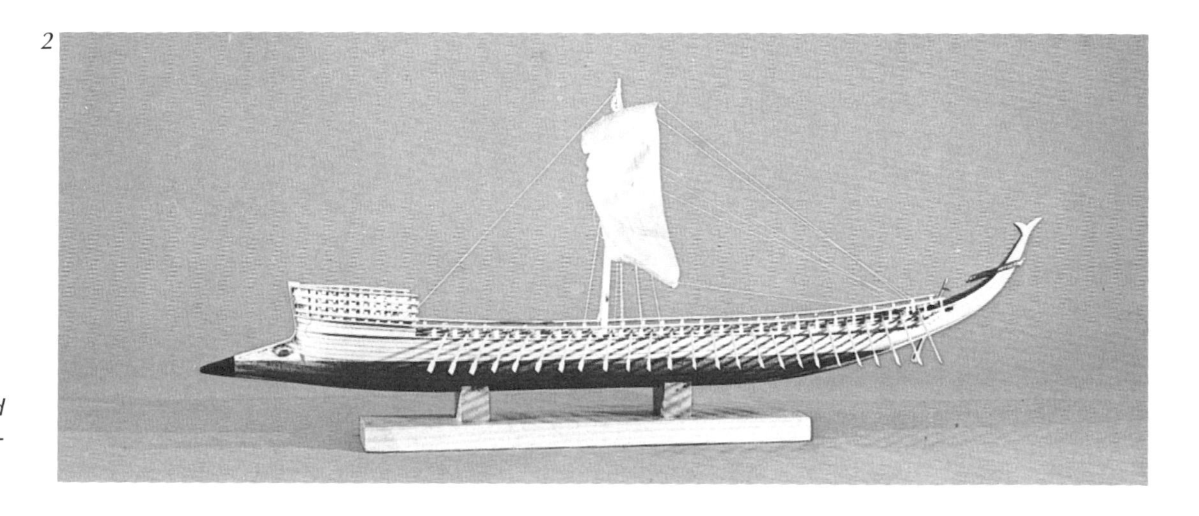

2. Model of penteconter from the period of colonization. Pireaus, Hellenic Maritime Museum.

were used for the transport of olive oil. There were also painted kraters and phiales for the luxury market, cast bronze weapons, especially swords and daggers and frequently craftsmen to make the clay (ill. 34) or bronze objects abroad, in the colonies that had set up there. Other items that were exported, though difficult for archeology to track down, must have included Greek wine, textiles, finished timber and even mercenaries.

The items that the Mycenaean ships brought back to their country were bronze, zinc and wine from Hanaan, women and copper from Cyprus, silver and perhaps horses and purple-dyed fabrics from the coast of Palestine and small porcelain objects, alabaster and gold direct from Egypt or from the towns along the eastern Mediterranean.

Trade with the West took on larger proportions with the Mycenaeans, as is shown by the remnants of vases and other archeological finds. The islands known as the Lipari are rich in obsidian and Liparian obsidian was found in abundance in the Mycenaean necropolises. Metal from Tuscany also played a role in Mycenaean sea transport, but to a lesser degree than that played by the metals from the East.

Besides the metals, many valuable articles were imported which were destined for royal or ritual treasures – as is shown by the tablets which have survived – or for the tombs of the wealthy. Of course, it is not easy to determine how vital sea trade was for Mycenaean life. The articles that were imported – Egyptian scarabs, wine jugs from Hanaan, gold and semi-precious stones from the East, zinc and rhyolite from the West – show these were not things that were used by people living in straitened circumstances.

In the tholos tomb of Mycenean IV, circle D, where three men and two women were found buried, the offerings are international in origin: ostrich eggs from Nubia – which must have found their way there from Egypt and Cyprus – lapis lazuli from Mesopotamia, alabaster and porcelain from Crete, unprocessed ivory from Syria, silver from the East, amber from Prussia – which arrived via the Adriatic or from Odessa. But no one can maintain that luxury items were the principal imports. The quantity of vases that have been found abroad shows that the ships were constantly traversing the eastern Mediterranean. One could even conjecture that the main imported item was, in reality, something perishable, like wheat.

If the vases constitute a guide as to where the Mycenaeans went then, it appears they travelled no further west that Ischia, the island in the bay of Naples.

When were these sea voyages made? Hesiod was briefly occupied with the question

3

3. Relief of the stern of a boat, carved in a rock. Base of a bronze statue, probably a work by the Rhodian sculptor Pythocritos, 180 B.C. Rhodes, Acropolis of Lindos.

of shipping and mentions the days when nature is in the mood to cooperate with the hard-working sailor. "During winter it is not possible to work at sea. When winter is approaching it is best for one to haul his boat on to dry land and keep it safe behind a wall, to open the stopcock so that water will not collect in the hold, to bring the rigging, the sails and the rudder in and for the sailor to await the return of good weather. When the good weather returns, the commercial sailor can resume his activity. Spring is another favorable, though brief, period for sea voyages"[7].

Colonization

In tandem with the first naval ventures of the inhabitants of the Aegean coasts, the first attempts at colonization also took place.

The naval dominance of Crete was expressed through a chain of towns which, not to mention the Cyclades and mainland Greece, were founded on the coasts of Syria, Palestine, Cyprus and Sicily. Ancient traditions place Minoan settlements in Cilicia and Lycia, Troy and Asia Minor.

In the myths of Heracles and the Argonauts one sees these voyagers founding towns in the Mediterranean and the Black Sea.

During historical times the first wave of colonization is observed around the end of the 12th century B.C.; the second was from the beginning of the 8th century B.C., and was followed by the one which established the dominance of Aegean shipping throughout the Mediterranean and even outside it. Led by Athens, Megara, Corinth, Chalkis from the metropolitan Greece, Phocaia, Smyrna and, above all, Miletus from the Asia Minor colonies, the Greeks spread out toward all the coasts of the Mediterranean and the Black Sea.

Colonies were founded on both banks of the Hellespont, in Propondis, the Bosporus and on all the coasts of the Black Sea, to the innermost part of the Sea of Azov. As Plato spoke of it: "The Greeks settled there like frogs around a swamp"[8].

Another group of colonists built along the Balkan coastline of the Adriatic. Southern Italy was so densely colonized that its was called "Magna Grecia".

The inhabitants of the Aegean were impelled to colonize for the following reasons: the defeat of a political faction which forced them to expatriate themselves as well as the over-population which as Plato observed: "...one race, leaving one country, settles elsewhere [...] forced out by lack of space..."[9].

But the principal motive was the development of merchant shipping activity. In both of the aforementioned cases the founding of the colony would have been the result of economic-political pressures, but the aim always remained the securing of the means of life through the maritime commerce.

The ship (ill. 2) was the same that was used for the founding of the colony; the ship was the umbilical cord with the homeland and the outside world. This is proven by the fact that the colonies were built along the coasts and their colonization was the work of maritime towns. Conversely, all the colonial towns which were able to develop and become prominent achieved this because they turned toward the sea and maritime commerce. Chios, Samos, Miletus, Phocaia, Ephesus and Rhodes among the oldest and Byzantium, Sinopi, Syracuse, Marseilles and Alexandria, among the newest, were large, perhaps the largest, maritime centers.

The creation of a commercial depot usually preceded colonization. These were installations that were built on the shore or on islands at a short distance from the coast

4

4. Silver four drachma coin from Alexandria, of Nero era, 54-68 A.D. On one side is a depiction of a grain ship of the period. The inscription ΣΕΒΑ[ΣΤΟΦΟΡΟΣ] can be seen. Mykonos, Aegean Maritime Museum.

where the sailors came into contact with the locals for the purpose of exchanging their goods.

These commercial depots were called "emporeia" and if their locations proved to be suitable and the harbor productive then the "emporeion" was extended into a colony.

The installations in these "emporeia" had the servicing of the ship and the sailors as their primary aim. Shipsheds and warehouses (arcades) were built in the "emporeion" for the collection of goods; structures were also built where the crew could spend the night, for the ancient ships offered few comforts for an overnight stay. A historian characterizes them as "structures by the sea built to receive ships when they were not at sea".

Starting in 800 B.C. and in the centuries which followed, the naval activity of the Greek population who inhabited the coasts and the Aegean islands increased. The Black Sea, the Aegean, the Mediterranean, the Persian Gulf, the Red Sea and even the Indian Ocean were continually traversed by numerous vessels which in the beginning connected the Classical world and later the Hellenistic. Down through the centuries which preceded Roman suzerainty, the Greek commercial push led to the creation of large shipping centers.

The products of the earth and human craft moved both to and from the homeland to the colonial ports. The wheat from the Black Sea and Sicily reached the inhabitants of the Greek towns and islands as far away as Marseilles. Dried fruits and nuts, legumes, leather, wool, timber and metals were the most common cargo on Greek ships. The various kinds of pottery travelled to all parts of the then known world. Greek pottery was produced in enormous quantities as it was used not only for household needs, but also to pack up or store olive oil, olives, legumes, wheat, wine and so on. The renowned Greek amphorae were the equivalent of contemporary "containers" for sea transport. Nearly all the cargo on the ships was transported in amphorae.

Interest was centered on two principal cargos: wine and wheat. The former was exported and the latter was imported into Greece from the colonies. The wine usually came from Chalcidice, Chios, Kos, Thasos, and elsewhere. The wheat was principally imported from the Black Sea (Cimmerian Bosporus) and Sicily. As soon as summertime began hundreds of ships set out from the harbors of the Crimea with loads of wheat for Pireaus. In Athens, strict laws were used to regulate the trade in wheat, its distribution by the wheat merchants and even the selling of bread. The Black Sea, together with Syracuse, was the largest granary of classical Greece.

It is worth noting the revival of the festivals on Delos in honor of Apollo. The initiative was originally taken by Peisistratos who endeavored to make the festivals occasions for commercial exchanges (ill. 29). This was eventually realized after the Median Wars. In 475 B.C. the Athenians founded the Amphictyony of Delos, in which the towns allied with Athens participated. This resulted in heavy maritime activity being centered on Delos until it developed into an international maritime transit station active until 69 B.C. when it was utterly destroyed by pirates.

In 408 B.C. the three Rhodian towns, Lindos, Ialysos and Kameiros, founded the town of Rhodes giving a powerful impulse to their own maritime activity while at the same time becoming crucial factors in the shipping trade between the western and the eastern Mediterranean (ill. 33). The town of Rhodes occupied a very convenient site. The ships that passed by were frequently obliged to spend the winter there, while others came there to unload or load. Thus, Rhodes developed into a port of refuge and center of transit trade. Rhodes flourished throughout the 4th and the 3th century B.C. Its decline occurred quickly when in 169 B.C. Delos was proclaimed a free harbor.

Classical Period

During the classical period the harbor of Pireaus was the center of all maritime activity in the Aegean.

In the commercial harbor, the "Emborio" ("Trade") there were five "stoas", that is, warehouses but with a different meaning than the present one because they were not only used for the storage of goods; the necessary negotiations were also conducted there for the buying and selling of the various goods which arrived from all the eastern Mediterranean and the Black Sea. The famous Makra Stoa was there as well as the "Deigma" ("Sample") which had been founded to facilitate foreign merchants in displaying the goods they had brought, principally wheat and wine. The wine merchants from Chios, Thasos and other wine producing areas brought samples of their products there. At the same time the merchants of Athens brought samples of their handicrafts that were for export. In this space set aside for merchants' negotiations, one also encountered bankers, eager to make loans with the ship or the cargo as a guarantee, something which during the 4th century made the port the main axis of maritime activity in the Aegean and caused Pericles to say with great pride: "Because our town is large, all the goods from all over the world are imported to it, and thus we can enjoy the goods that were produced by others as if they were our own"[10].

Besides the wheat which came to the port, we have information that other articles were offered for buying and selling as well, such as "stamnoi" with Attican olive oil or honey, empty vases painted in the familiar Athenian style, destined for export, "amphorae" with wine which were imported from Asia Minor, salted or dried fish from Byzantium and the Cimmerian Bosporus and timber and pitch from Macedonia for the shipyards and buildings.

Athenaeus tells us that in the harbor of Piraeus one could find "plants and cow hides from Cyrene, mackerel and all kinds of salted fish from the Hellespont, legs and sides of beef from Thessaly, pork and cheese from Syracuse, sails for the ships and papyrus from Egypt and incense from Syria, huge cypress logs from Crete, ivory from Libya, raisins and sweet dried figs from Rhodes... and so on"[11].

Hundreds of merchants of all sizes thronged to the arcades and this is where the moneychangers also set up their little tables to exchange the Persian dariens, the staters from Cyzicus or Sicilian coins for the Athenian silver tetradrachma coins stamped with the old image of Athena and her owl which throughout its entire acme Athens kept as a symbol of the strongest currency of that period.

From April on there was ceaseless movement in the Aegean with Piraeus as its center. When October came round and the bad weather began the period for voyages also ended. The moneychangers gathered up their tables, the foreign captains went back to their lands, the shipowners hauled their boats on to dry land or secured them to the piers and the stevedores went back to town. Like a summer theater maritime activity came to a halt and the harbors closed waiting for the following spring.

Roman Period

After the Roman domination of the Aegean and the fall of pre-Christian Hellenism, which coincided with the death of the last Greek king of central Asia, Ermaios – conquered by the Parthians – and the capture at the same time of that most Greek of cities, Alexandria, by Octavius and the torching of Corinth by Ceasar, one would expect that

5

5. Depiction of a ship on a Byzantine plate from 1200-1300. Corinth, Archeological Museum.

the maritime power of the Greeks would have disappeared for the 400 years of Roman occupation.

But exactly the opposite occurred. First, because the Greek maritime network (colonies, "emporeia") never ceased to exist and second because the Romans showed little inclination for the sea and as Polyvius observed: "They never thought about the sea, they first found themselves at sea" very slowly and specifically when it was necessary to confront Carthage and third because the large-scale provisioning and the other needs of the Roman Empire impelled the conquerors to seek out the Greeks who were specialists in maritime endeavors.

Thus, a happy combination of a variety of factors contributed to the preservation of the Greek dynamic on the sea, to the point where the many Roman shipowners would undergo true hellenization, taking refuge in Greek commercial centers such as Delos, Pireaus and Alexandria in order to avail themselves of the experience and the knowledge of Greek shipmasters.

The large grain freighters (ill. 4), which went back and forth between Egypt, the Black Sea and Puteoli or Puzzuoli, the harbor of Rome, had mainly Greek crews. The "Socii Navalis", that is, the sailors' alliances, was a stereotypical phrase in general use for the crews of every ship. Rhodes, Pergamon and other towns allied with Rome, supplied the crews for the Roman ships.

Let it be further noted that the boat building industry continued to be in large part in Greek hands. And even with the passage of time, when the investment of the Romans in sea transport took on a more serious character, shipbuilding orders were by preference given to Greek shipyards (which had been set up, primarily, along the coast of southern Italy) because of the excellent reputation they enjoyed.

The events during the second half of the Roman Empire heralded its approaching end. Civil wars, disturbances, social re-alignments and, finally, barbarian invasions, led to its dissolution, so that Hellenism again came to the fore in a new form, the Byzantine, which because of its naval tradition carried on the maritime works, both in the Aegean and the Mediterranean in general.

Byzantium

During the early Byzantine period the Aegean continued to play the most crucial role in the area of sea transport. Constantinople became an important commercial harbor. Shipping was conducted freely, particularly after Justinian's victories over the Vandals and the Goths. Byzantine merchant ships transported their cargo to the harbors of the West, while until the founding of Constantinople the Italians sent their ships to seek out and transport the products of the East to the harbors there or to Delos, which during the early Byzantine period was a kind of free port. Delos, besides its panhellenic holiness derived from the Temple of Apollo, was clearly a transit station, with harbors, wharfs, warehouses and shipowners societies. The Assembly of the Hermaistians, the Assembly of the Poseidoniastians of Beirut, the Society of the Apolloniastians or the shipowners of Tyre were nothing more than commercial and shipowning unions on the large, commercial center of Delos.

The dissolution of the Vandal's state in 548 and the dominance of the Goths in Italy made the Mediterranean secure for shipping. With Constantinople as the center, the ships went both beyond Gibraltar and to the East, to the shores of Syria and Egypt. Under Justinian one finds sea transport in full bloom, and frequently this was conducted by

6

6. Byzantine ship passing through the Hellespont. Illuminated manuscript from the 13th century.

ships of the line on yearly voyages. The "gallodromoi" carried out transport to French ports, the "spanodromoi" to the harbors of Spain while other ships headed for the Italian ports.

In the 7th century (634-638) the Arabs conquered Syria and Egypt. For that reason trade with the West, which was conducted from Syrian harbors and Alexandria, was hurt while conversely Constantinople profited. The commercial fleet of the Syrians was destroyed and trade in the eastern Mediterranean passed into Greek hands. The merchandise of the east was no longer sent to Syrian ports but to the harbors of Asia Minor and the Aegean as well as Trebizond on the Black Sea. In essence, the Black Sea was a closed sea and, as was natural, the Arab conquests did not influence the harbor of Trebizond which developed into the main port in the East. Transit merchandise was transported from there in Greek ships to Constantinople from where it was forwarded to its destination.

From the time of Justinian's reign (527 A.D.), certain maritime privileges were made into law, such as the privilege of the seller of the ship for its price and the lender for its construction or outfitting. The protection of the lender contributed to a preference for his satisfaction in the case where there was a throng of lenders; it was recognized as a special privilege with a pledge for all those who made expenditures for the repairs of a ship[12].

Justinian legislation also recognized the maritime loan (foenus nauticum) which was almost identical to the "maritime loans" of ancient Greek Law; this protected whomever used capital for maritime loans, for the purpose of strengthening the merchant marine of Athens and Pireaus. The sailors, "sea-worthies" ("ploimoi") as they were called then, were exempt from certain taxes.

Along with the regulations related to shipping found in the "Pandects" ("Digest of Justinian") and the "Basilica", the famous Rhodian Maritime Law was also applied from the 8th century on; this consisted of a collection of naval customs which were in force on the coasts of the eastern Mediterranean. This collection is considered to be the oldest

7. Byzantine ship. Pala Paolo Veneziano, 1345. Venice, Museo Marciano, Basilica of Saint Mark.

8. The dream of Saint Mark, mosaic, 13th century. Venice, Basilica of Saint Mark.

7

8

codification of Private Maritime Byzantine Law. It was divided into three parts. The first was the introduction, the second contained administrative regulations and the third included the legislative provisions which dealt with commercial shipping.

A key part of this law was the introduction of the institution of general average, that is, the share in the damage arising from the sea dangers to the ship, the cargo and the freight, an institution still in force today, practically unchanged. This codification was valid until the fall of the Byzantine Empire while starting in the 12th century the regulations of the so-called "Assizes" became valid, regarding relations created by sea trade, regulating the movement of commercial shipping in all the seas of the Mediterranean.

At the beginning of the 9th century, the emperor Nikephoros founded a kind of Maritime Bank in Constantinople, which lent every recognized captain or shipowner of Constantinople up to 12 gold pounds, with a charge of four "cerats" on the gold currency "...the official assemblies of shipowners in Constantinople are to be lent at a rate of 4 cerats the amount of 12 gold pounds, along with the usual customs duty..."[13], as Theophanes mentions (the cerats were a weight equal to the core of a carob tree fruit; they are what were later called carats, which showed the degree of purity of the gold in a given mixture).

When in 1081 Alexios I Comnenus ascended the throne of Byzantium, the state was nearly in disintegration, something which forced the emperor, through a gold bull published in May 1082, to recognize certain maritime privileges accorded to the Venetian colony in Constantinople, which was already heavily populated and flourishing. He then ceded to the Venetians an entire section of the harbor of Peran, with its wharfs, workshops, warehouses and so on. But the most important thing is that this type of ceding, a kind of "free zone", also occurred in other towns of the state where it was stipulated that the Venetians could sell or buy without paying any customs duty or harbor tax.

This strategy of ceding maritime privileges was continued, and in 1112 Alexios ceded similar privileges to the merchants and sailors of Pisa. Forty six years later similar privileges were ceded to the Genoese (1152-1158).

9

9. N. Kaloyeropoulos, "Byzantine dromon". Pireaus, Hellenic Maritime Museum.

The internal misfortunes, in combination with the ceding of privileges to the Italian cities, led to the merchant marine falling into foreign hands and in the end the definitive dissolution of the empire.

The ceding of the Aegean islands to the Latins constituted the main cause for the halt in all shipping progress in this area, because the Aegean islands, this broadest of Greek maritime areas, came for many years to constitute the "apple of discord" between the Latins and the Turks. The result of these clashes between the two belligerents – in which the inhabitants of the islands were forcibly conscripted, first on one side and then on the other – was an uninterrupted draining of the islands of their male population.

At the same time, the successive pirate raids also drained the islands of men and the women who were left, were sent to the slave markets of the East and to North Africa.

The Aegean islands were looted and destroyed long before the Fall of Constantinople and one can only wonder how they managed to avoid utter devastation.

The first large-scale destruction on the islands took place in 1247, after their conquest by the Franks, when the Byzantine emperor of Nicaea, Ioannis Vatatzis, in his endeavor to liberate the islands occupied by the Venetians, destroyed the largest part of the commercial ships of the Aegean fleet which were in the compulsory service of the Venetians.

The clashes between the continually warring Byzantines and Westerners, as well as the pirate raids, continued at the same pace until the first half of the 15th century.

In 1453 Constantinople fell into the hands of the Turks. The Archipelago suffered fresh attacks and the unfortunate Aegean islanders prepared for new tribulations.

During the period of the early years of the Turkish occupation, up to the beginning of the 18th century, the Aegean was a theater of battle between the Turks and the Westerners, so it was unable to develop any kind of maritime activity. The islands and the coasts were plundered. The inhabitants were conscripted for crews, first for the fleet of one of the combatants and then for the other, and the population was dragged off to the slave markets.

In the naval battle of Navpaktos (or Lepanto) (1571), for example, there are calculated to have been 8,000 Greeks killed on the ships of both combatants.

The Turkish Occupation

Toward the end of 1693, through the mediation of England and Holland, the war between Turkey on the one side and Austria, Russia, Poland and Venice on the other came to an end; it had lasted for fifteen entire years and on January 26, 1699 the Treaty of Karlowitz was signed in the Croatian town of the same name. This treaty provided that the subjects of the countries involved could trade freely in the dominion of the others. Only the Greek bondsmen benefitted from this, for they could now settle on Austrian soil and came to constitute the first core of the Greek communities of Austria which later played their crucial role in the preparations for the Greek War of Independence. Let it be noted that there were no Turkish merchants who could benefit from this specific term of the treaty.

A few years later, on July 21, 1718, the Treaty of Passarowitz on Commerce and Shipping was signed between Austria and Turkey which ceded the right to the subjects of the Emperor of Austria to trade in all parts of Turkey and the harbors of the Black Sea and the Crimea, paying an import or export duty of 3%. Austria was also given the right to appoint consuls, vice-consuls, consular agents and interpreters in all Turkish harbors. Conversely, Turkey had a difficult time in gaining the right to appoint a consul to Vienna.

Through the Treaty of Karlowitz, Turkish expansionism was brought to a halt and trade with Venice and the Austrian Empire resumed once more.

This definitive blow to Turkish expansionism, meant that the state through its inability to adapt to the new situation and to evolve, began to decline, slowly in the beginning and then more rapidly as all of its range of activities had been based on the force of weapons alone.

The oppression and the predatory exploitation of the bondsmen, which had always been the underlying pre-supposition of the entire Turkish administration, became even more intense resulting in a gradual geographic re-arrangement in the social groups within the Greek geographical area. Most of the dynamic and creative elements of the Greek population fled to areas abroad or far from the unremitting governmental oppression. These movements began in the 17th century and gradually grew in strength.

Among the areas which the oppressed emigrated to were those places which, for one reason or another, enjoyed a relatively privileged state of freedom, and this included the islands. In these areas the Turkish administration was rather vague for reasons connected to the very structure of the administrative mechanism itself, in combination with a non-existent road network and inadequate means of transportation. Thus, at some point in time, certain areas of Greece, the coasts and the Aegean islands in particular, were inhabited by both their permanent inhabitants, who had a traditional knowledge of the sea, and by the restless, creative and entrepreneurial elements which had arrived there and settled under the pressure of persecution and oppression in all its many forms.

One can consider this event as the internal factor in the great economic and shipping development in Greece during the 18th century. But there was also an external one. This was the slow but steady withdrawal of Venice from the eastern Mediterranean which resulted in the creation of a vacuum in sea transport and sea trade in general. The European powers hurried to fill this vacuum. After the Treaty of Karlowitz European merchants began to set themselves up in large, Turkish ports and to monopolize the foreign trade of the empire. In order to achieve this aim, they needed to have the cooperation of the local element; thus conditions developed for cooperation with Greek, Armenian and Jewish Ottoman subjects.

These European merchants, because of the adverse balance of the Ottoman economy, were able to import their industrial products at high prices and to buy its products, mainly raw materials, more cheaply than in the West. Another important role in the withering of Ottoman commerce was played by the currency and economic crisis of the 17th century. The most profitable enterprise then was the trade in precious metals and currencies. The ones who profited from this economic crisis were the European merchants and the Greek, Jewish and Armenian middlemen who as moneychangers, lenders, bankers, lessors of revenue and merchants had acquired control of trade in the East.

One could say that the 18th century was the period when the first preliminary work began and the first hesitant steps taken wherein the unclear prospects for a substructure began to acquire shape and form; this was the commencement of what later came to be called the Modern Greek Merchant Marine.

By the end of the 18th century, Greeks held away in local and internal trade. The Slavs and the Albanians were active in the north, mainly the Balkans, while the Armenians began to acquire control of the trade of Asia Minor. The Greeks supplied the entire Balkan peninsula with raw materials and controlled the largest part of the trade with Egypt, the Aegean islands and mainland Greece. From being simple transporters and local

Per Ordine di SUA MAESTA L'IMPERATORE
e AUTOCRATORE di tutte le Russie.
&c. &c. &c.

10

merchants, the Greeks developed into mandators in the markets of their final destination. In the beginning, however, their activity was limited in the field of international trade, since the largest part of sea transport was in the hands of European merchants.

Even though most European states took part in the trade in the East, at the beginning of the 18th century France was the country with the most advantageous and well-grounded commercial position. Its position was to support the Empire's territorial integrity. Soon, however, France's practically monopolistic position came to be contested in many commercial centers, first by its international opponent, England, and then by Austria and finally by the Greeks.

The wars between England and France in the 18th century assisted the Greeks since the western merchants installed in the various ports halted their activity. The Greeks grabbed this golden opportunity and replaced the European merchants.

Greek shipping gained strength from several privileges which arose from the Russian-Turkish treaties and particularly that of Kutchuk-Kainardji (July 10, 1774). This declared that the Black Sea and the Dardanelles had to be opened to Russian and Austrian trade, and it allowed the Greek subjects of the Sultan to fly the Russian flag on their ships (ill. 10). These privileges opened new horizons for Greek shipping. Some Greek merchants and captains were able to gather in their hands practically all the Turkish and southern Russian trade, as well as a good part of the brokerage trade of western Europe with the coasts of Asia.

The final and most impressive factor in the Greek economic and shipping renaissance was the French Revolution and the Napoleonic wars which followed. Throughout these wars the English and the French managed to practically annihilate each other's commercial fleets in the Mediterranean. Since these fleets had controlled most of the transport, a serious transport problem was created, as was to be expected. The Aegean Greeks snapped up this unique opportunity. Wherever a profit was to be made, Greek sailors and merchants were to be found (ills. 11-14, 17, 18). Ignoring the blockade of Spanish and, above all, French ports, they brought grain to hungry France and both the shipowners and the merchants accumulated enormous profits. By 1813 the Aegean island mer-

11

10. Russian ukase. Document, with the seal of Czar Alexander I (1819) granting free navigation to the brig "Alexandros I", property of "Philikos" Ath. Sekeris, and the right to fly the Russian flag. Mykonos, Aegean Maritime Museum.

11. "Kirlagitsi" flying the flag of Jerusalem (source: J.J. Baugean, "Receuil de petites marines", Paris 1817).

chant marine had increased to enormous numbers for that period: 615 ships with a capacity of 153,580 tons of cargo; they were outfitted with 5,878 cannons and manned by 37,526 sailors[14].

The cannon, which was to prove to be so useful later on in the Greek War of Independence, was then a standard part of the merchant ships in the Mediterranean to protect against piracy.

This situation led to the accumulation of enormous capital, for that period, in the hands of Greek merchants and shipowners. But these subject people had only two ways to invest their capital: abroad (Vienna, Pest, Venice) or in shipping. Only in this way could they avoid having it seized by the conquerors. On this K. Sathas writes: "...as the Chiotes said, even a chance meeting with a Turk always costs. You see a Turk? He wants money. You see another one? He wants some too"[15] and V. Kremmydas observes for the 19th century: "The amassed commercial wealth in the market of Greece had no other outlet than to be invested in Greek shipping"[16].

The contribution of the commercial fleet of the Aegean islands to the Greek War of Independence (1821-1827) is sufficiently well-known to make even a brief reference to it superfluous (ills. 44-47).

Liberated Greece

The price that the merchant marine paid for freedom in the Greek War of Independence was an extremely heavy one. Very few of the ships that took part in the revolution survived. A few of them made up the nucleus of the first war fleet and with this and about 50 other worn out ships, the Aegean islanders had to secure their position in shipping.

But besides the material damage, Greek shipowners had also lost their place in international freight hauling which foreign ships reaped the profit from. The profitable pre-revolutionary enterprises no longer existed and the State was unable to help out. Furthermore, during the revolutionary period the Greek shipowners had spent their reserve capital, because they were often obliged to run their ships at their own expense.

Despite all this, a return to the sea was a national necessity. The naval force of the country had to be upgraded. As the mainland part of the country was almost completely devastated, without fertile regions, and industry was non-existent, the sea once more became the only natural way for the Greek to make a living and particularly on the barren islands in the Aegean. The stages through which this Greek endeavor passed in order to re-create its lost shipping, compose an unrivalled picture of dramatic struggles and astounding achievements. Difficult working conditions and experienced and powerful adversaries were confronted with indomitable vitality and the hard work of shipowners, captains and crewmen. It was a period of unrelenting struggle. Finally, the Greek seamen (ill. 15) were able to again assume their place in the sea transport. Within a few years, they had surpassed their pre-revolutionary capacity and regained lost ground.

In 1834 the Aegean maritime centers, including Galaxidi, had 708 ships over 30 tons; in 1844, 1,014 and in 1866, 1,657.

Even during pre-revolutionary times, many harbors in the Aegean, and at Galaxidi, had developed small shipbuilding units, where a significant number of sailing ships were built. They functioned in the form of an ordinary light industry and usually covered the needs of the specific area. Immediately after the War of Independence, the new town of Syros, Ermoupoli, supplied renewed impetus to this sector. The assembled capitalists and entrepreneurs who had taken refuge there during the War of Independence, saw

12

12. *Captain from Kassos. Print from 1814 (source: E.D. Clarke, "Travels in various countries", vols. 1-7, Cambridge, 1810-1823).*

that in order for entrepreneurs to develop, there was need of organization and capital. They invested substantial amounts of capital for the standards of that period; they brought timber in large quantities directly from abroad, mainly from Rumania, iron and other shipbuilding materials from the places they were produced and built complete installations. Most importantly of all they gathered together craftsmen from everywhere, paying good wages. Thus, in a short period of time, wooden shipbuilding on Syros supplanted all the similar enterprises in other areas and took the form of a large, organized enterprise.

In 1835 around 2,000 workers were laboring in the Syros shipyards and sixty to eighty boats were launched a year. At the same time, the shipbuilders found everything they needed for the outfitting of ships in the market of Syros. The organization of the shipbuilding and the abundance of means were such that shipmasters not only from Greece but from throughout the East, from Smyrna, Beirut, Mersina, Crete, Egypt and even the Black Sea came to Syros to build their ships. From old contracts that have survived, we learn that a caique of 60 tons was delivered within a time limit of three months, while in Galaxidi it required twice the time, not to mention other delays before the boats could be completely outfitted.

But besides the rapidity of work and the proper construction, the one who was ordering a caique from a Syros boatyard knew that in the market of Syros he could easily take out a loan, if required to cover its value, something it was practically impossible to do in other parts of Greece.

All these factors contributed to the development of the Greek sailing ship fleet (ills. 48-52, 54, 56) to the point where 5,000 sailing ships were registered in the Syros ship register over a period of thirty years, an incredible number even today.

Soon, however, Syros was forced to surrender its place to the harbor of the capital, Pireaus. But before the end came for its naval activity, this Aegean island, in a final resurgence, once more held first place in the history of Greek shipping.

From the middle of the past century, when steam began to be systematically used as the driving force in ships, there can be observed a real upheaval in the prevailing order of things. The Syros shipmasters saw that things were not going at all well. The merchants, as well as the passengers, preferred the steam-driven ships. Work on sailing ships fell off, as did the profits, year by year. A change of course was needed. Faced with this

13

13. *"Sacoleva" (source: J.J. Baugean, "Collection de toutes les espèces de batiments de guerre et de batiments marchands", Paris 1814).*

situation, in 1857 a score of Syros capitalists founded the first Greek steamship company which they named "Elliniki Atmoploia" but which was known throughout Greece as "E Syriani".

It started off with three ships, the "Hydra", the "Panellinion" and the "Vassilissa tis Ellados" ("Queen of Greece"). Others were added to these, recently built or purchased from foreigners. Within ten years "Elliniki Atmoploia" had ten ships and conducted all the Greek steamship transport, with many routes abroad. At the same time, the company set up a dry-dock on Syros for the repair of their ships. A large complex for the construction and the repair of iron ships, the "Dockyard and Machine-Works of Syros" was later set up at the same site.

When in 1835 Loukas Rallis, a settler and notable of the area, left Syros and settled on the deserted shores of Pireaus, laying the basis for the future maritime capital of Greece, the Syros residents thought he was unbalanced. And they were not far wrong. He had abandoned an organized harbor, the largest commercial center of Greece, and gone off to create a new one, in a desolate and deserted area.

A typical reaction is found in an article in the Patras newspaper "Karteria"[17] concerning the discussion that was going on about which Greek harbor should become free. The paper wrote: "What kind of place is this that is supposed to become a free harbor? Pireaus! Why Pireaus? It is a desolate spot, still uninhabited, a remote place where commerce has no reason to gather... Furthermore, it is lacking in all the other advantages which could make for a good life and because of which the small merchant and the major profiteer would evince a desire to re-settle there. Besides that, the remote location of Pireaus is completely unsuitable for the concentration of commerce, especially that from abroad".

Despite all the pessimistic predictions of the Patras journalist, Pireaus began to slowly develop during the second half of the past century into a maritime and a shipping-industrial center. Of course, there was no local maritime tradition, but with the migration from all over Greece to the capital, Pireaus attracted the island population and those

14

14. Greek corvette flying the flag of Jerusalem (source: J.J. Baugean, op. cit.).

from the coastal areas, who brought the maritime traditions of their homeland with them.

During the decade 1840-1850, besides the traditional maritime centers, Andros, Kassos and Syros and others, also Galaxidi, Hydra and Spetses, began to emerge and develop and at a rapid rate came to capture the shipping area of the Aegean and Black Sea where almost day by day they ousted the foreign flags and replaced them in maritime transports first in the Black Sea and later in the eastern Mediterranean.

The trade in grain from Russia was now a monopoly of the Greeks and its transport was done in Greek sailing ships and the Greek flag was the predominant one in the harbor of Marseilles.

Soon these unpolished sailors-entrepreneurs, endowed with ability and faith, had a presentiment that the small boats, all those that had survived the War of Independence, were no longer of assistance in this new endeavor and they did not hesitate to build, or buy from foreigners, large sailing ships which would help them increase their profits.

In 1856 the Greek sailing ship merchant marine, despite the world-wide economic crisis of 1854, was able to favorably exploit the English-Spanish and, later, the Crimean War and came to number 4,000 ships with 300,000 tons of cargo and 32,128 sailors working on the boats.

The first shipping crisis to touch Greek sailing ships came in 1860, but it was overcome and the business reached the apex of its glory in 1875. But 1875 can also be considered as the time when Greek commercial shipping on sailing ships began to decline, for it was during that period that steam made its appearance.

With the growing supremacy of steam, things became difficult for the Greek sailing ships which up until then had ruled export trade in the areas around the Black Sea. From the time of the Napoleonic Wars, Greek grain merchants had preferred Greek ships so that for many decades the monopoly of the transport of grain to Italy and France was in Greek hands. Greek ships were continually arriving with loads of grain in the harbors of Genoa, Livorno and Marseilles. Later, their activity spread to the Atlantic coasts and England.

15

15. 19th century Greek sailors (source: magazine «Έσπερος», Leipzig).

16. *Plate of Minas Avramidis depicting a gorgon. Mykonos, Folklore Museum.*

Thus a great problem arose. There were few steamships and the shipping enterprise required large amounts of capital which neither the newly founded State nor the banks were able to offer to the future shipowners. Another obstacle was that the banks were unable to enter shipping enterprises in a dynamic way because the real insurance of the mortgage was not legislated by Greece until 1910.

The inability of the State and the banks to support this new type of shipping enterprise was somewhat alleviated by the large Greek commercial houses abroad.

Names such as the Vallianos brothers, the Scaramangas brothers, Rodokanakis, Negrepontis, the Koupas brothers, the Siphnaios brothers, Svoronos and others belonged to the Russian group of corn exporters who bought the first steamships (ills. 19, 20). To these must be added the large merchants of the Danube such as the Theophilatos brothers, the Stathatos brothers, Alkiviadis Embeirikos, Chrysovelonis, Mich. Embeirikos, Theodoridis, the Drakoulis brothers and so on. In their commercial activities all of them also acted as shipowners, shipping agents and frequently the assigne, and later as ship brokers. Their involvement in the purchase of ships gave Greek shipowners and captains the opportunity to get to know (and get to be known) the money market of the City which they would soon enter dynamically and become some of its best customers.

During the period 1880-1900 steamships were being purchased almost continually.

During the period before 1900 companies even appeared who reached an agreement with the state for the transport of mail in exchange for a reduction in, for example, lighthouse and harbor duties.

All the ships had Pireaus as a base where, besides the cargo that was received and delivered and the transport of mail, they could also do their repairs, take on supplies, change crew, coaling and so on. The field of action was southern Russia, the Danube, Marseilles and other Mediterranean ports and for the larger ships of the period the area of the Continent and England. They made few forays into the ocean. Shipping that some-

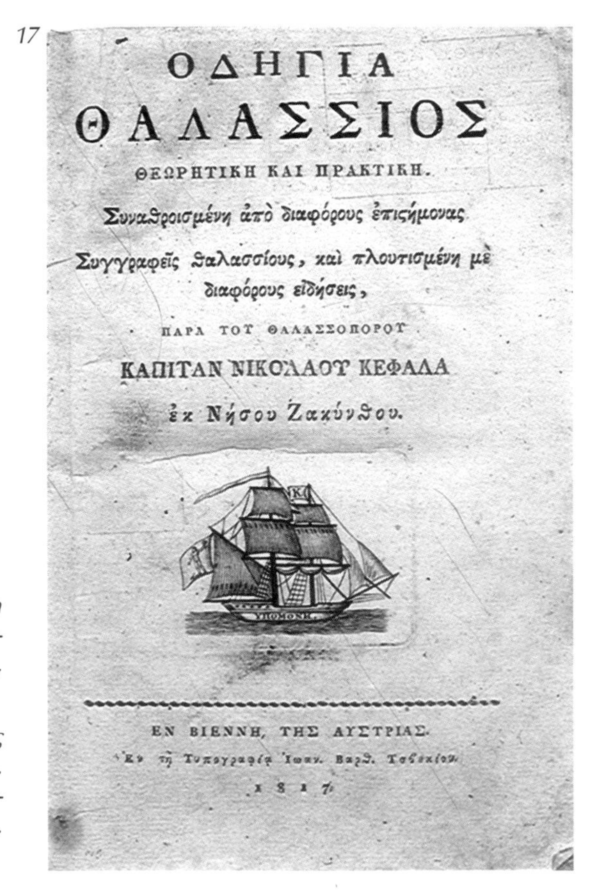

ΟΔΗΓΙΑ
ΘΑΛΑΣΣΙΟΣ
ΘΕΩΡΗΤΙΚΗ ΚΑΙ ΠΡΑΚΤΙΚΗ.
Συναθροισμένη ἀπὸ διαφόρους ἐπισήμονας
Συγγραφεῖς θαλασσίους, καὶ πλουτισμένη μὲ
διαφόρους εἰδήσεις,
ΠΑΡΑ ΤΟΥ ΘΑΛΑΣΣΟΠΟΡΟΥ
ΚΑΠΙΤΑΝ ΝΙΚΟΛΑΟΥ ΚΕΦΑΛΑ
ἐκ Νήσου Ζακύνθου.

ΕΝ ΒΙΕΝΝΗ, ΤΗΣ ΑΥΣΤΡΙΑΣ.
Ἐν τῇ Τυπογραφίᾳ Ἰωαν. Βαρθ. Τσεκίου.
1817.

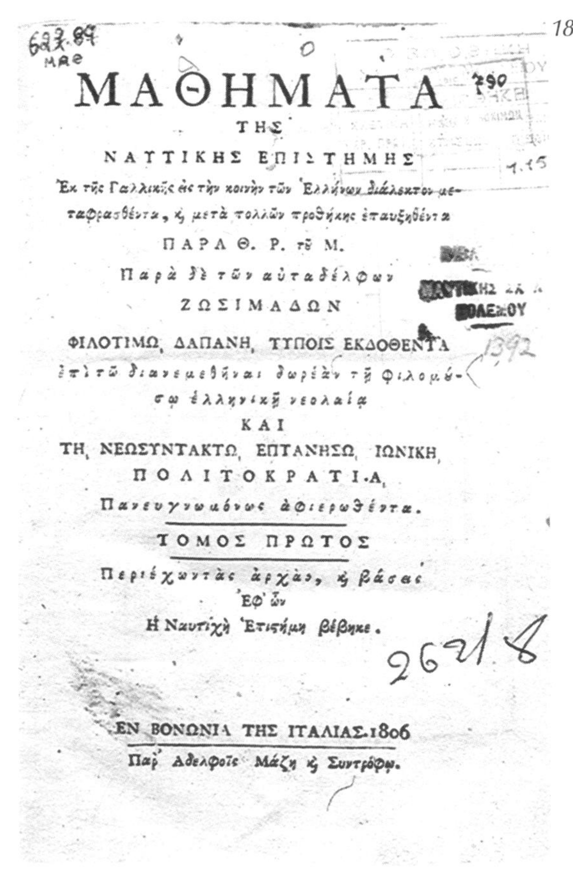

ΜΑΘΗΜΑΤΑ
ΤΗΣ
ΝΑΥΤΙΚΗΣ ΕΠΙΣΤΗΜΗΣ
Ἐκ τῆς Γαλλικῆς εἰς τὴν κοινὴν τῶν Ἑλλήνων διάλεκτον μεταφρασθέντα, καὶ μετὰ πολλῶν προσθήκης ἐπαυξηθέντα
ΠΑΡΑ Θ. Ρ. τοῦ Μ.
Παρὰ δὲ τῶν αὐταδέλφων
ΖΩΣΙΜΑΔΩΝ
ΦΙΛΟΤΙΜΩ, ΔΑΠΑΝΗ, ΤΥΠΟΙΣ ΕΚΔΟΘΕΝΤΑ
ἐπὶ τῷ διανεμηθῆναι δωρεὰν τῇ φιλομούσῳ ἑλληνικῇ νεολαίᾳ
ΚΑΙ
ΤΗ, ΝΕΩΣΥΝΤΑΚΤΩ, ΕΠΤΑΝΗΣΩ, ΙΩΝΙΚΗ,
ΠΟΛΙΤΟΚΡΑΤΙΑ,
Πανευγνωμόνως ἀφιερωθέντα.
ΤΟΜΟΣ ΠΡΩΤΟΣ
Περιέχωντας ἀρχὰς, καὶ βάσεις
Ἐφ' ὧν
Ἡ Ναυτικὴ Ἐπιστήμη βέβηκε.

ΕΝ ΒΟΝΩΝΙΑ ΤΗΣ ΙΤΑΛΙΑΣ. 1806
Παρ' Ἀδελφοῖς Μάζη καὶ Συντρόφῳ.

17. *Cover of the book by captain Nikolaos Kefalas, «Ὁδηγίαι θαλάσσιαι», in Vienna, Austria 1817. Pireaus, Hellenic Maritime Museum.*

18. *Cover of the book «Μαθήματα τῆς Ναυτικῆς Ἐπιστήμης παρά Θ.Ρ. τοῦ Μ. (Θεοδόση Ρώμπατα τοῦ Μουδανιώτου)», vol. I, in Bologna, Italy 1806. Pireaus, Hellenic Maritime Museum.*

20

19. *The steamship "S. Vallianos", 7,500 tons. Built in Glasgow in 1901 (source: E. Embeirikos in "La Grèce maritime", Athens 1907, 81-96).*

20. *The steamship "Vasileus Yeorgios", 6,400 tons. Built in Middlesbourgh in 1904 (source: E. Embeirikos, op. cit.).*

one characterized as "revolving between the Black Sea, the Mediterranean and England" with its home base always in Pireaus.

Entering the 20th century Greek shipping numbered, according to one set of statistics, 110 steam-driven freighters with a capacity of 344,756 tons, which represented 1,880,000 pounds sterling or 47 million gold francs. Some of these travelled under foreign flags (Turkish, Austrian, Russian, and so on).

Up to 1914 the area plied by the freighters was mainly the enclosed Mediterranean and the Black Sea. There were very few trips past Gibraltar and rarely overseas (ills. 58, 62, 63). The Greek shipping offices, which a few pioneering Greeks set up in London, are a significant contribution to these activities. The activities outside the Mediterranean were connected to the complete cooperation between shipowners, crews and merchants and in particular the wealthy and productive element of the Greeks abroad. It was because of these offices in London that Greek ships were hired to transport coal from England to Italy on their return to the Mediterranean.

Through these activities, Greek shipping, having the Aegean in its route, surrounded itself with related and multi-faceted enterprises and industries which composed, if not an elaborate, at least a satisfactory infrastructure, capable of serving and assisting its further activity (ills. 59-61). Syros, in the beginning, and then Pireaus, Andros and Chios developed into naval centers which served local shipping. The ships came to the home ports to re-supply, thus furnishing the market of the homeland with plentiful and badly needed foreign exchange. Moreover, the ships that passed through Greek waters, going to and coming back from the Black Sea, found the opportunity to go into dry dock and do their repairs in Syros or Pireaus, which had developed into repair centers, at a lower cost than anywhere else. These same harbors had important shipping offices which carried out insurance, chartering, sale anad purchase and financing the ships.

The results of these relationships was the influx into the Greek economy of significant amounts of the income realized by Greek shipping.

With the outbreak in 1914 of World War I, when Turkey allied itself to the forces of Central Europe and Russia to the forces of the Entente, Greek ships suffered from a lack of work. Turkey closed the Dardanelles and thus Greek shipping was cut off from the cargoes of the Black Sea. So it had to limit itself to the Mediterranean. Then it was offered wonderful opportunities for new and profitable activities. The need of the western forces for transport was enormous, so there was a great flow of cargo from all parts of the earth, particularly from the American continent to Europe and the war fronts.

Thus, it was natural for Greek shipping to turn in this direction, both from need and from a quest for profit. But this turn, which was positively reinforced by Greece entering the war on the side of the Allies, inevitably meant that the work of the Greek freighter was shifted outside the traditional areas of its activity and shipping was transferred once and for all to the center of international shipping, London.

This led to a reduction of jobs in the shipping offices in Greece, a limiting of the repair work and a lessening of the number of visits made to Greek ports. The maritime activity of Greece shrank instead of growing. Thus, Greece could not acquire large repair units, create a national insurance market or even maritime credit. The shift of the axis of our sea-going shipping from the Aegean led to the atrophying of all the offshoots here of the formerly flourishing and highly promising activities connected to shipping. This is the explanation as to why the Greek shipbuilding industry did not keep in step with the progressive rise of shipping, for with a complete lack of maritime credit the ship-

21

22

23

24

21-25. Figureheads from 19th century sailing ships (21, 23. Spetses Museum. 22. Hydra Museum. 24. Hydra, Kaminia. 25. Chios, Emm. Revithis family).

25

ping offices stagnated. The progressive rise of shipping, for with a complete lack of maritime credit the shipping offices stagnated. The internationalization of the ship and the shipowner was at the expense of the national economy.

From then on, the Aegean, "the cradle of shipping" as it was called, ceased to be the axis of movement for Greek ships and Greek shipping enterprises.

All those who pondered the future with a measure of experience, cold logic and awareness, thought that Greek shipping would disappear from the seas. The old, uneconomical capacity which sailed under the blue and white flag, the small strength and skimpily capitaled shipping company, a source of international reservation, are all elements which confirmed that, after that destructive war, with the markets lost to Greek shipping and the international economic recession, it would be highly unlikely for Greek shipping to be strengthened and there were many who awaited its demise. But the exact opposite occurred. Within a short period of time it rebuilt and surpassed its pre-war capacity and was finally able to escape from the narrow confines of the Aegean, the Mediterranean and the Black Sea, to conquer the oceans and in a brief period of time came to occupy one of the leading positions in world-wide shipping.

Greek shipowners and sailors often remind one of the mythical Anteaus, the only difference being that they are filled with life and grow mighty not by being in contact with the earth but rather the sea.

One could say that for Greek sailors the Aegean constituted the springboard from which they leapt in order to conquer the seas of the world and to bring Greek shipping to an enviable position in world-wide shipping.

The Greek maritime tradition, which was born in the Aegean, has been, and still is maintained for almost ten thousand years.

NOTES

1. Colin Renfrew, "Trade and Craft Specialisation", *Neolithic Greece*, ed. National Bank of Greece, Athens, 1973, 179.

2. *Op. cit.*

3. Colin Renfrew – J.E.Dixon – J.R. Cann, "Obsidian and early cultural contact in the Near East", *Proceedings of the Prehistoric Society*, XXXII (1966), 30-72.

4. Colin Renfrew – S.A. Durrani – H. A. Khan – J. Taj, "Obsidian source identification of Aegean obsidians", *Nature*, 237 (1971), 333-4.

5. Thucydides, *History*, A, 4.

6. Strabo, *Geography*, A, C-2.

7. Hesiod, "On Shipping", *Works and Days*, 624-631.

8. Plato, *Phaidon*, 103.

9. Plato, *Laws*, 708.

10. Thucydides, *History*, B, 38.

11. Athenaeus, *Deipnosophistai*, A, 49-50.

12. *Basilica*, 53, 5, 13, 14.

13. Λ.Η. Ποταμιάνος, "Ἡ ναυτική πίστις ἐν Κωνσταντινουπόλει κατά τόν Θ΄ αἰώνα", *Ναυτικά Χρονικά* 1 Ἰουλίου, 1951, 16.

14. Κ. Σιμόπουλος, *Ξένοι ταξιδιῶτες στήν Ἑλλάδα 1810-1821*, τόμ. Γ2, Ἀθήνα 1985, 405.

15. Κ. Σάθας, "Εἰδήσεις τινές περί ἐμπορίου καί φορολογίας ἐν Ἑλλάδι ἐπί Τουρκοκρατίας", *Οἰκονομική Ἐπιθεώρησις*, Ἰανουάριος 1879, 503.

16. Β. Κρεμμυδάς, *Εἰσαγωγή στήν Ἱστορία τῆς Νεοελληνικῆς Κοινωνίας (1760-1821)*, Ἀθήνα 1976, 114.

17. November 22, 1842.

BIBLIOGRAPHY

General

ARENSON, S., *The Encircled Sea*, London 1990.

BASH, G.F. (ed.), *A history of Seafaring*, London 1972.

ΓΕΩΡΓΟΠΟΥΛΟΣ, Γ.Ε., *Τό Ἑλληνικόν Ναυτικόν διά μέσου τῶν Αἰώνων*, Ἀθῆναι 1933.

HORNELL, J., *Water Transport*, London 1946.

KEMP, P., *The history of Ships*, New York, no date.

Navigation et Gens de Mer en Mediterranée de la Préhistoire à nos jours, ed. Centre National de la Rechershe Scientifique, Cahier No. 3, Paris 1980.

THROCKMORTON, P. (ed.), *The history from the Sea*, London 1987.

Prehistoric and protohistoric

CULICAN, W., *The First Merchant Ventures*, London 1966.

EDEY, M.A., *Lost World of the Aegean*, Time-Life Book, Amsterdam 1975.

EVANS, A., *The Palace of Minos*, vol. II, London 1928, 239-252.

GRAVE de M-C., *The Ships of the Ancient Near East (c. 2000-500 B.C.)*, Leuven-Belgium 1981.

JOHNSTON, P., "Stern first in the Stone Age", *International Journal Nautic Archaeology*, London 1973, 2, 1:4.

— *The Sea Craft of Prehistory*, London 1980.

MARINATOS, S., "La Marine Creto-Mycénienne", *Bulletin de Correspondance Hellènique*, Athènes 1933, 170-235 (fig. 13-17).

RENFREW, C., "Trade and Craft Specialisation", *Neolithic Greece*, ed. National Bank of Greece, Athens 1973, 179-192.

ΣΑΚΕΛΛΑΡΑΚΗΣ, Ι., «Ἐλεφάντινον πλοῖον ἐκ Μυκηνῶν», *Ἀρχαιολογική Ἐφημερίς* 1971, 188-233 (πίν. 34-51).

TAYLOUR, C.W., *The Mycenaens*, London 1964.

VERMULE, E., *Greece in the Bronze Age*, Chicago 1964.

ZIMMERMAN, G.T., *Bronze Age Ships in the Eastern Mediterranean*, Pensacola Flo, USA 1970.

Classical and Roman Periods

AMIT, M., *Athens and the Sea. A study in Athenian Sea Power*, Bruxelles 1965.

ANDREADIS, A.M., *A history of Greek Public Finance*, Cambridge Mass, USA 1933.

BASCH, L., *Le Musée Imaginaire de La Marine Antique*, Athènes 1985.

BOECKH, A., *The Public Economy of the Athenians*, London 1857.

CALHOUN, G.M., *The Business Life of Ancient Athens*, New York 1968.

CASOON, L., *The Ancient Mariners*, New York 1959.

— *Ships and Shipmanship in the Ancient World*, New Jersey 1971.

— *Travel in the Ancient World*, London 1974.

— *Ancient Trade and Society*, Detroit 1984.

ERICSSON, C.H., *Navis Orneratia*, Obo Finland 1984.

GARLAND, Q., *The Piraeus*, London 1987.

CARNSEY, P. (ed.), *Trade in the Ancient Economy*, London 1983.

CARNSEY, P. - WHITTAKER, C.R., *Trade and Famine in Classical Antiquity*, Cambridge 1983.

GÖTTLICHER, A., *Die schiffe der Antike*, Berlin 1985.

HASEBROEK, J., *Trade and Politics in Ancient Greece*, London 1933.

HÖCKMANN, O., *Antike Selfahrt*, München 1985.

HODGES, H., *Technology in the Ancient World*, Penguin Books, London 1970.

HOPPER, R.J.H., *Trade and Industry in Classical Greece*, London 1979.

HYDE, W.W., *Ancient Greek Mariners*, New York 1947.

ISAGER, S. - HANSEN, M.S., *Aspects of Athenian Society in the fourth century B.C.*, Odens 1975.

KNORRINGA, H., *Emporos*, Amsterdam 1926.

LANDERS, J.C., *Engineering in the Ancient World*, London 1978.

MEIGGS, R., *Trees and Timber in the Ancient Mediterranean World*, Oxford 1982.

MEIJER, G., *A history of Seafaring in the classical World*, London 1986.

MOIRAT, J., *Marines antiques de la Mediterranée*, no place 1964.

ROUJÉ, J., *Ships and Fleets of the Ancient Mediterranean*, Middletown Conn., USA 1981.

THUMBRON, C., *The Ancient Mariners*, Time-Life books, Amsterdam 1981.

VIERECH, H.D.L., *Die Römische Flotte*, Herford 1975.

WHITE, K.D., *Greek and Roman Technology*, London 1984.

Byzantium

AHRWEILER, H., *Byzance et la Mer*, Paris 1966.

— "Les ports Byzantins (VIIe-IXe siècles)", *La Navigazione Mediterranea nel Alto Medioevo*, vol. I, Spoleto 1978, 259-297.

ΑΛΕΞΑΝΔΡΗΣ, Κ.Α., *Ἡ θάλασσα δύναμις εἰς τήν ἱστορίαν τῆς Βυζαντινῆς Αὐτοκρατορίας*, Ἀθῆναι 1975.

ANTONIADIS-BIBICOU, H., *Études d'histoire maritime de Byzance*, Paris 1966.

BIBICOU, H., "Sources Byzantines pour servir à l'histoire maritime", *Quatrième Colloque d'Histoire Maritime*, Paris 1962, 121-136.

ΓΕΩΡΓΑΚΟΠΟΥΛΟΣ, Γ.Ε., *Οἱ λιμένες τῶν ξένων εἰς τό Βυζάντιον*, Ἐν Ἀθήναις 1935.

ΓΟΥΔΑΣ, Μ., *Τό Ναυτικόν τοῦ Βυζαντίου κατά τόν δέκατο αἰώνα*, Ἀθῆναι 1903.

ΡΑΔΟΣ, Κ.Ν., *Τό Ναυτικόν τοῦ Βυζαντίου*, Ἐν Ἀθήναις 1920.

TANGERONI, M. - GALLOPINI, L., *Navigare del Medioevo*, Firenze 1989.

VILLAINE-GANDOSSI, C., *Le Navire Mediévale à travers les Miniatures*, Paris 1985.

Turkish occupation

ΒΟΡΕΙΟΣ, Σ., *Τό Ἑλληνικό Ἐμπορικό Ναυτικό κατά τόν XVII αἰώνα*, Ἀθήνα 1940.

ΚΡΕΜΜΥΔΑΣ, Β., *Εἰσαγωγή στήν Ἱστορία τῆς Νεοελληνικῆς Κοινωνίας (1700-1821)*, Ἀθήνα 1976.

ΚΩΝΣΤΑΝΤΙΝΙΔΗΣ, Τ.Π., *Καράβια, καπετάνιοι καί Συντροφοναῦται*, Ἀθῆναι 1954.

LEON, G.B., "The Greek Merchant Marine (1453-1850)", *The Greek Merchant Marine*, ed. National Bank of Greece, Athens 1972, 13-56.

ΣΒΟΛΟΠΟΥΛΟΣ, Κ., «Ὁ ἑλληνικός ἐμπορικός στόλος κατά τάς παραμονάς τοῦ ἀγῶνος τῆς Ἀνεξαρτησίας», *Ὁ Ἐρανιστής*, τεῦχ. 59 (1973), 187-207.

ΤΖΑΜΤΖΗΣ, Α.Ι., *Ἡ ναυτιλία τοῦ Πηλίου στήν Τουρκοκρατία*, Ἀθήνα χ.χ.

ΦΙΛΑΡΕΤΟΣ, Γ.Ν., *Ἡ ἑλληνική ναυτιλία κατά τάς παραμονάς τῆς ἐπαναστάσεως*, Ἀθῆναι 1907.

Post-revolutionary period

ΕΜΠΕΙΡΙΚΟΣ, Ε., *Περί τῆς Ἐμψυχώσεως τῆς Ἑλληνικῆς Ναυτιλίας*, Ἀθῆναι 1890.

HARLAFTIS, G., "The Role of the Greek in the Black Sea Trade 1830-1900", *Shipping Trade 1750-1950*, Portofaret, England 1990.

ΚΡΕΜΜΥΔΑΣ, Β., *Ἑλληνική Ναυτιλία 1776-1835*, τόμ. Α', Β', Ἀθήνα 1985-6.

ΚΟΥΛΟΥΡΑΣ, Γ.Ν., *Περί τῆς ἱστιοφόρου καί ἀτμήρους ἐμπορικῆς ναυτιλίας*, Ἀθῆναι 1951.

ΜΕΤΑΞΑΣ, Σ.Α. - ΓΕΩΡΓΟΠΟΥΛΟΣ, Σ.Γ., *Ἑλληνικόν Ἐμπορικόν Ναυτικόν*, Ἀθῆναι 1925.

ΠΑΠΑΘΑΝΑΣΟΠΟΥΛΟΣ, Κ., *Ἑλληνική Ἐμπορική Ναυτιλία (1833-1856)*, Ἀθήνα 1983.

— *Ἑταιρεία Ἑλληνικῆς Ἀτμοπλοΐας (1855-1872)*, Ἀθήνα 1988.

26

27

28

29

26. Modern reed raft. Institute for the Preservation of Nautical Tradition.

27. Type of reed raft. Institute for the Preservation of Nautical Tradition.

28. Model of ship from Thera. Pireaus, Hellenic Maritime Museum.

29. Model of trireme from the 5th century B.C. Pireaus, Hellenic Maritime Museum.

30

31

32

33

30. *Model of a merchant vessel (Cyrenia vessel), 4th century B.C. Pireaus, Hellenic Maritime Museum.*

31. *Pyramid-shaped anchor, 6th-5th century B.C. Pireaus, Hellenic Maritime Museum.*

32. *Silver drachma piece from Thessaly, with a depiction of Artemis and her bow on the stern of a ship, 2nd century A.D. Mykonos, Aegean Maritime Museum.*

33. *Silver "stater" from Fasilis with a depiction of the stern and the stern decoration (of luston) of a ship, 400-300 B.C. Mykonos, Aegean Maritime Museum.*

34. *Clay model of a boat from Cyprus, circa 11th century B.C. Paris, The Louvre.*

35. *Odysseus (Ulysses) passes by the Sirens. Relief from the 2nd century A.D. Paris, The Louvre.*

34

35

36

36. Depiction of ships on a black-figured vase by Nicosthenes, circa 520 B.C. Paris, The Louvre.

37, 38. Laskaris Leichoudis, icon of Ayios Nikolaos (details), 1733. Athens, Benaki Museum.

39. Clay jar with an engraved depiction of a Byzantine ship. Pireaus, Hellenic Maritime Museum.

40. Mosaic floor with a personification of the sea, 578 A.D. from the Basilica of the Apostles in Madaba, Jordan. The inscription: Κ(ΥΡΙ)Ε Θ(ΕΕ) Ο ΠΟΙΗΣΑΣ ΤΟΝ ΟΥΡΑΝΟΝ ΚΑΙ ΤΗΝ ΓΗΝ ΔΟΣ ΖΩΗΝ ΑΝΑΣΤΑΣΙΩ ΚΑΙ ΘΩΜΑ ΚΑΙ ΘΕΟΔΩΡΑ Κ(ΑΙ) ΣΑΛΑΜΑΝΙΟΥ ΨΗΦΩ (ΤΟΥ) can be seen. Jordan, Amman Museum.

37

38

39

40

41

41. N. Kaloyeropoulos, "Byzantine dromon". Pireaus, Hellenic Maritime Museum.

42. The polacca of G. Kriezis, "Ayia Trias". A copy by A. Kriezis of the painting by L. Roux. She was built in Hydra and armed with 12 cannons. On the evening of 3/4/1810 she was attacked by four Algerian pirate ships south of Sardinia. After a fierce battle in which most of the members of the crew were killed, the ship was captured and taken to Algeria, where her wounded captain, A. Kriezis, and the few survivors, were put in chains. The painting was ordered and painted in Marseilles where it should have been picked up during the return of the ship but after everything that happened it remained in the hands of the painter. Pireaus, Hellenic Maritime Museum.

43. Polacca "Heraklis". Built in Spetses in 1815 by the brothers G. and Ch. Koutsis. During the period of the Greek War of Independence she was used as the flagship of the Spetsian fleet. Pireaus, Hellenic Maritime Museum.

44. The "Aris" of A. Miaoulis. Lithograph. Pireaus, Hellenic Maritime Museum.

42

43

44

15

46

48

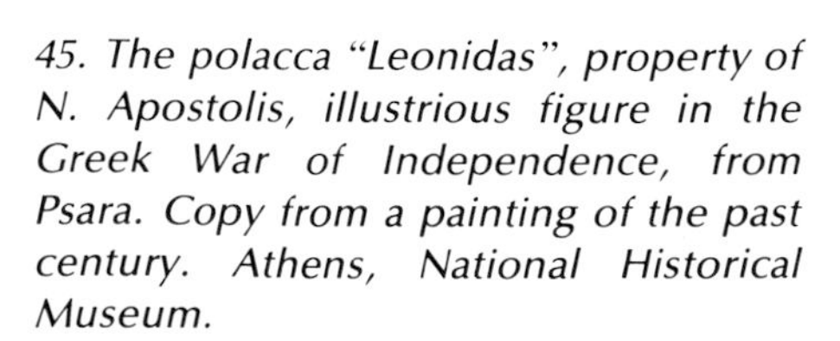

45. The polacca "Leonidas", property of N. Apostolis, illustrious figure in the Greek War of Independence, from Psara. Copy from a painting of the past century. Athens, National Historical Museum.

46. Model of the ship (brig) of A. Tsamados, "Aris". Pireaus, Hellenic Maritime Museum.

47. The brig "Periklis", property of A. Ch. Anargyros. Copy of the painting by L. Roux. Athens, National Historical Museum.

48. Model of a "barkentine" sailing ship from the 19th century. Pireaus, Hellenic Maritime Museum.

49

50

51

52

53

54

49. Model of the Kassian bark "Alexandros Ypsilantis", property of the Fragoulis brothers, capacity of 1,000 tons. She was built in Syros in 1892. Pireaus, Hellenic Maritime Museum.

50. Model of a schooner of Syros from the 19th century. Pireaus, Hellenic Maritime Museum.

51. Model of Aegean sailing boat with gaff sails. Mykonos, Aegean Maritime Museum.

52. Model of a Mykonian spritsail ("sacoleva"). Mykonos, Aegean Maritime Museum.

53. Model of A. Tsamados' sailing ship (brig) "Aris", capacity 250 tons. Built in Venice in 1819. Mykonos, Aegean Maritime Museum.

54. Model of the Mykonian bark "Philadelphos" belonging to G.P. Drakopoulos and L. Ambanopoulos, capacity 840 tons. Built in Syros, in 1868. Mykonos, Aegean Maritime Museum.

55

56

55. Model of a paddle-boat, the mail-boat "Enosis" which also helped break the blockade of Crete during the Cretan Revolution of 1866-68. Pireaus, Hellenic Maritime Museum.

56. Model of sailing ship ("perama") "Evangelistria" from the 19th-20th century. Mykonos, Aegean Maritime Museum.

57. Model of the steamship "Embros", capacity 3,500 tons. Built in Middlesbourgh in 1889. Mykonos, Aegean Maritime Museum.

58. Model of the ocean liner "Themistoklis", renamed the "Moraïtis" after it was purchased by the "National Steam Navigation Co Ltd. of Greece". Pireaus, Hellenic Maritime Museum.

57

58

59

60

61

59, 60, 61. Passenger ships from the beginning of the century (paintings by A. Glykas). Pireaus, Hellenic Maritime Museum.

62, 63. Advertisements for the ocean liner "Patris" of the "National Steam Navigation Co Ltd. of Greece". Built in England in 1908. Athens, archives of ELIA.

62

ΕΘΝΙΚΗ ΑΤΜΟΠΛΟΪΑ
ΤΗΣ ΕΛΛΑΔΟΣ
NATIONAL STEAM NAVIGATION C° LTD. OF GREECE
Η ΤΑΧΥΤΕΡΑ ΕΞ ΕΛΛΑΔΟΣ ΚΑΤ' ΕΥΘΕΙΑΝ ΔΙ' ΑΜΕΡΙΚΗΝ ΓΡΑΜΜΗ

63

ΕΘΝΙΚΗ ΑΤΜΟΠΛΟΪΑ ΤΗΣ ΕΛΛΑΔΟΣ
ΑΤΜΟΠΛΟΙΟΝ
«ΠΑΤΡΙΣ»
μέ διπλοῦς ἕλικας
ΚΑΘΕΛΚΥΣΘΕΝ
τῇ 10/23 Δεκεμβρίου
1908
ΧΩΡΗΤΙΚΟΤΗΤΟΣ 12000 ΤΟΝΝΩΝ
ΚΑΙ
ΤΑΧΥΤΗΤΟΣ 17 ΜΙΛΛΙΩΝ
Η ΤΑΧΥΤΕΡΑ ΓΡΑΜΜΗ
ΚΑΤ' ΕΥΘΕΙΑΝ ΔΙΑ
ΝΕΑΝ-ΥΟΡΚΗΝ
ΓΕΝΙΚΟΣ ΠΡΑΚΤΩΡ
Σ. Ξ. ΣΤΑΥΡΟΥΛΟΠΟΥΛΟΣ
ΕΝ ΠΑΤΡΑΙΣ
ΠΑΤΡΙΣ
ΕΝ
ΑΘΗΝΑΙΣ
ATHENS
NATIONAL STEAM NAVIGATION C° LTD. OF GREECE
Λιθ. Β. Παπαχρυσάνθου Αθήναι

64

65

64. Head from figurehead. Symi Museum.

65. Theophilos Chatzimichael, Gorgon, fragment from a wall painting. Volos, D. Gountelias family.

LAMBROS LIAVAS

The music of the Aegean

Translated by Philip Ramp

You cannot escape the sea which cradled you and which you seek...
with the reeds which sang in Autumn in Lydian mode...

G. Seferis

Nowhere else in all of Greece did music come to know, down through the ages, such wealth and such variety as in the Aegean Archipelago. Perhaps this was because, as Odysseus Elytis writes, "nowhere else has the triangle of mountains come down so naturally to the edifice; nowhere else have the mythic creatures of sea legend worn the two wings of the winds so convincingly...". Because in fact this music springs from the wind with its whispers and its cries, and from the sea with its myriad colors and the artistically crafted shapes of its islands, which has always remained "the sounding sea", just as in Homer's time.

The starting point for the musical history of the Aegean is lost in myth, interwoven with the birth of Zeus, the father of the gods, and Apollo, the god of music and light. Greek mythology ascribes the birth of music and dance to Crete. There is the well-known myth centered on the Couretes and the instruments they banged on to conceal the cries of the newborn Zeus, protecting him from his father Cronos, who ate his children. Later Zeus –by then the Lord of Olympus– made love to Leto and she, fleeing the rage of Hera, took refuge on a barren rock which floated perpetually in the sea. There she gave birth to Apollo, the god who dominated political and intellectual life in the ancient Greek world. As recompense to Leto, Zeus fixed the island firmly in the center of the Aegean and called it Delos ("Shining One"). From then on, as Callimachus mentions, all sailors who passed by had to stop there and take part in the songs and dances around the altar of the god. This is also what Theseus did when, returning from Crete, he danced along with his companions "the dance which, it is said, the inhabitants of Delos still dance today; an imitation of the sinuous twists and turns of the Labyrinth, done to a set rhythm with complex variations[1]. This type of dance is called *yeranos* (crane)..." (Plutarch). Even today one finds on many of the Greek islands a dance with the same name, though it is of a different type than the ancient *yeranos*[2].

The god of music made love to the muse of celestial harmony, Urania, who gave birth to the greatest musician of Greek mythology, Orpheus[3], also connected to the Aegean. Taking part in the Argonautic expedition he set a rhythm for the rowers, calmed the sea, while his melodies muffled the seductive song of the Sirens and thereby saved his companions. In Samothrace music was connected with mysticism; Orpheus and the Argonauts were initiated into the celebrated mysteries and ceremonies of the Cabeirja. Even in death Orpheus is connected to the Aegean. His head and his lyre, which the Maenads threw into the sea, were guided by the waves to Lesbos where the inhabitants set up a magnificent memorial while, according to tradition, his lyre was given to the great poet and musician from Lesbos of the 7th century B.C., Terpander[4].

Thus, Terpander bridges myth with history for –as Gevaert writes– "he set the definitive bases for Greek music and is worthy of the title of originator and founder". Indeed, he was the patriarch of an illustrious generation of innovative musicians and poets to which belonged:

– Alcaeus[5] the melodist (end of 7th/6th century B.C.) and the supreme representative of Aeolian lyric poetry, praiser of love, the good life and democracy as well.

– Sappho[6] the "tenth muse", a contemporary of Alcaeus (ill. 29), who was the first to use a plectrum for a lyre to accompany her renowned hymns and her wedding-lays (*Epithalamia*):

... And the sweet-singing pipe was mixed
with the lyre and the sound of cymbals,
and the maidens sang clearly a pure song,
and a wondrous echo reached to the sky...

– Arion (around 625 B.C.—?) from Methymna, Lesbos, who was the greatest musician of his time and is frequently depicted, with his lyre, on the back of a dolphin which –as Herodotus recounts– saved his life when pirates threw him into the sea.

– Phrynis the Mytilenaian (5th century) and Agenor the Mytilenaian (4th century) were revered for the innovations they introduced into ancient Greek music.

But the catalogue of the great musicians and poets of Antiquity, who were connected to the Aegean, does not end at Lesbos[7]. The word "rythmos" (rhythm) was used for the first time in the Aegean by Archilochos the Parian (7th century) who was also the one who established the free accompaniment of a song (instead of the instrumental) doubling of the vocal part which had held sway till then), giving a new dimension to music. During the same period Mimnermos, from Colophon or Smyrna in Asia Minor, sang of the joys of youth, while proving to be an excellent flute-player; he influenced his close friend Solon who was the first to introduce the teaching of music into the educational system of Athens (beginning of the 6th century).

At the same time, according to mythology, Thalitas from Gortys on Crete used music to save Sparta from the plague and had an influence on its musical education, transferring to continental Greece elements from the vast Cretan musical and dancing tradition.

Pythagoras, who had his roots in Samos (6th century), produced a number of theories to support the scientific basis of music and, as is commonly known, exercised a great influence on the musical thought of all ages right up to the present. Lycaon the Samian had his origins on the same island; he was a musician from the beginning of the 5th century of panhellenic repute. The great lyrical poet Anacreon (from Teos, on the coast of Asia Minor) distinguished himself in the court of Polycrates, the tyrant of Samos; according to Critias, he was "the charmer of the symposiums, seducer of women, friend of the *barbiton* –a kind of lyre– sweet, free of sorrow...".

During the same period Simonides and Bakchylides from Kea are considered to be the equals of Pindar; Melanippides from Milos (5th century) gave new dimensions to the art of the dithyramb and Ion from Chios was admired far and wide for being a great singer and lyrical poet.

Outside the written sources, the rich musical life in the Aegean during Antiquity is attested by a host of archeological finds (objects and representatives on vases, wall paintings and mosaics, ills. 20-24). The famous Cycladic figurines of the harpist and the flutist, made of white Parian marble (see p. 98, ills. 16, 17), which were found at Keros (an island near Naxos) are dated as far back as the Bronze Age, while there are also many related examples from Minoan Crete (3000-1400 B.C.). Among the most interesting are the sarcophagus which was found at Ayia Triada with the oldest known depiction of a seven-stringed lyre and a double flute, which are accompanying a ceremonial procession (ills. 20, 21), and the "Harvesters' Vase" with a representation of a group of harvesters who are dancing and singing while one of them is keeping the rhythm with a sistrum (rattle). This scene lends vitality to analogous depictions in Homer (*The Iliad*, XVIII, 569) and in Homer we also find a marvelous description of a dance at the palace of Knossos with which the poet wants to decorate the shield of Achilles (*The Iliad*, XVIII, 590-606): "... And there were young men on it [the dancing floor] and young girls, sought for their beauty... and holding hands at the wrist... while among the dancers two acrobats led the measures of song and dance revolving among them...". Cretan dances were also praised by Sappho, when she sang about the women of Crete who, "dance rhythmically on light feet around the magnificant altar lightly stepping on the delicately flowering grass...". Armed dances, military in character –such as the famous "Pyrrhic" dance– as well as funeral dances, are also mentioned in connection with Crete. Indeed, tradition mentions that Glaukos, son of Minos, was buried together with his flutes, which he loved so dearly and played with such skill. Aemilian informs us that the young people of Crete learned their laws through song so they would never forget them!

This rich musical life in the Aegean continued even after Classical times, when the area gradually came under the domination of Rome and Byzantium. Theocritus of Kos (3rd century B.C.) wrote about the songs and the dances of the farmers, the shepherds and the fishermen who carried on the tradition of Sappho through their wedding-lays, analogous forms of which will be found in Byzantium ("pastika" – bridal chamber songs) leading right on up to the modern "paraxypnimata", "awakening songs", with which newly-weds are awakened in the Dodecanese[8]. Mesomides, a lyric poet and musician from Crete in the service of the Emperor Hadrian, was well-known in the second century A.D. To him are attributed the hymns to Nemesis and –perhaps– to the Muse and Ilios, some of the few examples of ancient Greek music which have survived up to the present[9].

Even though during Hellenistic times the indissoluble combination of speech and music, a characteristic of classical antiquity, was broken (just as prosody shifted from quantitative to tonal), scientific research has proven that there was a smooth transition from the musical-poetic world of Antiquity to that of the early Christian period which led to Byzantine-medieval Hellenism. Thus, in the 3rd century A.D. one finds in the papyrus of Oxyrhynchus an early Christian hymn to the Holy Trinity, accented in ancient Greek alphabetic notation. The Aegean again came to the forestage when on Patmos Saint John the Evangelist "stood upon the sand of the sea" in order to write his Revelation in Greek: "And I heard a voice from heaven, as the voice of many waters, and as the voice of a great thunder: and I heard the voice of harpers harping with their harps" (XIV, 2).

And these musicians, with their instruments, who were rendered in the miniatures of Byzantine manuscripts, became part of the wall paintings in monasteries and churches (Mount Athos, Patmos, Salamis, Kythera, Crete and so on) and "lurked" in corners of portable icons, invaluable evidence concerning Byzantine secular music and dance[10] which the official church wanted to suppress, afraid of its links with the ancient world (ills. 25, 26).

But in the sector of Byzantine religious music as well, the Aegean was the place where a number of important chanting traditions developed such as at Mount Athos, Patmos and Crete[11] (where the renowned music teacher Georgios the Cretan was from).

Even though the islands and the coasts of the Aegean were the bridge which joined the musical world of ancient Greece with that of the East since Antiquity, at the same time they were also the place where, from the 13th century A.D., influences from the West were first manifested. The "Franks" (French, Genoese and Venetians) who occupied the Aegean during the Crusades, brought with them, among other things, melodies, musical and poetic forms (such as rhyme), dances (such as the *ballos*) and musical instruments (such as the violin).

Of particular importance is the dominance of rhyme, in the form of rhyming distichs, which first appeared at the end of the 14th century in the polished poetry of Crete and then gradually spread to the songs of all the islands. Here we have a very significant element of distinction between the music of mainland and insular Greece for –as Samuel Baud-Bovy has noted– in mainland Greece even the songs inspired by World War II and the Resistance have remained unrhymed with a "three half-line" structure (that is, a musical phrase corresponds to one and a half lines) while in insular Greece everything is in rhyming distichs[12].

The world of the Aegean, however, with the assimilating creativity which has characterized it down through the centuries, combined rhyme borrowed from foreigners with the Greek verse par excellence, the iambic fifteen-syllable line, which is already to be found in Aristophanes and which in Byzantium was called "politikos" ("public", in this case) precisely because of how widespread it was among the lower classes.

The French conquerors took this metre from the Aegean islands and introduced it into the folk songs of their own country. This is a clear proof of the reciprocal exchanges which went on between East and West, with the Aegean at the epicenter[13].

Thus, rhyme and the fifteen-syllable line were harmoniously adapted by the islanders in the "mandinades", distichs in verse form which were particularly open to musical and poetic improvisation, where the Aegean islanders have shown the power of their inspiration. Both at official, pre-determined occasions (feasts, local festivals, weddings, family gatherings) and in spur-of-the moment merrymakings by a group of friends, one could say that in the present-day Aegean the ancient "skolia" (banquet songs sung to a lyre) have been revived. A musician takes the basic motifs of the melodies (the "kontylies" as they are called on Crete) and "grafts" them with new rhythmical and melodic ornaments to show off his skill, signalling the start of a true poetic competition as the better *mandinada* players vie with each other, bantering, replying to and complementing each other while the party of people repeats half-line by half-line or line by line (in the Dodecanese) or the second half of the first line (in Crete). The subject matter of the *mandinada* is very diverse and is always adapted to the situation. Thus, one encounters amorous, social, historical, political, religious, satirical, laudatory, mourning and congratulatory *mandinades*, to name a few. On certain islands (such as Crete and Karpathos) the transmission of poetic improvisation is so widespread that frequently the inhabitants address each other, correspond or even write in the local press in *mandinades*. Thus, through the power of improvisation, the poetical and musical tradition of the Aegean is constantly renewed, despite the fact that one often finds older *mandinades* that have become "classics" and are repeated by the younger generation unaltered. In these pieces one sees the entire dynamic of folk elaboration which with the passage of time has shed everything

1, 2, 3. Three representations which clearly show the continual presence of the Greek tambouras *down through the ages, not only as an organological type with an analogous shape and names* (pandoura - thamboura - tambouras) *but also with a common technique for the playing of it (cross-legged).*
1. Muse playing the trichordon *or* pandoura. *Detail from a 4th century relief from Mantineia. Athens, National Archeological Museum (source: F. Anoyanakis, "Greek Popular Musical Instruments", p. 4). 2.* Thamboura *in a 16th century Byzantine wall painting (detail). Mount Athos, Koutloumousiou Monastery (source: "Music in the Aegean"). 3.* Tambouras. *Rethymno, Crete (period between the wars).*

1

2

3

4

5

4. Greek islander with tambouras (source: De Ferriol, "Recueil de cent estampes", Paris 1714).

5. Carol singers on Lesbos accompanied by a toumbeleki (source: F. Anoyanakis, op. cit., ill. 178).

superfluous or foreign to the community, producing masterly crafted, elegant gems, complete in form and in content:

With leaves of the rosebush a dress I'll make
and when I stroll past you, your heart will break.

The verse form as well as the content of many *mandinades* refer us to the "Epitaph of Seikelos" (1st century A.D.) the most complete and readable example of ancient Greek music that has come down to us and which was found at Tralles (on the coast of Asia Minor). On this tombstone Seikelos exhorts us:

Ὅσον ζῇς, φαίνου,	*While you live rejoice*
μηδέν ὅλως σύ λυποῦ.	*do not give sorrow voice.*
Πρός ὀλίγον ἐστί τό ζῆν·	*Life so very, very brief,*
τό τέλος ὁ Χρόνος ἀπαιτεῖ.	*and Time demands its due*[14].

The joy of life, interwoven with the imperceptible sorrow of death, has possessed the Aegean islander from Seikelos to Zorba and in modern Greece has once more become a song:

Dance on while you may
this earth will swallow us one day.
The grass upon the earth does wave
and leads away the young and brave.
(Cyclades)

Listen to the message a young man sent from Hades:
– Enjoy yourselves, you there in the upper world
because down here things are very tight.
There are no pretty girls in Hades, no fast livers,
nor a place for men to show their marksmanship...
("Rizitiko" song from Crete)

Furthermore, something else which shows the uninterrupted course of the musical tradition in the Aegean –which the language does as well– are the "helidonismata" ("swallow songs"), the carols marking the advent of Spring which, as Athenaeus mentions, date from the 6th century B.C. This selfsame song is still heard in Rhodes today, with a similar melody (as Samuel Baud-Bovy has proved) and only a few changes in the text. Nowadays, carolers (ill. 5) request:

The glass be full of wine
the scarf holds figs so fine
the basket with some eggs be lined,

just as the ancient Rhodians sang:

Παλάθαν σύ προκύκλει	*Bring figs hanging on a string*
ἐκ πίονος οἴκου,	*from the house with everything*
οἴνου τε δέπαστρον	*a cup of wine [would please]*
τυροῦ τε κάνιστρον.	*and in the basket, cheese.*

6. Greek dance accompanied by a tsambouna *(source: M. Guys, "Voyage littéraire de la Grèce", Paris 1783).*

Another proof is that "it is worthwhile for anyone who wants to learn about ancient Greece to study modern Greece, in all its expressions, and particularly in its outlying regions, such as the Dodecanese, where tradition has been faithfully maintained"[15].

Thus, in Aegean music one finds that the penetration of the western "major" and "minor" scales was resisted by the traditional Greek "dromoi" (literally, "roads"; here, "modes"), and modal scales (the dominant mode being the modes re, la and the chromatic re) which have a direct relationship to the ancient Greek "tropoi" and "ichoi" of Byzantine music.

We have already referred in general terms to the passage from the music of Antiquity to the music of Byzantium. Let us now look at certain elements that concern the influence of Byzantine religious music on folk music as this was expressed in the Aegean area.

These are the oldest surviving, written, musical scores of the *demotic* songs of modern Greece, which were found marked in Byzantine notation in manuscripts from the 17th century at Mount Athos (monasteries of Iveron and Xeropotamou). Their study, by D. Mazarakis, S. Baud-Bovy and B. Bouvier led to the conclusion that they were "rizitika" songs from western Crete, elements of which can still be found on the island today. They must have been inscribed by Cretan monks who had not completely renounced secular pleasures, for in the manuscripts that were found –among religious hymns and chants– there was the note: "and others for gaiety and joy"[16]. Moreover, it is a well-known fact that on the islands (and mainland Greece as well) the canters and the priests are among the best singers of *demotic* songs; the priest frequently leads the first dance and the wedding feasts commence with the related hymns ("The Beauty of Your Virginity" and others) – just as they still do today in Elymbos, on the island Karpathos.

Moreover, there are more than a few cases of islands (Lesbos and Samos, for example) where the church blesses the sacrifice of bulls; this is accompanied by dancing and singing just as in Antiquity (with the difference that now the sacrifice is in honor of a Christian saint). In the Dodecanese, on the feast day of Ayios Yiannis (Saint John), there is the custom of water divination which is accompanied by a special song[17], while on July 20 many islands have feasts in honor of the Prophet Elijah (Ilias) whose relationship to the god Ilios is not just limited to the name, but reaches all the way to the fiery chariot on which, according to tradition, he ascended to heaven[18]. At the same time we must make mention of the folk melodies which are directly reminiscent of Byzantine hymns, such as the "Pathos" ("Passion") on the island Kassos which comes down to us in the Songs of Praise ("eulogitaria") for Holy Saturday[19].

So, despite the repeated conquests and the foreign influences, the small communities in the Aegean managed to splendidly preserve their musical language down through time confronting the new with imagination and inspiration and guarding the traditional with nearly instinctual respect.

As one moves from the Middle Ages to modern Greece, a host of written and illustrated sources, mainly information from foreign travellers, bear witness to the rich musical life of the Archipelago. Despite the arrogance, the "graphic" bias and the "western" cast of mind which frequently characterize this data, it is nevertheless a valuable link which connects us to the Aegean music of the past.

In 1547 the French doctor, Pierre Belon, described the armed dances of the Cretans and in 1599 the Englishman Sherley spoke of the evening entertainment with lively dancing in the streets of Herakleion. In 1605 the French diplomat Jean de Contaut Biron was impressed by the dances and the musical instruments of Chios and in 1670 the Jesuit missionary Sauger wrote: "All the inhabitants of the islands, the women in particular, have a great fondness for dancing. On the eve of every great feast they come in groups and dance in the church enclosure. The aristocratic ladies arrive on horseback and their arrival is announced by the bagpipes and the drums which accompany them. The missionaries have tried to prohibit these festivals, but have not been able to..." (ill. 6).

Furthermore, Porter, Chandler and Savary (18th and 19th century) describe the dances of Greek sailors on the decks of their ships while other travellers (Guys, Montraye, Stackelberg and so on) array their books with etchings of island dances and musical instruments[20] (ills. 4, 6, 12, 27).

The various illustrated sources, as well as written testimony, from Antiquity right up to the travellers and the writers at the beginning of the 20th century (when a more systematic investigation of Aegean music commenced) convince one that musical instruments were also part of an uninterrupted tradition[21].

The flute –in its three forms: the *floyera* (open pipe), the *mandoura* (clarinet type with single reed) and the *souravli* or *thiamboli* (a ducted flute, ill. 7)– was the main instrument of the shepherds, together with the bagpipes (*tsabouna*, ill. 8, or *askomantoura* on Crete). The two joined reeds of the *tsabouna* are a re-creation of the double flute of Antiquity with an analogous technique for playing it: the musician plays the melody on one reed and uses the other to keep the drone.

The *tsabouna* along with the *toubaki* (a small drum) constitute the traditional island "zygia" (pair of instruments) suitable for celebrations in an open area because of the loud, penetrating sound made by these instruments (ill. 8). The second very common *zygia* in the Aegean is a combination of a *lyra* or violin with a *layouto* (lute) (ill. 11) while in certain of the Dodecanese (Karpathos for example) one still runs into the *zygia* of *lyra-tsabouna* under the name *liarotsabouna*.

The *compania*, the principal musical group in mainland Greece [clarinet, violin, *layouto*, *sandouri* (dulcimer) and the *defi* (tambourine)] even though it does exist along the coasts is not found on most of the islands. In actual fact the clarinet –the most important musical instrument on the mainland– is found only on Skyros, Chios and Lesbos, but it does not play a leading role in the musical groups[22]. Thus, the main melodic instruments in the Aegean remain the *tsabouna* (formerly), the *lyra* and the violin. Among the accompanying instruments are the *toubaki* (which besides the *tsabouna*, also accompanies the *lyra* in eastern Crete), the *layouto* (and, less frequently, the *tambouras* or the *outi* – the short-necked lute), the dulcimer, the *kanonaki* (psaltery) (formerly, along the coasts of Asia Minor) as well as a group of traditional membranophones (tambourines) and idiophones – brass *zilia* (cymbals), wooden spoons or even wine glasses which are struck against each other or rubbed with a string of worry beads. Instruments that can be played without accompaniment (solo) are the *sandouri* (dulcimer, ill. 9), the *kanonaki*, the *tambouras* (ill. 4) and the *outi*, particularly when the so-called "taximia" are being played (instrumental improvisations based on traditional modal scales) or accompany the *amanes* songs (vocal improvisations)[23].

The *laterna* (barrel-organ), even though confined to urban centers, made a decisive contribution to the uniform spread of tunes throughout the Aegean, bridging the folk and the urban musical tradition. A similar role was played, after 1920, by the phonograph, which in a number of cases came to replace the live, folk orchestra.

It is worth pausing for a while on an older technique for playing the Aegean *lyra*, which was in use before the appearance of the *layouto* as an accompanying instrument and which is still encountered in Kassos and Karpathos and, to a lesser degree now, in Crete. A row of small, pellet-bells used to be hung on the lyra's bow, which in Crete is known as the *yerakokoudouna* ("hawk bells") (from the fact that during the Byzantine period they were hung on hunting falcons) while in the Dodecanese they are called *asimokoudouna* ("silver-bells" because they used to be made of silver). These bells, with the proper, skillful movement of the bow, can be transformed in the hands of a good player into a second instrument of rhythmic and harmonic accompaniment as they under-

7

8

7. Shepherd from Crete playing the thiamboli *(*souravli*) (pipe). Geneva, Archives of S. Baud-Bovy.*

8. Tsambouna *and* toubi. *Pyrgi, Chios 1912. Athens, photographic archives of the Benaki Museum.*

score the rhythm, stressing the accented parts of the metre and accompanying the melody with the characteristic drone which gives their timbre[24] (ill. 10). This is an especially rare technique which, outside the island *lyra*, is only encountered in the case of the "sarangi", a stringed bowed instrument from India which belongs to the same family.

The *lyra* (vièle) in Greece goes back to the 10th century B.C. and despite the fact that it kept the name of the ancient instrument, it belongs to a completely different family of instruments (bowed instruments). Formerly, it was also played in mainland Greece while during our time it has been limited to the islands in the main (Crete, Kassos, Karpathos, S. Euboea, Limnos and some others). But on the islands the *lyra* (the same as the *tsabouna*) has been gradually replaced by the violin. There is evidence of the violin in Greece as early as the 17th century and it has a "softer" timbre suitable to indoor playing (where most entertainment has been transferred) and moreover has greater technical potential so that it corresponds to the new demands of the public and the musicians for ever-increasing virtuosity. This is because in the past a musician was considered to be good when he could play loudly and keep the dance going for hours, but during our time when amplifiers and songs played by "request" are the rule, virtuosity has become the main criterion. This change has profoundly affected not only the technique of playing, but also the construction of the musical instruments themselves. Thus, for example, we see the original model of the Cretan *lyra* (ills. 14, 28, 30) undergoing, after 1930, a series of radical morphological and functional changes (addition of a finger-board, change of tuning and so on), in order to adapt it to present-day social needs, but which have essentially transformed it into a violin (the extreme form of this was the *viololyra*) (ill. 18).

But the *lyra* has remained one of the principal ethnic symbols of the island of Crete, a function which makes one aware of the very important role that musical instruments play in the consciousness of the people. For they far transcend the level of "a simple object for the production of harmonious sounds" and come to embody music itself, expressing at all times –through their structure, the playing technique and their repertory– local, cultural identity[25].

Thus, the study of the "old" musical instruments of the Aegean islands leads us to another conclusion concerning the distinction between the music of the Archipelago and that of mainland Greece. Since the melodic range of these instruments (flutes, *tsabouna*, old *lyra*) is primarily limited to an interval of a sixth, the musical structure of traditional

9

9. Compania *in Mytilene. Postcard from the beginning of the century. Athens, photographic archives of the Benaki Museum.*

10
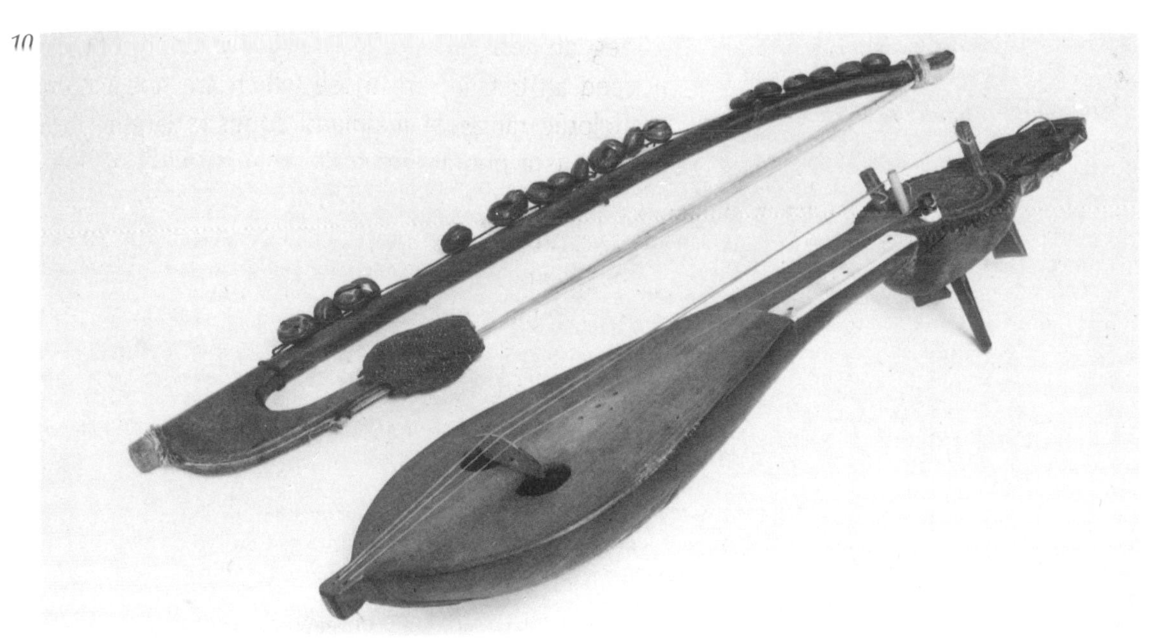

11

10. The lyra of S. Baud-Bovy. Made by Manolis Niotis, Karpathos 1910. Geneva, Musée d'Ethnographie.

11. Crete. Lyra and lute (layouto) (source: F. Anoyanakis, op. cit., ill. 192).

Aegean songs basically remains hexatonic (all the songs that reach or, more rarely, exceed an octave, are those which are not accompanied by instruments). Conversely, the melodic range of mainland songs is larger, most of the time, even in the cases where there is a pentatonic scale (that is, without semitones)[26].

Now we have reached precisely the point where contemporary ethnomusicological research has pinpointed the principal difference between the two musical worlds. On the mainland (Epirus, Thessaly and, to a degree, the Peloponnese, Roumeli and Macedonia) one encounters scales without semitones while, conversely, in the music from the island areas the semitone is dominant. It is noteworthy that this same difference also existed, as S. Baud-Bovy proved, in Antiquity; Doric harmony (no semitones) differed from the Ionian, the Lydian and the Phrygian (with semitones) which have since been dominant on the islands and along the coasts. Perhaps herein is concealed one of the principal "secrets" of the vastly different sound and "ethos" of the songs from the mainland and the islands[27].

We can make a similar distinction based on the rhythms found in the two areas. Nearly all the island dance songs are in 2/4 time and, less frequently, one finds a dactylic six-beat time (6/8 in the *syrmatiko* of Karpathos or some other "free" *balos* dances).

Conversely, in mainland Greece the dominant rhythms are: the three-time (3/4, as in the *tsamikos*) and the seven-time (7/8 of the *syrtos Kalamatianos* dance which comes from the ancient *epitritos*). The duple-time *syrtoi* ("on two" and "on three"-steps) are, as a rule, slower in their rhythmic expression than those of the islanders.

Moreover, along the coast of Asia Minor, on the islands of the eastern Aegean and in the Dodecanese one encounters –as early as Sappho's poetry– nine-time rhythms which in our time are represented by the 9/4 of the *zeïbekikos* and the 9/8 of the *karsilamas*.

These two rhythms, with all their variations and together with the 2/4 of the *hasapikos*, were the rule in the urban folk music of the Aegean which, by the closing decades of the past century, spread to all Greek harbors (with Smyrna as the epicenter), creating the marvelous tradition of the *rebetiko* song[28].

12

12. Dance from Paros (source: Choiseul-Gouffier, "Voyage pittoresque de la Grèce", vol. 1, Paris 1782).

13

Indeed, if one set aside its branch on mainland Greece (which principally represented by Vasilis Tsitsanis) *rebetika* were born and developed in the waters of the Aegean, expressing the longing and the yearning of the lower and the middle classes of the urban centers-harbors. If one examines the life of its most important representatives, one will see that all of them (composers, singers, musicians – even those who made a career in Greek recording in the USA) were connected to the islands or the coasts: Vangelis Papazoglou, Markos Vamvakaris, Marika Papagika, Rita Ambatzi, Antonis Dalgas... The list is a particularly long one. The Aegean *rebetiko* was born in tavernas, coffeehouses and the *café-aman*. "The tavernas in Smyrna and the other harbors are continually full of people drinking, dancing and singing; even on the decks of their ships they have managed to set aside little places for their longing to dance", as the traveller J. Bartholdy wrote at the beginning of the past century.

Rebetiko, particularly during its first two periods (up to 1940) retained all the characteristics of genuine folk creation and, more importantly, manifestly proved once more the assimilative and re-modelling power that has always distinguished the civilization of the Aegean when faced with foreign influences, and its unique adaptability to social conditions.

As early as 1702 P. de Tournefort observed that in Smyrna "the tavernas are open all hours of the day and night. There they play music, eat good food and dance à la franga, à la greca and à la turca". So the meeting of the East and the West in the Aegean area, to which reference has already been made, has *rebetika* as one of its most representative expressions. The harbors mentioned above were the areas where the age-old musical tradition of the Aegean passed through the filter of Italian, French, Rumanian, Serbian, Turkish, Persian, Armenian and Gypsy influences. In the back streets of Smyrna old Aegean ballads mixed with Italian canzonettas, French modish melodies, Rumanian "chores", Serbian tunes and Turkish "sarkia", while in the *café-aman* Greek musicians accompanied Armenian singers and Gypsy dancers, in front of a public which represented all the races in the eastern Mediterranean.

The result, recorded in the grooves of gramophone records (ills. 13, 15), is a partic-

14

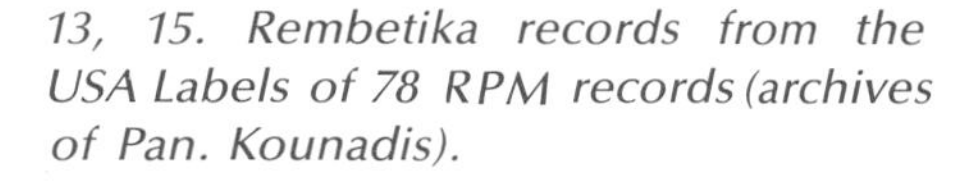

13, 15. Rembetika records from the USA Labels of 78 RPM records (archives of Pan. Kounadis).

14. Old type of Cretan lyra, 1954. Geneva, Archives of S. Baud-Bovy.

ularly eloquent one. It fits all this together in a music which comes to be embodied in and to harmoniously carry on the Aegean musical tradition. A music which is firmly based on the melodic and poetic structure of the Greek *demotic* song but which, at the same time, does not hesitate to use, with daring and imagination, both the harmonic language of the West and the artifices and the charm of the East. In his autobiography[29], Markos Vamvakaris emotionally describes the island festivals and feasts in Syros where he accompanied his father, who played the *tsabouna*, on the *toubaki*. Later he took up the *bouzouki* and the *baglamas*, those instruments that are spoken so ill of by the critics of *rebetika*, even though they were derived from the family of the ancient Greek "pandoura" or "trichordon" (three-stringed lute), the Byzantine "thamboura" and the "tambouras" of the freedom fighters of the Greek War of Independence of 1821 (ills. 1, 2, 3).

The rich musical tradition of the Greeks who lived on the Asia Minor coast (together with that of the Smyrnian *rebetika*) was transferred, after the Asia Minor Disaster of 1922, to all the areas where the refugees went, grafting the local musical traditions with the wisdom of the Greeks from the East and the same nostalgia and inner intensity that has been hidden in the wanderings over these waters since the time of "Captain-Dysseas" (Odysseus).

Since then, children have been born in new homelands which are changing almost day by day. The social and economic changes in post-war Greece are well-known. The causes and the results are many and complex and are unavoidably expressed in musical life as well. Tourism discovered the Aegean and the Aegean tourism while the *mandinades* of Greeks abroad always speak of the de-population of the islands due to emigration, but now to Athens itself rather than America or Australia.

In Athens (and other urban centers) as well as abroad, there are quite a number of island music "centers" (clubs), the societies and the associations which are addressed to emigrants and organize various forums, dance lessons, circulate books, records and tapes, all in an effort to keep in contact with their place of origin (with all the positive as well as negative consequences connected with these processes).

Some of the music of the Aegean may have been transferred to apartments and night

15

16

16. Cretan dance accompanied by bagpipe (askavlos), 1954. Geneva, Archives of S. Baud-Bovy.

17

clubs in the large cities or to record companies, but this does not mean that the islands and the coasts have lost their thread in the musical labyrinth: the summer festivals still collect their native islanders from overseas, the young go on singing carols, during Carnival the *koudounatoi* (bell-wearers) of Skyros continue to exorcise evil spirits while on Chios and Lesbos are heard the indispensible "ribaldry", with the spirit of Dionysos somewhere among the revellers. On Good Fridays women mourn around the *Epitaphios* ("bier of Christ") just as they still sing dirges for their own dead; at the same time other mothers are still lullabying their babies and children go on appealing to the sun in their games, as in olden times. In the eastern Aegean –though now in front of the tourist's camera-lens– bulls are still sacrificed every year, accompanied by dancing and singing. In Crete there is no way you can miss hearing about the battle of Digenis with Charon, always in fifteen-syllable verse which since the 10th century have told in epic akritan (border) ballads of the "sufferings of illustrious men". In the Dodecanese someone can always be found to sing ancient and tragic tales ("The Castle of Oria", "The Song of the Dead Brother", "The Bridge of Arta", "The Exile's Return" and so on). These are subjects which first appeared on the coasts of Asia Minor and spread not only into Greece but also into the broader region of the Balkans and South Italy. Furthermore, if you avoid tourist guides and keep your eyes open, it is not impossible that even today you might run into the old sea-dogs of George Seferis who, as he wrote, "resting on their nets... sang to me when I was a child the song of Erotokritos, tears welling from their eyes".

Seferis was not the only one who heard in the Aegean "the rattles of time" and lay comfortably "in the prow, next to the mermaid, her red lips singing as she gazed at the flying-fish...".

There have been many Greek composers who were directly inspired by the Aegean musical-poetic tradition. Chief among them was Yannis Konstantinidis who based the largest part of his compositional creation on the folk songs of the islands and Asia Minor, employing a harmonic language of delicacy and artistry. The exquisite harmonization of the five folk songs from Chios, in the collection of Hubert Pernot, that was done by Maurice Ravel, are similar in manner.

18

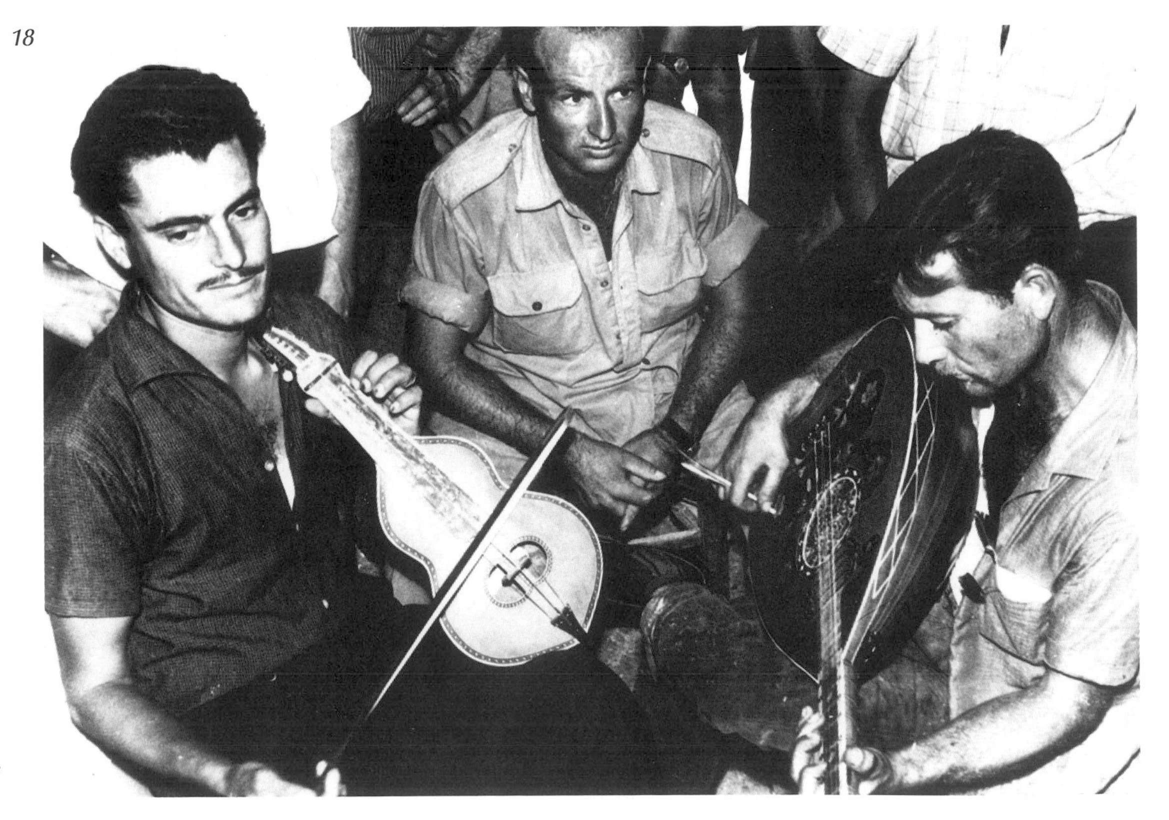

17. Chania, 1990. Society of the Musicians of Cretan Music (source: "Music in the Aegean").

18. Crete, 1964. Viololyra *and* layouto *(photo: Y. Hekaterinidis).*

19. Sheet of music by Nikos Skalkotas. Transcription of the rizitiko *song, "O Digenis" which was sung by El. Venizelos in 1930 for the Society of Demotic Songs. Athens, Archives of M. Merlier, Center for Asia Minor Studies.*

19

It is also worth noting the "Dance tunes of Kythera" for piano by Dimitris Mitropoulos, the transcriptions of Siphnian songs done by Nikos Skalkotas (ill. 19), for the Folk Music Archives of Melpo Merlier, the "Island pictures" for violin and orchestra by Manolis Kalomoiris, the "Concerto for piano and orchestra" (based on Cretan musical themes) by Mikis Theodorakis, the *sousta* for guitar by Dimitris Phabas and the "Melichomedhi" (based on the poetry of Sappho and Alcaeus) by Yiorgos Sisilianos. (This catalogue is merely indicative and it goes without saying that is limited to Greek and foreign composers who were directly inspired by the music of the Aegean, because if we wanted to extend it to those who used its natural wealth and history as a starting point, then a large, separate article would be needed).

So, the Aegean has been the womb of music and George Seferis, from a long line of Aegean poets, eloquently expressed the deepest essence of the musical vicissitudes of the Archipelago down through the centuries when he wrote: "... I know of a bent pine tree near a sea. At midday it casts shade as scanty as the days of our life and in the evening the breeze passing through its needles picks up a strange song, like sounds that have abolished death. I once spent a night under that tree. At dawn I was a new man, as if I had just been freshly cut from a quarry...". This is the message carried by the music of the Aegean. Let those with ears listen to it.

NOTES

This article, in its original form, was part of an album that was published in 1987 by the Ministries of Culture and the Aegean to accompany the exhibition "Music in the Aegean", whose object was the Aegean musical heritage down through the centuries. This exhibition was presented in Syros (Cultural Center of Ermoupolis), in Athens (Goulandris-Horn Foundation), in Brisbane, Australia (EXPO '88) and in Geneva, Switzerland (Museum of Ethnography), in 1987 and 1988).

1. Ι.Θ. Κακριδῆς, *Ἑλληνική Μυθολογία*, Ἐκδοτική Ἀθηνῶν, τόμ. 2, Ἀθήνα 1986, 139-144.

2. Record in the series "Greek Folk Dances – Dora Stratou", record no 110, side 1, no 8, "ayeranos from Paros".

3. Ι.Θ. Κακριδῆς, *op. cit.*

4. See the relevant quote in *Ἐγκυκλοπαίδεια τῆς ἀρχαίας ἑλληνικῆς μουσικῆς* by Σόλων Μιχαηλίδης, ἔκδ. Ἐθνικῆς Τραπέζης τῆς Ἑλλάδος, Ἀθήνα 1978.

5. *Op. cit.*

6. *Op. cit.*

7. *Op. cit.*

8. Παῦλος Γνευτός, *Τραγούδια Δημοτικά τῆς Ρόδου*, ἔκδ. «Πρίσμα», Ρόδος 1980, 79-83.

9. Record "Musique de la Grèce antique", Atrium Musicae de Madrid, Gregorio Paniagua, ed. Harmonia Mundi, HM 1015.

10. Fivos Anoyanakis, *Greek Popular Musical Instruments*, ed. "Melissa", Athens 1991.

11. Γ. Παπαδόπουλος, *Συμβολαί εἰς τήν ἱστορίαν τῆς ἐκκλησιαστικῆς μουσικῆς*, ἔκδ. «Κουλτούρα» (ἐπανέκδ.), Ἀθήνα 1977.

12. S. Baud-Bovy, *Δοκίμιο γιά τό ἑλληνικό δημοτικό τραγούδι*, Πελοποννησιακό Λαογραφικό Ἵδρυμα, Ναύπλιο 1984, 31-32.

13. *Op. cit.*, 33.

14. *Op. cit.*, 8-9.

15. *Op. cit.*, 11-12.

16. Δ. Μαζαράκης, *Μουσική ἑρμηνεία τῶν τραγουδιῶν τῆς Μονῆς τῶν Ἰβήρων* (πρόλογος S. Baud-Bovy, ἐπίλογος Β. Bouvier), Ἀθήνα 1967.

17. Γ. Μέγας, *Ἑλληνικές γιορτές καί ἔθιμα τῆς λαϊκῆς λατρείας*, ἔκδ. «Ὀδυσσέας» (ἐπανέκδ.), Ἀθήνα 1988, 227 καί Δημ. Λουκάτος, *Τά καλοκαιρινά*, ἔκδ. Φιλιππότης, Ἀθήνα 1981, 54-64.

18. Γ. Μέγας, *op. cit.*, 232-237 καί Δημ. Λουκάτος, *op. cit.*, 87-95.

19. Record "Songs of Kassos and Karpathos", in the series of the Society for the Dissemination of National Music (S. Karas), SDNM 103.

20. Κ. Σιμόπουλος, *Ξένοι ταξιδιῶτες στήν Ἑλλάδα*, τόμ. 3, Ἀθήνα 1970-75 καί Ἀλ. Γουλάκη-Βουτυρᾶ, *Μουσική, χορός καί εἰκόνα*, ἔκδ. Συλλόγου πρός διάδοσιν ὠφελίμων βιβλίων, Ἀθήνα 1990.

21. F. Anoyanakis, *op. cit.*

22. Δ. Μαζαράκης, *Τό λαϊκό κλαρίνο στήν Ἑλλάδα*, ἔκδ. Γαλλικοῦ Ἰνστιτούτου, Ἀθήνα 1959 (β΄ ἔκδ. «Κέδρος», 1986).

23. Μ. Δραγούμης, «Σχόλιο γιά τόν ἀμανέ», περ. *Τράμ*, ΙΙ, 2 Σεπτ. 1976, 151-7.

24. L. Liavas, *La lira piriforme en Crète et dans le Dodecanèse*, doctoral thesis EHESS, Paris 1986.

25. *Op. cit.*

26. S. Baud-Bovy, *op. cit.*, 28-30 and 38.

27. *Op. cit.*

28. Γκαίηλ Χόλστ, *Δρόμος γιά τό ρεμπέτικο*, Ἀθήνα 1977.

29. Μ. Βαμβακάρης, *Αὐτοβιογραφία*, 1973.

BIBLIOGRAPHY

ΑΜΑΡΓΙΑΝΑΚΗΣ, Γ., «Κρητική βυζαντινή καί παραδοσιακή μουσική», *Κρήτη - Ἱστορία καί πολιτισμός*, Ἡράκλειο 1989.

ANOYANAKIS, F., *Greek Popular Musical Instruments*, ed. "Melissa", Athens 1991.

BAUD-BOVY, S., *Τραγούδια τῶν Δωδεκανήσων*, ἔκδ. Σιδέρης, τόμ. I, Ἀθήνα 1935, τόμ. II, Ἀθήνα 1938.

— *La chanson populaire du Dodecanèce, Les textes*, ed. Les Belles Lettres, Paris 1936.

— *Chansons populaires de Crète occidentale*, ed. Minkoff, Geneva 1972.

— *Δοκίμιο γιά τό ἑλληνικό δημοτικό τραγούδι*, Πελοποννησιακό Λαογραφικό Ἵδρυμα, Ναύπλιο 1984.

ΓΚΙΚΑΣ, Γ., *Μουσικά ὄργανα καί λαϊκοί ὀργανοπαῖχτες στήν Ἑλλάδα (Ν. Εὔβοια-Σκύρος)*, Ἀθήνα 1975.

KALOYANIDES, M., *The music of Cretan dances*, doctoral thesis, Wesleyan Univ. (Ph.D.) 1975.

ΚΑΡΑΚΑΣΗΣ, ΣΤ., *Ἑλληνικά Μουσικά Ὄργανα*, ἔκδ. «Δίφρος», Ἀθήνα 1970.

LEYDI, R., *Musica popolare a Creta*, ed. Ricordi, Milan 1983.

ΛΙΑΒΑΣ, Λ., «Ἡ κατασκευή τῆς ἀχλαδόσχημης λύρας στήν Κρήτη καί στά Δωδεκάνησα», *Ἐθνογραφικά*, Πελοποννησιακό Λαογραφικό Ἵδρυμα, 4-5, Ναύπλιο 1983-85, 117-142.

— *Music in the Aegean*, Ministry of Culture - Ministry of the Aegean, Athens 1987.

ΠΑΝΑΓΙΩΤΑΚΗΣ, Ν., *Ἡ παιδεία καί ἡ μουσική στήν Κρήτη κατά τήν Βενετοκρατία*, Κρήτη 1990.

ΠΕΡΙΣΤΕΡΗΣ, ΣΠ., «Ὁ ἄσκαυλος (τσαμπούνα) είς τήν νησιωτικήν Ἑλλάδα», *Ἐπετηρίς Λαογραφικοῦ Ἀρχείου*, 13-14 (1961), 52-71.

PERNOT, H., *Ἑλληνικές δημοτικές μελωδίες τῆς νήσου Χίου*, ἔκδ. Ὁμήρειου Πνευματικοῦ Κέντρου Χίου, Χίος 1990 (ἐπανέκδ.).

ΧΟΛΣΤ, ΓΚ., *Δρόμος γιά τό ρεμπέτικο*, Ἀθήνα 1977.

ΨΑΧΟΣ, Κ., *Δημώδη ἄσματα Σκύρου*, Ἀθήνα 1910.

SELECTED DISCOGRAPHY

1. *Songs of Kassos and Karpathos*, Society for the Dissemination of National Music (research - recording Simon Karas), SDNM 103.

The same series by Ch. Karas contains the following:

2. *Songs of Rhodes, Chalki and Symi*, SDNM 104.
3. *Songs of Amorgos, Kythnos and Siphnos*, SDNM 105.
4. *Songs of Thasos, Limnos, Samothrace*, SDNM 108.
5. *Songs of Mytilene and Chios*, SDNM 110.
6. *Songs of Crete*, SDNM 114.
7. *Songs of Constantinople and the Propontis*, SDNM 118.
8. *Songs of Mytilene and Asia Minor*, SDNM 125.
9. *Τραγούδια τῆς Αἴγινας* (*Songs of Aegina*), Archives of Melpo Merlier - Historical and Folklore Museum of Aegina (2 records) - supervision Markos Dragoumis, Falereas Bros., FA 115-116.
10. *Grèce: Chansons et danses populaires* - Collection S. Baud-Bovy, Archives internationales de musique populaire - V.D.E., supervision Lambros Liavas, AIMP XII.
11. *Songs of E. Crete*, supervision Y. Amaryanakis, University Editions, Crete.
12. *Musica popolare di Creta, I. Violonisti*, supervision Roberto Leydi, ed. Albatros.
13. *Musica popolare del Dodecaneso*, supervision Wolf Dietrich, ed. Albatros.
14. *Kalymnos: many-versed songs, dances, distichs*, supervision L. Drandakis, ed. Lyceum of Greek Women, LCGW 106-107.
15. Nikos Oikonomidis: *Θαλασσινά περάσματα* (*Sea passages*), BMG.
16. Nikos Oikonomidis: *Πέρασμα στά Κύθηρα* (*Passage from Kythera*), Society "I Myrtia".
17. Irene Konitopoulou-Legaki: *Island songs*, Olympic.
18. Tassos Diakoyiorgis: *Νησιώτικο σαντούρι* (*Island dulcimer*), Alcyon.
19. *Κάρπαθος: Μελωδίες* (*Karpathos: melodies*), Marigoula Kritsioti - Man. Kostetsos, Falereas Bros.
20. *Δημοτική παράδοση: Νησιώτικα* (*Demotic tradition: Island songs*), EMI.
21. *Δημοτική παράδοση: Μπάλλοι* (*Demotic tradition: Island balloi*), EMI.
22. *Οἱ πρωτομάστορες τῆς κρητικῆς μουσικῆς* (*The masters of Cretan music*), (re-recorded from 78 RPM records) A.E.M.E.

20

21

22

23

24

20, 21. The two sides of the stone sarcophagus from Ayia Triada, Crete (1450 B.C.) with a depiction of a seven-stringed lyre and a double flute. Crete, Archeological Museum of Herakleion.

22. Apollo playing the lyre. Clay plaque from the 5th century B.C. Crete, Chania Museum.

23. Black-figured pelike *by the painter Eucharides with a depiction of a double flute (500-490 B.C.). Samothrace, Archeological Museum.*

24. Clay pyxis *(1300 B.C.) with a depiction of a seven-stringed lyre. Crete, Chania Museum.*

25. Tsambouna *and flute. Detail from an icon of the Nativity (17th century). Jerusalem, Church of Bethlehem.*

26. Concert with instruments and dancing: "Praise the Lord". Wall painting from the first half of the 18th century. Mount Athos, The Great Lavra, side-chapel of Koukouzelissa.

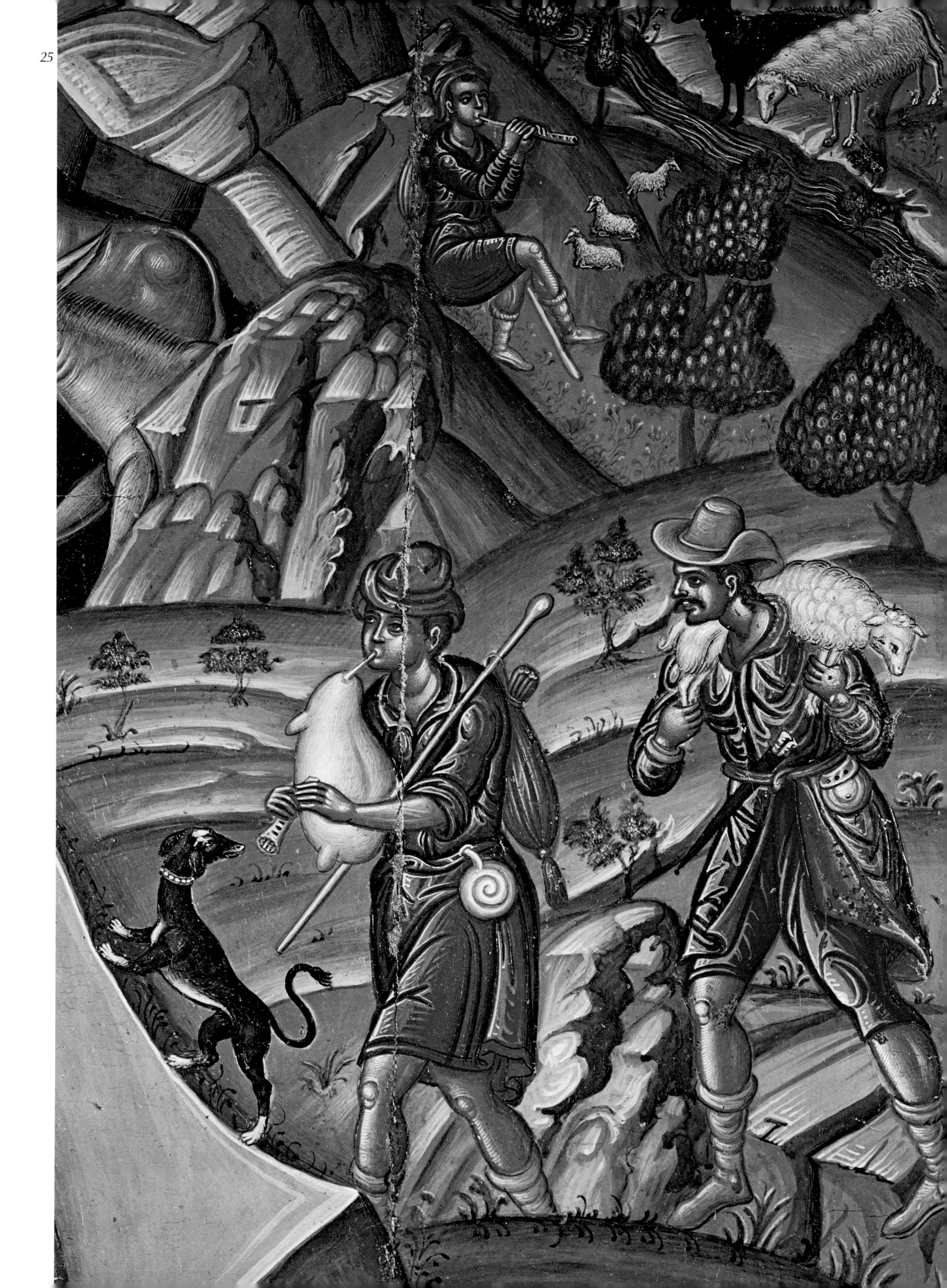

ΤΟ ΑΓΙ
ΟΝ

27. Greek sailor with lute (source: O.M. Stackelberg, "Costumes et usages des peuples de la Grèce moderne", Rome 1825).

28. Pear-shaped Cretan lyra (1743) and bow with bells. Athens, Museum of Popular Musical Instruments – F. Anoyanakis Collection.

29

30

29. Theophilos Chatzimichael, "The poet of Lesbos, Sappho, and the lyre player Alcaeus", 1932. Mytilene, Municipal Museum.

30. Theophilos Chatzimichael, "Limniot shepherd", 1933. Mytilene, Municipal Museum.

CHRISTOS DOUMAS

The early Aegean and its contribution to the development of western Thought

Translated by Alexandra Doumas

The pre-Socratic philosophers of Ionia were the first to attempt a reasoned interpretation of nature. Their strictly critical thought was not, however, the outcome of a momentary coincidence of circumstances. Early Greek science was not born in a vacuum. Long before the Ionian philosophers, the Aegean people had passed beyond the level of a closed traditional society. Both the archaeological evidence and, primarily, the texts – the Linear B tablets – reveal that the Mycenaean kingdoms of the fifteenth and the fourteenth century B.C. were true states with an army, a fleet, a bureaucratic system, division of labour and social stratification[1]. Moreover, there are indications in these tablets that some code of justice had been formulated in the Mycenaean world, which regulated relations between members of society[2]. Even though the Linear A texts of Crete, which date from before the arrival of the Mycenaeans on the island, remain undeciphered, there is convincing evidence that during the first half of the second millennium B.C. Cretan society had many of the diagnostic traits of a complex society. The Phaistos Disc, which dates from the early centuries of the second millennium, was, in the opinion of one scholar, a kind of almanac on which different phases of the constellations, useful for planning seasonal activities[3], have been recorded. This implies that important steps had already been made in the Aegean in the field of astronomy, even if these were the outcome of practical needs. The complexity of Cretan society during the so-called Palatial periods is also reflected in the imposing building aggregates. The range of functions they served, as P. Halstead has succinctly observed, combined under one roof roles which correspond to those of "Buckingham Palace, Whitehall, Westminster Abbey and, perhaps, even Wembley Stadium"[4]. The Minoan palace even functioned as an educational centre[5]. Last but not least, mention should be made of the generally accepted viewpoint that the famous Gortyn Code (fifth century B.C.) includes elements of familial, religious and civil law deriving from the Minoan period[6].

Archaeological research has shown that these two worlds, the Minoan and the Mycenaean, were in close and constant contact with the civilizations of the Eastern Mediterranean. This puts S. Sambursky's views on early Greek thought into perspective, namely that "it inherited material some of which had been worked upon and some not: the prescientific myths and cosmogonies of Greece and the accumulated treasures of two thousand years of Babylonian and Egyptian science". It was in this spirit that the Ionian philosophers embarked on their struggle of "logos" against "mythos", aspiring to a "rational interpretation of natural occurrences which had previously been explained by ancient mythologies"[7].

Archaeological evidence confirms that for thousands of years the Aegean and its archipelago served as a bridge for the transmission of goods and ideas[8]. It was the crossroads where the mentalities and civilizations of three continents met. The Aegean merchant and mariner was at the heart of this conflux, if not indeed its instigator. Thus he had the chance to judge and compare ideas and to form his own opinion. There is nothing excessive in the claim, therefore, that reasoned thought in the Aegean had been cultivated for many centuries before the appearance of the Ionian philosophers. They were simply able to classify and record it for posterity, thanks to the fact that writing had developed.

Thousands of years before the Colophonian Xenophanes attributed the origin of everything to Water and Earth, the inhabitants of the Aegean had found in the combination of these Elements the ideal solution to many of their problems. Using earth and water they created the shell –the dwelling, the settlement– within which their society evolved, directly after the abandonment of nomadic life and the founding of permanent installations towards the end of the seventh millennium B.C. A little later, in the sixth millennium B.C., with the addition of a third Element –fire– they were able to manufacture clay vessels and thus solve provisioning and dietary problems by improving methods for the preservation and preparation of food.

The major discovery, however, which radically changed people's lives, was metallurgy. In this were combined the four Elements the pre-Socratic philosophers considered essential for the creation of all matter: Earth, Fire, Air and Water. Earth, as an ore, with the aid of Fire, and assisted by Air (bellows), became liquid. When it cooled it had changed into something else, it had become metal.

Fully developed metallurgy appeared in the Aegean two and a half thousand years before Thales or Heraclitus sought the origin of all things in Water and Fire respectively[9]. At the beginning of the third millennium B.C. metal tools, which truly revolutionized the way of life, were evidently first used in the Aegean islands. In agriculture they both improved production methods and reduced the input of labour, leaving time for other activities: for recreation and reflection. In carpentry they contributed to the improvement of building skills and, consequently, the dwelling. The new tools enabled strides to be made in shipbuilding, thus giving a boost to seafaring. With better and larger vessels the Aegean islanders were able to undertake longer and more rewarding voyages. The earliest depictions of ships date from this millennium, the third[10].

From the moment well-built vessels ensured safe and speedy transport, the Aegean islands were permanently settled, the character of the economy radically changed and the centre of gravity was displaced from the productive North to the promising South. Aegean society moved from the subsistence economy of the Neolithic villages to transit trade, in which the islanders were middlemen. The large plains of Thessaly, Macedonia and the Peloponnese, which had been in the vanguard in the previous millennia, now withdrew to a secondary position. The islands came to the fore as important centres and it is there that the first tentative steps in proto-urban development were taken[11].

On their long voyages the intrepid islanders saw "towns with many people" and came to know "mind". Their home environment, with its open horizons, drove them to explore and broaden their minds. There was no potentially threatening or hazardous natural barrier, such as a mountain with its wild beasts for the mainlanders, to impede their progress. Thus there was no leeway for the creation of fantastic monsters or demons to explain away certain phenomena. A far-off, barely visible landmass slowly came into view as the sailor drew near. And when he arrived he discovered it was little different from where he had come from. Here too there was vegetation, there were animals and there were people, even though they spoke another language. For the well-travelled Aegean islander things were crystal clear and could be explained by reason.

Long voyages demanded more than just sturdy ships. Knowledge of meteorological phenomena and the currents, as well as of astronomy, were also required. There are indications that from very early on the Aegean islanders made use of wind power for propulsion of their craft[12]. And if we take into account the contacts with lands such as Egypt, Syria, Palestine and Cyprus[13], from the second millennium B.C., it can be readily concluded that the sailors of the prehistoric Aegean had already discovered the surface currents of the sea and exploited them accordingly[14]. These experiences, embedded in the memory and traditions of the people, are reflected in Hesiod's instructions to his brother Persis:

Ἤματα πεντήκοντα μετά τροπάς ἠελίοιο
ἐς τέλος ἐλθόντας θέρεος, καματώδεος ὥρης,
ὡραῖος πέλεται θνητοῖς πλόος . . . .
. . . . .
Τῆμος δ' εὐκρινέες τ' αὖραι καί πόντος ἀπήμων.
εὔκηλος τότε νῆα θοήν ἀνέμοισι πιθήσας
ἑλκέμεν ἐς πόντον φόρτον τ' ἐς πάντα τίθεσθαι,
σπεύδειν δ' ὅττι τάχιστα πάλιν οἰκόνδε νέεσθαι.
μηδέ μένειν οἶνον τε νέον καί ὀπωρινόν ὄμβρον
καί χειμῶν' ἐπιόντα Νότοιό τε δεινάς ἀήτας,
ὅς τ' ὤρινε θάλασσαν ὁμαρτήσας Διός ὄμβρῳ
πολλῷ ὀπωρινῷ, χαλεπόν δέ τε πόντον ἔθηκεν.

("Fifty days after the summer solstice, which is at its zenith then, an oppressive season, is the time for people to launch voyages... And when the sea breezes are constant and the sea safe, then with an easy mind trust to the winds and put the swift ship to sea, load it with all manner of cargo and look to returning to your home again, as quickly as possible; do not be caught waiting for the new wine and the first rains when winter strikes and the south winds rage and rile the sea, for the sea is made dangerous by the heavy rains of Autumn". Hesiod, *Works and Days*, 663 ff.).

According to the British astronomer M.W. Ovenden, the manner of depicting the constellations, as it has come down to us through the Alexandrian poet Aratos (315-250 B.C.), must have been conceived in the Aegean islands in the third millennium B.C. Ovenden deduces from the visual angle and the sequence in which they appear on the horizon that the relevant observations must have been made in this area *circa* 2700 B.C. The way the constellations were rendered did not serve any scientific purpose and it appears that they "were not designed because of fancied resemblances of star patterns with mythological figures, but rather as a primitive form of celestial co-ordinates"[15], the aim of which was "... to set up a simple navigation system, inaccurate and primitive it is true, but adequate for short journeys when the mariner is not long out of sight of land"[16].

With such a substratum of scientific knowledge, albeit empirical, of chemistry (pottery, metallurgy)[17], physics (hydrodynamics, aerodynamics)[18], astronomy and probably other fields which elude us at present, and with the open-mindedness fostered by their maritime ventures, the Aegean islanders of the third millennium B.C. proceeded to create institutions in which we find some of the ideals still common to humanity today.

The division of labour in the island communities at that time had reached the level which the great French sociologist Durkheim characterizes as "compound" or "specialization proper"[19]. Metal-workers, potters, artists such as sculptors and later painters, shipwrights, merchants and sailors were but a few of the categories of specialist craftsmen. This division was not simply economic, it had other ramifications too. It contributed to the organic cohesion of society where the job of one fitted in with the job of another and supplemented it[20].

The society of the Aegean in the third millennium B.C. was at a stage which could be qualified as "proto-scientific". It had transcended the stage in which there is "absolute unity derived from the intimate contacts of communal personal associations and participation in common values". It no longer belonged to what the sociologist F. Tonnies calls *Gemeinschaft*, in which the cohesion, characterized by sacredness, is mechanistic[21]. Here it is a case of *Gesellschaft,* in which the unity is individualized and differentiated and where "the parts of the whole are hardly more than physically juxtaposed, relations are impersonal, and the will of the individual is deliberate and rational"[22]. Such societies, where a community is dependent on other communities, as well as on its own division of labour, correspond to what Durkheim called a "social organ". Cohesion is organic and consists of "an integration dependent on differences, interdependence, and reciprocal usefulness, like the relationship between two organs in a body or two parts in a machine". In contrast to *Gemeinschaft, Gesellschaft* is distinguished also by secularity[23].

This secular element and the rule of reason can be traced back in the Aegean islands to at least the third millennium B.C. Not one building or site which could be automatically classified as a place of worship, a shrine, has been located in a settlement of this period. On the contrary, what is manifest in all aspects of material culture is an inherent anthropocentricism. Nowhere have monumental buildings analogous with those erected in Asia and Egypt in the same period been found. There are neither enormous temples nor magnificent palaces, intended to diminish man and impose upon him the authority of the god, and of his representative on earth, the ruler. In the buildings in the island settlements, the human scale prevails. Not power but reason (logos) was the motive spirit. The Aegean islander was convinced only by logical explanation and dialogue, not by recourse to the divine. That is why even though assembly areas appeared very early in the islands[24], royal palaces were never erected. The Aegean islands did not favour the concentration of wealth –and thus authority– in the hands of a few[25].

The anthropocentricism of Aegean civilization is also apparent in its art. From the Neolithic period till the present day, man and his occupations or preoccupations has been its reference point. Even the depictions of the deity assumed an exclusively human form[26]. Only in the Aegean did humans neither worship nor venerate animals. Only here were god and man, creator and creation, made in each other's image[27]. The speculation as to what is represented –god or man– in Neolithic, Cycladic, Mycenaean and Geometric figurines, the *kouros* and the *kore,* is characteristic of the humanization of god or the deification of man. Only in the Aegean was the promotion of the individual as the basic unit of human society achieved so early and defined with such clarity.

This anthropocentricism, which is reflected in the remains of the islanders' material culture, surely characterized their thought as well. The roots of the maxim: "Man is the measure of all things" assuredly delve deep in the early history of the Aegean. The naval code of the ancient Rhodians, according to which damage incurred by the jettisoning of cargo in the event of danger at sea had to be shared equally between all those who had cargo on the ship, is today one of the fundamental international rules of sea transport[28]. But this law was not drawn up by chance. It must have been applied in practice, as a custom, for several centuries before it was codified and written down. This too must have been one of the rules of human conduct of the early mariners of the Aegean.

In the light of the foregoing, we can better comprehend the emergence of the pre-Socratic philosophers, most of whom were, moreover, urbane merchants and seasoned seafarers. Only in a world where the processes we have outlined broadly above had already taken place could what the contemporary French thinker Jean-Pierre Vernant, have occurred: "De l'origine du monde, de sa composition, de son ordonnance, des phénomènes meteorologiques, ils proposent des explications débarrassées de toute l'imagerie dramatique des théogonies et cosmogonies anciennes"[29]. Through the discovery and the exploitation of the force of natural elements, the early inhabitants of the Aegean confronted their problems and perhaps they, before the Ionian philosophers –to quote Vernant again– "ils ont utilisé les notions que la pensée morale et politique avait elaborées, ils ont projeté sur le monde de la nature cette conception de l'ordre et de la loi qui, triomphant dans la cité, avait fait du monde humain un *cosmos*"[30].

In order to create this world, the Greeks had to devise a tool, which too appeared for the first time in the history of mankind: political thought. The central position of the individual in society was the main prop on which Greek political science was founded. A science which sought practical ways of organizing the society-state so that the individual could live better within it. As T.A. Sinclair observes, the Greeks viewed civilization "as the antithesis of barbarian despotism, the marks of which were Slavery for all"[31]. The freedom of the individual should not, however, jeopardize the concept of equality, because "the lust for wealth and power was so strong among them that they knew its dangers and feared its consequences"[32].

NOTES

This text was originally presented as a paper at the Three-Day Aegean Conference, December 21-23, 1989, *Παρνασσός*, ΛΒ΄(1990), 1-7.

1. J. Chadwick, *The Mycenaean World*, Cambridge 1976, 69 ff.

2. H. van Effenterre, "Droit et Prédroit en Grèce depuis le déchifrement du Lineaire B", *Symposion* 1985, 4-5.

3. L. Pomerance, *The Phaistos Disc: An Interpretation of Astronomical Symbols*, Göteborg 1976.

4. P. Halstead, "From Determinism to Uncertainty: Social Storage and the Rise of the Minoan Palaces", *British Archaeological Reports*, International Series 96, 1981, 201.

5. H. van Effenterre, "Les fonctions palatiales dans la Crète Minoenne", in E. Levy (ed.), *Le système palatial en Orient et en Grèce*, Strasbourg 1985, 181.

6. C. Davaras, *Guide to Cretan Antiquities 1976: Gortyn Code*. See also R.F. Willets, *Cretan Cults and Festivals*, London 1962, 112, 198, 306.

7. S. Sambursky, *The Physical World of the Greeks*, Princeton University Press, 1987, 3 and 4.

8. The exploitation and transport of Melian obsidian from the eighth millennium B.C. confirms early shipping in the Aegean, perhaps the most ancient in the world. See T.W. Jacobson, "17,000 years of Greek Prehistory", *Scientific American:* "Hunters, Farmers and Civilizations", 1979, 137.

9. K. Branigan, *Aegean Metalwork of the Early and Middle Bronze Age*, Oxford 1974.

10. Χ. Τσούντας, «Κυκλαδικά», *Ἀρχαιολογική Ἐφημερίς*, 1899, 90. Χ. Ντούμας, «Κορφή τ' Ἀρωνιοῦ», *Ἀρχαιολογικόν Δελτίον*, 20 (1965), 49 and 53. C. Renfrew, "Cycladic Metallurgy and the Aegean Early Bronze Age", *American Journal of Archaeology*, 71 (1967), pl. 3. L. Basch, *Le Musée imaginaire de la marine antique*, Athènes 1987, 79-83.

11. For example, at Poliochni in Limnos several characteristic traits of urbanism, such as a town-plan, public works (stone-paved streets, drainage system, public wells, fortification wall), the division of labour and so on had already appeared by the third millennium B.C., establishing the settlement as the most ancient town in Europe. See L. Bernabò-Brea, *Poliochni: Città preistorica nell' isola di Lemnos*, vol. I, 1964, vol. II, 1976 as well as Χ. Ντούμας, «Τό προϊστορικό Αἰγαῖο, κοιτίδα δημοκρατικῶν θεσμῶν», *Πατρέας*, 13 ('Απρίλης-Μάης-'Ιούνιος) 1988, 24-29.

12. If the two vertical lines on a ship incised on an Early Helladic sherd from Orchomenos constitute an attempt to render a mast, then this is the earliest

known indication of sailing ships in the Aegean. Early Minoan sealstones and sealings also show that the sailing ship was quite widespread before the end of the third millennium B.C. Cf. L. Basch, *op. cit.*, 83, ill. 172 (sherd from Orchomenos) and p. 99: B3, B4, B5 (EM seals).

13. V. Hankey, "Mycenaean Trade with the Southeastern Mediterranean", *Melanges de l'Université St. Joseph*, 46 (1970-1971), 11-30. R.S. Merillees, "Trade and Transcendance in the Bronze Age Levant", *Studies in Mediterranean Archaeology*, 39 (1974).

14. Recent studies have shown that a prehistoric Aegean vessel required only a 4-5 day voyage to reach Cyprus from Crete, if it exploited the surface currents of the Eastern Mediterranean. See, A. Theodorou and E. Mantzourani, "An attempt to sketch in the sea lanes between Cyprus and Crete during the Bronze Age", International Scientific Symposium: *The Civilizations of the Aegean and their extensions in Cyprus and the eastern Mediterranean, 2000-600 B.C.*, 18-24 September 1989, Larnaka 1991, 39-54.

15. M.W. Ovenden, "The Origin of the Constellations", *The Philosophical Journal*, vol. 3, No. 1, 1966, 8.

16. *Ibid.*, 14.

17. For example, the deliberate use of arsenical bronze in the early stages of metallurgy, because of its resistance to corrosion and oxidation, as well as its gradual replacement with tin bronze because of its high toxicity, bespeak quite a sophisticated knowledge of chemistry (see J.A. Charles, "Early Arsenical Bronzes – A Metallurgical View", *American Journal of Archaeology*, 71, (1967), 21-26). Similar knowledge is attested by the use of mica as a filler in the clay destined for the manufacture of cooking pots to make them more resistant to fire (for example, the cooking pots of Poliochni), or the choice of clay, depending on the specific required temperature for the firing of each kind of vessel (see Y. Maniatis and M.S. Tite, "Ceramic Technology in the Aegean World during the Bronze Age", *Thera and the Aegean World* (edit. Ch. Doumas), London 1978, 482-492.

18. Γ. Βῆχος, «Ἀεροδυναμική καί ὑδροδυναμική τῶν Πρωτοκυκλαδικῶν πλοίων πού εἰκονίζονται στά "τηγανόσχημα" σκεύη τῆς Σύρου», *Ἀρχαιολογία* 32 (1989), 21-23.

19. R. Biersted, *Emile Durkheim*, London 1969, 49.

20. *Ibid.*

21. R. Redfield, *The Little Community; Peasant Society and Culture*, The University of Chicago Press 1965^4, 141.

22. *Ibid.*, 142.

23. *Ibid.*.

24. For example, the so-called Theatre or "Bouleuterion" at Poliochni. See L. Bernabò-Brea, *op. cit.*, vol. I, 182.

25. Χ. Ντούμας, «Ἔθιμα καί θεσμοί τῆς Πρωτοκυκλαδικῆς κοινωνίας», *Ἐπιστημονική Σκέψη*, 41 (1988), 78.

26. See G.S. Kirk, *The Nature of Greek Myths*, Penguin 1974, 51.

27. K. Τσάκος, *Τό Μουσεῖο τῆς Ἀκρόπολης* (forthcoming).

28. Γ. Μιχαηλίδης-Νουάρος, «Μία ἔνδοξη σελίδα τῆς νομικῆς ἱστορίας τῆς Ρόδου», *Νομικό Βῆμα*, 33 (1985), 209-14, for the relevant bibliography.

29. J.-P. Vernant, *Les origines de la Pensée Grecque*, P.U.F., Paris 1962, 96.

30. *Ibid.*, 102.

31. T.S. Sinclair, *A History of Greek Political Thought*, London 1961, 3.

32. *Ibid.*

YIORGIS YIATROMANOLAKIS

The Aegean and Greek literature

Translated by Philip Ramp

The Aegean, outside its historical, ethnic and economic significance has for centuries been a highly important area for the production of literature, art and culture just like the Peloponnese, central and northern Greece, the Ionian islands, Crete and Cyprus. In this sense, the Aegean, like every other area of Greece, does not simply exist as a geographical space indissolubly connected to the history and life of the nation, but in addition it is the cradle for the production of a special cultural ideology and a distinct symbolism. Because of its geographical position and its natural formation, the Aegean constituted one of the original birthplaces of Greek civilization and, at the same time, through its sea lanes, forged a link between mainland Greece and both the Greek colonies of Asia Minor and the other civilizations in the region.

More specifically, the three main prehistoric civilizations, the Minoan, the Cycladic and the Mycenaean were born and originally developed within the boundaries of the Archipelago. In all likelihood, the Homeric epics were composed here and during historical times lyric poetry, philosophical thought, historical narration and mathematical and medical science flourished on these islands and the eastern shores of the Aegean. The first attacks of the Persians would be realized via the Aegean sea and their dreams of conquest would be extinguished once and for all in the waters of the Archipelago at the Battle of Salamis. So, it was not by chance that Delos was appointed the religious and political center of the first Athenian Alliance (477 B.C.) after the defeat of the Persians. In this manner the entire Aegean acquired, through the literature of the 5th century B.C. (see, for example *The Persians* and *Agamemnon* by Aeschylus) the aura of a place of vital importance for Hellenism, regardless of the fact that many of these literary allusions did not use historical events as their starting point but were more closely related to the concept of a super-historical and "mythical" Aegean as it is found in the Homeric epics. This feeling of a mythic-poetic and a real-historical Aegean continues to be expressed by its literature (written and oral). Indeed, after the so-called '30s generation of Greece, we are now able to refer to an Aegean literature which lends to the Archipelago a special aesthetic, ideological and moral importance (beyond its national one).

The present article cannot possible aspire to exhaust all the ancient, Byzantine and modern Greek literary references to the Aegean or to occupy itself with the entire range of literature that the Aegean has supplied us with for centuries now. Its primary aim is to touch on the high points — in the opinion of the author — of this literary creation and to note the ideological and cultural significance of the Aegean, as it emerges from its literature.

Ancient Times

Though neither *The Iliad* nor *The Odyssey* refers to the Aegean sea by name (the first mention of its name is in line 659 of *Agamemnon* by Aeschylus; cf. Herodotus 2.99, 4.85, 7.55) there is no doubt that the countless marine images of tempest or calm, the related maritime comparisons and the metaphors of the Homeric epics originated in this sea. Moreover, the etymology of the word Aegean itself (*aiges* = kymata, i.e., waves), refers to this great body of water, this eternally moving and continually transforming sea. This image of the sea (visual, acoustic), that is, the Aegean sea, can also be seen in the traditional adjectives one encounters in the epics which allude to various moods and views of the liquid element where Hellenism first travelled and achieved great deeds, such as, for example, the adjectives: «ἰχθυόεσσα» (full of fish), «πορφυρέη» (crimson), «πολιή ἅλς» (white-waved sea), «πολύφλοισβος» (loud-roaring), «εὐρύπορος» (where all may roam at will), «ἀτρύγετος» (yielding no harvest), «γλαυκή θάλασσα» (gleaming sea), «οἴνωψ» (wine-dark), «μέλας» (swart), «εὐρύς» (broad), «ἠεροειδής πόντος» (cloud-streaked sea) and «μέγα πέλαγος» (great sea). All these adjectives show that the eyes of the Homeric poet (who came from the coasts of Asia Minor or an island in the eastern Aegean) were filled and inspired by the same sea on which he lived.

Regarding the great, legendary sea voyages of the Argonauts, Odysseus and other mythical heroes, we can say that they were nothing more than the remodelled recollections of the endeavors of the first Greek mariners to conquer the Aegean and the seas that stretch beyond and around it. However, one should not lose sight of the fact that all the mythical, undetermined and unindentified lands in *The Odyssey* lie outside cap Maleas and Kythera island, that is, outside the borders of the Aegean of Odysseus (*The Odyssey,* X, 80-81). In the lands outside the Aegean are where the prodigious and supernatural events occur (Circe, Cyclops, Scylla and Charybdis, the Sirens and so on) and this is where the reality of Odyssian geography ceases, despite the fact that the flora and fauna referred to in these lands does not differ from the Aegean or, at least, the natural environment (again flora and fauna), of the broader Mediterranean area.

However, when the poet, by the nature of things, places his heroes within the known geographical area of the Aegean then these lands are real, as Homer appears to have had a first hand acquaintance with the topography of the Archipelago. This can be seen very clearly, for example, when the poet describes the crossing of the Aegean sea by the Acheans who are being repatriated after the war and particularly the reference to the return of Nestor and his comrades in the Book III of *The Odyssey.* This is the first description of the crossing of the Aegean from East to West and from North to South and one can easily confirm how the described passage of the Greek ships over the Aegean seems to precisely set down the first naval chart of the region (Book III, 153-183).

At dawn we dragged our ships to the lordly water,
stowed aboard all our plunder
and the slave woman in their low hip girdles.
But half the army elected to stay behind
with Agamemnon as their corps commander;
the other half embarked and pulled away.
We made good time, the huge sea smoothed before us,
and held our rites when we reached Tenedos,
being wild for home. But Zeus, not willing yet,
now cruelly set us at odds a second time,
and one lot turned, put back in the rolling ships,
under command of the subtle captain, Odysseus;
their notion was to please Lord Agamemnon.
Not I. I fled with every ship I had;
I knew fate had some devilment brewing there.
Diomedes roused his company and fled, too,
and later Menelaos, the red-haired captain,
caught up with us at Lesbos,
while we mulled over the long sea route, unsure,
whether to lay our course northward of Khios,
keeping the Isle of Psyria off to port,
or inside Khios, coasting by windy Mimas.
We asked for a sign from heaven, and the sign came
to cut across the open sea to Euboia,
and lose no time putting our ills behind us.

The wind freshened astern, and the ships ran
before the wind on paths of the deep sea fish,
making Geraistos before dawn. We thanked Poseidon
with many a charred thighbone for that crossing.
On the fourth day, Diomedes company,
under full sail put in at Argos port,
and I held on for Pylos. The fair wind,
once heaven set it blowing, never failed.

(*The Odyssey,* trans. by Robert Fitzgerald, Anchor Books, Doubleday and Company Inc., Garden City, N.Y).

Unfortunately, the original loses its elegance and power in translation and the small, but important details of the Aegean being described, along with the Homeric navigation, are also lost. But what clearly stands out is the classic passage of Greek ships from Troy to northern Greece and the knowledge and familiarity the poet has of the «μεγακήτεα πόντον» (cavernous sea), the «μέσον πέλαγος» (middle sea) and the «ἰχθυόεντα κέλευθα» (fish-road) the Acheans sailed over.

The first detailed and elegant description of the Aegean appears to have inspired all subsequent descriptions of the Archipelago and all Greek writers seem to have been moved by the same feeling of familiarity which runs through the Homeric text: the Aegean sea is a famous, enchanting and fruitful sea, sometimes dangerous but at the same time a friendly place in the Greek world, indissolubly linked to the history of the nation and the life of all who live or sail there.

One can observe this, for example, in the ancient Greek lyric poets, most of whom had their origins in the Archipelago. These poets, who could also be called the poets of the Aegean —without them referring to the Aegean by name— had, as can be seen in the few surviving fragments, a particularly intense relationship with their birthplace and were the first to consciously use the marine element for their personal, poetic needs. We will mention only three of these poets, Archilochus (7th century) from Paros, Sappho (7/6th century) and Alcaeus (7/6th century) from Lesbos.

The adventuresome life of Archilochus is well-known as is his participation in various naval operations in the Aegean where, according to tradition, he was killed in one of these military conflicts. Thus, it is only natural that the maritime, Aegean element is often encountered in his poetry. In one of his surviving fragments (56D = 105W), for example, he gives us a marvelous description of an impending tempest, the "mark of winter", off one of the coasts of the Aegean, most probably Tinos. But, as has been observed, this intense image of the approaching, dangerously bad weather simultaneously expresses man's fear when faced with some more general danger:

Glaucus, look. Already the deep sea is stirred
With waves, and about the Gyrean heights mistrises aloft,
Signal of storm. And suddenly fear comes on.

The daring metaptor for the sea (which would later become commonplace) holding the life of the shipwrecked in its embrace is also distinctive (21D = 213W):

Souls clasped in the wave's embrace.

Finally, one of the most original and daring poems, in subject matter, is the fragment where Archilochus, with pitiless aggressiveness, prays that a former friend of his will have a shipwreck on the shores of Thrace where naked and frozen and covered in seaweed, he will fall into the hands of the savage inhabitants of the area and spend the rest of his life as a slave (79a D):

Driven by the sea.
Naked in Salmydessos may the top-knotted Thracians
Seize him in their gentle way
(With them he will find a full career of hardships,
Eating the bread of slavery),
As he lies frozen with cold, may seaweed in abundance
Ooze over him from the brine;
May his teeth chatter as he lies like a dog,
Helpless on his face
At the very edge of the waves...
All this I would like to see
Because he wronged me and trampled on oaths,
He who was once my friend.

This must be the only poem in which the cruelty of a shipwreck on the coast of the north Aegean, is used by a poet in such impressive detail to punish the ungrateful and traitorous behavior of a former friend. The Aegean sea seems, one could maintain, to take on the role of a purifier and punisher — this role was undertaken by the same Aegean sea once again, but on a larger scale, when a few decades later, it would drown the invading Persians.

One encounters different images of the Aegean in some of the fragments of Sappho and Alcaeus. Thus, in one fragmentary poem (25D) Sappho seems to be imploring Aphrodite and the Nereids to bring her sojourning brother back unharmed to her native land, just as a present-day sister or mother of a sailor would, while in the so-called "poem of Arigno" (98D) the beauty of the beloved female friend is compared to the light of the moon which exceeds that of the stars. This is the heavenly light of the Aegean moon which falls on the salt sea and the flowering fields alike:

Over the salt sea
and over the richly flowered fields.

The linking of the sea and the earth under the light of the moon seems like a common enough image today, but this correlation, this "equation" of the earth-sea and the immutable and direct relationship of the two elements is realized for the first time by the great poetess from Lesbos; it will be carried on and repeated, in various ways, by later writers and poets from the Aegean.

The element of the sea plays a more important role in the surviving fragments of Alcaeus than in the poetry of his contemporary, Sappho, and here is where we can discern (not for the first time, but to a greater extent) the idea of the city-vessel, which will become another commonplace in Greek literature. The maritime metaphor or allegory, with its obvious political overtones, is naturally derived from naval activities and practices in the Aegean sea. Alcaeus writes (frag. 46a D):

I am baffled by the quarrelling winds.
One wave rolls up this side
another on that and we on our black ship
are caught in the middle,
struggling hard against the storm.

The bilge-water has already reached the mast-socket,
ande the sail is worn through as well;
there are great rents along it
and the sheets are slackening...

(*The Penguin Book of Greek Verse,* ed. by C.A. Trypanis, Penguin Books Ltd, Harmondsworth, Middlesex, England).

The same picture of a state in danger of sinking from the misdeeds of its inhabitants, enlarged and with more details, in found (though not exclusively) in a collection of poems, the "Theognideia", which is attributed to the Megarean poet Theognis. The interest here is that this extended poetic allegory of the political situation is focused on the stormy sea of Milos and the entire marine image offers us, even if indirectly, an idea of the typical conditions in the Aegean. Addressing himself to a friend, the poet says (668-682):

If I had money, Simonidis, it would not bother me to consort with the rich. Now, however, that I am aware my fortune has gone and I have been left speechless with poverty, I nevertheless know the state of things better than most. Outside the sea of Milos we pitched and tossed with our white sails lowered. The sailors refused to bail out the water and the sea washed over both sides of the ship. It is difficult for one to survive that. The good captain, who wisely knew how to keep us safe, has been cast aside. Money is snatched up, order has been lost to the world and nothing is shared out fairly. We are ruled by the merchants' cargo and the wicked now sit higher than the good. I am afraid our ship will be swallowed by the waves. I speak enigmatically and in parables for all the pure at heart, but even the wicked can comprehend this, if they have any sense at all.

From the above it appears that, outside everything else, the organic relationship that exists between the Aegean and its poets, and the influence that the sea exercises both on the growth and evolution of a special aesthetic (and ethic) and the development of a way of thinking, is what Odysseus Elytis would call, a great deal later, the "anti-slavish ethos" of the Aegean. This, of course, also holds true for the subsequent poets, the tragedians in particular.

This feeling of freedom emanating from the Aegean, the feeling of protection and security which it provides Hellenism as well as its cathartic role, which we have already alluded to, appears, we believe, very clearly and for the first time in Aeschylus. Thus in *The Persians* (472 B.C.) the Aegean seems to participate in the destruction of the invaders and the related references are not concerned with the Homeric Aegean (compare, *Agamemnon*) or the post-Homeric period (*The Women of Troy, Iphigenia in Tauris* and so on). This is the Aegean of the poet's period and its role in the events, regardless of whether the conduct of the naval battle takes on mythical dimensions through the language of Aeschylus (*The Persians,* lines 558-579):

For landsmen and seamen both,
the ships, dark-eyed and linen-winged,
led forth (woe!) the ships
laid them low (woe!) the ships,
under the deadly impact of the foe
and by the hands of Ionians.

(...) and those who were first to meet their
doom left behind perforce are swept along
about the Cychrean strand.
Groan and gnash your teeth;
in grievous strain shout forth our woes
till they reach the heavens.
(...) Lacerated by the swirling waters
they are gnawed (alas!)
by the voiceless children of the stainless sea.

We would say that we are given a similar feeling by the multiple maritime Aegean images found in Euripides (to limit ourselves to him). These images, which are derived from the natural and historical area of the Aegean, are not merely examples of the keen sensitivity and the attentiveness of the poet, but also reveal his aesthetic point of view and the image he has formed on the Aegean, both as a place of commerce and wealth and as an agreeable place to travel. Let us look at, for example, a part of the first chorus of *Iphigenia at Tauris* where the captive chorus sets forth its point of view in regard to the coming of the two foreigners, Orestes and Pelades, to the barbarian land of Tauris (lines 407-432):

Was it the jealous search for wealth to
Exalt their home
That drove their sails racing before the wind,
That plashed their pinewood oars, two wings as one,
To bring home riches over the wide waters?
Such hope is sweet to men:
Though it bring sorrow, it is not satisfied.
They wander over the waves, visit strange cities,
Seeking a world of wealth,
All alike sure of achievment;
(...) Trace the journey they have made:
Through the crags that close like jaws,
Past the swell unsleeping
Of the bay of Phineus,
Skimming, coastwise, Amphitrite's restless foam,
Where the fifty Nereid maidens
Dance and sing in the circling chorus;
Bellied canvas, the cleft ripples
Noisy round the turning rudder;
South wind, West wind urging onward night and day
To the myriad whiteness
Of the sea-birds on the gleaming island beach...

(*Penguin Classics,* trans. by Philip Wellacott, Penguin Books Ltd, Harmondsworth, Middlesex, England).

For those who maintain that the above quoted, vivid maritime description, with the circular dance of the Nereids, has to perhaps do with the sea that spreads beyond the Sympligades and not the Aegean, then the opening lines of the *Women of Troy* will convince them of what sea the poet is truly inspired by. As they are declaimed by Poseidon himself the lines take on even greater authority:

I come, Poseidon I, from briny depths
Of the Aegean sea, where Nereids dance
In lovely-woven passings of their feet.

(*Euripides Plays,* vol. I, trans. by A.S. Way, Everyman, 1959).

The descriptions of the Aegean by the ancient writers and the relatively poetic images could naturally be multiplied as all of them, poets and prose writers, historians and orators refer to both the physical glory and beauty of the sea and to its importance for the historical, economic and cultural development of the nation. From all this testimony (which could be easily multiplied) intensely projects, as has already been alluded to, both the organic relationship of the writers and the Aegean and the influence that it exercises over them which is finely honed until this special Aegean aesthetic has been fashioned as well as an overwhelming desire for freedom and creation. Furthermore, this is shown by the two final examples taken from two writers from early Christian times, the Evangelist John and Aelius Aristeides (2nd century A.D.).

To the Evangelist John, the Aegean and Patmos in particular, was the center of the world from where the enraptured writer surveyed the universe:

I, John, who also am your brother, and companion in tribulation, and in the kingdom and patience of Jesus Christ, was in the isle that is called Patmos, for the word of God, and for the testimony of Jesus Christ. Here on this island which would later acquire great importance (just as Tinos more recently and analogous to Delos in Antiquity) for the spiritual, moral and religious life of the area, what is envisioned will be broadcast to the seven churches: *I was in the Spirit on the Lord's day, and heard behind me a great voice, as of a trumpet.* Most probably "Revelation" was composed so that the Aegean, where most of the journeys of the apostles were also realized, would take on this spiritual and somewhat transcendent dimension which was to occupy the writers of the Generation of the '30s more than anything else.

The orator Aelius Aristeides (2nd century A.D.) in a short encomiastic speech of his which was superscribed: "To the Aegean Sea" summarizes, in a certain way, the poetic as well as the physical image that Antiquity had supplied. The writer wants to extol the Aegean which is why he puts aside any reference to another sea:

We will not speak for the moment about the other seas which are useful to people and which were made by God for all of them and will endeavor to express our due respects and praise for the Aegean. Its first excellence is its position [...] as it is in the middle of the entire universe and all sea having the Hellespont, the Propondis and the Black Sea to the north and the remaining sea to the south. It divides Asia from Europe at the point where the two continents were originally separated by the Hellespont. The races of people who dwell on its two shores are celebrated and peaceful; the one inhabits the land of Ionia and Aeolia and the other Greece. Thus only this sea can be said to lie in the middle of Greece, if, of course, one places the Greek race on both one coast and the other.

Thus, after referring to the superiority of the Aegean over all the other seas and praising its waters and islands, he ends by giving us an extensive picture wherein the Archipelago is likened to a perfect and harmonious human body:

The Aegean has a vast range of charms which unite the sea and the mainland, just as the ornamental deer and the pelts of leopards have the colors and the design intermixed. Thus, this entire sea is resplendent with glory while on the mainland lemon groves in full flower can be seen [...] and just as the sky is adorned with stars so the

Aegean sea is adorned with its islands, so that even one who does not need to travel by sea, will sail happily there, passing through the Aegean. And of all the oceans on earth and all the places, this sea is the most beautiful and its beauty is a symbol of the Aegean [...] Moreover, only the Aegean cannot be called infertile. Neither is it barren nor fruitless, but is distinguished for its fine wine and its fertile land [...] and contains all goods, all joys and all sights. It is full of harbors, full of sanctuaries, full of pipes and paeans, springs and rivers. It is the nurse of Dionysios but equally propitious for the Dioskouri and the Nereids. It provides a felicitous life and every kind of joy. For its inhabitants as well as the merchants who ply this sea it is lucrative and salutary and is favorable to all. But just as the beginning and end of a beautiful body is decorum, this sea also has a lovely beginning and end. It begins with the first series of islands to the south and ends at the Straits of the Hellespont which washes the peninsula on all sides and makes it worth seeing. Thus, as one says, its beauty begins at the head and extends all the way to the feet. When speaking of its channels and coves, one cannot begin to measure their number or beauty. And even those who have been terrified by the Aegean still want to go back to it again because people cross this sea for the supreme joy it offers them.

Modern Times

In order to find analogous descriptions of the Aegean sea, we have to move forward to much later times, practically the present. Nevetheless, during the centuries which define our modern literature, that is, from the first modern Greek texts (10th century), to contemporary literary production there is, of course, no lack of references to the Aegean. We could indeed mention a literature of the sailors and the sea which unquestionably has to do with the life and the work of people within the specific maritime area we are examining. The dangers of the sea, the shipwrecks and the difficulties faced by sailors in general, are subjects oft repeated in Greek *demotic* songs, along with the stories of corsairs, pirates and galleys, as for centuries the Aegean was the field for pirate raids and a variety of hostile actions.

From the many demotic songs which sing of the "white" sea we are presenting two (fragmentary) texts, which are indigenous to the broader area of the Aegean. The first is a fragment from a well-known variation of "To Kyr Northwind" (N.Y. Politis, *Ἐκλογαί ἀπό τά Τραγούδια τοῦ ἑλληνικοῦ λαοῦ*, 127-128) and the second is a dirge from the area of Thrace (*Τό δημοτικό τραγούδι τῆς Ξενιτιᾶς*, ed. G. Saunier, Nea Elliniki Vivliothiki, 105):

A

Kyr Northwind sent his orders out to all ships:
"You sailing ships, you galleys on the move,
head for your harbors, because I want to blow
to whiten fields and mountains, chill cold springs
and hurl upon the land what lies before me on the sea".
And all the ships that heard headed for the harbor
But Kyr Andria's galley sailed further on.
"I'm not afraid of you, Kyr Northwind, blow all you want
my ship is of walnut and my oars boxwood
I have bronze yards and masts of steel
I have silk sails, silk from Bursa
and my cables are of a blonde girl's hair;
I have a deck-boy who knows the weather
and once my course is set I'll not turn back".

"Deck-boy climb the middle mast
see what the weather's like, check the wind"
He went up smiling, weeping he came back down.
"–Boy just what was it you saw up there?"
"–I saw a troubled sky and stars that bled
I saw the squall flashing and the moon was lost
and hard bright hail falling on the mountains of Attaleia"
The fierce storm broke and the rudder groaned
the sea glowed and the masts screamed
the waves rose in mountains, the ship leapt
the storm struck one side, the storm struck the other
the storm hit from the side and the planks burst loose.
The sea filled with sail, the waves sailors
and the little deck-boy had forty miles to go.

B

Blow wind, southwind blow, lightly blow
so all the boats of Rodopi will come home.
All the boats came, they all appeared
only Fotaki's boat did not appear.
–You slave, you my girl, bring my veil
so I may wear it when to the shore I go
so I may ask the young men eighteen years old.
All the boats came, they all appeared,
why has Fotaki's boat not appeared?
–Fotaki's boat is gone, it's lost
the waves are pounding him upon the shore
and his black locks twine round his lean frame.

One could maintain that the variety and quite high quality of these maritime or nautical songs (The "nisiotika" songs) which are accompanied by certain musical tunes (*syrtos, balos* and so on) have their origins in this rich poetic tradition of the Aegean. This music which has been produced and circulated in the Aegean for centuries is no less important to literary production itself and research in this area by qualified specialists would help us gain a more complete understanding of this cultural aspect of the Aegean as well. An investigation concerning the Aegean landscape and the uniqueness of vernacular architecture as it has developed on the scattered islands of the Archipelago is of equal urgency. The economy of space, the small but functional building on a rock or a bare, waterless surface, the small courtyard, the two-storeyed units, the repeated boundary walls and the terraced fields, the whitewash or the charming colors which characterize the island houses along with every Aegean architectural element constitute a component of a cultural and aesthetic space, the same as one finds in the music and the songs of the Aegean. All are components of the same folk culture.

Of the well-known (and major) modern Greek poets, the first it appears to make use of the Aegean as a specific subject in the poetry, of particular importance and clearly symbolic, was Andreas Kalvos from the Ionian islands. In at least four odes, "To Chios", "The Ocean", "The Volcanos" and "To Samos", the poet referred to this ethnic area in order to praise the sea battles the inhabitants fought for their freedom.

The ode "To Chios" is dedicated to the uprising and the destruction of that island in March 1822. One frequently finds in the poetry of Kalvos, that before he mentions the historical or other events he wants to praise, he sets before us the natural environment in which these events were acted out, "psychologically colored". In other words, before the heroic figures are introduced and their emotional and psychic moods described, the natural landscape is itself charged with a similar, intense emotion. This is what happens in the following ode: the desolate landscape as well as the entire "sacred current" of the Aegean seems to be sharing the suffering of the human beings.

To the desolate
shores of the island
are brought the waves
and the complaints
of the Oceanides.

The milky limbs
of the maidens of Chios
no longer feel the spray
of your sacred current
Oh glorious Aegean.

Thus, the deepest inner relationship between the landscape and the person appears to be revealed and the recognized influence existing between the animate and the inanimate is defined, that is, the external and the internal landscape are of one and the same substance, a position that has remained a constant for modern Greek poets since the period of Solomos and Kalvos. This innermost relationship between land-person appears to be supremely favored by the Aegean which in Kalvos has taken on, besides everything else, a mythological dimension uniting the Homeric perception of the all surrounding Ocean or the land of dreams with the concrete but, at the same time, mythical "hieratic" space.

As over the bounless
sea of dreams
a few, despairing
souls of the dead make passage
unhurriedly;

Thus from the trees
of Athos to the rocks
of Kythera moved
the slow carriage
along the skyroad,

The trimorph Hecate
viewed the ships
in the bays of the Aegean
pulled up ingloriously, left
scattered.

Then you, oh most brilliant
daughter of Zeus, the only consolation
of the world,
you then remembered my land,
Oh Freedom.

The goddess arrived; she descended
to the illustrious
shores of Chios; she spread
out her hands and crying
said:

– Ocean, father
of the deathless dances
hear my voice
and consummate the great longing
of my soul.

. . . .

So said; and straightway blinding
brilliance was shed on the surf
of the Ocean, illuminating
waters wide-surfaced
and divine.

The waves sparkled
high as the heavens and cloudlessly,
serenely, the sun shines
revealing the many islands
of the Aegean.

This picture of the mythical Aegean, bathed in the "transcendent" light of an ancient tradition is complemented by the image of the epic and heroic Aegean in the ode, "To Samos". Employing a lofty style Kalvos refers to the "reality" of the geography and history of this island and first among modern Greek poets he reveals the crucially important position the Aegean has occupied, both in Greek history and Greek civilization and in the entire image, the multifarious manifestation of the Greek landscape.

Muse, you know
the Icarian sea. Look, Patmos
then Korassies and Kalymnos
which feeds bees on
unmowed flowers.

Then the island of aloe
and prosperous Kos
which gave Apelles to the world
and the immortal
Hippocrates.

Look, the great terror
of the land of Asia, Samos.
Weave it a wreath
laudatory and eternal,
lyric maid.

There, remember you filled
a merry krater
with the tea of Anacreon
and laid out cool roses
for the elder.

You taught Homer there
to let his fingers run
in harmonious agreement with the ode
when the works he narrated were
of gods and heroes.

It is interesting that this relationship of the Aegean sea with Kalvos was noted by a modern poet who could himself be characterized as the "poet of the Aegean" par excellence, Odysseus Elytis. Thus, in his study "The true physiognomy and the lyrical daring of Andreas Kalvos" (*'Ανοιχτά χαρτιά,* 86-87) he writes:

Indeed, Kalvos was the first modern Greek poet with a maritime awareness (in a superb combination of Aegean and Ionian nature) an awareness which on the one hand placed him at the center of Greek reality and on the other at the center of contact of present-day Greek poets with their European counterparts. I don't know if Kalvos was personally acquainted with life on the Greek islands. But what is important is that with a sensibility open to the purest elements of life he was influenced by the most representative nature of the land and gave it the leading place in his poetry.

The best known poet, after Kalvos, to use the Aegean as a physical environment or, more accurately, a "backdrop" against which certain poetic events were acted out, was the Phanariot Alexandros Rizos Rangavis (1809-1892) who in 1864 published that well-known poetic narrative, *The Voyage of Dionysus.* However the affected language of the poem, its obvious rhetoricism and, in general, its romantic tone, provide us with a completely different feeling and image of the Aegean, as can be seen from the opening lines of *The Voyage of Dionysus* which follow:

The whole immense
Aegean was asleep
and you saw two skies
the upper one azure
and the lower one plain blue.

The intermittent puffs
of spring breeze
uncertain and infrequent
and from afar the peaks of the islands
appearing as shadows.

In order to find the same (or at least similar) regenerative "maritime awareness" of Kalvos and the use of the Aegean as a symbol and the center of the world we must wait for the poetry of the Generation of the '30s. Prior to this, however, we have a series of writers who were distinguished (among other things) for their love of the sea and the Aegean in particular. The earliest were Alexandros Papadiamantis (1851-1911) and Andreas Karkavitsas (1866-1922) and they were succeeded by certain prose writers of the '30s, Photis Kontoglou, Stratis Myrivilis and Ilias Venezis to limit ourselves to these three "maritime" writers, all with Asia Minor origins.

Papadiamantis (as well as Karkavitsas to a great degree) "saw" and described the Aegean sea, regardless of whether he specifically named this broad geographical region each and every time. All of his sea scenes in his stories are from the Aegean, his inspiration is kindled by this specific sea and his sea-lashed heroes act out their roles in this place. For most of Papadiamantis' heroes the Aegean sea is a cradle and a maternal embrace as the young hero of the short story "Eros-Hero" imagines:

His other mother, the sea, still rocked him with her waves. She too had a cradle, she too had an embrace and many embraces. For his first mother he was now a grown and aging son. For his other great mother, the loving and liquid and perfidious, he was still little, her very small child.

This "biological" relationship of the people of the Aegean with their sea appears to exist in all the prose writers we have mentioned. Furthermore, after the loss of Asia Minor in 1922, the Aegean was to be charged with new significance, unknown up to then: this sea now constitutes the easternmost borders of Hellenism, it is what joins mother Greece to the lost lands of Asia Minor, a place at once both mythical and real. Through the descriptive sojourn to the Aegean sea by Kontoglou, Venezis and Myrivilis, as well as other prose writers from the period between the wars, a kind of metaphysical relationship is achieved with it, as the sea seems to transmit to them its own "demonic spirit" which seizes them and possesses them. The end of the short story by Myrivilis "The Marine Spirit of the Aegean" from the collection *Αιγαίο*, is an example of this:

Ever so slowly, before night ended, and while the morning star was sinking in the east, the sea, ending the Aegean dream of a summer night, drew it all inside itself — the love and the power, the passion and the hope. And it all became a voyage and an open sea. This was the marine spirit I saw while going to find the roots of the monk Theophilos Kairis, I saw it covering the Aegean, a green boat, brightly lit Andros. And then I was sure that [the monk] had worked in this spirit, had been tyrannized by it, had stood within it worthy and faithful, this monk who had become a legend of my homeland on the Asia Minor coast and who, wanting to obey the daimon of the Aegean to the very end, tried to grope his way to the very body of God.

Nevertheless, the development of the Aegean into a broader ideological and aesthetic center only occurred with the poets of the Generation of the '30s. This was a case of a new, one could say, perception of the world (Greek and European) as well as a new manner of literary exposition and evaluation of this world. Thus George Seferis, speaking in 1941 about the state of Greek poetry after Karyotakis and the new "sea" poets, wrote (*Δοκιμές*, A 167-168):

The poetry of Karyotakis' followers was without a horizon. But around 1930 things changed. What characterized the inquiries of the young was a kind of island idiosyncracy (emphasis ours). The horizons broaden. The dusty lanes and the rooms are left behind. The Aegean with its islands, the sea mythology, the voyage to all parts of the compass, are the things which move [them] and which they try to express.

A little further down Seferis, referring more particularly to his "friend", the poet Elytis, continues:

Elytis' poetry is also a poetry of the sea. But this sea is not an ocean, it is not a voyage, it is the sounding, luminous Aegean. When I consider the poetry of Elytis I always have the desire to call the Aegean by the name the old seafarers gave it and which our people still know it by, "The White Sea". The mirthful sea. And truly [...] in Elytis (something very rare in our country) there is just such a joy. It is the joy of a man who awakens at dawn with his nets or with his bird traps and is certain that he will return singing and bringing the most silver of fish or the gaudiest of birds [...].

Eros
the archipelago
and the prow of its foam
and the gulls of its dreams
the sailor perched on the highest mast
airing a song.

Precisely. This song of the archipelago, interwoven with the wind, the waves, the pebbles, with the stones and the vegetation of the island, with the courtyards of the snow-white houses, with the billowing sails, with the anchors on the bottom, this is the song that Elytis airs upright at the gunwale, heedless and happy.

The above observation by Seferis, despite the excessive emphasis on the "joy" and the "heedlessness" of Elytis –a view that is still held by many critics– constitutes, one could say, a kind of manifesto in regard to the Aegean and its importance to modern Hellenism. Elytis himself goes even further when he observes that the Aegean concentrates so many elements that it could be internationally established as a point of reference for art and civilization. Thus, in the same study of Kalvos (*op. cit.*, 88) he writes:

It is well-known that modern international art found on the Aegean islands many of the deepest elements which coincide with its own; that it also found the rules of ancient Greece, adapted with amazing precision to the creations of its modern-day islands. The representatives of this art, separating historical epochs into the pre-classical (where art marched on to conquests becoming more dynamic and more daring), the classical (when completing its conquest art became more balanced and measured) and the post-classical (when art is endeavoring to hold on to the past and is thus becoming conservative or, as we say today, academic) they have now been set, carrying along with their aesthetic, the aesthetic of the Greek islands as well, in a new pre-classical order. Thus, it would not be at all difficult for us now, by transposing the principles from the plastic arts to literature, to gain a new criterion which would permit us to classify in a analogous way the intellectual forms which interest us.

The extent to which Elytis was inspired by the Aegean, outside the fact that it engaged him as a spiritual and artistic space, cannot be analyzed to the proper extent here. Let us simply mention that the poem which opens the collection *Προσανατολισμοί* (1940) is "Aegean", to which reference has already been made. This seminal poem certainly expresses the "joy" and the "heedlessness" which Seferis notes but it is not simply that. In "Aegean" Elytis inaugurates his myth-making ideology and technique which sets him apart from those poets who, as he himself maintains, turned more toward classical mythology and less toward the personal practice of myth-making. The Aegean, in Elytis' poetry, is transformed into a living, throbbing, erotic, joyful and yet melancholic body (compare the poem "Aegean Melancholy" in the same collection) with all the characteristics of optimism and joy, —which one could certainly note— but also with the qualities of a formulated philosophical and moral "ideology", a regenerative "temperament" and an absolute freedom which can be of interest to and relate to the entire world.

All these intellectual and spiritual elements the Aegean can offer to poets as well as ordinary people are eloquently described in Elytis' essay: *Ἀναφορά στόν Ἀνδρέα Ἐμπειρῖκο* (p. 52 ff.) where the ideological, cultural and ethical importance of this age-old cradle of Hellenism can be clearly seen:

> *I am not a theoretician,* he writes, *and I often speak arbitrarily. But when one loves silver it is only natural that he should want to cover everything in silver. Didn't the islanders do the same thing with the Blessed Virgin? That's the kind of islander I am and still remain, Andreas; religious in regard to pomegranates and girls; and let all those who see "tree" and "unripeness" as symbols equal in power to the Cross and the sword accuse me as they will [...] this tree and this girl accompany us everywhere — accompany our thought, or better, the way in which we think: the power to plant, to bloom, to bear fruit from your innermost depths. And where was their first source, the genuine one, besides the Aegean? Maybe I've kept this sea over here and you've taken it over there; that isn't important. What is important is that both of us have tried to adopt its clarity and its anti-slavish composition — wishing to completely transform the material world and to completely liberate the moral one.*

BIBLIOGRAPHY

In writing this article, the following books were consulted:

BOWRA, C.M., *Greek Lyric Poetry. From Alcman to Simonides*, Oxford 1961.

ΕΛΥΤΗΣ, ΟΔ., *Ἀνοιχτά Χαρτιά*, Ἀθήνα 1974.

— *Ἀναφορά στόν Ἀνδρέα Ἐμπειρῖκο*, 2η ἔκδ., Ἀθήνα 1980.

ΜΕΡΑΚΛΗΣ, Μ., *Ἀνδρέα Κάλβου, Ὠδαί (1-20)*, ἑρμηνευτική ἔκδ., Ἀθήνα χ.χ.

PAGE, D., *History and the Homeric Iliad*, California Press, 1963.

ΣΕΦΕΡΗΣ, Γ., *Δοκιμές*, Α+Β, 3η ἔκδ., Ἀθήνα 1974.

ΣΚΙΑΔΑΣ, ΑΡ., *Ἀρχαϊκός λυρισμός*, τόμ. 1, Ἀθήνα 1979· τόμ. 2, Ἀθήνα 1981.

SNELL, B., *The Discovery of the Mind*, transl. from German by T.G. Rosenmeyer, Oxford 1953.

THOMSON, G., *Ancient Greek Society. The Prehistoric Aegean*, London 1949.

INDEX

B

C

D

E

F

G

H

I

J

K

L

M

Q

R

S

T

U

V

W

X

Y

Z